VITA AND HAROLD

Vita and Harold on the steps of the tower at Sissinghurst, 1932.

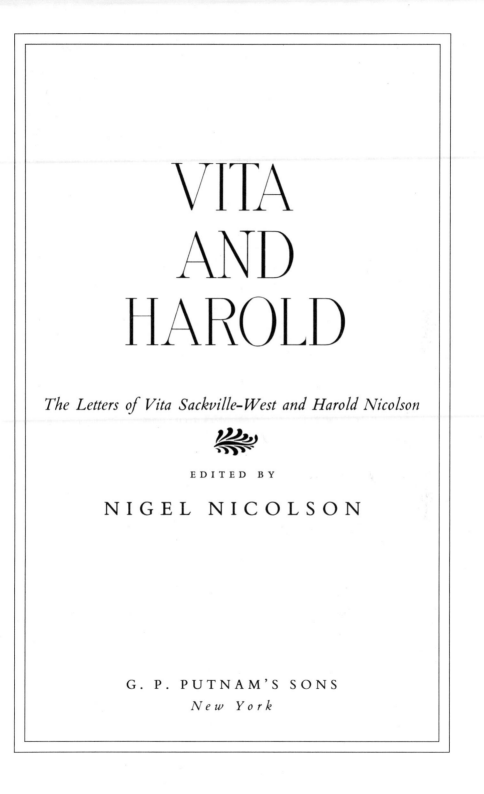

VITA AND HAROLD

The Letters of Vita Sackville-West and Harold Nicolson

EDITED BY

NIGEL NICOLSON

G. P. PUTNAM'S SONS

New York

G. P. Putnam's Sons
Publishers Since 1838
200 Madison Avenue
New York, NY 10016

Library of Congress Cataloging-in-Publication Data

Sackville-West, V. (Victoria), 1892–1962.
Vita and Harold : the letters of Vita Sackville-West
and Harold Nicolson / edited by Nigel Nicolson.
p.   cm.
Includes index.
ISBN 0-399-13666-5 (acid-free paper)
1. Sackville-West, V. (Victoria), 1892–1962—Correspondence.
2. Nicolson, Harold George, Sir, 1886–1968—Correspondence.
3. Authors, English—20th century—Correspondence.   4. Diplomats—
Great Britain—Correspondence.   I. Nicolson, Harold George, Sir,
1886–1968.   II. Nicolson, Nigel.   III. Title.
PR6037.A35Z493   1992   91-4340 CIP
823'.912—dc20
[B]

Designed by MaryJane DiMassi
Printed in the United States of America
1   2   3   4   5   6   7   8   9   10

This book is printed on acid-free paper.
∞

CONTENTS

ILLUSTRATIONS

VITA AND HAROLD

EDITORIAL NOTE

ON THE LAST DAY OF 1958, as Vita Sackville-West put away the letters that
Harold Nicolson had written to her during that year, she glanced through
some of the annual folders that had preceded this latest addition to her filing
cabinet, and wrote to her husband, "I hope that someday Nigel may publish
a selection of them." By the time of her death four years later, there were
fifty such folders, containing all, or nearly all, the letters he had written to
her since their engagement in 1912. He preserved her letters, too. Their
correspondence totaled 10,500 letters in all, many of them pages long.

For some years after my father's death in 1968 I kept them at Sissinghurst,
and made use of them in editing the three volumes of his diaries and writing
Portrait of a Marriage. I also lent them to his biographer (James Lees-Milne),
to Vita's biographer (Victoria Glendinning), and to the historians of their
gardens, Anne Scott-James and Jane Brown. Their books aroused the interest
of many other people, and as it was difficult to store the documents safely
in a private house and make them available to students, I decided in 1983 to
sell the entire collection, together with Lady Sackville's diaries, to the Lilly
Library, Indiana University, at Bloomington, Indiana, where they are kept
in conditions ideal both for preservation and access. I am much indebted to
William R. Cagle, the Lilly Librarian, and to Saundra Taylor, his Curator
of Manuscripts, for their hospitality, interest, and help.

Vita proposed a selection of Harold's letters only, thinking her own
unworthy companions to them, an opinion that I have ignored because I do
not share it. A one-sided correspondence is not a correspondence, and her
letters are of much interest, particularly in the early years, and essential for
an understanding of their remarkable relationship.

The majority of these letters have not been published before, and were
selected for that reason. But it would have been foolish to omit, for the sake
of claiming first publication for everything, certain letters previously quoted
in full or in part by myself or the two biographers, when they are key
documents in explaining important incidents or attitudes, or perhaps for no

other reason than that they are interesting or very funny. Examples are Vita's apologia for her affair with Violet Trefusis (pp. 66–67) or Harold's description of his first meeting with Charles and Anne Lindbergh (pp. 258–259).

My main purpose has been to show how the companionship of two very different people developed over these fifty years, and how their marriage survived crises, sexual incompatibility and long absences to become a source of profound happiness to both. They kept their work (Vita her writing, Harold his diplomacy and politics) separate from their personal lives, and seldom wrote to each other about it, unless one of them had just published a book or an event of great national importance, like the Abdication or both world wars, had occurred. I have retained enough to indicate the impact of these events upon them, but in the main their correspondence is the story of their maturing love for each other, expressed, for example, in their joint creation of the garden at Sissinghurst.

I have not thought it necessary to print the whole of every letter. Most letter-writers deal in the same letter with several subjects, and to isolate one or two of them for publication in a book that does not pretend to be a complete correspondence is, I believe, excusable. Nor have I annotated the letters fully, because to do so in a popular edition is likely to annoy the reader by telling him what he does not need or want to know. Only the first letter is annotated in the traditional way, to show him what he has been spared in all the others.

The addresses are given in full when they first appear, but thereafter they are truncated ("Long Barn," "Teheran," "Sissinghurst," "Berlin," etc.). Sometimes the greeting and signature are given in full, but more often they are omitted, because to repeat endlessly the endearments at the beginning and end of letters written by the same two people is to render their correspondence more saccharine than it seemed to them. Family expressions, nicknames, family jokes, and their habit of referring to each other in the third person ("Mar isn't going to like this: nor does Hadji") are only tolerable to an outsider if sparingly used, and they have been reduced by judicious excision.

I am much indebted to Mary Morgan for her sympathetic typing of the letters from photocopies supplied by the Lilly Library.

NIGEL NICOLSON
Sissinghurst Castle, Cranbrook, Kent

INTRODUCTION

HAROLD NICOLSON WAS the better letter-writer of the two, and not only because he had more to write about after 1930, the watershed in both their lives, when he changed his profession in mid-career and Vita left social Long Barn for reclusive Sissinghurst. He enjoyed writing letters more than she did, was eager to share experiences that would interest or amuse her, and he used his letters, as he did his contemporary diary, not just to record, but as a literary exercise at the start of each day, much as a man might knock up in a squash court before the match began. Thus he was given to set-piece descriptions of incidents and conversations (he had an exceptional aural memory), of moods and landscapes, of other people's clothes and houses, and how accent, gesture, mannerisms, and chatter reveal a person's background and taste. His letter-writing style, in fact, was little different from that which he adopted in his most loved book, *Some People,* and developed in his broadcasts of the 1930s, but less severe, less classical, less ornate than his articles and other books. He had no thought of publication as he wrote his daily letters to Vita, but some of them, like his description of the signing of the Treaty of Versailles on 28 June 1919 or his meeting with James Joyce on 4 February 1934, were undoubtedly intended for more than her eyes.

Vita, on the other hand, had no great wish to record or share experiences. Her diary, which she kept only intermittently, was little more than a retrospective engagement book. Nor was she gifted with Harold's effortless wit, or his ability to praise without flattery and mock without offense. In writing to him she didn't choose to exercise her narrative or poetic skills, which were greater than his, as she did when writing to other intimates, like Virginia Woolf. Indeed, I find it strange that the best of her books, like *The Garden, Passenger to Teheran,* and *All Passion Spent,* reveal a quite different, profounder, cleverer Vita than her letters to Harold. Perhaps it was because he understood her so well, and she felt so certain of his love, that she saw no need to show off a little, moan a little, exult a little, as he did in his letters to her. He threw his pleasures like confetti into the air, and craved sympathy for his sorrows. She nursed hers to herself. But this had not always been so. She became more reticent as she grew older. Some of her earliest letters, when they were engaged, indulged in mock scolding and flirtatious quips that she abandoned after marriage, but that she, too, was capable of the set piece, and did it well, is illustrated by her description of Rodin in his studio on 3 September 1913, and her humor (as well as her fortitude) emerges from the account of her escape from revolutionary Poland on 13 May 1926. Her most self-revealing letters were written to Harold in Persia, when she was struggling to reconcile her concurrent love for him and for Virginia Woolf, and at least two weeks would elapse before her letter reached him, and a month before she received his reply, the interval of time and distance reassuring her that she was not trapped.

Even before their wedding, Harold referred to "our amazing marriage" (28 July 1913), and indeed it was strange, so strange that many people could not resist questioning whether it was a marriage at all. When my account of it was published in 1973, a Sunday newspaper headlined its review of the book, "Portrait of a *What?*" The critic could not believe that a marriage that renounced sex after two sons were born could be anything more than a loving friendship, and that didn't count as marriage, particularly when both partners, by mutual consent, were unfaithful to each other with people of their own sex. But in every other sense Vita and Harold achieved a relationship richer and more enduring than most couples, replacing sex by something more binding and even more gratifying—mutual support, mutual sympathy, mutual forebearance, common enjoyments (gardens, books, children, travel, friends), and the generosity to encourage in the other separate achievements, separate pleasures, separate holidays, separate lovers, without loss of trust or affection. Neither felt any jealousy, envy, or resentment of the other. While they missed each other agonizingly during Harold's long absences abroad, it never occurred to them to suggest that Vita should sacrifice her independence by joining him permanently in his diplomatic posts. They wore their separation like a hair shirt. "It is rather good for us to have a chance of thoroughly missing each other," wrote Vita before their wedding had even taken place. And thirteen years later (slightly paraphrased):

> What is the point, in our enlightened world, of *marriage?* You see, if we had just lived together, we would be living together still, just as happily, and it would make no difference to our passion for our garden or our interest in the children. The whole system of marriage is wrong. It ought, at least, to be optional, and no stigma if you prefer a less claustrophobic form of contract. For it *is* claustrophobic. (26 December 1926)

Harold never found it claustrophobic. He liked marriage. It gave their union stability, legitimized their children, made Long Barn a home, not just a shared house, and their possessions common possessions. He was domesticated: Vita was not. He needed her love more than she needed his, because she was always sure of his and for many years he was not quite sure of hers. The slight tension that resulted is evident from his letters. He is always reassuring himself by dramatizing the happiness of their marriage and constantly re-examining its roots, and ultimately she caught the habit. ("I do think that we have managed things cleverly.") There is a note of self-congratulation about their correspondence that some readers have found puzzling.

Harold began by thinking that he could manage Vita. She responded with spirit, as if testing her blade against his before a duel. In his engagement letters he made tentative sallies to assert his masculinity: "I really must be the one who 'disposes' in these things . . . About big things I am to have the upper hand" (17 February 1913), but he did it in the manner of someone who, having once put his foot down, immediately lifts it up again. He ended the same letter, "Remember that whatever you do . . . I shall know that you were right." He was Victorian by birth, Edwardian by upbringing, Georgian by temperament, and the three influences conflicted in his character, the first authoritative, the third conciliatory, whereas Vita, even in childhood, had settled her priorities much more firmly. She would be liberated, iconoclastic, rebellious; and although she loved Knole with a sick passion, she was a wanderer, a gypsy—Pepita reincarnated—or so, for a time, she liked to think.

The duality of her character led to the great Trefusis affair. It has so often been described, even dramatized on film, that I need only repeat that it was the crisis of their marriage. In this volume I have included letters that tell the story from their two points of view as it was happening, and added later letters that make clear Vita's remorse for her part in it and Harold's fear of Violet's pernicious influence which persisted until the end of his life.

"You know what infatuation is," she wrote to him, soon after the crisis had passed, "and I was mad." And then, rather curiously, within two years of her death, "You were older than me, and far better informed. I was very young, and very innocent. I knew nothing about homosexuality . . . You should have told me" (23 November 1960). She was not all that young, not all that innocent. In 1920 she was twenty-eight, and although she may not have given homosexuality a name, she had had a taste of it with Rosamund Grosvenor long before her more torrid affair with Violet Trefusis began. We have no need to find excuses for her. Her behaviour was reckless and cruel. Violet's was worse. Her humiliation of her husband was an act of cynical wickedness compared to Vita's guilt-laden betrayal of Harold.

What of his part in it? As his dialogue with Vita was conducted almost entirely by correspondence (when alone together they could barely bring themselves to mention the subject), one can trace his terrible dilemma through all its mutations, undecided whether to bully Vita into submission or cajole her, act like Petruchio with his shrew or Bassanio with Portia. His nature was gentle, and it was gentleness that won in the end, but from time to time he simulated defiance, "Come back at once" alternating with "Come back when you can," and Vita took advantage of his vacillation, hating herself for doing so. But if he was gentle, Harold was not weak. It was not the performance of a weak man to woo and win, against formidable competition, so fiery a girl as Vita was in 1912, nor to gain an early reputation as the most brilliant diplomatist of his generation, the confidant of Lloyd George, Balfour, and Curzon, the adviser of Clemenceau, Venizelos, and President Wilson. He managed to retrieve Vita from Violet not just by being lovable, but because he was admirable, in spirit, intelligence, and fervor, and because, by that time, deep down, she *wanted* to be rescued from her insane adventure. Her ruthlessness had given the impression of strength, but it was she who was the weakest of the three, and afterwards the most repentant. She spent the rest of her life making up for him the brutality of those three years.

Yet a streak of mercilessness persisted in her. She could hate more violently than Harold: "Those filthy Germans! Let us level every town in Germany to the ground! I shan't care" (16 February 1944), and in the casual way she discarded lovers she displayed an arrogance worthy of generations of Sackvilles. Her shabby treatment of Geoffrey Scott is a striking example. But her short-lived affair with him was an aberration. She was born to be a lesbian lover. Though she bore three sons (one of whom died at birth), she was perpetually astonished that God should have devised such a peculiar way of begetting children, and her astonishment soon turned to disgust. With women lovers her only problem was to free herself of one love affair in order to begin the next, and she contrived this difficult task without ever inflicting a lasting wound. She did not regard sex as the most important element in her relationship with women, no more than she had with Harold, and once that phase was over, they could remain friends. Not all her lovers saw it in quite the same way. They were disconcerted by the frankness of some lines in her poem *Solitude* (1938):

> Those cheap and easy loves! But what were they,
> Those rank intruders into darkest lairs?
> We take a heart and leave our own intact.

Was that all they had meant to her?

With Virginia Woolf it was very different. Vita was flattered by her attention, awed; and it surprised her that Virginia could embark at the age of forty-four upon the only love affair of her life without trepidation, as if she didn't want to go to her grave without having done something really wicked. Vita was apprehensive (she didn't need Harold's warning) that their love making might trigger in Virginia a new attack of madness. It didn't. Both women were enriched by it. Vita found in their intimacy an inspiration that she gained from no other person. *Seducers in Ecuador* was one direct result of it, the most original of all Vita's prose works, written for Virginia, in her allusive style, and published by her, and from Virginia's side came *Orlando,* the longest and most charming love letter in literature.

Vita told Harold, who was in Teheran, a safe distance away, that she and Virginia had slept together, but it was the only occasion when she was so frank. Their unwritten marriage pact stipulated that each would tell the other about their current affairs. When it came to the point, they were too shy. They allowed the information to be surmised from dropped hints, that Harold had met "a funny new friend, a dress-maker," Edward Molyneux (15 September 1919), or Ivor Novello, the film star (14 April 1928), and Vita spoke lightly of Mary Campbell and Hilda Matheson, knowing that he would guess the true situation, just as she never needed to probe into his lifelong friendship with Raymond Mortimer, or his more casual affairs with young men like James Pope-Hennessy or John Strick. It was as if in this respect they were two unmarried friends, trained to leave each other's indiscretions unquestioned and not even to think of them as infidelities.

Vita's character changed more than Harold's as she grew older. The major transformation coincided with their move from Long Barn to Sissinghurst in the early 1930s. At Long Barn there had been weekend parties, constant expeditions to London and other people's country houses, but at Sissinghurst, a house twice the size of Long Barn, she determined to have no guest rooms, for guest rooms imply guests. Harold's gregariousness was satisfied in London during the week, and Sissinghurst with its "succession of intimacies" was his refuge as much as hers. So extreme was Vita's desire for solitude that she insisted on my brother and I sharing a bedroom until we were both at Oxford, because, she explained, if we had a bedroom each and one of us was away, Lady Colefax might find out and invite herself for the weekend. It halved the risk.

If this sounds eccentric, it gives a false impression of Vita's personality. She was deeply conservative. I have hesitated to print in this volume her letter of 7 February 1945, because her dislike of change, accentuated by the turmoil of a war that was just ending, is phrased in terms so reactionary as to defy belief. She would have preferred to call it her love of tradition, which she had expressed in very different ways in her novel *The Edwardians* and her poem *The Land.* She believed profoundly that the old order, including its class structure, was the best. People should stay in their villages, not demand buses to the nearest town. Tractors are no better than plough horses, and uglier. Retirement pensions are regrettable because they are a substitute for savings, and family allowances odious because they encourage the wrong people to breed. Wars, she thought, could be avoided if only enough people wanted peace, but when the Second World War broke out, she was exhilarated. Her love of England, the excitement of the air battles overhead and the threat of invasion on the Kentish coast, the involvement of both her sons on active service in Africa and Italy, and the danger to which Harold was nightly exposed in London cumulatively aroused her latent patriotism and induced in her a solemn contemplation of life and death, God and nature, which in the darkness of her tower she poured into her profoundest but most neglected poem, *The Garden.* How much one can sympathize with her complaint to Harold (1 October 1957) that, in contrast, her gardening articles in *The Observer* had gained her a reputation which she neither desired nor deserved!

Once she had written to him (26 September 1926): "What I really like is a severe life," by which she meant application, the industry needed to finish a book or perfect a garden, instead of frittering her time away socially. Harold did not agree. All his life he worked regularly and intensively, and his output on paper was doubled by his fluency, his retentive memory and quick imagination, but his well-regulated life allowed him equal time for conversation, parties, clubs, committees, meetings, broadcasts, lectures and love. His activity when he was in charge of the British Embassy in Berlin in 1928 is an example of the pattern of life which best suited him. Deeply engaged in analyzing for his Government the gradual resurgence of Germany as a great power, he entertained countless visitors, taking them at considerable risk to his reputation to the sleaziest nightclubs, mixed with the intellectual elite of Berlin, did his hated duty as host at formal diplomatic functions, lectured in Cologne, Munich, and Frankfurt, and yet found time to write what he considered the best of his books, his life of his father, Lord Carnock.

On retiring from diplomacy in 1929, largely because Vita hated it, he endured two disastrous years when he was involved first with Lord Beaverbrook's newspapers and then with Oswald Mosley's New Party, and only regained his poise by writing a best-selling novel, *Public Faces,* and his trilogy of books on diplomacy, the last of them a biography of an American, Dwight Morrow.

Harold's attitude to Americans was ambivalent. He could not

justly be called a snob. In England he had little sympathy with the Ascot or City sets, and chose his friends, as most people do, from among those who shared his interests, which in his case were undeniably elitist. He demanded a certain level of culture, taste, and intelligence before he could feel comfortable with them. He liked people who would recognize a Matisse on sight, quote the poets appositely and without showing off, wear a top hat without feeling or looking foolish, and when someone referred to Pinero's plays, didn't need to ask, "Who's Pinero?" In politics he hated the fake cordiality that a candidate has to assume. Therefore, he found himself as much at a loss in the workingmen's clubs of Leicester (his constituency) as in the smarter houses of Mayfair, Long Island mansions, and the drawing rooms of suburban Des Moines. His first visit to the United States, with Vita, was on a lecture tour in 1933, in the worst possible combination of circumstances for a first acquaintance with that exciting country— mid-winter, the depth of an economic depression, and an exhausting three-month tour by train and car of some of the most unappetizing of American cities. "There simply does not exist here the sort of person whom we like," he wrote to Vita. This nonsense he retracted when he went to Charleston, South Carolina, and a year later when he stayed with the Morrows and the Lindberghs, and met people like Thomas Lamont, Archibald MacLeish, and Mrs. Longworth. Yet the prejudice of the Old World against the New lingered in him. One of his funniest letters (30 August 1935) candidly describes how the New World had its revenge.

He sat in the House of Commons from 1935 to 1945, and for a year was a junior Minister in Winston Churchill's wartime government. He was an excellent speaker, a companionable colleague who never made a political enemy, and almost the only back-bench member who had had direct experience of the conduct of foreign policy. He would have risen to high office had he possessed one other quality, which Churchill once described as the most estimable in a man— mettle. Harold lacked it. He held no animosity in reserve, and displayed no political vehemence, except in one instance, his opposition to Chamberlain's attempts to conciliate the Dictators. His speech against the Munich agreement was his finest political hour. His training as a civil servant inclined him to seek compromise, see merit in his opponent's arguments, and avoid controversy. One of his parliamentary friends urged him to become more formidable. He replied that having been unformidable for fifty-five years, it was difficult suddenly to acquire the necessary techniques. In the end, he regarded his political career as a failure—too severe a verdict—and withdrew to his other life: the writing of books, the cultivation of his garden, and Vita.

They often reassured each other that the success of their marriage was due to "a common set of values," a blanket term that covered the whole range of moral and intellectual probities, an amalgam of Greek, Roman, Christian, and eighteenth-century virtues, among them, truthfulness, charity, industry, curiosity, decorum, and a capacity for friendship. Neither of them was formally religious. In one of these letters (7 July 1929), Harold expressed his astonishment at the "twaddle" that the English hymnal contained, and while Vita worried more about her lack of faith and actually wrote the lives of three saints (Joan of Arc, and the two Saints Teresa), both were content to describe themselves as good pagans. Their goodness was not quite absolute, their values not entirely common. They shared a seam of racism that could be uncovered not far beneath the surface, and the Sackvilles' "bedint" shibboleth, to which one clue was accent, often clouded their judgment. A young woman interviewed for the post of secretary at Sissinghurst ruined her chances by uttering in her nervousness the telltale phrase, "Our cow is a brown cow," and not one eye dared meet another.

Vita, like Virginia Woolf, was by temperament a pacifist and feminist, though neither satisfactorily worked out the implications of what they professed. Harold was neither. He believed unashamedly in the threat of war as an instrument of policy, and his attitude to women remained Edwardian: they were incapable of "thinking logically." There were also political differences between them. In 1948 Harold stood for Parliament as a Labour candidate: Vita's conservatism was unshakable. His "socialism" was the easy price he paid for the advantages he had enjoyed in life. Vita felt no guilt about her equivalent prejudices. Too well-bred to utter them publicly, in private she proclaimed them.

It was because she found it hard to come to terms with a changing world that her relationship with her two sons became uneasy. In our childhood her love for us was explicit and unforced (see, for example, her letter of 26 December 1926), but children were demanding, dirty, spies, pests, and disturbers of the peace. They interrupted terribly. In later life, the University, war, Parliament, scholarship, and business set us further apart from her in what she still considered male occupations, and we both drew closer to our father because he understood them better, and was more extrovert than Vita, more active, funnier, more demonstrably affectionate. I feel remorseful about this. I should have taken the trouble to know Vita better. I excused my partial withdrawal from her by what I supposed to be her partial withdrawal from me, but it was a sort of shyness on both our parts, a misguided fear of intrusion that vitiates the relationship between many parents and their children. At first it was Ben whom she loved the better; later it was me, for she considered me the rural son, Ben the urban, and though I was the younger, she bequeathed Sissinghurst to me, believing that I would care for it more. She misunderstood the adult Ben, and so did Harold, thinking his reaction against the domesticity and values of his family ungrateful, his erudition austere, and his untidiness and silences discourteous. They underestimated the position he won for himself as an art historian and his gift for friendship, and would have been surprised to know that at his memorial service in 1978, five hundred people crowded the church and Kenneth Clark gave the address.

In the last years of their marriage, their letters were shorter because they knew each other so well and spent almost every weekend together. There was nothing left to explain, and on Vita's side little to relate. "Another quiet day at Sissinghurst" became a constant refrain. Harold remained very active until her death in 1962, reporting the consequences of the war from Nuremberg and Paris, standing once again for Parliament, and writing the official biography of King George V, for which, to his slight dismay and Vita's, he was awarded a knighthood. Their bond was literature and the garden. For many years both wrote, or broadcast, reviews of current books, and published another dozen of their own. The garden was their sustained pleasure, expressive of their common attitude to nature, keeping it cool, Kentish, and indigenous, as Harold had counseled Vita from Teheran when she was making the garden at Long Barn. Flowers should not quarrel, no more than people. They had achieved at Sissinghurst a serenity that matched their own lives.

Looking back on their marriage, they came to consider it the perfect compromise. If Vita, from time to time (see, for example, her letter of 13 December 1928, a key document in this long story), confessed to a sense of inadequacy as his wife, or if he wondered (31 March 1941) whether she might not have been happier married to a more determined man, neither bothered to reply, for each knew what the reply would be. When she told him at the height of the German bombardment of London that she would kill herself if he were killed, she meant it. As it was, they lived into old age, Harold dying six years after her. He could have spoken for both of them when he wrote to her (9 April 1958), "When I die, nobody will think I failed to make the most of life."

arold and Vita first met at a London dinner party on 29 June 1910, and he was invited by Lady Sackville to spend the following weekend at Knole. He was twenty-four, Vita eighteen, each in their different ways a young star of Edwardian society. He was a junior official in the Foreign Office, of which his father, Sir Arthur Nicolson, became head in September of that year; and she, a beautiful though reluctant debutante, was the only child of a family that in February had become notorious by winning the famous Pepita legitimacy case. Knole was restored to its full grandeur, and Harold was invited to stay there more than once. He and Vita often met at London parties, and her first surviving letter to him records their friendly but by no means intimate relationship.

VITA TO HAROLD   *Knole [Sevenoaks, Kent]*

5 November [1910]

My dear Mr Harold,

I have been asked to "ask a man" to dine on Thursday with Mrs Harold Pearson[1] and go to a dance, so would you like to come? I promise you shan't be made to dance! I think it might be rather amusing. Would you let me know as soon as possible, to the St Petersburg Hotel,[2] North Audley Street, or better still come to tea

---

1. She was Agnes Beryl, a daughter of Lord Edward Spencer-Churchill. In 1905 she had married Harold (Weetman) Pearson, a Liberal M.P. and heir to the 1st Viscount Cowdray, whom he succeeded in 1927.
2. Knole had been half closed, pending the result of the legitimacy trial which could have deprived the Sackvilles of their inheritance, and they had been living in this hotel off Grosvenor Square for the best part of two years.

tomorrow at 6 South Street with the Rubens lady,[3] who is here and tells me to ask you. We are both going up to London tomorrow to go to *Macbeth*.

Do come to the dance.

Yours very sincerely,
Vita Sackville-West

Mr Vansittart is here.[4] How is Green Archie?[5]

---

3. Rosamund Grosvenor, Vita's childhood friend and current lover. She called her the Rubens lady because of her fleshy, roseate appearance.
4. Robert Vansittart (1881–1957), an early admirer of Vita and a friend of Harold. In 1910 he was on leave from Cairo, where he was a second secretary in the British Embassy. In 1930 he became head of the Foreign Office and was a major voice in warning the Government of the Nazi threat.
5. Harold's Morris Oxford car. Although he had learned to drive, he gave it up soon after his marriage, and it was always Vita who drove when they were motoring together.

N
o letters survive from 1911, although it was the year when Harold fell in love with Vita. He was parted from her for six months when he was appointed to the Embassy in Madrid, but spent Christmas and New Year at Knole, where their friendship developed rapidly. Shortly afterwards he learned that he was to be posted to the Embassy in Constantinople. He was determined to propose to her before he left, and took the opportunity at a ball at Hatfield House on 18 January 1912. Vita hesitated, then half accepted him, but when he left for Constantinople a week later, it was on the understanding (imposed by Lady Sackville) that they were not to correspond as an engaged couple nor even as lovers. Hence the apparent coldness of Vita's letters, and for the first year she did not keep Harold's. In 1913 their correspondence grew warmer, and they began to break Lady Sackville's rules, but Harold, though worried by Vita's varying moods, was quite unaware of the reason for them, that she was simultaneously much in love with Rosamund Grosvenor. The crisis came in May 1913, following her visit to Spain, when she hinted that perhaps they should not marry after all, but his anguished response convinced her, and she committed herself to Harold absolutely. He returned from Turkey in July, in time to witness the Sackvilles' triumph in the Scott inheritance case, and they were married in the chapel at Knole on 1 October 1913.

VITA TO HAROLD   *Knole*

23 January [1912]

My dear Harold,

The Saint has arrived. He is quite lovely, and has a gloriously flat nose. I like him quite, quite enormously, and he is going in the niche, and thank you ever so much. I suppose he is old?[1]

This letter is meant to catch you tomorrow morning between Ireland and Constantinople, though Providence alone knows whether it will. Anyway, if you receive it three months late you will know from this that the intention was good. As a matter of fact, I see that the Saint is really only a little boy, unless he is John the Baptist, who was a man saint at first, wasn't he? I have got influenza, isn't it a bore? Not very bad, but enough to keep me in bed with a temperature and neuralgia. This room is such fun to be ill in, there are so many things to look at. But it makes one long to get up and finish it.[2]

Goodbye and *buonissimo viaggio*.

Yours very sincerely
Vita Sackville-West

VITA TO HAROLD   *6 South Street,*
                                        London W.1
1 February [1912]

My dear Harold,

I am writing at the Rubens lady's house, with her pen, (which is vile), but she is not here. She is at the *Miracle,*[3] and I am by way of coming to tea with her. I am going to the *Miracle* myself tonight,

---

1. The saint was in fact female, St. Barbara, a sixteenth-century wooden statuette, 21 ins. high, which Harold bought for Vita in Spain. "Barbara" became a symbol of their marriage, accompanied them from house to house, even to Persia, and is still at Sissinghurst.
2. Vita and Rosamund were painting her bedroom in a mock-Italian style, blue and gold.
3. Max Reinhardt's play, in which Lady Diana Manners (later Diana Cooper) played the leading role.

hence my being in London at all. Then I am going for balls in the country, and then Knole, and parties. Perhaps I will go to Montana [Switzerland] with Uncle Charlie, *Schlittschuhlaufen* [skating]. I lunched with him today, and they told me they had heard of me at Hatfield. Don't you dislike being told you were heard of at various places?

Why I am really writing to you, besides that the Rubens lady is late, and I have nothing to do, and know her well enough to invade her writing table, is that Mother gave me a message for you, which is that the negotiations with the solicitors are being very tedious,[4] and that nothing will be 'proven' till the summer; but I *know* it is going to be all right, and so does she. How low and base and mean and altogether horrible money questions are, and how I hate the very word 'will', and how dreadfully long anything takes that has to do with the law. One ought to have a sort of whipping-boy, like child-kings used to have, to take upon their shoulders for one all the least pleasant parts of life, and then one would be free to revel in its joys like a lizard in the sun.

The lizards that lie on the red brick wall at the bottom of *my* garden in Florence, among the roses. When I was sixteen I used to write decadent poems about them, and I haven't forgotten them now, though I don't write decadent poems. They were so green and hot. The lizards, of course. And once I had a tame one. Then there were poor little overladen donkeys who couldn't drag their carts up the hill to Fiesole, and I used to go and help the little Florentine boys to push. Usually they had left the brake on. And if they were nice to the donkey I gave them *soldi*. My villa [Pestellini] there has a big garden, and the gardener's wife was called Aosunta. You have seen the picture of Florence in my room at Knole, done from my garden. I have the key of the garden gate even now, in my bag. Isn't that a pose?

Here is the Rubens lady, so I stop.

                                                                    V.S.W.

---

4. Over the disputed will of Sir John Murray-Scott. His brother and sister claimed that Lady Sackville had used "undue influence" on him to secure for herself a large part of his fortune.

VITA TO HAROLD   *Knole*

21 February 1912

My dear Harold,

Thank you ever so much for the Turkish delight. It is so bad for me, and I like it so much, especially with monkey-nuts in it like this kind. I also got a distressed letter which I couldn't understand, as I *had* written. What happened? I am so glad you danced. You must learn to go round the wrong way, because you are going to lots of dances next summer, which you will hate but which will be so good for you, and you will have to dance then. Do you know by the way that Ace[1] is coming home about the same time? Muriel [his sister] told me; we met skating at Prince's. Do you and Ace still correspond volubly as you used to? It will be fun having him again.

Here I have become an architect, and go about with two carpenters and a hammer and a yard-measure, and the result of much tapping of walls is that we are going to have another bedroom for people staying. I nearly made a bathroom too, but they said the house would collapse if we dug away the wall. Besides, Dada said Mother was bad enough about bathrooms without my starting too. I agree. But it is fun digging holes and making new rooms.

Tomorrow we are going to London. Mother may go to Paris on Sunday. At Monte Carlo Dada saw Anne (Stanley) and she had already made £100. Did I tell you that before? I am going to balls. Hitherto I have avoided them by banning all the invitation cards. I foresee a terrific season next summer. The other night we went to such an odd dinner you would have liked; there were queer untidy artist people, with a sprinkling of 'clever' young men like Patrick Shaw-Stewart.[2] Do you know him? he is the ugliest thing you ever saw, but very amusing. It is a recent friendship, but we have met quite often. Then there was Granby,[3] who is a curious rather morose person. I don't think I altogether like him. And there were playwrights and sculptors

---

1. Archibald Clark-Kerr, the diplomatist who became Ambassador in both Moscow and Washington. In his youth he was Harold's closest friend.
2. Harold's most brilliant contemporary at Balliol. He was killed in France in 1917.
3. The Marquess of Granby, heir to the Duke of Rutland, who was much in love with Vita.

and novelists and painters, and it was fun. I like that sort of people, and some of them came in quite vaguely after dinner, which I like too, but they were all quite clean. My erratic friend Violet Keppel[4] is coming home in April, so you will know her; I am so glad. She will amuse you more than anybody. You are going to know such crowds of people. And it will not be any use you saying you don't want to.

Tell me something to read. I am tired of the Italian Renaissance and Ranke's History of the Popes. Is it any use sending you English books by the bag? because of course I will if you would like. Have you got a horse? Call it anything except Pegasus. Dada's horse is called Trois Quartiers, but it is too long a story to tell you why. You would put your finger in your eye. Or didn't you know that was the family gesture for saying one is bored? One does it across the table at dinner, and nobody knows. One also does it when one has had enough and wants to go away. This letter is really quite short, but my writing straggles. And isn't it bad?

I don't want to go to London tomorrow.

Yours
Vita

VITA TO HAROLD   *Knole*

27 February 1912

My dear Harold,

Mother has gone to Paris, and I am all alone here for the moment, and all this big house is mine to shut up if I choose, and shut out all the rest of the world by swinging the iron bars across all the gates. But instead of doing that I have locked all the doors of my own tower, and nobody will come near me till tomorrow morning, or even know whether I am still alive. And it is so warm, and Micky [her dog] is dreaming in front of the fire, and the gold on my blue walls gleams in places in the light. And I think I have gone back five hundred years,

---

4. Violet (later Trefusis) had been spending a year in Ceylon with her mother and sister, following the death of King Edward VII.

to the days when the paintings on my walls were new. I heard from you this evening, about the Tschamlüja [outside Constantinople], and your arty pink handkerchief fluttering on the railings. If I sent you a rag, would you tie it on for me? only probably one can't wish by proxy, and even if one could I could not tell you what I should wish. Besides I am off wishing, since the day I fell into a wishing well as a child. I was fished out with a blackberrying stick. I was not pleased. I was an unsociable and unnatural mar[1] with long black hair and long black legs, and very short frocks, and very dirty nails and torn clothes. I used to disappear for hours up high trees, and they couldn't find me till I threw the eggs out of the bird's nests down upon their heads. Then I wouldn't do arithmetic, or scales on the piano. I had a governess who used to hit me across the knuckles with a ruler; you know her, Miss Scarth. She occasionally talks of you, and calls you Harry. In those days the Rubens lady lived quite near here, and that's how I knew her. She was sent for to console me when Dada went to South Africa. (I nearly wrote South Audley Street, with visions of Spealls![2])

The other day I went to a cotillon, and met a mutual friend of ours, who instantly asked why people hated him, and said you had not written to him. I said that wasn't my fault. I really almost did hate him, except that he was so ridiculous. Then Dada and I came down here, and 500 soldiers had a terrific battle in the park, and I saw the moment when I could defend a spiral staircase with an inefficient sword. If there was a war, could diplomats volunteer?

VITA TO HAROLD   [Knole]

18 March 1912

Suddenly, I have decided to go to Italy. Telegrams are flying to people who might possibly take me. Of course I should love to throw a toothbrush into a bag, and just go, quite vaguely, without any plans

---

1. "Mar" was the Sackville word for "small," hence a child. It was the name by which her mother, and later Harold, called her.
2. Lady Sackville's shop.

or even a real destination. It is the Wanderlust. And then I want the
sun so badly, and to get away too, right away. Wouldn't you like to,
in green Archie, from one little town with red roofs perched on a hill
to another, and never minding the fleas, and making friends with the
dirty children, and taking them all for drives in green Archie? And if
it was not warm enough in the North, you would drive Archie onto
a railway truck and go away down to Sicily. Isn't that much more than
travelling luxuriously with wagons-lits, and couriers, and rooms kept
for one in the best hotels in all the big towns? Mother can't understand
why I would *rather* go without a maid.

V I T A   T O   H A R O L D   *St. Petersburg Hotel,*
                                                     Grosvenor Square,
March [1912]   *London W.*

Harold, I am *not* rich, and even if I was, it couldn't possibly jar.
It is quite easy. So don't worry.

It is a good thing that we can always talk about anything without
minding, quite brutally. I am glad we fell into that way from the first.
It could never have been otherwise, though.

V I T A   T O   H A R O L D   *[Knole]*

10 April 1912

I used to hate Eddy[1] when he was a baby and I wasn't much more,
because he would have Knole, and I was vaguely jealous. But now I
don't want it, and he will be an excellent person for it, and when he
is twenty-two we will marry him to someone revoltingly rich. He will
be too gentle to mind. He will have long hair, and wear very low

---

1. Edward Sackville-West (1901–65), the writer and musician, who succeeded his father as
5th Lord Sackville in 1962. He never married.

collars with a large bow, and probably a velvet coat. He will be a soul [intellectual].

Mr Vansittart was here for Easter—he plays tennis wonderfully, but otherwise I don't care much for him. Patrick Shaw-Stewart I like; he is *so* ugly, but if one dresses him (in imagination) in Louis XI clothes his ugliness does not matter. He has the gift of condensing all one's vaguest and most intricate ideas into six words. It is like a flash of lightning on a dark night. But I think his qualities probably stop there, and beyond that I don't know whether he is really nice—a horrid word, but it exactly fits what I mean, so I must use it. He is going to Dorothy Heneage's at Coker[2] next Sunday, and so am I. And to Taplow[3] the following week, so by the time I start for Italy I ought to have all my ideas thoroughly well expressed, classified, and pigeon-holed.

VITA TO HAROLD   *34 Hill Street*
                                                      [London W.1]
6 June 1912

My dear Harold,

This morning I came home from a ball at 4, and I slept two hours only, and I'm so tired, so I dined all alone here off a bit of dry cold beef and a banana, and nobody is here because the B.M.[4] went to Knole today, and then I came in and found a letter from you. My room (where I am) is no longer macabre and like a hearse; it is rich and full of glowing sombre colours, and the light is very soft, and I love it, and I expect everybody else will hate it because it is *outré,* but up to now no one has seen it and it is quite, quite mine. Also in some odd way you are sprawling on the sofa saying how far off August is, and how you are bored with Constantinople, and I am cross with you for interrupting me while I am writing letters, and at the same time I am

2. Coker Court in Somerset, where Vita and Harold spent the first night of their honeymoon.
3. Lady Desborough's house on the Thames.
4. Bonne Mama, the family name for Lady Sackville. 34 Hill Street was her new house in Mayfair.

telling you—aren't I?—that August isn't very far, and *I* don't mind half so much as you do, and that I do really, only I pretend not,—it is all rather involved and has no more *queue* or *tête* than a dream, all because I went to a 100-years-ago ball and stayed up till 4.

Archie [Clark-Kerr] was there, in a smock like a shepherd! and I said he reminded me of the *Et moi j'aime mes moutons* tune and he didn't like it. But it is so good for Archie to be laughed at. He introduced me to a friend of yours called [Edward] Keeling, and we talked about you and whether you were liking Constantinople. It was quite serious, because I was Arabella Diana Duchess of Dorset, and had three nodding white plumes, and ring-miniatures of John Frederick the Duke on my fingers. There were other dukes there too, live ones, or rather future ones, and we walked about the Albert Hall together,[5] and I could see *"How suitable!"* in people's eyes as we went by. And I am asked to plays and to dinner-parties every night, and we are put next to each other, and I wonder if he thinks it as funny as I do. And he came to Knole. Please don't mind. And yet please do, a little. I tell you because I would rather you knew, and you must take it as I take it, and see how funny it is.

Now I am sorry I told you, because even if Lady Lowther[6] had a daughter how I should hate her, and you will torment yourself when you needn't. I am sorry, Harold.

This is very primitive, and unsubtle for literary people like us.

How I *loathe* writing this sort of letter, I mean half and half, don't you? It would be almost better to write about the weather. When you come back we will make other arrangements—if they will let us. Because after all . . . Oh how frightfully I want you to come back! and yet you must go on being pleasant to Lady L. and I must talk to dukes, and write you letters about balls. I never minded restrictions[7] so much as I do tonight. And, by the way, I am observing them extra-ordinarily little. Are you angry with me for it? especially when the B.M. is away which makes it worse.

---

5. With Lord Granby, the future Duke of Rutland and heir to Belvoir Castle.
6. Wife of Sir Gerard Lowther, Harold's Ambassador in Constantinople. Lady Lowther, who was an American, had two daughters.
7. Lady Sackville's, on the nature of their correspondence.

Now listen, Harold. You are not to mouch, and you are to sail your boat briskly, and be hearty on it, and in little green Archie all glorious with new shiny paint. Also remember there was a time when you wrote to me, "I have a motor, may I bring it to Knole?" and that was even worse than waiting five weeks.

But I can't be really cheerful because I mind so dreadfully myself the very thing I am telling you not to mind.

Write to me often.

V I T A T O H A R O L D   *Knole*

21 June 1912

Will you not write to me once, a totally post-Hatfield letter? I want you to. I ought not to ask you, but I *am* asking. Write it when you are inclined.

You see, sometimes I mind the stiffness—no, not stiffness, but I can't find the word, and you will know—of our letters so much, and that would alleviate it.

Harold, do.

I'll never ask you but this once.

V I T A T O H A R O L D   *34 Hill Street*

4 July 1912

You asked me about rugs and yellow amber. I would love a rug. No, we will never make *des façons* about presents.

I have never given you anything. When is your birthday? Are you generous?

After all, I am not sorry not to know you better, it makes it even more fun your being a *terra incognita*. We will find each other out gradually. You will be disappointed.

There is no fun equal to being *quite* at the beginning of things. Is there?

VITA TO HAROLD   *Knole*

23 July 1912

I got a long letter from you. It was rather a startling letter. I am alone here for today so I can answer it. Shall I? Conscientiously?

You enlarged upon the disadvantages before you left England, and *then* I made very light of them, not only to you, but also to myself, and since you went I've thought them over, and I can't say they frighten me very much. So we can leave them out of the question. You see, 1) as for finding the life dull, I am never bored; 2) as for poverty we shouldn't be very poor, because the B.M. has been splendidly frank with me about that, and I know we shouldn't—rather the contrary; 3) and as for being forgotten in England, the people who matter don't forget, and those who don't, don't count. And though it would be silly to pretend I should like spending two or three years in Rio, I shouldn't mind it so very dreadfully—and anyway you wouldn't enjoy it any more than I should, and it would be just a boring thing, to be made the best of. To compensate for that, besides, there would be years in splendid places like Rome, where we should have an apartment in a palazzo, and have little parties for the people we must be civil to, and be a success. Because if I marry you, everything has got to be a success all through.

(You see I have abandoned maddening grammatical evasions quite as honestly as you did.)

But, Harold, though for months I've kept going almost entirely on plans—the delicious plans we used to write to each other—and though I have been wretched on each of the numerous and separate occasions when your leave has been delayed, and though there isn't 'anybody else' to compare with you—in spite of all that, I don't think we can marry this autumn. Don't be depressed by this; it doesn't mean anything awful, or that I am paving the way to worse! I am not. It just means this: that this is the first year I have lived at all (because last year doesn't count), and begun to make friends, and that if I let you take me away this year it will all end—after all, I am only twenty. I suppose it is selfish of me, because you are away, abroad, and not having what one calls a good time, and I am just beginning to, but let me be selfish for myself till next June, or even April, and I'll spend the rest of my life being unselfish for you. Besides, there really is another reason. The B.M. would simply *hate* it. I know you will think that if I wanted it sufficiently myself I should not stop to think about that, but you are wrong: she has been wonderfully good to us both, and we do owe her that.

Oh Harold, you must be so depressed and so disappointed by now, but do read my letter several times as I did yours, and you will see that it is quite sensible. But then sense is never attractive.

So when you come back in September let us be merely unspeakably happy, and not think of when you have to go away again. Someday there will be no more away.

And you will probably get quite tired enough of me then, in the no-more-away-days, and be only too glad to have escaped six months of it at the beginning!

Because you don't know me either, I'll give you a category too, and then if you are frightened you needn't come home at all. What you will mind most is my forgetfulness, which is phenomenal—I mean I go downstairs to do something and then absolutely forget on the way what I have come down for. This will not amuse you in the least after a week of it. You will ask me to send the motor for you at the Embassy, and I shall forget it. We shall have people to lunch, and I shall forget to tell the servants. It will drive you quite crazy. That is the worst, I think. Then I am just as untidy as you are, and disgracefully happy-go-lucky and on the everything-will-turn-out-all-right-if-you-don't-fuss-about-it system. This is because I am very lazy. I will come out riding with you, but I won't gallop down hills, or jump, and do anything like that because I am frightened—and you will get very impatient about it. To make up for this cowardice, I don't fuss about my health, and you must appreciate that as an inestimable blessing. Then I am very selfish, and it bores me to do things for other people; I like having things done for me. And of course this is a lamentable characteristic under the circumstances.

Those are the drawbacks, to which you must add unpunctuality, which irritates you even now. You will have to get over that by putting the clocks on.

I don't know so much about my virtues. I'm very good-tempered indeed, and that's about all. I'll never worry you when you are tired, or give digs about your friends. And I shall probably like the books you like—except that you are more *décadent* than me, and I'm essentially breezy!—and I'm quite intelligent about them, and about tombs by Mino da Fiesole [1429–84]. I think that is quite a good list of virtues, all rather important ones. Up to now, too, I never have rows with the people I live with—and I'm very logical and very reasonable, and very amenable if people do it nicely, not if they try to compel. You are like that too. I think we should both *amène* each other quite easily. And of course, as we have always known, we are quite ludicrously suitable.

By the way, I'm atrociously jealous. So are you, and we may quarrel over that, especially you with me. But you mustn't make fusses about people I speak to more than once because I will always tell you about it, and we can laugh at them together.

And about your career—I will always be ready to go to dinner parties if you want me to, even if I am tired (will you be nice to me if I am ill?) and look nice, and you won't be ashamed of me.

And *surtout*—such a *surtout*—we will be wonderfully good friends.

After writing all this, and making pictures which are between the lines somewhere, I am half sorry I decided to be so firm about the autumn, but I'm going to keep to it, because it is fairer all round, to me, to you, to the B.M., and in September you will try to persuade me, and I shall say I won't. But in spite of that we will be engaged, if you like, even though people don't know about it. Then, some time we will have the tremendous fun of telling people like Anne [Sackville-West] and [Edward] Keeling—who has taken to writing me long letters about nothing at all.

If London gossip reaches Constantinople you may hear that I am engaged to someone [Lord Lascelles][1]—a new person this time—as simply everyone in London has been busy congratulating me about it, but it isn't true, and I didn't think there was anything in it at all, until to my intense astonishment he asked me (yesterday) to marry him. He must be mad; he hardly knows me, and I've never taken the slightest trouble about him. He's rather nice, poor thing, and a *parti!!* Don't tell the B.M. I told you about this episode, though. *How* I wish you were

1. Viscount Lascelles was, with Lord Granby, Harold's main rival for Vita's hand. He was heir to the Earldom of Harewood and the splendid house in Yorkshire that went with it. In 1922 he married Princess Mary, only daughter of King George V.

coming home on August 4th—in less than a fortnight. It's cruel, and I used awful Italian swear-words about it, which doesn't seem to have helped much.

Do you hate me for having sent such an unsatisfactory answer to your letter, or do you understand?

Goodbye, Harold, bless you.

VITA TO HAROLD   *Knole*

23 July 1912

You really won't like me much after a week or two, you know. You will hate coming home and finding me in rags and looking like nothing on earth, and you will resent my keeping beasts, and disgusting mongrel dogs. But that will only be in places like Teheran. In Rome or any decent place I should wear gorgeous clothes and jewels, and not be humble and dirty—except when we go to the one little ramshackle place which is all our own, near the sea. Harold, do you realise how happy we might be? We should bathe before breakfast on a deserted beach in the sun, and breakfast (unsociably) in the loggia, and read our letters to each other, and you would smoke horrid pipes, and I would wear green corduroy. We would take green Archie to pieces for the fun of it. And we would have a garden, because it would be in a climate where everything grows, and masses and masses of flowers. And a rather dark, very cool house. And in the evening we should sit out in the loggia, and read, or merely do nothing.

HAROLD TO VITA   *British Embassy, Constantinople*

14 January 1913

Vita darling,

This is written with a fountain pen as Reggie Cooper[1] is using my writing table. And I write badly with a fountain pen.

But it is rather fun, as I am sitting in the window seat, and it went

---

1. Harold's oldest friend, from schooldays, and his colleague in the Embassy.

and snowed last night and all the roofs are silent, unlike here, and it reminds me of Russia before I knew you and before I cared for life in the way I now do.

I wanted to get a frank opinion out of you about Vienna and I got it.[2] It is, of course, just what I feel myself. Even the snobbish feeling that it would be such fun to show you in a European place— sort of, "Look at this person, she is MY WIFE"—seems less attractive than having coffee with an untidy mar on the roof.

Of course Vienna is the very worst place of all socially. I mean they are all *touf touf* [snobbish] and uneducated and exclusive—and they won't at all like us taking up with grubby artists. But then we can have our two lives—one *touf touf* Embassy and one just Vita and Harold, and then we will go away often in a motor and sleep in little inns among the pines.

Vita darling, I should be happy wherever I was with you—and it is so splendid that we will always look at places in the same way—I mean you will know just what I hate, and just why I hate it, and I will know just why you are bored—and we will always want to go away at the same time.

And then, Vita—and this is to be pondered over—we will keep each other up to the mark. I don't think, poor darling, you have any conception how dull diplomatic dinners are—especially if you don't play bridge—which by the way you don't play. (Also what about golf—lazy.)

I have read this letter again up to where I have got. I see I have gone round the central subject, which is that we've jolly well got to go to Vienna anyhow. Don't you agree? More from the ghastly selfishness of it as regards my people [Sir Arthur and Lady Nicolson] than from any feeling that I would hurt my career by not going.

Anyhow there is time. If only we could get married by June we could come out to Therapia[3] for three months. Which would be awful fun—except we would have to go to the hotel. Vita, it would be fun, you and I, wouldn't it, at Therapia?

I don't think my people will go to Vienna till November.

---

2. He had written that his father might be appointed Ambassador to Austria, and he might have to go, too. Vita was appalled by the idea. In the end, neither went.
3. The summer resort of the British Embassy on the European shore of the Bosphorus.

Oh Vita, I've got such a cold in my head and I talk so funny. That's why this letter's so dull

HGN[4]

VITA TO HAROLD   *Hill Hall, Epping*

30 January 1913

I am horrid about Vienna, I know, not only because I couldn't be an Eastern potentate there, but because the whole thing would be so stodgy. And of course I shall hate diplomacy! You are always saying so, and I suppose you are right. But I love you, little Harold, so what are we to do about it? Of course the castle by the sea, and the vague expeditions in Archie, and our solitude *à deux,* were and are glimpses of perfection and Paradise, but, oh Harold, the rest! . . . And after a few years, when we had got tired of Archie, and the solitude *à deux,* and of everything being a new toy, as we *must,* there will remain— what? Rio de Janeiro, boring old diplomats, no English friends, no B.M. _ _ _ _ _ _ _ _ _ _ _ _ (as they do in French novels).

Aren't I being depressing about it?

I am wrong—aren't I, Harold? and the truth is a rose-coloured story culminating in you and me making a State entry into Delhi on an elephant with a golden howdah, and you receiving deputations of Indian princes, and me watching, and thinking, "If it hadn't been for me, he wouldn't be here now", because *j'aurai été pour quelque chose,* shouldn't I?

Write and cheer me up, and don't tell me I shall hate diplomacy. (I shall though).

HAROLD TO VITA   *British Embassy, Constantinople*

30 January 1913

There may be something happening today. It is rather complicated. You see the whole question is like this. Europe sent a letter to the

---

4. He often signed himself by his initials only, even in his most intimate letters.

Turkish Government saying 'make peace'.[1] They thought about it a long time and were just writing back "yes", when the revolution occurred[2] and the answer was never sent. The new Government were thinking what answer *they* were to send—and then they told us that the answer was to be at the Austrian Embassy by 11.0 today.

So we were all sitting with our cyphers ready to telegraph it to London when news came that the note had left the Sublime Porte and then suddenly a man ran after it and stopped it just at the door of the Austrian Embassy—and took it back.

Does this interest you? Do you know what it means? It may mean anything—war, revolution or peace.

And then again news that Romania is mobilising.

How dead and dim and distant this must all seem to you, darling: only one day it will interest you as much as it does me.

And thank God I am so busy that I have little time to sit in armchairs and ponder over big-eyed mars [Vita]—or even to write to them.

V I T A　T O　H A R O L D　　　　　　　　　　　　　　　　　*Knole*

15 February [1913]

I got such a blowing-up from you this morning. I'm not *décadente,* you little wretch, and I *was* ill, and I *never* faint, so when I do, it matters (I'm not your grandmother, and I won't be compared to her), and if you don't like me you had better marry somebody else, and see how you like it, so there!

And you know I'm not 'cultured' (how dare you!), but essentially primitive; and not 1913, but 1470; and not 'modern'; and you know I am nicer than anybody else, and you love me more than anybody in the world,—you know you do. And you know Ozzie[3] knows

---

1. With Bulgaria, Serbia, and Greece, whose troops had captured Salonika and were approaching Constantinople.
2. On 23 January, when Enver Bey seized power and the Turkish army mutinied.
3. Oswald Dickinson, a lifelong bachelor and patron of the arts. He was more Harold's and Lady Sackville's friend than Vita's.

nothing about it at all, and if I don't "seem to care much about any of the others", you know why; and you know if I leave my beautiful Knole which I adore, and my B.M. whom I adore, and my Ghirlandaio room which I adore, and my books and my garden and my freedom which I adore—it is all for you, whom I don't care two straws about.

Now you dare to deny a word of all that.

I will sit on the arm of your chair and read your dispatches over your shoulder, and rumple your curls, which will make you cross. And I want to be there when you are ill, and go out though you begged me to stay with you, so that you would appreciate me more when I came in. And I want to give dinner-parties in *our* house, when we will be so bored with the people because we would rather be alone. And it will be such fun becoming familiar with each other's possessions, and you will come into my room and use my brushes with "VITA" on them.

All this will be fun.

PS. I'm *not* decadent!!! You wouldn't like me if I was. I shall revenge myself by not burning incense in *our* house when we have parties, and you'll see how you like the smell of Brussels sprouts.

HAROLD TO VITA   *British Embassy, Constantinople*

17 February 1913

I see that it would be nicer to go to Rome or Tangier or to stay here. I notice that Vienna combines everything which we will both of us most dislike.

But then I *do* feel a *duty* to go—I would think less of us if we didn't go—I would think it a lack of discipline—morally 'sloppy' if we got out of it. Besides I really must be the one who 'disposes' in these things.

I tell you this because I want you to understand that this is the basis of our life that is to be. I will be invariably weak about trifles—but about big things I am to have the upper hand.

I know that in the bottom of your heart you think, "Oh yes, it's very well for him to say that, but he doesn't know what I give up."

But I *do* know what you give up. I know that by marrying me you give up vast worldly things—but they don't matter. And then any girl by marriage gives up her girlhood—which is so much.

Of course this is common to all, but then the diplomacy thing in your case is worse. Because, Vita, you will be admired (especially at Vienna) in the wrong way. You will be admired in the way that people will be surprised to find you can't dance better.

And this (though a tiny thing) is illustrative of the general irritation which their attitude will evoke. Darling Vita.

So you see, I admit the utter weakness of my position. I see how utterly you will hate doing what I am asking you to do, and yet I ask it, because deep down I know you will give this up to me, and that you will yourself not let me run away from it when I want to.

And, Vita, pull yourself together, you vague person: pull up all the blinds in your mind—and think whether you want it.

Darling, be *sure* about it before you decide. And remember that whatever you do—if you never speak to me again—I shall know that you were right.

V I T A　T O　H A R O L D　　　　　　　　　　　　　　　*Knole*

24 February 1913

Violet Keppel and I gave a party. It was *the* success of the year. The Rubens lady, who is jealous of VK, was furious. Especially when Violet and I acted afterwards, and ended up in each other's arms. I disguise from the Rubens lady when Violet comes here.

H A R O L D　T O　V I T A　　　　　*British Embassy, Constantinople*

26 February 1913

No letter from you for ten days. I know you are not ill, because B.M., in her last letter, says, "V. will have told you all about our last party." I know no letters can have been lost as I have got regular ones from my family.

Oh Vita, this is so dreadful for me—being left without letters. I know, I mean I *hope,* you will be saying, "Silly boy—why does he get into a state about nothing?"

But *is* it nothing, Vita? You must see how I look on it. I know you have nothing to do—and I am busy all day and yet find time to write to you four times a week. Oh Vita! And I know that in a case like this there can be no question of indolence. You can't be too *lazy* to write to me. At least if you are too lazy it means that you don't care one fig. It can't mean anything else. You see I always come up against that granite wall.

And there are lots of little things which make me feel it also. Little absurd things which mean enormously. Things like your never telling me about things that interest me—no I *don't* mean that, because everything you write does interest me—but somehow when I get some of your letters I feel you have not thought of the many things I would like to hear of—of your room, of your clothes, of the people you see—yes even of *Rosencavalier.* [1]

Oh Vita! Vita! I am making you angry and all because I am wretched myself. Yes wretched—and so frightfully disappointed to come back here early and to wait for the post because I feel sure there *must, must* be a letter from you today. I thought you would have *at least* written to say you couldn't get the Fortnum stuff. How I should love it if you made me get *your* stuff.

And then there is another thing—*not* a little thing—which has hurt me awfully, and in a point where you might have known me frightfully sensitive. You have only been once to see my mother since I left. Of course I know that it is shy-making and very tiresome. But still you know (or you ought to have guessed) that nothing in the world would give me more pleasure than that.

Is this a foolish letter to write, Vita? But it is only because my eyes are stinging with disappointment and my heart is sore—sore, Vita— and you are so far away, and I don't know what's happening.

Oh Vita, they are playing in my sitting room. (I write this in my bedroom with your photograph there), and, Vita, they are playing, *"Il pleure dans mon coeur comme il pleut sur la ville"*—and I feel it so, and I look over the wet roofs, and Mikky [dog] is by the fire—and

---

1. Harold was virtually tone-deaf throughout his life.

No! No! No! I can't bear it, you out there laughing with strange people, people I don't know, people who may have a power over your mind—and sometimes, before dinner, you write me a letter while Rosamund is having her bath, and it is written so lightly and goes so far, and is so important when it gets there.

HAROLD TO VITA   *British Embassy, Constantinople*

3 March 1913

I went to the front on Saturday. I went dressed up as a doctor with a red crescent and a fez like this, and they were fighting just behind the field hospital  and the maxims [machine-guns] made a noise like a motor bicycle, and I got so nervous and the wounded came in, and there were heaps of them and they sobbed when they were moved, and when their coats were taken off they screamed. And there were three officers who ran away, and they hid in the launch that had brought me up. And everybody said the Bulgars would be in at any minute and that we would have to bolt. And in the garden there was a cherry tree in full blossom and under it two pails full of bits of soldiers that they had cut off.

You would have liked it all, being a callous mar with big eyes, who has special note-paper for red-cross things.

And I took 22 wounded back in the launch with me and it was awfully rough and they were so ill. And they asked me about Adrianople, and when I said it was captured, they said "as God wills," which is what is written on the bit of embroidery I gave you.

Oh Vita, I sat there in the upper room making a splint for one of the people who were groaning below, and the rain slashed against the rattling window and the cherry blossoms shimmered in the failing light, and still the rattle went on beyond the village over the hill. And I thought of you warm and secure somewhere, my Vita, secure and unsuffering, and myself callous comparatively about the people downstairs, and thinking of you while I made the splint. I was left alone in the dark with the noise of the waves and the outline of the officer at the wheel against the glow in the sky.

But it was capable of me to get out—as no foreigner has been, not even the military Attachés, since when they got to Chavalia, they said they would shoot foreigners at sight.

So who says I am not capable!!

VITA TO HAROLD   *Knole*

4 March [1913]

Harold, you wrote me a long tempestuous letter [26th February], and it upset me so, I didn't know how to answer it, though I wanted to sit down straight away and write you a letter which would have consoled you altogether. I am sorry, miserable that I have hurt you, and don't, *don't* say, "She doesn't care," because she does, only things are so difficult sometimes, and to understand it all, you must think yourself into the atmosphere in which I am living, in which I hear nothing but case, case, case,[1] and when is it coming on? and the months it will be before it is settled, and the B.M. showing me (so kindly, but so inexorably) the impossibility of contemplating anything yet for you and me—it is all drops on a stone, and I get hopeless about it, and try to put it out of my mind, and to take an interest in parties, and then I suppose I involuntarily write *agacée* letters to you, until you write to me like you have done now, which brings me to my senses. Harold—you don't know, and how am I to tell you? but you are ever-present to me, and if I am slack and bored, it is because you are not here, and if I am cross, it is for the same reason, and if people bore me, it is because I want to talk to you,—don't you see? And then sometimes (this is so silly and rather BS[2] and I hate you for making me tell you, but I suppose I must) sometimes I think you are really quite happy there with your Gerry [Wellesley] and your wars, and I am not by any means all-important, and so again I write you a beastly

---

1. The Scott "undue influence" case, which began on 24 June in the High Court, London.
2. "Backstairs"—Sackville jargon for common.

letter, or I don't write at all. It is this long delay and separation that upsets our apple-cart, and gets on our nerves. I do see it is worse for you, much worse.

Then about parties, I think it can't interest you to get a week-old list, but since it does interest you, you shall have it, and I am glad you wrote that letter because it clears up a lot.

Go out for a ride with the wind in your face, Harold, and don't be morbid, and imagine I care nothing for you.

(This is me trying to be bracing.)

Of course I love you—you make untidy parcels, and read yourself into despair over *décadent* French poets, and you want me badly; and to other people you are just clever and someone who will get on. They don't know how far (you and I do), and we are going to do it together, and they will say, "She has helped him tremendously." Because I shall have.

But not if you write me morbid letters.

I wish you were here.

HAROLD TO VITA   *British Embassy, Constantinople*

10 March [1913]

My dearest Vita,

Your letter has arrived—the answer to my beastly one of which I am so penitent, and you have heaped more coals than ever, and I am a perfect idiot—and you are quite right about its all being morbid, and my oughting to go out and ride, and have the Black Sea wind in my hair.

I will do it tomorrow and I will take your letter with me, and I will ride to the sea's edge, and let you blow into me, and afterwards I will ride home into the sunset. Which will be like something by your friend [John] Masefield.

And Vita, I will wait and wait and wait for you—and be patient unendingly—and unendingly will I resolve not to bother you again or to be morbid.

Because you are firm and splendid, Vita—and all should be right with my world. My world that has been rather tremulous of late.

How feeble to be tremulous, Vita, when there is a splendid mar
over there in England—with the rooks tumbled against the grey sky.
And here, in little funny corners, snowdrops are coming.

Thank you V. for your letter.

VITA TO HAROLD   *Hotel De Inglaterra, Seville*

17 April [1913]

This is the life for me[1]: gipsies, dancing, disreputable artists, bull-
fights. Oh Harold, I can't paint to you the state of mind I am in by
now, I feel I can *never* go back to that humdrum existence; I am a
different being. Last night there was dancing at the house of a French
artist; imagine the little patio, open to the sky, with the fountain
trickling, and the moonlight, and the gipsies in their coloured shawls;
I know them all intimately! and go to their houses in *such* a slum, with
a strange creature who has come to live here and has 'gone native', and
won't speak to English people, but accepts me as a kindred spirit,
irritated by the tourists in perpetual search after 'local colour', Mrs
Hunter meanwhile thinking I am sight-seeing in the cathedral. Then
I got a letter from you and it was so in tune with Seville, and we might
have two rooms here, Harold, with a roof, mightn't we?, and my
gipsies will come and dance for us while we smoke cigarettes. It is the
feria here now. We go to bull-fights, and I wear a black mantilla and
a high comb and carnations, and hang my orange *manton* over the edge
of the box, and shout "yolé! bravo toro!" You would laugh at me so,
and be awfully good for me, and say I was more Spanish than the
Spaniards, and I shouldn't care.

VITA TO HAROLD   *Grand Hotel de Russie, Rome*

10 May 1913

I am absolutely alone in Rome! Not even a maid, and this evening
I start for London quite alone. I'm so frightened, but I mean to see

---

1. Vita had gone on holiday to Spain with Mrs. Charles Hunter.

Rome today. Mrs Hunter left today. Shall I get into the wrong train and come to Constantinople by myself instead of London? Or go right away where no one would ever find me? To my Sevillian gipsies? It is the chance of a lifetime and no one would ever hear of me again, and it would be in the *Daily Mail.* [1]

HAROLD TO VITA   *British Embassy, Constantinople*

19 May 1913

Vita darling—darling Vita

I got a terrible letter from you today [2] and it has quite crushed me with apprehensions. You put the fierce part into French, half because you were a little ashamed of it and half because you felt it sounded deadly earnest. But then it was so steely to use French.

Vita, I can't answer coherently about it. I have been trying to diminish the effect of it to myself. I have been explaining that you began the letter quite lazily in the garden—and quite thoughtlessly you put that in the end because you were alone, and had come back to England [from Spain] and found your house secure, welcoming and comfortable, and my letters in the bustle of arrival had seemed flat and impersonal, and you had read them in the wrong order, and while people were asking you questions, and they had left no after-glow— and so you ended your letter almost brutally, in an impulse of irritation and in the reaction to the home-coming excitement and the sort of feeling, "Well there is going to be nothing exciting now till Harold comes home, and will that be exciting? I wonder, now."

Oh Vita Vita, but did you think that those easy cruel little French sentences would go 1,500 miles—and knock the sun out of my days and make even the clock tick differently.

Oh Vita, if I could talk to you now I might do something—but what can a letter do if I have lost touch with you? I opened it in my

---

1. Harold replied: "I don't like one bit that you're going about alone like that. When you are my wife, I shall not allow you to go without Emily [her maid] to look after you."
2. It has not survived. Perhaps Harold destroyed it in his anguish. But obviously she was hinting that their semi-engagement should be ended.

room and Reggie Cooper came in and saw something was the matter, but he has no idea what is the matter, or how hard and terrible a thing it may be, and how vague and uncombatable.

And I, these last days, have been thinking, thinking, thinking, thinking about how it could be hurried up. And I was going to make a huge row about it and we were going to get married hurriedly—and quietly—and you were coming off to little autumn tours with me in Archie. And now it will be three days before I can get a letter from you and to know whether it was a mood.

I feel that you may be sounding the ground for worse news in your next letter.

Vita, surely you could not treat me like that. I feel I should kill you. And all those bright plan-edifices to be pulled down and shoved away by a few words at the end of a letter—like a Christmas tree the day after.

Vita, is it because I am flippant about us both—and don't talk heroics—that you think I won't mind? Why, it would alter the whole substance of things. You have worked in and out of the bits of me, and it would be such a fearful tangle to undo and it would hurt so awfully. (There I am using slang about vital things—which is a silly trick—but it doesn't make the things less vital.) And Vita, I was coming back so soon now—only six weeks—and I had planned it all out so. Oh Vita really really I get so angry—so repugnant about it all.

I suppose I felt too sure of you and this doubt shows me how thin the ice is. But at least, Vita, let me have some slight consolation for the moment—and wait till you see me before being really cruel.

And I love *you* so far more than ever before—the longing after you is like a stretched cord within me.

Of course it's all this damned artistic temperament that has been the muddle for both of us; the inveterate habit of seeing both sides.

And Vita, Vita, *why* on earth if the [Scott] case is won should we not get married at once? I always counted on that in my silly ass way. And now I have nothing to count on. Except that you can't have meant it, Vita; you can't have meant to write it to me out here: you would have kept it till I got home.

H.

VITA TO HAROLD   *Knole*

20 May [1913]

Mea culpa! mea maxima culpa! I come to you in sack-cloth and
ashes, and humble myself to the dust at your feet, a bad naughty mar
who hardly dares hope to be forgiven. Did you think, Harold, that
you had at last got the much discussed terrible letter, or at least a
warning? No, what you really got was just an ill-tempered storm from
a wanderer who felt caged again after weeks of liberty, and was cross
in consequence, and rebellious of iron bars—and, you poor, rash,
ill-advised Harold, that is what you so lightly contemplate undertaking
for life, something you know nothing about, which is liable to give
you these frights . . . but who would at least make up for it afterwards,
as you might see if you were here now. But how much happier and
more comfortable you would be with something more in the nature
of the Rubens lady [Rosamund], not the Rubens lady herself, *mais
enfin dans ce genre-là,* very gentle and dependent and clinging.

Oh Harold darling, I *am* sorry, I didn't mean to upset you, or
being strictly truthful I suppose I did at the time, but I don't now; the
only real true thing was that I do frightfully want you back. It is too
awful your always being away, and eight months is a lifetime, and I
don't know what I shall do if it has to happen again. I did write to
you the very next day, but I didn't dare send it, so I tore it up and
waited to see what would happen. Now your telegram has happened,
and I answered it, and by now as I write you must have got mine,
which is a comfort.[1] Also I got a letter from you so pleased to come
back, and in it you said you wouldn't let me travel alone (I shall,
though!), and you made me feel a beast. Which I am. Harold, darling,
I do want you to forgive me, you never will, and you will say I am
capricious and despicable, and no more reasonable than Gwen [Har-
old's young sister], for all I am twenty-one. I *wish* I had never sent
that letter, I do. Why do I do these mad things? and then I am sorry
afterwards. If only this could get to you quickly, quickly, but it will
take four days and all that time you will have only a miserable
telegram, and while you are playing golf you will remember there is

---

1. Vita's telegram, in reply to his which asked her if he was to take her letter seriously, read
   (in French), "No. Forgive me. Don't believe a word of it."

something wrong, without quite knowing what it is. But there *isn't* anything wrong, it is all all right, and soon you will come back to me, in the summer, and we will play in the garden and make the best of our two months. Write to me, and say I am a ridiculous mar, but that you aren't angry with me. Only before that I suppose I shall get an upset letter from you,—and then I shall beat my head against the wall.

Tu me pardonnes?

VITA TO HAROLD

29 May [1913]

34 Hill Street
Berkeley Square, W.

Today I went to such a *touf-touf* lunch at the Ritz. There were Rodin,[1] and Sargent,[2] and Mrs [Nancy] Astor, and others, and Lord Crewe,[3] whom I sat by. I love that sort of party, it is such a relief after the little silly pink and whites one sits by at dinner-parties for balls, who only ask one if one has been here, and is going there. After two days I am sick of it, except a very fine ball at Sunderland House, *un bal un peu propre*, not one of those scrimmages at the Ritz, but powdered footmen announcing duchesses. *N'est ce pas dégoutant d'être snob à ce point-là?* But I *do* like fit things, I do, I do, I do, I can't help it, and if I had the chance I would *faire les choses richement bien.* You know I would, and we will—someday. Then I went to an exceedingly amusing arty party at the Laverys,[4] given for Rodin, where I sat by a pianist called Mark Hambourg[5] who would talk to me about Bach— to *me! c'était bien trouvé.* And little Edward Keeling goes to balls, and I see him hovering shyly in corners. Next week there is an Albert Hall ball (one of the entertainments you say I shall miss in Vienna), where I am in the Louis XIV court as La Grande Mademoiselle; such good clothes, orange velvet and black, a riding dress with high boots and

1. Auguste Rodin (1840–1917), the French sculptor, who had fallen in love with Lady Sackville, and done several busts of her.
2. John Singer Sargent (1856–1925) had painted Lady Sackville's portrait, but she so much disliked it that he drew another in charcoal, which she thought sufficiently flattering. It is now at Sissinghurst.
3. 1st Marquess of Crewe, at that time Secretary of State for India.
4. (Sir) John Lavery, the fashionable painter.
5. Mark Hambourg, the pianist and composer. Vita, like Harold, was quite unmusical.

a *cravache* [riding-whip], and if you look in the illustrated papers you will find me probably.

Tonight there is a dinner of 70 at the Keppels to which I am going, so I am being conscientious about my season—my last? And how I hate it!

Harold, I have an awful feeling that this engagement of ours has so far brought you more worry than pleasure. Don't blame me entirely, but the exceptional circumstances. (Me too a little).

H A R O L D   T O   V I T A   *53 Cadogan Gardens, S.W.*[1]

28 July 1913

My family are in a perfect glow of enthusiasm about Knole, its owners, inhabitants and hospitality. I am glad they were so pleased. Father volunteered a statement that when you were in the room he could not look at anyone else. And I think he meant it, as it is a decorative Vita, with heavy eyes and hair as I said before.

But darling, I do feel so funny inside about you—oh my darling darling Vita who will be so absolutely mine one day—mine in a way that possession has nothing to do with—and which will be a sort of fire-fusion, darling—and there are such wonderful, terrifying abysmal things that will happen in our amazing marriage. I mean darling, that I feel giddy at the thought of you as my wife—giddy in a wider sense than the odd whirl-feeling that comes over one on your triangular piled sofa—oh my darling, you don't know how passionate I am—and how it frightens me—and how glad I am of it.

V I T A   T O   H A R O L D   *Knole*

28 July 1913

I think we are past mere words now, and I can only write to you about chairs and presents, but all the while my room is full of your

---

1. Harold returned from Constantinople on 3 July 1913 in time to hear Vita give her evidence in the Scott case, which the Sackvilles won easily. He stayed with his parents in London until his wedding in October.

presence as though you were smiling at me across my judge's desk,[1] and every possible receptacle is full of your nasty cigarette ends. Goodnight, my poor boy, so hating Buxton.[2] It *is* a shame, but rather good for us to have a chance of thoroughly missing each other, which we shan't have after this for many years.

HAROLD TO VITA   *Palace Hotel, Buxton, Derbyshire*

13 August 1913

Darling, it is so dull writing to you when I might be talking and looking at you. Vita, there are moments when the whole wind-swept sky seems to stagger at my happiness and at my hopes. No, it wasn't the same with poor dear Eileen.[3] It was less 'cosmic'. I fear it was less inspiring. Oh my darling, how I ache for that poor girl and the abominable way I behaved. I feel it more remorsefully now than I have ever felt it.

VITA TO HAROLD   *Hotel Meurice, Paris*

Wednesday [3 September 1913]

I have been spending the afternoon at Rodin's atelier. B.M., having worn herself out over sheets for us, and bath-mats for us to get out on from the bath which won't exist, was too tired to go, and I went alone (terrified) and bearded Rodin, by invitation, of course, in his nice messy atelier which used to be a convent, and which is now very dilapidated and where he is supremely happy. I was shown into his room, and waited there a few minutes—do you know how suggestive a person's room can be, before they come? It was rather dark,

---

1. The Italian desk given to Vita by her mother on her twenty-first birthday. It is now at Sissinghurst.
2. In Derbyshire, where Harold was staying with his parents.
3. Lady Eileen Wellesley, a daughter of the 4th Duke of Wellington, and sister of Harold's close friend, Gerald Wellesley (7th Duke). Harold had been unofficially engaged to her when he met Vita. Later she married Cuthbert Orde, the painter.

and there were huge roughly-hewn lumps of marble and a chisel left on a chair where he had put it down, and nothing else, and the suggestiveness of it grew on me more and more as I waited, and then he came in, very gentle and vague, and rather a commonplace little French bourgeois with long boots and the Légion d'Honneur in his buttonhole—rather an unreal little fat man, like a skit on the Académiciens in a funny paper, and the whole thing was a reaction and a come-down from the massive white marbles all round. But not when he talks about them, and points out lines to one with a real sculptor's sweep of his thumb, and he draws his finger lovingly across the marble brow of Mozart, and he and Mozart seem to smile at each other.

He gave me a bronze, signed, a statuette of a man, *une étude,* as he calls it. He has some magnificent things there at his studio. He has two people flying, which is supposed to be *l'aviation.* I admit that it sounds dreadful, but in reality it is beautiful, and rather the same idea as the Florence Mercury (that sounds like a newspaper, but I mean the Giambologna). And the head of Mozart, which is half strength and half-reverie, perfectly marvellous, and then two great clasped hands emerging out of a block of marble, and he says, *"Voyez les doigts entrelacés."*

HAROLD TO VITA   *Foreign Office*

19 September 1913

My dearest you know you have no idea how fond I am of you—because when things are really serious with me I become reserved about them. And I feel so dreadfully that you do not care nearly as much for me. There are such heaps of signs that you don't—your letting me go away so easily, and your being cross with me about getting my hair cut.

Darling, I know these things are absurd, and I don't mind really, as all I want is for you to let me adore you: and then, when we are married, perhaps you will get to care for me too. I mean really care—not just like. Except I know you care more than just like already, but it is not that absolute abandonment of self which I feel.

Darling, it was so nice when I was tired yesterday and you let me put my head on your shoulder.

Is this a depressed letter? But I am depressed.[1]

1. They were married, in the chapel at Knole, on 1 October 1913.

They spent their honeymoon traveling through Italy and Egypt (where they stayed with Lord Kitchener) and thence to Constantinople, where Harold resumed his duties as third secretary at the Embassy. They had their own house at Cospoli, overlooking the Golden Horn, and Vita made her first garden there. In June 1914 they returned to England, and their first son, Benedict (Ben), was born at Knole two days after the outbreak of World War I.

In 1915 they bought Long Barn, a tumbled-down fourteenth-century cottage near Knole, which they repaired and extended, and this was their country home till 1932, when they moved permanently to Sissinghurst. In London they lived at 182 Ebury Street, where their third son, Nigel (a second son was born dead in November 1915), was born on 19 January 1917. Harold was exempted from military service during the war by his essential work in the Foreign Office. Vita was beginning to write poetry and novels.

VITA TO HAROLD   *Knole*

9 July 1914

My darling Harold,

I am writing this in case I should die when Mikki III[1] is born instead of encumbering my will with small details. I know that you will carry out everything I want, and that no one will try to interfere with you so doing.

---

1. Mikki I and II were Harold's dogs. Mikki III turned out to be Benedict (Ben), born at Knole on 6 August 1914.

By my will I leave you everything of which I die possessed: jewels, furniture, pictures, books, *everything*. I want you to distribute certain things as follows:

If our baby is a girl, and lives, you must keep for her until you esteem her old enough to appreciate them:

1) my emerald chain
2) my string of pearls
3) my rope tiara,

and all my other jewels with the exceptions I will make below.

My other tiara, the one with the leaf pattern in emeralds and diamonds, is to go to Knole and be made an heirloom.

Give my diamond crystal watch, the one Sevenoaks gave me, to Rosamund [Grosvenor], also the diamond and crystal hat-pin, and any two of my rings that she may like to choose, except my engagement ring, which I should like you, Harold, to keep for yourself. If there is any other small thing that Rosamund particularly wants, give it to her, darling; you will have so much left for yourself.

Give Irene Pirie[2] some small jewel of mine; you can choose it.

Give Muriel Kerr-Clark my diamond wrist-watch on a black ribbon; and I should like you to send some small jewel to each of the following, and say it was at my request: Dorothy Heneage, Olive Rubens,[3] Lady Connie [Constance] Hatch, Aunt Maude, Aunt Cecilie, Aunt Mary, [Aunt] Eva, Anne Stanley, your mother, Emily [maid].

Give Gwen [Harold's sister] the seven big diamonds, the emerald ornament your mother gave me as a wedding-present, and one or two of my rings.

Will you keep my red amber [necklace] for yourself? and only let your daughter wear it if you would like her to, and if she is like me.

Now if the baby is a boy, you must dispose of the surplus jewels as you think best. Keep them, if you like, for your daughter if you marry again and have one. I should like her to have them. Or

---

2. Born Irene Hogarth, a childhood friend, whom Vita always called by the Italianized version of her first name, Pace.
3. Mrs. Walter Rubens, the singer, an intimate friend of Lord Sackville.

give them to Mikki III for his wife when he marries, if he does so with your approval and if you are convinced they love each other as we do.

Give Dada [Lord Sackville] a piece of furniture; perhaps he would like the big writing-table in my sitting room; he can use it without its platform.

B.M. would not care for any of my things, except the copies of Miss Linley, the Duke of Dorset, the Duchess his wife, and the three children.[4] Give her those. And any very personal thing she would like.

Everything at Constantinople goes to you. Please never get rid of the Kuba you gave me, or of Barbara [see note, p. 19]. I should like you to have Barbara always in your own room; she knew us both so well from the very beginning. Keep Mikki I [dog] with you, *please*. If you marry again, which I expect you will, and hope you will to save you from being lonely, don't be just the same with her as you were with me; give her a place of her own, but don't let her take mine exactly. I am not jealous of her, but I should like there to be a difference somewhere, and don't teach her our [family] expressions.

Darling, it is so lovely in the garden, and I hope I shan't die; I want years and years more with you as my play-fellow. I am not morbid, but I don't want to die a bit, and somehow today it seems impossible that I should. I love you so, my own darling husband; we are so mar, and we have such fun together always, I refuse to believe that it can be cut off.

All the same, in case it is, will you take care of all my manuscripts and ask Dada to have them put away in the muniment room at Knole, except the poems I wanted to publish; please publish these for me.[5] Rosamund has two books of mine which you must put in the muniment room too, and Violet Keppel has another.

Give Violet Keppel my small sapphire and diamond ring.

I can't think of anybody else just now, but if I have left anyone out, please supplement it.

---

4. All pictures at Knole. Miss Linley (by Gainsborough) and The Three Children (by Hoppner) were sold to American collections to raise duties on the deaths of the 3rd and 4th Lord Sackvilles.

5. These poems were published by Vita herself in *Constantinople* (1915) and *Poems of West and East* (1917).

Darling, I suppose I must say goodbye, because if ever this letter comes to you it will be after a bigger goodbye than we have ever said. Anyhow we shall have had nearly a year of absolutely unmarred perfect happiness together, and you know I loved you as completely as one person has ever loved another. There hasn't been a single cloud the whole time, and at least you will never have the torment of feeling that we might have made more of each other while we had each other because that would not have been possible. If I could have these months over again I would not alter a day of them—would you? I don't think many people could say as much.

You will never know how I have loved you, Harold.

Mar

God bless you, God bless you, my darling.

HAROLD TO VITA   *Foreign Office*

15 August 1914

I am afraid I won't be able to come down tonight—and it gives me a sink which even the consciousness of virtue and efficiency won't elate. Darling Mar, you would laugh if you could feel how depressed I get when I am not going to see my own darling. No one else in the whole world matters a halfpenny compared to you my angel, and it is only near you that I feel happy and at peace. When I have to go away I feel sore and sensitive as if the whole world has T.I.[1]—and I long to get back to my little black head. I don't know what it is, I never felt helpless before when I was alone—but now when I am without you I feel I can't cope with anything.

Oh my angel, I long for this most un-through-leaves[2] period to be over, and to get my own darling to myself again.

Give a hug from me to that odd little funny [Benedict] which happened the other day.

1. Thin Ice—a Sackville expression for an awkward or delicate situation.
2. Another Sackville expression, meaning difficult, unpleasant.

HAROLD TO VITA

11 September 1914

53 Cadogan Gardens,
London S.W.

My own darling Mar,

I have been blaming myself all day about my attitude to B.M.[1] It is a tremendous tug-of-war within me and I don't know which side is the stronger.

You see, darling, on the one hand everything in me cries out in loathing of B.M.—of her vain empty insincere nature—and I get hot with shame to think that I have allowed myself to pander to her vanity, to adulate her emptiness and to abet her insincerity.

And on the other hand I think of that soft gentle little head [Vita's], and I blame myself for even dreaming for one instant that anything you could love could be really vile, and I feel guilty that I have allowed my self-control to get cracks in it out of which all this jar and jangle has escaped into our sun-lit world.

And then again I feel, with you, my own gentlest, that this is a terrible thing to have happened, and that now at last has arisen something which comes between us—a thing about which you and I feel differently: on the one side your clean gentle love for B.M., and on the other my hatred for the vain egoist who has humiliated me.

And this can't go on, my dear one. We must make a treaty about it—a treaty of alliance not against B.M. and not in favour of B.M., but just a treaty of defence against the subtle difference and even discord that B.M.'s destructive personality might in the end intrude between us—between *us* my darling who love each other so passionately. Why the mere fact that she is the only thing on earth which could cause a cloud on our blue sky makes me hate her with a yet intenser loathing.

Darling, you must see that it will take me years to get over the wounds that B.M. has dealt to my pride, and I fear that never, never can I hope to form one of her sycophants. Without that ultimate

---

1. Lady Sackville had been insisting that Benedict be given the additional name Lionel, to which his parents agreed under protest. She had also abused Harold's parents, and he lost his temper, then apologized.

humbling of myself I fear that between her and me there can be no peace.

Little spirit of gentleness and love, don't think I am being a hard egoist about it: but really, darling, when I look down the vista of humiliation which my future co-operation with B.M. would entail, I realise quite calmly that I would emerge from each defeat with less self respect, and that our upper-air love for each other would get weighted with shame till it sank into the foetid atmosphere where she reigns supreme.

Darling, you are of finer stuff than I am and can afford to descend into these *bas fonds* as an administering angel. But I have not the strength of character.

And meanwhile our youth and peace are being given blows like the blows of a vulture's beak.

Oh my love I am not angry tonight, only smarting under the degrading letter[2] I wrote to her this morning.

Dear Mar, you know you used to say you would mind so fearfully if I and B.M. fell out—and darling, I do feel such a beast. In all the turmoils I go through, I get back to hearing my conscience say, "the one difficult thing you could have done for her you have failed to do."

Oh my love, my love!

Harold

VITA TO HAROLD   *Long Barn, Weald, Sevenoaks*

25 June [1915]

Somewhere I hear Detto [Ben] whimpering in his pram because he is bored, and you are in London, and it is all very workaday and commonplace, I suppose, to anyone else's eyes. One marries and has a mar, and settles down and you daily-bread. Only to you and me, darling, it does not mean that, because there is a great warm enveloping radiance, and Detto stands for wonderful things ("What does Mikki

---

2. Agreeing to the name Lionel. But Benedict never used it, and was known throughout his life as Ben only.

say?") and because every evening when you come back our minds and our hands rush together and merge and are happy to be one again instead of two, and everything which is dear and intimate to us is mutually so, and your life is mine, and mine is yours. Darling, please don't think I am sentimental, because I am not. I don't love you morbidly, but strongly, and tenderly, and passionately, and every way. It is all made up out of different sorts of love, and the result is something very companionable really, only there is something as well which makes me want to tell you about it.

[November 1915]

Harold, I am sad, I have been thinking of that little white velvet coffin with that little still thing inside.[1] He was going to give you a birthday present next Sunday [21 November]. Oh darling, I feel it is too cruel at times. I can't help minding, and I always shall; I mind more when I see Detsey [Ben], how sweet and sturdy he is, and the other would have been just the same. It isn't so much that I grudge all the long time or the beastly end, as everybody thinks. I mind his being dead because he is a person. Darling I do mind so: I can't be really happy. I love you and I know you love me and nothing can alter that except to make it more, but I do mind this and it clouds everything and I can't be happy. It is silly to mind so much. Detsey makes it worse as well as better. I can't bear to hear of people with two children.

Oh Harold darling, why did he die?

Why, why, why did he? Oh Harold, I wish you were here—I am meant to be asleep. I haven't got any more paper.[2] I try and stave it off not to think about it, and when I am alone it rushes out at me. I am frightened of being alone now. Darling, it isn't because I am ill, because I am not ill now any more; it is real. Harold, I want you so badly, I wish I could go to sleep.

---

1. Vita's second son was stillborn on 3 November.
2. She continued on the back of a map of St. Paul's journeys, torn from her Bible.

HAROLD TO VITA   *Foreign Office*

22 May 1916

My own dearest little one,

Dear heart, I do hate to feel that at the end of my beastly bustled days here, I don't get into that soft gentle haven—when I am alone with you, my gob, and when nothing outside fusses or worries or telephones.

Dearest, how happy we two are, when one gets outside ourselves, and think of our life and our two happy homes (Ebury Street[1] rather stern and prim and quiet, and the cottage [Long Barn] all untidy and tinkly), and of our baby, and the things we do together and like together, and all the many many things we will do and will like together in the future when this beastly war is over, and all Europe becomes a playground for the Mars to spend money in.

Darling, there are no clouds, are there? my sweetest, and when and if they rise, I feel we will just go indoors a bit, and sit together in front of the fire and wait till it clears up. Sweetest, it is such a deep strong river our love, isn't it? and there are great meadows on each side of it, and cows, and babies, and guinea pigs and newts.

Dearest, I am oh so busy—and I write now as there may be a rush at the end.

Ruffle that little head for his daddy.

Goodbye my darling.

                                                        H.

HAROLD TO VITA   *Royal Automobile Club, London*

24 December 1916

You don't know how I worship you, but I can't show you when you are there and it sounds sentimental, but when you are away from me I yearn for you with every fibre in my body, and with every beat

---

1. 182 Ebury Street, the house which Lutyens had remodeled for Lady Sackville in Pimlico, London.

of my heart, and with every pulsation of my brain. Darling, you are all in all to me, and if you ceased to love me the whole sun of life would be darkened, and all my joy in life would become a mass of leaden despair. Little Vita, you are mine, mine, mine and you have been mine for three years, and you will be mine as long as life remains for either of us—and even after death.

V I T A   T O   H A R O L D   *[Long Barn]*

[February 1917]

Come up and peep in at my door, and if I am asleep kiss me and creep away like a little mouse; and if I am not asleep, kiss me all the same, and then stay with me.

I shall not be asleep, and anyway you are more precious than sleep.

Darling, how undull love can be, even though it is married and has a little boy, two little boys, of its own.[1] I lie and wait for you with as much thrill as though you had never told me you loved me till yesterday, and had never kissed me, and I thought perhaps you might today, and half hoped you would, half hoped you wouldn't.

And I know you will.

H A R O L D   T O   V I T A   *Foreign Office*

22 August 1917

A busy day again—but I rather like it. George Clerk[2] is such an angel to work with: so appreciative and encouraging and stimulating. He never snubs one for being uppish, and oh dear, I was so uppish today: I suggested peace with Austria against everybody's views, and instead of just turning it down, he sends for me to discuss it all, and

---

1. Nigel had been born in Ebury Street on 19 January 1917.
2. Sir George Clerk (1874–1951) had been first secretary at the Embassy in Constantinople, where Harold had got to know him well. In 1914 he was appointed head of the new War Department of the Foreign Office.

I know how busy he is and how easy it would be for him just to put, "I think the moment inopportune." I don't care what Hardinge or Balfour say now.[3]

VITA TO HAROLD   *Long Barn*

August 1917

This is only to say how I miss you—it is all black when I think I am not going to see you. I love you, and you are absolutely the only thing that counts in the world. You are the vessel which contains the wine of life. My darling, I do appreciate you, and your lovely nature and eyelashes.

HAROLD TO VITA   *Foreign Office*

19 October 1917

I was at a loose end last night, so I telephoned to Macned[4] thinking he was a widower too, but oh dear, oh dear, he wasn't, so he had to ask me to Bedford Square, and I am sure it led to a row with Emmie.[5] Anyhow I went—and a terrible Theosophist friend was there, and poor Macned was such a darling. Emmie is a devil. She nags and jeers and sniffs and sighs at Macned as if he was a naughty schoolgirl, and the poor man is snubbed before that little swine of a Theosophist, who is not worthy to tie his bootlaces. There were only a few rissoles, and the rest, veg. Poor, poor Macned. She *is* a gloom. I do understand why

3. Lord Hardinge, the ex-Viceroy, had succeeded Harold's father in 1916 as permanent undersecretary at the Foreign Office. Arthur Balfour had been Foreign Secretary since December 1916.
4. Lady Sackville's name for Sir Edwin Lutyens, the architect, whose intimate friend she had become.
5. Lutyens married Lady Emily Lytton, who in 1907 fell under the influence of Mrs. Annie Besant, President of the Theosophical Society, with which he had little sympathy. He consoled himself with the constant company of Lady Sackville, but remained attached to his wife until his death in 1944.

B.M. cheers him up. Really, for once, there is a great deal in what B.M. says.

I love you.

I will write again.

I love you very much.

Kiss my two babies.

HAROLD TO VITA   *Foreign Office*

7 November 1917

Vita my dearest,

I wrote this afternoon and this is just another.

I love you.

You were such an angel in the little *too-too* [car], and you nearly ran over a man in St James' Street—and you upset a cart.

But I can't laugh over it all. I am so flight [frightened] about it.[1] It will be such an awful business if the [doctor's] report is not satisfactory. I simply *dread* it. Darling if you hated me today, how much will you hate me if it really does come? I haven't the courage to face it all.

Darling, I shall be so wretched about it if it goes wrong. I shall know what you will suffer and it will be my fault, my fault:—and that eats into my brain like some burning acid.

It is too horrible. Darling, I can't believe that our love and happiness would not survive even such a disaster.

Dear one—let's face it together and bravely.

All my whole love to you Vita—all my whole soul, my darling. Nothing in this whole earth counts for me but you.

Darling Vita

Hadji[2]

---

1. Staying with Vita at a smart weekend at Knebworth House, Hertfordshire, Lord Lytton's house, Harold had contracted a venereal infection from another male guest. He confessed it to Vita, and saw a doctor. See Victoria Glendinning's *Vita,* pp. 86–7.
2. Hadji ("pilgrim") had been Harold's father's pet name for him, and Vita adopted it for the rest of her life. To him she was usually "Mar," her mother's name for her.

19 *18–20 were the years of Vita's passionate love affair with Violet Trefusis, which nearly wrecked her marriage, but in a strange way stabilized it, because having jointly escaped this near disaster, Vita and Harold relied absolutely on the other's total support and love.*

The story has several times been retold in books about Vita, Harold, and Violet, and was dramatized for a BBC television serial in 1990. Only its outline needs to be repeated here.

Vita and Violet Keppel had been friends since childhood, and they became lovers in April 1918, first at Long Barn and then during an extended holiday at Polperro, Cornwall. Their affair soon became a mutual infatuation. They spent months together in Monte Carlo while Harold was in Paris wrestling with the complications of the Peace Treaty, and in spite of all his efforts to reclaim her, and Violet's marriage to Denys Trefusis in June 1919, the two women eloped in February 1920, intending to abandon their families and spend the rest of their lives together. Their husbands caught up with them at Amiens and persuaded them to separate. In July of that year Vita, now repentant, wrote the whole story, which in 1973 was published with a commentary by her son Nigel under the title Portrait of a Marriage.

HAROLD TO VITA   *Foreign Office*

23 April 1918

It was rather lucky that I stayed up tonight, as I have been made to write a Memo for the War Cabinet about Holland—of which I

know nothing, and I am wretched about it, and overwhelmed. Anyhow these things all straighten themselves out when one fights them.
I get Saturday off and we will have a nice holiday together and get
ourselves to each other.[1]

HAROLD TO VITA   *St James' Club, Piccadilly, W.1*

28 April 1918

My little girl,
        You can't think what London is like on a Sunday. Have you ever
been there? One's foot echoes on the pavements, and here, in the Club,
stretch fearful forms of fearful men in sleep.
        All this is not very cheery for a young husband who has just been
deserted by his wife, and whose two infant sons are marooned in some
distant village in charge of a hard featured stranger.

> Can the mother's tender care
> Cease towards the child she bore?
> Yes, she *may* forgetful be . . .[2]

Darling, you will get down there [Cornwall] and the bed will be
hard and the sheets will be coarse and the sea will come in at your
window full of huns and botolitis and submarines.
        I lunched at home. I dine at home tomorrow. They are both [his
parents] coming down for the *day* on Sunday! Thank God they don't
want to sleep.
        I shall dine here alone tonight and there will be the same fearful
men still asleep.
        Oh absence! le pire de tous les maux.[3]
        But I forgive you and hope you will be very very happy with your
new companion.

---

1. He did not know that Vita and Violet were alone at Long Barn, and had decided to go
   to Cornwall together.
2. William Cowper, *Olney Hymns 18.*
3. Paul Verlaine, 1885.

"TATLER. MAY 2 1918.

"Shrimping has always been a favourite pastime with me"

"and then I always do my own cooking."

Harold imagines Violet Keppel in Cornwall.

HAROLD TO VITA   *Foreign Office*

28 April 1918

Oh darling—*how* am I to get through these heavy black days in front of me? Poor Hadji! He does so hate being without his little one, and he feels no spirit left in him to do anything but mill and mope.

So if you see that the "body of an unknown man—stout and middle-aged[1] with plentiful curly hair and a snub nose" has been picked up at Wapping Stairs, you will know it's me and you can stay at Polperro a few days more.

Dearest—I do hope it is fine and warm—and that the blister gets all right—and that you are happy. That's all I want.

Anyhow it may make you like sea and moorland, and that will be something gained.

I adore you,
    and I miss you so.

HAROLD TO VITA   *Foreign Office*

2 May 1918

I hate being a bachelor—and it is most unwise from your point of view, as I get so miz [miserable], that I go and play poker with pretty ladies and then I lose that quiet balance which makes our life so happy, and I get a taste for excitement, and wine, women and poker, and become debauched and unfaithful and undomestic, and the divorce-court and Doctor Woods are the inevitable sequel.

Anyhow I am dining at home tonight which will be a damper.

I do hope Violet is not really ill—poor dear. She will mind feeling wretched in uncomfy surroundings and on boiled eggs. I am so sorry.

Oh my sweet, please don't go away and leave me again. I suppose I should get used to it in time, but it is so bloody for a short bit.

Darling, I feel so lonely without you—and it isn't really much fun playing poker with Diana[2]; only it makes one forget.

---

1. Harold was only thirty-one.
2. Lady Diana Manners, who married Harold's diplomatic colleague, Duff Cooper, in 1919.

VITA TO HAROLD   *[Long Barn]*

[11 May 1918]

Beloved, when I got home today I found your two letters, and although I shall see you this evening and all during tomorrow, I answer them because somehow it's easier.

Darling, you are such an angel, and nobody in this world will ever appreciate you more than I do. God knows I prefer your gentleness and patience and endurance to the violence you seem to covet. There is nothing, nothing, nothing I would alter in you.

Yes, I have got Wanderlust, and got it badly. I don't know if you've ever had it? It is real pain, you know—as definite as love, or as jealousy. You seem to muddle it up with what you call the desire for 'adventures'. You are wrong. I don't want that sort of adventure, having *you*. It is real Wanderlust I have—the longing for new places, for movement, for places where no one will want me to order lunch, or pay housebooks, or come with a grievance against someone else: yes, it is silly little things like that which have got on my nerves. Being interrupted, being available. I want to go away (with you) where no one knows where we are, where no letters can follow because no one knows our address. You see, it is a mixture of Wanderlust, the spring, and Westiness, and, as you say, probably liver.

Do you see now that it is not that I don't love you? Or that I want other people to love me?

I write this with my eyes fully open to the fact that to allow such things to grow upon me, of all people, is the most appalling form of selfishness—me who at this time of all others have got you safe (so far, *unberufen* [touch wood]) by an almost miracle of luck; who have you to love me; who have two little boys; a cottage; money; flowers; a farm; and three cows. It's absurd. I have everything I want, and my one real worry in life is Dada—no others. Whereas you, my darling, are tied to a beastly office, and yet you retain your sweetness, your charm, and your unselfishness for others. I feel ashamed now.

Of course I knew that you would trace it to Violet, but again you aren't right, because as I've explained, I don't covet that sort of life—in fact I should loathe it. No, I want to be free with you, that's all, a thing I can't have till the war is done. But in the meantime I feel that Violet and people like that save me from a sort of intellectual stagnation and bovine complacency, which is the very natural consequence of my present life. I *adore* my present life, but it is, after all, only one side of the medal, and on the other side is all the intellectual stimulus you and I both require and which we simply must not allow ourselves to neglect. So don't be jealous of Violet, my darling silly. You know you have always raved against the stagnation of Cadogan Gardens [Harold's parents' house].

Darling, one day we will go off with two little toothbrushes, and the bloody war will be over. If I can only keep you I am afraid I don't much care what happens to the war, if only it would stop. It is all such a fantastically tragic mistake.

HAROLD TO VITA   *Foreign Office*

16 May 1918

You have no conception how lovely the world looked this morning as I went up the hill. The fields swung great clouds of buttercups down the hillside, and every blade of grass stretched out its little green hands to the sun—and to our Weald which lay like a wet quilt below me. My walks up that hill [at Long Barn] have *qualcosa di sacerdotale,* and are indeed poems to nature and our own little nestling home there amid the meadows with the irises and the vine—and upstairs a little person who loves me like she used to, in spite of a terrible lapse within the last fortnight.

I went to lunch with Violet. Mrs K. [Keppel, Violet's mother] in a nice mood—she *raved* about you and said your yellow dress was too lovely and that never had you been so en beauté before. "She really is one of the most beautiful young women I have ever seen." Hadji put on his little face like this.

HAROLD TO VITA   *Foreign Office*

10 June 1918

Darling, I sit here and the sky is so blue and the little clouds sail across the window, so straight and direct, while underneath the trees show the whites of their eyes and bluster in all directions.

Even so, my sweet, I want our own life to sweep onwards to a clear old age, while other people's toss and touzle underneath. But that is a smug little thought, and Hadji is not going to be smug any more. He is going to be a Devil—a great blue and red devil with claws; and then his sweet one will love him again as once she did, and not feel that her own glowing youth is being wasted upon a curate.

Darling I feel dumb when I think of your 'sweet womanliness' as Gerry [Wellesley] would say. It is a sort of melody which harmonises all this jangle—and out of it all will come some assurance in the continuance of human things.

Darling, I fear it is all rather dull for you my sweet—but we will have another honeymoon at Herm[1] which will last for ever. Sweetheart, you know how I long for your happiness above all things—but it is so difficult to create the happiness of another: one can only destroy it.

HAROLD TO VITA   *Foreign Office*

18 June 1918

Darling, I did love the picture so.[2] It is so *absolutely* my little Mar: she's all there—her little straight body, her Boyhood of Raleigh manner, and above all, those sweet gentle eyes which are so familiar to me. I am really enthusiastic about it. It is, I think, one of the best portraits I have ever seen. It is so young and so grown up. It doesn't date. She is younger than the sham Chippendale chair on which she

---

1. One of the smallest of the Channel Islands, which they thought of buying.
2. A portrait of Vita by William Strang, R.A. It was commissioned by Lady Sackville soon after Vita's return from Cornwall, but she rejected it, and the portrait was sold to the Glasgow Art Gallery, where it still hangs. It is reproduced in *Portrait of a Marriage*.

sits, and the eyelids are a little weary.[3] And she has arrayed herself in strange webs from diverse merchants, and as Miss Vita has been the distant princess of my exile, and as Viti the mother of Ben and Nigel. That little head is that on which a thousand kisses have fallen—and she has been down to the sea at Polperro and come back just the same to the little cottage.

Olive [Rubens] telephoned to me about something—and she had been to see it too. She thought it wonderful but a little 'coarse'. I could see no coarseness—only a certain blatancy, which is contradicted by the beauty of the eyes. It really is a splendid achievement.

HAROLD TO VITA   *Foreign Office*

2 September 1918

Hadji has got a brilliant idea which she mustn't laugh at. It is this. Mar is to get a little cottage in Cornwall or elsewhere—and it is to be a Padlock[4] cottage: and the Padlock is to be that Hadji never goes there, or sees it. It will just have two or three rooms, and will be hers absolutely, and she can go there when she likes and be quite alone and have whom she wants. Then the Padlock is that Hadji never goes there and can't (by the rules of the Padlock) even be asked—or even know when she is there or who she has got with her. It will make it a real escape from the YOKE [of marriage]. And when I am rich, I shall have one too, just the same and on the same condition.

Darling, take the idea seriously and think over it.

HAROLD TO VITA   *Foreign Office*

4 September 1918

The following is the decision of Lord Denman's Committee[5] in my case:—

---

3. A parody of Walter Pater's famous description of the Mona Lisa.
4. "Padlock" was a Sackville term for an unbreakable promise.
5. Appointed to adjudicate on exempting civil servants from military service.

"Hon. H. G. Nicolson age 31, grade 1
Retained as indispensable.
Reasons: "Has dealt with certain subjects from the outbreak of the war, and has an intimate knowledge of many
difficult and intricate European problems. His technical experience and facility for writing memoranda render him quite
invaluable when information on the Balkans and other problems is called for by the War Cabinet at short notice. Mr
Balfour, whose opinion was solicited, stated that he did not
know how Mr Nicolson could be replaced: that, indeed, he
had no hesitation in saying that it would be almost impossible to do so."

So that's that—and I think I am safe for this war. I can't say that
I am really glad about it, or that I feel they had the facts put honestly before them. It was true in 1917. I doubt whether it is true
now.

HAROLD TO VITA   *St James' Club, Piccadilly, W.1*

9 September 1918

My little Viti,
    I was so rushed all today that I couldn't find time to write, and
this will come late and she'll think he doesn't love her any more.
    But oh he does! he does! he does! he's never loved her so much
as in the last few months when she has been slipping away from him.
Viti, my little one, you will never get anyone to love you as I do. I
know that, and one day you will know it. You see, all I want is for
you to be happy. Really I would go and live in a Martello tower[1]
all by myself with 2 bats and six mice—if it would make you happy.
I feel oceans of abnegations as regards you, my perfect.
    But then—I know—it is not that which counts: and Violet in her
clever way has made you think I'm unromantic. And oh dear! Oh dear!

---

1. A girdle of small round towers erected round the southeast coast of England in the early
1800s as defenses against the threat of a Napoleonic invasion.

how can an impoverished, middle-aged civil servant cope with so subtle an accusation? You see, if I was orfully rich I could have a valet, and an aeroplane and a gardenia tree, and it would all be very Byronic—but not being rich, or successful, it is just "poor little Hadji, he's such a darling and *so* patient."

But sweetheart—I am just *not* going to be a bore or touchy or sentimental. I'm not going to plant water lilies in the sea. It just *is* the sea—my love of you. My little one—you think you are so unaccountable, but you aren't.

Little one—I wish Violet was dead: she has poisoned one of the most sunny things that ever happened. She is like some fierce orchid, glimmering and stinking in the recesses of life and throwing cadaverous sweetness on the morning breeze. Darling, she is evil and I am not evil. Oh my darling, what is it that makes you put her above me? It is so difficult to realise. It is so poignant to think of. We seemed, you and I, to be running hand in hand on the downs (near Lewes), and now a fog has come and you have got into someone else's conservatory, and I am wandering about cold and rather frightened in the fog. And from the little valleys comes the laughter of past happiness and the shudders of the future (even *that* sounds forced).

Oh dear! oh dear! it was all so real and easy and natural, like the weeds on the terrace or the smell of Alyssum—and now, somehow, it isn't frank any more.

Yet I'm the same, my saint, and my love is the same. It burns so straight darling, it doesn't gutter. Oh darling, yesterday I wanted to kiss you as if I loved you, and you turned aside. Such a slight deflection—an *exiguum clinamen,* and yet it hurt me so, it sent me away so hurt, darling—and you meant to be so kind and nice and gentle.

Darling, is it all an Algy Hay[2]—or is it just a transitory thing, or is it more? You see, it may be your bloody Westie [Sackville] business, or it may be a sort of George Sand stunt [the notorious Sapphist], or it may be just that I am a bad, futile, unconvincing, evasive, unromantic husband.

And then against me I have that little tortuous, erotic, irresponsible, irremediable and unlimited person [Violet]. I don't blame her.

2. Algy Hay was an old Sackville friend who was notoriously accident-prone.

I don't hate her even—no more than I should hate opium if you took it.

But darling, what does it all mean?

Darling, what do your odd unconvincing bursts of affection mean? What do your intermittent and (alas) so convincing coldness mean? Little one, I am not a fool. I can forgive and forget anything, and understand a good deal.

But can't you tell me? Can't you write it to me? What has happened? You see it isn't *me*—so it must be *you*. And you, who are quite analytical too, should be able to tell—and to tell *me*.

You see, if it was tangible I could help, perhaps. But is it so untangible? I know it is more than that. Is it that I am not amorous enough? How can I even think such things? But what is it, darling?

It is raining tonight—and the winter is coming on.

Hadji

Burn this, my little friend, and don't ever speak of it.

VITA TO HAROLD   *34 Hill Street, London W.1*

[1 October 1918]

I know, as I know the sun will rise tomorrow, that I love you unalterably. I know it would survive any passing liking I might have for anyone else (It's all right! don't be afraid. I *don't* like anyone else!) I know now, after five years, what a difference there is between a thing with great long strong roots, all gnarled and Rackham-like, and a love which is merely an accident of the imagination, and the person one imagines one loves might just as easily have been somebody else.

You see, I don't think a love like ours often happens. Passion happens, and habit happens, but the knowledge that one is linked and welded and soldered by a mixture of passion *and* habit *and* tenderness *and* friendship *and* circumstance *and* memories *and,* above all, by the thing one calls love, which is essentially a sense of belonging, of choice, a sense of 'He is MINE'—I don't think that often happens.

HAROLD TO VITA   *Foreign Office*

11 November 1918

A strange, hectic, flag-waving [Armistice] day today, in which I have endeavoured to work on unaffected by the cheers and jubilation outside.

It began almost directly after we heard the news: a little knot of people had gathered outside No. 10—and the Prime Minister [Lloyd George] came out and told them. There were the wildest cheers—and they were silent—and they bared their heads and sang "God Save the King"—after which throughout the morning came cries and cheers from the [Horse Guards] parade—and at one moment I looked from an upper window to see a hatless white-haired and flushed Lloyd George, pushing himself backwards through a sea of hands, faces and flags into his little garden gate.

And then by luncheon the disorder had become more organised. Motor lorries filled with soldiers, women, and gutter urchins on the mud guards flew past yelling wildly. Everyone had flags—and as I went towards the Marlborough [Club], Pall Mall was festooned as never before. Again there was a rush of crowded lorries and people on the tops of taxicabs—wild heated hatless people.

I am so busy getting peace terms ready. It is rather fun, though I feel oddly responsible. I feel that what I do is so likely to be accepted, and that one tracing of my pencil in this familiar room and on my own familiar maps may mean the fate of millions of remote and unknown people.

I feel, almost an impulse [to say], "God guide me to the right." I feel quite solemn about it.

HAROLD TO VITA   *Foreign Office*

5 December 1918

You have stayed in Paris nearly a week without a word to me as to when you were going south or where.[1] The result is that I haven't

---

1. On 26 November Vita and Violet went to Paris for a week, and Vita paraded the streets dressed as a young, wounded soldier. They then went to Avignon, and from there to Monte Carlo, where they stayed for three months.

the least idea where to get hold of you. You really are quite *hopeless* about such things, and I put it all down to that swine Violet who seems to addle your brain. Oh you little idiot, I should shake you if you were here.

HAROLD TO VITA   *British Delegation, Paris*

10 January 1919

I know how extremely busy you are and how much of your time is taken up playing tennis and talking to your dirty little friend and your Persian Prince. Of course I know it is a lot to ask—but you might at least send me a postcard when you have no time to write. I am sorry to be a bore, and I know that your dirty little friend must chaff you about it a great deal, and that you must feel I am a tie and a responsibility. But try and remember that I am alone here, and anxious to settle about a flat which I can't do till I hear from you. Of course it must be much nicer in the South and I quite realise that you don't want to come up.

Damn! Damn! Damn! Violet. How I *loathe* her. I refuse absolutely to see her—and if you arrive with her I shan't meet you. I don't think I could trust myself to touch her. I feel I should lose my head and spit in her face.

HAROLD TO VITA   *Hotel Majestic, Paris*

[10 January 1919]

My own darling, dearest, sweetest one.

Another cross letter I sent you today and again I feel guilty. But darling, please don't mind them—don't think of them—it is only that at times I get quite racked with longing for you—and the slightest thing makes me angry and gives me a *crise de jalousie,* not jealous, dearest, of your loving other people (you know I am calm about that), but jealous simply of your *being* with other people—enraged, red-blood-surgingly indignant at the thought of other people, *dont je ne connais pas la puissance sur votre coeur*—of other people seeing you, hearing your dear modulated deep voice, and noting your splendid ways and movements—and oh dear the grace of you, and that little neck, that little neck with the pearl clasp all untidy, and the straight untidy tuque [cap]. And then I see red, darling, and the thought that you have spent two whole days without writing to me, running down unknown hotel steps into the sun with your racquet, and playing with unknown people on an unknown court, when you should have at least sent me a postcard.

Poor Hadji! I suppose it *is* jealousy—but I am not jealous, my own sweetheart, when you are there with me—and when I have at least a portion of your time.

Darling, I don't want to be a bore—but I do love you so. But *so* deeply darling—you understand.

VITA TO HAROLD   *Hotel Beau Rivage, Cannes*

27 January [1919]

My darling,

It is dreadful of me not to write to you. I know. Don't think it is just indifference, or forgetfulness, it is not. But as I've often said to you in talking, it's so difficult for me to write to you when I am staying with V.; it seems to me *indecent.* You can't say I have disappeared this time, because I have kept you *au courant* with my movements by means of telegrams, and I have written regularly to B.M.; this also I would much rather not do, for the same reason, but I have forced myself to. But you are different. It *is* indecent for me to write to you under these circumstances, oh, do, do, do try to see it!

Darling, I do hope you liked being in Paris.[1] It must have been rather exciting, but I am anti your conference because it has spoilt the exchange, and I hadn't yet changed any of my English money hoping it would go up! I sent you a telegram asking if you knew Lady

---

1. Harold returned to Knole, where he spent Christmas with his sons but no wife.

Lowther's[2] address in Cannes, but haven't had any answer. I am in Cannes now. I thought Lady Lowther would be a nice respectable person for me to see, and would gratify B.M. By the way, I think it is rather horrid of B.M. to be cross, when I gave up going to Spain which I was simply dying to do. It makes me feel "as well be hung for a sheep as for a lamb," and since you are in Paris I am not inconveniencing you in any way by being out of England.

Hadji . . .

Oh, nothing. But so many things, all the same.

I'm lonely, and have got a cold and wish I hadn't come here. I got an awful chill walking up a mountain and getting cold at the top. V. tried to get a cabin for Algiers and was promised one almost for certain last Monday, but it fell through. It was not her fault, or mine. It even got so far as paying for it.

What shall I do? I thought of going to Ajaccio, but thought you wouldn't like it.

Did you get dewdrops [compliments] in Paris? How could I have been any use to you there? darling. I fear you are better without me on those occasions. *C'est triste à dire* . . .

Your loving, and rather miz, and very snuffly

                                                                Mar

HAROLD TO VITA   *British Delegation, Paris*

1 February 1919

Yesterday I was at work from 9.30 to 12.30 and 1.30 to 8.0. I have generally a Committee all morning and then even lately I have been going down to the Conseil de Dix all afternoon. The latter is terrifying. A small but magnificent room, with armchairs arrayed both sides of a huge Régence writing table. At the table sits Clemenceau [France], and on his right are the 5 great Powers, Wilson, Lansing [U.S.A.]; Lloyd George, Balfour [Great Britain]; Orlando, Sonnino [Italy]; Pichon [France], and the Japanese.

---

2. Former Ambassadress in Constantinople.

Then comes Hadji—oh dear he looks so funny. In the middle are secretaries, and an interpreter.

This, of course, is the *real* Congress, where the work is done, but it doesn't look like one, as everyone is just sitting about, and they get up and lean against the mantelpiece.

The wretched small powers are brought in one by one and made to state their case. They are sat down opposite Clemenceau as if in the dock. It is an odd spectacle.

Hadji doesn't say anything except when he's asked—and then he gets pink.

HAROLD TO VITA   *British Delegation, Paris*

2 February 1919

I am feeling crushed, and sore, and sad today—because it's Sunday—and I had been packing some things to take round to the flat.[1] I packed them so tenderly as if they were bits of you, my saint—and I was so happy, *so* happy.

And then your letter came—and it was so dark and grim and horrible. I have never been so disappointed in my life—I didn't know it could come on one like that.

But it is childish, of course, and disappointment is after all a very transitory hurt—and nothing compared to poor V.'s [Violet's] tragic and hopeless position. Little one, don't think I am angry or sad about *you*. I always dissociate these things from you—especially when you tell me frankly what has happened.

But all the sun has gone from Paris—which has become a cold, grey meaningless city where there is a Conference going on somewhere, a conference which meant so much to me yesterday, and today is something detached, unreal and inanimate.

But tomorrow it will be all right again—and when you get this *I* shall be all right again. Only please get a new photograph done of

---

1. Harold had rented a flat in Paris for himself and Vita, who had promised to come, but she chucked him at the last moment.

yourself and send it me. I feel you are slipping away, you who are my anchor, my hope, and all my peace.

Dearest, you don't know my devotion to you. What you do can never be wrong.

God bless you, Viti.

HAROLD TO VITA   *[Paris]*

[9 February 1919]

I have torn up the rest of this letter. It was too cross and despairing to send.

I don't want to write to you at present much—as I don't want to say things which I shall regret.

You see, I have been quite terribly over-worked and all this sorrow and confusion has made me quite unnaturally upset—so I can't trust myself to write.

I don't want to say things which I shall regret. Only day and night there is a voice in my ear, "She lied to you! She broke her promise to you! She hurts you like this to spare the other!"

Would V. have suffered as I have this dark week? I wonder. If so I am sorry for her. But I feel quite different and aged—and all my joy in life and work has left me.

What frightens me so, is that I feel now I don't *want* to see you.

HAROLD TO VITA   *[Paris]*

[18 March 1919]

I want you to think: "Well, whatever I do, there is one person whom I need never consider, who always will understand—and that is my fat, ugly, red-faced, bourgeois, sentimental but *so* loving Hadji." I want you to feel that I shall always take your point-of-view and that I realise it is all as if you had been run over by a bus and broken your leg, and however bloody, it is *not* your fault.

34 Hill St.
                                            [London W.1]
[20 March 1919]

My own darling,

I got so dreadfully poisoned yesterday that I stayed the night at
Folkestone. I am all right today.[1] The crossing also was beastly,
although I wasn't sick. So I came on here today—B.M. has been *quite
too foul* for words to me. Dada has scolded me too, but he is so sweet
and sensible and un-violent that one doesn't mind, and of course I
know he is perfectly right and justified in all that he says, and I haven't
tried to pretend to him that I don't accept all his criticisms as perfectly
well-founded and just. He has not really really got a down on me. But
B.M. is impossible; she talks in a voice trembling with passion (you
know), contradicts herself the whole time, and is obviously even more
furious than one had gathered from her letters—she even refused to
take the little presents I had brought her—I HATE her tonight, I hate
her too much even to be unhappy about it. I want you so dreadfully
badly. I know I have brought it all on myself, and have got only myself
to thank, and all that sort of thing, and also I know B.M. has got a
real justifiable grievance this time against me, but all the same I don't
see why she should be such an utter beast to me, and *so* hard.

Well, darling, I mustn't bore you with it; I found a darling letter
from you here, which cheered me up lots; bless you. I wanted to leave
the house, but Dada said no. Oh, she *can* be horrid when she likes. I
expect she will write you a filthy letter; put it in the fire unread.

My sweet, I shall go to Brighton[2] tomorrow. Dada and Olive
[Rubens] have both talked about Ben to me; apparently he has missed
us quite dreadfully, and it isn't just repeating what the servants have
said to him. They are both extremely urgent that I should take him
over to Paris, and I trust them, even before I have seen him. I will of
course write and tell you about them both tomorrow.

Poor little Ben, it appears that no day has passed without his asking
for me, and that whenever they saw him he said at once, "Can we go

---

1. Vita joined Harold in Paris on 15 March, and on the 19th returned to England after nearly
   four months absence.
2. Lady Sackville's house in Sussex Square, where Vita's two sons had been temporarily lodged
   with a nanny.

and find Mummy now?"—isn't it dreadfully how?[3] and it does make
me feel a beast. Also he realises that there is a general theory that he
is naughty (the criminal!), and he says, "I know I am naughty, but
Mummy thinks I am good, and I will be good when Mummy comes."
Darling, it harrows me horribly. Olive says she could never have
believed it of so small a child. He is always talking of Long Barn, and
of how much he loves it. They say Nigel is most attractive, but it is
my own dark Ben I want,—oh I do want to see him, Hadji, and to
get away from B.M. who looks at me with eyes of stone.

I shall come back to you as soon as I can—with Ben.

I can't believe I ever loved B.M., or that she ever loved me. I think
Dada hates her and a good deal too.[4]

Darling, goodbye.

I could not be as hard as B.M., not to anyone.

Mar

HAROLD TO VITA   *British Delegation, Paris*

26 March 1919

My darling Vita,

I got such a sad letter from you today my dearest. What can I say,
darling? You know only that I love you beyond anything in this
world, and that my whole life will be devoted to shielding you against
unhappiness. Poor darling, how buffetted you have been by circumstances—and how terrible it is that I should not be available when I
am necessary to you: to protect you and heal you, and bring you back
to calm and security.

Darling, you know that one day you will be able to tell me all
about it—and that I shall love you all the more for what you have
been through; and do all I can to save you from such tragedies.

Of course I blame myself chiefly. I should have helped you more
from the first, and taken the decision out of your hands. I shall do so

3. "How" was the family expression for "pathetic," "touching."
4. It was on 19 May 1919 that Lady Sackville left her husband and Knole forever.

in the future, dearest, and not let terrible situations grow upon you and overwhelm you. But I have this excuse, that I have been so overcome by work—it is just as if I had been in the trenches. It is the war, darling, and the war is over, and now we are to have peace.

So try, my darling, to recover your confidence in yourself, and your serenity of life. Don't look upon yourself as a straw in the wind, but as a twig on some firm tree which waves and shivers in the wind but which is at least rooted somewhere to hope and solidity. My poor darling, I feel for you so. I got such a pang of sympathy when I read of Violet's engagement.[1] It is terrible for her. I hated to read it.

So try, darling, to recover *le beau calme de jadis*—and when we meet at last I shall help you, and support you and soothe you and fight all your battles for you. I promise, darling.

I feel so strong now—my work has made me feel that. I get my way about Europe by persistence. I shall get my way too about your life and mine.

Darling, I would give the world to be with you now. I feel I could help—by gentleness first, and by force later. All I want now is that you should still be strong these weeks. You are recovering from a terrible fever—and you can't quite walk across your room. But every day it will get a little easier—you will feel less tired—relapses will become less frequent. Only keep from doing anything foreign for these next weeks and you will heal.

The Council of Ten have realised their own futility and have dissolved into the Council of 4[2]—so that we really shall be at peace soon.

I have been turned on to getting an agreement out of the Americans on *all* South Eastern Europe questions. It is a *great* compliment, but also a terrible responsibility and entails appalling work. It is also a deep, deep secret, so don't say anything.

But it has made me happier about peace. I get my way with the Yanks generally.

---

1. Violet's engagement to Denys Trefusis was announced in *The Times* on this very day, 26 March.
2. The Council of Ten consisted of two delegates each from France, the United States, Great Britain, Italy, and Japan. It was now skimmed to Clemenceau, President Wilson, Lloyd George, and Orlando.

29 March 1919

My own darling,

I was so distressed by your letter today.

Let me make my own view quite clear.

(1) I don't want or expect you to 'break' with Violet. I don't expect you not to see her or write to her. I don't care how affectionate your letters are: I know how difficult is the position in which you are placed.

(2) I will not, however, allow you to go away again with Violet for any long period. I don't want you to allow her to completely monopolise your life—I don't mean it in a selfish or jealous way. What I mean is that the position is impossible—and that you simply can't go on sacrificing your reputation and your duty to a tragic passion. It is bad for you and bad for Violet—and it simply cannot be allowed.

If therefore Violet is completely unreasonable, and wants you to go away with her again, and refuses to see you unless you consent, then you are right to break with her.

If, ever, you find that seeing or writing to her leads to scenes, and leaves you both more wretched than before:—then also you are right.

But if you are taking the drastic line merely because you are not strong enough to take the middle line, then I think you are wrong.

I wish, darling, you could tell me exactly what you feel about it all. It makes me so wretched and miserable. Not so much the thing itself—but that you should be unhappy and I be powerless to help, or even to understand.

Darling, why did you ever leave our calm quiet road for this scarlet adventure? It is all a torment to me to think of—but above all that it should make you suffer. You dear gentle, loving, loyal saint— and I *did* want to make you happy, my own angel, and I have failed. I read your Constantinople poems—and they hurt me so dreadfully. Where are the happy feet that used to patter about our staircase over there? There is nothing but leaden sorrow and disease in our life now—and our love which is all that has survived is wild eyed and full of tears.

My poor poor darling!
poor poor Hadji.

HAROLD TO VITA   *British Delegation, Paris*

4 May 1919

I scribbled you a note yesterday in President Wilson's ante-room while a man was watering the lawn outside with a hose, under the eyes of an American sentry. Just as I had finished, Lloyd George burst in in his impetuous way: "Come along, Nicolson, and keep your ears open." So I went into Wilson's study and there were he and Lloyd George and Clemenceau with their armchairs drawn up close over a map on the hearth-rug. I was there about half an hour. The President was extremely nice—and so, I must say, was Lloyd George. Clemenceau was cantankerous, the *"Mais, voyons, jeune homme"* style.

But, darling, it is appalling those three ignorant and irresponsible men cutting Asia Minor to bits as if they were dividing a cake, and with *no-one* there except Hadji—who incidentally has nothing whatsoever to do with Asia Minor. Isn't it terrible—the happiness of millions being decided in that way—while for the last two months we were praying and begging the Council to give us time to work out a scheme?

Then decisions are immoral and impracticable—and I told them so. *"Mais, voyez-vous, jeune homme—que voulez-vous qu'on fasse? Il faut aboutir."*

The funny part is that the only part where I *do* come in—the Greek part—they have gone beyond, and dangerously beyond, what I suggested in my wildest moments—and everyone will think it was me.

Anyhow I was working up to 11.30, and got to bed dead to the world which was a good thing as it prevented me being miz. More Councils today—and I write this in violent haste.

HAROLD TO VITA   *British Delegation, Paris*

Saturday, 17 May 1919

There is *such* a thunderstorm brewing here against the P.M. [Lloyd George]. It is all about this Asia Minor business—and it is difficult for Hadji to guide his row boat safely in and out of these fierce Dreadnoughts.

Even A.J.B. [Balfour] is angry: "I have three all-powerful, all-ignorant men sitting there and partitioning continents with only a child to take notes for them." I have an uneasy suspicion that by the "child" he means me. Of course perhaps it may be Hankey.[1] I hope it is Hankey. After all Hankey is bald—but still he is younger by 25 years than A.J.B.

Then the P.M. had sent for the Indian Delegation from London—who took a special train—only to find that the question had been decided by the three men and the child and that Ll.G. had gone off on a motor tour.

I had better lie very low for a bit. Anyhow I have, I think, got my point. But it was playing with gun-powder.

HAROLD TO VITA   *British Delegation, Paris*

19 May 1919

When Mar has *nothing* to do, will she please think, sometimes, about the League of Nations?[2] She had better get a League temperament, ready to help Hadji and tonic him when he becomes too national and anti-dago. You see, if the League is to be of any value it must start from a new conception and involve among its promoters and leaders a new habit of thought. Otherwise it will be no more than a continuation of the Conference—where each Delegation subscribes its *own* point of view and where unanimity can be secured only by a mutual surrender of the complete scheme. But we must lose all that, and think only of the League point of view, where Right is the ultimate sanction, and where compromise is a crime. So we must become anti-English when necessary, and when necessary pro-Italian. So when you find me becoming impatient of the Latins you must snub me. It is rather a wrench for me as I like the sturdy, unenlightened, un-intellectual muzzy British way of looking at things. I fear the Geneva tempera-

---

1. Sir Maurice Hankey, Secretary to the British Delegation, and to the Council of Four. But he was forty-two, scarcely "a child." Harold was thirty-two, Balfour, sixty-seven.
2. Harold had been warned that after the signature of the Peace Treaty he would be temporarily detached from the Foreign Office to the League of Nations, which was established by the Treaty itself.

ment will be rather Hampstead Garden Suburb—but, dearest, the thing may be *immense,* and we must work for it. You can do as much as me by gentle proselytising. Think that you are a Salvation Army worker and when you hear the League abused and scoffed at, put on a gentle patient smile, and say, "But why?" They will have no *real* reason to condemn it, and you can then confound them by, "Obviously, it will fail if ignorant people attack it before its birth and without giving it a moment's thought."

But seriously, sweetest, when you hear the League thoughtlessly abused, think of yourself down in the cellar at 182 Ebury Street (without port) and with the guns going all round: and think how if there is another war that will begin again a thousand-fold: and then catch hold of the little thread of indignation which this memory awakes in you, and elaborate it to moral wrath at irresponsible gibing at what *may,* what really may, prevent all this. My feeling about the League is that it is a great experiment. And I want you to feel rather protective of it, just like you would rush to protect the unborn *Critic* [3] from the reviler and the cold-water thrower.

There is sun today—and it is splashing on the lawns at Knole, and over those gold brown roofs and into my babies' bedroom. And my darling—my sun is there—oh my sweet—how my love goes out to you, my darling. Dearest Vita, darling little one. I *do* hope you are less unhappy. Don't think of me my angel. I am feeling secure and confident again. Really I think love is the only *supreme* virtue—and covers all other ugly things. Nothing sad or beastly can do deep harm, I mean deep *moral* harm, if one loves.

HAROLD TO VITA   *British Delegation, Paris*

22 May 1919

Oh Viti—Viti—how I love you and cling to you and long to help you. But it *is* difficult and uphill work and I feel so discouraged sometimes. You see all I can do is to love you absolutely, and under-

---

3. *The Critic* was the title of a literary magazine that Vita proposed to edit in collaboration with Michael Sadleir, the publisher. The idea was stillborn.

stand you absolutely, and let you do whatever you like. That is easy. But it creates in you a feeling of debt to me, and that is in itself a bond. There are moments when I feel you would rather I gave you an excuse for going away for ever: when I think that you would rather I didn't love you and you didn't love me and that there was absolute liberty for you—moral as well as actual. I give you absolute liberty in fact—but in principle you are too loyal not to feel there remains an obligation. It is sad, because anyone else would be so easy to manage. I mean that to anyone else I should not be a burden and a responsibility. Dearest, I almost despair at times. You see, the weapons with which I can fight for you may make you hate me.

But I am feeling overworked, and stale, and depressed about this humbug peace, and I can't feel opty [optimistic] about things at present. Oh my dearest Vita, don't feel annoyed at this momentary despair of mine. But how can I, who only represent peace and security, cope with Violet who represents adventure? Of course I know that if you were wretched, or frightened, you would come to me. But by then it may be too late. You say you have no confidence in yourself. But you evidently have all confidence in me, in my patience and forebearance. I hope you are right. I think you are. But this can't go on for years! Oh darling, I have suffered so, this long dark year: have I got to go through another?

Darling, I am quite resigned to not seeing very much of you in my life. I quite see that for three months in the year you will go off alone somewhere—and you needn't even leave me your address. But does it do any good? We are getting on for half-year—and I have seen you 14 days! Do you realise that—14 days out of six months! And the babies have seen you less! You can't say that marriage is a bore to you, or motherhood a responsibility. I don't grumble at your having been away so long: what saddens me is that evidently you want to be away for longer. And we are so happy! at least *I* was. And then Violet came and all has been unrest and horror ever since.

And everybody envies me so! How little they know!

I think that V. has thrown the evil eye on all of us—on you and me and Dada and B.M. and Charlie and Maud [Sackville-West] and Walter and Olive [Rubens]. Don't let her see my babies.

Don't feel cross at this letter. My darling—it would be easier if

I didn't love you. I almost long for the peace and quiet of not loving you or caring what you do. How awful, though, if you just became a bore! It is funny to think of—but I suppose it will end like that.

I wish I knew where you were.

HAROLD TO VITA   *British Delegation, Paris*

23 May 1919

I read Celery[1] through from cover to cover last night in bed. It *really* is good. It is difficult to get outside it—but it leaves so strong a taste in the mouth, and the defects are merely a question of organisation, which is largely mechanical. All the un-mechanical part appears to have come quite naturally and that is what I suppose is called 'talent'. I have no doubt whatsoever that you will really become an important writer. You must keep your gravity of style. It is no use you trying to be funny—and you realise that. The only light business you could do well would be passages about children or animals or how [simple] people generally. I got annoyed with *The Observer* review about Ruth! To me she is a real achievement. The best thing in the book.

I hadn't realised its value quite, or its complete originality, till I read Celery again. In an emotional passage you really attain *Virtuosité*—you do really—and it is by gravity and simplicity. The passage when Malory tells her [Ruth] of love is as good a bit of prose as one could wish. And there is no 'precious' word in the whole business.

VITA TO HAROLD   *Long Barn*

Sunday, 1 June [1919]

Darling, something will absolutely have to be done about my coming to Paris, because V.'s wedding is tomorrow fortnight, and I know that there will be some disaster if I stop here. You may say that

---

1. "Celery" was his name for *Heritage,* Vita's first novel, which was published, to great acclaim, on 15 May.

I am superstitious, but I know, like Malory [in *Heritage*], fate will be too strong for me! I am really serious, Hadji. I am not just worried, I am ABSOLUTELY TERRIFIED. I feel as though I were being stalked. I tell you about it in order to protect myself from myself. I'm not afraid of anybody but myself. I shall do something quite irretrievable and mad if I stay in England. I shall probably try and do it even from Paris, at the last moment, but there I shall be prevented by just sheer distance.

O my Hadji, you oughtn't to have married me, I make you unhappy. But I do love you. That is the only anchor, as I told you. If it wasn't for you, I would give London something to talk about!!

Darling, the other night I sat next to Lord Hugh Cecil at dinner. He said he wondered why people didn't oftener do absolutely crazy things which would revolutionise their lives. I said probably because in doing them they would do infinite harm to the people they cared for and who cared for them. And also because most people weren't made that way, and simply didn't think about it. And Lady Hamilton joined us and said how often she had wanted to disappear, and I said how it was an instinct in people, a real instinct, which expressed itself in liking to dress-up, i.e. be somebody quite different for the time being, and they said it was quite true, and Lord Hugh got quite excited and eloquent.

O Hadji, I never ought to have married you or anybody else; I ought just to have lived with you for as long as you wanted me, because I am a pig really, and you are the dearest and sweetest and tenderest person in the whole world, and I only hurt you. I would have let you have a nice gentle affectionate wife who looked after your washing, which reminds me, have you got mine? Or else I ought not to have married till I was thirty. I think really that is the best solution for people like me, because not to marry at all is a mistake. We would have lost nothing, you and I, because we would have been every bit as happy unrespectably as respectably. Women ought to have freedom the same as men when they are young. It's a rotten and ridiculous system at present, it's simply cheating one of one's youth. It was all right for Victorians. But this generation is discarding, and the next will have discarded, the chrysalis.

You see, the mistake one makes is to expect youth to be consistent.

Youth is so fluid and impressionable that it will flow quite happily for
a given time through any mould one chooses to provide. But then
one's nature reasserts itself. That is why one oughtn't to bind oneself—
in other words, marry—when one is very young. That is why I say
that women, like men, ought to have their years so glutted with
freedom that they hate the very idea of freedom. Like assistants in a
chocolate-shop are allowed for the first month to eat as many chocolates as they like.

If ever we have a daughter we will bring her up to bring herself
up. And she will have a floater-mar [illegitimate child] which we will
have to pass off as the housemaid's.

O Hadji, if you knew how it would amuse me to scandalise the
whole of London! It's so secure, so fatuous, so conventional, so hypo-
critical, so whited-sepulchre, so cynical, so humbugging, so mean, so
ungenerous, so self-defensive, so well-policed, so beautifully legislated,
so well-dressed, so up-to-date, so hierarchical, so virtuously vicious, so
viciously virtuous. I'd like to tweak away the chair just as it's going
to sit down.

HAROLD TO VITA   *British Delegation, Paris*

3 June 1919

The letter I got this morning was so *rotten* that I think you had
better come here at once. (N.B. This is not meant to be cross.) You
seem to have no will-power at all—but just to drift and attribute the
muddle you have got into to the conventionality of the world. It is
as much good as a kitten who has fallen into the river blaming the
ground for having been too dry!

So you must come over at once and let me know by telegraph.
I shall get a room for you, and meet you.

Poor Hadji. If he looks after her he is infringing on her liberty—
and if he gives her her liberty she gets into a muddle. And what is the
use of his loving her so dreadfully?

But come at once my poor shattered Viti—and I shall be with you,
and help.

Now don't do anything excessive, but buy some black socks for me instead. And keep your head and your sense of proportion, and your self-respect, my sweet.

VITA TO HAROLD   *Long Barn*

[8 June 1919]

O Hadji, I couldn't ever hurt somebody as tender and sensitive and angelic and loving as you—at least, I mean—I know I *have* hurt you, but I couldn't do anything to hurt you dreadfully and irrevocably. What a hold you have on my heart; nobody else would ever have had such a hold. Darling, I will tell you something which although I say it quite casually in a letter is really very true and illuminating: the fact of loving you has made of me a quite different person, or rather it has entailed the renouncement of all in me that wasn't compatible with loving you. That part isn't quite dead yet, it's flickering and struggling to live, it struggles on its knees and puts its hands together, and says "O PLEASE!" and I say "NO," and it lies down again in its corner, very sick, and I look the other way and go to a dance.

O Hadji, it is so neat, the division in me, more neat than you'll ever know.

Darling, I suppose you needn't worry: I shan't do anything 'excessive', as you say.

I love you more than myself, more than life, more than the things I love. I give you everything—like a sacrifice.

I love you so much that I don't even resent it—which is rather contradictory, but you know what I mean, you've so often said it yourself.

I want to impress on you that it is all *you*, it isn't B.M., or Dada, or even the babies, or respectability, or peace and comfort (because I don't really like peace and comfort): it is only *you*. I should be pleased and flattered, if I was you.

The reason I am not coming till Saturday is that if I came to Paris several days earlier I should never stand it, but should go back to London and stop the whole thing [Violet's wedding], but if I cross on

Saturday I simply shall not have time to, however much I may want to—willy-nilly.

Hadji darling, I wonder how much you realise?

I can't tell you what I'd give to be this time next year!

O Lord, the weariness and length and *dread* of it all—It all seems to go from bad to worse, and this is the climax.[1] However, I suppose one survives everything.

This isn't meant to be a worrying letter, but a reassuring one.

HAROLD TO VITA   *British Delegation, Paris*

20 June 1919

I went to the front yesterday—to Noyon. It is less destroyed than I imagined—not Noyon, I mean, which is like the pictures, but the woods around, which are just like other woods. There is only one little knoll with the stumps of gassed trees like the remains of one's asparagus, but otherwise there are poppies and corn blowing over what less than a year ago was the fiercest battle-field of all. They are filling up the trenches and the shell-holes—and already the barbed wire is hidden by great crops of nettles.

HAROLD TO VITA   *British Delegation, Paris*

28 June 1919

It is over—the signature [of the Treaty of Versailles]—and as I write in my room at the Astoria the Arc de Triomphe is black with people watching the cars stream up the Avenue du Bois.

We were told to leave the Majestic at 1.30, so I had a small and early luncheon, put on my tail coat, lit a cigar, and started in one of our cars. My old black slouch hat came with me, as it has seen so much of the Conference that I thought it would like to see the end. Besides,

1. Violet married Denys Trefusis in London on 16 June while Vita was with Harold in Paris.

my top-hat is sitting quietly at Hill Street indifferent to the fate of Empires.

Along the road—under the trees at St Cloud—were posted soldiers in their grey helmets holding red flags and waving us along our privileged way. Little knots of people stood about with flags and babies and prams and rosettes and souvenir sellers. We swung suddenly into the main avenue leading to the Château. A sudden blaze of fluttering colours flashed out from the lancer-pennants of the cavalry who lined the road—and we bumped over the pavé of the great courtyard between thick rows of cavalry and infantry at the salute.

At the door the usual battery of official photographers and cinematographers—and a sudden rush in the cool hall, out of the crowd, with only one or two silent frockcoated plenipotentiaries blowing their noses before climbing upstairs.

The staircase was magnificent—on each step stood two Gardes Républicains in their helmets with drawn swords—and a splendid Aubusson splashed down it like a waterfall. My black hat began to feel a little ashamed of itself so I hid it under my arm. The two large salons before the Galerie des Glaces had been furnished with Aubusson, Gobelins and the gems of the Louvre. It was magnificent—the sense of dignity and order. At each door stood the Gardes Républicains like caryatids, at the salute—and we strolled in talking now and then to our friends and looking out on the terrace, where a privileged and ticketed crowd had gathered behind a close row of blue soldiers.

Beyond the second Salon opened the Galerie des Glaces, looking huge and barrelled with the gilt chairs in the middle, and rows of benches and *escabeaux* [stools] at the nearer end. I found my place at once—there were printed tickets, with a pin shoved through the card. For about twenty minutes we chatted with our friends and moved about. At the further end of the room the Press were already established.

Clemenceau was already *installé* in his presidential chair—and one after the other the Delegates began to arrive—Wilson, Lloyd George. It was like a wedding: no applause, but not what you would call silence.

At about three o'clock the *officier d'ordonnance* came from bench to bench saying, *"Asseyez-vous, messieurs—la séance commence,"* and in a few seconds there was a complete hush and everyone was seated.

Four Gardes Républicains then entered and kept the aisle clear. Suddenly there was an order from the Salon outside and with a loud click the Gardes Républicains flashed their swords into their scabbards ("We shall not sheath the sword", flashed into my mind). A silence among all those people so that you could hear a pin drop and faces turned towards the door into the anteroom. Suddenly a stiffening on the part of the four guards and the sound of slow steps on the parquet outside. First came two messieurs in silver chains, and then four officers—a French, a British, an American and an Italian in single file—followed by Müller and Bell,[1] upon whom all eyes were fixed, hostile and interested.

They passed close to me up the aisle, but they held their heads high and looked to the ceiling where Louis XVI sprawled among clouds and goddesses. Hardly had they sat down when Clemenceau began, *"Messieurs la séance est levée,"* and then just a few words, "We are here to sign the peace." The moment he had finished the Germans stood up suddenly—but sat down again abruptly as Mantoux [interpreter] began to translate into English. As soon as Mantoux had finished, St Quentin advanced to the Germans and led them to the table where the Treaty was. In breathless silence they signed—and walked back, their eyes still on the ceiling. Then Wilson rose, and his plenipotentiaries with him, and then began a *défilé* of the Delegations past the table of signature, like candidates filing past the Bishop at confirmation. America, Great Britain, Italy, Japan, while the tension relaxed. Suddenly from outside came the crack of the first gun which announced to Paris the signing of the peace—and in the intervals of the salvoes rose the cheers of the crowds outside on the terrace.

We were told it would last 3 hours—but almost at once it seemed that there came a loud "Sshh" from the ushers—and while an aeroplane rattled past the great windows, Clemenceau spoke again: *"Messieurs, le traité est signé. La séance est levée."* People kept their seats while the formal procession formed out again and the Germans were led from the room in silence. Then a general exodus while I went to one of the great windows and out on to the balcony. The fountain was playing and the crowds were waiting silently behind the troops. Suddenly a great cheer—and below me a group of top hats followed by generals

---

1. The two German Representatives.

in gold and blue with *grands cordons*. The crowd broke the lines and rushed towards them. It was Wilson, Clemenceau, Lloyd George—and I suppose Foch but I could not see him. They went mad: they yelled, "Vive Clemenceau": they threw flowers, and the guns by the Orangerie crashed out again. It was a wonderful fusion of enthusiasm—dust, flowers and uniforms—some soldiers came up at a double and rescued Ll.G. from the crowd and piloted him to his motor car which was drawn up between the fountains.

And then back again through lanes of cheering people—*"Vive l'Angleterre"* they yelled at our car—and the roses they threw always missed us.

I smoked my pipe and was happy and thought of you, my light and love.

VITA TO HAROLD   *Long Barn*

1 July [1919]

I wrote myself nearly sick yesterday.[1] I wrote poetry too. I have got a new system of writing poetry. I get such heaps of ideas that I just scribble them all down in prose and scraps of verse, and cast them into verse in calmer moments.

HAROLD TO VITA   *British Delegation, Paris*

4 July 1919

Hardinge[2] sent for me yesterday and after a pompous exordium which made all the people in the Champs Elysées stop and take off their hats, he said, "Now why are you so determined to go to this League of Nations?" I murmured something—'interest,' 'hope,' 'the new Europe' etc. etc. and he went on, "I can tell you frankly that it had been my intention prior to your decision to offer you an appointment

---

1. Her second novel, *The Dragon in Shallow Waters.*
2. Lord Hardinge of Penshurst, ex-Viceroy of India and Permanent Undersecretary of State for Foreign Affairs, 1906–10 and 1916–20.

of real importance. I am prepared to offer it you again—if you will abandon the League—I am prepared to make you MY PRIVATE SECRETARY." At these last words the crowds which had collected outside dropped on one knee—and not an eye was undimmed—even a poilu who had been through Verdun murmured the word "chouette" [splendid!] and burst into floods of tears.

I remained unmoved however—and while my head swam—I refused it. You can never say again that I am ambitious!

HAROLD TO VITA   *British Delegation, Paris*

14 July 1919

My darling,

Well the [victory] procession was a success. In fact it was a great success. There was a wonderful moment when Foch and Joffre came through the Arc [de Triomphe] like two pigmies. I have never seen such enthusiasm. But our men would have made you weep. A bright sun, with a cold wind and the flags fluttering: a long pause: and then a quite dull naval band coming through. Suddenly out of the diagonal shade of the arch another group—flashing with an enormous white ensign carried by a naval detachment. The Astoria [British Delegation's hotel] waved with enthusiasm while the British Grenadiers came from under the arch, and behind them hundreds and hundreds of British regimental flags—stiff, imperial, heavy with gold lettering, "Busaco" "Inkerman" "Waterloo"—while the crowd roared with enthusiasm, and our own tommies on the roof yelled "Good old Blighty", and Douglas Haig passed with his generals at the salute. Mar would have sobbed. Norman[1] cried which was a good mark. Hadji pretended to be looking at the programme—but he was rather weepy too. I have never had such a patriotic feeling. I never felt less League of Nations. There they were, the flags of British regiments—of people we know— people from Sussex and Bedfordshire and Kent and Houndsditch—in this blatant foreign capital—with flags emblematic of our past victories of which this is the most glorious, the most democratic and the most

---

1. Montagu Norman (1871–1950), Governor of the Bank of England from 1920.

final. The flags hung stiffly under their gold embroidery—whereas the
American flags had flattened, unweighted by history or past achievements. There were two tiny boy scouts at the head of one group, and
they saluted as they passed, stiffly like a Coldstream Sergeant-Major.
And behind them came the swirl of the bagpipes and the swinging of
the kilts. They walked quickly and rather shyly, and the officers rode
in front, and the air rocked with cheers and enthusiasm. What a *fool*
you were not to come.

VITA TO HAROLD　　　　　　　　　　　　　　　*Long Barn*

July 1919

Hadji mine,

　　I've got no news. I haven't been at the cottage the last two days,
I've been living on a delicious island in the Aegean, playing gooseberry
to the oddest couple . . .[1]

　　There has been a lot of fighting there, too, and I don't care what
you say: it is *damned good*. So there. Now you can think me conceited
if you like. (Don't tell anybody, for pity's sake.) They are really very
odd people: they have dreadful rows nearly all the time, *et comment!*

　　I am pleased, *really* pleased. (This cannot mean anything except
that it is extremely bad, on the analogy that what *I* think bad you think
good!)

VITA TO HAROLD　　　　　　　*Possingworth Manor, Sussex*

30 July 1919

　　I am at Blackboys.[2] Mrs K and Sonia [Violet's mother and sister]
came down to luncheon today. It was all so ghastly, they talked about

---

1. She had begun to write her third novel, *Challenge,* which was the story of Julian (Vita),
  a rich young Englishman who becomes President of a small republic on the Greek coast
  and falls in love with his wayward cousin Eve, who is, of course, Violet.
2. North of Lewes, Sussex. Violet and Denys Trefusis had rented Possingworth Manor for
  the summer, and Vita spent much of her time there when Violet was not at Long Barn.

people's incomes, and all the usually mean little London gossip. V. and I just looked at each other in despair, it was such a contrast from the conversation we had been having just before, which had been about the Iliad and Wagner's operas. Oh I *do* hate Mrs Keppel. She is a soul-destroying woman.

I love books and flowers and poetry and travel and trees and dragons and the wind and the sea and generous hearts and spacious ideals and little children.

HAROLD TO VITA   *British Delegation, Paris*

8 August 1919

My darling Viti,

I had a terrible day yesterday. A long 2 hours interview with Balfour and the new American (Polk) [1]—about the Greek business. Mr B. was rather weak at the last moment and asked me to come to an agreement with the Yanks and present it to the Council of Five. I refused to do so without first presenting it to Venizelos. [2] He agreed. We then sat down and drew up an agreement. I then went round with my American to submit it to Venizelos. It was very painful. I simply loathed it—and it was like letting Venizelos down. He was very indignant, and stormed for an hour. It was *bloody*. We then went away and I got A.J.B. to agree that we could not force a settlement on Venizelos. But I hardly slept all night (it was like Verdun), and at 9.0 I went round again to see V. and suggested a possible compromise. This he accepted. He had not slept either, and there were tears in his eyes. I then went to Tardieu [3] and got him to agree, and then to A.J.B. who also agreed. It comes up this afternoon at the Council and it will be

1. Frank L. Polk, a lawyer and diplomat, was leader of the United States Delegation after the departure of President Wilson and Robert Lansing.
2. Eleutherios Venizelos (1864–1936), the Greek Prime Minister with whom Harold, an ardent phil-Hellene, had established a cordial relationship. The argument concerned the division of Thrace between Greece and Turkey.
3. André Tardieu, a leading member of the French Delegation and close collaborator of Clemenceau.

decided one way or another. It is a *bloody* solution for Greece, but better than the American one. I am unhappy about it.

HAROLD TO VITA   *British Delegation, Paris*

15 September [1919]

I had a very busy day yesterday—chiefly with Maurice Hankey. I got some things done—at least I think I have. I must say Lloyd George is a dynamic person. I wish I could have a long talk with him, but he is too busy—and I have to do it through Hankey.

I have got such a funny new friend—a dressmaker,[1] with a large shop in the Rue Royale, a charming flat at the Rond Point (where I spent the *whole* of Saturday night—sleeping on the balcony) and about 10 mannequins of surpassing beauty. I am lunching at the shop today. My dressmaker is only 27—and it is rather sporting to launch out into so elaborate an adventure at that age. Mar would like my new friend, I think—very attractive. Such a nice flat too. I think I shall stay there when and if I come back and not go to the Majestic. There is a spare room and I would pay for my board.

VITA TO HAROLD   *Long Barn*

19 October 1919

My own own darling, my own beloved darling, I scribble this for you to read when I'm gone[2] and you are having your breakfast by yourself and are perhaps wishing I was there. My own precious love, I only want to say again what I said last night, namely that I love you immutably, sacredly, and rootedly—you're all the sacred secret things of life, my beloved, that's what you are, (the cottage, the babies, and all that), and besides that, you're *all* that I think clean and sweet and

1. Edward Molyneux, the well-known couturier and collector of Impressionist paintings.
2. On this day Vita and Violet, with Harold's consent, left for their second long visit to Monte Carlo. They were away until early January 1920.

good (*really* good, not priggy) and fresh and *tout couvert de rosée* and like apple blossom. My darling, my darling, I haven't got words to tell you how much I think of you in that way, or with what tenderness—and love. O my darling, I wish one could tell a person how much one loves them, it's one of the aggravating things of life that one shouldn't be able to.

Nothing in this world could ever alter my love for you, I KNOW THAT.

Darling, this letter is *packed* with love.

HAROLD TO VITA   *League of Nations*
                                        Sunderland House
25 October 1919   *Curzon Street, London W.1*

Darling, I've got a grievance against you—why did you tell B.M. the most intimate things about you and me? It is all right you telling her things about yourself—(though I think that very unwise)—but it is bad luck on me to tell her things about me, which are at once repeated to Ozzie [Dickinson] and via him *urbi et orbi*. But it's no use writing you grievances to 1200 miles away—and I love you.

I don't pretend that I'm happy, because I'm not. I feel I've thrown the precious vessel of my happiness into Niagara and it may either be submerged or taken out to distant and alien waters. I know that under V.'s influence you will think it very smug of me to worry. But you are all my hope, darling, and it is agony to think of your dear splendid nature being warped or hardened. You see she has all the weapons and I have none. The only ones I have represent for you what you hate. The ones she has are all that you most love and desire. So it's not a fair fight, darling, but *you* are fair and I am fair and it may be all right. I don't like the gossip—but it is only a detail and once I get over to Paris[1] it will all be easier. At present it drives me away from the haunts of man and woman. Oh darling! I feel so lonely and hopeless, and you are the only person who understands.

---

1. Harold left Paris on 21 October and began work on the International Secretariat of the League of Nations in London.

I long to get over to Paris and drench myself in work.

I feel rather selfish writing to you a grumble, when you will be so happy out there in the sun [Monte Carlo]. Darling, don't forget me—don't feel hard to me. Don't throw yourself too madly into an orgy of irresponsibility. Don't let little Smuts[2] reflect the cruelty of present circumstances. Keep Eve the little prig she is. Devotion is only really beautiful when it entails sacrifice: not when it becomes a bonfire on which the lives of others are chucked and broken.

Anyhow as you *are* there, enjoy yourself—and don't think of me as nursing grievances which I haven't got. I love you too much for that.

H A R O L D   T O   V I T A   *Paris*

4 November [1919]

I do envy you so your freedom and liberty—but don't let yourself feel it is a right, this self indulgence: it is merely a holiday. Oh darling, I am rather fussed about you—not about you or me, but about your getting sloppier and sloppier, till even having to wear stays will become a *corvée* [unpleasant duty]—and your life will become one long sluttish slatternly muddle. That's why it annoys me that you should *always* lose your luggage. It's so slovenly. I loathe slov (rather a good word that). But I know you think you don't do a slov about your work. But that's no excuse as you can sit down to that and not move, and it doesn't entail plans, arrangements, accounts, time-tables, arguments, accuracies, previsions, coming upstairs, telephoning, writing cheques, writing in the counterfoil of cheques, standing in queues, talking to bedints [servants], having to make up one's mind, pushing, having one's hair blown about in the wind—no, one just sits on a chair quite still and quiet with a cigarette, 2 tubes of lipsalve and a pot of powder.

Mind, darling, I want you back by Dec. 21—and no mistake about it.

---

2. His name for Vita's novel *Challenge*.

Monte Carlo

26 November [1919]

Oh Hadji, I don't think I am fit to love anyone, or for them to love me.

Darling, I do love your letters, and you can't think what a help your remarks about little Smuts [*Challenge*] always are, and such an encouragement. Eve is not a 'little swine', she is just all the weaknesses and faults of feminity carried to the nth power, but also redeemed by the self-sacrifice which is also very feminine. I do think she is left sympathetic at the end, in spite of what she has done. It will be fun to think you are reading it. Julian is a practical idealist. He is much better, and less a schoolgirl hero. (But still a little bit that, I'm afraid.) The end was very difficult. I have tried to keep it as simple as possible. But as a whole it is a bad book. I shall never write a good book; at least, I might write dozens of *quite* good books, but I shall never write a great one. And to be great is the only thing that really counts, whether for books or people. *The Idiot* [Dostoyevski] is great.

Paris

3 December 1919

I fear I am going downhill without you—and I get so awfully depressed that I drink too much, and I spend my time with rather low people, but I am ashamed to go into society, so I live in the demi-monde and I don't like it much.

Bordighera, Italy

5 December 1919

I feel it's such a mockery my writing you superficial letters, and I dread writing you *real* ones; that's really why I have written so little.

I hate unreality and convention, especially between you and me. It's an insult to us both. So I'm going to write you a real letter now, a long one, and, please, you must realise that I'm writing quite sanely, and not think that anything I say is hysteria or theatrical, or anything but the sober fact and truth.

You see, I don't think you realise except in a very tiny degree what's going on or what's been going on. I don't think you have taken the thing seriously. (Of course, I know you have hated my being away and all that, but I think you have looked on it all as more or less transitory and "wild oats"—your own expression.) But surely, darling, you don't think I would have gone away from you and risked all that I *have* risked—your love, B.M.'s love, Dada's love, and my own reputation—for a whim? (I don't really care a damn about the reputation, but I do care about the rest.) Don't you realise that only a very great force could have brought me to risk these things? Many little things have shown me that you don't realise it. For instance: you talked of "wild oats." You talked of my being away as a holiday. You write of V. as Mrs Denys Trefusis—don't you realise that that name is a stab to me every time I hear it? every time I see it on an envelope? Yet you write of her as that as a joke.

There is another thing you don't realise. When I come back this time, V. and I [will] give each other up for ever. It is the only thing we can do, but it is going to break me for the time being. I'm not grumbling about it, or suggesting any other course; only, simply, there it is . . . Please, darling, don't write to me and say why is this necessary? *please* don't do that, or refer to it; I know you are such an angel that you wouldn't ever want me to do anything so drastic, but you must let me decide this for myself, and I *have* decided.

This brings me to the question of my coming to Paris. It is quite true that I shan't be well, and I really won't travel sitting up all night under those conditions. Denys is coming to Cannes on the 15th. I will come back then. [She didn't.] I don't want to write any more about this. I am infinitely sorry to know B.M. will be in Paris. I should have liked to be alone with you, or failing that, by myself.

Then, oh Hadji, my darling darling Hadji (you *are* my darling Hadji, because if it wasn't for you I would go off with V.), there's another thing. You say you only want to *tromper* me with myself.[1] But that's *impossible,* darling; there can't be anything of *that* now—just now, I mean. Oh Hadji, can't you realise a little? I *can't* put it into words. It isn't that I don't love you; I do. I do! How much you will never know.

The whole thing is the most awful tragedy, and I see only too clearly that I was never fit to marry somebody so sane, so good, so sweet, so limpid, as yourself; it wasn't fair on you. If you had asked me to live with you, I would have done so. It is all I am fit for. But at least I love you with a love so profound that it can't be uprooted by another love, more tempestuous and altogether on a different plane.

Hadji, I don't want to hurt you, I can't *really* hurt you, can I, when I tell you I love you so infinitely much?

Oh dear, all the fount of anguish with which I started this letter seems to have exhausted itself and I must stop. Don't think it a 'rattled' letter, it's so much graver than that, if you only knew. And don't be afraid I shall do anything awful.

Mar

HAROLD TO VITA *Paris*

9 December 1919

Darling, your letter was so frank and splendid. So like the real you which I know. You see my love for you rests on such firm foundations of truth and frankness, that when, for a red few days, I thought you had deceived me, the whole edifice of life appeared to totter. You know I could forgive you (it is an absurd word to use)—but I could wipe out all things except meanness. And if you were mean it would be as if you were dead, and my love would die for all except the remembrance of what you once were. But now your letter has come and you are alive again. And my love is like a forest in spring.

When you come back to me, I shall get on your nerves and so will B.M. And it will all be a nightmare. But it has got to be gone through,

---

1. In this roundabout way (for she spoke French perfectly) Vita was suggesting that Harold wanted to make love to her.

and we will go through with it together. And you can count on me
to say nothing, and to go on as if nothing has happened.

And what's more, you can count on B.M. too. I really think you
can. She is in her best mood and anxious only to help you. She really
does love you deeply—below all the surface selfishness.

So my darling, you will have a month or two months of real
torture. I am dreading it for you. But you will be brave and splendid—
and you can be irritable to me and I should know it, and you can cry
to me and I shall say nothing, and you can laugh, and I shall know
what ashes your laughter is made of.

Oh my Vita—I know what you are sacrificing for me.

V I T A T O H A R O L D   *Long Barn*

[1 February 1920]

There is so much in my heart, but I don't want to write it because
à quoi bon? Only if I were you, and you were me, I would battle so
hard to keep you—partly, I daresay, because I would not have the
courage and the reserve to do like you and say nothing. O Hadji, the
reason I sometimes try to get you to say things, to say that you would
miss me and that sort of thing, is that I long for weapons to fortify
myself with; and when you do say things, I treasure them up and in
moments of temptation I say them over to myself and think, "There,
he *does* mind, he *would* mind, you *are* essential to him . . . It is worthwhile making yourself unhappy if it is to keep him happy," and so
on, but then when you say things like that you don't miss me in Paris,
and that scandal matters, I think, "Well, if it is only on account of
scandal and convenience and above all *because I am his wife* and
permanent and legitimate—if it isn't more personal than that, is it
worthwhile my breaking my heart to give him, not positive happiness,
but mere negative contentment?"

So I fish, and fish, and fish, and sometimes I catch a lovely little
silver trout, but never the great salmon that lashes and fights and
convinces me that it is fighting for its life.

You see, I know you can do anything with me; you can touch

my heart like no one, no one, no one (the nearest is Ben), and I try to *make* you fight for yourself, but you never will; you just say, "Darling Mar!" and leave me to invent my own conviction out of your silence.

And O Hadji, what you don't realise is that I am very weak, and that my life for the past year almost has been one resistance of bitter temptation; and that it is simply and solely love of you which has kept me. You are good and sweet and lovable, and you are the person I loved in the best and simplest way; but there is lots that is neither good or simple in me, and it is that part which is so tempted. And I *have* struggled, I *have* stayed; I tore myself away and came to Paris in June last year; you know I have. And it is only, only, only out of love for you, nothing else would have weighed with me the weight of a hair, so you see how strong a temptation it must be, to sweep everything aside, and you see also how strong my love for you must be.

My darling, my darling, I shall love you till I die, I *know* I shall.

HAROLD TO VITA   *Hotel Alexander III, Paris*

3 February 1920

My darling Mar,

I have just got your letter—my dearest one—and I am so moved by it, my darling. There are so many things that are difficult to explain but there is first one thing I want to clear up.

When did I say I didn't "miss" you in Paris? Darling, I miss you all the time—you must have misunderstood me. I suppose I said that I didn't miss you in Paris as much as in London, or England, but if I said that, it is only a question of relativity. I mean I simply couldn't *live* in England without you—it would be one big pang like the journey down to Dover on Sunday. In Paris it's rather like as if I were a soldier and said I didn't miss you in the trenches. It would be quite true—but it wouldn't mean that I didn't *want* you. I *want* you all the time and wherever I may be—and if I felt I was not to see you again, I can't contemplate what my attitude would be.

It would be despair like one can't imagine it—a sort of winter night (Sunday) at Aberdeen, and me in the streets alone with only a Temperance Hotel to sleep in.

Then about my general attitude. You see, what appeal can I make except that of love? I *can't* appeal to your pity—and it would be doing that to let you see what I feared and suffered. It would be ridiculous to appeal to your sense of duty etc.—that's all rubbish. So what is there left but to appeal to love—my love for you and yours for me? And how can *that* appeal be anything but inarticulate? How can I formulate in words how I love you? One has only the current coin of the English language—such used and battered currency—of course my love is dumb in that way. But you must feel it and see it—and all you have done and sacrificed shows that you have felt it.

I know that you think sometimes that if you left me I should recover in a year or two and not be unhappy. I think you are so wrong there. You see, you would have ruined my life—I mean my inside life—and all the joys you had given me would be stinking corpses. I should mind that acutely and permanently. It would poison my heart and ruin my character. You know it would.

Then I should never love any one else. I see that quite clearly. So I would be so lonely, so terribly lonely—think of Edward Johnson [Sevenoaks widower]—it would be worse than that, as even my memories would be painful.

Darling, I hate the thought of your feeling frightened. Perhaps I have thought you stronger than you are. You see, your excessiveness and your ruthlessness give the impression of strength. I am frightened myself at your being alone over there [Long Barn]. Can't you come here? My darling, I feel that if we are together it may be easier for you. *Can't* you come—I shall *choyer* [cherish] you so, my sweet, and I shan't be too busy to have to leave you alone all day.

It *is* bloody being here—with you over there and unhappy.

You know, Ben is like me in that way. I mean, his never mentioning the pantomime. I simply *can't* talk about inside things which go deep—the words won't come out, or come out different. I know I am a fool and I make up things to say and then I can't say them. It is my own particular looniness.

But darling, how I love and want you: oh my darling, I think of you every five minutes, and what a stab those thoughts would be if you were a beast to me! Even so I can't conceive of you hurting me deliberately.

What a hopeless letter!

Hadji

HAROLD TO VITA

League of Nations, Paris

4 February 1920

My dearest, I thought of you so much last night. I am so worried about you. You are all wrong in thinking that I look upon you as my *légitime.* You are not a person with whom one can associate law, order, duty—or any of the conventional ties of life. I never think of you in that way, not even from the babies' point of view. I just look on you as the person I love best in the world and without whom life would lose all its light and meaning. My darling, I do hope you can come over here—it would be bloody for you in a way, but I do so want to have you with me and you can write. The [Hotel] Alexander III is quite comfy, and very clean. I don't want to be here long—it is terribly dull if one hasn't got a lot of work, or doesn't plunge into debauchery.

VITA TO HAROLD

Saracen's Hotel, Lincoln

7 February 1920

I am not fit to consort and remain with ordinary nice people. I *hate* myself, as I have told you a thousand times over. I wish I was dead, and that you hated me and didn't care what became of me.

Forgive me for not having written before. Really it is because some latent honesty within me will not allow me to write when the future is uncertain and when I know that any day I may cross the

Channel on that desperate voyage.[1] Oh my sweet, simple, *clean* Hadji, how much I love you and look enviously at you from a long way off.

V I T A   T O   H A R O L D   *Dover*

[9 February 1920]

    Hadji, since I wrote to you this afternoon things have happened. I went out to send some telegrams and to post my letter, and then I was standing looking at the sea when I saw Denys [Trefusis] coming towards me. He asked me where Violet was.[2] I said I had promised not to tell him. He said he would find out, or stay with me till I left Dover and come wherever I went because he knew I would join her sooner or later. So I told him, as it seemed useless to conceal it. So he and I are going there [Amiens] tomorrow, and he is going to ask her whether she will go back to him. I shall try my utmost to make her, O God, O God, how miserable and frightened I am—and if she refuses, he says he will never have anything to do with her again. I do not for a moment think she will consent, as I urged her *so* much this morning and she refused so positively; she said she would never live with him even if I did not exist. I will try to make her, I will, I will, I will; I will only see her in front of Denys, and he shall see that I will try.

    If she consents, and goes with him, I shall come to you. I am trying to be good, Hadji. I want so dreadfully to be with her, and I cannot *bear* to think of her being with him, but I shall try to make her. We are going to France. I nearly had a fit when I saw him. I can't help seeing the ludicrous side of this journey with him—will we go in the same railway-carriage or what? The whole thing is so unreal; everything is unreal except the pain of it. He has spent all the afternoon and most of the evening walking up and down my room in this filthy little

---

1. Vita's affair was approaching its climax. She had gone to Lincoln with Violet ostensibly to tour the Fens for her new novel, but in fact to plan their elopement. Harold, in Paris, did not know that Violet was with her.
2. Violet had crossed the Channel earlier that day, and Vita was to follow her on the 10th. They were to meet in Amiens. By this time, each had pledged to the other that they would abandon their families and spend the rest of their lives together.

hotel. I do not believe she will go back to him, and he says he will have nothing more to do with her if she won't. Hadji, it is the most extraordinary situation I have ever been in; I think you would think so too if you were me.

But the point is that if, after all his arguments and all my persuasion, she still refuses, he will go away leaving her for good. And she *will* refuse, I am almost sure she will refuse.

Hadji, I will try, I swear I will try, both for your sake and a little bit for his as I think he is too fine a person to be broken, but of course it is for you really. I *will* try, I feel strong, I did this morning and I can keep it up.

Poor Denys, he is really a very splendid person, though I know you think he is mad.

O darling, there's such an awful wind and the sea is so dreadfully rough.

How terrified she will be when she sees me arrive with him.

How worried you will be by all this. I am thankful you are not in the middle of it, as things always seem a little less vivid when one isn't there.

O darling, it's awfully lonely here.

I must write to B.M. now and Dada.[3]

Your Mar

---

3. No more is revealed in their correspondence, but the sequel is clear from Vita's and her mother's diaries, and Vita's narrative published in *Portrait of a Marriage*. Vita and Denys did cross the Channel together the next day, and found Violet unexpectedly in Calais. All three took the train to Amiens, where Denys abandoned his wife, giving up hope. But on 14 February he and Harold flew to Amiens and persuaded the two women to part. Eventually Vita and Harold returned to England, and Violet and Denys to the South of France.

*V*ita *and Violet continued to see each other, and even travel abroad together, for another year, but the confrontation at Amiens had defused their affair, and Vita's marriage was never again in danger. She and Harold had agreed that each could enjoy sexual independence of the other, and in 1923 she had her only affair with a man, the writer Geoffrey Scott, which ended more easily for her than for Scott, for he was divorced by his wife, while Vita abandoned him for the most important lover of her life, Virginia Woolf, whom she had first met in December 1922. This was the period when Harold, in the intervals of making a brilliant reputation as a diplomatist (notably on Lord Curzon's staff at the Lausanne Conference of 1923), had begun to write his first books—biographies of Paul Verlaine, Tennyson, and Byron, and his novel* Sweet Waters—*while Vita was writing fiction, poetry (she began* The Land *in 1923), and the history of her family,* Knole and the Sackvilles. *At Long Barn, and in London and Paris, both were enjoying a brilliant social life.*

VITA TO HAROLD   *Long Barn*

21 July [1920]

I got such a triumphant letter from you today about your [Austrian] treaty: you *are* brilliant and successful and clever and all that, damn you—and P.V.[1] is so good—it's not fair, whereas I am nothing

---

1. Harold's biography of the French poet Paul Verlaine, published by Constables in 1921. It was his first book.

but a muddling failure, damn you again. It will be envy and not infidelity that splits up our little ménage.

Your friend [Denys Trefusis] and Violet are separating completely, and I have much to tell you. She is going abroad almost at once. I have refused to go.

HAROLD TO VITA   *Foreign Office*

8 February 1921

My own darling silly,

I telegraphed to you twice—to Hyères[1] and to Cannes, begging you to fix a definite date for your return. This morning I get a reply to the effect that you "want to stay on a bit"—and ending in some rigmarole about a housemaid. But darling, that wasn't in the least a reply to my question. I never asked whether or not you wanted to stay on a bit (I took that for granted). What I asked was the length of the bit you wanted to stay on. To that I shall get no reply. Why? Because you are more selfish than Agrippina[2] in her worst moments, and because you are more optimistic than the Virgin Mary at her most light-hearted, and more weak than some polypus floating and undulating in a pond. You see, (a) you refuse obstinately to look at my side of the case. If you think of it at all, you evoke a picture of me bending by day over new maps of the Balkans; guiding the hands of Prime Ministers and statesmen towards a saner and better world: occupied, adulated, content. By night your picture shows me radiant in immaculate clothes, bandying the bouquet of wit with the bouquet of Veuve Cliquot—and returning at last ambrosial and refreshed to my warm and honourable bed. On Sundays you picture me relaxed and paternal, playing with my children among the tapestries of your ancestral home, or directing with gay and measured eye the structural alterations on my own estate.

Such is the picture you draw of me, and if, at moments, it seems

1. Where Vita had been staying with Violet since mid-January.
2. Mother of the Emperor Nero.

a little unconvincing, you quickly switch off the light with a "Poor little Hadji, I'll be so nice to him when I get back. I'll make it up."

(b) As regards yourself there is, first, the abiding squalor of dates. What was Saturday February 28th to Hernando de Soto[3]—or what was Hernando de Soto to Saturday February 28th? But secondly, and more important, is the thought that a date means an obligation, and an obligation a scene. Besides, it is throwing away a very useful stick wherewith to stir the troubled waters of your present life. You see, when the fur begins to fly it is splendid to be able to say, "Well really, Fatushka (or whatever it is),[4] I shall leave you tomorrow"—and then one has a reconciliation and it's all quite delightful. But if there are dates in front of one, one's departure becomes a mere fact, and not a threat which one can wave as a red flag at dramatic moments. And finally there is the thought, that little friendly thought of yours, "Oh something will turn up."

But on this occasion it isn't going to work. You are to be back in England on Friday, Feb. 25. On Saturday we shall go down together to the cottage. So please take your tickets at once. And please also realise that this is definite. I shall be more angry than I have ever been if you do not come back on that date. Don't misunderstand me: I shall really cut adrift if you don't. It is a generous date: it is longer than you promised: but it is a *fixed* date and you must keep to it.[5] If it is inconvenient to you, *tell me at once* and I will alter it. Otherwise it must be accepted.

I honestly believe you think that to write to me is 'indecent'. I know that the real reason is (a) V. doesn't let you write, (b) if you do write it makes you think of me and that produces a guilty feeling. But tell me this: if it is indecent of you to write to me when you are with V., isn't it far more indecent to write to V. when you are with me? And telegraph, and telephone, and meet in hotels, and churches, and galleries—and even at Hildenborough Station. How grotesque you are, darling!

Don't think I blame you. I love you too much for that. I know

---

3. The Spanish explorer who marched from Florida to beyond the Mississippi, 1539–41.
4. Vita called Violet "Lushka."
5. Vita returned to England on 9 March 1921, her 29th birthday.

that when you fall into V.'s hands your will becomes like a jelly-fish addicted to cocaine. All I ask is *please* don't make excuses. They don't take me in. I know that they are a little cold cream for your sore conscience. But keep them for yourself. Don't give them to me. They only sadden me the more, and *telegraph* when you have got tickets.

God bless you, my looney.

H.

HAROLD TO VITA   *Sussex Sq., Brighton*

18 September 1921

After all, it's no use writing novels which are only the observations of life. Journalism and the movies will do that for us. The point is to write books which are the explanation of life—and that is where you come in and I go out.

There is a light high up in the house opposite, and the spire of the church against dark wind-scudding clouds. The babies are asleep in their little beds. There are bath salts waiting for me. And there are you out there somewhere[1]—who will always love and stimulate, God bless you, and always, oh God bless you, understand.

HAROLD TO VITA   *53 Cadogan Gardens, London S.W.3*

16 November 1922

This is just a little scribble to reach you when you come back to Long Barn[2]—so that when you arrive you won't feel lonely or deserted, but will feel warm and so terribly loved and protected by our little mud pie [Long Barn], which we both love so childishly and

1. Vita was on a tour of Italy with Dorothy and Lord Gerald Wellesley.
2. Harold left for the Lausanne Conference the next day and did not return to London until February 1923.

which for both of us is the place where we have been so happy, darling.
I don't think we could ever leave the cottage: there is not one crook
in the wall, or one stain in the carpet, which does not mean something
to you and me which it could never mean to strangers: something
which has been built up gradually—little cell by cell, as Mr [Walter]
Pater would have said—and which means you to me, dearest, and me,
dearest, to you.

And with it all a sense of permanence so that as you sit in your
room tonight I shall think of you there, I dashing through the Ile de
France in a train. And I shall think of the Rodin, and the blue
[Egyptian porcelain] crocodile and the figure of St Barbara—and the
London *Mercury* [magazine] upon the stool. And it will be for both
of us as if I were there, and love still hangs, as well as smoke, about
the room.

It is beastly going away—but I think of £1,500 [salary] and liberty
at the end of it, and next summer, and Tennyson[3] coming out and the
revisions you will be sending me of the Knole book.[4] We are always
stirred and excited by the same thing—and oh my sweet we *do* love
and understand each other so absolutely that being parted is really only
like standing back from the picture to see it better.

Darling, you musn't be miz, will you—and you will make Chalk
Stone[5] the best book you have done.

And please don't run away with anybody without giving me time
to get my aeroplane ready.

VITA TO HAROLD   *Long Barn*

25 November [1922]

The garden is all dug over, and I have been so unslops; nearly
everything is done. The little devil polyantha are replaced by pink

---

3. Harold's *Tennyson* was published on 15 March 1923.
4. *Knole and the Sackvilles* in November 1922.
5. This was Vita's next novel, *Grey Wethers*. It received favorable reviews, but later in life
she so much disliked her early novels that she mentioned only *Heritage* in her *Who's Who*
entry.

roses; the tennis court is surrounded by roses; there are new archways
with Guirlande up near the chicken run; the lilacs are moved; the roses
are weeded out in the little enclosed gardens; the bed under the
big-room window is dug up and empty waiting for the roses to come;
next week there will be hedges planted down by the right of way and
up above the tennis court; there are new Guirlande roses by the
entrance; masses of new orange lilies in my border; lots of manure or
leaf-mould; a new strawberry bed; new roses in the oil-jars; no more
Dorothy Perkins; Irish yews ordered for the top of the steps, both
flights; so there really remain only the poplars to move now. Don't
you long for the spring?

HAROLD TO VITA   *Lausanne [Switzerland]*

25 November 1922

Curzon's valet got drunk and went down to the hotel ballroom
where people were dancing, and danced with the lovely ladies of
Lausanne. With the result that he was sacked. In revenge he hid the
Marquis's trousers, and the latter appeared in Allen's [Leeper] room in
his dressing-gown. It was some time before they were recovered.[1]

HAROLD TO VITA   *Lausanne*

6 December 1922

I was a little fussed by hearing in one of your letters that Violet
was coming to London. I can't help worrying over that a bit. I can't
help being afraid that she will bother you to see her and then mesmerize you, and that then it will all begin again. You see, now that you
have finished chalk-stones [*Grey Wethers*] and are going up to London,

---

1. This scene was described in the most famous chapter of Harold's most famous book, *Some People*. There he named the valet "Arketall." His real name was Chippendale.

you will be at a loose end and *so* available. And you will imagine that it will be quite safe to see her, and it *won't* be safe, and she will get hold of you again. She is so absolutely unscrupulous, my darling: and you, my darling, are so gullible and so weak. *Promise* me that you will be careful, and that if you get into a muddle you will jump into a train and come out here before it gets bad again.

Not that I care in the least how you behave: that's your business. It's simply that I don't want us both to be drawn into that vortex of unhappiness which so nearly overwhelmed us. So you will *promise,* darling, to be careful and not to go and get mesmerized; or take drugs; or go into smallpox areas; or eat too many sweets between meals? My darling—it is rather a fuss for me to have you there in London with that panther sneaking about waiting to pounce upon you.

I love you. I also love Lady Curzon. So if you go to Amiens with V. I shan't get into an aeroplane *this* time: not I: I shall get into a dinghy and row across to Evian with Lady C.

I wrote a poem today:

The expert attached to Lord Curzon
Is a strangely inferior person,
   When the Marquis rebuts
   His opinions, he puts
An expression of boredom—or worse—on.

VITA TO HAROLD   *Long Barn*

8 December [1922]

I have just come home from London and found a poor little worried letter from you about Violet, and have instantly sent you a telegram to set your mind at rest; I curse myself for having told you she was coming to London, and so having given you even a moment's anxiety.

Darling, my own darling, *not for a million pounds would I have anything* to do with V. again; I hate her for all the misery she brought upon us; so there. She did ring me up, (only I *beg* you not to say so to anyone), and I made Dots [Dorothy Wellesley] stay in the room as a witness, while I told her that nothing would tempt me to see her, and that she was utterly indifferent to me; which is true. You can ask Dots if you like. She has not tried to ring me up since, and I don't think she will again, after what she got from me! As a matter of fact, she is going back to Paris any day. But *don't worry*, oh don't, my little boy; word of honour, padlock, don't. I wish I could convince you.

And above all, I would *never* have anything more to do with her; the boredom of it . . . and the lies . . . and the rows . . . oh no, no, NO. Even if you didn't exist, you whom I love so fundamentally and deeply and incurably.

Oh yes, I know you will say, "But you loved me *then,* and yet you did." It's quite true, I did love you, and I always loved you all through those wretched years, but you know what infatuation is, and I was mad.

HAROLD TO VITA   *Lausanne*

2 January 1923

I went yesterday to Montreux and then changed and went in a funny funicular to a place called Gstaadt where we arrived at 7.30. I read Byron all the time.[1] We were met by a big sleigh with bells and went up to the Hotel. There was a dinner and a fancy dress ball afterwards, at both of which the school-boys whom your friend Neville Lytton[2] sends over to Switzerland all got drunk and noisy. I was rather bored and felt out of it. Next morning I skied. I don't think I have ever fallen about so much or so often. I rolled over and over like a rabbit. It was great fun. I was very careful. I was divided between trying to show off to the other members of the delegation and trying not to be chanticleer to my own sweet. The delegation won in the end. It was because there was a jump. One goes down the hill and then there

1. Harold had started researching for his book *Byron: The Last Journey.*
2. Later (1947) the 3rd Earl of Lytton, a portrait and landscape painter.

is a little nick in it and one goes right up in the air and then one falls down and rolls to the bottom. It is great fun.

By luncheon time I was dripping with heat and snow like a *bombe surprise*—and very excited. I started to go back to the hotel. I thought I should go alone just to surprise them. So I got into a little path and went on and on till suddenly I came across the railway line or rather the funicular. At a bound I had jumped it and was dashing down the slope beyond. The houses of the village rushed up to meet me: it was like coming down in an aeroplane: I thought how right you had been to warn me against winter sports: and where I had put my Will: and whether I had been good enough to Mummy: and then just as my whole past life began to rise before me, I saw that a barbed wire fence was also rising to meet me. I flung myself on my back: there was a shower of snow and skis and Hadji—and I came up crash against one of the supports of the fence.

Got up and shook myself. Very carefully felt myself all over. Limped along to the village street. The hotel was about half a mile above me. It was one-thirty. Wet, frightened, bruised and hungry I limped up the hill carrying my skis with me. It was as if Christ had been asked to carry his cross back from Calvary or like Mr Oates[3] going off to die at the South Pole.

HAROLD TO VITA [TELEGRAM]   *Lausanne*

9 January 1923

Letter just received. Delighted to expect you at Lausanne on Friday morning. Don't fail as Marquis is counting on you to help him at huge official dinner on Saturday. Lady Curzon comes today. I haven't written lately in view of your arrival. Oh God I long to see you, so bring pretty clothes and jewels. Keeping very snobbish about you and want to show you off. Isn't this an extravagant sort of telegram to send. Hadji.[4]

---

3. Lawrence Oates, who sacrificed his life in an attempt to save his comrades on Scott's expedition to the Antarctic, 1911–12.
4. Vita arrived in Lausanne as arranged, and stayed nine days.

VITA TO HAROLD   *182 Ebury St., S.W.1*

10 January [1923]

Tomorrow I dine with my darling Mrs. Woolf[1] at Richmond, "a picnic more than a dinner, as the press has overflowed both into the dining-room and into the larder." I love Mrs. Woolf with a sick passion. So will you. In fact I don't think I will let you know her.

VITA TO HAROLD   *Long Barn*

12 January [1923]

I dined alone with Virginia Woolf last night. Oh dear, how much I love that woman. Mrs [Julia] Cameron was her great-aunt, and she has lots of Mrs C's photographs, so I suppose I will have to let you meet her after all. She says Mrs C used to say to Tennyson, "Alfred, I brought my friends to see a lion, but they have only seen a bear." And she used to cut his hair.

HAROLD TO VITA   *Lausanne*

24 January 1923

I am so angry, that I am not in a fit state to write. I don't remember having been so angry in my life. It is about the Turks. They had the impudence to say that they must be allowed to dig up our graves at Gallipoli and put them all in one cemetery. I simply saw red. I told them that it was incredible that a beaten country should raise such a question. Then they climbed down, but they did not climb down far enough and I refused to go on discussing. Really they are quite, quite mad—and if they want war they will get it. I feel I won't speak to them again. I told them that the British Empire would never NEVER evacuate Gallipoli until our graves were safeguarded.

---

1. Vita had first met Virginia Woolf on 14 December 1922, dining with Clive Bell, who until then had been the Nicolsons' only link with Bloomsbury. Virginia and Leonard Woolf were then living at Hogarth House, Richmond, and it was there that they installed their printing press and published their first books under the imprint "The Hogarth Press."

HAROLD TO VITA   *Lausanne*

1 February 1923

I really think now we shall leave on Sunday *and with a Treaty*. I do really. Of course it is *entirely* the Marquis [Curzon] absolutely entirely. When I thought he was wrong, he was right, and when I thought he was right, he was much righter than I thought. I give him 100 marks out of 100 and I am so proud of him. So *awfully* proud. He is a great man and one day England will know it.

But you see Britannia *has* ruled here. Entirely against the Turks, against treacherous allies, against a weak-kneed cabinet, against a rotten public opinion—and Curzon has *won*. Thank God.

All this is after an interview with Ismet[1] when he collapsed in spite of Poincaré telling him not to collapse. And it was just due to the Marquis sitting there solid and *grand seigneur* and amused and brutal.

HAROLD TO VITA   *Foreign Office*

24 May 1923

My poppet,

They have mended my typewriter, and as I must try to see if it works, I shall write to you.

It does work.

I am rather worried about your speech tomorrow,[2] and the feeling that you will go there in your dear opty [optimistic] way, saying, "Oh No, they won't expect a speech from little me." And then suddenly when you are talking about water-wagtails to Lord Grey of Fallodon, you will be startled to hear a man, with a very grave face and a very distinct voice, say: "YOUR ROYAL HIGHNESS, YOUR EXCELLENCIES, MY LORD DUKE, MY LORDS, LADIES AND GENTLEMEN, PRAY SILENCE PLEASE FOR Miss V.

---

1. Ismet Pasha, the leader of the Turkish Delegation at Lausanne. Harold described the Conference in great detail in his *Curzon, The Last Phase* (1934).
2. At the English Association's annual dinner at the Trocadero Restaurant, London. Lord Grey, the former Foreign Secretary, was in the Chair, and Vita and the Spanish Ambassador responded for the guests.

Sackville-West." Then you will get up and feel very tall suddenly, and then very small suddenly, and in a voice like the bleat of some very distant lamb upon the mountain-side, you will begin, "YOUR ROYAL EXCELLENCY, HIGHNESS, MY DORD LUKE, MY LADIES, MY GENTLEMEN, PRAY SILENCE PLEASE . . . PLEASE . . . NO I mean . . . unaccustomed as I am to public speaking, yet I cannot restrain myself from thinking what I say about the Englosh assiciation, no I mean the Englash associotion, no I mean— well you know what I mean. Thank you very much. I HAVE ALWAYS THOUGHT . . . I HAVE ALWAYS THOUGHT . . . I have always thought . . . I HAVE ALWAYS THOUGHT . . . I have always thought . . . AND I THINK Today . . . today that that . . . AND I SHALL ALWAYS THINK . . . always . . . always . . . think . . . I think today, I have always thought and I shall always think . . . That . . . THAT . . . THAT . . . the English Association is the most english association that England has ever associated with. My Dord Luke, my excellent royal, my gentlemen, thank you very much. That's all I have to say. Thank you very much . . . great honour, unexpected pleasure . . . unaccustomed as I am. The heir to all the ages   the heritage of unfulfilled renown . . . the sallenge to Sirius . . . Orchyard . . . Sorry . . . Please may I sit down."

That sort of thing won't do at all. You must have something ready and learn it by heart. And have a little hot rumpled bit of paper with notes on it to remind you how your sentences begin.

Oh my sweet.

Hadji

HAROLD TO VITA   *Marlborough Club, S.W.1*

15 June 1923

They have shot poor old Stambolisky.[1] I don't think you know him. He was like a great bison with little red furtive eyes and a great massive frame. His hands were like large dimpled hams, and he painted

---

1. Alexander Stambolisky (1879–1923), the Bulgarian Prime Minister, who had represented his country at the Lausanne Conference. He was assassinated on 12 June after the fall of his Government.

his face, and roared like a bull and all his buttons came undone. He was a fine man, in a capricious way, and I can't help being sorry. He disliked me intensely—so that I am not speaking from personal prejudice. I hate the idea of someone whom I knew and abused and worked with and rather liked, lying in some dusty roadway with his tongue cut and his hair clotted with blood.

What swine the Balkans are! My pig farm. But how glad I am that they are my own speciality.

HAROLD TO VITA

2 September 1923

The Royal Automobile Club, London S.W.1

At noon the Embassy telephoned to say that the Marquis had left Paris. At six they telephoned to say he had arrived at Dover. Tyrrell,[1] Allen [Leeper] and I went to Victoria to meet him. The train was an hour late. We went to dine at the station buffet and returned to the platform. There was a large crowd and mounted police. The posters had got "The new War" on them, and "Lord Curzon's hurried return."[2]

There was a large space railed off for his arrival and a crowd of police, reporters, photographers and detectives. The white faces of the crowd bobbed beyond the barrier under the arc-lights. Slowly the train came in and his saloon drew up opposite the enclosure. First came a procession of red boxes and the green baize foot-rest. Then slowly and majestically came the Marquis. The reporters got out their note-books. The photographers set flame to their magnesium. The detectives detected: the police policed. The crowd crowded.

"Where is Nicolson?" said the Marquis, but the rest was lost in a burst of cheering from the crowd. He walked across and "entered his waiting motor."

"Nicolson?" he exclaimed again. I came to him, and leant into the motor. The crowd peered. The detectives kept them back. The report-

---

1. William Tyrrell, Assistant Undersecretary at the Foreign Office, and Curzon's senior civil servant at Lausanne.
2. The crisis had been caused by Mussolini's sudden seizure of Corfu after a dispute with Greece. Curzon, the Foreign Secretary, was ill with phlebitis, and rapidly returned from his holiday in France to London.

ers again took out their note-books. I pulled myself together for the instructions which were to settle the fate of Europe.

"I have been reading *Grey Wethers* [Vita's novel]," said the Marquis—"a magnificent book. The descriptions of the downs are as fine as any in the language. Such power! Such power! Not a pleasant book of course! But what English!"

He was still muttering "What English" as he drove off with Tyrrell. The latter, as he told me afterwards, was longing to ask what Poincaré had said—but no! He was given your literary biography all the way to Carlton House Terrace. "Poincaré?" pleaded Tyrrell as they arrived. "Oh, we talked about Rénan—goodnight Tyrrell."

HAROLD TO VITA   *Athens*

5 October 1923

Poppet,

I worked all yesterday like a little lamb whose fleece was white as snow, which was more than Byron's was, poor man. Atchley is really immensely useful and helps me a great deal. Suggesting there, correcting there. It was worthwhile coming here if only for him.[1] In the evening I had to go out to Kephisia bump bump bump along a dusty pepper-lined road under the stars: the goats, now and then, were frightened of the motor lamps. But Charles Bentinck [Chargé d'Affaires at the Legation] lives there and he begged me to go and dine and sleep. He has got a Villa with oleanders and a gramophone and a shower bath which sighs at one when one pulls the handle because the water has run out. So does the other thing: I was never an expert at pulling plugs but this one just said "fancy that" in a deep bass voice and nothing more. There was a japanned tin pail to help one out with water in it, and a horrid little bristly brown brush. I had a mosquito net. I don't like Kephisia. There is not even a view, and I was glad to get back to my violet-crowned Athens this evening. And I love this place. It beats Rome hollow.

---

1. Harold had gone to Greece to research for his book *Byron: The Last Journey*. S. C. Atchley had been attached as a translator to the British Legation, Athens, since 1909.

Today I went over the Acropolis alone with Wace[2] who is head of the English School at Athens. I am not in principle a good sightseer, but I remained there three hours without noticing and I asked intelligent questions. I didn't ask questions about Corinthian as I doubted whether I could render them very intelligent. Then we lunched together, and afterwards Atchley showed me the bits of Athens that remained from the time when Byron knew it. Just a little cluster of cottages round the Acropolis hill and the smell of drains. And I have got to go to Kephisia again tonight. DAMN. I go to Missolonghi[3] on Tuesday and come back here on Friday.

HAROLD TO VITA   *Garrick Club, London W.C.2*

12 February 1924

I had the most extraordinary experience here tonight, which I must record at once unless it be, or to prevent it being, disbelieved afterwards. It was this.

I dined at the Marlborough [Club]. It was dark and dull. I talked to Admiral Pakenham who is fat and dreary. I couldn't bear it. I came here. I spoke to Admiral Hall who asked me to stand as a Unionist (Good God! but why not?) candidate. Then he went away. I had some beer. I said I would have light beer and not heavy beer. This point is important. They brought me Bass.

Then I went to the lavatory. And beyond the lavatory is the little room in which they keep the sofa which was in Byron's room at Missolonghi. A sudden temptation seized me. The room was quite dark—lit only by the coke embers of a very economical fire. The lights were unlit. I knew where the sofa stood. I threaded my way between the few leather chairs which separated me from it. I bumped a bit, but still I threaded. And then I got there. I lay back and tried to make my mind a blank. I thought of sheep going through a gate: No! that was something else: I thought of nothing: I tried to make my mind as blank as possible. I thought of things like Ochs [Herbert Asquith], and clean

2. Alan Wace, the archaeologist. He was Director of the British School, 1914–23.
3. Where Byron died in 1824.

water, and Reggie Cooper, and your friend Mrs Pirie [Irene Hogarth]. Only by this means could I attain the necessary anaesthesia. I clasped the wooden parts of the sofa. The fluffy parts might be new: but the wooden parts were Byron, Missolonghi, Missolonghi, Byron, Byron, Missolonghi, Missolonghi, Byron. I repeated the words, since that (I believe) is the psychic thing to do.

Well, nothing happened. I tried again. I thought back on all the last pages of my book, I thought myself INTO Byron. And then gradually a sort of strange, unknown, feeling came over me. Really it was very uncanny. The room was very dark. It was absurd, but something white and phosphorescent began to glimmer opposite against the curtains. I wasn't in the least bit taken in. I *knew* it was imagination. But NO! the thing took shape. It really did: it emerged quite definitely, darling, as a FACE.

It was a face, a white magnolia face, that looked at me across the room. You *know* that I don't make things up: and I *swear* to you that at that moment I saw the face of Byron looking at me. I wasn't in the least frightened. I just sat and watched it. It didn't disappear. It got clearer and clearer. There was a sort of drapery (or was it protoplasm?) round the shoulders.

Then I got frightened and dashed to the electric light switch. I turned on the light. There was a bust against the curtains, with a brass plate underneath:—

> WINIFRED EMERY
> BY ALBERT TOFT
> Presented by Cyril Maude

HAROLD TO VITA   *Foreign Office*

4 December 1924

I have been worrying all day about Violet.[1] I couldn't bear it in the end, and sent you a silly telegram. I hope you weren't cross. But

---

1. Vita was going to dine with friends in Paris, and Violet Trefusis was to be another guest.

my darling, I do so dread that woman. Her very name brings back all the aching unhappiness of those months: the doubt, the mortification, and the loneliness. I think she is the only person of whom I am frightened—and I have an almost superstitious belief in her capacity for causing distraction and wretchedness. Of course I know that it's all over now, but what I dread is your dear sweet optiness—just, "Oh but it's quite safe—and rather fun"—and then she will mesmerize you and I shall get a telegram to say you are staying on in Paris. If I *do,* I shall fly over at once—I'm not going to trust to luck this time.

Oh my darling—do please be very careful and take no risks. You don't know how anxious I am.

I lunched with Mrs [Margot] Asquith. What a splendid woman she is! I am really fond of her. It was a nice luncheon and I sat next to her and she told me stories about Kitchener. But all the time I was thinking of that basilisk [reptile] over there and my poor sweet opty at No. 53 rue de Varenne.[2]

Oh how glad I shall be to hear you are coming back!

---

2. The house of Walter Berry, their host.

*arold was appointed Counsellor (and Chargé d'Affaires be-
tween two Ministers) at the British Legation, Teheran. Vita
did not accompany him, but twice made the long and hazard-
ous journey to Persia to stay with him for a couple of months. Her
first visit was from January to May 1926, when she attended and
helped organize the Shah's coronation (which she described in her
book* Passenger to Teheran), *and the second from February to May
1927, which ended with an arduous trek across the Bakhtiari Mountains with Harold. While he was in Persia, Harold occupied his
leisure with writing* Some People, *and Vita at home and in London
developed her friendship with Virginia Woolf into an intimacy. She
was writing* The Land *and completed it in Persia. She and Harold
wrote to each other every day, posting their letters in a single
envelope to catch the fortnightly diplomatic bag.*

VITA TO HAROLD   *Long Barn*

5 November [1925]

It's a ¼ to 9—you must be thinking of arriving at Trieste. You
have gone over that strange calcined Carso country which I thought
so dramatic, only I saw it in full-moon light, and you will have had
no moon. Do you remember a moon-landscape walk we had at
Schluderbach[1] after dinner? how lovely it was? How happy we have
been, whenever we have got away together like that, and we had a

---

1. Now Carbonin in the Italian Dolomites, where Harold and Vita went on a walking tour
in July 1924.

bare wooden room under the three peaks and there was a storm—no I'm muddling it: the storm was at Tre Croci.[2] Oh Hadji! . . . shall we ever do those things again? Everything that we have done together comes back to me with such poignancy: I am dreadfully lonely tonight, I don't mind telling you so, because it will all be so safely distant by the time you can read this and know about it: I thought I would be able to work, but the only relief I can find is in writing to you. I have already written you one long letter this evening. Now I have had my dinner, or rather Pippin [her spaniel] has had most of my dinner, and it is dark and the house is silent, and the book of Elizabethan lyrics which I have been trying to read seems to be all about love—(blast it)—so I threw it across the room in anger because it made things worse. I feel all at sea, Hadji; I cannot get a hold upon myself; but of course I shall before very long. If it was just your going away, I think I could cope with it; but you see it will be three weeks before I know you are safe.

HAROLD TO VITA

6 November 1925

In the Adriatic
Piroscafo Helouan

Oh my dear, how I wish you were with me—you know how I love the sea, and Greece, and I shall get both. But it all seems rather meaningless without my own darling. I am all right during the day. But when night falls and the electric lights come out, and the sea is something realised only by its sound, then a wave of home-sickness comes over me and I walk up and down the deck thinking, "Viti, Viti, Viti." I have not had the spirit yet to go on with MY NEW BOOK [*Some People*]. I have felt upset and jaundiced by being so unhappy. But I have taken some camomile and should regain my buoyancy tomorrow. I shall take a lot of exercise, and I hope that my intelligence, which at present is hiding hurt and muffled in a hole, will come back to me. So far I just feel bruised and stupid and terribly tired.

---

2. Between Cortina and Misurina.

VITA TO HAROLD   *Long Barn*

16 November [1925]

An enormous excitement that I found when I got home was that
the Encyclopaedia had come[1]—Oh darling it is going to be quite
invaluable to me. So far I have only *durch-blättered* [skipped through]
it, but I have seen quite enough to know that the georgics will swell
in volume and in information. It looks blue and impressive in my
shelves. I flung out the works of Corneille to make room for it. You
were a perfect angel to have ordered it for me. I shall never be able
to tell you how touched I was. I'm really going to settle down to work
now. I wonder what your new book is? Oh Hadji . . . I just go stupid
with missing you and wanting you.

HAROLD TO VITA   *Kermanshah [Persia]*

24 November 1925

At 9.30 p.m. we hooted out of Jerusalem.[2] One drops five thousand feet down to the Jordan. It is a lovely road, but rather hair-pinned.
One could see the lights of the car in front lighting up the rocky sides
of the gorge, and twisting in and out down the mountain. It got
warmer and warmer and then suddenly the sound of frog-croaking and
the lights of a guard house by a steel bridge. We had reached the
Jordan, and bumped across from Palestine into Transjordania. From
there on, the road was bad and it was past midnight before we came
to the poplars and running water of Amman. Beyond the town is a
large enclosure shut in with barbed wire, full of lorries and motors and
bell-tents. In one tent we had supper. In the other, we slept four of
us on camp beds. It was there, by the light of the flickering candle,
that I opened your birthday letter, my saint. The trucks on the Hedjaz

1. A four-volume Encyclopaedia of Agriculture, which Harold had ordered for Vita to help
her with the technical information for her poem *The Land,* which she first called "The
Georgics."
2. In 1925 travel to Bagdad and onwards to Teheran was by motor convoy from Jerusalem
across the desert.

railway above me clinked and clanked all night, and all night the dogs barked.

At 5.0 a.m. a face opened the flap of our tent. "Passengers for Bagdad get ready please." With grunts and snorts we undid ourselves, had some hot tea, and climbed back into our cars while the dawn was breaking. There was a large sort of charabanc which held six people. I and an employee of the Anglo-Persian [Oil Company] were on the back seat of a Cadillac touring car, having the chauffeur and a spare chauffeur in front. A convoy going the other way had come in early in the night and as we jerked out of the wire enclosure there was much private soldier badinage and witticisms. From Amman one gets almost at once into the open country. Wide sad downs like the short cut above Rottingdean. Then ten miles or so of shale. Then ten miles of bumpy little sand hussocks, over which we swayed and lurched. Then the rising sun and the distant silhouettes of Volcanic mountains—small Vesuvius formations and table-mountains. Then forty miles of lava boulders, bump, bump, bump, then twenty miles of mud flats and puddles, then shale again. Luncheon (turkey, hard boiled eggs, tea) on a rug in the burning sun. Then start again. Flying for two hundred miles over a hard tennis court at 60 miles an hour. Then five more hours of jerking over bad country, an amazing sunset, Jupiter and Venus in conjunction doing a double evening star, and then complete darkness with the head-lights straining in front of us. We had done 400 miles and passed only one human being, and he was dead—a dead man by the roadside with his guts disarranged by vultures. On and on through the night until suddenly we pulled up with a jerk in front of an extraordinary jumble of white wood and aluminium, looking like some vast and expensive toy which had been smashed in the post. It was a wrecked aeroplane de luxe, and we lit a fire from the wreckage and had supper. Then on again after supper through the dark. I blessed my cushions and slept well enough. Woke to feel cold and found we had stopped. An armoured car detachment was encamped there. They gave us whisky and there was more badinage. A wonderful sunrise and by ten o'clock we were at Ramadi the air-station. Here we had breakfast. Left at noon and flew at 70 miles an hour across another hard tennis court, till we reached the Euphrates. Then another two hours sprint and by 3.0 p.m. we were crossing the bridge at Bagdad.

Washed, shaved, I went off to The High Commissioner. A telegram from my darling and letters from Loraine. Dashed in to see Gertrude Bell.[3] She was charming. Then dinner and off to the station. A reserved carriage or rather saloon with a bathroom. Slept like a top and woke up at 7.0 a.m. at Khamkin. Foul little motor for me. A dreadfully protracted fuss over passports, customs etc. and off at nine. A beastly road to the Persian frontier—bump, bump, bump. Then a grand house and some barbed wire, and a darling Persian official who gave me cigarettes in handfuls and delicious tea. Then off again, very uncomfortable—no room at all in the car for my feet. All my luggage in a motor long behind. Three people at the back (two Imperial Bank people and myself) and in front the driver (Irish) and the Legation orderly. The road was good enough—but the car was so rotten that we crawled and crawled. We should have got here by 5.0 p.m. but by then we were 100 miles away and it was dark and bitterly cold. On and on very slowly, till suddenly *crash* and we collapsed into a hole in the road. We all climbed out, extricated the car, and found that the front axle was bent and the exhaust pipe broken. Very slowly we limped onwards—getting here at 10 p.m., five hours late.

The Consul and his wife did their best. But they have no spare room and I slept on a camp bed in their drawing-room, too small for me, hard, and incredibly cold. My one consolation was your dear letter.

This morning we were to start at nine. I waited and waited till 12.0 and then sent a message to see what had happened. The car was too badly broken to continue. So I shall have to stay here another day and have another day in that beastly refrigerator. You can imagine how furious this makes me. If the car had been even averagely good I should have got through easily. The road itself is excellent—just as good as the road from the village to Sevenoaks.

Of course I expect that people here get used to never knowing when one starts and when one arrives. But to me this hanging about is really maddening—and destroys the pleasure I should get from the amazing beauty of the scenery.

---

3. The traveler and writer. She was then Oriental Secretary to Sir Percy Cox, British Commissioner in Iraq, and Director of Antiquities.

HAROLD TO VITA   *Teheran*

28 November 1925

The Chancery is exactly like all other chanceries—even to the smell of sealing-wax and mail-bags. The staff is enormous (soldiers, archivists, interpreters, dragomen)— but the only two diplomatic members proper are Warner and Jebb.[1] The former erudite, slightly uncouth, efficient, rather attractive. The latter of great beauty (half Hugh Thomas and half Lady Curzon) and possessing a gentle charm. Rather shy at first.

HAROLD TO VITA   *Teheran*

3 December 1925

This morning early I dressed in my tail-coat and was taken by Percy [Loraine] to see the Foreign Minister. The Foreign Office is rather a jolly old building with a courtyard and a fountain and the most heavenly picture running right across the top of the staircase. A life-size (or over-life-size) fresco of a Foreign Ambassador being received by Fat Ali-Shah.

Then we went into a little room with a wallpaper of yellow chrysanthemums and red damask curtains. And there were little red arm-chairs with tockles [lamps] and cigarettes: they brought us tea. The minister is a copper-coloured man, or rather bronze-coloured, and after a long discussion about my nativity,[2] we settled down to business, which meant just silence and sighs. I see that this is no place for impiness [impatience], and that I must realise that what took 5 minutes at home must take two hours here. So we smoked and drank tea and talked at very distant intervals about the weather, and then the M.F.A. [Minister for Foreign Affairs] fished in his frock coat and brought out a tiny bit of paper which the interpreter translated and which was all

---

1. Christopher Warner and Gladwyn Jebb, respectively Second and Third Secretaries.
2. Harold was born on 21 November 1886 in the Legation Compound in Teheran, where his father was Secretary.

about a river I had never heard of and the iniquitous treatment accorded to that river by the Government of Iraq. And so by easy flatulent stages one passed on to more serious business.

VITA TO HAROLD   *Long Barn*

8 December 1925

I am reading Proust, and dislike his mentality more and more. I get the sense of that flabby, diseased, asthmatic man, all frowsty in bed till evening, and preoccupied with such contemptible things—nothing but women and snobbery. It makes me angry that he should write so exceedingly well, having nothing worthwhile to write about.

HAROLD TO VITA   *Teheran*

10 December 1925

In the afternoon I went to see Reza Khan [the Shah of Persia]. He lives in a little white villa in a garden. We went in by the street door, as the garden-door was crowded with guards and lancers. We were shown into a little white room with a huge fire and atrocious Louis XVI furniture. The room gave on to a sort of balcony or loggia and we hadn't been there long before the windows were darkened by an immense figure passing in front of them. The end-windows opened and he came in. He was in Khaki uniform with a peaked Khaki hat— slashed at the corners. He hadn't shaved very well and glowered out of the corner of his eye at us. He was quite alone. He is about six-foot-three and inclined to corpulence. He has fat red hands like Gerry [Wellesley]. He has bad teeth, fine eyes and chin, and a determined nose. A clipped greyish moustache. But he looked cross and tired and dirty. Then he sat down.

I told him of the interest he aroused in England and how we hoped he would make a nice good kind Shah. He was pleased by these assertions, and relaxed. He gave us cigarettes and cakes and tea. Suddenly he took his hat off—disclosing a tiny little shaven head like a Russian Cossack. He looked more of a scallywag than ever. But then gradually he began to talk quite calmly about becoming Shah, and his arrangements for his coronation, and how cross everyone was, and how he had felt his collar too tight at the opening ceremony, and how Farman Farma[1] had been photographed sitting on the steps. And then he laughed a sort of non-commissioned officer laugh—and asked me how old I was. He wouldn't believe it when I told him[2] and said evidently I had had no troubles in love or politics. I thought of my darling digging away over there at our mud-pie. Then he laughed a great deal—and for the rest of the interview was simple and jolly and with a certain force and dignity. But I am not so sure about him. I haven't seen enough Persians yet to compare him with. Anyhow he was very cordial and told me to come and see him as often as I liked when he was Shah. He adores Percy[3]—and Percy is rather pleased with himself (and with justice) at having backed a winner from the start—and *such* a winner.

VITA TO HAROLD   *Long Barn*

17 December [1925]

Well, I took my letters for you to the [Foreign] office, and I took my box of rosemary, and I sent off my puppy from Waterloo to Winchester, and I fetched Virginia, and brought her down here.[4] She is an exquisite companion, and I love her dearly. She has to stay in bed till luncheon, as she is still far from well, and she has lots of writing to do. Leonard [Woolf] is coming on Saturday—(oh dear, how meaningless all these Saturdays and so on must be to you at that distance. The only thing is to go on writing, day by day and to allow you to

1. A Qajar prince of the old regime.
2. Harold was just thirty-nine.
3. Sir Percy Loraine had been Minister in Teheran for four years and, although a somewhat conventional and ponderous British diplomatist, he had won the confidence of Reza Khan who regularly consulted him even on domestic affairs.
4. It was on this visit that Vita's love affair with Virginia Woolf began.

fill in the dates from your imagination,—just living my life from day to day and let you re-live it at a month's remove.)

Oh, the doves are cooing. It is midnight. The doves cooing *always* make me think of you because you love them, and they are so much the cottage.

Please don't think that

(a) I shall fall in love with Virginia

(b) Virginia will fall in love with me

(c) Leonard   "   "   "   "   "   "

(d) I shall fall   "   "   "   Leonard

because it is not so. Only I know my silly Hadji will say to himself, *"Allons, bon!"* when he hears V. is staying here, and *"Ca y est,"* and so on.

Loud coo from the doves.

I miss my puppy, which was the nicest I ever had.

I am missing you dreadfully. That is why I am writing to you last thing at night. I am missing you specially because Virginia was so very sweet about you, and so understanding.

Oh darling, I do love you SO AWFULLY. It doesn't get any better as time goes on. I hoped it would. But it doesn't.

VITA TO HAROLD   *Brighton*

26 December [1925]

I lunched at Charleston[1]—very plain living and high thinking. I like Virginia's sister [Vanessa] awfully. There were two huge, shaggy, rather attractive boys [Julian and Quentin Bell] who call their father and mother Clive and Nessa. There was Clive, and Virginia and Leonard. Virginia discoursed about the Georgics [*The Land*] till I was shy. She does this to everyone, I find—a good preliminary advertisement! I drove them over the Downs. So lovely in the mist, and I longed for Hadji. Virginia *loves* your mar. She really does. It is a soul-friendship. Very good for me; and good for her too.

---

1. The farmhouse under the Downs near Lewes, Sussex, which Vanessa Bell and Duncan Grant had made their home.

I find that not one person in six knows where Persia is. Vanessa could say only that it was "not in America." Oh my dear, they do live in such squalor! How luxurious they must think the mars.

VITA TO HAROLD   *Long Barn*

29 December 1925

Geoffrey [Scott] rang me up suddenly this evening in a state of hysteria (or so it sounded), and said could he see me tomorrow. I said I was sorry, I was too busy. He said, "I want to say goodbye to you." I said, "Why, are you going to Mexico after all?" He said, "No, I mean I want to see you for the last time, but of course if you are too busy to accord me a quarter of an hour, it doesn't matter: I'll say goodbye here and now"; and slammed down the receiver. So I don't know what the position is. He has been furious ever since you left because I wouldn't see him, or scarcely. Really, Hadji, I should be relieved, except that I would rather have remained good friends with him if possible. But he minds too much for that. I don't know why I bore you with this. It must all seem very remote. And indeed it seems very remote to me. I am too concentrated on you—little pig. And you have gone away.[1]

HAROLD TO VITA   *Teheran*

8 January 1926

I am not really bothered about Virginia and think you are probably very good for each other. I only feel that you have not got *la main heureuse* in dealing with married couples. And how dare you say you won't tell me what she said about the Georgics—when you know that is such an excitement to me? Don't get them put into print until I have

1. Vita felt guilty about her abandonment of Geoffrey Scott, the writer, because she had smashed his marriage by their brief affair. He went to live in New York, where he died in 1929, aged forty-six.

seen them, and you have been able to put in some purple passages from the East. (Like the Lebanon honey, and the Tuscan wine.) Oh dear, what fun we shall have sitting there in our beastly little room reading them over again! Have you yet coped with the vast problem of who is to publish them?[1]

HAROLD TO VITA   *Teheran*

15 January 1926

The Military Attaché is called Fraser. His wife is called Mrs Fraser. She is rather a jolly woman really and you will like her. Only she came in here today to see whether she would buy any of Monson's[2] things, and on the Po-stand she saw that piccy of you holding Benzie [Ben] when he was in his christening clothes. She looked at it for a long time and then she said: "I like that woman; she knows how to hold a baby." And oh my sweet I thought of what a ridiculous piccy that was of you—so I have drawn one of what that phrase awoke in me. I always make you look like Venetia Montague in my piccies—I must try another:—

Pretty!   Oh dear!   Eddie!   No! I can't
               Grecian!   do it.

1. *The Land* was published by Heinemann, to whom Vita was bound by contract, not (as she would have preferred) by the Woolfs' Hogarth Press.
2. Edmund Monson, Harold's predecessor as Counsellor.

HAROLD TO VITA   *Teheran*

3 May 1926

When you get this it will be at Brighton[1] and we shall both have
a great iron chunk of misery behind us. Dearest one—what an odd
thing it all is: the whole centres of us both aching for each other and
then going off in opposite directions. Oh my dear—I do hope that
when you read these words we shall both be happy again or at least
not unhappy. I know now that I can't really be happy without you
being there, or being imminent. These months will be waste months
in my life—arid thirsty deserts. That's why I turn to the thought of
work as my only solace. I feel quite ill this evening with it all. And
the sun setting among the planes looks as if it were doing it in some
different way—like when one has cotton-wool in one's ears.

HAROLD TO VITA   *Teheran*

12 May 1926

Tray is writing his article about alternatives to chastity.[2] It is very
good—perfectly simple and closely reasoned. He concludes (having
watched the Mars and knowing how much they love each other) that
the best life is marriage plus liaisons. Or rather his argument is:—

(1) Passion, i.e. being 'in love', can only last a certain number of
    years.
(2) After that both sides instinctively search for variety.
(3) If the doctrine of fidelity is too rigid, then they both have a
    sense of confinement and frustration, and irritation results.
(4) But if there is mutual physical freedom, this sense of bondage
    does not arise: good relations are maintained—and from this
    emerges community of life, and *'love'* (with a big L)—which
    is something quite different from passion, and far deeper than

1. Vita was about to leave Teheran after her first visit to Harold. She traveled to the Caspian,
   thence to Baku-Moscow-Berlin-Holland.
2. "Tray" was Raymond Mortimer, who remained Harold's guest in Teheran after Vita's
   departure. His article was a pamphlet about liberal attitudes to sex, but Leonard Woolf
   thought it too frank for publication.

Vita in 1910,
the year when
she first met Harold.

Harold in 1911,
as a junior official
in the Foreign Office.

Lord and Lady Sackville, Vita's parents, in 1913, setting out for the courts to defend themselves in the famous Scott case.

Vita on her way to give evidence in the Scott case, accompanied by Harold (left), Rosamund Grosvenor, and her father, Lord Sackville.

Vita and Harold are married in the chapel at Knole on 1 October 1913.

*Vita at about the time of her elopement
with Violet Trefusis (1920).*

*Violet Keppel (Trefusis) in
the early 1920s.*

*In Persia, 1926. Vita and Harold are in the front row, with Raymond
Mortimer (left) and Gladwyn Jebb behind.*

Virginia and Leonard Woolf, in a photograph taken by Vita at their country cottage, Monk's House, Rodmell, Sussex, in 1926.

Vita at Long Barn in 1928, photographed by Leonard Woolf for Orlando.

Her sitting room at Long Barn, where she wrote The Land *and* The Edwardians.

The Nicolson family at Long Barn in 1927, when Harold was on leave from his diplomatic post in Berlin. Left to right, Ben, Harold, Nigel, Vita.

affection. He says that only really fine characters and deter-
minedly intellectual people can attain to this. But that the
confusion of 'love' and 'in love'—and the idea that "Love
equals merely affection"—leads to great confusion. There is
something in all this, but I expect there is a snag somewhere.
You see, our love is something which only two people in the
world can understand. The first and dearest of these two people
is Viti. The second, poor man,

is your own
Hadji

VITA TO HAROLD   *[In the train Moscow–Warsaw]*

13 May 1926

Now I will tell you what my impression of Russia was. It was one
of terror. Everyone seems to go in fear of being overheard; everyone
looks furtive and afraid. All the people at that dinner-party at the
[British] Mission [in Moscow] said to me, one after the other, and not
in reply to any prompting on my part, "You see, it is so dreadful living
here. One never knows who will disappear next." There are arrests
nearly every day. If they cannot or will not bring a political accusation
against someone they want to catch, they cause false money to be
slipped into his pockets and then arrest him on that charge. The
Russians hardly dare to consort with foreigners. Of course the obvious
thing to say is that one is 'suggested' into these impressions, but truly
I believe I should have felt the same even had I known nothing about
the state of the country. Baku was quite different—quite gay and
lively—but Moscow is terrible. One sees people sitting or standing at
the street corners in attitudes of despair; and yet they say it is better
than it was a year or two years ago.

Dear me, I hope they won't open this letter! I shall post it from
Warsaw if I can get a stamp, otherwise it will have to wait till I reach
Germany. Oh my darling, what a long way it is, to go half across the
world like this! country after country unrolling itself, frontier after
frontier—and all so ugly.

Polish frontier. Here is a pretty kettle of fish! There is a revolution

in Poland, and no trains can go through Warsaw. So we have to be
sent round—some people say by Cracow and Prague, others say by
Königsberg. The officials seem to be extremely vague. I hope there
won't be an accident, that's all. In any case I fear it will mean a great
deal of delay. How I wish now that I had gone by Riga. The train
has started. It consists of only two carriages, and we are apparently
making for a place called Bialystok. Anyway I am seeing the world.
There are two nice Germans in my carriage. I find the way to talk
really lovely Persian is to try to talk German. I feel rather a waif, and
wonder where I shall sleep tonight—if anywhere.

Saturday, May 15th Königsberg station, between 2 trains.

My precious Hadji, well, anyway I am in Germany, having escaped
from Poland on a railway engine, so with any luck I may get home
before long. It's been one of the most absurd experiences I ever had;
I wish I could reproduce it all for you, and above all, oh above all,
I wish you had been there. If I had had anyone to laugh with, it would
have been the best possible joke. Now I'll go back to yesterday.

The train pulled up with a jerk at Bialystok, which is a little
junction somewhere in Poland, and there it became necessary to devise
a plan of campaign. There were a great many soldiers, and everybody
in a fluster, and no news from Warsaw as the telephones were all cut
and no train had come down the line from Warsaw that day. All that
the officials would promise was to take us (in the Russian train) to a
station ten miles from Warsaw; after that they would guarantee nothing.

So, with ten other people, we made up a party determined to get
to the nearest German frontier. (I am now no longer at Königsberg,
but in Berlin. It's a muddling life. Here, after the infinite squalor of
the last few days, I sit at the Kaiserhof, having ordered the best dinner
and the best wine from a crowd of obsequious waiters. But I antici-
pate.) Behold me, then, at Bialystok, ejected with my little packages
into the middle of revolutionary Poland, in company with 7 Germans
(commercial travellers I should think), a Russian, and two Austrians—
one of them a young woman with cropped golden hair, no better than
she should be, and the other her? husband. Anyhow we all went and
ate Wienerschnitzel very merrily in the station buffet, not knowing
when we should get our next meal. And then the little train came in,

and we launched off, meandering about Poland, seeing troops in occupation of every station, and finally after dark we came to Grajewo,
which is the German frontier. A tiny place, with a shed for a customs
house. There were, it seemed, no more trains that night, and very
doubtful whether there would be any at all next day. So, being
determined to get out of Poland at all costs, we got the promise of
our engine to take us across the frontier. But it was not available till
after midnight. How, then, to spend the hours from 8 to 12 at Grajewo?
a charming village doubtless, but not offering much resource. Stay!
there was 'ein Kino'. We made for it, through the quiet village streets
under the new, sickle moon.

But Kinos, apparently, are as popular in Grajewo as elsewhere, and
it was full. So we set out to return, sadly, to the station, with four hours
to put away. I confess that I was by then so tired that I could have
gone to sleep on a table. However, on the way we passed some little
shack which flaunted the word 'Restaurant' in the fan-light over its
door. We went in. We were shown into a little narrow room with
a coloured lithograph of Millais' Angelus and a coloured print of a
Russian sleigh stopped by wolves in the snow; also ibex horns, a falcon,
and other trophies. Next door, some Polish officers were drinking at
a little table. It was all very Slav. We sat, the ten of us, at a long narrow
table, like the Last Supper. We were all tired and gloomy. Then a
bottle of vodka appeared as though by magic. Tongues were loosed.
(Not mine; I was tired beyond vodka, but vastly amused in a quiet
detached way.) One of the Germans leant across the table and suddenly
said to me, "I have travelled Singer's sewing machines one hundred
thousand kilometers over Manchuria." And indeed his luggage was
plastered with Chinese labels. The golden-haired Austrian woman,
who had been asleep on her arms on the table, woke up and drank six
glasses of vodka straight off, and began to dance while one of the Polish
officers crashed out a czarda of sorts on a crazy cottage piano. The
atmosphere became thicker every minute with Slav-icism and cigarette
smoke. Every language fluttered across the room—Russian, Polish,
German, English, Chinese. Everybody wanted to show off. The traveller in Singer's sewing machines beat a spoon on the table and shouted,
"Ich Komm aus China." They asked me what *Guten tag* was in Persian,
and the familiar *Salaam aleikem* echoed in unfamiliar voices. They

poured the vodka generously, and all got very drunk. Somebody played the Blue Danube on the cottage piano. The two Austrians made love openly. Then they all swayed swinging into the village street, irrupting noisily into that sleeping place under the stars and the young moon. And there was our engine puffing in the station. Passports; luggage. We clambered in, and puffed away, down the shining silent line. They burst into *"Deutschland über alles"*; then looked suddenly at me and said they hoped I didn't mind. The conquering race said it didn't mind at all. And so we came into Germany.

The place we slept at was called Prosten, I think; another little sleeping village. We reached it at 1 o'clock. I was *dead;* and fell asleep in a strange little room. At 4 I had to get up again. We caught another train, and after several changes arrived at Königsberg, where I went on with this letter. Then another train, and finally Berlin. I went to the Embassy; but as it was then after 8, everyone had gone. So I came to the Kaiserhof, where I have now dined extremely well, and in a quarter of an hour must catch the train to Flushing.

I have telegraphed to you, my darling, as you will have heard of the Polish business, and may perhaps be worried if you realise that just on that day I was due at Warsaw. I still feel slightly bewildered. I fear this letter will give you no idea of the fantasy of this journey, but it has been written so disjointedly; you won't be able to follow my movements at all! I can scarcely follow them myself, as I re-read it. I have no wagon-lit, of course, and shall have to sit up all night. I think I must have a constitution of iron, as I am not really very tired. The Kaiserhof has a really Ritz-ian atmosphere, which forms an odd contrast with that little restaurant at Grajewo, where I was only 24 hours ago.

I am due in London at 8.30 tomorrow night, and have wired to Dotz [Dorothy Wellesley] to meet me. But as it is Sunday tomorrow, she probably won't get the telegram.

Oh my darling. There is a pot of pink azaleas on my little solitary table. One of the Germans has just rung me up to know if I am all right. Their niceness and efficiency was beyond praise. Also they lent me money, as of course I couldn't use my ticket, and had only £10 with me. I hope I can recover my ticket money. Or is it the King's Enemies?

Please tell me if you get this letter. Goodbye my beloved; you can see that my thoughts are always of you, from the way I start writing to you whenever I have 10 minutes. Though I admit it produces a tiresome disjointed result.

VITA TO HAROLD *Long Barn*

22 May [1926]

The garden is lovely; the wood-garden especially is a dream. Everything is so tidy; everything looks so healthy. I will tell you in detail, now that I have had time to go round.

The limes are alive. Your new poplar-walk is alive. The wood is a blaze of primulas, anemones, tulips, azaleas, irises, polyanthus. The horse-chestnut is alive. The apple garden is a mass of lupins and irises. The walls are still rather bare, but everything doing well. The turf is perfect. The new, lower lawn is almost the nicest thing of all—so smooth and green and level. All the edges are straight and tidy. The top of the wall is better than I have ever seen it. The roses are beautifully pruned; the lilac is smothered in blossom. Your honeysuckle by the big room door also. Your Hugh Dickson [rose] under your bedroom window is up to the roof, and covered with buds. The tennis court is a disaster. The new orchard is a tig [triumph]. The greenhouse is full of tidy boxes, with seeds. The hedges are all alive and shooting. There is not a weed to be seen. The doves are alive. There are seven grey puppies and four yellow kittens. Four yews in the new garden are dead, but the rest flourishing, and not really too silly. The new box trees are all alive. I shall take lots and lots of photographs for you tomorrow; I have got two films.

I have got my proofs [of *The Land*], and will send you a set by this bag.

I should be so happy if only you were here; but, my darling, there is no happiness for me without you, none, none, none. I can only think of when I shall bring you here next year. That thought is the one thing which makes me able to enjoy the garden now.

HAROLD TO VITA   *Teheran*

31 May 1926

I went to tea with the Shah. It took place at his summer Palace near Pashkolé. There was a huge long gravel path along the terrace and at the end of it I saw the Shah. But at the beginning of it, out of sheer

nervousness, my bootlaces came undone—all four of them. Now why does this always happen when I go to see the Shah? I had known it would happen and had tried on my button boots instead. But three of the buttons had come off, so I put on my Oxford shoes instead and tied the knots as no knots have ever been tied before. On getting out of the motor I glanced at the knots:—there they were, firm and tidy. But when they saw that long vista of garden path, a hundred yards of garden path, they got nervous and untied themselves. I knew that the Minister was watching from beside the Samovar. It was a trying ordeal. I said, *"Hoda hafiz i alahazret,"* which means "Goodbye your Majesty"—but I said it so humbly that I don't think he could have borne me much resentment. Then I went and stood beside the Samovar and watched the other guests arriving.

VITA TO HAROLD *Long Barn*

31 May [1926]

Tray's theory[1] is all very well so far as it goes. But he leaves out the stipulation that the two people who are to achieve this odd spirito-mystico-practical unity must start with special temperaments. I.e. it is all very well to say the ideal is "marriage with liaisons." But if you were in love with another woman, or I with another man, we should both or either of us be finding a natural sexual fulfilment which would inevitably rob our own relationship of something. As it is, the liaisons which you and I contract are something perfectly apart from the more natural and normal attitude we have towards each other, and therefore don't interfere. But it would be dangerous for ordinary people. Besides, you cannot make laws about emotional relationships: either you love, or else you don't love, and that's that.

VITA TO HAROLD *Long Barn*

12 June 1926

The Woolfs are not coming today after all, because Virginia has started one of her attacks of headache again, but I am going to Rodmell[2] tomorrow for two nights; Leonard will be away and she doesn't want to be alone. Your cabbage doesn't want to go much, thank you, and would rather stay here. I have come to the conclusion that I should like to be very eccentric and distinguished, and never see anybody except devout pilgrims who rang the front door bell (which doesn't ring), and remained for an hour talking about poetry, and then went away again. But the eccentricity is easier to acquire than the distinction. The eccentricity, indeed, is native. I am quite alarmed at the rapidity of its growth; that I don't want to see even Virginia as a dreadful symptom, for not only am I very fond of her, but she is the best company in the world, and the most stimulating.

1. For Raymond Mortimer's views on marriage see pp. 138–139.
2. Monk's House, Rodmell, near Lewes, Sussex, the Woolfs' country cottage.

VITA TO HAROLD   *Monk's House, Rodmell, Sussex*

Monday, 13 June [1926]

My own darling Hadji,

I am, as you see, staying with Virginia. She is sitting opposite, embroidering a rose, a black lace fan, a box of matches, and four playing cards, on a mauve canvas background, from a design by her sister, and from time to time she says, "You have written enough, let us now talk about copulation," so if this letter is disjointed it is her fault and not mine. I arrived yesterday. They have put in a bathroom and a b.s. place [lavatory] on the proceeds of *Mrs Dalloway*. [1] They both run upstairs every now and then and pull the plug just for the sheer fun of it, and come down and say, "It worked very well that time—did you hear?" rather as the mars might do if their standard of luxury were lower than it is. Leonard had to go back to London last night, so I remain alone with Virginia. There is a woman from the village who washes up, but otherwise we boil an egg and make coffee, and I have brought 2 bottles of Allella [a light Spanish wine] and a box of cherries, and that's all. Darling, you would love the country round here: water-meadows and green tracks, Downs and buttercups, plover and larks, ricks and a river. One day we must walk along the Downs in the opposite direction. I mean, away from Chanctonbury,— oh my dear, I wish it was next summer!

Later

I went over to Rottingdean to see Enid [2]; Virginia sat in a tea shop and ate Sally Lunns [buns] meanwhile. Enid is very bovine and lactiferous, but very happy. Then I took Virginia to White Lodge [3] (B.M. being in London), where she was rivetted with amusement. She 'got' B.M. in the twinkling of an eye of course, and made a number of illuminating observations which I had never thought of. I can't write this letter properly, because V. who is an outrageous woman keeps on getting up and reading it over my shoulder. She says you are to give up diplomacy and find a job from £600 a year onwards.

---

1. Virginia Woolf's novel had been published in May 1925, and was a best-seller.
2. Enid Bagnold, the novelist, who was married to Sir Roderick Jones, head of Reuters.
3. Lady Sackville's house between Rottingdean and Brighton.

VITA TO HAROLD   *182 Ebury Street*

16 June 1926

I dined with Virginia and Leonard in one of their Bloomsbury pot-houses; and then went on alone with her to the ballet. She had got on a new dress. It was very odd indeed, orange and black, with a hat to match—a sort of top-hat made of straw with two orange feathers like Mercury's wings—but although odd it was curiously becoming, and pleased Virginia because there could be absolutely no doubt as to which was the front and which the back. We had press tickets, and sat in the dress circle. Virginia made up stories about everyone in the audience, but not so audibly as B.M. The ballet was Carnival, Pulcinella (a new one—not very good), and Igor.

We came out into the misty Haymarket. Virginia was shivering, I thought she was cold; but no, it was excitement. I couldn't get her away from the theatre at all, and we strolled up and down, with the dark blue sky overhead, and groups of well-dressed people talking, and it was all very like Mrs Dalloway; and then, to complete the likeness, we saw a dwarf on crutches, under a street lamp, with locomotorataxy. That frightened Virginia, so we went to the Eiffel Tower [restaurant], and drank coffee, and were joined by Viola Tree[1] and the fashion editress of Vogue.

HAROLD TO VITA   *Teheran*

26 June 1926

Don't think, dearest, that I'm unhappy. Only sort of suspended neutral feeling. You see this sort of life is really what I like best: Work, riding, hot weather, reading, writing, bathing. But it seems to have no point without you. I get through the days quickly, contentedly, mechanically—but it is only when something like Tray coming back jerks me into being myself again and not a machine that I realise how automatic and perfunctory is my general existence.

---

1. Author of *Castles in the Air,* published by the Hogarth Press in April 1926.

VITA TO HAROLD   *Long Barn*

28 June 1926

The Laureate[1] breakfasts at 8.30. I was brought early tea, which Hadji would have liked, but which I scorned; rose and dressed. I descended. The Laureate was playing the clavichord which his admirers—me amongst them—had presented to him on his 8oth birthday. I peeped through the curtains; he was dressed in his evening shirt of the previous evening, a tweed Norfolk jacket, and grey flannel trousers. There he was, tinkling away at Handel. I crept away unobserved, on my crepe soles. I went and got the motor out of the garage and brought it round to the front door. By then Mrs Bridges had appeared. There were eggs and bacon for breakfast. After breakfast the Laureate said, did I still want to consult the Oxford Dictionary? I said I did. He took me into his library, and left me there sitting on the floor. I had my proofs [of *The Land*]; and verified my odd words to my satisfaction. Presently the Laureate returned, his spectacles pushed up on to his forehead, very indignant. "It is perfect nonsense," he said, "the way these people *will* edit Chaucer." He sat down on the floor beside me, and helped me to look up 'droil'. "What's this?" he said, taking up my proofs. I simpered. He took them out into the garden, spread a rug very carefully on the grass, and began to read. I fled upstairs and packed. After an hour I re-appeared. The Laureate was still reading. He got up and came towards me. "Have you," he began, "read Virgil a great deal?" I said no, I didn't know Latin; had, however, read the Georgics in a translation. "But how," he said, staring at me very hard with a fierce blue eye, "but how, then, have you got this Virgilian *bite?* eh?" I quailed. "It's VERY GOOD," he said, still staring at me, "I'm VERY PLEASED—very pleased indeed—you've got your feet on the ground—nothing woolly there—not a woman's writing at all—damn good—I congratulate you." I said, I, too, was pleased that he should think so. "Send it me," he boomed, "when it comes out." Mrs Bridges appeared. "Good STUFF," he said to her, striking the pages angrily with his hand, and looking at me meanwhile as though

---

1. Robert Bridges, the Poet Laureate, at whose house near Oxford Vita had been staying the night.

I had committed a crime. I was overcome with confusion, and to cover it up said should I photograph them both for their daughter? The Laureate posed happily amongst his pinks. Suddenly he grabbed his wife by the wrist. "Do you think," he whispered, "that she would photograph THE CURTAIN?" They both looked apprehensively at me. Of course, I said; fetch the curtain! They fetched it—at a run. They hung the curtain, a Jacobean crewel-work affair, over a dry-wall, standing themselves at the top and each holding a corner. I solemnly photographed them and it; pray God it may come out. Then I rescued my proofs, and climbed into the motor; they urged me to come again. They opened the gate for me, and stood there waving.

I went down into Oxford,—a lovely morning,—out to Summer-fields[2] and there were the babies in grey flannels with Eton collars. They took me into chapel, and between the two of them I worshipped God. They were very serious, and sang loudly, if out of tune. I shared Nigel's hymn book. Then we came out,—"Oh Mummy, didn't you think it was a lovely service?" They changed their collars for soft ones, and we started off. All the way Ben taught Nigel Latin.

VITA TO HAROLD   *Long Barn*

28 June 1926

No, I am in no muddles [love affairs]. Pat[3] writes, occasionally, but I don't answer. Geoffrey [Scott] writes, but I have refused to see him, and he has accepted that. He now writes me sentimental letters about "Remember what I was once . . .," and hints darkly at troubles with Dorothy.[4] Dorothy I have not seen. Louise, no muddles (either Genoux or Loraine[5]), Vera,[6] no muddles. Lady Hillingdon, no muddles; don't know her; don't want to. Violet [Trefusis], no muddles; don't even know where she is; don't want to get into touch, thank you.

---

2. More correctly written, Summer Fields, the preparatory school on the outskirts of Oxford.
3. Margaret ("Pat") Dansey, who had been Violet Trefusis' most intimate friend.
4. Dorothy Warren, who had been simultaneously in love with Geoffrey Scott and Vita.
5. Louise Genoux was Vita's French maid; Louise Loraine, the wife of Sir Percy.
6. Vera Cardinal, who farmed the land at Long Barn.

Virginia [Woolf]—not a muddle exactly; she is a busy and sensible woman. But she does love me, and I did sleep with her at Rodmell. That does not constitute a muddle though.[7]

H A R O L D　T O　V I T A　　　　　　　　　　　　　　*Teheran*

1 July 1926

Well I have had my party.[8] There were 36 people. I sat one end of the table and Percy [Loraine] the other end. The whole staff was there, plus the heads of the colony. There was a balalalalalalaika orchestra on the lawn and a great number of little miffy chinese lanterns. We had soup, trout, cutlets in aspic, turkey and an apricot ice. My wine had arrived two days before. I made a nice English-public-schoolboy sort of speech. Percy replied very slowly and with some emotion. I was rather pleased with my speech and when it was all over I went up to Tray [Raymond Mortimer] and said, "Well how did it go?"—expecting praise. He said it had made him almost sick. He was really angry about it. Funny Tray. Because really the speech was quite moderate and devoid of undue sob-stuff. But I admit that it was rather an Empire builder's speech and aroused Tray's anti-virility complex. Also I think he thought it rather shaming: he said it had irritated him as much as I would be irritated if I saw him dressed up as a woman at some Paris dancing-hall. I think this really was his attitude, and he is right in feeling that I loathe the *tapette* [gay] side of him as much as he hates the Kipling side in me.

Well, feeling rather crushed by this attack, I led the way to the second part of my party—which took place in my own house. It really looked rather well, and there was another band there and a good buffet and heaps of drink. It really *was* a success; people danced and drank and enjoyed themselves. It went on till 2.0 a.m. Oh my Viti, how I missed you! The Minister was impressed, I think—and I have at a stroke removed all criticism of my not entertaining. Also whatever

7. Harold replied (7 July): "Oh my dear, I do hope that Virginia is not going to be a muddle. It is like smoking over a petrol tank."
8. For the British colony in honor of the Minister, Sir Percy Loraine, who was leaving Teheran the next day. Harold remained in charge of the Legation.

Tray may say, I think the colony were impressed by my noble uplifting patriotic sturdy homily. Perhaps it *was* a little revivalist in tone—Yes? No?

VITA TO HAROLD   *Long Barn*

1 July 1926

My own Hadji,

I seem to be drawn into doing a lot of things these days, which I don't really want to do, and really only want to be here by myself quietly; but I suppose they do amuse me, and I suppose they are good for me in that they do prevent me from becoming a complete cabbage.

Well, you see, I went to the Sitwells' show[1] with Virginia [Woolf]. We dined first at the Eiffel Tower, and talked about literature. So absorbing a subject was it, that we were very late for the Sitwell party. We had one complimentary ticket, and one promise from Edith (Sitwell) that we would be admitted on mention of our names. We mentioned our names, and were ushered to a back seat where even the megaphone failed to reach us. Virginia was not satisfied with this, nor was I. We began pushing. There were some empty seats, and to these in the interval we elbowed our way. Virginia made me go first, much as the German troops pushed the Belgian civilians before them during the war. So I bore the brunt and got all the blame; encountered Sachie [Sacheverell Sitwell]: "Oh, Sachie, you know Mrs Woolf, don't you?" *I* wasn't going to be made wholly responsible. Finally we were ensconced, under the wing of Sachie, in good prominent places. The audience was the best part of the show. Long-haired young men, short-haired young women; you never saw such a collection. And Augustus John's picture-show hanging on the walls. There was a sort of embryo Ottoline [Morrell] in an 1840 dress with a train, and a young man with hair like Struwel-Peter [shock-headed Peter], and an obscene red lily in his buttonhole,—a red plate of a lily, with

1. A performance of *Façade* at The Chenil Galleries in Chelsea. The poem was by Edith Sitwell, the music by William Walton. The words were spoken from behind a screen through megaphones.

a pink penis sticking out of it—you must have seen them at Knole—
that was a sample of the audience. Now and then Osbert's [Sitwell]
voice said down a subsidiary megaphone, "Ladies and gentlemen, I do
like to be beside the seaside," and then to the crash of gongs and
cymbals the poem began. But nobody knew when they (the poems)
were meant to come to an end; therefore the applause always came in
the wrong place, either too soon or too late; either the poem came to
an end unexpectedly and was received in complete silence because the
audience expected it to continue, or else there was a deafening applause
in the middle, where the reader had merely paused for breath. Anyhow
it was a great success; and one clap from a vague pair of hands was
enough to make Osbert's megaphone say, "Ladies and gentlemen, with
your permission we will now repeat that number," and duly repeated
it was. But you know, Hadji, I am quite sure that in 50 years from
now no one will ever have heard of those frauds the Sitwells, any more
than they will have heard of George Robey.[2]

I saw everyone I had ever known. I was quite impressed by the
number of people I knew. Then when I had dragged Virginia away—
but she gets drunk on crowds as you and I do on champagne—we went
back to Bloomsbury. On the way, through one of those dark squares,
we overtook Mrs Bell [Vanessa, Virginia's sister]. We stopped. Virginia hailed, "Nessa! Nessa!" She loomed up vaguely, and said, "Duncan [Grant, the painter] is in the public house." We drove on. Presently
we overtook Duncan, hatless, and very carefully carrying one hard-
boiled egg. We drove on to Clive's [Bell]. There were Leonard
[Woolf] and [Maynard] Keynes. Presently came in Mrs Bell and
Duncan. Clive produced vermouth and more eggs. The conversation
became personal and squalid. I was amused. At half past twelve Clive
and I departed for Argyll House.[3] There I met Dada [Lord Sackville],
very fish-out-of-water. There was an immense party, with everyone
you have ever heard of, from Mr Balfour (Arthur, not Ronnie) to
Mary Pickford and Douglas Fairbanks. Really a triumph for Sibyl
[Colefax]. Mr Balfour was sitting on the floor. Very convivial altogether. I had supper with Desmond [MacCarthy, literary critic]. Then
there was Ruth Draper [the actress]—oh my darling, does it make you

---

2. The comic actor (1869–1954).
3. In the King's Road, Chelsea, the home of Sir Arthur and Lady Colefax, the London hostess.

long for London? or merely feel superior? Anyhow it was great fun: and the garden was illuminated, but not so nice as the Gulistan and no fireworks. And I lost no emerald.

HAROLD TO VITA   *Gulahek, Teheran*

10 July 1926

I have got two Virgins staying with me. They came in a Ford car from Isfahan. The smaller one is called Miss Richardson. She has an inquisitive little face like a ferret. She has lovely deep copper hair—all oily and smooth like women should. But like women should *not*, she has bobbed it, after the manner of the Sassanid dynasty, so that it looks like a hay-field which has been nibbled at by a small pair of blunt nail-scissors. The other is called Miss Winifred Eardley, known to her friends (of whom Miss Richardson is one) as Winnie. She has either got very acute indigestion or else an inferiority complex. Anyhow she sniffs.

Now, how comes it that I, who loathe women in general and virgins in particular, should for three whole weeks have to entertain these types? How comes it that I who am rendered rather ill by the thought of the church, who don't like missionaries, and who hates society, should entertain these vestals of the Church Missionary Society? Will you please explain all this to me? Like Wordsworth, I "wonder at myself like men dismayed." [1] I suppose it is the white man's burden. And the maddening thing is that Trott, [2] who rather likes them, being a white man all through, gets all the credit. And that I, who am bored stiff and have to make an effort to be polite, am just thought an amiable pagan. And last night Trott's motor broke down and I had them alone for dinner: and I had toothache. And they said, or rather Miss Richardson said, "This is heavenly—one might be anywhere but in Persia." She said it in a wistful way, poor little bitch, gazing at *The Field* spread out on the table under a lamp with a red silk fringe to it. One could see the poor little sparrow-mind fluttering

1. The quotation should be, "We wonder at ourselves like men betrayed." Wordsworth, *The Borderers.*
2. Alan Trott, one of the consular officials at the Legation.

back to the rectory drawing-room. "Too Too Too," went the owls: the fountain splashed on the blue tiles: the durbar tent bulked billowly against the white hot stars; and yet that effect of red light on *The Field* took her away back to the Eversley [Surrey] Rectory. I was touched by this, and went to bed with that evening-service feeling, trying to feel more hospitable about them—had I put Bromo for them? Would they like a book?

But really I don't mind much. I see, as I write, a flash of white muslin going towards the tent. "Winnie!—breakfast's ready—there's honey." "Coming, dear!" Oh England—my England—how I *love* you. That's why I don't mind having them.

VITA TO HAROLD   *Long Barn*

27 July 1926

Virginia [Woolf] was very charming and amusing. She had been to see old [Thomas] Hardy, and had come back impressed by the Great. "I felt, here's a great man, and I'm only so damned clever." She says he talked about his writing in a sort of puzzled way, as though he had done it all in the dark, and as though his life was really important only in so far as it affected his tea and his dog. He told her he had had to write all his novels as serial stories: that was why there were so many moments of crisis, because each instalment had to end on an exciting note. But I can't, myself, see many crises in that slow broad stream. She says he is a simple, ugly, insignificant little old man, and almost illiterate; also that literature, as such, has no interest or importance for him at all.

Well, then, today I took her over to Rodmell, which was nice of me, and Clive and Leonard arrived from London with one of Clive's shaggy sons [Quentin Bell], and there was a thunderstorm. On the way back I went to see Plankino who was working on the woodcuts for *The Land.* [1] Then I dined with Dada alone [at Knole] and now am not awake at all. Besides, I talked to V. till dreadfully late last night. I gave

---

1. George Plank, the American artist who worked mostly in England and was an intimate friend of Lady Sackville.

Leonard one of Pippin's [spaniel] puppies. He *was* pleased, he adores dogs.

Goodnight, my sweet, my darling. I told V. how much we loved each other. Oh yes, and I gave her Tray's essay on chastity. She is pleased with it. Why don't you write a Hogarth Essay? She would like you to. Oh darling, she is so funny, she does make me laugh! And *so* sane, when not mad. And *so* how [pathetic], about going mad again. What a nightmare it must be.

HAROLD TO VITA   *Teheran*

1 August 1926

My darling,

The Bishop *in* Persia came to dinner. He said, "I should like to give you a little service while here. I generally celebrate all the Legation when I come." That word 'celebrate' should have warned me—but I am (in spite of the *Golden Bough* [1]) obtuse to ritual. I said, "Oh that would be delightful." So he came. It was rather fun arranging a church for him. We did it on the wide veranda upstairs. The Warren Hastings arches looked like some Saxon church once the chairs had been arrayed with an aisle between them. There were cushions to kneel on—and flowers and a table covered with an Italian brockade (I mean brocade) as an altar. A screen arranged behind the altar gave the appearance of a triptych. I had put candles on the altar, but Trott, being low church, made me take them away. It looked terribly naked and grim so I borrowed a bible and put beside it a copy of *Vogue* and *Gentlemen Prefer Blondes*. Trott objected to these also, so they were taken away. The bible remained: rectangular, English, misleading.

I had written to the Bishop asking (a) whether he would mind if I didn't communicate (the word reminded me of my book on Swinburne) myself. (b) Whether he wanted any wine or stuff. He replied to both in the negative.

---

1. *The Golden Bough* by Sir James Frazer, published in twelve volumes, 1890–1915, a study of mankind's magical and religious thought.

The service was fixed for 11.30. A Persian had come to see me at 9.45 and was of course still there. I had to get rid of him. I went upstairs and on the staircase I met Gladwyn [Jebb] suitably arrayed in black. He said that the Bishop wanted (a) wine (b) bread (c) a napkin (d) a champagne glass. I shouted *"Biar!"* Taqhis appeared and I told him what was required. He got terribly fussed and disappeared flopping in his slippers. It was then 11.45. Finally Taqhis emerged with 15 glasses on a tray and a bottle of champagne. Also some toast. This had to be coped with, and by 12.0 we were ready. The congregation consisted of nine people. I sat in front. Henry [Harold's dog] yelled pitiably from the room where I had shut him up. The Bishop preached a sermon about how even as when we shed our nice fleecy great-coats when the referee whistled and appeared in shorts, so also when Christ whistled should we cast off the vanities of this world and engage in the strife. As always when I hear sermons I wanted to contradict. I wanted to point out (1) that we only take off our greatcoats because, so I am told, it is irksome to play football thus encumbered; (2) that the motion of the said game produces a circular warmth which compensates for the nice fleecy greatcoat; (3) that, therefore, once you decide to play football there is no apparent virtue in doing so without a greatcoat; and above all (4) that any decent religion, as Christ, being a man of sense, kept on pointing out, allowed one to exploit the flesh as well as the spirit. (5) that people who went about in shorts were either (a) exhibitionists (b) eccentrics or (c) liable to get pneumonia. (6) that if some people went about in shorts . . .

Well, well, we can leave it at that. Then came the communion service. Never have I heard such lovely prose! "We do not presume to come to this thy table." It wasn't his table, it was mine. And none of them knew that Barbara,[2] hidden by the Italian brocade, was chuckling underneath. Anyhow, Mrs Durie, Warner, Humphrey [officials of the Legation] all went up and became Christophagists. They returned to their places in an aroma of sanctity and Messrs Berry Bros' port. Then they all went away.

I went and read the Greek Anthology before luncheon. I am glad that the Christian religion is on the decline.

---

2. See p. 19, note 1.

8 August 1926

Here is a story—a true story—which will amuse you. You know that after the war we occupied northern Persia and even extended our operations against the Bolsheviks. In this way a British detachment under a Colonel Thompson occupied Baku where the White Russians flocked to meet him. In the harbour of Baku was the Russian Caspian fleet who had surrendered at the first appearance of Col. Thompson and who declared themselves to be White Russians. They were thus regarded as allies and left where they were. It slowly dawned on them however that Col. Thompson had only 500 British troops in Baku and that there was no need for them to have surrendered at all. So one morning Col. Thompson woke up to find that the fleet had gone Bolshy, had left its moorings, and had taken up a position a mile out at sea where his field guns could not reach them but from where their heavy guns could blow Baku to bits. From this position of incontestable advantage the fleet gave Thompson two hours to surrender failing which they would bombard the town.

Thompson called a council of war. He had a captain and a lieutenant and the man who looked after the motor boats. There were two motor boats and they each had one torpedo. It was decided that the faster of the two motor boats should take the two torpedos and attack the Russian fleet. The torpedos were the very latest sort from White-heads and nobody knew quite how to work them. Anyhow they started off and circling round the biggest of the Russian gun-boats they discharged the first torpedo. It went straight at the gun-boat and then dived elegantly right underneath it coming up the other side. The motor boat dashed back under fire to within signalling distance and informed Thompson that they had fired the first torpedo and missed. "Fire the other," he replied, "and don't miss." So they went back, again circled round the flag-ship, and fiddling carefully with the mechanism sent off the other and only remaining torpedo. Its behaviour was identical with that of its predecessor. It made a bee-line on the surface of the water towards the flag-ship and when twenty yards away, kicked up its tail and dived neatly underneath. The motor boat dashed back to the harbour. It was slowly followed by the whole Caspian fleet flying the White flag. They surrendered to a man. It was only when the crews had been locked up in barracks and British platoons had occupied the several warships that Col. Thompson disclosed to the Russian admiral that those two torpedos were the only two we possessed—and that they had been fired in earnest and not as a warning of worse to come. A few days later the Russian ships were towed out and blown up at sea.

So we did sometimes have luck on our side.

VITA TO HAROLD   *Long Barn*

17 August 1926

You have never understood about Violet [Trefusis] (a) that it was a madness of which I should never again be capable—a thing like that happens once, and burns out the capacity for such a feeling; (b) that you could at any moment have reclaimed me, but for some extraordinary reason you wouldn't. I used to beg you to; I *wanted* to be rescued, and you wouldn't hold out a hand. I think it was a mixture of pride and mistaken wisdom on your part. I know you thought that if you tried to hold me, I should go altogether. But in this you were wrong, because I never lost sight of how you were the person I loved in the sense of loving for life. Only I suppose you either didn't believe this, or else you wouldn't take the risk.

But anyway that is a thing of the past, and not worth going over, and only the present remains.

Darling, there is no muddle at all, anywhere! I keep on telling you so. PADLOCK! And padlock I would tell you if there was. You mention Virginia: it is simply laughable. I love Virginia, as who wouldn't? but really, my sweet, one's love for Virginia is a very different thing: a mental thing, a spiritual thing if you like, an intellectual thing, and she inspires a feeling of tenderness which I suppose is because of her funny mixture of hardness and softness—the hardness of her mind, and her terror of going mad again. She makes me feel protective. Also she loves me, which flatters and pleases me. Also— since I am embarked on telling you about Virginia, but this is all absolutely padlock private—I am scared to death of arousing physical feelings in her, because of the madness. I don't know what effect it would have, you see; and that is a fire with which I have no wish to play. No, thank you. I have too much real affection and respect. Also she has never lived with anyone but Leonard, which was a terrible failure, and was abandoned quite soon. So all that remains is an unknown quantity, and I have got too many dogs not to let them lie where they *are* asleep. Besides, *ça ne me dit rien;* and *ça lui dit trop,* where I am concerned; and I don't want to get landed in an affair which might get beyond my control before I knew where I was. So you see I am sagacious—though probably I would be less sagacious if I were more tempted, which is at least frank! But, darling, Virginia is *not* the sort of person one thinks of in that way; there is something incongruous and almost indecent in the idea . . . I *have* gone to bed with her (twice), but that's all; and I told you that before, I think. Now you know all about it, and I hope I haven't shocked you.

Oh, darling, send away Iago, or I shall think you don't even begin to realise how absolutely I love you. It *is* a little hard, to have Iago thrown at me, when all the time I am miserable about not being with you. Don't you know, you silly, that the whole of this summer is as meaningless to me as it is to you? I, also, am only half alive.

Please make a comment on all this, and say you understand. But don't say you understand unless you really do. My darling, you are the one and only person for me in the world; do take that in once and for all, you little dunderhead. Really it makes me cross, when I am eating out my heart for you; and it makes me cry.

HAROLD TO VITA   *Teheran*

30 August 1926

I had a nice day yesterday lying out under the trees in a deck-chair reading Bertie Russell's *On Education* [published 1926]. A good firm book. I don't think we have made any mistakes [with their own children]. Most of what he advises we have done instinctively. There is one point however which he makes much of, that one should never show fear in front of children. As a matter of fact you are particularly good at that and try to restrain your panics. But I think he is right in preaching that principle. He also believes in allowing children to absorb sex facts naturally and in letting them see grown-ups naked. I daresay he is right, but my incest complex is too strong for me. Of course I think one may be optimistic about one's own children. Both Ben and Niggs [Nigel] seem perfectly clear and open with no knots now. And I really think they are. He also says one should not expect any response in affection at least until the age of puberty. But we were never morbid on that score—and I think they both love us very warmly and intelligently. In fact the book cheered me a great deal since so many of our principles (i.e. never telling them a lie or breaking a promise) are cardinal with him. You see, I think what guided us was your instinct to treat them as potential men and never as pretty little kittens. We have probably formed their characters much more than we imagine.

Oh my darling, it makes me homesick to write of us four.

HAROLD TO VITA   *Teheran*

7 September 1926

My last letter was written at Pelur. I sat there scribbling to my darling under the tent and with a blanket over my knee. I had just finished when I saw Gladwyn [Jebb] coming down the path with a rifle slung over his shoulder—gaunt and slightly bearded. I was so delighted to see him as I was getting rather bored with Patrick Hepburn.[1] I do hope Ben isn't *too* good looking. Hepburn is really amazingly beautiful, but it gives him the self-consciousness of a professional beauty. Which is tiresome. He is not in the least b.s. [homosexual] but he has got so used to being made-up-to that he rather expects it. Gladwyn and I teased him dreadfully. We said he was like Mrs Langtry [mistress of Edward VII]. Apart from his looks he is a rather soft and colourless

---

1. Patrick Buchan-Hepburn, then aged twenty-five, was attached to the British Embassy in Constantinople and on temporary secondment to the Teheran Legation. After a distinguished career in politics he was created Lord Hailes and became Governor General of the British Caribbean Islands.

youth with a lack of vitality and a great many rectory corners in his mind. One has the impression of his having been a mother's darling, and he has a lot of undigested ideas about having to keep up one's position: "Of course I like some of those clever people but it's a bad thing to see too much of them." He is not exactly a fool—but a youth who is at moments coyly skittish. Thus he is beginning (oh so slightly) to get on my nerves, and I regret the time when he lay there as a beautiful corpse.[2]

All these reflections are provoked by thinking how glad, that grey Scotch morning, I was to see Gladwyn. He makes Hepburn, poor boy, look merely a little (or rather a huge) fancy piece. He makes him look terribly bedint—which is odd in a descendant of Bothwell.[3] Poor Patrick, I fear he is the "charming boy" and will become less so each year. But the contrast between him and Gladwyn was very striking: Gladwyn so absolutely real: Patrick so beautiful and so second-hand. Oh I *do* hope Benzie won't be like that.

Mar will smile at all this and think it is merely because Patrick was so stand-offish and that Hadji was re-buffed. Not so. Don't like sleeping with Archdeacons' daughters and didn't want to in the least, the moment the Deanery began to obtrude with his retreating fever. But it shows one how bloody critical we all are, and how we really don't like people who have no personality inside. Poor Patrick!

VITA TO HAROLD   *Long Barn*

26 September 1926

It is really autumn now. A week ago the thermometer was at 83 and this morning there is frost on the ground! But such lovely days, with that lovely light over the ridge at sunset. I don't dislike it, only my nose and knees are cold when I wake up. I am busy taking the garden to pieces, pulling out the dead annuals, cutting down the dead stalks. And everything I plant now in their places is for you. This makes me incredibly happy, because you will like it, and "I can't be

2. He had become very ill on first arriving in Persia, and Harold looked after him.
3. Mary Queen of Scots' third husband, from whom the Hepburns claimed descent.

happy unless you're happy too." I am planting more azaleas in the wood, more scarlet anemones, a row of plum-trees in the new orchard, lots more roses in the top garden, turning one of the Michaelmas daisy beds up there into a big bed of *Moysii,* and putting 100 Madonna lilies into the border where it runs along the tennis-court wire. Also replacing some roses on the Calvary, and making a honeysuckle arch into the apple garden, where that crazy little gate used to be. Planting 100 more *iris sirilica* round the pond. It is all great fun and I love it. Barnes [the gardener] is as keen as I am, and keeps on saying, "I must do this and that before Mr Nicolson comes back." Yet he never prepares horrors as a surprise for me—like Goacher, who while Dotz [Welles-ley] was away, filled six tubs with scarlet geraniums and set them all round the house.

Then I come in and work—i.e. do my lecture—and Pippin [span-iel] snores, and I have a fire. If only you were locked away into your little room it would be the perfect life. Oh darling, if you are an aubergine, I am a cabbage. I drink nothing at all, eat very little, and feel extremely well. So now you know all about it, and I only wish it could last longer, but I have the threat of poor dear B.M. coming to stay here. However, that is not yet certain.

You know, Hadji, I think I can analyse why I have this obsession about being here alone. It is because (a) I put myself together again and become a unity instead of a patchwork, and (b) I know I go soft when I am with people, idle my time away, talk too much, eat and drink too much. What I really like is a severe life, but have too weak a character to withstand the dissipations of company! I never spoke a truer word than

> the heart, the very heart of me
> That plays and strays, a truant in strange lands,
> Always returns and finds its inward peace,
> Its swing of truth, its measure of restraint,
> Here among meadows, orchards, lanes, and shaws.[1]

Forgive me quoting myself, but it puts the matter in a nutshell. And that is why it is so odd and wrong that you should not be here, because you are so intrinsic a part of the inward peace.

---

1. From Vita's poem *Orchard and Vineyard* (1921).

Darling, do you know what I did last night after writing to you? I meant to finish my lecture, but fell to reading the Georgics (mine, not Virgil's) [*The Land*], and really I thought they were rather good.

HAROLD TO VITA   *Teheran*

1 October 1926

I have just typed out a telegram to you. First, many many happy returns to us of this lucky day.[1] (Oh dearest—I have thought and thought about it all. How mar we were! Rather sweet really and how. My angel, we *have* grown close together since then. Little weedy saplings we were then. We are oaks today.)

Well then the second part of my telegram was about your Persian book,[2] and as it is rather about that than about what happened 13 years ago that you want to hear, I shall now drop the sob-stuff.

Well, *en somme* I think the Persian Book *absolutely first class*—infinitely better than I had expected.

What is really interesting about it—or what is *arresting,* rather, and so original—is that one feels all through that there is an interesting mind trying to mould all these pictures into shape. It is all the difference between looking at coins or cameos in a museum, or being shown them by some sort of Roger Fry who explains the point. I don't quite know how you have achieved this effect, but it is very striking: it makes the book wholly different from other travel books: it gives it a psychological interest far above the Cook's tourist part. The tone, of course, is set by the Introduction: but where Mar has been so tremendously clever is that she never diverges for one instant from the same key. The book is the same colour throughout; it leaves the same colour-tone in the mind.

It is this which gives it its continuity. (I read it through at a sitting—but that of course is not a good test in one Mar about the other's book.) One gets the dominant impression of a very real and

---

1. Their wedding anniversary.
2. Vita's *Passenger to Teheran,* about her first journey to Persia, earlier in 1926.

sincere person accepting nothing second-hand and feeling everything. One feels that all those emphatic landscapes have been given a personal interpretation. It makes all the other travel books I have read look just like coloured picture-post-cards.

"The wise traveller is he who is perpetually surprised." Oh my sweet—you have got something of the essential Vita into this book. Rather an alarming Vita. But so aloof and independent and real. One thing which I particularly relish is your rapid fore-shortening. India in one page—five pages to little Dilijan![3] *That's* the way to do it!

I won't talk about the beauty of the style—or the real conviction carried by the description—because that I expected. I let Colonel Haworth read a bit of it. "By God!" he said, "this is the first book I've read on Persia which gives one the slightest idea what it's like." All *that* part is excellent—but I expected that.

No—it's just the writer's personality which makes it such a good book. I think it is lucky you had to write it in a rush: it has helped to produce that smooth uniform surface which is so effective.

Of course there are things which I shall never forgive. NEVER. Poor Hadji—in his mind remains for ever that night when he waited under the moon, listening to the dogs barking, straining his ears for the sound of a motor.[4] She acted well: she pretended to be pleased to see him: But No!! It is clear now. It was all put on. She was, in fact, "Sorry when she saw the lights of Kermanshah."

Well, well: one gets used to such wounds I suppose.

It is a pity also that she should have called the Ali Kapi the Ali Carpi—thinking of Capri I suppose. Or that she should have said Chel Setum, when she meant Chebel Sirtoon, or that, when once she breaks into Persian, she should say it wrong. Also there is no Isphahan gate—it is called the Gate of Shah Abdul Azim. And oh! *Viti*—"Say something in Persian," they demanded, and I repeated a verse from Hafiz!"—oh Vits! Vits! But I will cease Ali carping: this is nothing

---

3. A village on the road to Isfahan, where they had spent the night.
4. It was at Kermanshah, western Persia, where Harold awaited Vita's arrival in the car from Bagdad. Vita in her reply explained that her apparent indifference was a joke.

to carp about. It is a splendid lovely book; it has given me such an up on life.

Your Hadji

VITA TO HAROLD   *Long Barn*

2 October 1926

Ronnie [Balfour] and I were climbing over the gate into the orchard, when we heard Dottie [Wellesley] call out, "Look at that aeroplane!" We looked up, and saw a huge machine just overhead, with a long blood-red plume of fire streaming from it. It swerved away as though it were making for Penshurst; Ronnie and I stared at one another, appalled; after a minute we heard the engines stop; after another minute (though it seemed an eternity) we heard the crash. Of course we thought it had come down quite close, and ran for all we were worth; then we saw a column of black smoke rising up out of the Westwood trees. Well, we rushed across the fields, and there was the ruin in a field, still blazing, an appalling sight. You will read about it in the papers, of course. There was absolutely nothing left of that machine but a blackened circle of grass, some twisted iron, some fluttering coloured silks, and seven sinister heaps covered over with sacking. They had got the bodies out with hay-rakes—just charred stumps, and the same smell as at Potter's Bar when we went to see the Zeppelin [crash]. The most poignant thing of all were the clothes, they had been in the luggage and consequently had not had time to burn; they lay strewn all round the wreck, pathetic frivolous things, bright silks and bits of fur, intended to adorn those charred remains.

There was of course nothing to be done, and we walked home. Plankino [George Plank] nearly fainted when we got back, and we had to pour brandy down his throat.

Now this morning the papers are full of the Weald names: West-wood, Geffers, Marchant, Ketney—it will look so strange to you when you read it. I am *thankful* the thing did not fall in one of our fields, though I can't think why it didn't, as in the end it turned upside down and fell like a stone. I shall never forget that blazing thing flying over the trees of our orchard and staggering away to its death. Glad the babies weren't here.

12 October 1926

I hear from Dotz [Dorothy Wellesley] that all my Persian bulbs (irises and tulips) which I left in her greenhouse are coming up. This excites me to madness. If you see any exciting vegetation, dig it up and send it *now,* while it is dormant. Some of the wild broom? Sage? Lavender? Oh please, Hadji, some of the lavender with the big pink flowers. But wrap it in something damp (moss, tissue-paper) and put it in a biscuit tin.

26 October 1926

Ouf! I breathe again. Lecture over.[1] Did you think of me? I hope so. I thought of you thinking of me, even as I stood terrified and with tremulous voice before the audience in the R.S.L. room. People I knew in said audience: [Sir Edmund] Gosse [the literary critic] (in the chair), John Drinkwater, Philip Guedella, Dotz, Irene (Cooper-Willis), George Plank, your mummy, Eric!! Katherine[2]!!!! And, in the back row, grinning at me, ironical, *émue,* Virginia [Woolf]. Others were strangers. A sea of faces—Gosse speaking—the sensation of being on one's feet—"Ladies and gentlemen . . ."

Then the sensation of speaking, speaking, speaking . . . The blessèd sensation of coming to an end. Applause. The refuge of sitting down again. Then Gosse . . . Silly old ass. Silly little arch bows towards me. *The Land* flattened open on the desk before him. "A poem of which

---

1. Her lecture was on *Tradition in English Poetry* to the Royal Society of Literature.
2. Eric was Harold's older brother, later 3rd Lord Carnock, and Katherine his wife.

neither Tennyson nor Wordsworth need have been ashamed." "This truly Virgilian solidity . . ." "This most important contribution to English literature . . ." Silly ass, silly soapy old ass. Gosse intoning my lines. I shrank behind my desk. I escaped at last with Virginia who put me properly in my place in the mists of Bloomsbury Square. She wants to print my paper as a Hogarth Essay.

I love you endlessly. I feel bruised and raped; an odd feeling. As though I had been stripped publicly naked. Yet I suppose I ought to be pleased. I shall write to you tomorrow from home, where I am myself.

You are the only reality. Oh darling, darling . . .

HAROLD TO VITA   *Teheran*

7 November 1926

Dearest—you don't know what *The Land* means to me! I read it incessantly—it has become a real wide undertone to my life. I forget absolutely that it is by you: it is such a lovely thing, darling, so beautiful a thing. It gives one a sense of permanence. It seems infinitely better each time one reads it. I keep on coming with surprise on lines I hadn't noticed:

"How delicate in spring they be / That mobled blossom and that wimpled tree."
or:
"Some concord of creation that the mind / Only in perilous balance apprehends."
or: "She being beautiful, and Leah but tender-eyed."
Lines which one could instance as the very stuff of poetry—lines which are memorable as catching a swallow-wing of thought which would have been lost by the trudge of prose. Oh my dear, if there was ever a work of art about which I felt *certain* it is this. So certain, that, except for fun, I don't care what other people say. So certain that I feel shy about it, like I feel shy about all my profounder feelings. My darling—it is so absurd—but I feel *grateful* to you for it. I don't mean to exaggerate, but it has added a pleasure to life. It is so firm, reliable.

It never lets one down. Dearest, the fact that it is by you (a fact which is too incredible to be realised) really does not weigh with me. But I know that the side of you which wrote that poem is detached from all mundane things—that it is above all exterior connections. You will get outside it in the same way some day. You will think, "Did I really write that?"

Of course naturally I want it to be a public success. But intrinsically I don't care. I simply know that it *is* a part of English literature, whereas all the other stuff is just like *Vogue* or the *Daily Mail*. Funny Mar! [1]

VITA TO HAROLD   *Long Barn*

7 November 1926

It is such a lovely day, so warm that we (Leonard, Virginia, and I) have been sitting in the sun by the big-room door all morning. The woods are golden, the distance deep blue—a blue and brown day. The garden looks incredibly neat; all sharp edges to turf and hedges everywhere, dug borders, black earth. It was fun waking up this morning and seeing what had been done during the past week. Such a nice dinner last night, with Eddy [Sackville-West] and Desmond [MacCarthy], the latter at his most amusing. But I agree with Virginia: he is really too mild. It is becoming too much of a stunt. Too negative. But very charming and amusing he is all the same.

Leonard is perfectly happy with a crowd of puppies. He has brought his own, and she and her sister are tearing madly up and down the lawn. The three elk [hound] babies try tentatively to join in. Leonard is a funny grim solitary creature. Virginia an angel of wit and intelligence. Leonard goes back to London this evening and she stays on with me till tomorrow, which I enjoy more than anything, as she then never stops talking, and I feel as though the edge of my mind were being held against a grindstone. Hadji not worry, though. It is all right.

---

1. *The Land* was awarded The Hawthornden Prize in 1927.

Later. We went to tea with Eddy at Knole, and then took Leonard to the station. A young moon, which Hadji must be seeing through the planes, oh dear. I think today has been one of the most beautiful days I ever remember; our Weald was looking its best, and such a sunset burnishing the brown trees. It made me absolutely long for you to be there.

VITA TO HAROLD   *Long Barn*

9 November 1926

Oh dear, Virginia . . . You see, Hadji, she is very very fond of me, and she says she was so unhappy when I went to Persia that it startled and terrified her. I don't think she is accustomed to emotional storms, she lives too much in the intellect and imagination. Most human beings take emotional storms as a matter of course. Fortunately she is the sensible sort of person who pulls themselves together and says, "This is absurd." So I don't really worry (Rather proud, really, of having caught such a big silver fish.) I look on my friendship with her as a treasure and a privilege. I shan't ever fall in love with her, *padlock,* but I am absolutely devoted to her and if she died I should mind quite, quite dreadfully. Or went mad again.

HAROLD TO VITA   *Teheran*

10 November 1926

My own darling Viti,

Sweetest, it's rather awful but I don't think I like Mrs Clive[1] at all, at all. It's so bedint not to like one's chief's wife (like the wife of the Colonel being snuffy about the wife of the brigadier), that I don't say so to anyone else—and Mar [must] not repeat it. Besides I may

---

1. Robert Clive had come to Teheran as British Minister on 5 November. His wife was Magdalen, daughter of Lord Muir Mackenzie.

change my mind. It is far better to start disliking someone than to start liking them—that is, when one has *got* to have close relations over a long period. I will scarcely get to *dislike* Mrs C. more and I may get to like her more. Whereas the reverse process would be a diminuendo.

But in the first place I think her affected. Now what on earth do we mean when we say 'affected'? Clive Bell I suppose is affected, and Raymond [Mortimer], and Virginia, and Vita and Harold. So all one means is that her mechanical habits (whether mental, moral, aesthetic, or merely laryngeal) are not the sort of habits I like. One means also that the mechanism is a little too obvious. That certain habits of attitude occur with too regular a precision. Now she has a form of affectation which irritates me particularly and which I have met before in women of birth, education and ill-health. It is a trick (1) of pinning situations to a phrase, (2) and of doing so in an off-hand way, with a sort of flicking gesture—to show how easily such apothegms come to one, that they are but the hors d'oeuvres of the banquet of one's soul. The victim of this habit thinks, I suppose, that it gives to situations and their own comments thereon a light and amusing effect. Thus I say I must be going off to the chancery—"Robot!" she says. The catch-words of the day are applied by her to the incidents of daily life, but they are the catch-words of a world I don't like at all, the world that lives in Hans Place, and dines at Prince's Restaurant, and goes to the best plays, and reads *Punch,* and has relations in all the countries, and simply revels in the Army and Navy Stores.

Then her meanness is simply terrifying. He may be just as stingy as she is, but he hides it better. She has no shame at all. Following [was the] dialogue yesterday while I was in his study going through telegrams. Enter *Mrs Clive:* "Daddy, sorry to interrupt you two important people (oh yes I know I'm a bore) but just fancy, one has to pay 1 Rial 25 for the most rotten little note-book here. Isn't there some rough government paper on which Mimi [her daughter, aged 15] can do her lessons?" *Clive:* "But after all, 1 Rial 25 is only just sixpence." *Mrs Clive:* "But my dear man, you should see the note-books. Why at the Stores one could get something far better for 5d. Of course I sent Mimi back to the shop to return them . . ."

And then her voice is dreadful. A sort of brave whine—courage struggling against ill health: a sort of plaintive tolerance, superior

No. 185.
November 10. 1926
(Wednesday)

Dearest darling Viti,

Sweetest its rather awful but I don't think I like Mrs Clive at all at all. Its so tedious not to like one's chief's wife (who the wife of the Colonel being smutty about the wife of the Brigadier) — that I don't say so to anyone else — & may not repeat it. Besides I may change my mind. It is far better to start disliking someone than to start liking them — that is when one has got to have close relations over a long period. I've scarcely got to dislike Mrs C. more & I may get to like her more. Whereas the reverse process comes by a diminuendo.

But in the first place I think her affected. Now what on Earth do we mean when we say "affected"? Clive & Bell & Raymond, and Suffice is affected, and Virginia, & Vita, Harold. So all one means is that her mechanical habits education tolerating a world of fools—("one must keep one's sense of humour . . .").

He is amiable and not a bit pompous—but I fear a light-weight.

Oh Viti Viti—I fear the Mars are not easily satisfied. Of course it is an impossible position being forced to live in subservient intimacy with people unlike oneself. The only basis for such a relationship must be one of blind admiration.

VITA TO HAROLD   *66 Mount St., London*

15 November 1926

After breakfast I was caught by the old man,[1] who glowered at me from under his eyebrows and said didn't I want to know his opinion of my poem? I wasn't at all sure that I did. I wanted to write to Hadji, I wanted to put on my fur coat, I wanted to say goodbye, Dr. Bridges—however I sat down meekly, as near as possible to the bit of smouldering peat which did duty as the fire, and composed myself in an attitude of proper respect, a nice blending of (1) Little Lord Fauntleroy, (2) the younger generation, (3) the young Swinburne at the feet of Victor Hugo. I was then treated for two hours to a lecture on English prosody. Chaucer, elision, syllabic verse, the diatonic scale, Shakespeare, Milton, the iniquity of daring to exist at all—all this was thundered at me in true Tennysonian manner. I huddled myself together, getting smaller and smaller, longing for a coat-collar, an umbrella, anything to creep behind and hide.

HAROLD TO VITA   *Teheran*

19 November 1926

I went to Clive's opening reception for the Persians. In the middle of it all Mrs Elgood came and told me that they had thrown Henry's

1. Robert Bridges, the poet laureate, with whom Vita had again been staying the night at his house on Boars Hill, outside Oxford.

body on to the dust-heap outside the Russian Embassy.[1] I don't think I have ever been quite so angry in my life. I absolutely saw red. I left the Legation and dashed across to my house. I quite unconsciously seized the two sticks you used for your ankle and called for Bogber. He must have thought his last hour had come—seeing me standing there in a frock-coat transfigured with rage and waving two sticks in my hand. He got as white as a sheet and dodged behind the table. I spoke to him in Persian at first. He said, of course, that it was the fault of the Dispensary people. He had told the latter exactly what to do, but had had to come back here because of his work. I then stopped talking Persian and spoke to him in English. I then sent him out with lanterns and a man to rescue that poor little corpse and bury it decently.

It is things like this that really exhaust me—I felt as if I had been beaten all over—like you, my sweet, after a scene with B.M. It is things like this also that show one what savages these people really are. I walked back to the reception, and looked at all those polite frock-coated people with a feeling of loathing.

VITA TO HAROLD   *Long Barn*

20 November 1926

I got a letter from Virginia, which contains one of her devilish, shrewd, psychological pounces—so true that I'll transcribe it for you:

"You'll be tired of me one of these days (I'm so much older), so I have to take my little precautions. That's why you say I put the emphasis on 'recording' rather than feeling. And isn't there something obscure in you? something that doesn't vibrate? It may be purposely—you don't let it, but I see it with other people, as well as with me: something reserved, muted. It's in your writing too, by the by. The thing I call central transparency sometimes fails you there too. I will lecture you at Long Barn."

Damn the woman, she has put her finger on it. There *is* something muted. What is it, Hadji? Something that doesn't vibrate, something that doesn't come alive. I brood and brood; feel that I grope in a dark

---

1. Harold had been obliged to have his dog put down when Henry developed incurable sores.

tunnel, persuaded that somewhere there is light, but never can find the way to emerge. It makes everything I do (i.e. write) a little unreal; gives the effect of having been done from the outside. It is the thing which spoils me as a writer; destroys me as a poet. But how did V. discover it? I have never owned it to anybody, scarcely even to myself. It is what spoils my human relationships too, but that I mind less.

She ends up her letter by saying, "Do you know this interesting fact: I found myself thinking with intense curiosity about death. Yet if I'm persuaded of anything it is of mortality. Then why this sense that death is going to be a great excitement?—something positive, active?"

There is no doubt about it, Hadji: that as one grows older one thinks more: Virginia worries, you worry, I worry.

Oh dear, what a solemn mar—that's what comes of living alone in the rain and reading Wordsworth. Yet I would rather do this, and become introspective, than rattle about London, while people's voices become more and more devoid of meaning.

VITA TO HAROLD   *Long Barn*

23 November 1926

Sibyl Colefax told Virginia you had the most delicious nature she had ever known. There now! I always told you she was an intelligent woman. V. was impressed at Sibyl corroborating what *I* had told her. I'm a little bothered about Virginia, but fortunately she is a sensible and busy person, and doesn't luxuriate in vain repinings. She is an absolute angel to me, and the value of her friendship is not to be measured in gold. Oh my dear, *what* intelligence! it is amazing—what perception, sensitiveness in the best sense, imagination, poetry, culture; everything so utterly un-shoddy and real. I long for you two to know each other better. I hope to God she won't be too unhappy when I go away; she told me that last year she was terrified by her own unhappiness and I fear this will be worse. Darling, this all sounds very conceited, but I don't mean it like that, and it is *padlock* anyway. She is very much on the crest of the wave, which pleases her vanity, but so *how* always: "I want you to be proud of me." I think she's coming here for the weekend as Leonard has to go away—or perhaps weekend after next.

Oh my darling, how well I know that feeling about "how can a fountain-pen express my ache for you?" I simply cling to the idea that the time is going by. But I cannot believe that next summer will ever come, it is too good to be possible.

VITA TO HAROLD   *Long Barn*

30 November 1926

I'm alone. It is very cold and wet. I have got Virginia coming for the weekend. Darling, I know Virginia will die, and it will be too awful. (I don't mean *here,* over the weekend; but just die young.) I went to Tavistock Sq. yesterday, and she sat in the dusk in the light of the fire, and I sat on the floor as I always do, and she rumpled my hair as she always does, and she talked about literature and Mrs Dalloway and Sir Henry Taylor, and said you would resent her next summer. But I said no, you wouldn't. Oh Hadji, she *is* such an angel; I really adore her. Not 'in love' but just love—devotion. I don't know whether it annoys you that I should write so often about her? One has to be so careful at this distance; but really Hadji shouldn't be annoyed, because her friendship does enrich me so, and she is so completely un-silly. I absolutely long for you to know her better. I don't think I have ever loved anybody so much, in the way of friendship; in fact, of course I haven't. She knows the mars adore each other; I've told her so, and so has Tray. Oh my sweet, they do, don't they? God, how I want to *talk* to you; just talk and talk and talk. Yes, 'the time' is a real personal thing—like a snowman that dwindles very, very slowly. But still dwindles.

HAROLD TO VITA   *Teheran*

3 December 1926

You *do* promise to tell me if there is a muddle with Virginia! I am so worried about that. It is *such* a powder magazine. I am far more worried for Virginia and Leonard's sake than for ours. I *know* that for each of us the magnetic north is the other—and that though the needle may flicker and even get stuck at other points—it will come back to the pole sooner or later. But what dangers for them![1] You see, I have every confidence in your wisdom except where these sort of things are concerned, when you wrap your wisdom in a hood of optimism and only take it out when things are too far gone for mending.

H A R O L D   T O   V I T A   *Teheran*

17 December 1926

No my sweet—it doesn't annoy me that you should talk so much about Virginia. From your point of view I know that the friendship can only be enriching. I am of course a little anxious about it from her point of view as I can't help feeling that her stability and poise is based on a rather precarious foundation. I mean it would be rather awful if your coming out here made her ill. That is my main consideration. Attached to it, like a little ivy growing at the foot of a castle, is the feeling that she will make me seem dull to you. Not jealousy, darling—only an instinctive movement of self-defence. But my dominant idea is one of pleasure that the rich ores in your nature should be brought to light—I *know* that it does you moral and mental good to be with her and be loved by her, and that is all that matters. I think you are very akin—the marriage of true minds to which I will not allow myself (even to myself or to you which is the same thing) to admit impediment.[2]

And as for *my* relations with Virginia—I shall never forget how she was kind to me when I was smarting from Lytton's rudeness.[3] There was no reason why she should have been nice about it except that she saw I was flustered and in real pain. So at the bottom of my

1. He was, of course, fearing that their love affair might trigger a new attack of insanity in Virginia Woolf.
2. "Let me not to the marriage of true minds / Admit impediments." Shakespeare, Sonnet 116.
3. Lytton Strachey had been disdainful to Harold at their first meeting at a Bloomsbury party on 15 March 1923, the day when Harold's *Tennyson* was published.

terror of her glimmers a little white stone of gratitude. Which can only be increased by her loving you.

VITA TO HAROLD   *Long Barn*

17 December 1926

I have read so much of the 19th century lately that I can scarcely restrain myself from writing in that manner—whether in prose or poetry—and the more I read, the more I am convinced that I was born out of season: I should have lived in an age when seriousness and noble thoughts found an echo. Not that I like it; and I dislike it the more, now that I recognise in myself the natural tendency to precisely such earnest bombast; so, as we dislike in others what we mistrust in ourselves, I annotate my Wordsworth with angry comments and throw my Arnold across the room. I have now taken to Jane Austen, but although the genius of Proust forces me to tolerate a fiction founded upon snobbery, materialism and hypocrisy, her mere sly pokes of humour cannot persuade me to the same enjoyment—*I can't do with it;* she seems to me only a degree removed from Galsworthy. I agree with Charlotte Brontë about her.[1]

In fact, I don't know what I want from literature; I don't hold with the dunghill despair of Eliot; I don't like the hearty Victorianism of God's-in-his-heaven, all's-right-with-the-world; I, even *I,* can't stomach the self-righteous sententiousness of Wordsworth (although I think *Tintern Abbey* one of the finest poems in the language, and some of his sonnets the same). The 18th century is out of the question. There remain only the metaphysicians (who are obviously limited) and the Elizabethans. I'm not sure that they don't have it every time, with their *awakeness* and virility—yet even they had their affectations: the Italian tragedy, and all that. There seems to be no escape from affectations, of one sort or another, in literature; perhaps inevitably; every one

1. In a letter to G. H. Lewes of 12 January 1848 Charlotte Brontë wrote of *Pride and Prejudice:* "What did I find? An accurate daguerreotyped portrait of a commonplace face; a carefully fenced, highly cultivated garden, with neat borders and delicate flowers; but no glance of a bright, vivid physiognomy, no open country, no fresh air, no blue hill, no bonny beck."

seems conscious of a mission, whether to introduce new concepts (as Donne and Herbert and Vaughan and Co) or to redeem the language from a conventional groove (as Coleridge and Wordsworth), or again as Eliot and his kin. All a question of reaction; never a question of approaching LIFE, through the medium of poetry, with a true personal attitude—save in people like Blake, who rapidly become such cranks as to become bores. Yet what should poetry express, but an attitude towards life? Fresh, thought-out at first hand, uncoloured by fashion (least of all!) or by what has gone before? But a damned difficult thing to do. (I mean *major* poetry of course; the Herricks and Sedleys always have their place—a different one.) All this comes of reading *Mansfield Park;* I try her [Jane Austen] periodically, and always with the same result—*I am sure* she is for the Desmonds [MacCarthy] and Eddie Marshes, and such littérateurs.

Tired out now with temper and going to bed—this is the third letter I have written you today. I wish I understood what life and literature was all about.

Your own puzzled
Mar

PS. It usually seems to me that serenity is the only thing worth aiming at, yet what is the Eliot school but the opposite facet of the same conviction (the sour grapes sides of it), and then one knows all the time how false one's serenity is—how instantly it would be shattered by the touch of personal tragedy. What *is* it all about?

Vita to Harold   *Long Barn*

21 December 1926

My own, *nothing* is wrong. PADLOCK. What 'reservations' or 'half truths' have you detected in my letters? There have been none, I have told you everything day by day exactly as it has happened. I swear to tell you at the first sign of "muddle with Virginia." My dearest, how can you speak of reservations and half truths when I have told you all about that business? Even that I *did* sleep with her, which I need never have told you—but that I wanted you to know everything that happened to me while you were away. (If you had been at home I might not have told you.) There is nothing I will not tell you, that you want to know. I am absolutely devoted to her, but not in love. So there. Oh my darling, has all my wretchedness at being separated from you then failed to convince you of my absolute love for you? It can't, it can't; you *must* know. It was only that you had 'flu, wasn't it? Oh darling, I get frantic when I think of you having even a moment's anxiety.

VITA TO HAROLD   *Knole*

26 December 1926

Ben is in bed in Cranmer's dressing-room—your room!—and I am in bed in Cranmer's bedroom, and we have the door open between us, so that we can talk. I can hear him saying to himself, "The mild continuous epic of the soil,"[1] like somebody rolling a sweet round and round his tongue. Niggs [Nigel] is the same little clown, a born comic. He has got his bicycle, and is as happy as a king. He is infinitely *serviable,* unselfish, and affectionate. Also sturdy, practical, resourceful, independent, humorous. I see *no* flaw in him, as a character; everybody loves him. I have had to institute scrubbage, as never was there such a little guttersnipe. Otherwise he is perfect; not an intellectual, but we shall have enough to spare of that in Ben. My darling, we are very, very lucky in those two boys. They will, respectively, satisfy all that we could wish for: Ben our highbrowness, Niggs our human needs. Or, at least, so I read them. Ben may be selfish to us, though I think we are both intelligent enough to cope with that; Niggs may be conventional and English but, again, we are intelligent enough to cope with that. It remains, that we are very lucky in them, and that they are very lucky in us. What I really do look forward to is having them next summer, as Ben will be just at the age then when you will be most valuable to him, and your influence most important.

---

1. From Vita's own poem *The Land.*

Eddy [Sackville-West] wandered in and interrupted, but I have decided that I am fond of Eddy, so I don't mind. He is gone now, and I have had my luncheon, and presently I suppose I must get up—I should like to stay in bed today, but it is not fair on Dada, whose Olive [Rubens] has got boils.

What is the point, in our enlightened world, of *marriage?* You see, if the mars had just lived together, they would be living together still, just as happily, and it would make no difference to their passion for their garden, or to their interest in their mars. The whole system of marriage is wrong. It ought, at least, to be optional; and no stigma if you prefer a less claustrophobic form of contract. For it *is* claustrophobic. It is only very, very intelligent people like us who are able to rise superior; and I have a suspicion, my darling, that even *our* intelligence (about which there seems to be a good deal in this letter), wouldn't have sufficed if our temperamental weaknesses didn't happen to dovetail as well as they do, e.g. my impatience of restraint and Hadji's constitutional dislike of scenes. In fact, our common determination for personal liberty: to have it ourselves, and to allow it to each other. (There is no *arrière-pensée* about all this; just thinking aloud, and just a smug satisfaction with the way we have solved the problem.)

But of course the real secret is that we love each other—one always comes back to these simple human things in the end, and 'intelligence' goes on the scrap-heap.

HAROLD TO VITA   *Teheran*

31 December 1926

Darling, I don't like rhododendrons—I am sorry. I don't mind them in a big place round a big lake. But I think they are as out of place at our cottage as a billiard-table would be. To me it is exactly the same. Then I don't like putting in big things (as distinct from small flowers) which are not indigenous: I am opposed to specimen trees. You see, I think our stunt at Long Barn is to keep the Kentish farm background, and on that background to embroider as much as

we like. But rhododendrons would spoil the background. I feel sure
you agree really—only you think, "He doesn't understand that the
pond garden has to be backed and enclosed by something large and
bushy and dark." But I do understand this, and I agree that if rhododendrons were natives to Kent they would be exactly and absolutely
what we want. But they are *not* natives and we should spoil our
lovely Kentish atmosphere. I'm sure I am right. But what then can
we have? Well, cob nuts, and hazel, banked right at the back, with
holly as a background to them—and in front some syringa and
flowering shrubs. Yes, I know it's difficult. Shrubbery is a great
problem if one is to avoid the suburban. But it's not a problem
which can be solved by rosie-dendrons. I don't mind holly so long
as it's not variegated. But be clever and think of all the indigenous
things and get an idea of derivatives. What about more flowering
peaches against a background of holly? I think that the pond garden
wants a great deal of dark background. In fact I think the nuttery
should be made with a plantation of dark trees. One wants the pond
to look like a clearing in a wood: not like a piece of water in a rock
garden.

HAROLD TO VITA   *Teheran*

7 January 1927

Such a marvellous day yesterday. An absolute stillness. It is so odd
that cloudless days should differ so much from each other. I think this
place is so excellent for training the observation. There is the vast
uniformity in space and even time: the feeling that it will all be the
same colour and contours right away to China: the feeling that it was
the same colour and contour five thousand years ago: that is the first
background. The second background is the climate. The fact that one
really does get about 300 days in the year which are absolutely cloudless—and thus in appearance absolutely the same. The fact that there
are no breezes in Persia—rare gales only, howling against an absolute
stillness. All this produces a monochromatic background against which
little changes—the sound of a dry leaf pattering on a tin roof, the trail

of smoke against the umber plain, take a far intenser significance. I think it is this which has made me so sensitive to nature-sounds. Persia in effect is a great stillness: that really is its charm. And darling, how immense that charm is! Now that my happiness has come back to me I savour it with joy. I ride out over the hills and look back on that amazing design of plain and mountain. And I shout—so that Bay Rum [Harold's new horse] pricks his ears—"Viti!—Viti!"

VITA TO HAROLD   *Long Barn*

22 July 1927

My own precious Hadji

It seems so funny to be writing to you again,[1] and the pot pourri is such an awful coffee cup [reminder].

I have lots to tell you:

I went to lunch with the priest. Talk about Clive [Bell] having a Restoration appearance! it is nothing to the Rev. Summers.[2] Dressed in black, hung with amethyst crosses and bits of jet, black suéde shoes, fat white hands, a fat dimpled face, oiled black curls, very carefully disposed—he is just like a Lely. He gave me a very good lunch and lots of information, then when I asked him to tell me the way, he said he would come to the end of the street, and put on a top-hat with a curly brim, and black silk gloves. You never saw such an old sod in all your life.

Then I went and met Virginia, who had come down with Leonard to Richmond Park where V. was to have a driving lesson. Leonard and I watched her start. The motor made little pounces and stopped dead. At one moment it ran backwards. At last she sailed off, and Leonard and I and Pinker [dog] went for a walk at 5 miles an hour. Every five minutes Leonard would say, "I suppose Virginia will be all

---

1. Harold and Vita, having walked across the Bakhtiari Mountains to the Persian Gulf, returned to England together on 5 May. On 21 July Harold went to Paris with Raymond Mortimer for a week's holiday.
2. Rev. Alphonsus Summers, the expert on Restoration plays. Vita visited him in connection with her book on Aphra Behn published in 1927. He lived on The Green, Richmond.

right." We walked round a plantation and he told me how once he had walked there with Desmond [MacCarthy] on a moonlight night, and the night got mistier and Desmond got more and more romantic, and was pouring out all the secrets of his heart, when they came to a clearing in the midst of the plantation, and there, gleaming in the moonlight, was a white, solitary, enormous chamber-pot.

Well, then we got back to the trysting place and there was Virginia taking an intelligent interest in the works of the car. So Leonard drove off back to London, and V. and I went to Kew (in *my* car), and walked about and sat there till 6.30—and then came back to London and tried to go and see Ruth Draper but there were no seats, so we dined at the Petit Riche and had a lot of Chianti and went back to Tavistock [Square] and sat in the basement and talked more.

HAROLD TO VITA   *Long Barn*

12 September 1927

My own own darling Viti,

Dearest—isn't it absurd that after all these years of marriage and all these delicious months of constant companionship I should feel a wrench, a cleavage, a real gulf and gap—just because you go away for one night? The afternoon is all still grey and purple: there is a faint sun: the poplars stand straight and unwanted: the house seems empty and broods on its little untidy self. My dear, my dear, what *would* happen to me if you really went away? Such desolation. I couldn't survive it. I wonder what I should do and from what part of myself I could dig up the stores of courage required. Has one reserves of fortitude? I feel that my present stock of it would be but as a tea-cup capacity compared to all the tanks and cylinders of Abadan. And he was cross to her about the Income Tax! And it *is* such a lovely soft and silent day here, whereas at Brighton there will be a wind, and hard colours, and the feeling of cement against shingle, and shingle against a cold and noisy sea.

Your own
Hadji

HAROLD TO VITA   *Long Barn*

23 October 1927

Viti—I am sitting in my rabbit hutch and you are in reach of me.
But when you read this I shall have no dear neighbour.[1] Little one,
be not angry with me for being so obstinate and selfish. It *is* Othello's
occupation [diplomacy]—and however much it may depress and irritate me, I feel that without it I would become *not* a cup of tea but
a large jug of tepid milk.

Darling, do you remember saying once that you had never established an absolutely satisfactory relation with anyone—not even with
me? That was years ago. I don't think you would say that now. I feel
that our love and confidence is absolute. I mean in the technical sense
of absolute: it is relative to nothing but itself: it is untouched by
circumstances, emotions: it is certainly untouched by age. Darling—
isn't this a great comfort? *Cosa bella mortal passa: ma non d'arte.*[2] I feel
that our love is something as detached from circumstance as the beauty
of a work of art. This gives one security in all this transience. If one
of us died, this love would live, although in agony. Our love will only
die with both of us.

---

1. He was about to leave home for Berlin.
2. "Human beauty fades: but art never."

*H*arold remained in Berlin for the next two years as Counsellor in the British Embassy and Chargé d'Affaires between two Ambassadors. Vita visited him there quite frequently, hating Berlin and its diplomacy, and it was partly because of her unhappiness at their recurrent separations that he took the decision, after much self-questioning, to resign from the Foreign Service at the end of 1929. Vita at Long Barn was busy writing poetry and her book on Andrew Marvell, and took to regular broadcasting for her new friend Hilda Matheson, the BBC's Director of Talks. Her love affair with Virginia Woolf culminated in 1928 with the publication of Orlando, Virginia's mock-biography of Vita. Harold in Berlin wrote the life of his father, Lord Carnock, who died in 1928, the same year when Vita's father, Lord Sackville, also died, at Knole.

3 November 1927

I love foreign politics and I get them here in a really enthralling form. If I chucked them merely for emotional reasons I should feel a worm—unworthy of what is one of the few serious and virile sides to my nature. "Yes," you say, "that's all very well—but what about me?" I know, my saint, and I am bothered by that consideration. But somewhere right deep down in you you must realise that Hadji's willingness to do hard drudging work merely because it is interesting is a very respectable form of looniness. It should give you, somewhere, somewhere deep down, a twiddle of respect. Doesn't it? So bear with me, my sweet. I won't undergo anything *intolerable* for this idea: but Berlin is not *intolerable* and I can't pretend that it is.

VITA TO HAROLD   *Long Barn*

4 November 1927

Well, I've got home, you see, and there were two letters waiting
for me from Hadji—also an array of photographs of the perfect
diplomatist. Oh my darling! I *don't* like perfect diplomatists, no I
don't. I like Hadji's soft collars—and his laughing eyes—not that
white cardboard round his neck and that severe expression. Oh my
darling, where have you gone? and what become? Where's my own
neighbour with his tousled head?

HAROLD TO VITA   *Berlin*

7 November 1927

My angel,

I had Noel Coward[1] to luncheon yesterday. Then we went on to
a review at the big Music Hall here. It was rather an odd thing to do
but Coward has little time and is anxious to pick up something original
for the review which he is himself producing in London [*This Year
of Grace*]. I must say, he *is* rather remarkable. Completely self-educat-
ed—and producing a review in which he acts, sings and dances himself
and of which he has written the plots, the words and the music. When
you add to this the fact that he also writes excellent social satire, one
can't help treating him with respect. He is a bounder of course—but
I really don't mind that when combined with real talent and energy.

We left at about 4.30, and went to a party at Mrs Albert's. Mrs
A. is the American wife of Dr Albert who was the man who invented
poison gas. They are very rich and have a large house with damask,
Dutch pictures, tapestry and very heavy Italian furniture. Mrs Albert
turned to me: "I didn't see you in church today, Mr Nicolson."
"No—I hate church." "But the Bishop was there." "I loathe Bishops."
Complete consternation on the part of Mrs Albert. Change of subject:

1. Noel Coward, who was then only twenty-seven, had just achieved his first major success
with *The Vortex* and *Hay Fever*.

"Don't you play bridge Mr Nicolson?" "No—not on Sunday after-noons." Whereat Mrs Albert became so puzzled that she gave me up and returned to the subject of servants. Never, *never* will I set foot in that house again.

VITA TO HAROLD   *Long Barn*

7 November 1927

Roy[1] returned from London after two nights of debauch, and is now very ill. I have sent for the doctor. Mary, poor child, looks like death. He has been drinking, and sleeping with Dorothy Warren. Keep this to yourself. I think he is absolutely crazy. I feel most frightfully sorry for Mary. He went for her last night with a knife. But I suppose that after he has got over the effects of drink he will quiet down.

VITA TO HAROLD   *Long Barn*

10 November 1927

Roy, after a series of incredible scenes and rows, in which he has alternately threatened to commit suicide or disappear to S. Africa, and invited Mary to commit suicide with him, offering his razor for the purpose, has recovered his senses. Fortunately I have a calming effect on him, and he now rushes down here instead of venting it all on Mary. It is very odd altogether. I have the strangest conversations with him, which always end in expressions of mutual respect, and he goes home beaming. But really he is a strange creature—weak and violent. I got quite alarmed at first, as I didn't want him to drown himself in our pond or anything like that, but I soon saw that he was quite incapable of action, and indeed he admits it himself. His two days of orgy in

---

1. Roy Campbell, the South African poet, to whom Vita had lent the gardener's cottage at Long Barn. She had fallen in love with his wife, Mary, and Roy had found out, both facts that Vita conceals from Harold.

London thoroughly upset him, and he came home in frenzy and despair. He's all right now.

HAROLD TO VITA   *Berlin*

9 December 1927

I lunched yesterday with the Military Attaché to meet the four Chiefs of the German Military Staff. It was a curious experience. They came in uniform and clicked their heels and were very polite and stiff. The military attaché (Colonel Sandilands) is an absolute peach. He *is* Colonel Bramble.[1] I am sure of it. You must get him to tell you the story of the Calais rebellion. It is too marvellous. You see, in 1919 some troops—about 5,000—declared a Soviet at Calais, arrested their officers and captured the whole camp. Sandilands was sent "to deal with the situation." He went there. "Well you see—er—it was—er er—difficult to know what to do. So I—er—just—er—told them to bugger off." "And what did they do?" "Oh—er—well, they did bugger off." He is a gem.

I went in the evening to tea with Frau [Lalli] Horstmann. Her husband is head of the English section of the Foreign Office. He is a rich Jew and their home is the only 'fashionable' centre in Berlin. She, *mirabile dictu,* is some relation of Maud Cunard.[2] He is a fat, vulgar, lecherous, self-indulgent scoundrel—with a faint dash about him of something adventurous which prevents one from really disliking him. She is a dark, clever little woman who "likes books and things" and has a "small circle." The small circle seems to centre round Mario Pansa,[3] but all the same it *is* the most interesting house here and one feels less provincial there than in other places.

She was alone and we had a heart to heart. She told me that Princess Lichnowski[4] is acutely miserable and that he ill-treats her. The

---

1. In André Maurois's *Les Silences du Colonel Bramble,* sketches of a British officers' mess.
2. The American-born London hostess.
3. Formerly Mussolini's private secretary, he was then on the staff of the Italian Embassy in Berlin.
4. The wife of the German Ambassador in London at the outbreak of the First World War.

Princess is always falling desperately in love with people who are
frightened by her passion and run away. I think myself that she would
have found greater happiness had she been b.s. [lesbian] and not fallen
in love with men, who don't like amorous tigresses. She also told me
that the Princess had been really plain as a young woman and that her
beauty has only come to her at 48. That in itself is rather tragic.

HAROLD TO VITA   *Berlin*

27 December 1927

A few nights ago there was a large subscription dance at the
Central Hotel in aid of the British Relief Fund. A feature of this dance
was the Tombola organised by Lady McFadyean.[1] Several English
firms had provided prizes, and there were 500 tickets of 1 mark each,
and about 300 prizes. As everybody took at least ten tickets they each
got at least two prizes. The prizes had already been arranged by Lady
McFadyean all in their right order and numbered to correspond with
the tickets. She had arranged a sort of counter, and behind it she stood,
backed by mountains of prizes—pyramids of cocoa-tins, obelisks of
Pears soap tablets, huge triumphal arches of pineapple in tins. Everybody clustered round to get their presents and a hundred outstretched
arms waved tickets at the firm but harassed face of Lady McFadyean.

It was then that, most unwisely, I offered to help. I leant across
and said, "Lady McFadyean, can I come and help you?" Fool that she
was, she said "Yes." Fool that I was I climbed in under the counter.
The first thing that fell was a pile of those little soap-tablets which one
puts in guests' bed-rooms. Each tablet had been numbered separately
and the whole had that afternoon been arranged by Lady McFadyean
in a neat sort of façade, a pyramid, a slightly baroque façade. This, I
fear, crumbled at my approach, and as I stooped to pick them up I
banged Lady McFadyean's bottom with my own. "Oh *do* be careful,
Mr Nicolson, you know it's a tight fit behind here." It was. I got very

---

1. The wife of Sir Andrew McFadyean, the British Representative on the Reparations
   Commission in Berlin.

hot rearranging the soap, but when it was finished, I took a ticket from one of the outstretched hands. No. 406 it was.

Now the 400's were up Lady McFadyean's end of the counter, and to get to them I would have to push past her. I pushed. She said, "Easy on," and picked up a covey of candle-shades which she (or perhaps I) had noticeably disarranged. Now 432 was there all right and a little to the left of it was 389. Between them shivered a high and slender tower of Three Castle cigarettes. Each diminutive packet had a separate number, and 406, of course, was near the base of the pile. I thought I could jerk or flick it out without really disturbing the rest of the structure. But I thought wrong. It took me a good time picking them up again, and when I had finished I realised that once again I must push past Lady McFadyean to present this guerdon to the holder of No. 406—to the man who, earlier in the evening, had handed me his ticket. So much, however, had passed since then, that I had forgotten what the man looked like. I pushed oh so gingerly behind Lady McFadyean—and got back to my point of departure. I held the packet of Gold Flake (it must have contained at least six cigarettes) high in the air and asked if anyone claimed it. No one did. Obviously that was the wrong method.

The thing to do was to choose an object first and then ask who had the number. Now the best object was a receiving set presented by the Marconiphone Company. There it was on the top shelf behind me—in the place of honour behind two pyramids of pineapple tins. Its number was 387. I memorised the number carefully and then turned with engaging brightness to the crowd which by then was becoming a little out of hand. "Who," I cried, "has No 387?" *"Wer,"* I translated, *"hat den drei hundert sieben und achtzig gewählt?"* A short little man began to wave frantic fat fingers from the back. "Please, please . . ." I said to the front ranks, indicating that the man at the back should be allowed to step forward. He stepped. I then turned to get the receiving set. It was a nice square box with two dials in front. All I had to do was to lift it down from the shelf, turn round, and hand it with a certain style to the recipient. Such actions are only graceful if done in a single motion, as it were; if done, as it were, with swift ease. I turned. I grasped the box. I turned rapidly again, holding the box in both hands, smiling generously on the lucky recipient. I felt a slight tug as I did so and then followed a noise like a bombardment.

I was struck in several places by tins of pineapple: tins of pineapple leapt the counter and rolled out into the ball-room: tins of pineapple fell battering down on the lowering form of Lady McFadyean. You see, some ass had attached two ear-pieces to the receiving set by a long flex at each end, and some greater ass had draped the flexes and ear-pieces behind the pyramids of pineapple. Now an ear-piece is a prehensile object—and my particular two gripped the pineapples in what was, in fact, a grip of death.

I apologised to Lady McFadyean. I crept under the counter again, and mingled hot and bruised with the crowd.

VITA TO HAROLD   *Knole*

18 January 1928

I went down to Long Barn today and was telephoned almost immediately by one of the nurses, as Dada's temperature had risen and they were alarmed. I came back at once, and have sent for Horder.[1] He is *very bad,* and I am terrified. Horder should be here in an hour or so—God grant that he may be in time. Hadji, I feel really desperate. He (Dada I mean) is under morphia now and asleep—I found both Sichel and Burnett [Sevenoaks doctors] here—Sichel says his condition is critical. Hadji, I would mind so dreadfully if he died. Oh I *wish* you were here. He mustn't die. I feel Horder can save him if anybody can, but beyond sending for Horder I feel absolutely helpless. It is so awful to see anybody ill like that, and to be able to do nothing for them. One *feels* so strongly that one thinks one ought to be able to perform a miracle, but one cannot. Oh I do wish you were here—so sane as you always are, bless you my own Hadji, you must never, never get ill. I do long for you now—but I expect Horder is the better substitute, a more practical substitute, I mean. We have got a lung specialist coming too. I have not telegraphed to you yet today as I simply don't know what to say.[2]

---

1. Sir Thomas Horder (later Lord Horder), who was the senior physician in St. Bartholomew's Hospital, and doctor to several members of the Royal Family.
2. Lord Sackville died at Knole, of pericarditis, on 28 January 1928.

HAROLD TO VITA   *Berlin*

11 February 1928

Sinclair Lewis[1] is an odd red-faced noisy young man, who called
me Harold from the start, and wouldn't leave me. He insisted on me
going to a bar with him and then he insisted on coming back to dinner
with me. He talked the whole time and drank and drank. At 9.30 he
remembered that he had got to take his fiancée to a ball, and off he
went dragging me with him as he said he was too tight to dress. He
then spoke of Anglo-American relations. What could be done? Were
we drifting into war? Good God!—what was there to do? Would I
write a joint letter with him to the Evening Standard? And yet what
could we say? Perhaps it would be better to leave it alone? And yet
he did so love England. No wonder we hated America. And would
I come round with him to Edith Thompson's?[2] She might be annoyed
at his being so late. And of course I wasn't ill—why, he could feel my
pulse. Yes, I must come. And oh yes he was sleeping with Edith tonight
and must take his pyjamas round. And would I telephone for a taxi?
And did he look very tight? Because Edith minded.

I went to see Edith. She was a nice wise woman with charm and
good sense, and I packed them off together to a ball and went to bed.

HAROLD TO VITA   *Berlin*

14 April 1928

I went to the Puccini Abend at the Staats Oper. It really was very
good. I enjoyed it hugely. In the intervals Ivor[3] and I ate more and
more sausages. I like him so much. He is completely un-spoilt by his
success and absolutely *thrilling* about his life. He has contracts which
will bring him in £35,000 by November year. He calculates that if his
health lasts he should be able to make about £500,000 before he is

---

1. Sinclair Lewis (1885–1951), the American novelist, whose *Main Street* (1920) had been an
   immense success. He was awarded the Nobel Prize for Literature in 1930.
2. In fact she was Dorothy Thompson, the American journalist, whom Lewis married as his
   second wife in 1928, and divorced in 1942.
3. Ivor Novello, the Welsh-born composer, actor, dramatist, and film star, then aged thirty-
   five.

forty. He is rather appalled by this—and is very sensible about it. Says it makes one feel such a fool to be worth so much money solely because of one's profile. He suffers dreadfully from the worship of flappers. Every day there are two or three of them who wait outside his house just to see him. There were twelve of them at the station to see him off! All this must be terribly bad for a person—and he is himself terrified of becoming fatuous about it.

VITA TO HAROLD   *Long Barn*

18 April 1928

This morning I went down to Pemberton's [solicitors], and was doing my business with him, when a messenger came in to say B.M. was downstairs and wanted to see me. Well, I went down to the waiting-room, and there was B.M. in a towering rage—"I wish to see you in Mr Pemberton's presence." I said I would call him. "Give me your pearls!" screamed B.M., "twelve of them belong to me, and I wish to see how many you have changed, you thief." Then young Pemberton came down. He went to shake hands with her, and she put both hands behind her back. Then the scene began in real earnest. Darling, never, *never* have I heard such floods of the vilest abuse, aimed at both Pemberton and me. She was like a mad woman, screaming Thief and Liar, and shaking her fist at me till I thought she was going to hit me. It was quite impossible for either P. or me to speak, and equally impossible to make out what it was all about—the jewels, mostly. In the middle, the Commissioner for Oaths arrived, before whom I was to sign the papers—I cannot begin to tell you all the dreadful things B.M. said, none of them with even the elements of truth or reason in them. Then she started abusing Dada, at which I simply walked out of the room, and went upstairs with young P. and the Commissioner and signed the papers. B.M. followed, and broke into old P.'s room, where he was engaged with a client, and started calling him names too. Finally she went away, after a very long scene, but Bull [Lady Sackville's secretary] came up in a minute and said she wanted me to go with her to a jeweller to get her 12 pearls cut out of my necklace. I refused to do this but said I would cut them out myself in her presence. So I went down to the street where she was in the car, and cut them out. She then started off worse than ever. Said I was to return to her all the jewels she had ever given me, and the Isfahan rug—that I was to bring them up to London next day and send them to her room at the Savoy by a waiter, and that I should "wait outside her door like a servant while she looked over them to see how much I had stolen from her while she was ill." I said that I would do nothing of the sort, but that as I had no wish to keep anything she did not want me to have I would take them over to Brighton and give them to Bull—but that I would not see her to be insulted again. She screamed that she hated me, and wished I would die—wished, indeed, that I might be run over and killed that day—in fact there is no end to the horrors she shrieked at me through the window. She then began abusing you—at which I hailed a passing taxi and drove off. All this lasted from 12.30 to 2.15.

Darling, I fear that all this gives you but a faint idea of the scene. It was really dreadful. But apart from that, there are two important points which I have left to the end, (1) that she refuses to pay my allowance any longer,[1] and (2) that she wants everything sent back from Berlin [furniture lent for Harold's flat]. Now these are two very serious things. As to the allowance, of course legally we can insist on it—as she knows, and she dares us to do so—but I have a strong disinclination to accept a penny, except enough to cover the boys' education. As to the things from Berlin, this is more serious, and I propose to ignore the suggestion until she raises it again. She may forget about it, or she may be ashamed when she thinks everything over. Anyhow I shall take no steps for the moment. But heaven help us if she adheres to it!

When I finally escaped, I went to meet that little angel Tray [Raymond Mortimer], with whom I was lunching anyhow and to whom I had telephoned, and we went into a restaurant and he poured half a bottle of champagne down my throat—bless him.[2]

1. Lady Sackville owed Vita £2,400 a year as her marriage settlement.
2. Harold replied to this letter: "You must refuse to see her again under any circumstances. You must not expose yourself to such a scene again. If she comes to Long Barn, you must tell Louise to say you are out—and then you must bolt out of the back door and take to the woods."

HAROLD TO VITA   *Berlin*

16 May 1928

It must have been simply awful for you going to Knole. My poor sweet—it *is* beastly about Anne[1]: and I feel for Eddy almost as much as I feel for you. It wouldn't be so ghastly if Charlie had died first and if Eddy was now the owner. But it ought, it ought, to belong to you my sweet. *Personally* I am glad it doesn't, as it would be a bore for Hadji who doesn't like being a Prince Consort, and who loves his mud-pie. But Mar would love it—bless her dear heart—and Hadji would be allowed to build a little cement cottage for himself at the Mast-head [in Knole Park]. But best of all would be if Lionel [Sackville] had not died. What a shock and a blow that was! I feel it acutely even now. The tissues of my mind are bruised all round that part.

Cyril Connolly[2] came yesterday. Like the young Beethoven with spots—and a good brow, and an unreliable voice. And he flattered your husband. He sat there toying with a fork and my vanity, turning them over together in his stubby little hands. He tells fortunes. Palmistry. But the main point of him is that he thinks *Some People* an important work. IMPORTANT!! And it was just scribbled down as a joke.

VITA TO HAROLD   *Long Barn*

16 May 1928

My own Hadji

I allowed myself a torture-treat tonight: I went up to Knole after dark and wandered about the garden. I have a master-key, so could get in without being seen. It was a very queer and poignant experience; so queer, and so poignant, that I should almost have fainted had I met anybody. I mean, I had the sensation of having the place so completely

---

1. Vita's father was succeeded as 4th Lord Sackville by his brother Charles, who had married Anne Bigelow, an American, in 1924. Eddy Sackville-West, who was to become the 5th Lord Sackville in 1962, was Charles's only son.
2. The author and literary critic (1903–74).

to myself, that I might have been the only person alive in the world—
and not the world of today, mark you, but the world of at least 300
years ago. I might have been the ghost of Lady Anne Clifford.

V I T A   T O   H A R O L D   *Long Barn*

24 June 1928

Robert Harris read [on BBC radio] the *Ode to the West Wind,* part
of *Adonais,* and the *Ode to a Nightingale,* and I sat with the tears
pouring down my face. Oh Hadji, what poetry! What pure gold of
poetry! What a heritage—*damn* T. S. Eliot, bloody American that he
is, with his 'combinations drying in the sun'. I could not have believed
that I should be so moved by anything so familiar. Those lovely, lovely
lines seem to be floating round the room still—

Then more than ever seems it rich to die,
To cease upon the midnight with no pain. . . .

I don't care what you say about Shelley; he was divine when he
wrote.

H A R O L D   T O   V I T A   *Berlin*

28 June 1928

Yesterday I lunched with President von Hindenburg. It was rather
fun. The Ambassador[1] went on ahead as he had a private audience to
hand over his letters of credence. Lady Lindsay and I followed at 1.0
p.m. In the hall we were met by Hindenburg's son, surrounded by
about six footmen and a man with a large cocked hat and a silver mace.
Escorted by these we went upstairs. There was another man with a
silver mace at the top of the stairs, and when we reached the landing
he brought his mace down crack! As if by magic *(c'est magique,
Excellence)* two huge doors flung open in front of us and there were

---

1. Sir Ronald Lindsay, who was retiring as British Ambassador in Berlin, leaving Harold in
   charge of the Embassy. In 1930 Lindsay was appointed Ambassador to the United States.

a group of figures in a great saloon. We advanced towards them. The President advanced towards us. He kissed Lady Lindsay's hand: he shook mine warmly. The Chancellor [Herman Müller] was there and the Von Schuberts [Foreign Secretary]: a ghastly silence, broken only by the distant hum of traffic, descended upon us. Suddenly the man with the mace, who alone of the party displayed any initiative, beat the floor again—and the Victor of Tannenberg [Hindenburg] advanced towards Lady Lindsay and very slowly started, with her arm in his, to go to luncheon. We followed. I sat opposite the President, and between the Chancellor's wife and the wife of the President's sort of Chamberlain man. We spoke in German. *"Was für schöne Rosen haben sie hier in Berlin!" "Ja—sie sind schöne Rosen."* And so on, and so on. The President is an old darling: he has a trick of raising his eyebrows and laughing like a school boy: he talks very simply, almost boyishly, but is pretty shrewd: he is wonderful for his age [81]— neither deaf nor blind. I don't wonder that they all worship him. After luncheon we all sat round a table and had coffee. This time I sat next to Hindenburg. He spoke about father [Lord Carnock], and asked where I had learnt German, and how when he was a boy, there were still many English expressions current at Hanover, and how he remembered the Embassy here before it was an Embassy, and how he had gone up in the first Zeppelin. A splendid old man, and I wish Mar had been there. She was asked.

Then a walk with Henry [spaniel]—and in the evening comes a telegram "Don't fly!" Oh my sweet, my sweet, of course I won't fly without permission. I didn't count just going up over the aerodrome as *flying.* But I do want terribly one day to do the flight Berlin–Vienna– Venice. But I promise *absolutely padlock* not to do any such thing without your permission.

VITA TO HAROLD   *Long Barn*

6 July 1928

Virginia has just gone. She was absolutely enchanting. We talked a lot about poetry and she said it doesn't matter a bit about not being modern.

Darling, really the Wolves are funnies. You see, they haven't got a garage, and it goes to Leonard's heart to pay garaging fees for the umbrella.[1] So for some time past he has been saying what a good garage Virginia's studio would make, but she didn't respond very much because she didn't want her studio taken away from her. So Leonard didn't *quite* dare to suggest taking it away altogether, but finally he said, did she think they could poke a hole in the wall which abuts on to the mews [in Tavistock Square], and get the motor in that way, if it wouldn't disturb her to work with a motor in the room? So now she and the umbrella are going to share the studio between them. A funny pair.

VITA TO HAROLD   *Long Barn*

12 July 1928

My own darling Hadji,

    I was plunged into despair this morning by your letter saying you might have to stay in Berlin till 1930. I had come to count really on you getting away in the spring of next year. I see the point about staying with Rumbold[2] till he has settled down, but it can't take him two years to settle down! and from now till 1930 is two years, or nearly. I can't believe that IF Lindsay knows you want to come home, he will leave you there all that time; but I don't trust Hadji a yard about what he has said or not said to Lindsay. I really do get into despair about it; you would too, my sweet, if I went and lived in a place you loathed in pursuit of a profession you really deprecated because it took me away from what you considered to be my legitimate pursuits; and a profession moreover which (as practised abroad— *not* in London), entailed a great many obligations which you thought utterly *infra dig* [humiliating]. No, Hadji would not like it either. No, he wouldn't.

---

1. Leonard Woolf had just bought a Singer car, which he and Virginia called the umbrella.
2. Sir Horace Rumbold, who was to succeed Lindsay as British Ambassador in Berlin.

VITA TO HAROLD   *Long Barn*

26 July 1928

I have got Clive [Bell] staying here. He came last night and we talked without stopping from 5.30 to 12.30. About life, middle age, love, books, drugs, Mary,[1] and Virginia. He is very gloomy, and wants Mary back, but she is in the throes of a *béguin* for some man unknown. They have, however, met again quite recently; and it was a success. Not as lovers, but as friends, and he hopes that some day it will come right again. It is really rather sad that a liaison of 14 years standing can be knocked out by a mere *béguin*. She doesn't even *like* the other man. Clive says he has made no provision for his middle-age, and asked if I had? My darling, I thought of our love for each other and how firm a foundation that was. I told him occupation was the only thing. He said that was a makeshift like everything else. I said I thought the only occupation which one couldn't look on as a mere makeshift was science.

And so on.

He is going this morning.

Talking of Jean Cocteau, Clive saw him recently in Paris, and says he has taken to cocaine. He knows it will kill him in a few years, but he is happy in the meantime, and doesn't care how much he has to increase his dose. Clive seemed to think this a good plan. Altogether I fear poor Clive is very low.

HAROLD TO VITA   *Berlin*

3 August 1928

At seven I had to get up in order to meet old [Sir Horace] Rumbold. I put on my top-hat and tails, and motored in on a lovely clear morning feeling rather cross and uncomfortable in my stiff clothes. There is no doubt moreover that I do *not* like Ambassadors

---

1. Mary Hutchinson, wife of St John Hutchinson, the barrister. She had been the intimate friend of T. S. Eliot and Clive Bell.

arriving when I am in charge. They had opened the special waiting rooms at the Friedrichstrasse [station]—and there was the whole staff there looking very lovely, and two representatives of the German Government. The train came in and old Rumby bundled out rather embarrassed with an attaché case in one hand and in the other a novel by Mr Galsworthy. I introduced him to the German Representatives and to the staff, while the crowd gaped and gaped and the policemen stood at the salute. Photographs were taken, and then very slowly we passed through the waiting rooms preceded by the Ober-bahnhofführer [station master] to the waiting cars. I carried the attaché case. We drove round to the Adlon [hotel] where he is staying until the Embassy is in order. We were greeted by the whole Adlon family.

Rumby was confused. "Never," he said, "have I felt so odd." You see, the last time the poor man was in Berlin was exactly fourteen years ago to the day almost—on August 4 1914—when he was Counsellor and crept out of Berlin under cavalry escort and amid the booings of a crowd. It is odd thus to return. He is a nice old bumble bee—and I am quite happy with him. But he is *not* Lindsay—no no.

VITA TO HAROLD   *Long Barn*

4 August 1928

Read Leonard's review in this week's Nation of a book called *The Well of Loneliness.* [1] I agree with all he says. It is a perfectly serious attempt to write a quite frank and completely unpornographic book about b.s.ness [lesbianism]. The pity is, that although serious and not sentimental, it is not a work of art—he says this. I have got the book and will bring it if it would interest you. Let me know. Perhaps Cyril [Connolly] or Tray have given it to you already. More than ever do I feel that a really great novel remains to be written on that subject. This is not a great novel, but it is quite a decent piece of work, and

1. By Radclyffe Hall. It was prosecuted for obscenity and banned until its republication in 1949.

it is a miracle that it should ever have got published by a publisher like Cape.

Heinemann refused it! They would!

HAROLD TO VITA   *Berlin*

9 August 1928

We had a long argument last night as to what was a test of intelligence. Cyril [Connolly] said that if he found a woman had *really* read through the whole of Proust he would think her intelligent. I said that was rubbish, as I felt sure that Lady Gosford had read through the whole of Proust. That I tested intelligence not by knowledge or culture but by imagination and ability to draw quick and original associations. Raymond [Mortimer] stuck up for culture: he said that one could tell by what a person had read how intelligent they were. The discussion, I felt, was about to become angry. The figure of strife stood gaunt and impatient at the next cross-road.

So I changed the subject to day-dreaming. Cyril and I both agreed that we had had day-dreams. I said I dreamt of doing brave things—of shooting ibex from a very far distance, of behaving with conspicuous courage at fires, or revolutions, or during a debate in the House of Commons. Cyril said that his day-dreams were largely stories in which he himself figured as the Sheikh Senoussi and in which, disguised in white scarfs, he captured European tourists and put them all to death with the exception of Bobby Longden,[1] who, on his side, would be grateful for this privileged treatment. Tray, for his part, said that he never day-dreamt: that he thought it "shocking" to do so—a relaxation of intellectual fibre which was worse than drugs.

Again the figure of strife loomed in the distance, so the conversation was diverted once more, from personal experience to culture. Cyril said that the difference between Bloomsbury and Chelsea culture was that the former would think the *Oedipus Rex* better than the

---

1. He was on a visit to Berlin from Magdalen College, Oxford, of which he was a Fellow. He became Master of Wellington College in 1937, and was killed by a German bomb in 1940.

Epictetus, and the latter, for their part, would prefer the *Epictetus* to the *Oedipus Rex.* Tray was a little disconcerted at this and retreated into the French XVIIth century: where he was fairly safe. I, for my part, said I must take Henry out to pee.

VITA TO HAROLD   *Long Barn*

10 August 1928

Got a pi-jaw from Hadji this morning.[1] I quite agreed about Acid X [eccentricity]: that it is impossible, and indeed undesirable to eliminate altogether, and that absorption is the only method. But your initial premise is mistaken. You think I mind the inevitable interruptions of life: I don't. They can be organised and so become no bore at all. I don't notice them. The boys are a different matter. No one, not even Hadji himself, would want to have entire charge of two children for four months of the year. I should like to see you try it; you would be screaming by the end of a week. You see, one is not permanently in the mood for children—even you wouldn't be. It is really quite reasonable on my part, Hadji, and not entirely a question of being willing to waste two months.

HAROLD TO VITA   *Berlin*

17 September 1928

I asked Ben how much he knew, and he said that Williams[2] had told him "some details." I then explained how when one came to a certain age one had new physical powers and pleasures—and that these

---

1. Harold had written to her: "Oh my love, it would be such a good thing if you could throw a little more eccentricity into your writing and a little less into your life. How I wish I could get at the fool (was it Violet?) who gave you the idea that responsibilities, instead of being stepping-stones through a marsh, were something to evade and regard with shame."
2. Dr. Cyril Williams, headmaster of Summer Fields school. Ben was fourteen and about to leave his preparatory school for Eton.

pleasures if properly controlled were the best in the world. But I kept on getting out of my depth—and I *hated* it. Anyhow I told him he must work it all out for himself, and that if he got puzzled he could always ask us, as we should always understand. I said that about masturbation he must put it off as long as he possibly could—and that then he must only do it on Saturdays. But I loathed talking to him about it. I have the incest inhibition very strong. He was very sensible and sweet, and said that he would never worry about those sort of things as he could always talk to me or you about them.

Poor boy—I don't suppose he understood much. By the way I wrote to Chute[3] just a polite letter—and saying that I should like his advice about Ben being confirmed, adding that I would prefer sooner than later. I mean, he will *have* to be confirmed and I think it would be a good thing to get that nonsense over as soon as possible. It will be a great bore for us—but we can't get out of it.

VITA TO HAROLD   *Saulieu [France]*

25 September 1928

My own darling Hadji

I am lying on the grass in a field, with Burgundy spread out before me. It is warm; it is sunny. There is a fair going on in Saulieu, where Virginia bought a green corduroy jacket for Leonard.[4] I nearly bought one for you, but I was sure you would not wear it. So I bought a blue bottle instead, with full-stops, marks of interrogation, marks of exclamation, and commas all over it.

But the point of Saulieu is not the fair, which is just a chance, but the restaurant. It is kept by a chef who was the chef for some Embassy in Berlin before the war—I have not yet found out which—and it is as good as Boulestin [Covent Garden]. Really it is. Yet Saulieu is a

3. The Rev. J. C. Chute was to be Ben's housemaster at Eton.
4. Vita and Virginia Woolf went to Burgandy together for a week's holiday. It was their only expedition abroad together, and the only occasion when Virginia had a holiday without Leonard.

tiny place—a mere village. Nobody seems to stay in it, but people motoring through stop for lunch.

We left Paris early this morning—got up at 6, so I am not quite awake—and drove through empty streets to the Gare de Lyons. I feel very much tempted, with the south lying so to speak just over the hill . . . and if it were not for the BBC on the 2nd [Vita's broadcast] I would go on down into Provence. I foresee that if we stay here for two days eating *canneton en croûte* and *crème double,* washed down by *Bourgogne mousseaux,* we shall get dyspepsia.

Darling, it is very nice: I feel amused and irresponsible. I can talk about life and literature to my heart's content—and it amuses me to be suddenly in the middle of Burgundy with Virginia. I like doing expeditions with you. But failing you, I could not wish for a better companion than Virginia.

Your own Mar

VITA TO HAROLD   *Long Barn*

2 October 1928

From Vézelay we went to Auxerre, where we stayed one night, and left next morning very early for Paris. Lunched in Paris, and went on to Rouen, where we were met by Ethel Sands'[1] motor and taken to Offranville. A lovely little chateau, done up, as you may imagine, with the most faultless taste. Ethel and Miss Hudson[2]; Vanessa [Bell] and Duncan [Grant]. The last two have painted a loggia for Ethel, which made me long to have one here, and I thought that when we built our summer house we would get them to decorate the inside? They have done six scenes of rustic employments—vintage, haymaking, harvest, and so on—in a manner mixed between idyllic-pastoral, romantic—and the very modern: the result is absolutely enchanting. After dinner, (a delicious dinner), Virginia read us her memoir of Old Bloomsbury.[3] She had read it to me already at Saulieu, but I loved

1. The American painter, who lived part of the year in London and part of it at her house in Normandy, at Auppegard near Dieppe.
2. Nan Hudson, also an American painter, and Ethel's lifelong friend.
3. She had read it to the Memoir Club in 1922, and it was first published in *Moments of Being,* ed. Jeanne Schulkind, in 1976.

hearing it again; I want you to hear it. It is very amusing, and terribly improper; the two old virgins bridled with horrified delight. I wondered whether V. was going to shirk any of it; but she didn't shirk a word. Then, as they had no room to put us up, we motored into Dieppe—passing through Sauqueville[4] on the way—and stayed at a hotel, and left by the boat next morning. It was rather rough, so I made V. drink the best part of a bottle of Burgundy with the result that she went to sleep as I had foreseen.

HAROLD TO VITA   *Berlin*

11 October 1928

Virginia is quite right about your ridiculous diffidence. It is the same part of you that makes you shy at parties, makes you creep into corners and hide there, and stay there all evening so as not to be seen. But it is absurd you being diffident about your writing since you have such a compelling literary gift. I think you are a late flowering plant in the sense that it will be your fruit which will be important rather than your blossom. But I would rather produce nectarines in September that burst in April with all the blossom of our crab-apple.

VITA TO HAROLD   *Long Barn*

11 October 1928

My own darling, I write to you in the middle of reading *Orlando*,[5] in such a turmoil of excitement and confusion that I scarcely know where (or who!) I am. It came this morning by the first post and I have been reading it ever since, and am now half-way through. Virginia sent it to me in a lovely leather binding—bless her. Oh Lord, how I wonder what *you* will think of it. It seems to me more

---

4. Where the Sackvilles came from in 1066.
5. *Orlando,* by Virginia Woolf, was published on 11 October. It was a novel in the form of a mock-biography of Vita, Virginia's longest love letter to her. Vita was not allowed to read a word of it until it was published.

brilliant, more enchanting, more rich and lavish, than anything she has done. It is like a cloak encrusted with jewels and sprinkled with rose-petals. I admit I can't see straight about it. Parts of it make me cry, parts of it make me laugh; the whole of it dazzles and bewilders me. It maddens me that you should not be here, so that we could read it simultaneously. I scarcely slept with excitement all night, and woke up feeling as though it were my birthday, or wedding day, or something unique.

Well—I don't know, it seems to me a book unique in English literature, having everything in it: romance, wit, seriousness, lightness, beauty, imagination, style; with Sir Thomas Browne and Swift for parents. I feel infinitely honoured at having been the peg on which it was hung; and very humble. Oh I do want to know what Hadji thinks.

HAROLD TO VITA   *Berlin*

27 November 1928

I have no desire whatsoever for fame, and would really be bored to feel that the people in a Harrogate Hydro knew about me in the sort of way they know about Hugh Walpole. "There's H. Nicolson," they would exclaim as a ham-faced arthritic limped through the palm-court. No thank you very much. I want *influence,* and to be esteemed by the people I like.

HAROLD TO VITA   *Berlin*

28 November 1928

I am terribly busy with my father's papers.[1] Of course it is all absolutely thrilling to me, but I can't get outside it, or estimate how

1. Harold's father, Lord Carnock, who had been the British Ambassador to St. Petersburg and civil head of the Foreign Office, died in London on 5 November 1928, and Harold immediately began to write his biography, which later in life he considered the best of his books.

interesting exactly it will be to others. For instance the Persian part is of real importance to the development of the book, but may seem an interlude to the casual reader. Anyhow I shall go ahead and see how things fall into shape. There is a real wealth of material—all that I want. Oh God! how I wish life were twice as long and that the days consisted of 100 hours each!

Every morning I wake up thinking how I want to write a book about Puritanism, and spend a winter in Tahiti, and learn how to fish for salmon, and go a walking tour through Patagonia, and try and get at the secret of Cézanne's landscapes (I am really wild about Cézanne just now), and do nothing for six weeks except visit the Greek islands with my darling and the boys, and build a home in the anti-Lebanon, and visit Australia, South Africa, and America, and do a fuller life of Byron, and Ludwig II, and through all this to go on being a diplomat, and having Long Barn, and seeing, every autumn, the wood-smoke drift across our dear remembered woods. And God has given me only a little handful of years—a little attaché case into which to cram the furniture of Knole. I seriously thank God, bless his heart, that these 42 years so far have not been so empty after all—love and life and literature and politics—work and old brandy, gardens and adventures, a thousand friends and one deep love, the whole essence of liberty and the whole essence of security, as if one had one's own writing table on a yacht crossing the Pacific.

All this lyricism is induced (a) by reading my father's papers and realising how much he missed; (b) by having had a good night; (c) by going to lunch with a Bishop.

HAROLD TO VITA   *Munich*

8 December 1928

My darling Viti,

Sorry to type, my dearest, but there is no ink available, and as little Mr Remington [his portable typewriter] has come down with me to Munich, he may as well write my letter for me.

I had an odd luncheon party yesterday, consisting of Emil Ludwig[1] and Mrs Ludwig, Ethel Smyth,[2] Eddy [Sackville-West], Sir Horace Rumbold and [his daughter] Constantia. Emil Ludwig is really rather a disgusting creature. Ethel arrived late in a fine to-do. Her tricorne kept on falling over her eyes in her excitement, and she screamed loud in her indignation against the Jewish republic that Ludwig and his friends had elevated in Germany. He was rather hurt by this. He said that the old gang had done nothing except land Germany into the Great European War. She said that his friends had destroyed the Old German culture. He said, "Not at all, not at all." She said yes, they had, and ("God! Harold, why do you give me cold sauce with sole, I hate cold sauce with sole"), "what about the Grand Duke of Weimar?" Ludwig said which Grand Duke? "Weimar!" said Ethel triumphantly. Ludwig asked whether she meant the Goethe one? She said, No, she meant the Ethel Smyth one, the one who had been Grand Duke at Weimar when she had been there as a girl. Ludwig said that that one had been gaga. She said that of course he had been gaga, but that at least he had cared for art, and did not think a book was a good book merely because it had sold 13,000 copies. Ludwig said that he didn't see why he should be scolded merely because the Grand Duke of Weimar hadn't sold 13,000 copies, and if it came to that the number was nearer 130,000 than 13,000. Ethel said, "The number of *what?*" He said that he had supposed (and with justice) that she had been referring to his 'Napoleon'. She said (oh woman!!) that she had not read his Napoleon and did not intend to. At which, throwing her head back with a challenging gesture of defiance, the tricorne, wobbling for a minute, fell, not *off,* but right *down* over her face, and for a moment her torrent of invective was stilled.

The Ambassador [Rumbold], who had been vaguely aware that all was not proceeding with that amity to which he is accustomed at table, asked, "Had she been in Berlin long?" She said that she had only arrived the day before and that was why she was so out of temper. The Ambassador did not know what to say to that, and just bubbled silently for a bit. Then Mrs Ludwig, a tactful woman, began to talk of the

---

1. The German author and playwright, born in 1881. He wrote biographies of Goethe, Wagner, Bismarck, Napoleon, and Christ.
2. The English composer and suffragette. She was then aged seventy.

servant problem at Lugano. By the end of which, Ethel, having swallowed three glasses of Rieslinger Auslese, was able to talk, not with calm, but with less violence. And so, almost amicably, the luncheon party drew to an end.

I took the night train down here and slept like a top, or pot, or whatever a dead sleep is.

Your own,

Hadji

VITA TO HAROLD   *Long Barn*

12 December 1928

On Monday I met Hugh and Hilda Matheson[1] at the Savoy grill at 7, where Hugh had sausages and coffee, and I had oysters and coffee. Then we adjourned to Savoy Hill, Studio No. 6. Two armchairs (very luxurious); two microphones; small table between us, with a siphon, a bottle of whiskey, two glasses, cigarettes, matches, ash-trays. Red light flickers. Silence, please. "Miss V. Sackville-West, the poet, and Mr Hugh Walpole, the novelist, will now hold a discussion on The Modern Woman. Miss V. S-W. is well-known to listeners by her talks on modern poetry; Mr Hugh Walpole is broadcasting this evening for the first time. Miss V. S-W.: Mr Hugh Walpole." And the British Isles waited breathless. Mr Hugh Walpole and Miss V. S-W. confronted each other; Miss Matheson sat on the floor,—a small, but efficient, impresario.

Mr Hugh Walpole led off. "Well, Vita, *you* begin,—it's your prerogative as a woman."

Miss V. S-W., "I don't see why you should say that, Hugh; I don't see why the prerogative should be mine any more than yours . . ."

All went swimmingly. For what seemed a long time. Then Miss V. S-W. looked at her watch. 8.30. Half the time gone. The room

1. Hugh Walpole, the novelist (*Rogue Herries,* etc.), and Hilda Matheson, the Talks Director of the BBC, who became Vita's most intimate friend in the years 1928–32.

began to swim. There was Hugh's nice rubicund face; there was Hilda's nice reassuring smile; but there, also, was the microphone and four million homes listening all agog to the Modern Woman. The room swam wildly. Miss V. S-W. lost all sense of what Mr Hugh Walpole was saying. She thought, "Whatever happens, I must not faint. I must not get up and rush from the room. I must not exclaim, 'I can't keep it up!' At all cost, I must not let Hugh, Hilda, and the BBC, down."

So she neither fainted (though she felt near to it), nor rushed from the room; but she did signal despairingly to Mr Hugh Walpole to go on, at all costs, to go on talking. And Mr Hugh Walpole rushed nobly into the breach. He talked; he talked. He said a million things Miss V. S-W. in calmer moments would passionately have disagreed with; but as it was, she let them all pass.

VITA TO HAROLD   *Long Barn*

13 December 1928

Women love too much; they allow love to over-ride everything else. Men don't. Or, rather, men see to it that the people who love them should submit themselves. I love you too much. You are much more important to me than anything else. That is the long and short of the matter. But, darling, I am not a good person for you to be married to—said she, avoiding the word wife. When people like you and me marry—*positive* people, when men and women ought to be positive and negative respectively, complementary elements—life resolves itself into a compromise which is truly satisfactory to neither. But I love you; I can never never never cure myself of loving you; so what is to be done? And you love foreign politics. And I love literature, and peace, and a secluded life. Oh my dear, my infinitely dear Hadji, you never ought to have married me; and I feel my inadequacy most bitterly. What good am I to you? None. What with one thing and another.

But at least I do love you, incurably, ineradicably, and most oddly. That remains, fixed. Immutable.

HAROLD TO VITA   *Cologne*

15 March 1929

After writing to you yesterday I went to see the Oberbürger-
meister. His name is Adenauer[1] and he is a rather remarkable figure
in modern Germany. There are some who say that if Parliamentarian-
ism really breaks down in Berlin they will summon Adenauer to
establish some form of fascismo. For the moment he rules Cologne
with an iron hand, and is responsible for such things as the new Rhine
Bridge and the Presse exhibition. There was some sort of fuss going
on around his room when I got there, private secretaries dashing about,
people opening doors, squinting in, then shutting them again rapidly.
I was asked to sit down while bells buzzed and people hurried in and
whispered to each other, and then hurried out again. I am to this
moment unaware what had happened, but the contrast between the
scurrying and whispering outside, and the sudden peace of his own
large study, was most effective, and this strange Mongol, sitting there
with shifty eyes in a yellow face, sitting with his back to the window,
talking very slowly and gently, pressing bells very slowly—"Would
you ask Dr Pietri to come here?"—snapping with icy politeness at the
terrified Dr Pietri when he arrived—possessed all the manner of a
Dictator. It is not a manner which I like, but it is a manner which once
seen is never forgotten. I feel I could adopt it at once. I shall try to
do so. One of the main stunts is to create an atmosphere of rush and
flurry around one and to be oneself as calm as the hollow in the centre
of a typhoon. Another stunt is to talk to one's subordinates in a very
gentle voice but with a sudden flash of a shifty eye.

He was very expansive on the subject of town planning. I told him
how impressed I had been by the garden suburbs at Frankfurt, and he
was not pleased at this, knowing that his garden suburbs were not up
to the same level. He said in the first place that the Frankfurt people
had lost a great deal of money by extravagance in garden suburbs, and
in the second place that his own aim was not to bring the town into
the country but the country into the town. It was at that stage that

---

1. Konrad Adenauer, Chancellor of the Federal Republic of Germany, 1949–63. He was Lord
   Mayor of Cologne, 1917–33, when he was dismissed by Goering and temporarily imprisoned.

he summoned the agitated Dr Pietri and told him to show me all that
there was to be seen.

HAROLD TO VITA   *In the train Munich–Berlin*

17 March 1929

I have had a health-panic this evening, and before I die I should
like to record it on paper.

As you know, for the last fortnight, I have had a cold in the head
and in the chest which I originally caught from you. Damn you, my
own adored darling Mar, to whom I can pour out all my silliness and
know that I shall provoke only a gentle smile, "Silly Hadji." Oh My
God! what a wonderful day that was when I decided to marry you
for your money.

Well you see, tonight I got a health-panic. It happened this way.
I went to call on Thomas Mann.[1] He had asked me to call on him as
he had been unable to attend my lecture, and thus very civilly he had
telephoned to ask me to tea. So I went. He was alone. He talked about
how lovely life was, and how polite they had been to him at the P.E.N.
Club, and how much he admired Mr Galsworthy. And I, being snuffly
but interested in life and death, asked him how long, generally, as a
fellow *littérateur,* it took him to get rid of his colds. He said three days
to prepare, three days suffering, and three days to get rid of it. Being
quick at *le calcul,* I made that out to be ten or even nine days, that
is five days later or longer than my own disease, I mean five days
quicker than my actual present cold. Having worked out this sum I
became alarmed. My cold was not a cold, it was PNEUMONIA—
that's what it was. SCEPTIC PNEUMONIA. I could feel the sceptici-
tis growing within me. I felt a wave of fear pass over me. There was
a large mirror on the wall opposite and in it I saw my distorted and
pallid features. Yes, I was looking very pale. That meant consumption
of the galloping variety. I talked feverishly to Thomas Mann about
the younger generation in England, and when I next glanced at the
mirror, my face was flushed. "Fever," I quaked, "fever, high fever.

---

1. The English translation of his best-known novel, *Der Zauberberg* (The Magic Mountain),
   had just been published.

Sceptic pneumonia, as I thought from the start." So then I took leave of Thomas Mann. I was sorry to leave him knowing that he was the last man I should see on earth. But I said goodnight.

HAROLD TO VITA   *Berlin*

2 April 1929

I went for a long walk with Peter Clive.[1] The latter is a good, handsome, but very dull young man. He believes in virginity. I said I believed in it too, but only for people of unexampled ugliness who never had a chance of anything else. He was silent at this, and we walked along the side of a lake in the rain while Henry [dog] cast his goggly-eyes at two ducks at the edge of the ice. The ice had broken up a little and tinkled against the edge of the lake, like sleigh-bells among the reeds. I do hope that I do not have a bad influence on young men. I should hate that. I obviously have an influence, but there is nothing that would fill me with deeper remorse if I felt that I had led them astray. I imagine that I teach them to be active, interested, happy, kind, and filled with the zest of experience. But I may really be destroying some of the scaffolding of their beliefs without putting anything in its place. Then I always want them to enjoy themselves so much, that I am bad at discouraging them from any experience even if I know it to be bad for them. But my intentions are beyond praise.

HAROLD TO VITA   *Berlin*

16 April 1929

I went to H. G. Wells's lecture in the Reichstag. One simply could not hear a word. Not a single word. It was rather a disaster. After that there was a dinner at the Adlon. Einstein presided. He looks like a child who for fun has put on a mask painted like Einstein. He is a darling. He made a little speech for Wells which I then translated. I began by saying, "I have been asked to translate Professor Einstein's speech. I

---

1. Elder son of Sir Robert Clive, Harold's Minister in Teheran.

may add that it is the first thing of his I have ever understood." They thought that a funny joke.

HAROLD TO VITA   *Berlin*

18 May 1929

Cyril [Connolly] is not perhaps the ideal guest. He is terribly untidy in an irritating way. He leaves dirty handkerchiefs in the chairs and fountain pens (my fountain pens) open in books. Moreover it is rather a bore having a person who has *nothing* of his own—not a cigarette or a stamp. In fact the poverty of this colony[1] is heart-rending. Christopher and David[2] are both absolutely bust. But I really am firm about it, and won't take them all to Pelzer's [Restaurant] to eat plover's eggs. In other ways, however, Cyril is a pleasant guest, easily amused, and interesting about things. I don't trust him a yard and I think he makes mischief. He is very thick with Violet Trefusis, and I imagine that he is very disloyal about me when with her. I rather mind that, as she is so unscrupulous and appears never to have got over the desire to revenge herself on me. But what does it all matter so long as none of these people can make trouble between you and me?

HAROLD TO VITA   *Berlin*

25 May 1929

We motored the Yorks[3] out to the golf-course for luncheon. She is really a delightful person, incredibly gay and simple. It is an absolute tragedy that she should be a royalty. Moreover she is no fool. She talked to me so intelligently about *Some People,* whereas he had clearly

1. Harold's flat in 24 Brücken Allee in northwest Berlin, where he put up his transient and sponging friends.
2. Christopher Sykes, the author and biographer, was then aged twenty-two and a temporary attaché at the British Embassy in Berlin; David Herbert, the son of the Earl of Pembroke, was twenty-one.
3. The Duke and Duchess of York, later King George VI and Queen Elizabeth (still later, Queen Elizabeth, the Queen Mother).

only read the Arketall story and had got it wrong. But she and Cyril Connolly are the only two people who have spoken intelligently about the 'landscape' element in *Some People*. She said, "You choose your colours so carefully—that bit about the palace at Madrid was done in grey and chalk-white; the Constantinople bits in blue and green; the desert bits in blue and orange." Of course that may be second-hand, but I don't think so—and even if I am making a mistake about her intelligence, I am making no mistake about her charm. It is quite overwhelming. He is just a snipe from the great Windsor marshes. Not bad-looking—but now and again there is that sullen, heavy-lidded, obstinate dulling of the blue eyes which is most unattractive.

VITA TO HAROLD   *Long Barn*

25 June 1929

My darling,

What is so torturing, when I leave you at these London stations[1] and drive off, is the knowledge that you are *still there*—that, for half an hour, or three quarters of an hour, I could still return and find you; come up behind you, take you by the elbow, and say, "Hadji."

I came straight home, feeling horribly desolate and sad, driving down that familiar and dreary road. I remembered Resht [Persia] and our parting there; our parting at Victoria when you left for Persia; till our life seemed made up of partings, and I wondered how long it would continue.

I got home, and all the way was strewn with coffee-cups [reminders]: specially the road through the beeches on the [Sevenoaks] common. I remembered how you had said that so long as you were alive they were there for you, and when you were dead it wouldn't matter.

Then I came round the corner onto the view—our view—and I thought how you loved it, and how simple you were really, apart from your activity; and how I loved you, for being both simple and active, in one and the same person.

Then I came home, and it was not consolation at all. You see,

---

1. Harold had been on a fortnight's home-leave from Berlin.

whenever I am unhappy for other reasons—Knole, or Dada, or B.M., let us say—the cottage is a real solace to me; but when it is on account of *you* that I am unhappy (because you have gone away), it is an additional pang—it is the same place, but a sort of mockery and emptiness hangs about it—I almost wish that just *once* you could lose me and then come straight back to the cottage and find it still full of me but empty of me—then you would know what I go through after you have gone away.

Anyhow, you will say, it is worse for you who go to a horrible and alien city, whereas *I* stay in the place we both love so much, but really, Hadji, it is *no* consolation to come back to a place full of coffee-cups—there was a cardboard-box-lid full of your rose petals still on the terrace.

You are dearer to me than anybody ever has been or ever could be. If you died I should kill myself as soon as I had made provision for the boys. I really mean this. I could not live if I lost you. Every time I get you to myself you become dearer to me. I do not think one could conceive of a love more exclusive, more tender, or more pure than that I have for you. It is absolutely divorced from physical love—sex—*now*. I feel it is immortal, I am superstitious about it, I feel it is a thing which happens seldom. I suppose that everybody who falls in love feels this about their love, and that for them it is merely a platitude. But then when one falls in love it is all mixed up with physical desire, which is the most misleading of all human emotions, and most readily and convincingly wears the appearance of the real thing. This does not enter at all into my love for you. I simply feel that you are me and I am you—what you meant by saying that you "became the lonely me" when we parted.

Darling, there are not many people who would write such a love letter after nearly sixteen years of marriage, yet who would be saying therein only one-fiftieth of what they were feeling as they wrote it. But you know not only that it is true, every word, but that it represents only a pale version of the real truth—I could not exaggerate, however much I tried—I don't try. I try sometimes to tell you the truth and then I find that I have no words at my command which could possibly convey it to you.

Your Mar

HAROLD TO VITA   *Berlin*

7 July 1929

Cragg is the parson here, and on him fell the duty of arranging the mumbo jumbo for King George.[1] Now the whole point of that show was that it was to be identical with what was being said in London and throughout the Empire at the same time. But Cragg added and altered it. Damn him! Of course, as I take no interest in his bloody church, I cannot complain to him, but if I were the Ambassador who attends regularly, I should have made a row. The service was silly enough anyhow—just imagine that with all the prayer-book, bible and hymn book to choose from, they selected a ditty which contains the following verse:

> The Lord, ye know, is God indeed;
>   Without our aid he did us make;
> We are his flock, he doth us feed,
>   And for his sheep he doth us take.

Now lines as bad as that would be rejected by Niggs from the Summer Fields magazine. The first line is meaningless, the second indecent and singularly untrue, the third is a direct misrepresentation of social conditions, and in the last line alone is there a glimmer of irony and truth. I looked over my shoulder—row after row of English mouths singing this rubbish. It passes my comprehension how any person can be religious and an Anglican. At the end they did the Blake poem which pleased me:

> Bring me my bow of burning gold!
>   Bring me my arrows of desire!

And I do not suppose that one soul in the congregation realised that Blake's twaddle was any better than the twaddle of "All people that on earth do dwell."

Well I was cross. "O enter then his gates with praise, Approach with joy his courts unto." Now I suppose most people think that His courts UNTOOOO are some summer residence of God outside the capital. "The court moved to Untoo in the first week of May."

---

1. A service of thanksgiving for the King's recovery from a severe illness.

VITA TO HAROLD *Long Barn*

10 July 1929

My voluntary exile from Knole is very curious. I think about it a lot. I feel exactly as though I had had for years a liaison with a beautiful woman, who never, from force of circumstances, belonged to me wholly; but who had for me a sort of half-maternal tenderness and understanding, in which I could be entirely happy. *Now* I feel as though we had been parted because (again through force of circumstances and owing to no choice of her own) she had been compelled to marry someone else and had momentarily fallen completely beneath his jurisdiction, not happy in it, but acquiescent. I look at her from far off; and if I were wilder and more ruthless towards myself, I should burst in one evening and surprise her in the midst of her new domesticity. But life has taught me not to do these things.

HAROLD TO VITA *Berlin*

22 July 1929

My sweetest,

Tikki [his typewriter] must write this letter as it is VERY IM-PORTANT and I want you to be able to read it easily and calmly. Without those efforts of decyphering, without that personal emotionalism, which I fear and hope are evoked by my beastly scribble. Bless you my sweetest Mar.

But never have I more wanted to consult you calmly than at the present moment. If you were at the cottage I should telephone although that would not be of much value since a long discussion is what I want and I cannot wait till the end of the month.

The PROBLEM is as follows:—

(1) I have spoken to you I believe of Bruce Lockhart, an attractive scamp who was our Chargé d'Affaires in Moscow and is now the Londoner of the Londoner's Diary of the *Evening Standard* of the Lord Beaverbrook.

(2) Well I have got a letter from him.

(3) In this letter he writes as follows:—

My dear Harold,

When I was in Berlin in April, you hinted that you might not stay indefinitely in the diplomatic service. I did not take you very seriously, but it may be worth while to put the following before you. Please treat what follows as very confidential and for yourself only.

Beaverbrook is looking for a man of your ability (jub-i-jub) and your knowledge (JUB-i-jub) of men and affairs, and would offer a very considerable inducement for his services. His job would be to write and edit a page like the Londoner's Diary in the *Evening Standard*.

As far as you yourself are concerned, you would do it admirably. It would bring you into close touch with politics and the politicians again. It would also leave you time to write your books and would leave the door open for a literary or a political career. And, as I have said, it would be well paid.

I have already suggested your name to Beaverbrook and he would be glad to 'capture' you. The object of this letter is to ask if you would be prepared to consider such a proposal. Please let me have your views on the subject as soon as ever you can.

Yours ever
Bruce Lockhart

Well, my poppet, obviously this is very tempting. It means London, liberty, scope, salary, freedom of time and opinion, plus a tremendous score over the Foreign Office. But I must not allow these mixed feelings to affect my judgement, and would put the thing as follows:—
Objections to accepting this offer.

(1) Beaverbrook is not a man of very savoury reputation. I am not sure that I should like to be identified with the dirty politics of the *Evening Standard*.

(2) I do not wish to abandon my radical opinions, or to be forced to write things which I do not believe. I am prepared to provide them with facts and fancies, but I am not prepared to express views with which I do not agree.

(3) It might entail a great deal of lobbying. I am bad at that. You know how bad I am at asking people the way or the time. The job might degenerate into a constant process of accosting Cabinet Ministers and worming things out of them. A great deal of my time would be employed in talking to people whom I do not like and in suffering

fools gladly. I fear I am too 'proud' and in a way too 'upright' for this sort of work.

(4) If I ever wanted serious work in the future it would do me harm having been connected with the Beaverbrook group. My stunt is not that sort of stunt. If I ever went in for politics I should succeed only in terms of being a high-brow of unquestioned integrity. I could never succeed on the basis of brazen-faced pushing. I feel it is like playing poker when one had very little capital and does not care much for cards.

(5) I feel therefore that if I accepted I might regret it later, and regret that I had yielded to a momentary temptation which had not turned out a success and which had prejudiced my general prospects.

What I am doing therefore is (A) To write today to Lockhart saying that I should be prepared to consider the proposal, but must know what the salary will be and what the job entails. (B) To write to Leonard [Woolf] putting the above objections, but more modestly, before him and asking his advice.

What I want you to do my sweetest is to telegraph on the receipt of this letter, "Advise accept" or "Advise refuse." I do not suppose that you will be able to group your feelings under any one of these two formulas. But if, on thinking over the advantages and disadvantages, you are quite clear one way or the other, please telegraph. Consult Hilda [Matheson] but under the seal of confidence. I do not undertake of course to follow your opinion or to blame you for it in after years. But I trust your judgement enormously when you sit down and think a thing out.[1]

HAROLD TO VITA   *Berlin*

8 August 1929

Today, for all I know, may be a decisive date in my life. I feel rather wretched. Whatever happens—whether I get this [Beaverbrook] job or not, I shall feel rather gloomy. If I fail to get it, then

1. Vita replied, advising acceptance.

I shall feel *blamiert* [ridiculous]. If I get it, however, then I shall feel depressed at leaving diplomacy. Gloom in either case. But it may simply be liver.

I daresay that the main cause of my gloom is fuss about money. My poverty is really getting on my nerves. I mean it is awful not to have any money in the bank. Of course I have got enough to go on with and I am not in serious difficulties. But it is just the feeling of having spent so much money here and having absolutely nothing to show for it. Anyhow I funk all bills. *J'ai peur des notes comme d'une abeille.*

I heard from the Ambassador that there are five Legations to be filled—Mexico, Athens, Belgrade, Bucharest and Oslo. Now it is *quite* likely that they will offer me Athens, Belgrade or Bucharest. If they don't, then I shall have no qualms at all about resignation. But if, a week after accepting Beaverbrook's offer, I get appointed to Athens, then I admit that I shall think that fate has played me a scurvy trick. Five years in Athens, and then an Embassy. I should probably think of it in those terms. Poor Hadji—not much of a success in life. Everybody will think me quite, quite looney.

You see, my darling, supposing I hear, after I have resigned, that they really were about to offer me Athens. Supposing that, having become a hack journalist cadging interviews from people, I think of the man who got my job at Athens sailing from Aegean island to Aegean island. Supposing that when Beaverbrook has chucked me out after four years, I hear that my successor at Athens has been appointed to Rome. But perhaps I'm doing a White Queen [in *Alice in Wonderland*] and getting all my regrets over in anticipation.

VITA TO HAROLD   *Withyham, Sussex*

11 August 1929

Yesterday I went to Rodmell to see Virginia. Much to my amusement, they both asked me searchingly whether they were the only people to whom you had written about Lord B [Beaverbrook], the truth being that they were exceedingly flattered and rather touched.

"Are you sure," they asked, "that he didn't consult Raymond? or Eddy? Or anybody?" I assured them that they alone had received your confidence. They are really making Monk's House very nice. Leonard has thrown three rooms into one, and made himself a lovely room to work in. He invited me gravely upstairs to come and see it. I *do* like Leonard.

By the way, I have been induced by him and Dotz [Wellesley] to put together a handful of poems for their series this autumn—and having done so am a little worried about them. I shall have to show them to you before they are published.[1] It is not on the score of their goodness or badness that I am worried, as I think they are quite passable enough, but you see they are love poems, and purely artificial at that—I mean, *very* artificial, rather 17th-century most of them—and although I should have thought this would be sufficiently obvious (that they were just 'literary', I mean), it has since occurred to me that people will think them Lesbian. I should not like this, either for my own sake or yours, more especially as (unlike Shakespeare's sonnets) they are really literary exercises. I shall send you a copy of the complete lot, and would like an honest opinion please.

HAROLD TO VITA   *Berlin*

26 August 1929

You say in your letter that Ernest Gye[2] must have upset me by telling me not to leave the [diplomatic] service. No, my sweet. My perplexity and hesitations are deeper than that. You see, Diplomacy really does give me leisure to do literary work of my own and it *does* have advantages such as leave, nice people etc. Moreover (and this is the essential point), if I stay in diplomacy I am certain of being 'successful', or, in other words, of getting to the top. You say, with justice, that it is not a very glorious top. I quite agree. Yet I have

---

1. They included a series of sonnets addressed to Mary Campbell. Harold advised against publication, but Vita did publish some in *King's Daughter.*
2. Ernest Gye entered the Foreign Office in 1903, and became Minister in Tangier, 1933–36.

sufficient knowledge of human nature to realise that it is more satisfactory to succeed on a small scale than to fail on a big one. If I end up as an Ambassador I shall always feel (and say) what a wonderful career I could have made for myself in the open market. But if I climb down into the open market and then fail to make good there, I shall regret bitterly not having remained in my armchair and ended as an Ambassador. I shall feel that I was absolutely mad to chuck a certainty for an uncertainty, and at an age when my supply of violent energy must shortly begin to give out.

I don't think I shall be affected by the present [Foreign Office] moves, but I shall certainly be affected by the new ones. There is even a prospect, if I stay on, of my being a Minister next year with £4,000 a year.

Naturally I put against this (1) B.M. (2) Being separated from you. In the end these two factors will probably be determinant. But you must understand, my love, that the decision is a grave one to have to take, and you can't quite expect me to chuck my job at my age [43] in a spirit of light-heartedness. I feel *very* heavy hearted about it, and whatever decision I do take will not have been taken without hours and hours of very anxious thought. If I were ten years younger the whole thing would be different.

HAROLD TO VITA   *Berlin*

14 November 1929

Feeling rather miz at the moment as I have been reading three days worth of the *Express* and *Evening Standard*. They really fill me with alarm. I simply shall be unable to write the sort of sob-stuff they want. They seem to have an unerring eye for just the sort of thing I loathe—*Journey's End*, Orpen, *Jud Süss* [1]—all the *faux bon*. There are columns of sob-stuff by R. C. Sherriff about Armistice

---

1. *Journey's End,* R. C. Sherriff's play about life in the trenches of World War I; Sir William Orpen (1878–1931), the fashionable portrait painter; and *Jud Süss (Jew Süss),* the novel by Lion Feuchtwanger about eighteenth-century Germany, published in 1927.

Day and the V.C. dinner. I don't think I am intellectually fastidious but I do loathe slush. Then there is a ghastly article by my colleague Mr James Douglas entitled, "Why do the Heathen rage against me?" in which he explains how he tried to defend "the homespun ideals of humanity" against the new "cloacal school of literature" ('cloaca' is Latin for drain).

Now what shall I do in such a *galère?* I shall be thought highbrow and cloacal. For this reason I shall be glad when my *Express* and *Standard* reach me by post in small doses. I really feel ill when I consume a whole pile of them at a time.

Then about the money. I should really mind if I had tied myself to Shoe Lane [the *Standard's* office in London] and got nothing in return. You see, my sweet, it is rather a blow to my pride to work as a hack on a newspaper, and the only thing that counterbalances that is a gain to my pride not to take money from B.M. So that you must make it quite clear to her that once she has repaid the Knole capital, we shall take nothing more from her. Not one penny. If she insists on paying something, then it must go into a fund for the boys. Also you might take the occasion to hint that she must not tell any lies about us.

VITA TO HAROLD   *Long Barn*

7 December 1929

I wish I knew what you were really feeling these days. I am afraid you will have an awful heart-sink when it comes to the last days; you will look at the red boxes, and the green bootlaces, and the draft-papers, with a real wrench at the heart. But when I open the door of K.B.W.[1] for you, I shall feel as though it were *our* wedding day.

Your own (after 16 years)

Mar

---

1. 4 King's Bench Walk, Inner Temple, London, the flat which Vita had been preparing for Harold's return.

HAROLD TO VITA *Berlin*

16 December 1929

At the Buccaneers [Club] dinner[1] there were nearly 40 people—including old Rumbie [Rumbold] and the American Ambassador. Speech by Rumbie which gave me a lump in my throat. Speech by me—very restrained but gulpy. Musical honours. All went off very well. It is quite extraordinary how nice people are to me here. They really are sorry I am going.

Rumbie made a rather provocative speech saying that the Foreign Office ought to have been able to keep me "had they possessed more imagination." As all the Press were there, this was rather odd.

I was exhausted by the whole thing, and sank into my bed with relief. Luncheon with the [Carl von] Schuberts today. Tomorrow dinner at the Embassy—and then my farewells are over.

My darling, I know what she has done at K.B.W. She has put his modern pictures in the bedroom. Well, I expect she's right. Get a large basin for me to be sick into.

Tomorrow will be my last letter.[2]

---

1. A farewell dinner for Harold given by the British Embassy.
2. He left Berlin, and diplomacy, on 20 December.

H arold joined the staff of the Evening Standard *on 1 January 1930, writing paragraphs for the "Londoner's Diary." He hated the work, finding it trivial and debasing, but enjoyed a little more his weekly talks for the BBC, which made him for the first time a well-known figure to the public. In 1931 he resigned from the Beaverbrook Press, stood for Parliament as a candidate for Sir Oswald Mosley's New Party, and edited its journal,* Action. *From this too he resigned when the paper failed to pay its way and Mosley turned fascist. It was an inauspicious start to his "market-place" career. Vita, on the other hand, wrote two best-selling novels,* The Edwardians *and* All Passion Spent, *and bought the ruins of Sissinghurst Castle, near Cranbrook in Kent, where she and Harold restored some of the buildings and began to create a new garden. They moved there permanently from Long Barn in 1932.*

Evening Standard, *London E.C.4*

2 January 1930

My own darling.

   I have no pens here and have to do this on Tikki.[1] Just a few kind words, my sweet, to wish you good morning again.

   Came up with Desmond [MacCarthy] who was very charming and full of talk. Rather too full of talk as I wanted to do my lessons,

---

1. From now until Vita's death in 1962, Harold almost always typed his letters to her.

which now consists in reading all the papers in the hope of finding a good paragraph. I suppose that I shall get into the way of finding these paragraphs leaping ready-armed to the mind. At present they are rather a bother to think of, rather a bother to write, and terribly feeble when written. But I shall settle down in time.

Got here soon after ten. Found [Bruce] Lockhart fussing about in a rush as usual. I rather like all this rush business. Read French and German newspapers. Wrote three paragraphs. Fiddled about.

The Editor rushed in to say that the Duke of Westminster was engaged to Loelia Ponsonby. He asserted that his information was absolutely correct. I rang up Olive: "Mrs Rubens left this morning for the Continent." Now what does it mean? I begged him to be very careful.[2]

Bless you my sweet. Off to luncheon with Tray.

Your own
Hadji

HAROLD TO VITA   *4 King's Bench Walk,*
                                  London E.C.4
24 April 1930

Well, my view is:—

(a) That it is most unwise of us to get Sissinghurst.[3] It costs us £12,000 to buy and will cost another good £15,000 to put in order. This will mean nearly £30,000 before we have done with it. For £30,000 we could buy a beautiful place replete with park, garage, h and c, central heating, historical associations, and two lodges r. and l.

(b) That it is most wise of us to buy Sissinghurst. Through its veins pulses the blood of the Sackville dynasty. True it is that it comes

---

2. The 2nd Duke married Loelia Ponsonby on 20 February as his third wife. This marriage ended in divorce in 1947, when the Duke married a fourth time.
3. Vita had first seen Sissinghurst Castle (more the ruins of an Elizabethan house) on 4 April, and Harold visited it the next day. They bought it, together with 400 acres of land, on 6 May 1930.

through the female line—but then we are both feminist, and after all Knole came in the same way. It is, for you, an ancestral mansion: that makes up for company's water and h and c.

(c) It is in Kent. It is in a part of Kent we like. It is self-contained. I could make a lake. The boys could ride.

(d) We like it.

VITA TO HAROLD   *Sissinghurst*

23 October 1930

My darling love,

The moat wall is going to be very superb. They have uncovered its foot a bit, and I think there is no doubt that there was originally water there too. There are lovely big stones at the foot of the piers. The piers are going to be lovely—quite a 'feature'. Those nasty little thorns at the end have gone, and it is now open to the view; much nicer. It will be a lovely walk. The wall will look much higher than you think.

The Hayters[1] have cleared a good deal of the nuttery, which now looks like a series of avenues. That is nice too.

I planted a fig, and lots of roses.

I think the yew hedge will be planted by the time you come. The yews are all here, and it won't take long to put them in.

I can see that we are going to have heaps of wall-space for climbing things. I have already ordered some choice shrubs, including a pomegranate and a mulberry.

I am not sleeping in that horrid farmhouse. I have got a bed in the oratory off my sitting room [in the tower], which increases the squalor but also my sense of security. I have also got Canute [elkhound].

Your own Mar

---

1. Tom Hayter and his son George were living in the derelict south wing when the Nicolsons bought Sissinghurst, and remained there for several years as its first working gardeners.

HAROLD TO VITA   Action, 5 Gordon Square, W.C.1

28 September 1931

I went down to Denham yesterday after writing to you. Tom[1] was alone. We discussed the paper [*Action*] first. He will agree to our taking out shares together. He gives me an absolutely free hand about all editorial stuff. Off we go with a bang on Thursday week. Our orders to date are 110,000 but the advertisements are a bit sticky. We have got six of our twelve pages but shall want six more. This rather worries me, as it is said that one can always get advertisements for the first copy of a paper. But I hope that we are in for a slight trade boom and that may help.

We then discussed the future of the party. The [General] Election has of course caught us bending. We had made all our plans to fight a campaign in February and we are simply not ready to fight one now. I told him that what I dreaded was that no-one would be elected except Mr Kid Lewis [the boxer], and the resultant ridicule would kill the party stone dead for ever. He admitted this but confessed that he was not optimistic about any single one of us being returned to Parliament except perhaps Cimmie.[2] The problem is, therefore, shall we fight a few seats and risk complete annihilation or shall we retire completely from the contest, proclaim that this is a ramp election and withdraw from political life—concentrating our energies upon becoming a movement rather than a Parliamentary party? We still cannot make up our minds on this.

HAROLD TO VITA   Action

1 October 1931
Day of joy and day of good omen [wedding anniversary].

Little one, how young we were those eighteen years ago, how uncertain, how unlike our present selves. And in all these years we have

---

1. Sir Oswald Mosley, leader of the New Party.
2. Cynthia Mosley, a daughter of Lord Curzon and Sir Oswald's first wife. She was also standing as a New Party candidate.

grown into a complete harmony—which seems now so inevitable and so indissoluble but which I suppose was really a very intricate and intelligent thing to have achieved. I have a theory that a happy personal relationship is based upon a dovetailing of the static and the dynamic in people. One day I shall work it out. What I mean is that the active and passive forces in each have to be mingled in equal proportions. There must be an equal proportion of rest (confidence, security, no nagging) and an equal proportion of motion (interest, stimulation of ideas, etc). That's what we have got. We are both static and dynamic in our mutual relations.

Oh my darling, what a lucky man I am to be able to look back on eighteen such years. Whatever happens tomorrow or today nothing can take from us all the great enjoyment we have had together. I do not suppose that two people have ever retained such a high level of happiness for so long a time. I am so grateful to you. It is all your sweetness that has done it. During all those years you have been so loving and gentle. It makes me feel that I have been selfish all the time just to take so much and give so little and then to stand for politics and rush about and be a bother generally.

HAROLD TO VITA   *Hotel Excelsior, Rome*

3 January 1932

I wrote from Pisa station and sent two postcards to the boys. But after Pisa I got into new territory. For a long time the Carrara mountains flashed above the umbrella pines. Later on we came opposite Elba, and as sunset came we entered the Piombino-Orbetello region— lean flanks of hills and dykes and lagoons catching the sunset. The sun flamed down into the sea and lit up the Isola del Giglio. I insist on going there one day with you. It is small and mysterious and en- trenched. My love, we shall go there one day when troubles have ceased and I do not find my hair crackling to grey with worry.

I read *Mansfield Park* [Jane Austen]. Proust applied to *la petite noblesse de campagne.* I also read Aristotle's Ethics, feeling that it was really high time, before I got to Rome, to know what was meant by 'good'. I arrived at the Terme [station] before I had quite decided that point.

Christopher[1] met me and we drove to this Edwardian caravan-serai. They had engaged a suite for us and are charging us absurdly low prices. A vast drawing room replete with palms and little gilt tables. A double-bedded room for me and bathroom. Ditto for Tom [Mosley]. And Christopher in a *chambre de demoiselle* along the passage. Tom arrives tomorrow.

Gladwyn came in.[2] He took us off to dine in his flat. For the moment he is occupying his mother-in-law's little flat looking out on the Castel San Angelo. Very Anglo-Italian. A hard night, steel stars. Not very cold. Christopher has returned from Munich having seen Hitler. He says that the Führer contends that we British Hitlerites are trying to do things like gentlemen. That will never do. We must be harsh, violent and provocative. I do not care for this aspect of my future functions. I fear that it will be very bad for Tom to go to Munich. Oh dear! Oh dear!

Thereafter we had a drink called Nectar which tasted like the sort of hair-wash you would get at the coiffeur at Sauqueville. And then to bed. Being both a little tired.

I woke this morning to find sun pouring in and to see, opposite, a red villa adorned by statues of Emperors and a miffy palm. Above this crenelated cornice swept the deep blue sky. "I am," thus did I address myself, "in Rome." And at that I rang for a *Caffè completo*. Already I am feeling better in the head and heart. My dear—how worried I have been the last three months! How much more worried I *ought* to be now! But there it is—I shall not bother these days and try and enjoy myself.

What a strange expedition this is! Oh my dear, when I saw that Island of Giglio I thought how far better would it have been had I lived there all my life with you. Giglio non Gigolo. But then I have been active—that is something to be said—even if it has given me a sore head and brought me into disgrace with fortune and men's eyes.

---

1. Christopher Hobhouse, aged twenty-one, a New Party devotee, who had just come from Munich filled with pro-Nazi fervor.
2. Gladwyn Jebb, now serving in the British Embassy, Rome.

HAROLD TO VITA   *Hotel Excelsior, Rome*

4 January 1932

My own darling,

I cannot tell you how lovely it was yesterday. A cloudless sky and that light which only Rome can give—a gentle brilliance. We walked in the Borghese gardens observing the equestrians trotting together in the row. Then along the Pincian and down Trinità dei Monti. What a marvellous staircase! Then we went and sat in the sun in the Piazza del Popolo and finally to St Peter's. At an open window on the façade lounged three papal guards in their uniforms. It was exactly like some Velasquez sketch. We went into the Cathedral. Christopher [Hob-house], who is drawn to Catholicism, was rather shocked. He found it flippant. As indeed it is. And showing off. Which it does. And irreverent. Which it may be. He refused for these reasons either to kiss the pope's toe, or to cross himself.

At 7.45 I went to meet Tom [Mosley]. He arrived looking most unwell. He said that Paris and *réveillon* had knocked him up. He recovered a bit after his bath and we had dinner here at the hotel. They treat Tom with the utmost deference—regarding him as a *duce in erba*. After dinner the editor of the *Lavoro Fascisto* came round to interview Tom. He was not much of a man as editors go, nor did he possess such a knowledge of the English language as might have been helpful to us. But we managed all right, and he told us about the Fascist electoral system which is in fact not electoral at all. We were much impressed.

HAROLD TO VITA   *Hotel Prinz Albrecht, Berlin*

25 January 1932

I did not write yesterday as I was so rushed. It was not a noble rush. It was an ignoble rush. It came from the fact of oversleeping, in its turn induced by too much festivity. For on the previous night I dined at the Embassy. A vast banquet. Rows of state liveries, and the

porter going flump with his mace when one came in. The Papal Legate
in scarlet, the new French Ambassador with a conceited swing to his
head. And all the usual appurtenances of a diplomatic dinner. I wore
my little flag [his CMG decoration]. Old Friedländer Fuld was there.
She was dressed in a dowdy little shift—none of the emeralds and
diamanté of the past. This is because she is afraid of Hitler who has
said that if he comes into power he will get rid of all the Jews. Which
includes Jewesses. Most disturbing. That little fiend, her daughter, is
hiding in the country.

I was warmly welcomed by my ex-colleagues. I sat there looking
up the table through the gold candelabra upon those shirt fronts and
ribbons. Well, well . . . I keep on reminding myself that if I had stayed
in Diplomacy I should now be Minister at Montevideo and not pleased
at all. Yet I cannot hide the fact that when I last sat at that table I was
a person of consequence. And now I have lost all the reputation that
I had. My own fault—and I daresay it is not irremediable. But I
certainly have made myself a motley to the view during the last two
years. Reckless of me. I had too many irons in the fire. I was in too
much of a hurry.

Thinking gloomily of these things I left the banquet having said
goodbye to the Papal Legate and proceeded to the Jockey [Club].
There I met Francesco[1] by appointment. He is less wild and extravagant than formerly. He thinks only of his plays—which are doing
well. He took me on to the rough bar in the east end. It is pathetic
how hungry everyone is here. I stood them all sausages. Their eyes
became like wolves.

Yet the result of all this was that I only got to bed at 4.0 a.m.—and
that I woke with a start at 10.30 to the telephone saying that the car
was at the door. It was to take Christopher and myself to Potsdam.
It did. We visited Sans Souci [Frederick the Great's palace]. We
walked through the park. We returned to lunch with Francesco. He
has constructed a bathroom in a very odd style. The walls are of
chromium steel and the bath is a huge Roman sarcophagus. It is spoilt

---

1. Francesco Mendelsohn, a rich, musical lover of the arts and a dramatist, who knew all Berlin
   society.

in its effect by a neat little white lavatory in the corner. Hitler is the sole topic of conversation. [2]

This sort of life is, I am told, interesting and exciting. Yet I am too old for it. I long for home and quiet. Not that I have been bored. I have learnt a lot.

---

2. Harold recorded in his diary of this visit, "My general impression is that Hitler has missed the boat."

During the summer of 1932 Harold wrote Public Faces, *a novel about diplomacy, which had an instant success, and he and Vita were persuaded, as the best-known married couple in English letters, to undertake a lecture tour of Canada and the United States. They were away nearly four months, January to April 1933. For both of them it was their first (for Vita her only) visit to America, and they stood the physical, mental, and social ordeal with undiminished buoyancy. Sometimes they spoke from the same platform, discussing such subjects as "Marriage" or "How to Bring Up Children," but for much of the time they were lecturing apart, and wrote each other letters that released some of the tensions that they managed to conceal from their hosts.*

HAROLD TO VITA   *British Embassy, Washington*

28 January 1933

My own darlingest,

Tears of a widower—oh my sweetheart—how young you looked as you came down the stairs last night with your little bag. Such a mar. So alone. So wanted and so alone. My heart ached. I talked to the Ambassador[1] for a bit about politics. He is a sensible man. And then dreading it, I went upstairs. There was a cigarette stump in your ashtray and tissue paper about. And the iodine and cough lozenges on my table. Really it is absurd how we go on exposing ourselves to these *déchire-*

---

1. Sir Ronald Lindsay, who had been Harold's first Ambassador in Berlin. He was Ambassador in Washington, 1930–39.

ments. I do not ever want to be separated from you ever again. Not for an hour. My dearest, dearest, dearest marki.

This morning is fine and clear, and I can see the Washington obelisk and the dome of the Capitol. I have finished my breakfast, done my diary, washed, dressed—and here I am settling down to write some letters. Then I go off to Baltimore and the old smile will be set again upon my *pomettes.* But I shall not be really glad till today week when our reunion comes closer.

What an odd life! But it is useful for us not merely as an experience but as a break with vegetationing. I scarcely dare to think of Sissinghurst. I see that they are having very heavy weather in England. Frost and snow. Our poor garden.

Goodbye my own angel—all my love

Hadji

VITA TO HAROLD

Hotel General Brock,
Niagara Falls, Canada

31 January 1933

Niagara on closer inspection is after all rather more impressive than the waterfall at Sissinghurst. When I wrote this morning I had seen only the American falls, not the Canadian ones. Since then, I have been taken round by Dr Harry Grant. Dr Harry Grant is a darling old boy of 73, with the whitest hair I have ever seen; half scholar, half philosopher, with a real passion for Niagara. He has built himself a house just opposite the Falls, where he lives quite alone, and reads, so he tells me, for ten hours a day sometimes, his only companions being a dog, a parrot, and some pheasants. *Face* [1] is one of his favourite books; so there. He simply loves it. Also your book on your father. He says *All Passion Spent* has had a bad effect on him, in so far as he used to be burdened by 50 nephews and nieces, but now never sees them unless he feels inclined.

I was amused. He began cautiously by asking me to go back to tea with him after seeing the sights. On our way round the sights (driven by a chauffeur called Ben as old as Dr Grant himself, and as

---

1. Harold's novel *Public Faces.*

silvery-haired), he informed me that the way to be happy was to expect only a tenth-part from life; i.e. if you read one book in ten that you liked, or met one person in ten that you liked, you ought to be satisfied, and to feel that you had achieved your quota. After tea, he made me the oddest little bow, and said, "I know now that you are my quota. I trust that you will return to dine with me. The car will call for you at 7.15." So there I am landed with having to go out to dinner. I can scarcely plead a previous engagement in Niagara Falls—although I *have* actually been invited by the Scarlet Quill Club, who in some miraculous way have already nosed me out—and anyhow he is such a darling that I couldn't refuse.

HAROLD TO VITA   *Hotel New Weston, New York*

1 February 1933

We went to Harlem. It is the real thing there—one mass of young black men and black women. They danced the Lindy Hop with intense seriousness. It is unlike any other dancing. The absence of self-consciousness. The absence of any smiles or conversation—grim earnestness. And the subordination of sex to movement. One feels that in this they have a form of self-expression which we whites cannot understand. Something voodooish or religious. Whatever happens Mar must go there. It is a wholly new experience—something which opens out a background which is as alien to us as the real east.

HAROLD TO VITA   *The Drake, Chicago*

7 February 1933

I have just come back from seeing you whirl in a whirl-door into a whirl of blizzard. No, I didn't like it in the least. I wish now that I had insisted on coming to the station as once you are in the train, you will be safe and warm. But then if I had come to the station you would now be fussing about how I would get back—and that would make it all worse for you. Darling, the Mars are really rather silly about each other. I feel now as if a helpless mouse had been turned out into the snow. Whereas really you are the most competent of people and will be travelling in a *train de luxe*. And you feel that a rabbit has been left behind exposed to whirlwinds and gangsters. Whereas in fact I am here in my room tikking away and as safe as safe. But we do love each other so, my dearest. We know that the whole of life is enshrined in the other. I shall see you the day after tomorrow. I shall be separated from you one whole day. I have heaps to do. I feel as if I were a mongoose stuck in the middle of the ice-floes of Lake Michigan.

VITA TO HAROLD   *Minneapolis*

14 February 1933

The whole of Minneapolis seems to be out for Red Lewis' blood; I responded with some mild remark, and that came out in all the papers too.[1] I hope neither he nor Dorothy [Thompson] sees it. There were also several descriptions of my personal appearance; my eyes, you will be pleased to hear, are (1) blue, (2) deep blue, (3) brown, (4) hazel. So you can take your choice. They got very puzzled as to what my name was, and there is a touching reference to my modesty in preferring to be called Miss S-W. instead of Lady "which is her rightful title." I think they thought I was being tactful in a democratic country. I don't feel I can stand many more women. America is rapidly curing me of any weakness I may ever have entertained for my own sex.

HAROLD TO VITA   *British Embassy, Washington*

16 February 1933

Such a miz letter he got from her written in the train. I am not surprised. Wisconsin at 4.30 P.M. on a February afternoon is not *folichon*

---

1. Vita had said, "It is too bad Sinclair Lewis is so widely read abroad and his caricatures are taken as real American people. It is entirely unfair to you."

[festive]. There are few things more depressing in this life than a lonely sunset in a train.

We went to lunch with Alice Longworth.[1] My word! how I like that woman! There is a sense of freedom in her, plus a sense of background. That, I feel, is what is missing in this country. Nobody seems to have anything behind their front. Poor people, they feel it themselves, and hence all those pitiful gropings after Manor Houses in Wiltshire and parish registers and the Daughters of the Founding Fathers. But Alice Longworth has a world position, and it has left her simple and assured and human. Yes, there at least is an American who is unquestionably a woman of importance. It was a pleasant luncheon. You know—those sort of luncheons where one feels mentally comfortable and warm.

After that I walked to the house in S Street where President Wilson died. It is a large neat modern house in good taste. Nothing grim about it. Excellent plumbing, I feel sure. I then walked down to the site of the old [British] Embassy. It has been completely cleared of buildings and the large triangular site is now occupied by second-hand cars standing cheek by jowl in the mud. I felt rather sad about poor B.M.[2]—and those distant happy days when she was young and successful and a belle. I stood there reflecting on the mutability of human affairs, and thinking of that encumbered bedroom at Brighton, and all the rage of disappointment hanging in the air. Oh my sweet!—pray God that you and I will not prepare for ourselves so tragic an old age.

HAROLD TO VITA   *Fort Sumter Hotel,*
                                        Charleston, South Carolina
18 February 1933

Charleston is really delightful. It has personality—which is a thing most American towns and people lack. It is not merely that there are a few old bits and lovely old houses—it is that the whole place is old in character and southern. The old atmosphere is lazy, untidy, digni-

---

1. The eldest daughter of President Theodore Roosevelt. Her husband, Nicholas Longworth, Speaker of the House of Representatives 1925–27, had died in 1931.
2. As a girl Lady Sackville had acted as hostess for her father when he was British Minister in Washington, 1881–88.

fied, lotus-eating, anti-noise and rush. Even their voices are as soft as the feet of the negro women selling narcissus in the streets. It is the most unamerican thing I have met. Mar absolutely must come here. It would be impossible to understand America's falling off unless one sees this place.

It is not that they are pro-English, or like the English; it is that they *are* English of a peculiar sort—a sort of West Indian, plantation flavour has remained undiminished. They talk of the Americans almost as of enemies. They dread lest "the Yankees" may come and spoil their lovely little town. They refer to the Civil War as 'The Confederate War'. They still long for secession under the British crown with Dominion Status. Even in details the difference is apparent. They loathe 'taste' which they call 'Lady's Journal'—and they keep old Victorian things in their houses so as not to 'become period'. Their servants are all black nannies like in the magazine stories, but they refuse to sentimentalize about them. They are infinitely less affected, more proud, than the denizens of Rye [Sussex].

From my window I look out across the glittering harbour to the thin line of the Atlantic. Over there, but 500 miles away, is Barbados and the Bermudas. One is conscious of their proximity. As I write I can hear soft voices calling 'spring flashers'—all else is padded and silent. From my other window I look down upon the town. Just low roofs and white balconies from which emerge white steeples and little neat lanterns in the Wren manner.

Miss Pinckney picked me up. She is from one of their oldest families. She writes poetry. She is well-read and intelligent but takes it as a matter of course. There are gardens everywhere. Public squares with statues of Pitt among palm trees. Green grass. Azaleas in flower. No, I mean in bud. Little quiet cobbled streets with the neatest of houses. Like the back streets of Westminster except that all the houses have a Barbados feel. And above all they have walls everywhere and iron gratings and fine iron gates disclosing lovely gardens. And round it all stretches water.

Dubose Heywood[1] [*sic*] picked us up. A very thin quiet interesting man. He motored us out to Middleton Place—some fifteen miles

---

1. Du Bose Heyward was born in Charleston in 1885. His novel about the Deep South, *Porgy*, was published in 1925.

away. We drove through avenues of huge ilexes draped in Spanish Moss. This moss is characteristic of the whole country. It isn't moss in the least but a hanging creeper like old man's beard. It drapes every branch, hanging down like huge cobwebs. The effect is as if every tree were draped in widows weeds of grey. In detail it is ugly and untidy: in the mass it is strange and impressive.

Middleton Place was one of the great plantation seats. It still belongs to the family who are cousins of Miss Pinckney. It is as romantic in its way as Sissinghurst. The main *corps de logis* was burnt in the Confederate war. Only the little brick kitchen wing remains. In this they live. But the wide avenue approach and the ensuing terraces and gardens still have their axis on the main frontage, and are on a fine wide scale. Enormous ilexes—eighteen-foot round in the trunk—flank a wide lawn cut up into high beds of camellias in flower. This terrace drops down to dark lakes 30 feet below to right and left. In front stretches a wide marsh intersected by a broad river. The skyline is intersected some fifteen miles away by low hills with forests. The marsh used to be a rice field. Six elderly negroes in blue were mowing the vast lawns with little tiny mowing machines. The camellias blazed. The air was damp and heavy with the smell of *Olea fragrans* or scentive olive—a sprig of which I sent you. I couldn't make out what it reminded me of. We went into the little house. All very simple. Three rooms with Empire furniture and shuttered as if it were blazing hot. Not a touch of *The Lady's Journal*. The gardens were beautifully kept up and when the azaleas are out it must be amazing. I am not much of a one for camellias even in the mass. But there was no nonsense about it. A few old stone benches. No statues. And from every tree hanging shrouds of moss.

We came back, and I came face to face with Elizabeth Lindsay. We fell into each other's arms. I said I had been to Middleton. She said, "Now what did it remind you of?" I said it had reminded me strongly of something but I could not say what. She said, "Well it's Vita's poem—*Sissinghurst.*" Of course it was; she is no fool that Elizabeth.

I gave my lecture in a lovely Adams hall with old pictures. The whole thing is so effortless and unaffected here. No strain. No noise. I delight in it. We MUST come. They are all longing to see you. Great passion-spenters.

23 February 1933

Darling, it was so nice settling down into my rather hard little Victorian bed last night and to feel that when I woke up I should see you again the day after tomorrow, and that thereafter we would not again be separated for more than two days at a time. It was also nice to see that you had traversed your great ordeal without any visible signs of exhaustion. My sweet—what a strong old horse you are, touch wood (I gave the desk here such a loud rap at that, that I had to say "come in"), but really you are a marvel of endurance and good temper. I confess that I myself find all this slushy adulation very trying, and irritating in the sense that all unrealities are irritating. Of course I know that you and I are very gifted and charming. Only we are not gifted and charming in the sort of way these people suppose.

One should remember however that if we were lecturing at Cheltenham, Roedean College, Bath and Harrogate we should be faced with just the same vapidity of compliment, by just the same uniformity of faces. I try to concentrate on the really nice people we have met, who don't gush but are just quietly and competently kind. It is not that these people are really less civilised than similar sorts of people in England. It is just that at home we should be bored stiff by that sort of person, and here we have a feeling (which may or may not be justified) that there simply does not exist the sort of other person whom we like. If you cut out the territorial aristocracy and the types which have gathered round them in England, and also cut out our scholars and our intellectuals, one would be left with a residue which would be no better than, and possibly worse than, our audiences. What appals me is the sense that the only alternative to these audiences is either the vulgarity of big business or the morons of the farming community. America seems to have so few alternatives: England so many.

Anyhow, my sweetest, I slept the first unanxious sleep I have had for ten days. It was the first night that one way or another I have not had an anxiety dream about you. I feel this morning so cheerful—a sense that we have broken the back of our tour, that we have turned the corner, and that we can now look forward to the second lap, aware that we have gained a rich experience, much money, a confidence in our own oratorical powers, and that you at least have done some real good for our beloved country. Oh my sweet, I am so proud of you! Your gentleness, your magnificence, your intelligence. You looked so lovely last night with your red velvet and gardenias. They adore your shy dignity, your regal modesty.

On returning from America, Harold devoted the next two years to his diplomatic trilogy: Peacemaking, Curzon, The Last Phase, *and the life of the American statesman Dwight Morrow. The third of these books took him once to Mexico and several times to the United States, where he stayed with Charles and Anne Lindbergh (Anne was Morrow's daughter) at crucial stages of the trial of Bruno Hauptmann for the kidnapping and murder of their baby. Although they were in frequent financial difficulties, Harold and Vita somehow managed to keep two sons at Eton, employ three domestic servants and three gardeners, travel frequently abroad, and develop ambitious plans for extending the garden at Sissinghurst.*

HAROLD TO VITA

4 *King's Bench Walk,*
Inner Temple, London

7 November 1933

H. G. Wells's dinner party was not, perhaps, an unqualified success. I gather that its intention was to announce his engagement to Moura, but then Odette got nasty[1] and there are breaches of promise in the air and no announcements of immediate marriage. That was the first error. The second error arose from the fact that the titled cousin of Moura who was to play to us on the harp afterwards has an only child, and this child developed a temperature with the result that the titled cousin of Moura failed to come. The harp was there all right as once

---

1. Baroness Moura Budberg, born in Russia, had been the mistress of Maxim Gorki and for many years of H. G. Wells. Odette was Odette Keun, the daughter of a Dutchman and a Greek lady from Constantinople, who was also loved by Wells.

in Tara's Halls[2] but there was no one to play it. The third error was
that we dined in a little restaurant called Quo Vadis where there was
a large horseshoe table in imitation of the Last Supper. There were also
little snippets of lobster in tomato cocktails, which were among the
least successful of zakouska that I have ever known. Then the company
was mixed in the sort of way that companies could not, or should not,
be mixed. There was Emerald Cunard looking like a 3rd dynasty
mummy painted pink by amateurs. And there was Christabel who is
going to have a baby. And there was Hazel Lavery who looked as
though she had stuck on top of her face a caricature mask done by
someone else. Very ill she was poor woman. And there was Enid Jones[3]
who has an outbreak on her face and arrived veiled like the Beghum
of Bhopal. Owing to these disabilities the smarties were not smart
enough. The intellectuals were below standard also. There was Stutter-
heim late of the *Berliner Tageblatt,* David Low the caricaturist, [Sir
Frederick] Keeble the botanist, Gip Wells, the son, with his bedint
wife, and Brendan Bracken [financier and politician]. After that we
adjourned to Wells's flat which is like a fountain-pen box split into
cubicles by the designers of Broadcasting House. Maurice Baring
appeared and Max Beaverbrook. We sat around looking at the harp.
No, it was not a successful party. But I rather enjoyed it. Lady Keeble
is hell.

V I T A   T O   H A R O L D   *Il Castello, Portofino [Italy]*

31 January 1934

Enchanted, yes; but idiots, no.[4] It is *divine.* You must admit that
I acted promptly, for I only fixed it up definitely on the telephone at

---

2. "The harp that once through Tara's Halls
      The Soul of Music shed
    Now hangs as mute as Tara's Walls
      As if that soul had fled." *Thomas Moore*
3. Christabel McLaren, later Lady Aberconway; Lady Lavery, second wife of Sir John Lavery
   the painter; and Enid Bagnold, the novelist, wife of Sir Roderick Jones, head of Reuters.
4. Vita and her sister-in-law, Gwen St. Aubyn, had gone to the Italian Riviera, where in a
   spasm of romantic extravagance they took a fortnight's lease of the castle that overlooks
   the harbor of Portofino. It was the setting of Countess Russell's novel *Enchanted April*,
   published in 1922.

7 last night, and by 11 this morning we were here, Gwen's trunk and all, and a demi-john of *vino del paese,* with a complete household of servants waiting for us and mattresses hanging out of every window and the garden-boy with a large bunch of irises at the gate. And if you walked in now, you would not believe that we had not been here for weeks, even to the wireless playing away. Damn, I wish we'd been here on Saturday night to listen to you.

We had luncheon on the terrace and then went down the olive-terraces to the sea. There are bulbs coming up everywhere, but only irises, narcissus, and roses in flower as yet. Oh yes, and we've got a party on Friday. The Beerbohms.[5] In short I can't tell you how perfect it is, and how pleased I am at having been such an idiot.

HAROLD TO VITA   *Munich*

4 February 1934

I have not been very virtuous. I found that Jim Lees-Milne[6] was going over to Paris so I decided to go with him as it was more or less on my way. It was beautiful in the extreme. Cloudless and cold. I have seldom seen Paris looking so crisp and clean. Jim had never been to Versailles so we went out there to lunch. It was quite empty and very cold and magnificent. We walked to the Trianon and then up through the park to the Chateau. I picked up several hints for Sissinghurst. The Bassin de Neptune would do well in Mr Nicolson's rondel. We went over the Palace. I had not been to the Gallerie des Glaces since the great day of 1919. Very odd it was. Then back to Paris.

Jim is such a charming person. He has a passion for poetry and knows masses about it. I like my friends to be well-read and well-bred. Jim is such an aristocrat in mind and culture. You would like him enormously.

Then I walked to James Joyce's flat in the Rue Gallilée. It is a

---

5. Max Beerbohm, the novelist and essayist, lived close by at Rapallo.
6. The biographer and historian of architecture. In 1980–81 he wrote Harold's biography in two volumes.

little furnished flat and stuffy and prim as a hotel bedroom. The door was opened by the son. A coarse young man in a huge greatcoat which he kept on the whole time. A strange accent he had, half German, half Italian—an accent of Trieste. The sitting room was like a small salon at a provincial hotel, and the unreal effect was increased by there being florist's baskets about with arranged flowers—a large basket of mimosa tied with a broad ribbon. We sat down on little hard chairs and I tried to make polite conversation to the son. He got up and offered me an ashtray in the form of a saucer. Then Joyce glided in. It was evident that he had just been shaving. He was very spruce and nervous and natty. Great rings upon little twitching fingers. Huge concave glasses which flicked reflections of lights as he moved his head like a bird, turning it with that definite insistence to the speaker as blind people do who turn to the sound of a voice. The son sat there hunched in the chair and his vast greatcoat. Joyce was wearing large bedroom slippers in check, but except for that, one had the strange impression that he had put on his best suit. He was very courteous, as shy people are. His beautiful voice trilled on slowly like Anna Livia Plurabelle.[7] He has the most lovely voice I know—liquid and soft with undercurrents of gurgle. He told me how the ban had been removed from *Ulysses* (Oolissays, he calls it) in America. He had hopes of having it removed in London also and was in negotiation with John Lane. He seemed rather helpless and ignorant about it all and anxious to talk to me. One has the feeling that he is surrounded by a group of worshippers and has little contact with reality. This impression of something unreal was increased by the atmosphere of the room, the mimosa with its ribbon, the bird-like twitchings of Joyce, the glint of his glasses, and the feeling that they were both listening for something in the house—a shriek of maniac laughter from the daughter along the passage.

He told me that a man had taken Oolissays to the Vatican and had hid it in the shape of a prayer book—and that it had been blessed in such disguise by the Pope. He was half-amused by this and half-impressed. He saw that I would think it funny, and at the same time, he did not think it wholly funny himself. It was almost as if

7. A character in Joyce's novel *Finnegans Wake.*

he had told me the story in the belief that it might help to lift the ban in England. And yet, being uncertain about it, he smiled deprecatingly as he told it, whereas his eyes behind his glasses were almost appealing.

I suppose that if I had been lunching with him at a restaurant, I should not have felt so strange. But the impression of the Rue Gallilée was the impression of a very nervous and refined animal—a gazelle in a drawing-room. His blindness increases that impression. His shy courtesy, his neatness, his twitching fingers with the rings. I suppose he is a real person somewhere—but I feel I have never spent half an hour with anyone and been left with an impression of such brittle and vulnerable strangeness.

HAROLD TO VITA   *Svenska Lloyd* Suecia *in the North Sea*

13 May 1934

My disinclination to Sweden[1] increased rapidly as Copper [chauffeur] with marked disapproval negotiated the bumps and crevices of our lane. It was so warm and lovely. The horse-chestnuts were beginning to light their candelabra.

This is a nice clean boat with dryad chairs and waitresses instead of stewards. I washed. I brushed my thinning hair. I entered the saloon. *"Skiljetecken Utstrykning sasom sarskilda konditor bud,"* said the head waiter. "That," I answered, "would be delightful." So I sat at the Captain's table. He, poor man, was threading the intricacies of the Thames estuary and did not appear. But two Swedish matrons appeared and a Doctor man, and, I rejoiced to find, Lord Peel[2]—whom I like very much indeed. No food came. *"Gong-gongen gar ej,"* said the head waiter. I translated to Lord Peel (I have picked up Swedish quite quickly), "The gong," I said, "has not sounded yet." We had a nice meal. Then I read. Then I went to bed. The fog-horn hooted in the night. "Danger," I murmured to myself, "drowning and death." But I did not wake.

---

1. Harold was on his way to Stockholm to lecture on Democratic Diplomacy.
2. The first Earl of Peel, Secretary of State for India, 1922–24 and 1928–29.

HAROLD TO VITA   *British Legation, Stockholm*

16 May 1934

I really am a little worried about Tina and Archie.[1] The former has taken Sweden *en grippe*—and I sympathize with her. Apart from everything else, she does not get the admiration she deserves. She is really a museum piece and ought not to be confined to the provinces. It is not merely her very original beauty (which they cannot see) but her intelligence. It is hard luck on her to be in a place for so long where her qualities fail to shine at all. I fear also that she loathes diplomatic life, thinks she is a drag on Archie's career and altogether feels a failure. Archie still treats her as a toy—and you know how bedint and tactless he is. She is far more distinguished and intelligent than he is. I see her squirm when he is snobbish or crude. Yet she still adores him. There are angles in her face which suggest sulkiness, and a spoilt-child ill-temper. There are other angles which are very gentle and rather fine. They both loathe this place with a fierce intensity. I reproved Archie for his sloppy way of living. He has breakfast at 9.30 in his dressing gown and is not dressed till 11.0. Tina stays in bed reading till 1.0. "Well you see," she said, "it makes the day go quicker. The only pleasure we get here is when we feel another day has gone." Archie tells me that she cries a good deal.

HAROLD TO VITA   RMS *Berengaria*
16 September 1934   en route *for the United States*

A male film star approached me rather tight. An ageing Apollo he was, and he said to me, "Where can one get a drink?" I looked at him with marked distaste—pointing with a blunted Royal Sovereign pencil in the direction of the bar. He staggered with an uncertain but still undulating movement of the hips towards a high contiguous stool.

Darkness was descending and the *triste patience des phares* throbbed painfully along the parapets of Europe. Observing that the film star

---

1. Archibald Clark-Kerr (later Lord Inverchapel) was British Minister in Stockholm, 1931–35. In 1929 he had married a beautiful Chilean girl of nineteen, Maria Salas, nicknamed Tina.

had left his stool, I myself entered the bar and ordered a martini. That made me feel better, and when I felt the throb of engines again I faced my departure with emotion but not in despair. For half an hour I paced the deck seeing the lights fling out sudden appeals. And then I said goodbye to my really beloved continent and retired to my cabin.

I cannot tell you how luxurious and self-satisfied that cabin is. The walls are panelled in chinese silk depicting lotus and dragons. The mirrors flash to concealed lights: the twin beds look like neat little twins; cupboards open on all sides with hangers on which my steward (a talkative man of the name of Emerson) had already hung my clothes. Cameras and binoculars hung upon platinum pegs; a sprig of heather reposed in an ornamental vase; and upon the tables were my books and the Lenare photograph [of Vita].

I then washed in my private bathroom redolent with the rose geranium which B.M. had given me. I then dined at our small table with Victor Cazalet.[1] He has just been motoring in France with Sibyl [Colefax] and cannot speak too highly of her intelligence and charm as a companion. They had ended up at Aix where they had spent the time with Mr and Mrs Baldwin. Teenie [Cazalet] likes Prime Ministers in any form. Mrs B. was hostile to Sibyl and feared she might get hold of her husband. Teenie decided that the visit must not be prolonged and they thus left for the Dordogne.

He is a strange and I fear slightly despicable man. He said, "What I like about journeys such as this is that one can invite people to dinner and not have to pay for their meals." "Yes," I said, "but one has to pay for their drinks." He became thoughtful at this and after a while he said, "We might ask Philip [Lord Lothian] to sit at our table tomorrow evening and then he will ask us to dine with him and the two Astor girls." The whole of Morgan Grenfell and Co rose within me in protest at such meanness. "No," I said, "No, Teenie, we shall ask Philip, Alice Wynn and Nancy Tree to dine with us tomorrow night and we shall give them champagne." He giggled hollow-like.

After dinner (which consisted of grouse and sole ordered fussily by Teenie) we discussed Christian Science which is the centre of his life and the purpose of his visit to the U.S.A. He is not unintelligent

1. Conservative M.P. for Chippenham since 1924. A neighbor of the Nicolsons' at Cranbrook, Kent, he was killed in 1943.

about it. But I do feel that a Christian Scientist should not abuse the head waiter because his grouse is an elderly bird and not an adolescent. But he is an agreeable companion full of information about people. His views of things are deplorable in the extreme. He has no ordinary common sense about politics. He advocates an alliance with Japan. Now that is just wrong-headed, and with wrong-headedness I have small sympathy and little patience.

We then went upstairs to the lounge where a band played and where Teenie played piquette with Alice Wynn. She failed to wyn. I talked to Philip about his Knole scheme. He is really keen about it and has gone into the subject thoroughly. His idea is to get the Government to accept certain places (there is a list of some 20 first class and some 430 second class national monuments) as a national possession in their entirety—including park, furniture, gardens and general 'condition'. The Treasury would accept as payment for death duties the transference of an equivalent value in these possessions. The objects thus transferred would belong to the state who would lend them on trust to the owners. Thus Eddie [Sackville-West] could pledge the furniture of Knole as payment in death duties: the furniture would remain there, and all the Government would ask would be that it should not be sold or otherwise dispersed, that the public should be admitted, and that the owners, as guardians, should take all proper precautions for maintenance etc. He thinks he will persuade Neville Chamberlain [Chancellor of the Exchequer] to accept this scheme. It would be a magnificent thing for Knole if he could.[2]

HAROLD TO VITA

20 September 1934

RMS *Berengaria*
One day from New York

We had Professor Catlin and his bright little wife to luncheon. Her name is Vera Brittain. She wrote a book called *Testament of Youth.*[3] He is an austere and vain type. She is like a thin robin pecking with

2. Lord Lothian's scheme was carried out by the National Trust Act of 1937. His own house, Blickling in Norfolk, passed to the National Trust in 1940, and Knole in 1946.
3. Her book, published in 1933, was an eloquent exposure of the horrors of the First World War, seen through a woman's eyes. Her husband, George Catlin, was appointed Professor of Politics at Cornell University in 1924 at the age of twenty-eight.

bright eyes. He is lecturing to an American University on political theory. She is lecturing upon the *Testament of Youth* to several women's clubs. I gave her much sound advice. So sound was my advice, so friendly and paternal my attitude, that they both consulted me separately regarding the education of their son aged seven. Catlin wanted to send him to Eton since he feels that it is the best education, being confirmed in that supposition by what his academic friends tell him. She wants more experimental methods and co-education. I said that co-education was calculated to make boys homosexual for life, whereas Eton was only calculated to make them homosexual till 23 or 24. She said she didn't mind about that, but she felt Eton was 'narrowing'. I said, "What do you mean by 'narrowing'?" She had no idea what she meant and made a vague and most unsuccessful gesture indicative of how narrowing the effect of Eton really was. I said it wasn't narrowing at all, and that she could take it from me, and if she didn't want to take it from me she could take it from you. I said that you loathed Eton from the depths of your noble soul, but that if we had a third son now aged seven, I believe that (under much protest and snorting, and after pinching Rebecq [dog] twice, hitting Abdul [donkey] on the nose, removing all food and drink from the budgerigars, sending Tom [gardener] to dig up the rondel and plant artichokes in it, telegraphing "Beast—so there" to Christopher [Hobhouse], and sending Dottie [Wellesley] a small pot of cheese from Woolworth) you would agree.

HAROLD TO VITA

23 September 1934

*Deacon Brown's Point,
North Haven, Maine*

I woke as we were approaching Rockland.[1] I pinched the clip of the blind and pulled it up. A Scotch mist, and by the railway embankment masses of stunted Golden Rod with rain-drops hanging. Rockland itself is a small place, a sort of log-cabin Shoreham [Sussex]. We

1. On the coast of Maine. North Haven is an island off it, where the Morrows had their summer home. This was Harold's first meeting with Elizabeth Morrow, whose husband's biography he had undertaken to write.

were met by the captain of the Morrows' *St Michael,* by a man I could not make out, by another man I could not make out and by a third man I could not make out. The retainers who attach themselves to American millionaires are disconcerting. There are always people hanging about who may be friends or under-gardeners or private detectives. Anyhow I shake hands all round, and if I include a chauffeur here and there, what does it matter in this egalitarian country?

There was a taxi at the station which took us to THE COPPER KETTLE where we breakfasted—George Rublee and I. Now that man George Rublee is an angel. About 63 I should think, huge and lank, the type of an American H.A.L. Fisher. A thoroughly nice man and we got on like anything.

The Copper Kettle was a wooden structure with neat tables in a veranda and a neat proprietress doing accounts at one of them. We had coffee and eggs and dough-nuts. I then walked across to the cable office and sent B.M. a many happy returns cable.[2] The man there was helpful in the best American way. "Now see here," he said, "when exactly do you wish this dame to receive your message?" I said that her birthday was September 23. "Is that so?" he commented. "But you see," I said, "I am not sure whether in England they deliver telegrams on a Sunday." "Is that so?" he said. "Well now, you just leave it to me. With our deferred rate, we can make certain sure that the lady gets her message before she retires for the night." I must say, there is something about this side of American manners which attracts me strongly. It has nothing about it of the prim self-consciousness of the English petty official.

We then went down to the little pier where something between a yacht and a steam launch awaited us. The Scotch mist hung over the little harbour and the spars and rigging of a little yacht at anchor were hung with heavy drops. We hummed out into a satin sea, accompanied by a soft circle of fog. The islands are some eight miles from the mainland and I enjoyed the forty odd minutes which it took us to creep cautiously towards them. We passed a school of porpoises. Among marine monsters, they give me the effect of hawks. They treat their element in so individual a manner, differing from the blind fumblings

2. Lady Sackville was seventy-two.

of lesser fish. Sharks are as eagles: porpoises as hawks. They flopped along slowly in the muggy satin sea.

Then a buoy appeared with two cormorants on it, and directly afterwards the dim outline of pine trees stepping gingerly down to the very edge of the rocks where the sea lapped. We swung in between two islands and across to a third where there was a landing stage. There we landed *O venusta Sirmio* [Catullus]. There was a little pier house and an inn with shingle sides. A station car was waiting for us—one of those cars which have yellow wood for sides and give a wagonette effect, and recall the Tyrol and shooting parties in East Prussia. We drove in and out of little bays with pines down to the water and eventually the pines became tidier and there were sweeps of mown grass between the plantations. "That," said Rublee, "is where Lindbergh lands." Then we swept down to the house. It is charming. It is of wood with shingle sides. The views all round (since the fog had begun to lift) are superb. Rocks and islands at every angle and the sea splashing in and out of dahlias.

Mrs Morrow advanced to meet us at the gate. A little woman— neat and ugly. We were given coffee in the drawing room. The whole thing is rather *House and Garden,* but not aggressively so. I have a dear little room on the ground floor with pink curtains and a super-bathroom next door. I had a bath and changed into more untidy clothes. I then went round the place with Mrs Morrow. The lawns run down between quite adequate flower-beds to the sea.

Mrs Morrow was in quite a state of excitement at my arrival. She had not slept all night. I feel that this book means so very much to her. I pray that I shall not disappoint her. She worships her husband's memory, but is intelligent enough not to wish to control what I write. I do not think that we shall have any differences.

V I T A   T O   H A R O L D   *Sissinghurst*

25 September 1934

I am afraid it may be being rather painful for you, living in the Lindbergh milieu with this revived business about the baby going on.[1] It must be so horribly painful for those two nice people to have the whole question re-opened now. Personally, I would like to put the man into the electric chair with my own hands, and give him two minutes agony, to pay him out for the months of mental agony he made them endure. Ben and Gwen both say they can't understand this. But then you know that I am very revengeful when I love, and so I can understand other people being revengeful too. It seems to me that people are mostly very tame—but I daresay I'm wrong. Anyhow I know I would gladly torture anybody who had hurt anybody I really loved. "Revenge is a wild kind of justice."[2] It seems to me a right kind of justice.

HAROLD TO VITA   *Hinsdale, Massachusetts*

27 September 1934

Minna[3] was voluble and informative. She was a great friend of Constance Morrow [Anne's sister] and had often stayed there. She was interesting about Lindbergh. She said he is really no more than a mechanic and that had it not been for the lone-eagle flight [to Paris, 1927] he would now be in charge of a gasoline station on the outskirts of St. Louis. Although the Morrows were themselves of humble origin, yet they were always cultured people and distinguished. Thus Lindbergh is really of a lower social stratum and they treat him with aloof politeness as one treats a tenant's niece. He is himself simple and 'not easy'. Anne has a difficult task. It will be a strange experience being with them all for so long and in such intimate circumstances.

Dwight Morrow junior [b. 1908] is a tragedy in their lives. He was sent to a 'private' school—in fact to the American Eton. He was bullied during his first term there and went off his head. He heard

1. The Lindbergh baby was snatched from his cradle on 1 March 1932. A ransom was paid, but the baby had died within an hour of being kidnapped. The police arrested Bruno Hauptmann, a German carpenter, as a suspect two days before Harold landed in New York.
2. Francis Bacon, *Of Revenge*.
3. Minna Curtiss taught in Northampton College and ran a farm in the Berkshire Hills, where Harold was staying with her.

voices calling him, which is a thing no sane person ought to hear. Remember that, my poppet, and when you start hearing voices you must go to a doctor. Anyhow they shut him up in a private asylum and in the end he recovered. But today he is still nervous and un-developed and unstable. This is a mortification to Mrs Morrow, who is not really kind to the boy. When the baby was kidnapped one of the news-service people on the radio put out that one theory was that the crime had been committed by the Morrows' 'lunatic' son. This was not a pleasant thing to have broadcast, nor did it diminish the self-consciousness of young Dwight. One way or another, therefore, I expect my three months at Englewood to be rich in human problems.

We climbed up in the heat and it became cooler and gradually the woods increased both in thickness and colour and there were mountain streams tumbling under wooden bridges. We stopped at Archie Mac-Leish's farm.[4] A nice wooden house with green shutters and the shadows of vines upon long deck chairs. It is on the ridge of a hill with fine views over wooded mountains. We sat there on the lawn and had cocktails. Mrs MacLeish was in a bathing dress, and as she looks like Siegfried, Sieglinda and Odin all rolled into one, it was an expansive sight. Archie was in corduroy and a singlet.

He has lost all his money and supports himself by journalism. He is now very famous in this country as he won the Pulitzer prize. He is writing a play in free verse on the subject of the great depression of 1932–33. He says it is the best thing he has ever written. He also experiments in the ballet, and says that it is the perfect form of expression. We discussed the American character. He said that the essential thing to remember was that American men are essentially cerebral. The fact that they are not intellectual makes foreigners think that they are unconcerned with things of the mind. This is a mistake. The brain of an American works all the time, but it works in terms of fact, not in terms of ideas. They have no sensuous perceptions. I enjoyed the conversation. People like Archie are really of far more value to me than the average 'class-mate of '95' who has not noticed the differences between people. I really like that man and admire him. He admires Auden hugely. Stephen [Spender] also.

---

4. Archibald MacLeish, the American poet, then aged forty-two. His poem *Conquistador* had won the Pulitzer Prize in 1933. Harold had first known him in Teheran.

Minna told me her life story after dinner which took place in a very odd room lit by candles in old iron-work stands and off a table painted with the arms of the Curtiss's from a design in the Musée de Cluny. Afterwards we sat in her big room and discussed her life, her brother's life, her father's life, Duncan Grant's life, Miss Bingham's life, Mr Bingham's life (which is indeed odd),[5] Bunny [David] Garnett's life, Stephen Tomlin's life—but NOT, I am glad to say, my life. I went to bed at midnight in the little hut across the lane. There is a bed in the room and a bed outside in the porch surrounded with meat-safe stuff to keep off flies. Frogs croaked from the stream. I could see stars. I slept beautifully.

Today we had arranged to go and see Robert Frost. I discovered however that he lived 60 miles away and that it would take us five hours to go there and back. It was so pleasant here this morning when I woke up—that I struck at Frost. I sent Minna a message to say could we get out of it. She was delighted.

HAROLD TO VITA   *Englewood, New Jersey*

30 September 1934

I confess that these entries into New York [Grand Central Station] are impressive. There was this vast onyx cathedral, bathed in subdued lights, soft to the foot, soothing to the eye, impressive to the sense. Great limousines slid in upon india-rubber flooring, and magnificent lifts moved passengers from one level to the other. It is like the subway at Piccadilly Circus but enlarged to the scale of the baths of Caracalla. The red-caps were, as always, solicitous and fatherly. I did not know where to find the car. "Now don't you worry about that—that'll be all right—you just stay right here." The vast Cadillac of the Estate of Dwight W. Morrow then slid glistening and enormous into my ken. I entered it. It crackled out between onyx and marble into the superb plutocratic canyon of Park Avenue. On and on we crackled, down Fifth Avenue, through Central Park, on the Riverside Drive. The

5. The United States Ambassador in London and his beautiful daughter Henrietta, who was much taken up by the Bloomsbury Group. Stephen Tomlin, the sculptor of Virginia Woolf, was much in love with her.

skyscrapers above the park flashed and winked from a million windows. It is impossible to renounce the exhilaration of such triumphant human energy. London seems in comparison to shrink untidily and to become like Hildenborough Station compared to Versailles. The *metropolitan* can scarcely go further, and on such a scale that the lack of history and organic development does not irritate and depress. After all the Pyramids are standardised, but when you standardise monoliths, their very repetition is impressive. I admit that New York at night is one of the most impressive visions in the world.

A terrific thunderstorm crashed over us as we crossed the Hudson. But it was no good God trying to show off in that way. He cannot do it in New York. I grant you that as a thunderstorm it was one of the best I have ever seen God indulge in. But it just didn't work. It was no more disturbing than the night-flash of a tram wire when a car crosses the points.

We approached Epping Forest (since it is in such terms that you must visualize this place)—the same distance as Epping [from London], the same effect of street lamps in stunted trees, the same idea that in the recesses of those trees lie sardine tins, rain-soaked copies of the *Daily Mirror,* and the corpses of unwanted babies. There is a long approach to the house through a gate. At the gate a man kept guard and waved us on with an electric torch. To be accurate, there is no gate, only two piers and a little hutch in which the detectives group and grouse. The car hummed up the hill between dripping trees, and splattered upon the sweep in front of the house.

Banks, the butler, was waiting. "Mrs Morrow," he said, "is dining out with Mr Lamont. Colonel and Mrs Lindbergh are here." He led the way through the *Home and Garden* hall to the *Home and Garden* boudoir. There were Anne and Charles. Anne like a Geisha—shy, Japanese, clever, gentle—obviously an adorable little person. Charles Lindbergh—slim (though a touch of chubbiness about the cheek), school-boyish yet with those delicate prehensile hands which disconcert one's view of him as an inspired mechanic. They are smiling shyly. Lindbergh's hand was resting upon the collar of a dog.

I had heard about that dog. He has figured prominently in the American newspapers. He is a police dog of enormous proportions. Martin [Vita's alsatian] in comparison is a mere martinette. His name is Thor. I smiled at him a little uncertainly. Not for a moment did

Lindbergh relax his hold on the collar. It is this monster which guards Lindbergh baby no. 2. "What a nice dog!" I said.

"You will have," he answered, "to be a little careful at first, Mr Nicolson."

"Is he very fierce?"

"He's all that. But he will get used to you in time."

"Thor is his name, is it not? I read about him in the papers." I stretched a hand towards him. "Thor!" I said, throwing into the word an appeal for friendship which was profoundly sincere. He then made a noise in his throat such as only tigers make when waiting for their food. It was not a growl, it was not a bark. It was a deep pectoral regurgitation—predatory, savage, hungry. Lindbergh smiled a little uneasily. "It will take him a week or so," he said, "to become accustomed to you." He then released his hold upon the collar. I retreated rapidly to the fire-place, as if to flick my ash away from my cigarette. Thor stalked towards me. I thought of you and my two sons and my past life and England's honour. "Thor!" I exclaimed, "good old man . . ." The tremor in my voice was very tremulous. Lindbergh watched the scene with alert, but aloof, interest. "If he wags his tail, Mr Nicolson, you need have no fear." Thor wagged his tail and lay down.

I had a stiff whiskey and soda and talked to Anne about Mrs Rublee. Feeling better after that, I turned to Lindbergh. "What happens," I asked, "if Thor does not wag his tail?" "Well," he said, "you must be careful not to pass him. He might get hold of you." "By the throat?" I asked—trying, but not with marked success, to throw a reckless jollity into my tone. "Not necessarily," he answered. "And if he does that, you must just stay still and holler all you can." Well, well—I must grin and bear it. By the time you get this I shall either be front page news, or Thor's chum.

HAROLD TO VITA   *Englewood, New Jersey*

1 October 1934

I got your telegram yesterday, bless you. Twenty-one years have we belonged to each other. That is a long period of time. My darling, you know when I pause and look back upon that stretch of time, I feel such gratitude to you. I know you loathe marriage and that it is not a natural state for you. But I also know you love me dearly. And I am grateful to you right inside myself and right through myself and as part of my inner core for having been so gentle to me and so unselfish. Whatever happens, nothing can take from me those twenty-one years. I know that I shall die in agony tomorrow and that Ben will fall down the well and Niggs be run over by a helicopter. I know all that. But there is *la chose acquise*— those twenty-one years of perfect life. You know when I look back upon my life since 1913 I feel almost frightened by my own felicity. Think of it only in terms of laughter, my dearest, how much we have laughed together! Or in terms of the little things we share as memories—the Dolomites and Resht [Persia] and that night at St Cergues and our early gardening efforts and the day at the F.O. when I gave you Turf [a dog]. A million delicate memories which only you and I can share in this world and which will remain with us when the other dies as a ground-swirl of the perished leaves of hope.[1] Just gratitude to fate and you.

Yesterday, I drove out with Mrs Morrow to the Palisades above the Hudson river where Tom Lamont[2] has a villa or home. It was all typically American millionaire. No sign when one had entered the property, just mown grass and neat trees and a tarred sweep. Then as we approached the house there was the detective in his hutch, scrutinising and then taking off a shabby trilby slouchily. Then the sweep in front of the house with four or five grand cars parked. Then the hall, white and black marble floor and a huge coromandel screen. Then the living room, pitch-pine, Raeburns, huge dahlias, *petit point,* the latest books. Then the porch—elaborate deck-chairs and wire-netting to keep off flies. No garden near the house but a bit of Italian nonsense on the way to the swimming pool. Fine views up the Hudson River. All very good taste and depressing. No inner reality.

But what can they do, poor people? After all, nothing is real here except the sky-scrapers. If I were an American I might desire to evolve a domestic architecture on Le Corbusier lines which would bear some

---

1. "The ground whirl of the perished leaves of Hope." Rossetti, *The House of Life.*
2. Chairman of J. P. Morgan and Company, then aged sixty-four.

relation to the sky-scrapers. But would I? I have no wish at all to live among steel arm-chairs. When it comes to comfort, William and Mary goes best with chintz and flowers and books. It is rather like an Atlantic luxury liner. Once one starts going modern it becomes a restless stunt. The only alternative is to copy the English gentleman's home and not mind about the fake. Yet my heart sinks when I think of all those millions of period rooms, correct, tasteful and uniform. We are better at that sort of thing, you and I. I do not see any of these millionaire libraries being diversified by a bit of stone from Persepolis, some bass left about, Martin's latest bone, Tikki, a hammer, a Rodin, a tobacco tin full of seeds, some loose films, a back number of the *New Statesman,* an evening shoe on its way back to the bedroom, and a soda-water syphon. Yet it is these varied and illuminating objects which make our rooms real and personal.

Mrs Lamont is an ass, as you know. Tom Lamont is a nice intelligent man. I walked with him. Norman Davis was there. He is the big noise now in American diplomacy and the adviser of Roosevelt. He is to be their delegate at the Naval Conference [in London, 1935]. At tea, he talked. Now the oddest thing about Americans is that they never listen. Davis was telling us what he felt would be the prospects of the Conference. He was talking seriously and earnestly. His idea is that the Franco-Italian pact and the Russo-French understanding will force Germany to come to heel. He discussed whether the true pacifist should not be strong and forceful rather than weak. What he said was thoughtful, well expressed, and immensely important as coming from him. But did they listen? Not for one moment. "Now let me give you another cup of tea, Mr Nicolson. I am afraid that our tea here is not as good as the tea you get in England . . ." Chatter, chatter; interrupt, interrupt. If I understood the explanation of this, I should understand more about American civilisation. Is it utter frivolity of mind, or merely a complete lack of all sense of real values? I suspect it has something to do with the position of women, or rather with the vast gulf which separates the male and the female in this continent. Women are supposed to discuss art, literature and the Home. Men are supposed to discuss business. Whatever it may be, it irritates me beyond words. It is as though Sir John Simon were lunching at Sissinghurst and explaining his policy to Venizelos and then you interrupted by talking about the Russian ballet. You would not do such things. But why do they?

Mrs Morrow has gone up for two days to Cleveland to see her mother. I am alone with the Lindberghs. He amuses and puzzles me. On the one hand, he is a mechanic and quite uneducated. On the other hand he is shrewd and intelligent. He has also got a sense of humour. Mrs Morrow mentioned that Mrs Lamont, who is not air-minded, said she would only fly if he took her up. "Now that is just like these old dames," he said, "just because I flew alone to Purris they think I am a safe pilot. That's just silly." He has an obsession about publicity and I agree with him. He told me that when [President] Coolidge presented him with a medal after his Paris flight he had to do it three times over—once in his study which was the real occasion, and twice on the lawn of the White House for the movie people. "The fust time," he said, "I was kind of moved by the thing. After all, I was more or less of a kid at the time and it seemed sort of solemn to me to be given that thing by the President of the United States. But when we had to go through the whole damned show over again in the yard, I mean lawn—me standing sideways to the President and looking an ass—I felt I couldn't stand for it. Coolidge didn't seem to care or notice. He repeated his speech twice over just in the same words. It just seemed a charade to me." I asked him whether he also repeated his own little speech. "Well, I mumbled something—but I was kind of sick about the thing and sore about it and I just murmured as low as I could in order to do in the movietone."

He adores that dog. I must say it is a magnificent animal. He trains it in a way I have never seen a dog trained. He says to it, "Now, Thor, you go and be nice to Mr Nicolson," and Thor trots across to me and puts his chin on my knee. He says, "Now, Thor, go and get a magazine for Anne." And off he trots into the library returning with a magazine in his teeth. "Now, Thor, you take Anne upstairs," at which he rushes at Anne, seizes her wrist gently in his teeth, and tugs her from the room.

Another odd thing. We have breakfast together. The papers are on the table. The Lindbergh case is still front-page news. It *must* mean something to him. Yet he never glances at them and chatters quite happily to me about Roosevelt and the air-mail contracts. It is not a pose. It is merely a determined habit of ignoring the press. I like the man. I daresay he has his faults but I have not yet found them. She is a little angel.

9 October 1934

Yesterday Hauptmann was identified by Lindbergh as possessing the voice he had heard calling in the cemetery.[1] Yet this dramatic event did not record itself upon the life here. Lindbergh was at breakfast as usual and thereafter helped me to unload my Leica camera. He is very neat about such things and I am clumsy. He then said, "Well, I have got to go up to Noo Yark—want a lift?" I said no. Then I worked hard at my files and at luncheon there was only Anne and me as Mrs Morrow had gone to some charity committee. Towards the end of luncheon Lindbergh arrived and we chatted quite gaily until coffee came. We had that in the sun parlour, and when it was over I rose to go. The moment I had gone I saw him (in the mirror) take her arm and lead her into the little study. Obviously he was telling her what happened in the court. But they are splendid in the way they never intrude this great tragedy on our daily life. It is real dignity and restraint.

At 3.0 I went out for my walk in the garden. The paths wind in and out of the property and over the stream. Anne and Jon [her younger son] joined me. Jon is bad at going down steps and has to turn round and do them on his tummy. He is a dear little boy, with the silkiest fair curls. I think of his brother's little head being bashed by Hauptmann. They *must* realize that what happened was that the child began to yell and they tried to knock him unconscious. It is a ghastly thing to have in one's life and I feel profoundly sorry for them. The best way I can show it is by manifesting no curiosity. But it is awkward and rather farcical when I take up the paper at breakfast and it is full of nothing else. "Things seem to be getting rather dangerous in Spain," I say. But I am sure that is the best attitude.

---

1. Where the ransom money was handed over on 2 April 1932.

HAROLD TO VITA　　　　　　　　　　　　　　　　*Englewood*

10 October 1934

In odd moments when I am at a loose end (about eleven minutes in the day) I read Emily Dickinson. Now why on earth should your old buttock find such enjoyment in Emily Dickinson I really do not know. She is everything I ought by logic to loathe. She was pretentious, overweening, mystic and fey. Yet my admiration for her mind and personality throbs through this routine treatment. I know why it is. She is Virginia [Woolf] in 1860. "Then," she writes to Colonel T. W. Higginson, "there is a noiseless noise in the orchard which I let persons hear." "And so much lighter than day was it," she writes to Louisa Norcross, "that I saw a caterpillar measure a leaf down in the orchard . . . It seemed like a theatre, or a night in London, or perhaps like chaos." This was when a barn burnt at Amherst. But it is all superb, and gives me the excitement and increased awareness that Virginia gives. Has she read the book? Has she written about Emily Dickinson? Ask her. It is exactly her subject. Beg her to do an article. Really, darling, if there is such a thing as genius as definitive and recognisable as a cigar lighter—then this frail ugly little trout possessed it. "I am no portrait," she writes, "but am small like a wren; and my eyes, like the sherry that the guest leaves in a glass." That is superb. The whole little frail egoist is superb. Mrs [Elizabeth Barrett] Browning is just a charwoman in comparison. She means so much to me here in this instinctive but uneducated country that I wish you were here to talk about her. I know that in England I should loathe her. Over here, she seems Blake without the prophecy stunt. I am deeply grateful to her.

VITA TO HAROLD　　　　　　　　　　　　　　　　*Sissinghurst*

14 October 1934

Raymond [Mortimer] was very sweet. He is a nice person so far as he goes, but soft. Really incorrigibly soft. He said Eddy had invited him to spend the whole of October-November at Knole, but he was afraid that "the beauty of Knole would overwhelm him and make him lazy." Now this seems to me funny, coming from Tray. When has he ever been anything but lazy? You will be surprised to hear that he has actually written two-thirds of his book on suicide. He is inordinately proud of having accomplished this much. I have refrained from asking him how long he has been at it.[1]

Then Charles Siepmann[2] arrived. I know you don't like him much, but really he is a stronger person than Tray, and a more real person. Gwen [St Aubyn] doesn't like him either, but rather came round to him today, which pleased me, because I do like Charles, and I mind when people I love don't like the people I like.

HAROLD TO VITA   *Englewood*

23 October 1934

New York looks superb as you approach it on an autumn evening over the Washington Bridge. It was clear last night and I could see the lights like fire-flies all round me. You know how fantastic is that Christmas-tree effect.

I drove to the club and dressed. I then drove to the River Club to dine with the Kermit Roosevelts. Marthe[3] appeared magnificently dressed and bejewelled. We dined. We drove to the theatre. It was a sort of pre-first night benefit performance for charity. The real first night is tonight. But the theatre was packed and I rather loathed it. I am not good at plays—they *take* so long. Yvonne Printemps was very charming and effective. But she sang rather bad Noel Coward songs rather badly, and there was too much 'charm' about it for my tastes. There was one large young man who wore a tight uniform with white trousers. They were too small for him. His bottom was like the dome of the Salute [Church, Venice]. When he turned round people sniggered, and for the rest of the play the poor man tried to back out of it. My heart went out to him, knowing how gross it is to be too large for one's clothes.

---

1. It was never finished, and consequently never published.
2. He had succeeded Hilda Matheson as Director of Talks at the BBC.
3. Princess Marthe Bibesco (1886–1973) was born in Rumania and married a cousin of Antoine Bibesco in 1901. She was a literary figure of distinction, as much at home in New York, London, and Paris as in her native country.

In the interval Marthe leant across to me. "Harold," she said, "will you take me round to see Yvonne Printemps?" Well you know, I am not good at this sort of expedition. But was I going to leave a beautiful princess in the lurch? I was not. I took her arm, tripping over my great-coat, and forgetting hers. We went out into the street. I asked a policeman. He said, Sur, he didn't know. So we went up an alley where there was much orange-peel, a smell of horses, and a vast iron ladder going up the side of the wall. But no stage door. Then we emerged again and tried the other side of the building. Marthe, flashing emeralds and diamonds, shuddered slightly. I felt like a knight errant— only the errant part of the proceeding was more marked than the knightly part. Anyhow to my astonishment and relief we got to a door marked "STAGE DOOR." I knocked. It was opened by a negro. "We want to see Princess Printemps," I said—being confused by the whole incident. He took that quite naturally and we were taken along a passage. We knocked at a door. An Algerian woman emerged. I said who we were, or rather who Marthe was, since I wasn't anything by that time worth being. And—would you believe it—we were received. Chrysanthemums and a huge mirror and Yvonne in an ivory dressing-gown. She was terribly nervous, on the verge of tears, but so glad to be able to talk French for once. She almost cried. *"Dieu, que c'est gentil de votre part, Madame—je me sentais tellement abandonée."* I was introduced as *"l'écrivain bien connu."* Yvonne swallowed both her tears and her ignorance of that fact, and gave me a hot, still tear-drenched, hand. Then we went back—and the silly billy of a play went on to the end.

HAROLD TO VITA   *Englewood*

5 November 1934

I spent the week end on Long Island. I think it was a good thing that your ancestors disposed of their possessions in this continent[1] since

---

1. In 1637 Edward Sackville, 4th Earl of Dorset, obtained a grant from Charles I of Long Island and other islands off the New England coast "not inhabited by any Christians."

I do not feel you would care for Long Island in the very least. You know that I am a social little cove, but I am not, I find, gregarious. I cannot conceive how these people endure the life they lead. Nobody ever seems to know who is lunching with whom and whose house is which. They drift in and out of those white porticoes howling at each other in merriment and neighbourliness.

I stayed with Mrs Kermit Roosevelt. Kermit is away. The house is a typical home, with a nice big library, and more untidy and less heated than other similar homes. I like the whole Roosevelt clan—they are at least thoroughly real people with no affectations or conventions. But they all live in a heap together on this point of Oyster Bay and their friends agglomerate round them. It is all very like Surbiton or Southampton Water. And it poured with rain. But I enjoyed it, and have returned this morning feeling soothed and well. Not that I was nervy or ill before. But of course the atmosphere of incense which floats here above the memory of Morrow is a trifle suffocating at moments. The Roosevelts are fresh air.

Teddy Roosevelt (the eldest of the clan) came to dinner with his wife. He has all the Roosevelt charm. Then on Sunday morning we went across to the Marshall Fields' place to play tennis. It is a huge house in a real park running at the edges down to the sea. The house is William and Mary—like Reigate Priory. There was no one there—but we went in. Very like an English stately home with coromandel screens, wood work, Raeburns and topographical pictures from Legatt. Fine carpets, magnificent massed chrysanthemums, a sense of enormous wealth. There was a closed racquet or tennis court with little rooms opening on to it. Italian gardens, bathing pools—and not a leaf allowed to disfigure the sweeps of grass. But as always in this country a terrible sense of UNREALITY robs it of all meaning. It has just been bought with money. It has never grown an inch by itself. There is none of that sense of the Raeburns having played among the woods as children which gives to our houses the aroma of continuity. Something horribly provisional mars this continent even at its most lovely.

The Marshall Field family itself is a dissolving view. The first wife was got rid of with a pretty little settlement of £200,000 a year. Audrey Coates, the second wife, is now in Reno also being got rid of at an approximate figure. I find all that depressing and unstable.

But the Roosevelts are real all right and rooted. Mrs Kermit took me to Theodore Roosevelt's house to see her mother-in-law, the old President's widow. A gentle, dignified, alert but untidy old lady—her hair in wisps. That in itself was a relief after all the rag-tag, bob-tail white heads I have seen. She was like old Lady Carnarvon. Ungainly and yet beautiful. The house is old fashioned and interesting. Enormous elephant tusks—some shot by T.R., some presented by various African potentates. What thrilled me most was a little case containing snapshots of the famous Döberitz review which Roosevelt attended in the Kaiser's company in 1911.[2] There were about 12 of these photographs mounted between sheets of glass and on the back of each the Emperor had scribbled remarks. These remarks are typical of his arrogance and indiscretion. "The Commander-in-Chief of the German Army and the Colonel of the Rough Riders discuss strategy together. A blow for that old peace-fool Carnegie." "Mr Roosevelt explains to the Emperor how if America and Germany stand together they can defy the world," and so on and so on. Mrs Roosevelt told me that these snapshots were sent round to their hotel by one of the emperor's aide-de-camps. Next morning a man came from the Foreign Office asking if they might have them back as they wanted to mount them in an album. Obviously they had guessed that the Emperor had scribbled indiscretions. T. R. refused to give them up, but said they would never go outside the family. At least he had the decency not to publish them.

I enjoyed all that. And the atmosphere of the place—rather like Clandeboye [Lord Dufferin's house in Ireland]—of an exuberant personality stamping his enormous range of interests upon his house.

HAROLD TO VITA   *Englewood*

13 November 1934

You have been to long barn (not worthy of capitals any more) and hadn't minded in the least. I wonder whether you would have minded

---

2. Theodore Roosevelt, who retired from the Presidency in 1909, reviewed the Imperial Guard at the Kaiser's side, the first civilian to do so.

had the bees been humming in at the big-room door. But Sissinghurst is more your spiritual home since it contains birthright and that sort of thing and a donjeon and a moat and the tower springing like a toolip. By the way, my sweet, in the American edition of Sissingbags[1] there is a Miss Print. At least I think so, but with you one can never tell. "Here," you exclaim, and fittingly, "tall and damask as a summer flower, Rise the brick gable and the *spring* tower." Now the word 'spring' strikes me, being illiterate in such things, as a Miss Print. I think it should be either 'springing' or 'springouth', 'springelth', 'springheld' or some dissyllabic anyway. But of course you may have meant to indicate that you had one tower for each season of the year (a thing of which you are fully capable), a winter tower, an autumn, and a summer tower plus spring ditto. Only, apart from the meaning, the word 'spring' just doesn't scan. Of course you may have felt that to put 'springing' in that line would clash with the next line in which "invading Nature crawls" all creepy crawly. But still I merely refer to the point.[2]

HAROLD TO VITA   *107 East 70th Street, New York*

22 November 1934

I wrote yesterday from Yale. After I had written I walked across to the lecture hall and mounted the tribune. There were about 300 undergraduates there—rows and rows of eager young faces. I talked for 45 minutes and then had 15 minutes for questions, which were intelligent and acute. When I had finished, they started clapping and then they started cheering. Seymour[3] said he had never heard them do that before. I confess to a great pleasure when I can hold the attention and stimulate the ideas of the rising generation. One feels at once that it is really worthwhile and that one is transferring something of one's experience. How different from lecturing to old women in pearls!

I have the definite impression that the new house system as adopted

---

1. *Sissinghurst,* Vita's poem published by the Hogarth Press in 1931.
2. It was a misprint. The word was "springing."
3. Charles Seymour, Master of Berkeley College, Yale University.

at Princeton, Harvard and Yale is going to revolutionize American
education. They are all aware now that the former system, while it
imparted superficial knowledge on a great many topics, did not produce educated men. I must say that the young men who asked me
questions yesterday were convincingly acute. I have a deep feeling that
America is abandoning its old quantitative standards for more qualita-
tive standards. And this will be of immense value to the human race.

After my lecture I visited the university with Seymour. Collegiate
gothic can go no further. It is really beautifully done, and I am not
sure that this style is not really more suitable to universities than the
bright brisk Georgian of Harvard. The Library is superb and all the
facilities put at the disposal of these young people are lavish, opulent
and not unwise. I went into some undergraduates' rooms. They are
better than ours, and the washing facilities are tremendous. But how
strange is the gregariousness of the American race! Each boy has a
bed-sitter in theory. In practice however they share bedrooms, sleeping
cheek by jowl, and keep the other bedrooms as joint studies. In
England no undergraduate would willingly share a bedroom with
another undergraduate. In America men are never quite happy unless
surrounded by other men. This is one of the crude sides of their
civilisation. But I like them—especially the professorial and academic
class.

HAROLD TO VITA   *Englewood*

14 February 1935

Last night's experience was very strange.[1] Dinner was rather
strained. You see, that morning Judge Trenchard had summed up in
the Hauptmann trial. He did it very well and his statement was one
of which even an English judge need not have been ashamed. Lindbergh tells me that it reads more impartial than it sounded. For
instance, he kept on saying to the jury, in going over some of Haupt-

---

1. Harold had been in England during December and January, and now returned to America
   to complete his book on Dwight Morrow. He reached Englewood on the very day when
   Bruno Hauptmann was found guilty of murdering the Lindbergh baby.

mann's evidence, "Do you believe that?" Now that sounds all right when read in print. But what he actually said was, "Do *you* believe *THAT?*" Anyhow, the jury had been in consultation five hours when we sat down to dinner and a verdict was expected at any moment. They knew that the first news would come over the wireless so that there were two wirelesses turned on—one in the pantry next to the dining-room and one in the drawing-room. Thus there were jazz and jokes while we had dinner and one ear strained the whole time for the announcer from the court-house. Lindbergh had a terrible cold which made it worse.

Then after dinner we went into the library and the wireless was on in the drawing-room next door. They were all rather jumpy. Mrs Morrow, with her unfailing tact, brought out a lot of photographs and we had a family council as to what illustrations to choose for the book. This was just interesting enough to divert, but not to rivet, attention. Then Dick Scandrett[2] came over to see me. It was about 10.45. The Lindberghs and Morgans and Mrs Morrow left us alone. We discussed Dwight for some twenty minutes. Suddenly Betty [Mrs Morrow] put her head round the huge coromandel screen. She looked very white. "Hauptmann," she said, "has been condemned to death without mercy."

We went into the drawing-room. The wireless had been turned onto the scene outside the court-house [at Flemington, New Jersey]. One could hear the almost diabolic yelling of the crowd. They were all sitting round—Miss Morgan with embroidery; Anne looking very white and still. "You have now heard," broke in the voice of the announcer, "the verdict in the most famous trial in all history. Bruno Hauptmann now stands guilty of one of the foulest . . ." "Turn that off, Charles, turn that off." Then we went into the pantry and had ginger beer. And Charles sat there on the kitchen dresser looking very pink about the nose. "I don't know," he said to me, "whether you have followed this case carefully. There is no doubt at all that Hauptmann did the thing. My one dread all these years has been that they would get hold of someone as a victim about whom I wasn't sure. I am sure about this—quite sure. It is this way . . ."

And then quite quietly, while we all sat round in the pantry, he

2. Dwight Morrow's nephew.

went through the case point by point. It seemed to relieve all of them. He did it very quietly, very simply. He pretended to address his remarks to me only. But I could see that he was really trying to ease the agonised tension through which Betty and Anne had passed. It was very well done. It made one feel that here was no personal desire for vengeance or justification; here was the solemn process of law inexorably and impersonally punishing a culprit.

Then we went to bed. I feel that they all are relieved. If Hauptmann had been acquitted it would have had a bad effect on the crime situation in this country. Never has circumstantial evidence been so convincing. If on such evidence a conviction had not been secured, then all the gangsters would have felt a sense of immunity. The prestige of the police has been enormously enhanced by this case.[3]

Poor Anne—she looked so white and horrified. The yells of the crowd were really terrifying. "That," said Lindbergh, "was a lynching crowd."

He tells me that Hauptmann was a magnificent looking man. Splendidly built. But that his little eyes were like the eyes of a wild boar. Mean, shifty, small and cruel.

HAROLD TO VITA   *Cuernavaca, Mexico* [4]

22 February 1935

Such a marvellous morning. I woke up in my little cottage and flung open the door. A blaze of sunshine and plumbago greeted me. The datura in my little patio smells even in day time. There is a feeling of something more tropical than Tangier or Sicily. It is given, I think, by the banana trees which are in fruit. A Gauguin effect with the soft footed gardeners in their huge hats. The hoses have sprinklers, and sparkle on the grass. I go up terrace after terrace on wide tiled steps

3. It is only right to add that considerable doubt has since been thrown on the evidence, and that Hauptmann may have gone to the electric chair an innocent man. See, particularly, Ludovic Kennedy's *The Airman and the Carpenter,* 1985.
4. Dwight Morrow was American Ambassador to Mexico, 1927–29, and he bought this house at Cuernavaca.

edged with huge vases of geraniums and heliotrope. The swimming pool on the central terrace reflects oleander and a blue sky. The awnings are lowered over the upper patios. It is more than summer.

After tea last night we walked in the little town. There is an old baroque cathedral rather tumbled down. There is the palace of Cortes who lived here after the conquest. There are the gardens of the villa inhabited by Maximilian and Carlotta.[5] For the rest, it is exactly like some small Spanish town—Ronda or Algerciras. Along the lane behind the house trot rows of donkeys like at Fez. Thud thud thud thud.

The disadvantage of this place is that it is a weekend resort for Mexico City. I foresee that we shall be overwhelmed with visitors. But here in my cottage (which reminds me of the Villa Pestillini [Florence] cottage) I am detached. I hope to work well here.

We dined out of doors. After dinner we went up to the mirador and looked out over the dark little town to distant shapes of mountains. Popo [catepetl-volcano] was not visible. He is extinct. But what a terrible menace he must have seemed flaming up there among the stars.

Bless you my own darling. I wish you were not six thousand miles away. I cannot get rid of the loneliness and home-sickness which that thought produces. And I hate not to share these vivid pictures with you.

HAROLD TO VITA

11 July 1935

Deacon Brown's Point,
North Haven, Maine

We had an almost perfect day yesterday.[6] The sun was very hot but the air was scented with fresh seaweed and pines. I must say this island is a divine spot. It must be exactly like the Western Highlands, with distant mountains, a whole archipelago around one, morning mists, and heavy rain-drops on the pines.

---

5. Ferdinand Maximilian of Austria, Emperor of Mexico, 1864–67, and his wife, Princess Charlotte of Belgium.
6. Harold had returned to the United States to work on his proofs of *Dwight Morrow,* and brought his elder son Ben with him, then aged twenty.

Ben and I worked all morning in our little cottage. He is doing Bismarck. I was doing the final revisions to my proofs and starting on the index. After luncheon we watched Lindbergh doing stunts in his little scarlet aeroplane. It is a divine little instrument, and he plays with it like one plays with a canoe on a swimming pool. Up there in the high air he flashed and dived and circled above the sea and islands just like a boy plunging in the sea. The scarlet wings flashed in the sun and then darkened to shadow.

Then he came down and we played tennis, or rather Ben and the Lindberghs played tennis. I sat and watched with a book. Ben plays a good style but inaccurately. Like my handwriting, it looks efficient from a great distance.

Our dear Benzie—what a strange person he is! He is so absolutely himself. He isn't shy exactly, since he never appears embarrassed or awkward. But he is very silent, intervening but seldom in the conversation. Yet his agreeable smile saves him from appearing morose.

It was a lovely day and we sat on the terrace looking down on the sea and the islands. Anne said to him, "Would you like to come sailing this afternoon?" "No," said Ben, "sailing bores me." I confess that I was rather taken aback. I reproved him afterwards, but he said, "I think it wrong to pretend to like a thing which I don't like. You always say, Daddy, that you hate music." I then explained that he had put on his 'voice', and that his remark sounded not merely like a curt refusal but like a snub. He was terribly distressed by this and brooded over it. I asked Anne afterwards whether she had thought him rude, and what was one to do between telling people to be absolutely frank and yet training them to observe social conventions. She said that she liked him for it. But all the same Ben does lack zest: it is so beautiful here, and the bathing and tennis and general charm of the place render him happy: but he does not show it; he just mouches around looking bored. I know that he is not bored in the very least. But they, who expect high spirits and affability in the young, must feel him very 'dumb' and 'effete'. But perhaps not. One is unduly sensitive about the impression people of whom one is very fond make on other people of whom one is fond. He loves Anne, who is angelic to him. He likes Mrs Morrow. He is thrilled by Lindbergh.

HAROLD TO VITA *Ritz Hotel, Paris*

30 August 1935

On the train from Dieppe I found myself in a compartment with three Americans—aged father, middle-aged mother, and much bespotted son. The mother was of the talkative type and kept on drawing the attention of her son Junior to the beauty of France. "Junior," she said to him, "you reeely must look. You remember Mrs Furnivall said that the part between Dieppy and Purris was vurry vurry interesting." Junior merely grunted and went on reading *Time*. And I, pretending to read Charles Lamb, wondered how a woman of over forty could still suppose that Dieppe was called Dieppy. Then the passport man came in. "Les passeports, s'v'plait, M'ssieurs, mesdames." "Junior," screamed the old lady, "go and get your father: he is in the washroom." And in truth the old man had disappeared. "Pass! Pass!", said the conductor breaking into English. When the incident was over, she leant back and with dreamy eyes said, "I reely must learn that word for passport—I reely must—it was 'pass-pass' that he said, Junior. Let's remember that."

Now you know how I always determine to be kind to Americans, especially the dowdy sort. But I did not help on this occasion. I think she thought I was French as I was reading the *Matin*. But when I picked up Lamb which was obviously an English book, she began throwing out leading questions. "My," she said, "look, Junior, that house had Mairie written on it. Now that can't be like our Mary, can it? How I wish that someone could explain these things to me. I find them so *interesting*." But I did not offer to explain.

Then the father came back from the washroom and slept heavily so that the mother had to cease her chatter. I crept out and went and had some tea. When I got back, we were only some forty minutes from Paris. I wanted to smoke my pipe and the father had woken up. I thought it time to emerge from my reserve. "Madam," I said, "would you object if I smoked a pipe?" "Why no," she answered, as if I had pulled the plug of an enormous lavatory, "go right ahead. I always say to my son, don't I, Junior?—I always say, a pipe is a *clean* smoke—now a cigar . . ." and on that she let forth a perfect Colorado River on the subject of cigars. The ice having thus been broken, she paddled ahead exuberantly. They were going to Geneva, for the Conference of course, so difficult to get rooms—so on, so on. I identified him as the rather insignificant correspondent of some Methodist journal in Milwaukee. The old man eyed me sleepily. I had told the old lady that I was off to Venice for a week. "Why," said the husband, "for only one week?" So I explained to him that there was a crisis over a country called Abyssinia, that we took one point of view and Mussolini the other—in fact I explained the whole situation to him in clear, but very simple, terms. "Is that so?", he said from time to time. He was a nice old bedint and my heart warmed to them. I would help them at the station and see them to their hotel—after all I was in no hurry and they would be so utterly lost.

By that time we were running into Paris. "Batignolles," read the old lady on a signal box, "Now whatever can *that* mean?" I assured her that it meant much the same sort of thing as Englewood meant Englewood. "Fancy that, now," she answered, nodding her head wisely. "St Lazare Poste I" flashed by. "Now that, I suppose, means Lazarus like in English, the raising of Lazarus you know, Junior!" "Perhaps," I said, "you will allow me to help with your luggage and things?" "Well that's reel kind of you, mister, but they are coming to meet us."

They were. For as we emerged onto the platform there were three obvious American secretaries from the Embassy and some photographers. The eldest of the secretaries advanced and raised his hat. "Senator Pope?" he enquired of the old man.[1] I bolted to a taxi.

I jumped inside. "Grand Hotel," I shouted. Then I lay back and thought it over. Had I really said anything foolish? Since Senator Pope, as you know, is Roosevelt's Colonel House and has been spending the last three days locked in the embraces of Sam Hoare [Foreign Secretary] and [Anthony] Eden. Had I said anything very foolish? Now why is it that I am exposed so often to situations as absurd as this? I blushed at the thought. I slid the little window aside. "Non pas le Grand Hotel," I shouted, "l'Hotel Ritz, Place Vendôme."

As a matter of fact I did not show off in front of Pope. But ten years ago I would have.

---

1. Senator James P. Pope was then aged only fifty-one. He was a lawyer by profession, U.S. Senator from Idaho, 1933–39, and then Director of the Tennessee Valley Authority. He had married Pauline Horn in 1913, and they had two sons.

In October 1935 Harold was adopted as National Labour candidate for West Leicester, and on 14 November he was elected to Parliament with the narrow majority of eighty-seven over his Labour opponent. Immediately he became involved in great issues of foreign affairs. Hitler reoccupied the Rhineland and Mussolini invaded Abyssinia. Vita, as the following letter shows, did not share his political interests, preferring her garden and her books (Saint Joan of Arc, Pepita, and her poem Solitude were published in this period) to the social and political dramas like the King's Abdication, which Harold was experiencing in London. They wrote to each other every day when they were apart, and spent the weekends alone together at Sissinghurst. Lady Sackville's death in January 1936 gave Vita more financial security, and she refurnished much of the house with her mother's treasures.

28 October 1935

My darling Hadji—I fear you have gone away hurt—and I mind that dreadfully. It is no good going over old ground, so I won't—only to say that apart from what you called 'principle', I do genuinely think that an isolated appearance [in Leicester] would be worse than none, because of its inconsistency, and that it would lead to bazaars and things *after* the election, if you get in, as I do very truly and sincerely hope you will. Still I am more sorry than I can say to have hurt you, but do remember, darling, that we had always been agreed on this matter even before you got adopted, and I quite thought that your views coincided with mine—as I still think they did, until agents and people started badgering you. Do remember also what I said last night, that I had always cared very very deeply about your writing and even your broadcasting (don't murder me!), and my admiration for your very rare gift, which I rate *far* higher than you do, is great and has always been accompanied by the very deepest interest, so don't run away with the idea that I "have never taken any interest," as you said, in the things which mattered to you. You know as well as I do, if you stop to think, that this is an absurd contention!

Darling, don't let this make a rift?

Mar

H A R O L D   T O   V I T A   *Leicester*

10 November 1935

Yesterday I spent the morning canvassing. You know that I am not very good at intruding into other people's lives—and this was in my own interests. "Good morning, Mrs Brown, may I come in for a moment? I hate to disturb you, but as I was visiting round here, I thought you might wish to have a look at the candidate." Mrs Brown has a look in which the emotion of disgust struggles unsuccessfully with the emotion of contempt. "My vote's my own," she snaps. "Good morning, Mrs Brown, and a nice day isn't it? Quite a brisk snap in the air this morning." "My vote's my own, anyway, and I won't tell even the old man which way I'm using it." "Quite right, Mrs Brown, that's the spirit, and I wish all the electors felt the same. Goodbye to you, Mrs Brown." The latter makes no answer, and we then knock next door at Mrs Smith.

Of course I do not have to do much of that side of the business myself, and really only did it as there was nothing else to do at the moment and I wanted to give a good example to my workers. One cannot expect them to do the work one hesitates to do oneself.

Then in the afternoon I attended two football matches. There was tea at half time and my two opponents Crawfurd [Liberal] and Morgan [Labour] came up and talked to me. Crawfurd is hell—very slimy and unreliable. But Morgan is a delicious sturdy man whom I liked at once. I am glad that if I do not get in, he will get in.

I got back late to my office. The woman downstairs said, "Oh Mr Nicolson, a gentleman has just been in to see you—a friend he said he was." "What was he like?" I asked. "Oh, he was very tall and thin and a little blind I should say from the glasses he wore, and he is round at the hotel waiting for you." So round to the hotel I went, and there was Aldous Huxley wearing the strangest clothes. I gave him some tea; and he talked for an hour. I have never heard him talk so readily or so brilliantly. It was like the most perfect hose compared to a tea-pot with a broken spout. He seemed to think it perfectly natural to find me standing National Labour, and he encouraged me enormously just by taking it all for granted and saying that he admired me for doing it. I shall always like him more for that visit. He took me right away from the Turkey rugs of the Grand Hotel and the mud-baths of ignorance and meanness in which I have been wallowing of late.

Then in the evening was one of those bloody working men's clubs and a bright little speech from me.[1]

HAROLD TO VITA   *4 King's Bench Walk*

20 November 1935

We went into dinner. I found that being the only man who has ever *gained* a seat for National Labour I was regarded as a museum piece. I talked to Ramsay.[2] He is a fine battered figure and I love him. He was so *pleased* with my success. "My dear Harrold—that was a grrrand fight—a grrand victory—and mark you, I *know* Weest Leicester—you must have had an ungodly task."

Afterwards over coffee in a private room he discoursed to us in the old campaigner style about the future of the National Labour Party. I confess that it was somewhat like King Charles I addressing

1. On 14 November Harold won the seat, after a recount, with 15,821 votes over Labour's 15,734 and Liberal's 4,621.
2. Ramsay MacDonald, former Labour Prime Minister, now leader of the National Labour Party.

the Cavaliers from the Whitehall scaffold. Yet out of all the muddled truculence of the thing there did in fact emerge an idea. It was this. "In your hands rests the future of Tory Socialism. You eight people are the seed-bed of seminal ideas. The young Tories are on your side. Work hard: think hard: and you will create a classless England."

HAROLD TO VITA   *4 King's Bench Walk*

20 February 1936

When I got to the Londonderry party, there was a dear little patapouf in black sitting on the sofa, and she said to me, "We have not met since Berlin," and I sat down beside her and chattered away all friendly thinking meanwhile, "Berlin? Berlin? How odd? Obviously she is English, yet I do not remember her at all. Yet there is something about her which is vaguely familiar." While thus thinking, another woman came in and curtsied low to her, and I realized it was the Duchess of York.[1] Did I show by the tremor of an eyelid that I had not made her out from the first? I did not. I steered my conversation onwards in the same course as before but with different sails: the dear old jib of comradeship was lowered and very gently the spinnaker of "Yes Ma'am" was hoisted in its place. I do not believe that she can have noticed the transition. She is charm personified.

HAROLD TO VITA   *4 King's Bench Walk*

11 March 1936

Hitler has behaved with a completely reckless regard for morals, and yet he probably thinks he is behaving splendidly. Anthony Eden's statement on Monday was superb and last night we had good speeches from Winston and Lloyd George. There is no doubt that we should refuse to negotiate with Germany until she evacuates the Rhineland and should force her out of it. It is really essential to demonstrate that

---

1. For his first meeting with the Duchess (later Queen Elizabeth) in Berlin, see pp. 214–215.

Treaties cannot be torn up by violence.[1] But the difficulty is that public opinion in this country is really afraid. Terrified of war. Actually frightened. And the result is that we shall give way to Germany and let down France—from sheer lack of courage. Not that I regard courage as a high virtue. But the fact remains that when one country is brave and the other cowardly, the latter is apt to get the worst of it in battle. Anyhow we shall scramble out somehow and achieve peace with dishonour. You can count on that.

VITA TO HAROLD   *Sissinghurst*

29 April 1936

How people can say life is dull in the country beats me. Take the last 24 hours here. An extremely drunken man had left his pony to be tried in the mowing machine. So it was put in the mowing machine; I watched; all seemed satisfactory; I went away. So did the mowing machine. Kennelly [gardener] sent it away without saying a word to me or to Copper [chauffeur] who is supposed to be responsible for it. Copper arrived in a rage in my room and abused Kennelly. I went and cursed Kennelly, who indeed was in the wrong. In the evening at about 9, I was told that Punnett [builder] wanted to see me. I went out. He was in tears, having just found his old father drowned in the engine tank, and a note written to himself saying it was suicide.

Next morning, i.e. today, George [Hayter, manservant] came to fetch me: Copper would like to speak to me. I found Copper in the garden room, covered in blood with a great gash in his head. Kennelly had come into the garage and knocked him down without any warning. He had fallen unconscious, and had come round to find Kennelly throwing buckets of water over him. He had then tried to strangle Kennelly, and they had only been separated by the arrival of Mrs Copper. So I sent Copper to the doctor in George's car, and meanwhile sent for the police. Accompanied by the policeman I went out in search of Kennelly, whom we found very frightened and white. He was

---

1. Hitler's seizure of the Rhineland territories on 7 March 1936 was in violation of the Treaty of Versailles and the Locarno Pact. Britain and France took no action to oppose him.

ordered to go and pack his things and leave at once. So that was that, and we are now without a gardener.

Copper is in bed with a splitting headache, and I fear a touch of concussion. If he hadn't been so knocked out I really believe he and Kennelly would have half killed each other.

HAROLD TO VITA   *4 King's Bench Walk*

11 June 1936

The great event of the day was Sibyl's [Colefax] dinner-party. Poor Sibyl—I had a feeling that it was her swan-song, but nonetheless it was a very triumphant one.[1] I arrived to find everything lit up lovely and the guests assembling—the Stanleys, the Brownlows, the Lamonts, the Rubinsteins, Bruce Lockhart, the Vansittarts, Buck De La Warr. I sat between Lady Stanley and Lady Brownlow. There were two tables. Our young King [Edward VIII] and Mrs Simpson sat at one, and the [Thomas] Lamonts sat at the other. Then when the women went, we all sat at the King's table, and I talked to Stanley about the Navy. Afterwards I took the King downstairs. He said that the Lindbergh dinner had been a great success. Anne had been rather shy at first, "but with my well-known charm I put her at ease and liked her very much."

Then we returned to the party. Rubinstein[2] started to play Chopin. More people drifted in—the Winston Churchills, Madame de Polignac, Daisy Fellowes, Noel Coward, the Kenneth Clarks.[3] Madame de Polignac sat herself down near the piano to listen to Rubinstein. I have seldom seen a woman sit so firmly: there was determination in every line of her bum. It was by then 12.30 and Rubinstein (who is sadly losing his looks) had played his third piece. It was quite clear that he was about to embark upon a fourth, and in fact Madame de Polignac was tapping her foot impatiently at the delay. Then the King advanced across the room: "We enjoyed that

1. Her husband, Sir Arthur Colefax, an eminent lawyer, had died on 19 February, and his widow was selling Argyll House in Chelsea.
2. Arthur Rubinstein, the Polish pianist, then aged forty-eight.
3. Kenneth Clark was Director of the National Gallery, 1934–45.

very much, Mr. Rubinstein." So that was that, and he then said goodnight all round. But by then more guests had arrived, Gerald Berners and others, and by the time H.M. had got half through the guests, we at our end by the piano had forgotten his presence, and Noel Coward started to strum a jazz tune and to croon slightly. At which the King immediately resumed His Royal Seat. And I much fear that Rubinstein and Madame de Polignac must have thought us a race of barbarians. Nonetheless it was very welcome when Noel sang *Mad Dogs and Englishmen* and *No, Mrs Worthington,* and even if Madame de Polignac failed to smile throughout, the rest of us relaxed somewhat. So that when an hour later the King really did leave us, the party had gone with a swing.

I was glad for Sibyl's sake, since I fear it is her last party in that charming house and never has it looked so lovely. She managed it well. She only made one mistake, and that was to sit on the floor with Diana Cooper to give a sense of informality and youth to the occasion. But Sibyl, poor sweet, is not good at young *abandon.* She looked incongruous on the floor, as if someone had laid an inkstand there.

But the important part, my dearest, is the following. I talked to Kenneth Clark. After December there will be a vacancy as Honorary Attaché at the National Gallery. Would Ben take it? After a year he could look about for a paid job. Clark suggests that in the interval he ought to go to Munich, Dresden, Berlin etc. and really master the galleries of Europe. What do you think about all this?[4]

VITA TO HAROLD   *Sissinghurst*

16 June 1936

While I was at Brighton yesterday I found some papers which absolutely thrilled me.[5] These were the depositions of the Spanish witnesses taken before the Knole succession case. They are *exactly* like the Jeanne d'Arc witnesses: all labourers and suchlike people, living in a little village in Spain. I have not read them through yet, but have

---

4. The proposal matured. It was the first step in Ben's career as an art historian.
5. Lady Sackville had died in her house near Brighton on 30 January. The papers that Vita found formed the basis of her book about her grandmother, *Pepita.*

read enough to make my mouth water. They are all people who knew Pepita and her mother.

VITA TO HAROLD   *Sissinghurst*

2 July 1936

I got such a nice letter from you this morning. I quite see what you mean about not minding if they [The House of Commons] think you dynamic, vitriolic, and violent. But I do think it would be a pity if you gave them any handle for thinking you unbalanced. What I mean is, that judgement is what really counts in the long run—not 'safety first' exactly, but a considered judgement delivered as vigorously as ever you like, so long as it *is* considered. I think that in the long run this is what wins respect in public life, more than any amount of brilliance and wit, both of which you have. And in your case, you have so much of both that people might be liable to mistrust you—you know what English people are. Take Winston as a warning. You see, it is very easy for a person like you to acquire a position and a reputation for brilliance, but very difficult to reverse it later on into a reputation for good sense and sobriety. I think one ought really to start the other way round—build your house first, in fact, and then add the ornamentation. This pi-jaw is not because I think you *have* made any mistakes, but just because I don't want you to do so. You see, again, you have got such a long solid career of work behind you—F.O., Persia, Berlin, and your books—that you have a marvellous foundation to build on. Of course the part of you that I really love best is the part that goes wild, Utopian, and indignant. But everybody doesn't know you as well as I do.

HAROLD TO VITA   *4 King's Bench Walk*

16 July 1936

Lunched with Sibyl [Colefax] yesterday. Somerset Maugham, the Winston Churchills, Mrs Simpson, Prince de Monaco. Mrs Winston talked to me so sadly about Randolph [Churchill], saying he was losing his looks, his mind and his heart. She was very despairing poor woman, and I liked her more than I have liked her before. Willy Maugham was very pleasant as usual. He said (stammering), "I-I-I am the m-m-most interesting person here. I knew Mrs Simpson when she was *a* Mrs Simpson and not *t-t-the* Mrs Simpson."

HAROLD TO VITA

22 September 1936

St Martin, Im Innkreis, Austria

I confess that I find my host and hostess a trifle vulgar.[1] But kind—so kind—so kind to impoverished royalties.

But Chips is really not a snob in an ordinary way. I suppose everybody has some sort of snobbishness somewhere, just like everybody has a few keys somewhere. Even you have a Sackville snobbishness, just like you have a huge key which you put down (together with Sarah's lead and a piece of groundsel and a worm-powder) upon the table in my sitting room. Some people have a whole lot of keys on trusses. But what makes Chips so exceptional is that he collects keys for keys' sake. The corridors of his mind are hung with keys which open no doors of his own and no cupboards of his own, but are just other people's keys which he has collected. There they hang—French keys, English keys, American keys, Italian keys and now a whole housekeeper's room truss of Central European keys. The word 'mediatized' is frequently on his lips: could he pronounce the word *Durchlaucht* [Serenity] that also would figure in his conversation, but the German 'ch' is not within his scope. So it is all Fritzy Lichtenstein and Tuti Festitics and the Windisch-Grätz twins and Cuno Auersperg ("My favourite man, absolutely my favourite man").

Today he goes over to Naziland to lunch with the Törings.[2] They foresaw that I would not want to come. "I am," I explained, "not good

---

1. The host was Henry ("Chips") Channon, the M.P. and diarist, and the hostess was his wife, Lady Honor Channon.
2. Countess Töring was the daughter of Prince Nicholas of Greece and the sister of the Duchess of Kent.

at that sort of thing." "Nonsense, Harold, what do you mean by 'that sort of thing'?" "Greek Royalties." "Well, of course, if you won't, you won't." I think they are rather glad, really, as I expect they want to talk to Countess Töring (who sounds less böring than her bloody father and her shy shambling sister of Kent) about the said Kents. And they might feel that I was looking on and listening in that tiresome way I have.

But how gay and lovely is this rich and ancient country. The villages have baroque frontages in blue and pink with pretty stucco work. A Fürstenstein and a Schillingfürst came to dinner and to sleep. Young men very full of smart English society. I suppose it was always like that, and the Austrians always did regard the *Gräfliches Taschenbuch* [Dictionary of Aristocrats] as the very pillar of life. Chips calls Honor "Frau Gräfin" to the servants. He is not very good at German but he has got that bit quite correct. "Frau Gräfin zurück?" he asks. And they bow. Well, I suppose that's all right, and I do not quite see what else he could call her. All I know is that it would never enter my head to call you Frau Baronin any more than it would enter your head to call me Herr Baron. Shall we start?

HAROLD TO VITA

28 September 1936

Villa Mauresque,
Cap Ferrat, France

I do not believe (if I recollect aright) that you have ever been fired out of a cannon. I have. It happened last night in the station yard of Monaco. Having glanced behind him, the chauffeur turned a switch, at which the car trembled slightly and then shook and gave six loud reports like fifty horsemen of the Apocalypse. It then sprang into the air, cleared the barrier, hurtled sideways past a tram, and flung itself with reckless abandon up the hill by Château Mallet. The moon on my left hung over a silent sea and seemed to swing rapidly westwards as the earth flew below us. Snorting furiously with great raucous snorts, the car crashed through Beaulieu and on to the corniche road. Other humbler cars going in the same direction flashed past my window with a woof as if they were in fact going in the opposite direction.

And then we came to the curves. Round we went, the chauffeur leaning out sideways to fling his weight on the inside, in and out, round and round. The precipices, the tunnels, the rock-arches, the great caverns cut above the sea, roared back at us. I thought of you and Ben and Nigel and my poor widowed mother and my little sister. I know I ought to have said, "Please do not go so fast: j'ai une petite *phlébite.*" But I have got Scotch and Ulster blood in my veins. I clenched my teeth. I clung on in grim terror, and suddenly there were the lights of Villefranche swinging round to the right as if someone were swinging them at the end of a string, and with a scrunch of brakes and a rattle of gravel we crashed into the drive and actually stopped at the front door. Staggering slightly, I entered the white hall, and there were Willie and his nephew[1] and Osbert Sitwell.

HAROLD TO VITA   4 *King's Bench Walk*

4 November 1936

I went to a party given by Mr Baldwin [Prime Minister] to the junior Ministers at No. 10. We all sat round the Cabinet Table and old S.B. read out the King's Speech. He then talked to us about what to say, and we had some delicious sherry and it was all rather fun. I cannot conceive how I ever disliked old Baldwin. He is such a dear old thing and so amusing. I asked him whether in my speech I should mention the King. He said, "Yes, but if I were you, I should not mention Mrs Simpson—not in so many words."

I woke up with a sinking feeling and at 12 I went to the opening of Parliament. It is a fine sight. The King looked like a boy of eighteen and did it well. But his accent is really worse than Philippa's [Harold's niece] at her most cockney stage. He referred to the "Ammurican Government" and ended, "And moy the blessing of Almoighty God rest upon your deliberoitions."

I then lunched at a snack bar and got into my [diplomatic] uni-

---

1. Somerset and Robin Maugham.

form. I joined Miss Horsburgh[1] in the Chief Whip's room and we were conducted to seats exactly behind the Prime Minister and Ramsay MacDonald. The Speaker then read the Speech and called upon Miss Horsburgh. She delivered her little piece quite beautifully, in a slow voice and without a tremor. She was very warmly applauded.

The Speaker then called on me. I had been told to follow the precedents, and the precedents prescribe that one must allude to one's constituency and then mention previous holders of the seat who have won distinction. This made it essential for me to mention Ramsay. I knew that this might not go down very well, so I prefaced it by saying, "My constituency, which maybe in a moment of blindness, refrained from electing the Rt. Hon. Member for Epping" [Churchill]. Winston at this flashed out, "They also refrained from electing the Rt. Hon. Member for the Scottish Universities" [Ramsay MacDonald]. At this the Labour Party let forth a hoot of triumph and thereby broke the solemnity which is supposed to reign on those occasions. Thus it became increasingly awkward when I passed on to my eulogy of Ramsay. They yelled. They hooted. Our people shouted, "Order! Order!" On I went, heaping upon Ramsay's head, which was exactly below me and bowed in acute misery, the compliments which I had prepared. Will Thorne, who is a decent old boy, tried to quiet his companions by shouting out, "This is not controversial," but the clamour did not die down until I had finished my bit about Ramsay and passed on to the rest of my speech.

That went well enough. But the incident was unfortunate since it created an impression of a floater whereas it was really an act of courage.

HAROLD TO VITA   *House of Commons*

5 November 1936

All the talk as usual was about Mrs Simpson. The extreme view is that the Cabinet should employ a gangster to murder her. I regard

---

1. Florence Horsburgh, Conservative Member for Dundee. She was the first woman to move the Address, and Harold was to second it.

that view as too extreme. But there is no doubt that they fear his marriage, and that there will almost be a revolution if it occurs. The main feeling is one of fury that this empty-headed American who has twice been divorced should bring this great Empire to the brink of a very grave crisis. My own view is that I am sorry for her and blame him. How can one expect a Baltimore girl to appreciate the implications of her action? Sibyl [Colefax] tells me that Mrs Simpson is getting rattled and that there is terrible ill feeling between her and the Royal Family. Not only will she split the Empire but she will put her David [the King] against his brothers and mother. What a mess!

HAROLD TO VITA   *House of Commons*

10 December 1936

We expect the blow to fall today.[1] I dread it. It is horrible. But I am sure that abdication is the only course. We may have to take a new oath of allegiance on Saturday. What a little ass the man is to plunge us into this disorder! I cannot but suspect that Mrs Simpson has convinced him that she is in a family way. Otherwise he could scarcely be so obstinate. But none the less, as things have turned out, abdication is his only card. I feel so sad about it, since it will take years for Albert the Good [George VI] to build up a legend comparable to that of his brother, and during those years the socialist feeling in this country will have grown beyond proportion.

HAROLD TO VITA   *House of Commons*

15 December 1936

I lunched at the Club with Tommy[2] who is so relieved at the fall of his master that he was almost indiscreet. He said that some disaster

---

1. The King's Abdication.
2. Sir Alan Lascelles, Private Secretary to the Prince of Wales, 1920–29, and to King George VI, 1936–43.

was certain to arrive sooner or later. He suspects indeed that the King and Mrs S. had laid all their plans to run away together last February and that the death of King George did them in. He says that the King [Edward VIII] is like the child in the fairy stories who was given every gift except a soul. He said that there was nothing in him which even understood the intellectual or spiritual sides of life, and that all art, music, poetry etc. were dead to him. Even nature meant nothing except forms of exercise and his garden at the Fort [Belvedere] meant nothing beyond a form of exercise. He enjoyed nothing at all except through his senses. He had no friends in this country, "nobody whom he would ever wish to see again." He called all respectable people 'Victorian', and all educated people 'high-brows'. When he succeeded, he shirked his duty terribly. The Private Secretaries had a devil of a time. He would disappear every Thursday to Tuesdays to the Fort and they could not get at him. Even when he was in London he shut himself up in Buckingham Palace with Mrs S. and they giggled there together for hours.

Tommy told me of the great row he had had with him when he was his Secretary in Canada and the United States. Tommy resigned the position, and then for one hour and a half he told him what he thought of him. The King took it well. "Yes, Tommy," he said, "I was not made to be Prince of Wales." I really believe that Tommy is glad he is gone. "He was without a soul," he kept on saying, "and this made him a trifle mad. He will probably be quite happy in Austria. He will get a small *schloss;* play golf in the park; go to night-clubs in Vienna; and in the summer bathe in the Adriatic. There is no need to be sorry for him. He will be quite happy wearing his silly Tyrolese costumes (there was a note of fury at that), and he never cared for England or the English. That was all eye-wash. He rather hated this country since he has no soul and did not like being reminded of his duties."

I daresay that this is all true, and it is some comfort to me. Tommy is a very sane and loyal person and I trust his judgement in these things. "The new King," he said, "will be first class—no doubt about it."

Well, thus encouraged I went down to the House and took my oath to George VI.

VITA TO HAROLD   *Sissinghurst*

18 January 1937

I do wish Sissinghurst were not quite so inflammable. It's as bad as Dottie. I was washing peacefully in the bathroom before breakfast this morning, when Pat [Hayter] came knocking at the door to say the tower was on fire. It was. Smoke was pouring out from between the cracks in the bricks, so we sent for Punnett who tore out the fireplace in my sitting room and discovered a huge beam glowing red all through. We poured minimaxes [fire extinguisher] on to it, and the danger was averted, but it has been an awful business getting the beam out and my poor room is in an awful mess.

The smoke has made my room uninhabitable, so I shall spend a useful afternoon doing the books in the big room. It is pouring and blowing a gale, so there's no temptation to go for a walk. The fire insurance people will begin to think we do it on purpose!

VITA TO HAROLD   *Touggourt [Algeria]*

26 February 1937

Darling, I think Touggourt is one of the most magical places I ever struck! On arrival by full moonlight I thought the hotel was white, but next morning discovered it to be the colour of a ripe peach, with bright blue shutters and balconies. It has a big garden, mostly palms, but next door is the *jardin publique,* which is full of flowers—stocks, marigolds, flox, nasturtiums—and also contains wire cages with hyaenas and a little local animal called a fenouk, which is something like a tiny fox only with enormous ears. The town is pure white, and the sand honey-colour; the population dressed almost entirely in white, with occasional cloaks of blue, red, russet, and orange. The sun is so hot that, like everyone else, we have been obliged to buy solar topees, and Gwen [St. Aubyn] is wearing cotton frocks. It is like a hot August in England.

But the best of all was last night. We gave, rather unintentionally, a party. It included Lord Beauchamp,[1] who has turned up here accompanied by a sulky, embarrassed and bored young man called George, whom I take to be the footman you saw on the P. and O. The party came about in this wise: I asked the local guide (a most charming nomad Arab called Dadi), whether there were any dervishes here, and he said that he would get one to come and do his stunts for us in the garden after dinner. It would cost 60 francs. We agreed. But on going out after dinner we found the entire sect of dervishes squatting grouped round little fires, and most of the population of Touggourt as well, with a band of some four or five musicians with drums and flutes—a savage looking lot with their dark faces and white turbans. Even the presence of a Spahi in his scarlet cloak did little to reassure Gwen, who is convinced that there is about to be a revolution.

Then the music struck up, and an old man like a coal-black monkey crept out of the circle and began to dance. Meanwhile the others were heating long needles in the little fires, and when these were red-hot he stuck them into his cheeks, through his ears and into his arms, till as he danced he rattled like a porcupine. Before long he was joined by others; you could see which one was going to creep out next, for they would start to shiver all over, and sway, and crouch. One horribly skinny object flung himself on the ground and started digging with his hands in the soft sand like an animal. They thrust a stick between his teeth. I asked Dadi why. *"C'est pour l'empêcher de mordre quelqu'un,"* he replied casually; *"il est complètement fou, il ne sait pas ce qu'il fait."* Luckily Gwen did not overhear this remark. Then he sprang up and seized two flaming palm-fronds from the fire; he danced and twirled, holding them close to his face, close to his naked chest, close to his throat just under the chin, while the flames streamed all over him in the night. There was worse to come. The young chief of the sect suddenly joined in, stripped to the waist; a piece of wood with about 12 or 15 steel nails, about 5 inches long, was produced, and with a wooden mallet he banged the row of nails right into his stomach. Yet when they had torn it out of him there was not a mark, not a drop

---

1. An immensely wealthy, popular peer, who had been a member of Asquith's Wartime Cabinet. His wife, a sister of the Duke of Westminster, had died in 1936.

of blood. The most horrible of all was when another man plunged a long curved dagger into his stomach.

HAROLD TO VITA *Cairo, Egypt*

27 February 1937

Dear me, I was sorry to leave Khartoum. I found Gordon College fascinating as a problem and the roof of the Palace the best roof there ever was. The administrators were intelligent and friendly, and the weather divine. Now it means farewell to topees and tropical suits, and that cold shiver which will last till June. I was not made for northern climates. I am a child of the Sun—Akhnaton, Ammon, that sort of thing.

I wonder whether you have derived from my [diary] carbons the intense enjoyment I have got out of this commission.[1] Not only has it been enthralling in itself, but it has taught me a great deal that I did not know before. Oh God! Age, age, age! How intolerable it is not to be young. Time's winged chariot has become an aeroplane (not Imperial Airways but a RAF bomber), and I feel that there will not be nearly enough time for me to do all that I want to do. Darling, what a consolation it is for people of fifty to feel that they have at least not wasted one hour of life in the past. Had I strolled through my middle years I should feel enraged today. As it is, I say, "It sinks—and though not in the very least ready to depart[2]—at least I have not dawdled on the way."

Fifty has been a terrible landmark for me. A great gallows upon my primrose path. I suppose I shall get over it. But God doesn't understand somehow that I was not intended to be old. I am a young man by nature. I cannot make him see that. He allows me to get old just as if I was Lord Salisbury. Which I am not. But no grumbles, darling. Only gratitude for being able at the age of fifty to fling into a visit to the Sudan all the energy and zest of a boy of 23.

---

1. He was a member of a Government Commission to report on African education.
2. "I warmed both hands before the fire of life;
   It sinks, and I am ready to depart." Walter Savage Landor

HAROLD TO VITA   *4 King's Bench Walk*

22 April 1937

Poor Mrs Koestler came to see me and cried on the bench of the lobby. She is the wife of a *News Chronicle* correspondent who has been missing for a month in Spain.[1] We suspect that Franco has done him in, although all enquiries are met with, "He is alive and well." But of all atrocities it seems to me that the worst is this keeping of widows in suspense. Anyhow I said I would do what I could, and got hold of Vansittart who was good about it and admitted that our Seville Consul was slack and timid, and sent him there and then a snorter to say, "This must stop. You must insist on seeing Koestler if they claim he is alive." In such matters it is of great advantage being in with the F.O.

Then off I went to a dinner in the French Embassy. Very grand and good. It was in honour of Daladier, the Minister of Defence.[2] He is to be Prime Minister one day. A dreadful little man he seemed, and so bedint in comparison with our own people. There was Halifax, Duff Cooper, Stanley, Philip Sassoon, Derby, Inskip and the rest of our Cabinet, whom I have never regarded as beauties or patricians, looking like Roman Senators compared to this little Iberian visitor.

HAROLD TO VITA   *4 King's Bench Walk*

29 April 1937

The Guernica bombardment was really horrible.[3] It looks as if it had been carried out by the Germans without the consent of Spanish headquarters. They deliberately swooped down on the escaping women and children and machine-gunned them. The feeling in the

---

1. Arthur Koestler (1905–83), author of *Darkness at Noon,* etc. He was imprisoned by Franco for four months, March to June 1937, daily expecting execution. His first wife, Dorothy Asher, campaigned vigorously and successfully for his release. He divorced her in 1950.
2. Edouard Daladier, French Minister of Defense, 1936–38, and Prime Minister, 1938–40.
3. Guernica, a small town in the Basque province of Vizcaya, was totally destroyed by German aircraft on 26 April. 1,654 people were killed and 889 wounded.

House is very bitter—and only that ass Teenie [Victor Cazalet] goes on sticking up for Franco. I could have boxed his silly ears. Anyhow, we are trying to rescue as many women as we can before a similar fate overwhelms Bilbao. The Foreign Office have behaved splendidly.

I do so loathe this [Spanish civil] war. I really feel that barbarism is creeping over the earth again and that mankind is going backwards. It is terrible that the invention of the aeroplane should have given such an advantage to ruthlessness and placed pity and gentleness at its mercy. I feel very deeply about this—right deep down in myself among the hidden shynesses and other things. I wake with it as one wakes with some dread or sorrow.

VITA TO HAROLD   *Sissinghurst*

30 April 1937

I do so agree with your feelings about the war and the other wars for which everyone is preparing. I really feel at moments that Bertie Russell is right and that we ought to retire from the competition, not merely for our own safety but to give a lead away from this insane barbarism. Quite obviously, *in the long run,* we would some day be acknowledged as the first to take a step towards true civilisation—but would anybody follow our example? I doubt it. After all, they wouldn't disarm when we wanted them to. And what about the peoples for whom we have made ourselves responsible? Yet for the sake of civilisation it is the only thing to do. How difficult it is to decide between such things as our national pride and our much advertised sense of responsibility, and our real desire for peace in Bertie Russell's meaning of the word. Would we be really justified in letting other nations partition our Empire, in letting India cut her own throat? Or do we only pretend to ourselves that we wouldn't be justified, just because we want to keep our proud possessions?

It makes me cross when the House spends days discussing Cabinet Ministers' salaries, when there are these appalling problems—and others such as strikes and poverty and cancer and unemployment.

HAROLD TO VITA   *4 King's Bench Walk*

21 July 1937

My speech [on Foreign Affairs] seems to have gone better than I
had supposed. Many people have come to congratulate me upon it. It
is extraordinary how these things seem to affect temperature. If one
makes a good speech even the policemen at the door seem to salute
with greater deference. After a failure, it is as if the very pigeons
avoided one's eye. This is of course mainly subjective. But I think there
really is something in the fact that no institution on earth shows so
much barometric variations as the House of Commons. Nor can any
triumph be more sweet than a real oratorical triumph in the House.
I wonder if I shall ever have one.

I lunched with Mary Spears.[1] Maggie[2] was there like a fat slug.
She said, "You know, Harold my dear, the one thing I cannot stand
in life is unkindness in any form. Especially people who say unkind
things about other people behind their backs." With that little exordium she began to take out her fountain-pen-fillers one by one and
inject oily poison into everything. She is now very much the *Reine
Mère.* How comes it that this plump but virulent little bitch should
hold such social power?

HAROLD TO VITA   *4 King's Bench Walk*

8 December 1937

I breakfasted with old Baldwin[3] at his house this morning. We
were alone. He was sweet, and we talked of literature and politics for
an hour and a half. He was generous about everyone except Lloyd
George who, he said, had done his best to debauch British politics and
"had never led a party or kept a friend." He showed me the little

1. Mary Borden, the novelist, wife of Sir Edward Spears, soldier and historian.
2. Mrs. Ronald Greville, who from 1906 until her death in 1942 entertained lavishly in
London and at her house Polesden Lacey, Surrey, now a property of the National Trust.
3. Stanley Baldwin, Prime Minister, 1923–29 and 1935–37. On his retirement he was created
Earl Baldwin of Bewdley. He died in 1947.

pencilled note which was the last communication sent him by King Edward VIII. Such a childish scribble. He is leaving it to the British Museum.

I have never enjoyed a breakfast more. I take back everything I have ever said against that man. He is a man of the utmost simplicity and therefore greatness.

HAROLD TO VITA   *4 King's Bench Walk*

15 February 1938

I had a word with Sibyl [Colefax] about Ben. She said that he had seemed in tremendous spirits, chattered the whole time and was a most delightful companion. She also said that Berenson[1] had said he was the best student he had ever had. I said, "But surely not?" She said, "Those were his words—and you know that B.B. is not apt to be agreeable."

What a mystery Ben is! Wretched at Eton, and one of the greatest social successes Oxford has ever had. Hopelessly lazy, and then he gets so good a second [class degree] that he almost got a first. Incompetent and dreamy, and yet manages to impress Berenson. I can't make him out. Are we too sceptical, or others too credulous? I wish I knew. Bless you, my dearest, who shares with me these worries as no one else does or ever could. Because they are worries to me. I love my sons so deeply. It is my domestic instinct.

HAROLD TO VITA   *House of Commons*

9 March 1938

I had a depressing day yesterday. We had a private meeting at Chatham House[2] to discuss the present situation. We came to the

---

1. Bernard Berenson, the American art historian, with whom Ben had been working at I Tatti, his house outside Florence.
2. The Royal Institute of International Affairs.

unhappy conclusion that now that Russia has dropped out we are simply not strong enough to resist Germany. Or rather we did not come to so extreme a conclusion. But we did feel that 80 million fully armed Germans plus the Italians were more than we and France could safely take on. What tremendous things have happened in these five years! We are suddenly faced by the complete collapse of our authority, our Empire and our independence. Poor England.

Then I dined with [Sir Edward] Spears. Vansittart[3] was there. He was most gloomy. He thinks that we can scarcely prevent Germany collaring Eastern Europe, and that when she has done so, she will turn round on us and demand our submission. Well, it may not work out like that. But opinion is at the moment as gloomy as in the days after Austerlitz [1805]. Nobody who is well informed believes that there is any chance of negotiations with Germany leading to anything at all. We may get some little scrap out of Italy but it will be a mere crumb of comfort and quite unreliable.

Jolly, isn't it? My dearest, do not worry about these things but cultivate your lovely garden. I wish you were here nonetheless. You always soothe all my ruffled feathers, and make me as sleek and gay again as any Bantam.

HAROLD TO VITA   *British Legation, Bucharest*

17 April 1938

As I walked upstairs I felt strangely giddy.[4] The staircase seemed to shift and wobble. I was appalled. Supposing I came over faint during my luncheon? That would be hell. I arrayed myself miserably in the tail-coat of Rex Hoare [British Minister] which would not, I regret,

---

3. Robert Vansittart, who had been permanent Undersecretary at the Foreign Office since 1930, was demoted to "chief diplomatic adviser" to the government, after he lost the confidence of the Prime Minister, Neville Chamberlain, for opposing the policy of appeasing the Dictators.
4. Harold was on a lecture tour of the Balkans on behalf of the British Council, and had been invited to lunch with King Carol of Rumania. Having left his own frock coat behind, he was obliged to borrow that of his host, the British Minister in Bucharest.

Harold Nicolson in 1930, the year when he abandoned diplomacy for journalism and politics. (Photo courtesy Howard Coster)

The entrance range of Sissinghurst Castle, built in 1490 and restored by the Nicolsons in the 1930s.

The Nicolsons at Sissinghurst in 1932.

Vita and Harold at Smoke-Tree Ranch in California, 1933.

The Elizabethan tower at Sissinghurst.
Vita's writing room was behind the
first big window above the archway.
(Photo courtesy Country Life.)

With her dog Rollo in the
orchard at Sissinghurst.

Charles and Anne Lindbergh, 1934.
(Photo courtesy The Bettmann Archive)

The yew "rondel" at Sissinghurst in the center of the rose garden, which Harold designed and Vita planted. (Photo courtesy L. & M. Gayton)

Harold with Bertrand Russell (left) and Lord Samuel at a broadcast discussion on the BBC's Overseas Service in 1951. (Photo courtesy BBC)

Vita in 1955, aged sixty-three.

Vita and Harold outside the South Cottage, Sissinghurst, in a photograph taken in 1959, three years before her death.

Three generations in 1962, in a photograph taken a few days after Vita's death. Harold, Nigel, and Nigel's son Adam. (Photo courtesy Edwin Smith)

meet in front. But it looked all right. Then I espied the bottle of Sal Volatile which I had bought at Cambridge when I had to deliver the Rede Lecture after an all-night sitting. I corked it tightly and put it in my pocket. Then off I went.

At the Palace an aide-de-camp in stays and aiguillettes arrived and made polite conversation. Then a lift hummed and two little pekinese darted in barking followed by the King in naval uniform. I bowed. He greeted me with affection and respect. We passed into the dining-room. I sat on his right. The aide-de-camp sat on his left. The pekinese sat on his knee. We started conversation.

He had ordered, he said, a purely Rumanian luncheon. God, it was good! In spite of my feeling so faint, I gobbled hard. I sat there on my pink plush chair and ate the *marimagi* and the *olovienic* and the *gruzaka*. We talked agreeably. He is a bounder but less of a bounder than he seemed in London. He was more at ease. His Windsor-blue eyes wistful, and he had something behind them. Was it sadness, or overwork, or mysticism? He spoke with intelligence about Chamberlain and Eden and the Italian Agreement and the French Cabinet and the League of Nations. He was well informed and most sensible. We kept all debating topics away.

I had been asked nonetheless to try and tackle him about his dictatorship and the Hungarian minorities. I got on to the former subject by saying how difficult it was for us not having a good Opposition; how the basis of a democracy was an alternative Government; how the Labour people did not offer a possible alternative; and how bad that was for everyone concerned. He rose to the bait. He said that he also was experiencing that difficulty. It had been necessary for him to clear away the old party politicians (and indeed they were a poor lot), and he must now build up again three more parties. "Why three?" I asked, my mouth full of *lutchanika*, "Your Majesty," I added. He replied that two parties were apt to share the spoils between them, and a third party was necessary to restore the balance. Quite a good idea.

I was beginning to enjoy my conversation when I became aware of a cold trickle and the smell of ammonia. I thrust my hand into my pocket. It was too late. The Sal had indeed proved Volatile and my trousers were rapidly drenched. I seized my napkin and began mopping surreptitiously. My remarks became bright and rather fevered, but quite uninterrupted. I mopped secretly while the aroma of Sal Volatile rose above the smell of *gruzhenkoia*.

This was agony. I scarcely heard what he was saying. "Have you," he was asking, "recovered your land-legs yet? After three days in the train one feels the room rocking like after three days at sea." So that was it! Why on earth had he not told me before, and now it was too late. I recovered my composure and dropped my sodden napkin. The conversation followed normal lines. At 2.45 he rose abruptly. I rose too, casting a terrified glance at the plush seat of my chair. It bore a deep wet stain. What, oh what, will the butler think? He will only think one thing.

HAROLD TO VITA   *4 King's Bench Walk*

2 May 1938

My luncheon to meet Ethel Smyth[1] was not really successful. She arrived in a state. Her hair was coming down and she mistook her muffler for a handkerchief. I knew that she was frequently and inordinately committing this mistake, but I forebore to say so. One must forebear on such occasions, since it is difficult to say, "Do you realise you are blowing your nose on your muffler?" when one has to say it through a machine that looks like a cinema apparatus. She is really stone deaf. She carries this machine about, but she always turns it the wrong way round, and she interposes between her headphone and her ear a whole wad of untidy grey hair. Not one word does she hear. Moreover, her train had arrived one-and-a-half hours before luncheon, so she had gone to the Paddington Hotel and sat in the lounge reading P. G. Wodehouse. She had drunk sherry after sherry and was quite biffed. But what a magnificent fighter all the same! It is like a Moscow veteran in 1852 telling stories of Borodino.

---

1. Dame Ethel Smyth, the composer and suffragette, was then eighty.

HAROLD TO VITA   *4 King's Bench Walk*

30 May 1938

It was nice seeing those hulking young men[1] together. I am always impressed by their relations with each other. Although utterly different in character, they have for each other a sort of amused respect. Isn't it ghastly to imagine that two people who deserve and get so much from life may be nipped off by a bullet? That is a terrible thing.

I cannot really believe that humanity will not see before it is too late that there is nothing heroic about war but only a foul foolishness. To that extent the Canton bombings are a lesson. I do not mean that I wish this lesson to be inculcated upon the Chinese, but I do think it is less fatal to civilization that Canton should be bombed than London or Paris. I do really believe that we shall unite in this country and in other countries to say, "This thing must cease." But the anomaly of it all is that we can only do so by arming. Strength and justice has worked in the Czech crisis. Perhaps we can extend it.

HAROLD TO VITA   *Waddesdon Manor,*
                                  Aylesbury
17 July 1938

Oh my God, how odd my arrival here was! I was all untidy after a long train journey, and I was ushered into a vast saloon sprinkled with bridge tables occupied by the racing set—Hillingdons, Bessboroughs[2] and God knows what. There was not a soul I really knew. I was greeted warmly by Mrs Rothschild and then presented to Princess Mary who was gracious—gracious me she was gracious. Then I sat down and watched them playing poker. Hillingdon was tight, which was rather awkward.

I can't tell you what this house is like. It is vast, 1870, Italianate stucco. But hardly a thing has been changed since the old Baron's

1. Ben, now twenty-three, was Deputy Surveyor of the King's Pictures under Kenneth Clark; and Nigel, twenty-one, was still at Balliol College, Oxford.
2. 3rd Lord Hillingdon, banker, soldier, former M.P.; and 9th Earl of Bessborough, Governor General of Canada, 1931–35.

time.[3] There are marvellous pictures and Sèvres, but execrable taste. Jimmy[4] hates anything being altered, and the lavatories still have handles you pull up instead of chains you pull down. There is no running water in the bedrooms, and although it is all very luxurious as regards food and drink and flowers, it is really less comfortable than our mud-pie in the Weald.

I came down to breakfast. Hillingdon was there, very red about the gills. Then Harry Lascelles[5] came in. Hillingdon asked him if he minded a cigarette. "Yes I do," answered Lascelles. "Well now I know," said Hillingdon, continuing to puff his cigarette. A slight strain descended upon the breakfast room. I think on the whole (miserable as your decision was in its consequences) that it would have been even more fraught with disaster if you had married Harry Lascelles instead of me. Oh my dear Mar, really you would not have liked it in the very least.

H A R O L D　T O　V I T A　　　　　　　*4 King's Bench Walk*

26 July 1938

My own dearest,

I had time yesterday to read your poem.[6] In fact I read it three times. Once in the train. Once after luncheon in the library. And once before I went to bed.

I had rather dreaded that I should find it vague and metaphysical. I also had a sort of fear that it might be too ambitious in the way that *Genesis* [Dorothy Wellesley's poem] was too ambitious. That was silly of me. Your greatest gift is perhaps an extraordinary sense of propor-

3. In 1874 Baron Ferdinand de Rothschild built this elaborate house on a Buckinghamshire hilltop, and surrounded it by a Victorian formal garden. It is now a property of the National Trust.
4. James de Rothschild, M.P. for the Isle of Ely, 1929–45, and a Trustee of the Wallace Collection.
5. Henry Lascelles, 6th Earl of Harewood, who had been much in love with Vita before her marriage, and married Princess Mary, daughter of King George V, in 1922. He was a Steward of the Jockey Club and a Trustee of the British Museum.
6. *Solitude.* Hogarth Press, 1938. Its themes were reflections on love, God and the universe, beauty and truth, life and death.

tion in all important things. It is very odd. In little things your s. of p. is almost as bad as B.M.'s. But in big things it is the best I know.

Now instead of a metaphysical or didactic poem, I get one of the loveliest things I have read for years. It is 'pure poetry' in the sense that it makes no appeal to sentimentality or mere lilt. When I say 'pure poetry', I mean a passage like that on page 16, "Then strength and beauty came into my hands . . ." That very sentence is pure poetry. The use of simple words in the right order, so that each one takes on a special value. The whole of that passage is superb.

But what a strange thing poetry is! Why are the first four lines on page 12 so lovely?[7] I mean they might so easily be ridiculous— Brendan Bracken and a bird. And yet somehow they are lovely lines. Absolute poetry.

It is a lovely sombre poem, beautifully written, absolutely sincere, and poetry rather than verse. I should put it No. 3 of your poems. *Sissinghurst* comes first. *The Land* second. This third.

I am so proud of you, my darling. I think you are someone apart from all the rest of the world. But I don't think that blurs my judgement. If I had read this poem as if it were by someone else, I might have approached it in a more critical mood. But I should certainly have felt when I had finished it that I had had a new experience—something as sombre and sincere as a meadow at night.

Bless you my dearest,

Hadji

VITA TO HAROLD   *Sissinghurst*

3 August 1938

I went to Rodmell last night, and very nice it was too. We sat out in the garden watching the late sunlight making the corn all golden over the Downs. Then I had a long talk this morning with Virginia

---

7. "As once Saint Brendan cast his harp aside
   When he had heard
   Gabriel in the plumes of a white bird
   Singing within the Temple as day died."

[Woolf], who was in her most delightful mood. Tell your host [Somerset Maugham], if you think it would please him, that she much admired his autobiography, *The Summing Up*. She had liked the clarity of his style, and also the honesty with which he tried to get at the truth. She liked his analysis of his own methods of writing. And you know that she is *peu facile,* so, as he knows it too, he might be pleased.

She went so far as to say that although she had first got his autobiography out of the circulating library, she now intended to buy it for herself for keeps, but for goodness sake don't tell him this, or he will send her a presentation copy, and I shall be *blamiert* for having repeated what she said.

Oh my dear, what an enchanting person Virginia is! How she weaves magic into life! Whenever I see her, she raises life to a higher level. How cheap she makes people like Teenie [Cazalet] seem. And Leonard too. I know he is tiresome and wrong-headed, but really with his schoolboyish love for pets and gadgets he is irresistibly young and attractive. How wrong people are about Bloomsbury, saying that it is devitalised and devitalising. You couldn't find two people less devitalised or devitalising than the Wolves—or indeed more vitalising than Roger Fry for example. I think where Bloomsbury has suffered is in its hangers-on like Angus Davidson[1] and equivalent young men, and of course the drooping Lytton [Strachey] must have done its cause a great deal of harm. I hated Lytton.

HAROLD TO VITA   *Villa Mauresque,*
                                                 Cap Ferrat, France
4 August 1938

I am glad I came here. It really is the perfect holiday. I mean, the heat is intense, the garden lovely, the chair long and cool, the lime-juice at hand, a bathing pool if one wishes to splash, scenery, books, gramophones, pretty people—and above all, the sense that it is not going on for long.

I was met by the car and told the man that my *phlébite* was very

---

1. He had worked for the Hogarth Press for three years until 1927, and was now living in Cornwall writing a biography of Edward Lear.

bad this year, so would he go slowly. He did. Then I was met by Willy [Maugham] at the door. He has an old-fashioned courtesy about these things. Rather bedint about it. There has been a terrible drought and I expect Willy is selfish about water. Anyhow the garden was as cool and as green as could be and I had a lovely bath. I sat and read for a bit as Willy went off to work. Then the Paravicinis appeared. He is Willy's son-in-law and really beautiful. The daughter is just a mar.[1] I have not made her out. Very pretty in a way.

I am afraid that this household is on the capitalist side, and they do not feel for Leon Blum[2] those emotions of respect and admiration which are felt by others. They regard Communism as the greatest of all dangers, and their conception of the German menace is, "Well, why not give Hitler Togoland and the Cameroons and Tanganyika if only he allows us to keep our yachts and villas." Of course I may exaggerate all this. On the one hand my loathing for fascism is due to the fact that I hate the type of mind that believes in brute force. It is not nobility on my part but a sort of physical loathing which I suppose is based on cowardice. Conversely, we doctrinaires have not come across Communism in fact. Willy and Gerald Haxton[3] have. Down in the harbour at Villefranche there is acute Communism and they see what harm it does to the decent people. For instance, the Italian boats used to put in here on their way back to America. The dockers refused to handle their stuff so that they now cut out Villefranche—with the result that the whole port loses about £200,000 a year. This means real loss to all the little people. I think Gerald Haxton (who knows the people here intimately) is quite sincere in hating the reds for this alone.

I had a lovely afternoon. I went out in his little yawl to bathe. We crossed the bay, anchored under the rocks opposite, got out the harpoon gun, gazed into the depths for fish, found none, bathed in warm water, sat on deck and drank in the sun and the sea and the sky. I do not want to do that for ever, and I should die of ineffectiveness if I spent my whole time in delights of the body. But really, when one has a clear conscience about public work and so on, it is a halcyon thing to do just to sit and bask. We had with us Jojo and Lulu. Jojo's function

---

1. Elizabeth (Liza) Maugham, aged twenty-one. Her husband, whom she had married in July 1937, was Vincent Paravicini, son of the Swiss Minister in London.
2. Socialist Prime Minister of France, 1936–38.
3. Somerset Maugham's companion and secretary until Haxton's death in 1944.

I understand—he is the sailor who works the boat. Lulu's status in life was less evident. Gerald Haxton described him as "a friend from Nice." But when Gerald was swimming round with his harpoon, Lulu told me that he had been a miner in Lens, that Gerald picked him up, brought him down here, and he was now very happy training to be a tailor. *"Oui, monsieur, et quand je dis tailleur, c'est bien entendu de la haute couture que je parle."* He was himself exquisitely dressed or rather undressed. Perfectly manicured and decapilatorised.

When we returned to the shore, Lulu leaped into a beautiful little two-seater and buzzed off. "Tailors' apprentices," I murmured to Gerald, "must be very well paid in Nice." "They are," he answered.

HAROLD TO VITA   *Villa Mauresque, Cap Ferrat*

5 August 1938

I had a bath, shaved, and put on my best clothes. Because the late King of England [the Duke of Windsor] was coming to dinner. Willy Maugham had prepared us carefully. He said that the Duke gets cross if the Duchess is not treated with respect.

When they arrived Willy and his daughter went into the hall. We stood sheepishly in the drawing-room. In they came. She, I must say, looks very well for her age. She has done her hair in a different way. It is smoothed off her brow and falls down the back of her neck in ringlets. It gives her a placid and less strained look. Her voice has also changed. It now mingles the accents of Virginia with that of a Duchess in one of Pinero's plays. He entered with his swinging naval gait, plucking at his bow-tie. He had on a *tussore* dinner-jacket. He was in very high spirits. Cocktails were brought and we stood around the fireplace. There was a pause. "I am sorry we were a little late," said the Duke, "but Her Royal Highness couldn't drag herself away." He had said it. Her (gasp) Royal (shudder) Highness (and not one eye dared to meet another).[1]

---

1. King George VI had informed his brother that the Cabinet had advised him that the title Royal Highness could not be extended to the Duchess.

Then we went into dinner. There were two cypresses and the moon. I sat next to the Duchess. He sat opposite. They called each other 'darling' a great deal. I called him 'Your Royal Highness' a great deal and 'Sir' the whole time. I called her 'Duchess'. One cannot get away from his glamour and his charm and his sadness, though I must say he seemed gay enough. They have a villa here [at Cap d'Antibes] and a yacht, and go round and round. He digs in the garden. But it is pathetic the way he is sensitive about her. It was quite clear to me from what she said that she hopes to get back to England. When I asked her why she didn't get a house of her own somewhere, she said, "One never knows what may happen. I don't want to spend all my life in exile."

HAROLD TO VITA   *4 King's Bench Walk*

10 October 1938

My Leicester speech went off well. There were 2,500 people in the de Montfort Hall which is its full capacity. I was very loudly cheered. I spoke on democracy and made no allusion to the crisis.[1] But the audience were all Workers Educational Association and that sort of person. Left-wing and therefore pro-me. The people against me are the ladies of Leicester. Isn't it terrible that the destinies of the Empire should rest in the hands of such as them? I feel terribly sad about democracy. I do not think we can survive. And now Hitler tells us what Ministers we are to have and what Minister will be disagreeable to him. What a terrible speech and what a slap in the face! That is the worst of Germans. Once they have knocked you down they cannot resist kicking you.

I found Bertie Jarvis[2] very distressed. There is a meeting of the Association on Thursday and I shall have to come up for it. A frightful bore. They will probably ask me to pledge myself to support Cham-

1. The crisis provoked by Hitler's threat to annex Czechoslovakia, and the meeting at Munich on 29 September between Hitler, Mussolini, Chamberlain, and Daladier. Hitler had obtained almost everything he wanted without a war. Harold strongly criticized Chamberlain.
2. The Chairman of Harold's Constituency Association.

berlain. I shall do nothing of the kind. It is just possible that the women will turn me out. If that happens, I think I shall regret not having resigned my seat as a noble gesture. But Bertie seems confident he can keep me in. I expect I shall get away with it.

VITA TO HAROLD   *Sissinghurst*

14 November 1938

I know you will never forgive me, but I *can't* go to this party.[1] I wrote to Jay's and discovered that an evening-dress would cost at least £30, and the adjuncts (shoes, underclothes, gloves etc.) another £10. Well, that seems to me wicked to spend on personal adornment for one evening. It was silly of me ever to say that I would go to it. Gwen [St. Aubyn] says that it would be wrong of me to funk it, and that I *must* go. But I am too shy. And if I went to this party, I should be being false to myself. I am writing this letter with my jewels littered all around me—emeralds and diamonds, just taken out of the bank— and they make me feel sick. I simply *can't* buy a dress costing £30 or wear jewels worth £2,000 when people are starving. I *can't* support such a farce when people are threatened that their electric light or gas may be cut off because they can't pay for their arrears.

HAROLD TO VITA   *4 King's Bench Walk*

7 February 1939

Really Chamberlain [Prime Minister] is an astonishing and per-plexing old boy. This afternoon (as you will have heard) he startled the House and the world by proclaiming something like an offensive

1. A dinner at Buckingham Palace on 16 November in honor of the King of Rumania. At her death in 1962, only one evening dress was found in Vita's wardrobe. It dated from 1927.

and defensive alliance between us and France. Now that is the very thing that all of us have been pushing for, working for, writing for, speaking for, all these months. And the old boy gets up and does it as if it was the simplest thing on earth. The House was absolutely astounded. It could not have been more definite.

Now what does it all mean? Is he really so ignorant of diplomacy as to assume that this means little? I cannot believe that. The F.O. would never have allowed him to make the statement without his being quite certain what it meant. Moreover, he spoke so resolutely and so deliberately. The House cheered loudly. It was superb. I felt happy for the first time for months.

But this is a complete negation of his 'appeasement' policy and of his Rome visit. He has in fact swung suddenly round to all that we have been asking for. What does it mean? I think it can only mean that he realizes that appeasement has failed. It is at this stage that his value as a diplomatic asset becomes operative. No ordinary German or Italian will ever believe propaganda telling him that Chamberlain is a 'war-monger'. I feel so pleased about it since I feel that our constant unexpressed opposition has had some effect. I am so glad that we all lay low all this time and allowed facts to speak for themselves.

Yet still I have the awful doubt lest he (being so abysmally ignorant of foreign policy) may not have understood what was meant by his statement. But if he did understand what he said, and if he did mean what he said, then all differences are over. I know very well that he will say, "But how foolish of you to doubt me." I know very well that in saying this he will be talking rubbish. There must have been some very unpleasant information that drove him to make this statement. But how odd these things are. My line was, "You are mad to trust the Dictators." His line was, "Appeasement is the only policy." Now that he sees we were right and he was wrong he can say, "Wasn't it clever of me to try appeasement first? I always knew that it would come to this. You tried to force me into a breach before I had convinced the world how pacific I really was!" He may say that. But it isn't true. He is a convert—not an original believer. But so long as he does the right thing, God knows all personal scores or triumphs mean nothing.

Happy for once—since I think *this* may give us peace.

VITA TO HAROLD   *Sissinghurst*

13 February 1939

I have really nothing to say at all except that Mr Armstrong is coming to look at the orchids this afternoon. And that's of no interest, compared with the full life you lead.

I do feel so dull always, compared with your life.

I like my life, and don't envy yours, but at the same time I often feel how dull and rustic I must appear to you.

Anyhow, I have spent the whole morning writing poetry (though no doubt Spender, Auden, etc. wouldn't call it poetry at all), and that gives me some sense of justification. *"On fait ce qu'on peut,"* as the French priest said.

Je fais ce que je peux—which is very little, I know, but if I can write a few decent respect-worthy verses I am doing of my best. And I suppose that if one means to be "a good sweet pea," in your phrase, one must be the best sweet pea one can.

Darling, you are such a very *right* person in everything you do. I was so struck by your saying you had re-written your review last Saturday, because you thought it was slops. How many people would have let it go, even though slops, when they were as tired as you must have been? *How* I respect you for that probity! It is one of the many things that makes me respect you as I do. You know, or perhaps you don't know, I respect you (quite apart from loving you) as the most respect-worthy person I have ever known. I think you go wild and injudicious on occasion, but fundamentally I know that your values and standards are permanent and honest and indeed noble.

HAROLD TO VITA   *House of Commons*

7 March 1939

I had to dash up to Leicester yesterday. Jarvis wanted me to take an early opportunity of saying that I agree with the Government's present policy. Which indeed I do. So up I went and spoke to a woman's meeting.

They do not really understand what it is all about, and I spoke more for the local press than for my audience. What it really boils down to is that the ordinary elector does not want to be worried. He *loathes* fuss, anxiety, apprehension or even being obliged to think. Thus what he really wants to do is to say, "Leave it all to Chamberlain," and he is therefore annoyed if anyone throws doubt upon Chamberlain's infallibility. Moreover (and this is what inflames peoples' tempers) they have a subconscious feeling of guilt. They feel dimly that we behaved badly to the Czechs and that we did not conduct ourselves with our usual courage and calm. Now Chamberlain has rendered cowardice and treachery respectable. This is why people get so cross.

HAROLD TO VITA   *4 King's Bench Walk*

8 May 1939

How lovely it was this week-end! It was such a happy time for me, beginning with my silly little boat[1] (oh my dear—how I love the sound of foam against a boat!) and fortified by the fact that squalid little tub though she be, she is really quite habitable, and has taken a distinct liking for myself—and then the beauty of the garden afterwards. I really do think that you have done a great work in that garden. It is so like yourself.

I have got an up on Benzie. He is so keen on his present job[2] and so determined not to be dilettante about it. He says he will get to know every print and picture in Buckingham Palace before his little Queen [Elizabeth] comes back. I thought it rather moving all the descriptions of their departure.[3] They are a great asset. Just think how miserable we should all feel today if our national feeling were symbolised by Wallis Simpson. The Queen (and he also in a way) are really representative of what is best in our national character. I have always been a

---

1. Harold bought a yawl, which he christened *Mar,* and hired a crew of two to sail her at weekends.
2. Deputy Keeper of the King's pictures.
3. It was the first visit of a reigning British monarch to the United States.

monarchist. And when I saw the *Europa* creep into Southampton against all the background of the *Victory* and the *Repulse* and the flags and the simple people feeling so happy, I felt that we were in fact invincible.

V I T A   T O   H A R O L D   *Sissinghurst*

19 June 1939

I must write to tell you how excellent your speech was yesterday afternoon.[1] It was really a work of art in the beauty of its construction and development; its simplicity, logic, and reasonableness in the sense of the 'reasonable man'. I was deeply impressed. It was like watching a beautiful piece of architecture grow before one's eyes, in a quick-motion way, rather like those films which show one a nasturtium attaining its full development in an hour. As I listened to you, I felt that you were not only my charming Hadji, but also a creative artist moulding your clay into a shape like a chalice.

I don't think I had ever realised before how deeply you reflected the truly Greek and also the Christian spirit.

Darling, what a combination! What an influence you are, and ought, to be! 'The Good Pagan'—yes, you are that, but also the Good Christian although you don't subscribe to any orthodox religion. How far more Christian you are than many so-called Christians!

Of course I have always realised this about you, but it is odd that a speech of 40 minutes should have made me realise it even more vividly after 25 years. I suppose it was because I was seeing you and listening to you objectively, as 'the speaker', not as Hadji who takes Martin down to bathe and folds his pyjamas neatly before catching the 8.50 train. It produced a queer division in my mind—you, so familiar, standing on the platform, dressed in the neat stripey suit I know so well, the handkerchief I have so often rescued from the laundry sticking out of your pocket, and then the public Harold Nicolson

---

1. At the Barn Theatre, near Tenterden, Kent, on "Foreign Affairs and Public Opinion." Harold wrote in his diary, "I did not enjoy it at all."

standing up to address an audience, becoming a stranger, a public figure, and yet remaining Hadji just the same, blinking at the lights.

Darling, it was a beautiful speech. I say 'beautiful' with intention. You will laugh, because you make similar speeches all the time, and this letter will sound to you like fan-mail. But I do mean it; out of the deeps of my soul.

HAROLD TO VITA   *4 King's Bench Walk*

17 July 1939

Benzie rang up. He said, "Daddy, I have been asked to the Buckingham Palace Ball on Wednesday and I suppose it is all right to refuse?" I said, "No, you cannot possibly refuse." He said, "But I am dining out that night for another dance." I said, "Well, that may be, but you had better not refuse." He said, "But couldn't I go to the Master of the Household and ask to be let off?" I said, "No—any hostess will understand that a command is a command, and that you as a member of the household have got to go." He said, "But I shall be so *bored.*"

That fairly got my goat, and for once in my life I cursed him. I said that if he had a first class appointment he must put up with the rough and not merely take the smooth. That if he did not do his duty in every way he would lose the job. That in any case to describe a court ball as something odious and intolerable was showing lack of intelligence. Anyhow, it proves that he has some qualms of conscience that he should have consulted me at all. But what are we to do about the boy? He has no *savoir faire* at all.

HAROLD TO VITA   *Yacht Mar, Guernsey*

15 August 1939

We had a gay time in Cherbourg since there was a fair on and we watched the merry-go-rounds and fired at the shooting galleries. Niggs was rather good at it and won a little woolly monkey. Then this morning we put out of the harbour and came on here on our way to Brest. It was without question the perfectest of sailing days that I have ever seen. A light following wind, blue dancing seas and not a cloud in the sky. We read and joked and basked in the sun and were wretched when we began to see the outline of the Islands in front of us. We passed very close to Sark and it is in truth a fine sight. Then we passed Herm and I smiled rather sadly at the thought we once had of taking it. I do not think we should have liked it. Then in we came to the harbour here and while Niggs and John [Sparrow] are busy tidying up the deck, I am here in the little cabin writing to my dearest eponym.

HAROLD TO VITA   *4 King's Bench Walk*

25 August 1939

Yesterday's meeting of the House was glum in the extreme.[1] None of the speeches reached the level of the occasion. Chamberlain was like a coroner summing up a murder case.

I had a long talk with Lloyd George and Winston. They said that it was hopeless to expect Parliament to speak out except in a secret session. We should have such a session at once and tell the P.M. what a hopeless old crow he was. I gather that he at last realizes that fact and has offered to resign, but the King (rightly) has refused to accept his resignation. Obviously the man cannot leave the ship which he has run on to the rocks. He must for the moment remain in command. But the reception which he had in the House yesterday must have convinced him that we know how much he is personally to blame for this disaster. Naturally I feel sorry for him. Who would not? but his refusal to take into the Cabinet those who had criticised appeasement has demonstrated his mean and vain side and has lost him all sympathy. The reception yesterday (compared to the ovation last September) was so cold that he must have felt it as a douche. Poor man! Poor man!

---

1. Parliament had been recalled when Russia announced a Pact of mutual support with Germany.

I cheered as much as I could, having a weak spot for lost causes. But it is a lost cause. Nor is it concerned with personalities. It is concerned with realities. We have said since 1935, "Be careful, Germany is plotting our destruction." He said, "Trust me and I shall make friends with Germany." The result is that we are today in the most dangerous position we have been in since after Austerlitz.

The Second World War began on 1 September 1939 with Hitler's invasion of Poland. Britain and France declared war on Germany two days later. Harold's first wartime task was to write, in two weeks, a 50,000-word book, Why Britain Is at War, which was published on 7 November and soon sold over 100,000 copies. He was immensely active in this period, broadcasting regularly, writing a weekly column for the Spectator, reviewing books for the Daily Telegraph, and speaking at meetings all over the country and sometimes in France. Vita remained at Sissinghurst and joined the Kent Committee of the Women's Land Army. Both their sons were soon in uniform, Ben with an anti-aircraft battery at Chatham and Nigel as an officer cadet at Sandhurst. After Hitler's conquest of Poland in less than a month, there was a lull (the "Phoney War") throughout the winter, while the British Expeditionary Force manned a section of the fortified Franco-Belgian frontier. Hostilities began in earnest in April 1940 when the Germans invaded Denmark and Norway.

VITA TO HAROLD   *Sissinghurst*

28 September 1939

I very much enjoyed seeing the Wolves. It was a lovely day and the Downs looked very beautiful in the sunshine. Virginia seemed well in health, though naturally unhappy in mind. She says the only good thing which has come out of the war for her so far is that Ethel (Smyth) has fallen in love with her next-door neighbour, who, like herself, is aged 84. For years they have lived side by side avoiding each other, but the war caused them to talk over the garden fence, with the result that they discovered they were twin souls.

Leonard told me to warn you about Kingsley Martin.[1] He says he is the worst scare-monger and rumour-monger in London, far worse in talk than in the N.S. and that half the 'stories' that go about originate with him. Allowing for wolfish exaggeration, I daresay there is something in it.

I do like the Wolves so much. They always do me good. Virginia was so sweet and affectionate to me. I was touched. She told Ethel that she only really loved three people: Leonard, Vanessa and myself, which annoyed Ethel but pleased me.

HAROLD TO VITA   *4 King's Bench Walk*

2 November 1939

We had Lord Trenchard[2] to dinner last night. He is angry with the Air Force for not attacking Germany. He says we have an immense geographical advantage and ought to use it. It is very difficult indeed for them to bomb us across the North Sea and very easy for us to bomb them across France. For instance a great many machines which get away, get away 'wounded'. Now our wounded machines can land in France. The German wounded machines have to go back across the North Sea and a very large proportion must drop into the sea before they get home. It is for this reason that he thinks the Germans are almost certain to attack Holland. But they have mighty little time to do it in. The weather has been on our side. If they do not start their attack at once they will have to wait till the Spring by which time we shall have more aeroplanes than they have.

He was most optimistic.

---

1. Editor of the *New Statesman*, 1931–60.
2. The Marshal of the Royal Air Force, who was appointed its first leader in 1918 when it became a service independent of the Army.

V I T A   T O   H A R O L D   *Sissinghurst*

12 December 1939

The Lion Pond is being drained. I have got what I hope will be
a really lovely scheme for it: all white flowers, with some clumps of
very pale pink. White clematis, white lavender, white Agapanthus,
white double primroses, white anemones, white camellias, white lilies
including *giganteum* in one corner, and the pale peach-coloured
Primula pulverulenta. [1]

H A R O L D   T O   V I T A   *4 King's Bench Walk*

1 March 1940

I had such a rush yesterday I couldn't write. I had to revise my
speeches for France, dictate a speech for Glasgow, dictate a broadcast
for France. I also had to go and see Vansittart. He is worried about
the Home Front. Not merely are the Peace Pledge Union people and
the Communists creating much havoc, but the rich right-wing appeas-
ers are getting active. Both are being much assisted by Jo Kennedy and
Maisky [2]; particularly Kennedy (who is about to return) is very dangerous. He is essentially a stupid man but he has a swollen head and
thinks he can play a great part in world politics. I see the danger of
such people. Everything is so hush and secret that the rulers can really
dictate policy without question and it is very difficult to have a good
parliamentary opposition.

I lunched with the lobby correspondents. Winston made a magnificent speech. I have never seen him in such form. He did not speak
about the war but about the House of Commons. The Prime Minister
[Chamberlain] was there and Winston could not resist teasing him. He
did not like it at all.

---

1. This idea was carried out after the war, not in the Lion Pond, which was small and sunken,
   but in the old rose garden beside the Priest's House. The "White Garden" is now the best
   known of many separate gardens at Sissinghurst.
2. The Ambassadors of the United States and the Soviet Union.

*O*n 10 May 1940, the day when Hitler attacked in the West, Chamberlain resigned and Winston Churchill succeeded him as Prime Minister. Harold Nicolson was promoted from the back benches to become Parliamentary Secretary to the Ministry of Information, under his friend Duff Cooper as Minister. Thus during the critical retreat of the British Army to and from Dunkirk, the collapse of France, the air battles over southern England, and the bombardment of London, he was in the center of events and in considerable danger, as was Vita at Sissinghurst, which lay in the path of the German bombers and on the route to the capital which the Germans would have taken if they had invaded Kent. Harold's main duties concerned civilian morale, war-aims, relations with France and the United States, and advice to the public on how to act if invasion came. His short period as a junior Minister (May 1940 to July 1941) was ended by Churchill's curt demand that he vacate his office in favour of a Labour Member.*

HAROLD TO VITA   *Ministry of Information*

19 May 1940

Things seemed a little better this morning. Duff [Cooper] went off to luncheon in the country and Winston dashed down for two hours to Chartwell. I went to lunch at the Travellers and then returned here. In the hall I met Ronnie Tree and saw from his face that something awful had happened. He took me to my room and then said that he had been to No. 10 to pick up Brendan Bracken for luncheon, and just as they were leaving, Anthony Eden and Ironside[1] flew up with

---

1. Field Marshal Sir Edmund Ironside, Chief of the Imperial General Staff, 1939–40.

NIGEL NICOLSON

haggard faces and said that Winston must be summoned back immediately. It is all terribly grave. We know no details as yet.[2] Poor Winston—having to speak on the wireless tonight!

Darling, we share together this unutterable sorrow.

VITA TO HAROLD   *Sissinghurst*

22 May 1940

My darling

How ghastly it all is. How thankful I am to think of your dug-out.[3] I begin to wonder when I shall ever see you again. Supposing Kent is evacuated, as seems increasingly likely, and I have to go? In that case I suppose the Government would be evacuated too, so we may next meet in Bristol!

I dread the possibility of Niggs being sent out [to France]. But what's the good of going on like this?

Darling, to think we should come to this! And the eventual outcome—victory, or defeat? Anyhow, you and I have always foreseen the possibility of defeat, since the beginning of the war and even before that. The only thing for us to do now is to reverse that idea and make the most of such poor hope as remains to us.

HAROLD TO VITA   *Ministry of Information*

22 May 1940

We hope to pinch the German bulge and to throw them back from the Channel. They are not there in strong force and we have already retaken Arras.[4] But you are right to feel we should be prepared. I do not know whether the Government have prepared any scheme for evacuation [of Kent] but I shall find out and you can be certain that

---

2. The Germans had broken through the French defenses and reached the Channel coast on 20 May, thus cutting off the British Army.
3. The reinforced basement of the Ministry of Information.
4. Arras was not "retaken," since it had not yet been captured by the Germans, but Allied attempts to pinch out the bulge ended in failure and the retreat to Dunkirk continued.

I shall let you know. Meanwhile you should think it out and begin to prepare something. You will have to take out the Buick and get it into a fit state to start with a full petrol tank. You should put inside it some food for 24 hours and pack in the back your jewels and my diaries. You will want clothes and anything else very precious (Barbara?), but the rest will have to be left behind. After all, that is what the French did in 1915 and we have got to do it ourselves. You might make for Devonshire. This all sounds very alarming, but it would be foolish to pretend that the danger is inconceivable.

VITA TO HAROLD   *Sissinghurst*

24 May 1940

Beale[1] came here yesterday with the officer in charge of all the searchlights in this district. He wanted to inspect the country from the top of the tower. He was very frank. It is not only parachutists that they are afraid of, but troop-carrying planes landing on our own Sissinghurst fields and the fields at Bettenham. If this happens, our tower-guard rushes downstairs, informs Beale who telephones, and shock troops are produced. They have pickets all over the district. The officer was obviously longing for German planes to choose Sissinghurst or Bettenham to land on; personally I wasn't sure that I shared his longing. Nor was Beale. "My wheat . . ." he remarked ruefully.

HAROLD TO VITA   *Ministry of Information*

27 May 1940

I am afraid that the news this afternoon is very bad indeed and that we must expect the Germans to surround a large proportion of our army and to occupy the whole of the area of Belgium and Northern France. We must also face the possibility that the French may make a separate peace, especially if Italy joins in the conflict. I warn you of

---

1. Oswald Beale, the tenant farmer at Sissinghurst.

this so that you will prepare your mind for the bad news when it comes and be ready to summon all the courage that is in you.

V I T A   T O   H A R O L D   *Sissinghurst*

29 May 1940

I am so appalled by thinking of the Belgians that I don't know what to say.[1] Not only is it a major disaster, but a real soul-hurt. I could no more have believed it of him than I could believe it of our own King. One is so shocked and incredulous that Duff's [Cooper] plea to suspend judgement is scarcely needed. He *cannot* have been a merely 5th column traitor to his own country and his allies. Yet it looks horribly like it.

V I T A   T O   H A R O L D   *Sissinghurst*

3 June 1940

Last night was one of the most beautiful nights I ever remember. I was out late by myself getting some of Beale's sheep back into the field from which they had escaped. One lamb got *égaré* into another field and I pursued it through the long wet grass, led by its bleatings and the faint glimmer of its little body. The rim of the sky was still pink with sunset, Venus hung alone and enormous, and the silhouette of the sentry appeared above the parapet of the tower.

H A R O L D   T O   V I T A   *4 King's Bench Walk*

4 June 1940

I was terribly rushed yesterday as I had to get out a memo for the Cabinet about invasion. We do not know whether to warn people

---

1. The Belgian army, on the instructions of King Leopold, capitulated on 27 May.

now or to wait until it becomes likely. It is 80 per cent probable that the enemy will attack France first and only go for us afterwards. Yet we must be prepared for the invasion when it comes and the public must be told what to do. We have got a long list of instructions, but do not like to issue them without Cabinet orders. As Duff was over in Paris I had to do all this myself.

My dearest Viti—I suppose it is some comfort to feel that it will either be all over in August or else we shall have won. Hitler will not be able to go on into next year. The whole thing is, "Shall we be able to stand it?" I think we shall. And if we do win, then truly it will be a triumph of human character over the machine.

I force myself to see things at their worst. I do not really believe in my soul that the Germans will make a successful invasion of this country, but I do think they may bring off a smash and grab at several points. But I force myself to foresee what will happen if they land at Hastings and Faversham and make a pincer movement to cut off our forces in Kent. This will mean that there will be fighting at Ashford. It means that you will be in danger. Now that thought makes my heart stand still with a sick pause. But then it beats again. You are a brave person and you have a sense of responsibility. It would not be you to run away and leave your people behind. If you are told to do it, then you must go. But I see, and you see, that you must stick it out if you are allowed to. And finally there is the bare bodkin.[1] That is a real comfort.

But actually I do not think it will come, especially if the French are able to put up some show of resistance on the Somme. How I long for the spirit of Verdun to revive! It may—you know what the French are. I feel so deeply grateful for having hard work to do in these days. And now comes Italy.[2] My dearest, what a mean and skulking thing to do. The French have offered them practically all that they want in Tunis etc., but they want more and more. They are like the people who rob corpses on the battlefield. I forget what those people are called. The Greeks had a name for it [Necrosylia].

Bless you my poppet—courage and hope.

---

1. The "bare bodkin" was a lethal pill that Harold and Vita had acquired from their doctor, for suicide in the case of capture by the German army. See *Hamlet,* Act III, Scene I: "He himself might his quietus make with a bare bodkin."
2. Mussolini declared war on 10 June.

HAROLD TO VITA   *4 King's Bench Walk*

10 June 1940

I looked in at our Duty Room to see how the map of the battle was getting on.[1] To my horror I saw that the Germans had got to Pont de L'Arche on the Seine. But it must only be a thin spear of armoured columns and we must try to cut them off. The French, we hear, are fighting absolutely magnificently. But it is dreadful that we cannot help them. We simply must do something. It is all very well getting the announcer to say, "This is our battle," and so on. We must do more than that.

If the French can only hold them up, what a triumph it would be! The Italians are playing the dirtiest game ever played. I sat down in my bath last night and said to myself, "Now be a sensible person and try and see the Italian point of view." But try as I could, I could see nothing more than the point of view of a man who waits till the merchant drops on one knee before attacking him and stealing his goods.

Darling, do you feel as I do? Never have we been threatened with such separation as we are threatened with today: and never have we been closer to each other. I feel no need to say anything to you. I just know that you and I think the same. I have found in these weeks that a love such as ours really is above space and time.

HAROLD TO VITA   *4 King's Bench Walk*

19 June 1940

We still do not know what terms the Germans intend to impose on France.[2] If they were wise they would give good terms and treat the French population very well. This will not only enable them to exploit French resources but also increase defeatism over here. I think it is practically certain that the Americans will come in in November, and if we can last till then, all is well. Anyhow as a precaution I have

1. The Germans had crossed the Somme to renew their attack on the French Army, and entered Paris on 14 June.
2. The French Government had sued for an Armistice on 17 June.

got the bare bodkin. I shall bring down your half on Sunday. It all looks very simple.

How I wish Winston would not talk on the wireless unless he is feeling in good form. He hates the microphone and when we bullied him into speaking last night he just sulked and read his House of Commons speech over again.[3] Now as delivered in the H. of C., that speech was magnificent, especially the concluding sentences. But it sounded ghastly on the wireless. All the great vigour he put into it seemed to evaporate.

HAROLD TO VITA   *Ministry of Information*

26 June 1940

I must say that the French have behaved with intolerable cowardice and treachery. They gave us their word of honour that whatever happened they would not allow the French fleet to fall into the enemy's hands but they seem to have surrendered it already. We have taken steps to prevent the rot going further. But what a collapse for a great nation! Henri Bernstein[4] told me that most of the upper classes were almost delighted at Hitler's victory since they imagined it would save them from communism. He said that nothing in Shakespeare could equal the complete moral collapse of French society. He feared that this would mean the end of France. *"Ils nous ont trahis avec une bassesse inconcevable."* They are of course trying to excuse themselves on the grounds that it was all our fault.

VITA TO HAROLD   *Sissinghurst*

9 July 1940

The army came here yesterday, looking for large country houses to use as headquarters if necessary. They were much taken with Sissing-

---

3. The "finest hour" speech.
4. The French dramatist. After the fall of France he lived in New York until 1946.

hurst, I fear, for this purpose. I don't at all relish the idea, as headquarters are apt to become the favourite target of German bombers. The army was two young officers and an N.C.O. in a lorry. One of the officers was an absolute dream of beauty and elegance, in a black cloth beret and pale tight riding breeches. Very polite they were, and I left them talking to Beale.

HAROLD TO VITA   *4 King's Bench Walk*

15 July 1940

I had such a curious and distressing experience this evening. André Cheradame came to see me. In the period before the last war he was a famous journalist and wrote books about Pan-Germanism and was quite a figure. What he wanted was that we should get him a passage to the U.S.A. and arrange about his money. Now getting him a passage means that we have to requisition a berth and turn out some wretched person whose claims may be greater than we know. Arranging his money means trouble with the Treasury. It all boils down to influence and favouritism which I loathe. Thus when Cheradame came to see me this evening, I was none too well disposed. He tottered in and said that he must take his secretary with him. All he wanted was a letter from me to say that he and his secretary were essential for national service. There was no real reason why he should not remain here.

I then realised that I had lost all sense of pity. Having adjusted my mind to the loss of my own life, I had become so hard that I did not care for the lives of others. I felt only contempt for a person twenty years older than myself who could not *"faire la mort du loup."* [1]

Anyhow this smelly trembly old man came and fiddled with papers at my desk. I was correct and calm. But I was as hard as nails. And then I felt a beast and the memory of it hangs round me. I feel ashamed of myself. It is easy to be brave if one suppresses one's own sensibilities. But it is not so easy to be brave if one tries to keep a perfect proportion between one's hardness to oneself and one's softness to other people.

---

1. Alfred de Vigny's poem (1838), which proclaims that man has a lesson to learn from the wolf, which, when cornered, licks its wounds and dies silently.

There is a tendency to feel that Hitler may hesitate to attack us now that we are so strong. But I do not believe this. I think he is bound to attack us.

VITA TO HAROLD   *Sissinghurst*

17 July 1940

I was amused by your story of Cheradame. But I am sure you were right, and what you call your hardness was merely a sense of proportion induced by the changed scale of values by which we now order our lives. Not that our essential values would ever change, but the top ones do and must. We are forced to become less soft and sentimental about personal convenience and safety. This is one effect of Nazi theories raging through Europe, and I am not at all sure that it is not a salutary effect. It may lead us to consider our personal security and prosperity a little less, and to realise the insecurity and anxieties of other people a little more. (By 'our' I mean the well-off classes.)

I see that the invasion is now announced for Friday. Don't worry about me down here if we should get separated. If the worst comes to the worst, well, there it is. Like you I have adjusted myself to the idea of losing my own life. I don't in the least want to lose it; but if I must, I must. I should worry about you, naturally. But we both have the bare bodkin. I prefer the idea of doing a Jeanne Hachette[1] on the top of the tower with Dada's shot-guns.

HAROLD TO VITA   *Ministry of Information*

19 August 1940

It was fun yesterday wasn't it—watching the aeroplanes fighting for Britain in the sunshine.[2] Our people here (I mean our air experts)

---

1. Jeanne Hachette saved Beauvais in 1472 when it was under attack by Charles the Bold. One of his soldiers had scaled the battlements, when Jeanne cut him down and flung him into the moat, thus reviving the courage of the garrison.
2. The Battle of Britain started on 13 August, and much of it took place above the Weald of Kent.

think it the best day we have had mainly because we brought down so high a proportion of German fighters in which they are weaker than bombers.

I got caught by the siren at Tunbridge Wells. We were herded into the waiting room. There were all types of people and many women and children, but there was no trace of nervousness. Generally people when they are frightened talk and laugh abnormally, but there was no sign of that at all. They read their magazines and newspapers quite quietly. Eventually my train came in and I looked out to see if I could see any damage. But none at all. There was a bomb at Dunton Green but I saw no signs of it. Also one at Tenterden. People are beginning to feel that there is no possibility of even seriously impeding this country by air bombing. I whisper to myself, "Yes, but he will start gas." But really yesterday he had 600 over, and for the damage created, we could stand 6,000. Our losses were really very slight. In this week we are as good in the air as Drake's men were at sea. It is a heartening talk. God! I feel so proud of my country! Bless it.

Vita to Harold   *Sissinghurst*

28 August 1940

We had such a raid last night: the whole of the South Cottage shook, and I am told that 6 bombs were dropped at Frittenden falling in fields only but making a horrible row. The sky over towards Tenterden was lit up with a red glow—so I suppose they must have started a fire there—I saw flares falling through the darkness.

Today, so far, we have had 3 warnings and some bursts of machine-guns overhead this morning behind the clouds.

Darling, I am appalled by something which has happened. You know I told you Violet [Trefusis] was coming here today—well, she rang up this morning to say she couldn't because her mother was returning to London, but might she come on Saturday for the night instead? I lost my head and said yes—but you will be here, and you didn't want to meet her. Anyhow I daresay it won't come off. I devoutly hope so.

HAROLD TO VITA   *4 King's Bench Walk*

3 September 1940

I read the Keats letters coming up in a belated and dawdling train. His letter to [Charles Armitage] Brown from Naples is one of the most terrifying things that I have ever read. The knowledge of his own genius ("an intelligence in splints") and the certainty of his approaching death are bad enough—but one has to add to these the obsession about Fanny Brawne. What a beast one feels her to be! The whole story is obscure. When he was staying next door to her at Hampstead she seems to have been kind; she visited him regularly and showed herself at the window since it gave him pleasure; but thereafter she appears to have become irritated by his passion, and it is clear that from his bed of sickness he writhed in agony at the thought that she was going out into the world and seeing people whom he did not know. But what essential dignity he had! That fierce integrity about poetry and his own art. He is too great even to be jealous of Byron.

Darling—if only one could have told Keats that one hundred and twenty years after his death people like you and I should in a great crisis (with death hurtling at us through the skies) write to each other in respect for him? That, I suppose, is one of the benefits of war. One ceases to think of the topical or the fashionable or even the contemporary, and falls back for comfort (which one finds) upon the beauty and the dignity of the human imagination and character. One feels the sinews of one's soul grow hale. It may be this factor which in this year of suffering has made my love for you tower like Everest above the shabby hills of self-indulgence.

HAROLD TO VITA   *Ministry of Information*

16 September 1940

We did far better yesterday than was given out. Our people decided to throw in a proportion of their reserve fighters. We got down 185 for certain but there were another 80 'probables'. This excludes the further 40 'possibles'. One can be certain that of the 60 probables, fifty were done for. That means a loss to them of 235.[1]

Everybody here is rather cocky today. It was a real defeat for the Germans yesterday and the American press is taking it up hot and strong. My dear, what a world we live in. Ugly, heroic and mad. I am ugly but I am not mad. Therefore I shall be heroic. It is very odd that I should not be more frightened. It rather worries me, since I fear I may be suppressing fear and will end in a nervous collapse. But truly I am not conscious of any fear. I am conscious only of immense curiosity and a strong desire not to die.

I shall be careful, dearest, truly I shall. I saw Vansittart today. He was 5 to 1 on invasion three weeks ago. Today he is not so sure, if it does not come tonight or tomorrow.

HAROLD TO VITA   *Ministry of Information*

2 October 1940

I attended the Cabinet Committee on Home Policy this morning. We all had to go down to the basement at one moment. We should have been a big bag as six Cabinet Ministers were there. The odd thing is that the people in the East End refuse to budge. We had expected something like panic evacuation and in fact the infidels ran away as quick as they could. But the cockney sticks to his ruins to an embarrassing degree. He doesn't want to be given a basement in Belgravia. Not he. He just wants to stay put.

HAROLD TO VITA   *Ministry of Information*

8 October 1940

I went to supper with Julian Huxley[2]. Poor man, he is rather worried by his animals. They are always bombing round Regent's

---

1. This was the day when the Luftwaffe made their supreme effort to overcome the RAF. The true figure of their losses was not 235 planes but 56.
2. The author and scientist. He was Secretary of the London Zoo, 1935–42.

Park, and the other day they hit the Zebra cage and one of the Zebras bolted as far as Marylebone. "At any rate," he said, "I think the carnivores are pretty safe." But he saw no humour in the situation. He was clearly much worried.

I like him so much. We discussed peace aims and a raid began in the middle. The whole flat shook. I was relieved when he offered to drive me home. We walked round to his garage. It was a perfect night. The moon showed through mackerel clouds and the guns were booming splendidly. The streets were all silent under the noise of the bombardment and suddenly the whole sky was lit up by a flare which sailed down gently under a parachute with tracer bullets after it. It was beautiful in the extreme but I was glad when I was safe again inside the Ministry.[3] One really cannot dine out these days.

HAROLD TO VITA   *Sissinghurst*

VITA TO HAROLD   *Sissinghurst*

8 October 1940

Lord! we have had a lot of raids this morning. They began at 8.30 and are still going on at 11. There was a most lovely sight: ten white machines climbed absolutely sheer, leaving perfectly regular white streaks of smoke like furrows in a cloudless blue sky, while a machine lower down looped smoke like gigantic spectacles before shooting up to join its friends. We saw one catch fire and fall. "That's one less to go after Hadji," I thought.

HAROLD TO VITA   *Ministry of Information*

16 October 1940

Last night was the worst I have had. Bombs boomed all round. The whole place shook. I slept fairly well but it was none too good. When

---

3. At this most intense period of the night raids on London, Harold slept in the tower of the Ministry of Information, where he was less exposed to the bombs than at King's Bench Walk.

I walked down to K.B.W. this morning there was a smell of burning in the air.

There had been a heavy bomb on the poor little Temple. The whole of Middle Temple Lane was down and the Middle Temple Hall (where Shakespeare acted in front of Queen Elizabeth) was badly hurt. Not destroyed but just knocked about and the windows blown out. My own little K.B.W. was all neat outside, but when I got in, I found that two of the pictures had been blown down and that the panelling behind them had been splintered. Nothing bad really, but I was glad I had not been sleeping there at the time. The whole place was full of soot and ashes like Pompeii.

I had a Cabinet Committee in the morning and then the House. People were grim but not in the least gay. The new tactics of the Germans in sending over fighter bombers in twos and threes all night certainly faces us with a problem.

In the afternoon I had to address the American correspondents. It did not go well at all. They are enraged by our censorship. Poor people, they feel that the bombardment of London is the hottest news ever and they get furious at our stopping their stories. I am not good at coping with that sort of thing.

HAROLD TO VITA   *Ministry of Information*

6 November 1940

I was so happy this morning when I heard of the Roosevelt result.[1] I had steeled myself to pretend not to mind either way, and I think it was true that three months ago it would not have mattered so much if wee Willy Winkie had got in. But in the last month Roosevelt had become identified with our cause and Willkie (unfairly perhaps) with the German cause. Although the German papers have been very cautious about it all, the French papers in occupied France have not been so cautious at all. They have openly rejoiced at the apparent decline

---

1. President Roosevelt was elected for his third term with a majority of five million votes. He carried thirty-eight States, and Wendell Willkie, his Republican opponent, ten.

in Roosevelt's popularity and said that it shows that America has no faith in our victory. Now they will have to swallow their words.

HAROLD TO VITA   *Queen's Hotel, Leeds*

7 January 1941

We had a ghastly drive here, or rather the country through which we drove [from Manchester] was hell. Great rolling moors under a grey sky, not unhedged or unvintaged enough to be magnificent, but like soiled grey counterpanes. Then in between and all along the valleys dark mills belching smoke. God, how I wish man had never invented the machine! I sympathise with the Nottingham frame-breakers. They saw the light.

I dined with Billy Harlech,[1] the Regional Commissioner. He had been spending the day with the Queen visiting Sheffield. He says that when the car stops, the Queen nips out into the snow and goes straight into the middle of the crowd and starts talking to them. For a moment or two they just gaze and gape in astonishment. But then they all start talking at once: "Hi! Your Majesty! Look here!" She has that quality of making everybody feel that they and they alone are being spoken to. It is, I think, because she has very large eyes which she opens very wide and turns straight upon one.

HAROLD TO VITA   *Ministry of Information*

21 January 1941

I wonder whether you fully realize what it means to me coming home. It is like what a motor must feel having fresh water in its radiator. I have got enough petrol. But it is the cooling drafts I need.

---

1. Lord Harlech, the North-East Regional Commissioner for Civil Defence. He had been Secretary of State for the Colonies, 1936–38.

Your love for me is a thing which always surprises and delights me as the beauty of Knole takes one by surprise.

I got to what remains of the station[1] in time. It poured with rain and we cowered in a tin hut looking out on the remains of the snow as if we were refugees on the Finnish frontier.

I lunched with de Gaulle. He is less horrible with his hat off since his hair is young and spruce and his eyes look tired although not benevolent. He attacked me on the ground that the Ministry were not sufficiently anti-Pétain. I held my ground. [Hugh] Dalton and [Clement] Attlee were there. De Gaulle told me that he had received a letter from unoccupied France telling him that the whole country was with him. His correspondent had put at the top in red ink that he had written the letter from a desire to express himself, but he well knew that the Vichy Censor would not approve it. Written across was a message in violet ink—*"La censeur de Vichy approuve totalement."*

HAROLD TO VITA　　　　　　　　　　　*Ministry of Information*

25 February 1941

Winston came here today to inspect us and to see some of our films. We showed him 'Cambridge'. That was my idea. He loved it. He said, "That is fine stuff." He also saw all our posters and stuff and was very kind about them. We had kept his visit dark, but the whisper went round and all the typists leant out of the windows and cheered and cheered. He was rather touched. The Press cheered him also. What popularity that man has got!

Kenneth Clark and I took Sibyl [Colefax] to dinner. It was not really a success. She wanted to talk gossip, and we wanted to talk shop. In the taxi coming back, I asked K. whether Sibyl was becoming a bore or whether we were so deeply concerned with the war that all trivial conversation seemed tiresome. He said that it did not work out that way. He loved nothing more than getting away from the war and

---

1. Staplehurst station (five miles from Sissinghurst), which had been destroyed by a fighter plane that crashed on it in flames.

talking about other things. I said that was why I looked forward to coming to Sissinghurst, as you never bothered me about war subjects but talked about the boys or the garden. You always listened when I wanted to talk my war things. So then we decided that Sibyl was not as intelligent as we thought. Then we corrected that, and said that why she bored us was that she was really out for inside information, and wanted us to tell her things the repetition of which would increase her self-importance. Then we felt we had been unkind about her. But were we? There is such a greedy look in her eyes when she scents inside information. I think this war is like a sieve. All the dross appears. I suppose that really K. himself is an ambitious and worldly person. But all that has gone. He works twelve hours a day[1] for purely impersonal reasons. So do I. Although I was pleased at the little pat Winston gave me on my bald head. But that is not ambition. It is just admiration for a great man.

HAROLD TO VITA   *Ministry of Information*

31 March 1941

It is always a gloomy moment for me when I unpack the *panier* which we packed together. I take out the flowers sadly and think of you picking them and putting the paper round them. But today it was worse, as I feel such a failure as a help to you. I do not know what it is, but I never seem to be able to help you when you are in trouble. I loathe your being unhappy more than I loathe anything. But I just moon about feeling wretched myself, and when I look back on my life, I see that the only times when I have been really unhappy are when you have been unhappy too.

I wonder whether you would have been happier if married to a more determined and less sensitive man. On the one hand you would have hated any sense of control or management, and other men might not have understood your desire for independence. I have always

---

1. Kenneth Clark was not only Director of the National Gallery, but Director of the Film Division of the Ministry of Information.

respected that, and you have often mistaken it for aloofness on my part. What bothers me is whether I have given way too much to your eccentricities. Some outside person might imagine that I should have made more of my life if I had had someone like Diana De La Warr to share my career. There are moments when I think you reproach yourself for not having been more interested in my pursuits and for not having pushed against my diffidence. I never feel that myself. I have always felt that the struggle in the market-place was for me to fight alone, and that you were there as something wholly different.

But what has always worried me is your dual personality. The one tender, wise and with such a sense of responsibility. And the other rather cruel and extravagant. The former has been what I have always clung to as the essential you, but the latter has always alarmed me and I have tried to dismiss it from my mind—or, rather, I have always accepted it as the inevitable counterpart of your remarkable personality. I have felt that this side of you was beyond my understanding, and when you have got into a real mess because of it, you have been angry with me for not coping with the more violent side in yourself.

I do not think that you have ever quite realised how deeply unhappy your eccentric side has often rendered me. When I am unhappy, I shut up like an oyster. I love you so much, darling. I hold my head in my hands worrying about you. I was nearly killed by a taxi today. I only missed an accident by a hair's breadth. And my first thought was, "If I had really been taken to hospital in a mess, then Viti would have been shaken out of her muzzy moods." I love you so much.

VITA TO HAROLD   *Sissinghurst*

31 March 1941

My darling

I have just had the most awful shock: Virginia has killed herself. It is not in the papers, but I got letters from Leonard and also from Vanessa, telling me. It was last Friday. Leonard came home to find a note saying she was going to commit suicide and they think she has drowned herself as he found her stick floating on the river. He says she had not been well for the last few weeks and was terrified of going mad again. He says, "It was, I suppose, the strain of the war and finishing her book and she could not rest or eat."

Why, oh why, did he leave her alone knowing all this? He must be reproaching himself terribly, poor man. They had not yet found the body.[1]

I simply can't take it in—that lovely mind, that lovely spirit. And she seemed so well when I last saw her, and I had a joky letter from her only a couple of weeks ago.

She must have been quite out of her mind or she would never have brought such sorrow and horror on Leonard and Vanessa.

Vanessa has seen him and says he was amazingly self-controlled and calm, but insisted on being left alone—I cannot help wondering if he will follow her example. I do not see him living without her.

Perhaps you better not say to anyone that it was suicide, though I suppose they can't keep it out of the papers. I suppose there will have to be an inquest.

What a nightmare for L. to have to go through. When they find her body, and all that.

Your Mar

HAROLD TO VITA   *Ministry of Information*

2 April 1941

I am glad I came down last night since I was so worried about you and it was a relief to see you taking the shock so well. I hope you can manage to dismiss the physical aspect from your mind and to concentrate only upon the great joy that friendship has been to you. But, my dearest, I know that Virginia meant something to you which nobody else can ever mean and that you will feel deprived of a particular sort of haven which was a background comfort and strength. I have felt sad about it every hour of the day.

---

1. Virginia Woolf's body was found three weeks later in the River Ouse, Sussex, a short distance downstream from where she had drowned herself.

H A R O L D   T O   V I T A   *Ministry of Information*

17 April 1941

The Blitz last night was the worst we have had. Even I slept badly
listening to the chatter and jabber of the bombs and guns. There was a
moment when I thought I should never get to sleep and that it would be
interesting to go down and see what was happening. But that meant
putting on bedroom slippers and a British Warm [overcoat] and I felt
that I might look foolish. The alternative was to dress completely, but I
knew that if I did that I should remain up all night. With the result that I
stayed in bed and slept fitfully. I am sorry now. On the one hand the
view from our upper stories was superb. And on the other hand we had
some 40 casualties from the Victoria Club opposite who were carried in.
Five of them died in our hall.

London today is rather muzzy and distraught. The damage is very
bad indeed. Selfridges has gone and most of Jermyn Street and the
R.A.C. and other clubs. Windham's has collapsed, and the London
Library has escaped by a hair's breadth. In fact it is a Coventry and
has made people half angry and half worried.

H A R O L D   T O   V I T A   *Ministry of Information*

30 April 1941

How difficult this world is! I quite like it in a way, but I wish
the Germans were less successful. And I wish our own people were less
foolish. Bless their hearts.

I have got into a row with Herbert Morrison [Home Secretary]
because Lady Astor lost her head at Plymouth and started screaming.[1]
I quite see that Lady Astor had survived five raids in nine nights and
had the right to be unstrung. But why the censor should have stopped
her ululations I do not quite see. Anyhow I am to be put on the mat
by Morrison tomorrow and it amuses me having to defend Lady Astor.
I think she was wrong. Plymouth as a result is almost totally destroyed.

---

1. She had said publicly that Plymouth, her constituency, had been so badly bombed that the
people were panicking, with the result that the Germans bombed it again.

Kingsley Martin came to see me this evening and talked defeatism. He wants to make peace with Germany. He calls my opposition to that suggestion 'emotionalism' whereas his panic point-of-view is called 'facing realities'. He is a shattered worm. I left him feeling that I could fight the whole panzer divisions of Germany armed only with a fountain pen. Nothing does me so much good as cowardice in other people.

VITA TO HAROLD   *Sissinghurst*

4 June 1941

My darling,

I write this after dinner. A big thunderstorm is circling round somewhere: a pale flash comes, and then a dim rumble some appreciable time later. I was up in the potting shed, getting out the dahlias from under the bench. (I have not dared to plant them out before now, because of the frosts.) I was thinking to myself, as one does think when one is alone and doing something mechanical like putting dahlias into a trug, I was thinking, "How queer. I suppose Hadji and I have been about as unfaithful to one another as one well could be from the conventional point of view, even worse than unfaithful if you add in homosexuality, and yet I swear no two people could love one another more than we do after all these years."

It *is* queer, isn't it? It does destroy all orthodox ideas of marriage?

Yet it is true, so true that I know our love to be like a great oak tree with lots of acorns, or like a tulip-tree with lots of flowers.

I do think we have managed things cleverly.

I was sorry I had said to Cyril[1] that I wanted you to divorce me for the sake of economy; I thought he might misunderstand so I wrote to him and put it right. I don't think he would misunderstand, but I wasn't taking any chances.

Goodnight, my darling.

Your

Mar

---

1. Professor Cyril Joad, the philosopher, and one of Harold's partners in the popular radio chat-show *The Brains Trust*.

In compensation for his loss of office, Harold was appointed by Churchill a Governor of the BBC, and this was his only public duty until the war ended. He resumed his journalism (mainly book reviews and his weekly Marginal Comment *for the* Spectator*) and found time to write two books,* The Desire to Please *and* The Congress of Vienna. *Politically his chief concern was in reconciling de Gaulle and the Free French to the British Government. Vita remained at Sissinghurst, writing* The Eagle and the Dove *and her long poem* The Garden. *Both their sons went overseas as serving soldiers, Ben to the Middle East and Nigel to Tunisia.*

HAROLD TO VITA   *4 King's Bench Walk*

22 July 1941

I dined with James and Guy Burgess.[1] I do not think that that affair is going very well, and James looks white and drawn. I am seeing him alone on Wednesday and he will tell me all about it. Guy is a bit of a scamp, and James is far too sensitive and affectionate for that sort of relationship.

Well here I am in K.B.W. as a private individual.[2] If only it were not for the raids I should be glad to be back, but it is really impossible to stay here when the bombing begins since the shelters are quite inadequate and the place exposed. I shall go to Atheneum Court and

---

1. Guy Burgess had resigned from the BBC in 1938 and joined the Secret Service. He defected to Russia with Donald Maclean in 1951. James Pope-Hennessy, the author, had been Nigel's friend at Oxford, and now became Harold's.
2. He meant losing his job in the Ministry of Information.

VITA AND HAROLD · 341

see if I can get a room there. It is by far the largest and strongest of those sorts of building.

The Times has a rather disobliging paragraph today suggesting that a job had to be found for me and that this was invented.[3] I really do wish that I could have afforded to refuse it. I hate the idea that I should be bought off with favours. Dearest Mar—such a nice letter from you today. What should I do in life without you? I would be lost and lonely, like a jam-jar floating in the North Sea.

HAROLD TO VITA   *4 King's Bench Walk*

21 August 1941

I went to the funeral.[4] It was moving and short. But please, at my funeral let there be no moaning at the bar,[5] and no anthems. I cannot abide anthems. When one thinks that they are all over, suddenly some fool starts yelling out the opening words all over again. They had Cecil Spring-Rice's, "I vow to thee my country." I should like that at my funeral. It is not so much my attitude towards foreign policy. Is it not strange that that brilliant man who lived so long and did such good work will be remembered only because he wrote a really rather ordinary little poem one morning at Government House, Ottawa, after he had been sacked and only a fortnight before he died.[6]

HAROLD TO VITA   *4 King's Bench Walk*

12 September 1941

I have had Dylan Thomas [the poet] to see me this morning. He wants a job in the BBC. I told him that he must not drink if he wanted a job there. They did not care for drunkards. He took it well.

---

3. The Governorship of the BBC.
4. The funeral of Lord Willingdon in Westminster Abbey. He had been Governor General of Canada and Viceroy of India.
5. "And may there be no moaning at the bar
   When I put out to sea." Tennyson, *Crossing the Bar*
6. Sir Cecil Spring-Rice (1859–1918) had been British Ambassador in Washington, 1913–17, and was on leave in Canada when he died suddenly.

HAROLD TO VITA   *4 King's Bench Walk*

22 October 1941

I have got so fond of my Leicester people. They are glum and shy and rude; but so loyal. If there were an election tomorrow, I should get in by a large majority entirely upon my Munich stand.

I went to see Maisky.[1] How you would like that little man! He talked to me with the utmost frankness, and I think he feels that I am safe and sympathetic. He does not think they will surrender, but they may be knocked out for a bit.[2] He said that of all our statesmen Anthony Eden was the one he trusted most. He said, "He understands. Churchill does not wholly understand." Now isn't that odd?

I like life being odd. I like hearing Maisky praise Eden above everybody. But one must not allow one's liking for strange patterns to develop into a taste for the arabesque. But truly, how odd it is. Brendan Bracken[3] had a long talk with me in the House about the Ministry and the BBC. Suddenly he said, "God! Harold, how I wish you were at the Ministry still—what fun we would have!"

That's pretty odd.

HAROLD TO VITA   *4 King's Bench Walk*

10 December 1941

I lunched with de Gaulle yesterday. I cannot make out whether I like him or not. There are sides of him which are as attractive as a Newfoundland dog. There are other sides which are arrogant and hostile. He is obviously a clever and a powerful man. He thinks the Germans have failed badly in Russia and that they will have to compensate their public opinion by an early and large success elsewhere. This can only be in the Mediterranean and we must expect heavy fighting in North Africa.

---

1. Ivan Maisky, Ambassador of the Soviet Union in London.
2. Hitler's attack on Russia had started on 22 June. Few experts had thought that the Red Army could resist for more than a few weeks.
3. He had succeeded Duff Cooper as Minister of Information. Harold had been succeeded as Parliamentary Secretary by an insignificant Labour Member, Ernest Thurtle.

The Americans were badly caught. I gather that the damage done to their fleet at Pearl Harbor and above all to their sea-planes was serious.[1] But not really serious enough to make it worth Japan's while to have put upon the American people so vast an affront. They will not rest until they have avenged it. But I hope that whoever was responsible for the light-hearted way in which they allowed the Japanese fleet to approach so near to Honolulu will get it hot. I am sure that the Japanese trick, however successful for the moment, was a mistake. People here think that Japanese intervention will do us much harm and bother for six months, but after that its advantages will be greater than its disadvantages.

HAROLD TO VITA   *4 King's Bench Walk*

28 January 1942

I wish you had been in the House yesterday. There really had been considerable opposition[2] and many members had been boasting openly that they would vote against the Government unless Winston changed his Cabinet. But after Winston had been speaking for five minutes one actually felt the opposition dropping like a thermometer. He also sensed it, and began to enjoy himself more and more. He thrust his hands deep into his trouser pockets and turned his tummy now to the right and now to the left, revelling in his own mastery. He is so sturdy and so lucid. He told us that further horrible blows were to come, and we loved it instead of being depressed. It is like a doctor in whom one has got total confidence saying, "I expect your temperature will go up to 104 tonight and tomorrow night, after which it will drop." In a way it was his most successful speech although it contained no fireworks. But if the purpose of a Parliamentary speech is to change the opinion of one's auditors, then surely Winston did it. He was so patient, so polite, so modest. I revelled in it.

---

1. The Japanese attack on Pearl Harbor on 7 December sank four of the finest American battleships.
2. The campaign in North Africa had been going very badly. Rommel's attack on 21 January had led to a rapid British retreat and the loss of Benghazi.

HAROLD TO VITA   *4 King's Bench Walk*

24 February 1942

The debate today went on and on. Running through it was the idea that our troops had not fought well in Malaya.[1] There were only two Japanese divisions engaged and our men retreated and surrendered more readily than they ought to have. This is a most alarming thought. It gives me cold shudders in my heart. The left-wing people say that it is because we have not got a cause. The right-wing people say that it is because we have not got sufficient discipline. Cause be hanged! What keeps men in the front line is fear of being shot if they run away. On the other hand we have the behaviour of the civil population in London, the conduct of the Air Force, the Navy and the Mercantile Marine, and the real guts shown by our people in Libya. We have captured a German army order there saying that our generals may be stupid but our men fight well. But Malaya is the blackest mark in the whole history of the British army. Why? Why?

Some people think that it is because we have allowed the Press to put such stress upon equipment. That gives the private soldier an excuse for cowardice. He can always say, "But we had not enough aeroplanes or tanks: what else could I do?"

HAROLD TO VITA   *Dublin*

16 March 1942

The High Commissioner's car picked me up and I drove with him into the Wicklow mountains. Rain and sunshine over moors and streams gushing. We drove to the famous waterfall in the Powerscourt demesne which I remember so well from childhood. Behind us in another car rode four detectives, since Maffey[2] has to be guarded. It was lovely by the waterfall and the grass all around is springy and

---

1. Singapore had fallen on 15 February and 60,000 men surrendered to the Japanese.
2. J. L. Maffey, later Lord Rugby. He had been "British Representative" in Eire since 1939. The Irish did not use the term "High Commissioner."

green from the spray. Then we turned back and drove to Powerscourt House[3] where we lunched. A great ostentatious eighteenth century mansion with a most elaborate Italian garden and a superb view of the Wicklow mountains. Viscount Powerscourt, whom I remember as a young guardee forty years ago, took me into the garden. We leant upon a gilt balustrade over the fountains looking down upon the great pool between the statues. He said, "Here I am marooned—the last of the Irish aristocracy with nobody to speak to." And I remembered when the place was the centre of social life in Ireland and when two brass bands played upon the terrace and the great marquee seemed to provide innumerable ices for little boys. My granny[4] would not let me have more than one ice. She was a firm woman.

I gave a lecture in the evening. It went well. There was one man afterwards who made an impassioned speech saying that there was only one thing which should be subject to government censorship and that began with the letters 'c.o.n.' I imagined of course that he was attacking the cruelty of Great Britain and all the wrongs that we were still doing to Ireland. I looked down my nose. I merely said, when panting with passion he had resumed his seat, that I did not wish to comment on controversial matters. It was only when I was walking away that I was told what he had meant was 'contraceptives'.

HAROLD TO VITA   *House of Commons*

23 April 1942

I am feeling cheered tonight. We have had our secret session and although I must not say what transpired, yet I can say that Winston had a great personal triumph.[5] He spoke for nearly two hours and he avoided all oratory, jokes or brilliance. He just stood there at the box telling us one alarming thing after the other and piling up a huge

---

3. The great house and Italianate garden of the Slazenger family, twelve miles south of Dublin.
4. Catherine Rowan Hamilton, who died in 1919 in her ninety-ninth year.
5. His speech dealt with the surrender of Singapore, retreat in the Libyan desert, and losses in the Battle of the Atlantic.

pyramid of adversity, mischance and danger. And then like some God of War he stood, stout and stubborn, upon the pyramid he erected and the House knew that he was far greater than themselves. To do them justice they rose and cheered as I have never seen them cheer since that dreadful Munich scene. He must feel that whatever the country may think, he has re-established his ascendancy over the House. It was a magnificent triumph.

After that the debate really collapsed. Nobody felt they could speak after that and the thing petered out.

HAROLD TO VITA　　　　　　　　　　　　　　*House of Commons*

24 September 1942

Ben said to me today, "How happy I have been these days!"[1] I said, "But you have done nothing." He said, "But I am always happy when I am at home with Mummy and you."

Now truly that is a compliment (fresh with all his great sincerity) which I cherish more than any other. It is really an achievement on our part to have created an atmosphere which is more congenial to a fastidious young man like Ben than all the glitter of the Gargoyle [a London club]. It gives me pleasure that he should have said this so spontaneously, since I know that it was true. Of course one can modify it by saying that he is sedentary by nature and likes his files and books. But the fact does remain that poor old Sissinghurst (which offers no entertainment) does offer something which his sensitive and exacting criticism enjoys.

It is you, my darling, who have made this atmosphere (a) by great integrity; (b) by hating rows; (c) by a sense of real values. I do not think that, except for Winston, I *admire* anyone as much as I admire you.

I remember you saying (years ago) that you had never established a complete relationship with anyone. I don't think you ever could—

---

1. Ben was then on embarkation leave, but did not leave England for the Middle East till 4 October.

since yours is a vertical and not a horizontal nature, and two-thirds
of you will always be submerged. But you have established, with your
sons and me, a relationship of absolute trust and complete love. I don't
think that these things would be so fundamental to the four of us were
it not that each one of us four is a private person underneath.

I have often wondered what makes the perfect family. I think it
is just our compound of intimacy and aloofness. Each of us has a room
of his own. Each of us knows that there is a common-room where we
meet on the basis of perfect understanding.

If Ben were killed or drowned, I should always remember that
remark. And I should know that from the difficult web of human
relationship (now a spider's web, now a mass of steel hawsers) we—
thanks to you only—have made a pattern which is taut where tautness
is wanted, and elastic where we need to expand on our own.

HAROLD TO VITA   *4 King's Bench Walk*

2 October 1942

Benzie has had instructions to leave [for Cairo] early on Sunday
morning. He is rather excited. Lists all over the place—socks 3, pants
2, and so on. But the point is that he will not see you again. I do not
suggest your coming up to London. What is the point of these last
farewells? We four understand and love each other so deeply that there
is no need for conventionalities. Ben will telephone.

The three of us dined at the Greek restaurant. Nigel seemed in very
good form. But I was sad and Ben was sad and it was not the gayest
evening I have passed. And then this morning they are both here
together—enormous khaki shapes in my little room—cleaning their
buttons and chaffing. Then it is time for Ben to go to Paddington.
"Well, goodbye Niggs—we may meet somewhere." Then it is Nigel's
turn to return to Perth. "Goodbye Daddy." His voice was gay but he
had tears in his eyes.[1]

---

1. Nigel embarked at Gourock, Scotland, on 14 November to take part in the invasion of
   Algeria and Tunisia. Both sons remained overseas for nearly three years.

VITA TO HAROLD   *Sissinghurst*

10 November 1942

The American invasion [of North Africa] is indeed wonderful.
One does feel that anything may happen now anywhere and at any
moment. What a superb moment of history to be living at! It makes
one feel again as one felt during the Battle of Britain, only the other
way round—the exhilaration of victory, not of a high despair. But in
quality the feeling is the same.

One understands the feelings of St George when he saw the dragon
beginning to bleed, the black-blooded worm of evil oozing under his
lance.

HAROLD TO VITA   *4 King's Bench Walk*

24 November 1942

I came up from East Grinstead with Mr Dewar and his charming
daughter. She is to be married on Saturday to Michael Astor,[1] and he
is a lucky man. She is gay and clever and charming. Dewar is rather
a stiff sort of man, but it may be that he is averse to M.Ps. We had
to change at East Croydon and get into a bedint train which had only
one class and no corridors. As soon as I realised that I was stuck with
no possibility of escape, I began to suffer from agonies of Secret
Sorrow. I felt that the worst was bound to happen. A cold sweat broke
out upon my highbrow. The train stopped at Norwood Junction, and
in despair I murmured to Mr Dewar that I must get out. "Not here,
surely?" he said, perplexed as well he might be. "Yes, here," I wailed,
and as I wailed, the train started again. "How far is it," I murmured
to him with clenched teeth, "to the next station?" "It depends on the
fog," he answered—and shame and disaster danced before my eyes. I
summoned up all the moral courage and physical muscles of which I
am capable. The train stopped because of fog. In an agony of mind
and body I made feverish conversation. The train went on. After an

_____

1. She was Barbara McNeill (her mother subsequently married a Dewar) and her fiancé was
the son of 2nd Viscount Astor.

aeon of internal pangs it stopped at London Bridge. I bumbled out. But my Secret Sorrow (which is a sneak and a thief) ceased to be a sorrow at all the moment it saw GENTLEMEN. I just ignored it, and replaced in my pocket the penny which I had held there, anxious that there should be no slip between the slot and me. Then I took a taxi to King's Bench Walk and spoke quite calmly to Miss Niggeman[2] on various matters before I retired to that place which but half-an-hour before had glimmered as the bourne of all human desire.

VITA TO HAROLD   *Sissinghurst*

2 December 1942

I wonder what you thought of the Beveridge Report?[3] I think it sounds dreadful. The proletariat being encouraged to breed like rabbits because each new little rabbit means 8/–a week [in Family Allowances]—as though there weren't too many of them already and not enough work to go round, with 2 million unemployed before the war, and everybody being given everything for nothing, a complete discouragement to thrift or effort, and not a word said about better education. Lloyd George gave them old-age pensions, and what do they do? They grumble about having to contribute to the stamps, and then grumble because they don't get enough money. Oh no, I don't hold with Sir William Beveridge, and it all makes me feel very pre-1792.

HAROLD TO VITA   *4 King's Bench Walk*

9 December 1942

Why do you say "it is silly to think that anything in life matters much"? I think everything in life matters terribly. I feel that this war

---

2. Elvira Niggeman, Harold's secretary from 1938 till 1965.
3. Sir William Beveridge's plan for universal social security, which was largely implemented by postwar governments.

is a test of our character and I rejoice that all those I love have come through it enhanced and not diminished. I want to live through this war with my courage unabated, my faith firmer, my energy increased, and my hopes and beliefs lit by a sun that has never lit them before. I have much pride in my own people and much faith in the future. I really do believe that we in England have set an example to the world. I think that we may solve the social and economic problems of the twentieth century with as much wisdom and tolerance as when we solved the political problems of the nineteenth. Surely this is worthwhile? Surely your dignity and calm and uncomplainingness and courage are an example to all who see you? Not worthwhile! Why, everything is ten times more worthwhile now than ever before!

VITA TO HAROLD   *Sissinghurst*

10 December 1942

When I said that it is silly to think that anything in life mattered much, I suppose I meant one's personal life. Of course I think with you that the war and after-the-war matter. But, darling, you are a goose to talk about my "uncomplainingness and courage," because (a) I have nothing to complain of, and (b) my courage is a very poor thing. I am sure it would go phutt if put to the test. My calm is really my cabbagey nature. Luckily for you, you have never seen the more tempestuous side of my nature. You have only seen an occasional bubble rising to the surface, which has startled you and made you realise vaguely that I feel passionately, and am vindictive and uncontrollable when my emotions are aroused, but as you do not like that sort of bubble, you have always wisely looked the other way. The emotions I give you are deep and strong. You are about the only person in whose love I trust. I know that we will love each other till we die.

By the way, you said we ought to ask de Gaulle to luncheon. Shall we give a joint luncheon party? You ask the guests, and I will go shares with you. Shall we?

VITA TO HAROLD　　　　　　　　　　　　*Sissinghurst*

3 February 1943

I am rather excited about this book[1] which entirely absorbs my mind. I think that you will like it even though the subject is not at all your cup of tea. I think that I am dimly beginning to understand the saints and what they were after, far better than I did when I was writing about Joan of Arc. It is rather like trying to grasp relativity, and every now and then getting a flash of understanding. It is such a totally different world, and the first point to understand is that all ordinary values are reversed. You will understand better what I mean when you come to read it; and if you don't, it will merely mean that I have done the job badly.

I have got a grand phrase as an epigraph for the beginning, by Cardinal Newman: "There is a God—the most august of all conceivable truths."

HAROLD TO VITA　　　　　　　　　　　*4 King's Bench Walk*

12 May 1943

I wish you had been in the House yesterday. Attlee had to make a statement on Tunisia.[2] It would seem almost impossible to render that amazing campaign dull—but he succeeded fully. It was as if, when one expected an eagle-swoop, one had the pecking of a tiny quail in a bamboo cage. It was so extraordinary that a man could be so ineffective that if he had gone on for another five minutes, the good manners of the House would have broken down. One felt that a *fou rire* was about to burst, and had one man tittered, the whole House would have rocked with guffaws.

Anyhow, it is all practically over—and if Niggs is alive he has had

---

1. *The Eagle and the Dove,* a study of the two Saints, St. Teresa of Avila and St. Teresa of Lisieux.
2. The British First Army had captured Tunis and Bizerta on 8 May, and on the 12th forced the capitulation of the entire German-Italian Army in Tunisia. 250,000 prisoners were taken. Clement Attlee was deputizing for Churchill, who was in the United States.

the satisfaction of delivering the *coup de grace*. What the *Daily Telegraph* calls "the famous Sixth"[3] broke through at Hammam Lif by sending their tanks into the sea and just splashing through the waves.

VITA TO HAROLD   *Sissinghurst*

12 May 1943

Violet [Trefusis] is here. It is extraordinarily unreal and rather embarrassing. It is rather like speaking a foreign language that one has once known bilingually and has not used for years: idiomatic phrases, and even bits of slang, come back to one suddenly, yet one finds that the foundation has gone.

She discovered that she would be alone in the Priest's House and declared that she would be terrified, so I gave her my room (but did not share it with her). It was all very odd, and we were both acutely conscious of the oddness. Luckily we were able to say so, which eased it into amusement instead of embarrassment.

VITA TO HAROLD   *Sissinghurst*

26 August 1943

I am glad that we see so completely eye to eye about the new world. I am not a very public-minded sort of person, as you know, but this is a point on which my personal idiosyncrasies and public tendencies touch and correspond with yours. The reason they correspond is of course that we have fundamentally the same standard of values. And this is probably one of the reasons why we are so happy together. Over essentials we invariably agree—and indeed over minor matters too. We differ only in that you are a more public and active person than your skulking old stodge of a Mar.

---

3. 6th Armoured Division, of which the First Guards Brigade (in which Nigel was serving) was the infantry element.

Darling, I love you so much—so very, very, very, very much—more than anything—so dearly, so protectively, so respectingly, so much more than anything else, so eternally.

I do hope that you will like my new book [*The Eagle and the Dove*]. I think it has some merit, but of course, as one always does, I wish that it were better. I do so want you to have the leisure to write another book yourself. I have such enormous belief in your writing, and regret always that you should by force of circumstances regard it always as a sort of sideline. My idea of heaven on earth would be for you to live here and bury yourself all morning and evening in your room and write, with perhaps one very interesting job that took you to London once every six months. But you would not like that. Perhaps when you are eighty you may come round to my point of view.

HAROLD TO VITA   *House of Commons*

23 September 1943

Darling,

I shall be rushed tomorrow, so I write to you late tonight. I thought this evening that supposing I were killed in a raid, the nurse would lean over me and I would feel a block of cold cement rising from my knees to my thighs. Before it reached my heart I should want to send you a message. Yet (even if I had been as detached as Socrates) how could I compress into a few minutes of obituary communication what I would really feel? You admit that this is an interesting conundrum.

I worked it out as follows:—

a) Your knowledge of what I feel (and how gawky and slipfaced I am about it) is the axiom.

b) Therefore I need never *explain* anything.

c) Therefore I need never *express* anything.

d) Therefore if (to my nurse taking down my dying words) I merely gasped out the family phrase, "Loving thoughts," you would see that phrase not as a small map of the environs of Ventnor, but as Mercator's Projection.

And having realised that my last words could (without offence, disappointment or misunderstanding) be reduced to this code-formula, I thought just this, "Hurray!" Because, my saint, after thirty years that does really imply a certitude of understanding. And God knows I am muddled and confused enough!

Your own,

Hadji

HAROLD TO VITA *Stockholm*

19 October 1943

On all fours I crept below and out of the aeroplane to be met by a blaze of arclights.[1] A neat little man came up to me and took off his hat: "Good evening, Mr Nicolson. I am Leadbetter of the Legation. I hope you had a good journey." I shuffled across to the adjoining customs shed and got rid of my beastly [flying] clothes. I was passed through immediately and taken to a huge car with a kettle on the luggage-rack which makes gasoline out of wood. We drove into Stockholm through brilliant peacetime streets.

I was shown to my rooms [in the Grand Hotel]. It is a royal suite. Anyhow, I don't have to pay for it. There are five windows looking out on the Palace and the river, with a view of the tower of the town-hall, surely the loveliest thing in modern architecture. I had a bath. I dined. I went to the flat of the Press Attaché, Peter Tennant, where I found many other members of the Legation. The Minister [Sir Victor Mallet] is away, having gone to Gothenburg for the exchange of disabled prisoners with the Germans. I sat talking till midnight.

It is really very odd sitting in this palatial room looking out on Stockholm. I feel as if my body had been flung through space and that my mind had been left in Dundee. I suppose it will follow on later.

---

1. Harold had flown from Dundee to Stockholm in a RAF Mosquito to give a series of lectures for the British Council.

HAROLD TO VITA

27 October 1943

The coast of Denmark—the coast of the enemy—glimmered in the sunshine and the towers of Elsinore stood up above the woods. I went to see the graves of our airmen who have been washed up on the coast. Four little white crosses. The Consul who was with me had lost his boy off Pantelleria [near Malta] and seemed to be distressed that his body has never been found. I do not understand that. I should not feel any better about a dead person if he or she were put in the ground than if they melted gradually into the great purity of the sea. I should far rather be buried in the Mediterranean than in earth. But the poor man minded, and he cried as he looked at the neat graves.

I fear that the Swedes regard me as far more important than I am. My meetings have all been crowded and people who do not know a word of English come to honour. I have met with more than kindness; I have met with enthusiasm. I am sure it was worthwhile. They are flattered that a middle-aged buffer like myself should have faced the discomfort and danger of a Mosquito to come and talk to them. They do *admire* us so. I am glad I came. Tremendously glad.

VITA TO HAROLD

5 January 1944

Sissinghurst

My own darling Hadji,

I cannot tell you how touched I was by the letter Elvira [Nigge-man] brought me, nor how pleased I was that you should have liked that little poem,[1] written with so much love. I was so extravagantly pleased, too, by your saying I had got control of such literary powers as I possess, and was writing better than I ever had. I was pleased about this, because I do feel that something has happened—or is in process

1. The poem, addressed to Harold, began, "I must not tell how dear you are to me. / It is unknown, a secret from myself / Who should know best." It was read by the Poet Laureate, Cecil Day-Lewis, at their joint memorial service in 1968. For the full text, see *Portrait of a Marriage,* pp. 192–3.

of happening—within me, and that I may write better in future. It is as though something had gone, or was about to go, click. I think that this possibly happens to people of talent in their middle age; I mean, flaming genius may be a thing of youth, e.g. Shelley, Keats; but failing that, experience teaches, only it takes a long time to come to fruition. Like *Chimonanthus fragrans* (Winter sweet) which doesn't flower till it is years old. I *know* that in the little poem I wrote for you I was setting myself to compress a complicated story into a short space, and that in its small way it was a tour de force to do so with any clarity. I feel like a juggler who has hitherto been able to spin only three plates into the air at a time, and who now can spin twenty. But this is only one thing. This is merely getting control of one's medium. Apart from this, I feel I have lost my shallowness; and if I can put both gains together I may yet do something worthwhile.

Oh darling, what an egotistical letter—but you will forgive me. Your own letter provoked it.

Your Mar

VITA TO HAROLD   *Sissinghurst*

18 January 1944

My own darling Hadji

Considering that Niggs will be twenty-seven tomorrow and Ben thirty in August, it is remarkable, isn't it, that I should love you so much more now than I did when we made them? And you me, I think. Of course I was much in love with you then, in a very young and (also) uninformed way; it was young and fresh like Greek poetry, (I have just been reading some translations from the Greek Anthology), but it was like a spring then, like the mountain springs we used to drink from in Persia; but now it is like a deep deep lake which can never dry up. Darling, I don't honestly think that as much can be said for most marriages, do you? Of course I suppose it could be said of the bourgeois bedint marriage founded on habit; but not for a difficult unorthodox marriage like ours, with rather subtle and difficult people involved. Of course it is largely due to your own sweetness of nature;

I don't think any man but you would have put up with me; but there is something more to it than that even. Oh I don't know and I can't express myself—and this letter will reach you on a busy morning—and Hadji sheers off from anything like emotional expression anyhow—and my quiet room with the pink tower seen through the window is so different a place from London—but I did want to say these things to you on Niggs' birthday somehow, when everything is so precarious and we may either of us get killed at any moment, and Niggs too. A little record of thirty-one years of love.

from Mar

VITA TO HAROLD *Sissinghurst*

16 February 1944

Darling, Knole has been bombed. All the windows on the front of the house and in the Green Court and Stone Court, and on the garden side (including a window in the chapel) have been broken. A special sort of bomb fell just in front of the wicket—no, not just in front, but slightly to the left. Eddy [Sackville-West] rang me up to tell me. Then I rang up Uncle Charlie [Lord Sackville] who says he has written me a long letter about it today, which I suppose I shall get tomorrow. I mind frightfully, frightfully, frightfully. I always persuade myself that I have finally torn Knole out of my heart, and then the moment anything touches it, every nerve is alive again. I cannot bear to think of Knole wounded, and I not there to look after it and be wounded with it. Those filthy Germans! Let us level every town in Germany to the ground! I shan't care. Oh Hadji, I wish you were here. I feel hurt and heartsick.

VITA TO HAROLD *Sissinghurst*

23 February 1944

As I read the *New Yorker* article (getting more and more indignant) I thought, "This man, although he is saying some exceedingly foolish things, is a man of intelligence who also writes very well."[1] Then I looked for a signature and found Edmund Wilson. It is of course absurd to say that you are shocked by Byron or Swinburne, and where he goes wrong over criticising you for so obviously belonging to a definite class, by birth, education, experience and consequent outlook, is that he ought to have stated it as a fact and not as an adverse criticism. He is falling into a common error of critics, which is to demand that a writer shall be something he is not. It is no good expecting a gentle person of sensibility and culture to care for the rough and tumble. I think that your almost morbid dislike of emotion is at the root of much of what E. Wilson is trying to say.

VITA TO HAROLD   *Sissinghurst*

13 June 1944

"One enemy raider was destroyed during the night." It was indeed. I thought it was going to destroy Sissinghurst Castle in the process. We had a series of warnings and all-clears (three, to be exact) and then a solitary plane came along, with a sudden burst of machine-gun fire, so close that I leapt from my bed and rushed into your bedroom to look out of the window; and there, beyond the roses, was a stream of scarlet tracer-bullets rushing up into the sky and a plane all in flames, apparently about to descend on Beale's stock-yard.

VITA TO HAROLD   *Sissinghurst*

4 July 1944

Poor old Rosie has been killed.[2] I got a telegram from Jack Lynch, and then I saw it in *The Times,* as no doubt you did too. Well we

---

1. The article, by Edmund Wilson, was titled "Through the Embassy Window; Harold Nicolson" and was published in *The New Yorker* of 1 January 1944.
2. Rosamund Grosvenor, Vita's first love, had married Captain Jack Lynch in 1924. She was killed, with many others, when a bomb fell on the Savoy Chapel.

always teased her about her passion for attending memorial services, and now she is going to have one for herself. It has saddened me rather, that somebody so innocent, so silly, and so harmless should be killed in this idiotic and violent way.

VITA TO HAROLD   *Sissinghurst*

19 December 1944

I have lost all pleasure in the lake and indeed in the woods, since soldiers came and invaded them and robbed them of all the privacy I so loved.

I shall never love the lake or the wood again in the same way as I used to. I mind about this—more than you would believe. It was a thing of beauty, now tarnished for ever—one of the few things I had preserved against this horrible new world.

I wish I could sort out my ideas about this new world. I feel one ought to be able to adapt oneself—and not struggle to go back to, and live in, an obsolete tradition.

All this makes me very unhappy, Hadji. And my back worries me too.[1] I don't mind its hurting—but the *weakness* it brings to my limbs worries me. You see I used to be so strong, but now I dare not make a rash movement and am also frightened of falling down.

If only I thought I could write good poetry I should not mind anything, but even over that I have lost my convictions.

HAROLD TO VITA   *4 King's Bench Walk*

21 December 1944

I do so understand your unhappiness at the moment. I think that everyone in these dark autumn days is truly unhappy. Partly war

---

1. She had arthritis in the spine.

weariness, partly sadness at things not going right, and partly actual malnutrition. But I also know that yours is a deeper unhappiness. You do not ask much from life but you do desire passionately privacy and the respect of your independence and quiet. The tanks in the wood were a real symbol; the boats being sunk by carelessness or actual malevolence is another symbol. The world for people like you and me is becoming a grim place. Then of course added to this is your arthritis which makes everything seem dim through a cloud of pain. I pray to God that the treatment will improve it.

But there is one thing which I do not agree about—namely your poetry. I do not think you have ever written better than you are writing now. Even if you never wrote another line of poetry your fame as a poet is anchored to *The Land.* Not a day passes almost in which someone does not mention that poem to me. At the Club on Tuesday Tommy Lascelles said, "I suppose *The Land* is about the only truly classic poem written in our times." But I believe *The Garden* will be as good and certainly the cradle poem is among the finest you have ever written.

Oh my sweet sweet Mar—how it hurts me that you should be unhappy. You are all my life to me. The thought of you is a little hot water bottle of happiness which I hug in this cold world. When people behave meanly and badly (as they did in the debate yesterday) I think of you—so serene and lovely—and it all seems to smooth itself out. As I said to Duff [Cooper] the other day when he said that he thought the Government had treated me rather shabbily, "Well you see someone who has had my happiness in life has no right to feel bitter about anything." "You mean Vita," he said. He understands.

V I T A　 T O　 H A R O L D　　　　　　　　　　　　　　　 *Sissinghurst*

7 February 1945

Darling, listen; there is an agitation on foot to get a bus service between Biddenden and Cranbrook. This is horrid for us, as it would pass along the road skirting our wood, but it would be nice for the inhabitants of Biddenden and Three Chimneys who are entirely cut off from the world—the world in this case being Cranbrook. We cannot resist it, so we had better co-operate. Why people have this passion for moving about passes my understanding, but there it is.

What a world! It's like drawing up one's own death warrant and is all on a par with the tanks coming into our wood.

Manifesto: I hate democracy. I hate la populace. I wish education had never been introduced. I don't like tyranny, but I like an intelligent oligarchy. I wish la populace had never been encouraged to emerge from its rightful place. I should like to see them as well fed and well housed as T.T. cows—but no more thinking than that. (It's rather what most men feel about women!)

Oh—à propos of that, I've been absolutely enraged by a book about Knole, in which Eddy is described as "author and musician," and I am described as "the wife of the Hon. Harold Nicolson C.M.G."

I don't grudge Eddy being described as an author and musician— but I do resent being dismissed as merely somebody's wife—with no existence of my own—especially in connexion with Knole, and my name.

Very very cross about this. You know I'm not a feminist, but there are limits . . .

HAROLD TO VITA   *4 King's Bench Walk*

9 May 1945

The whole of Trafalgar Square and Whitehall was packed with people and I had some difficulty in pushing my way through.[1] At last I got to Palace Yard and as it was a few minutes to three I thought it would be a good thing to stand there and listen to Winston's Broadcast before entering the House. And then as the clock struck 3.0 an immense hush descended on the crowds and Winston's voice boomed out over the loud-speakers. When it was finished the B.B.C. played God Save the King and I went into the House. They were going through questions at the ordinary pace and when 3.15 came they kept

---

1. May 8 was Victory in Europe Day.

them going by sham questions. All that was amusing and dignified. Then there was a slight bustle at the door and Winston, a little shyly, came in. The whole House rose and yelled and yelled and waved their order papers. It was by far the most triumphant demonstration I have ever seen.

HAROLD TO VITA   *Leicester*

21 June 1945

The election campaign continues. Yesterday I had a deputation from the anti-vivisectionists in the morning. They are also anti-vaccinationists. I said that to my mind the life of 10,000 guinea-pigs was less important than the life of one human. They contend that we have imposed "untold agony" on millions of guinea pigs without having discovered a cure for cancer. So there!

In the evening I had one bad meeting and one not so bad. The first one was small and sparsely attended. But it was dominated by a slightly intoxicated workman who kept on yelling, "You're a liar, you are!" That meant that I had to raise my voice. But what was worse was a sort of Madame de Krüdener [1] and Lady Macbeth all in one who rose all the time and waved her arms aloft and uttered incantations. One of her incantations was that I was a bloated landowner who lived in a Castle and ground his tenants down for rent. No good at all my saying that Sissingbags wasn't a castle but only the remains of it; that it didn't belong to me but to you; and that Beale was not being ground into the earth. But I did not at all like Sissinghurst, that shrine of quiet and loveliness, being dragged into this squalid controversy. It was like seeing a piece of Tudor embroidery in the mud.

Darling, truly it is not as bad as last time [the 1935 Election]. In the first place I have far more experience and am not in the least nervous at meetings. I have infinitely more self-confidence as a speaker. In the second place it makes a difference to know Leicester people well. On the one hand it makes me feel that the apparent animosity, hatred,

---

1. The Russian mystic (1764–1824) who conceived a passion for Czar Alexander I.

scolding etc. is confined to a tiny minority. And in the second place I am surrounded by friends and supporters who really do want me to get in. I have been allotted a LOVELY girl to be my chauffeuse; she has white hair but is quite young.[2]

2. Polling day was on 5 July 1945, and the result was declared on 26 July. Labour won a majority of 180 seats, and Harold lost his seat by over 7,000 votes.

The war ended. Ben (damaged by a road accident in Italy) and Nigel (unwounded) returned to Sissinghurst, and for some years Harold shared a house with his sons in Kensington, having been obliged, to his great chagrin, to give up his flat in the Temple. Having lost his parliamentary seat in the General Election, he hoped for a peerage, which to some extent would restore it. In this he was disappointed, and he joined the Labour Party in a moment of aberration. His income, mainly from journalism and broadcasts, was more modest than his tastes, and it was Vita who again came to the rescue of the family finances by her weekly articles on gardening for The Observer *and a novel,* Devil at Westease, *which she would only allow to be published in America. Harold was the more active of the two. He lived a vigorous social life in London, went to Nuremberg to witness the trial of the Nazi war criminals, and to Paris in 1946 to broadcast twice weekly for the BBC about the Peace Conference. His books of this period were* The English Sense of Humour *and* Benjamin Constant.

14 July 1945

Ben said that he was going to the Ordinary.[1] I cut in at once as if the idea had just occurred to me: "I pray to God, Benzie, that you will, if you find yourself next to a dull person, not just sit in a heap

---

1. The "Ordinaries" were large dinner parties at the Dorchester Hotel organized by Sibyl Colefax for friends, who were discreetly asked to contribute to the cost.

with your mouth open." Here I gave him an imitation of himself that made him laugh. I went on to say that such an attitude was unkind to the dull neighbour, and unkind to Sibyl who would spot the well of loneliness sitting over there. Moreover there was always something interesting in everyone, and a man who could talk as well as he could when aroused could always, with a very little effort, find something at least to get out of even the dullest neighbour. He would be surprised, if he once tried, to find how easy it was, and how afterwards it gave one a small satisfaction to have made what might have been a dull dinner-party interesting by one's own efficiency in talking to bores. Then (such is my tact) I immediately changed the subject and asked him to help me with an article on the National Gallery pictures. I proposed to mention only three pictures which I specially liked, and I explained to him what I was going to say about them. He lit up at once. He agreed with my comments and added a whole mass of fascinating detail to complement them. I do not think I ever met a man who can talk so interestingly as Benzie does about pictures. So thus I was able (a) to reprove him for being a well of loneliness; (b) to stimulate him by showing how brilliantly he could talk.

HAROLD TO VITA   *British Embassy, Athens*

27 October 1945

After luncheon the Leepers drove me out to Penhelicon.[1] There are Mediterranean pines and little byzantine chapels and slim autumn croci in the pine-needles. And a view, darling, such as only Attica can give. The great sweep of the Attic plain and then the mountains of the Peloponnesus and the islands. And below, Athens bathing in a clear light. My God! I am not surprised that from this wonderful air and setting should have come the greatest lucidity of mind.

---

1. Harold had flown to Greece to give two lectures, on Byron and democracy, and stayed in Athens with the British Ambassador, Sir Reginald Leeper.

HAROLD TO VITA   *4 King's Bench Walk*

29 November 1945

Look here, my sweetest. Madame Massigli[1] is giving a "small but interesting dinner" for Winston and Clemmie [Churchill] on December 19 and wishes us both to go. Now Mar will say that she does not go out and that she has no clothes. That is rubbish. She can easily evolve the sort of tea-gowny stuff that women wear for dinner parties. There is no need of an *ausgeschnittenes kleid.* Mar must have some sort of draperies she can affix or get the Belgian seamstress to affix. I think she would regret it if she missed the chance of meeting Winston again in congenial surroundings. So be firm with yourself and not a cabbage stalk. You could stay the night here. I should have telephoned had it not been that I knew such a suggestion would fling you into a flutter, and it was best to put it to you calmly and in writing so that you could recover from your first panic-stricken instinct to say "No."

Oh my love! what a crazy loon she is, bless her![2]

HAROLD TO VITA   *10 Neville Terrace,*
                                         Onslow Gardens, London S.W.7
14 February 1946

I went to Beaconsfield to lecture to the Germans there. It is a sort of course which they arrange at which selected prisoners are to be taught civic values. A mansion in the park surrounded by wire and huts and more wire. All very grim and grey.

We started by having dinner in mess. The Commandant, who is an elderly Australian, had been there ever since it was a prison camp in 1940, and it was astonishing to him to find himself surrounded suddenly by professors and school-masters and odd visitors like me. He had not yet recovered from his bewilderment with which mingled a touch of resentment at he knew not what. Anyhow he was

---

1. Wife of the French Ambassador, René Massigli.
2. Vita did go to the party at the French Embassy, and in his diary for that day Harold described her as "looking quite beautiful in diamonds and emeralds."

polite to me and even offered me a glass of port (which was not forthcoming) and then I walked through the barbed wire and into an enormous hut which was packed with Huns. The idea is to get together some of the older ones (who are anti-Nazi) and some of the cleverer Hitler Jugend. It is a good idea. I spoke to them about "An Englishman's View of the German Character," and they listened entranced. They laughed very loud indeed at my jokes. Then there were questions for one hour and a half! Poor people—I felt so sorry for them. I had a feeling that I had cheered them up by treating them as civilised human beings.

HAROLD TO VITA   *10 Neville Terrace*

25 April 1946

I am afraid I have a nasty for you. It is now confirmed that I am to go with George Clerk to Nuremberg next week.[1] We fly there on Tuesday morning and ought to get back late on Friday. I am sorry about this as I know it casts over you a cloud of anxiety. But I should always blame myself if I funked going to Nuremberg (which quite honestly I do) since it would be like having a chance to see the Dreyfus trial and refusing it. But I do dread it so. I know I am squeamish about that sort of thing, but I hate the idea of my sitting all comfy in a box with George Clerk and staring at men who are certain to be hanged by the neck and who are in any case caught like rats in a trap. You know as well as I do that my feelings for Ribbentrop have always been cold feelings. But I do not want to see the man humiliated. And Schacht was a friend of mine.[2] I do not want to see him a prisoner in the dock. Nor really do I want to see Germany in its present state. But I should never forgive myself if I shirked this opportunity.

---

1. He went there, at the invitation of the Foreign Office, to write about the trial of the major Nazi war criminals. George Clerk had been British Ambassador in Paris, 1934–37.
2. Dr. Hjalmar Schacht, Hitler's Finance Minister, had been President of the Reichsbank when Harold was Counsellor in the British Embassy.

HAROLD TO VITA   *10 Neville Terrace*

15 May 1946

I went to the Flower Show yesterday. I could not see any *Cheiran-thus* displayed at all. What really happens is that things become fashionable and nurserymen concentrate on such things and ignore the other things. I mean there were no herbaceous things at all except for Delphiniums. The azaleas were no good, the rhododendrons good but not up to Bodnant standard, and the Alpines no better than what we have got. In fact I saw little there which we could envy or even desire. But there were very beautiful tulips. I enclose the list of those I ordered. When you see "24" or "three dozen" do not be upset. It means that half goes for my life's work[1] and half for Mar's garden. The Barr parrot tulips were really wonderful, enamelled like Battersea china. Then there was the finest delphinium I have ever seen—a most beautiful Eton blue with a dash of Oxford blue. It was expensive. It was 30/– a plant. But I ordered two plants as a birthday present and we can take seeds from them.

I like spending money in this way. I mean, I believe that before we die we shall make Sissinghurst the loveliest garden in Kent. And we can only do this by getting better and better varieties of things we like. It is no good trying to have things which we do not get on with. Rhododendrons are to us like large stock-brokers whom we do not want to have to dinner. But there are certain things which are adapted to Sissingbags and those things should be improved and improved and improved until they reach the perfect standard.

HAROLD TO VITA   *10 Neville Terrace*

5 June 1946

I lunched with the Walter Elliots to meet Smuts.[2] He is an amazing old man—so gay, so young, so full of optimism and faith.

---

1. The Lime Walk, or spring garden, at Sissinghurst, which Harold designed and planted himself.
2. Field Marshal Jan Christian Smuts, who was then seventy-six, was still Prime Minister of South Africa, and had been in San Francisco helping to create the United Nations.

He greeted me as if I had been his oldest friend. He talked well. He spoke of his visit to Germany and of how the Germans had not yet acquired repentance. Hatred and self-pity enervated their will. He had, arrayed as a Field Marshal, addressed the Senate at Hamburg. He had told them that Germany would in all certitude perish if they did not help themselves. "I also," he said, "have belonged to a defeated nation. I also have looked around and seen the ruins of my country and felt that no human energy would ever suffice to repair them. But we set to work. We made friends with our enemies; and God has spared me to witness the birth of a country more rich and prosperous than we ever dreamed. A great South Africa which is now a power in the World."

He said, "Your England is not an old country; she is a young country—far younger than the United States or Canada. And I shall tell you why. Because you absorb new ideas into your blood stream; you keep your arteries elastic; you change the whole time. Never have I seen so many gifted and energetic young men as I have in England. You have a great future before you."

Oh yes, darling, a lovely man, a lovely man. He asked in a funny old-fashioned bowing sort of way about you. I said you were thriving, and then I put my hand behind me to touch wood in case some fatal illness had attacked you during the night.

HAROLD TO VITA   *Ritz Hotel, Paris*

30 July 1946

You will see that I have been busy enough and very happy and passionately interested.[1] Looking down upon Gladwyn [Jebb] sitting as a delegate in a plush armchair did give me a slight twinge; but not of envy; merely the 'elderly failure' twinge. But as a matter of fact I am glad to be free of responsibility and these slight twinges at being out of official life are as nothing to the great tugs of misery which I feel when I go to my beloved but unwanting House of Commons.

---

1. Harold had gone to Paris to report the Peace Conference for the BBC, and remained there till mid-October, when the Conference ended.

What is odd is that I am not lonely or depressed. Now why is this? Partly I suppose because I am surrounded by friends and fans, that I love Paris, and that I am doing something which I know to be important and which I believe I do well. That I take for granted. But there is something more than that. The ghastly home-sickness and depression which usually assail me when you go, are not present this time. My God! how I suffered at Lausanne (why on earth was that the worst barring Persia?), and how I suffered in Berlin! But this room is in an odd way more friendly to me since you have been there, and with the rosemary and the sweet geranium and the violas in front of me. Of course it is mostly because I am active and interested and surrounded. But I think it is also because your coming gave me such extraordinary pleasure that the pleasure lasts even after the cause of it has been removed. I feel I am so lucky to have you and Niggs and Benzie in my life. How empty poor little Pierre de Lacretelle[2] is compared to me! Nobody really cares if he is run over or not.

VITA TO HAROLD   *St Antonin (Tarn et Garonne), France*

5 September 1946

We did not get to Albi today after all. We got to Toulouse instead—and by mistake. After we had driven for about 50 miles we reached a village, and Tray [Raymond Mortimer] said, "Where are we now?" "Caussade," I said, having just seen the name in the *poteau*. Tray collapsed into a heap with his face in his hands. "My God," he said, "so it *was* the wrong bridge we went over. We have gone west instead of east."

So then we decided to go on, and we got to Montauban where there is a vast episcopal palace entirely devoted to the culte of Ingres. We arrived there to find, much to my relief, a notice on the gates saying, *"Le musée Ingres est fermé."* But did that defeat Tray? Not a bit. He got hold of the concierge and sent in his card to the director, with the result that an enormous *trousse de clefs* was produced and the

2. His old bachelor friend whom he had first met in Constantinople. Harold called him "one of the most brilliant people I have ever known." Opium and gambling were his undoing.

gates unlocked and we were admitted. Now of all great painters Ingres is the one I most dislike. And then a bright young woman appeared and said she was working on a complete catalogue of Ingres in eight volumes, and would we like her to show us over? There were about 3,000 drawings by Ingres in the museum which she would be delighted to show us . . .

When, exhausted, I emerged two hours later into the street again, Tray exclaimed *"Wasn't* that a bit of luck?" Personally, I thought it a disaster.

HAROLD TO VITA   *10 Neville Terrace*

6 March 1947

I must break the fact to you that I have joined the Labour Party. I have done this because in the end it was inevitable and I had better do it when the night of misery is on them rather than when they are basking in the sun of popular acclaim. I did it quite quietly by joining the local branch. They registered me as 'H. Nicolson', and it is probable that there will be no publicity. I told Elvira [Niggeman], who emitted a short sharp scream. I told the boys, who received the news in horrified silence. I shall get into a real scolding when I come down on Saturday. But I know I was right. This is NOT (repeat NOT) an impulsive gesture. I have been worrying over it for months.

VITA TO HAROLD   *Sissinghurst*

7 March 1947

I am not sure about the Labour Party, though not wholly hostile, especially if it leads eventually to Lord Cranfield.[1] Of course I do not really like you being associated with these bedints. I like Ernest Bevin [Foreign Secretary], I have a contemptuous tolerance of Attlee, but I *loathe* Aneurin Bevan, and Shinwell is just a public menace. I do not

---

1. The title that Harold had decided to assume if he was offered a peerage.

like people who cannot speak the King's English. The sort of people I like are Winston and Sir John Anderson. I like Jowitt personally, but now think him to be a windbag and a broken reed.

H A R O L D　T O　V I T A　　　　　　　　　*10 Neville Terrace*

22 May 1947

I went to the Salisburys' party at Montpelier Square. We were told to be there at 6.0 as the Queen was coming. There was the American Ambassador and Mrs Lou Douglas and lots of younger people. The Queen arrived on the stroke and remained for two solid hours standing the whole time. She was looking radiant. She said in her lovely clear voice, "How nice to meet old friends again." Then she shook hands with us one by one. Then she established herself in the corner of the room and we were brought up for a chat. She asked after you and I said we had been down to Panshanger. Then we got on to St Helena. She is all very easy and simple. Lady Harlech, who went round South Africa with her, said that she possesses a sixth sense. She can tell when someone is feeling hurt or left out or frightened. She can spot them even when they are skulking or sulking at the back of a crowd. She will pass through the crowd and talk to them and all is sunshine again. She says it is some magnetic faculty. The one thing wrong with the Queen is that she is a bad leaver. "Like Pharaoh," said Lady Harlech, "she won't let the people go."

V I T A　T O　H A R O L D　　　　　　　　　*Sissinghurst*

5 June 1947

I am amused. You know the absurd thriller story I wrote in 4 weeks for an American magazine and got £3,000 for? [*Devil at West-ease*] not that it was £3,000 by the time Dr Dalton [Chancellor of the Exchequer] had finished with it. Well, I said on no account was it to be published in England but I didn't mind it being published by Doubleday in the U.S.A. (I have got copies; but I won't inflict it on

you.) And now I hear from Curtis Brown [literary agent] that they
have applications for translation rights into Spanish, Portuguese, Italian, German, and 'English Continental' whatever that may be. I think
they must have had even more than those, because they say "numerous
enquiries, *including*" . . . the ones mentioned.

I re-read it. It is quite readable, and as I had completely forgotten
it, I was able to read it quite objectively. But it is only a nonsense.

HAROLD TO VITA   *10 Neville Terrace*

22 July 1947

No darling—I do not agree about the azaleas. And why is that?
First because I don't feel that azaleas are very Sissinghurst in any case.
They are Ascot, Sunningdale sort of plants. Not our lovely romantic
Saxon, Roman, Tudor Kent. I know you will say, and rightly, that
nor are magnolias. But you know what I mean. Anything with the
suggestion of suburbia should be excluded. But secondly because I
think we want something formal. You have the wall; you have
Dionysus [statue]; you have the strip of mown grass; you then have
the bank; and along the top I want something different from the bank
and different from the nuttery. Something dividing the formality of
the moat walk from the comparative informality of the nuttery. I
should rather have a row of stiff Irish yews than a flurry of azaleas.
But we may find something. It is a very important site. [1]

HAROLD TO VITA   *Hotel Richmond, Geneva*

7 September 1947

I spent most of the time in the library of the University poring
over their amazing collection of manuscripts. [2] They were frightfully

---

1. Harold did not get his way. The bank was planted with azaleas, underneath which wild
   bluebells were allowed to flourish.
2. Harold was in Switzerland gathering information and impressions for his book on Benjamin
   Constant, the French intellectual banished by Napoleon for his political activities.

kind and I sat in the librarian's room at a little table and had in front
of me all the letters from and to Constant that they possessed. I had
of course not time to read more than a small percentage of them, nor
in fact do I want my book to be a work of research. I have no time
for that. I want it to be a study. An 'interpretation' if you like. But
of course to handle all these letters gave me added insight. As a child
Constant was a regular calligraphist. He wrote to his grandmother at
the age of ten in a hand which is like that which B.M. used to affect
when she wrote the names of guests for the bedroom doors. I was
lucky, I think, as each of the letters I selected for special reading gave
me some information of value.

The librarian was a nice man and an intellectual. He had read several
of my works. He did not call me "cher maître," which I thought remiss
of him, but in other respects he was waggy-tail, and handling things
with neat fingers, and pointing out things I might miss. Then he showed
me the manuscript of the *Contrat Social,* and what was more interesting,
that of the *Confessions* [both Rousseau]. The latter is written in the tiny
hand which people adopt when they want to write the Sermon on the
Mount on a five-shilling piece. Beautiful it was in its neatness. *"On voit
bien,"* said the librarian, *"qu'il était fils d'un horloger."*

Well I enjoyed that and thereafter I strolled through this Calvinis-
tic city and had luncheon alone with Lysistrata (a fine strapping girl),[3]
and then went to the museum where there is an extraordinary picture
called 'Le Lever de Monsieur de Voltaire'. Voltaire has just tumbled
out of bed and is struggling out of his night-gown. White naked thighs
stamp in impatience, and with his free hand he is dictating furiously
to a secretary sitting all prim at a table by the window.

HAROLD TO VITA   *10 Neville Terrace*

19 November 1947

I had foreseen the Violet [Trefusis] difficulty and ought to have
discussed it with you before I left. I remember that she is frightened

---

3. Not a person but a book, the play by Aristophanes that described a women's revolt.

of sleeping alone. The solution is that she should have my room and I will go into Ben's. I should really loathe feeling I was alone with her in the cottage, and I do not think she would like it either. Why I should hate it so much I cannot begin to say. But the idea fills me with horror. Real horror. In fact I refuse absolutely to do it. So Violet has my room and I go to Ben's. I will not truly accept any other solution. But why the idea of sharing the cottage with Violet should make me tremble with real panic I have no idea. I shall have to be psychoanalysed about it. But make no mistake at all. I would rather walk the fields all night.[1]

HAROLD TO VITA   *10 Neville Terrace*

11 December 1947

I met Tommy Lascelles in the Club. He said to me, "Was Vita pleased?" I said, "Yes," not wishing to expose to the private secretary of the fountain of honours [King George VI] that my own beloved is a nit-wit about such things. But I did say to him, "Tommy, who was it who suggested V. should get the C.H.?"[2] "The Prime Minister," he said. I said, "Yes of course I know that formally it has to come from the P.M., but who was at the back of it?" "The Prime Minister," he repeated grinning—and then he told me that Attlee had a passionate admiration for THE LAND and had tried to get you this last year but the list was full. So the little rat whom you so despise is a persistent little rat.

I wrote our names down at the Palace. I told Tommy that if he was a true friend he would see to it that the announcement was V.S.W. with (Mrs Hadji) in brackets. He said it would have to be Victoria in any case as full names have to be given. He did not know about the V.S.W. coming first. But he promised to see what he could do. I hope

---

1. Violet Trefusis did not come to Sissinghurst after all.
2. Vita was made a Companion of Honour in the New Year's Honours of 1948.

he will. He will be all friendly about it I know, but I doubt whether he realizes the importance you attach to it. Poets still and patriots deck the line.[3] But I couldn't explain all that to Tommy at the Beefsteak. But I did my best.

3. "And patriots still, or poets, deck the line." Pope's epitaph on the tomb of Charles Sackville, 6th Earl of Dorset, at Withyham, Sussex.

Harold was nominated by the Labour Party to contest a bye-election in North Croydon. He did himself no discredit, but failed to win the seat, and the experience effectively ended his political career. Vita (who was on a lecture tour in North Africa during the election) was secretly delighted, particularly when Harold was invited to write the official biography of King George V, his magnum opus, *which occupied him till 1952 and gained him a knighthood. In the intervals of his researches in the royal archives at Windsor, he continued his weekly journalism, his membership of several committees including the National Trust and the London Library (of which he became Chairman), and gave many lectures, three of them in the devastated city of Berlin. Vita became a local Justice of the Peace, and explored the idea of a White Garden, her greatest horticultural triumph at Sissinghurst.*

HAROLD TO VITA   *10 Neville Terrace*

19 December 1947

It was nice of you to telephone about Croydon. Niggs also telephoned on his return from Leicester. I was touched by this solicitude. I meant to treat Croydon as my own private worry and not impose it on my family. Like a dog going into the dark when ill. But I was touched by their interest and sympathy. Niggs is so sweet about it all.[1]

I dined with Rab Butler last night. He says that Winston is a grave

1. The problem was that Nigel was standing as Conservative candidate in Leicester while his father was the Labour candidate in Croydon.

liability to the Party. He does not consult them and is always making speeches which let them down. But they can't get rid of him. "It is a question of which dies first, Winston or the Tory Party."

H A R O L D　 T O　 V I T A　　　　　　　　　　　*10 Neville Terrace*

8 January 1948

I went yesterday to hear Chaim Weizmann give an address on Palestine. He is a fine man, like a large Lenin, and with a sort of sad dignity which is impressive. He was more optimistic than I expected. He says that we are apt to judge the Zionists by the Stern gang which is nothing but a tiny gangster minority. That is all very well, but Haganah is not a minority and they do nothing at all to control the Stern gang. Poor Weizmann—he will live to see his independent Jewish State—but instead of it being a nice comfy little home like Luxembourg, it will be a fierce camp, riven with hatred, and red with blood. A sad thing to achieve the aim of one's life and find it a thing of horror.

V I T A　 T O　 H A R O L D　　　　　　　　　　　　　*Algiers*

19 February 1948

Well, I went to Radio-Alger and did my little piece in a strange studio whose walls and floor were made of cork. It had a vaguely Egyptian look, like a chamber in the centre of the Pyramid. You could poke holes in it with your fingers; and as everybody had apparently amused themselves by doing so, it had a honeycomb appearance. I expect you went there too, when you were here.

Darling, I go on scribbling my little doings to you in spite of realising how silly and remote they must seem in the middle of an election campaign. Listen, I wish you would get yourself a really good tonic for this election. Will you? To please Mar? Metatone is as good as anything, I think, if you can get it; unless you would like to ask

Dr Goadby to prescribe something which he knows would suit your make-up. Do, *please,* Hadji. You will need it. Oh my darling, you're going to be so tired and bothered, I can't bear to think of it.

HAROLD TO VITA   *The Queen's Hotel, North Croydon*

24 February 1948

This is, or was, a hydro—like one of those many hydros in Tunbridge Wells—but has fallen on evil days. There is no heating, no running water, a bath along the passage with a tepid drip, a gas-fire in my room which I have to work by inserting a shilling into the metre. I know that I shall return frozen to find that I have no shillings. The other inhabitants of this hotel consist in broken old ladies and epileptics.

My Committee Room is a disused and requisitioned building. Most of the windows have holes in them, the doors won't shut, and it is very cold and draughty. I have to sit all day in my greatcoat with a muffler. But they are getting me another electric stove and the thaw has begun. Great icicles drip from my window-ledge. Huge posters of myself decorate the walls with exclamatory gestures. No, I do not like it one little bit.

The staff are charming and gay and efficient, and that makes a great difference and relief. But the hours are ungainly. I mean, I don't know when I get my meals. There is a tiny bedint restaurant near here where one can get fish-and-chips and a cup of coffee. But somehow that is not a diet to which I am accustomed.

I met my opponents.[1] Harris is stout, common, naive, young, rather attractive I thought. Bennett is young-looking, smart, determined, speaks with a faint Australian accent, very composed. Harris speaks glibly but evidently he has learnt one gramophone record and will play it over and over again. Bennett made a set speech quite well. I follow with an ordinary little talk. The whole theme is, "What, in

---

1. Harold was the Labour candidate; F. H. Harris (who won) was the Conservative; Air-Vice-Marshal Donald Bennett, a war hero, the Liberal.

your opinion, should be done for the smaller trader and businessman?"
Now, the Croydon Chamber of Commerce are entirely composed of
small retailers and businessmen, and are enraged by all the restrictions
and forms which the Government have imposed. Thus Harris and
Bennett were very popular when they said, "We are for freeing the
small man," and I was not at all popular when I said, "We must retain
controls." But up to that point it went well enough.

Then came questions. They were all addressed to me. As always
happens, they were based upon a detailed grievance and not upon a
definite principle. "Why has the Croydon Council requisitioned a
house at the corner of the Bellevue Road?" "Why was I not allowed
to get hides from Sweden?" "Why does one not have a rebate on
purchase-tax for unexpended stock?" Now, of course, I could not
answer these questions, but Harris could. So in the end he and Bennett
scored heavily.

I drive back at 9.45 to my hotel. It is bitterly cold. I find the whole
place in semi-darkness and cannot get anything at all to eat—not even
a glass of water. I go up to my room and light the gas-fire. It is not
a cheerful contrivance. I then go to bed, but I sleep badly, as I am cold
and nervous. And rather hungry. I shall buy some Ovaltine tomorrow
to drink when I get back from meetings.

Well, that is the end of the first day. I found such a sweet letter
from you here, darling. It did cheer me up. I have got the Lenare
photograph [of Vita] in the office, and all the Sissinghurst ones in my
hotel bedroom. The silver pot is in the hotel, as it will be useful for
the Ovaltine.

HAROLD TO VITA   *Croydon*

1 March 1948

I am so glad I belong to the [Labour] Party now. I really feel much
more comfortable as a Labour man than I ever did as a hybrid. There
is a quality of mutual confidence which is moving and rare.

The Tories are evidently very frightened of losing the seat. I do
not think they have any cause for alarm. Air-Vice-Marshal Bennett is
not cutting very much ice. And unless he seriously splits the Tory vote,

then Harris is bound to get in. You know that I shall not mind much being beaten although it would be a terrific triumph to win. What I do not want to do is to make a fool of myself. But the Tories have gone all out. They have imported cinema vans, and loud-speaker vans, and the whole of their Central Office, and the whole of their shadow Cabinet. Anthony Eden is coming, and Oliver Lyttelton, and Harold Macmillan, and Rab Butler and all the rest. I am glad of that. It will make my defeat less humiliating and my victory more triumphant.

HAROLD TO VITA   *Croydon*

10 March 1948

Well the battle is over and I am alive and well. It has been the most lovely weather and promises to be fine tomorrow. Quite summer warm it has been and I am thinking of the Magnolia and almonds at home. I shall see them on Saturday. And then on Saturday week we are united again, thank God, and resume our happy private life without publicity or angry crowds.

I can honestly say, darling, that there has not been one moment in the last three weeks which I have not hated to a large or small degree. The only contented moments I have had is when I have got back to my room and my Ovaltine and written to you. However much one tries, there is always a falsity about elections. I mean, one simulates friendship and matiness with people whom one does not wish ever to see again. My hands are still aching (and have to be washed) after shaking hands with a hundred enthusiastic workers. Something of their excitement does communicate itself. But it does not go deep down. And always the censor watches and murmurs in my ear, "Hadji—you are putting it on and showing off."

But truly, darling Viti, I can look back with some satisfaction upon this campaign. I have not spared myself and have not shirked a single odious task. I have spoken well enough and answered questions frankly. I have not descended to any abuse or tricks; I have not made a single pledge or promise which I shall be unable to fulfill; and I have not, even in the heat of controversy, said a single word which, in the after vacancy, need cause me shame.

Of course I am aware that there have been those among my supporters who feel that I have exaggerated the superior and noble line and that a more dynamic and popular candidate might have done better. I do not regret the line of moderate decency which I have taken. From the practical point of view, the Labour vote was mine anyway; the reason I was chosen was that they felt I might attract some floating votes. I think I might have done so and may have done so. But I do not think I shall get in.[1]

HAROLD TO VITA   *10 Neville Terrace*

7 May 1948

Another lovely May morning and I think of the view over the lilacs to the azaleas which I get from my bedroom window. I think I gain more from Sissinghurst than anyone else. (1) My sitting room is the nicest room in the estate. (2) My bedroom is the nicest bedroom in the castle. (3) My Life's Work is the finest part of the whole garden.

Anyhow I go to Oxford today and it will be nice to see it on a May evening. I am going for the opening meeting of the Oxford Philhellenic Society. A most inauspicious moment to have chosen, since the Greek Government are massacring their [Communist] prisoners by the shoals. So conscious of this was I that I went and saw the Greek Ambassador who was to have presided and told him he must contract an immediate diplomatic illness. It would not do at all if there were to be boos at the Greek Ambassador. He was much relieved at my insisting that he should chuck.

On my way there I called in at the Roosevelt memorial.[2] The statue itself is a nightmare but the surround with its two pools and little fountains is quite successful. But how difficult the proletariat are! In principle I like to see such gardens thrown open to them. But they destroy the grass and there were little ragamuffins sailing cigarette

---

1. The result was declared next day: Harris (Conservative) 36,200; Nicolson (Labour) 24,536; Bennett (Liberal) 6,321. Conservative majority 11,664.
2. In Grosvenor Square. The Memorial (by Sir William Reid Dick) had been unveiled by the King in April.

cartons in the two pools. Yes I fear my socialism is purely cerebral; I do not like the masses in the flesh.

HAROLD TO VITA   *10 Neville Terrace*

14 May 1948

I went to [Laurence] Olivier's *Hamlet* yesterday. It is built on the theory that Hamlet was a man of weak decision. But I agree with [Salvador] Madariaga that this is not possible as an interpretation. He was a tough. After all he murdered Polonius and Ophelia and Rosencrantz and Guildenstern without a qualm. But in any case Olivier cannot act a *weak* man. He is himself a tough. So the thing is more unconvincing than ever. It remains an insoluble problem. Shakespeare must have known it was one of his finest plays, and yet he was terribly careless about it. For instance Hamlet is 20 when the play opens and then one discovers that he is really 30. And all those stiffs at the end are pushing it too far. Anyhow the film is a very competent piece of work—but not more. It lacks that touch of April which made *Henry V* so unforgettable a film. I went three times to see *Henry V*.

HAROLD TO VITA   *10 Neville Terrace*

8 June 1948

I walked across the park to Buckingham Palace. I was taken at once into Tommy Lascelles's room. He had been delegated to approach me to write the life of George V. I said that in principle I did not like writing biographies when I could not tell the whole truth. Tommy said (well, I thought), "But it is not meant to be an ordinary biography. It is something quite different. You will be writing a book about a very ancient national institution, and you need not descend to personalities." He said that I should not be expected to write one word that was not true. I should not be expected to praise or exaggerate. But I must omit things and incidents which were discreditable.

Well, that is the proposition. I have not got clear in my head what I really feel about it. I see the balance-sheet as follows:

Advantages: A definite task, taking me three years at least and bringing a large financial reward. Access to papers of deep interest and importance. Close collaboration with charming people such as Tommy and Morshead.[1] The opportunity of writing the history of my own times. Added to which, I suppose, is the compliment of having been chosen.

Disadvantages: To have to write an 'official' biography. The lack of charm in the King I am dealing with. My inability (and indeed my unwillingness) to poke fun at the monarchy. My not being allowed to mention discreditable or foolish things. My having to be mythological.

I shall like to hear your reactions to all this. What you will hate, as I hate, is the idea of having to write 'to order'. Rather like a painter being forced to paint the official royal portraits. But being a writer, you will also see the fascination of the challenge. Is it possible to write such a life in a way that will be really interesting, really true, while keeping to the convention of royal portraits? I do not feel that my integrity is involved. I need not say one word in praise. All I have to do is leave out the funny bits. Nor shall I consent to distorting a single passage.

I told Elvira [Niggeman]. She was delighted and as usual most intelligent. She said, "But it is just what you need—an anchor. It will keep you busy for three years and prevent you doing silly things like Croydon. People say that young men need anchors. That may be true—but people of later middle age need anchors far more than the young."

After we had discussed this, Tommy said, "Must you rush off at once? Can you spare me another ten minutes?" He then gave me the speech he had been writing for the Duke of Edinburgh at the Guildhall. I pointed out that certain phrases would be difficult to get across clearly. He then took up the telephone and said, "Get me the Duke of Edinburgh." "Could you come down, Sir, for a moment?" So the young man came in like a schoolboy. He is far better looking than his photographs. We made him go through it. He did it so seriously and so well. "What a bit of luck," said Tommy when the boy had gone, "such a nice young man, such a sense of duty, not a fool in any way,

---

1. Sir Owen Morshead, the Librarian at Windsor Castle, 1926–58.

so much in love, poor boy—and after all, put the heir to the throne in a family way all according to plan."[2] Yes, Tommy is the least courtly courtier I have ever known.

VITA TO HAROLD   *Sissinghurst*

8 June 1948

I am divided in my mind about George V. I do see that he would be a good solid peg on which to hang a very interesting study of the period. Very interesting indeed, if you were allowed a free hand. But would the King want you to concentrate principally on his father? Or would he allow you excursions all round? Tommy L. of course would understand exactly how you wanted to write it, but Tommy's employer probably has a Divine Right attitude, and might not understand. Anyhow it was a great compliment, and I expect Queen Mary was the originator.

VITA TO HAROLD   *Sissinghurst*

26 September 1948

It was such a relief to get that telephone message to say that you had arrived safely in Berlin.[3] It was just like you to have taken the trouble to get it sent, but really you would have been rewarded for your trouble if you could have known the relief it gave me. I slept soundly all night, whereas I hadn't slept much the night before. It is a perfect day here. Hot, like summer, and you among the ruins. You will hate all that: I know how much you will mind it. Oh Hadji, how much I wish you were here instead of in Berlin! With the world in such a mess, I cling more and more to the serenity and happiness of Sissinghurst and our life—our way of life, as we have made it.

2. Prince Philip, Duke of Edinburgh, was then twenty-seven. He had married Princess Elizabeth on 20 November 1947, and Prince Charles was born on 14 November 1948.
3. He had flown there via Hamburg, since all other forms of transport were cut off by the Russian blockade of West Berlin. Harold had been asked to give four lectures as a demonstration of British solidarity with the Berliners.

HAROLD TO VITA   *Berlin*

29 September 1948

I had a long talk alone with Lalli [Horstmann] yesterday, and she told me the whole story. She says that we have no idea of the extent of rape the Russians carried out. She herself had to jump out of her window and hide in the hay in the barn night after night. The officers made no pretence at all to stop their men. Not a single woman, whatever her age, in her own village was not raped some ten or twelve times by different soldiers. Then after a month of these nightly orgies, discipline was reestablished. But for that month the thing was hell. Lalli, who has endured so much, now feels that she must really get away to safety. She hopes to go to Portugal and remain there a year.

I lunched with the Acting Lord Mayor of Berlin [Friedenburg] in a clubhouse on the Wannsee. I met most of the leading Berlin politicians and was glad to find that my German was coming back to me. They were delighted that their city was the centre of world attention. But except for one of them [Reuter], I thought them a poor lot.

When I got back, old Graf Limburg Stirrum was waiting for me. He used to be a very rich landowner, but all his properties are beyond the iron curtain and he is left with one room in Berlin, a Boucher, and not a bob. He is dreading the winter. He has no light except for two hours a night. No candles. He just sits in the dark. And what happens when the cold comes? The prospect for them is really terrible.

HAROLD TO VITA   *10 Neville Terrace*

26 October 1948

How cold and lovely it was this morning. I walked about the platform of Staplehurst station and watched the leaves turning. I thought how much nature has meant to me in life. I do derive intense pleasure from the loveliness of my whole world of Kent, and above all of Sissinghurst. I am sure we are right about that. Sissinghurst has a quality of mellowness, of retirement, of unflaunting dignity, which is just what we wanted to achieve and which in some ways we have achieved by chance. I think it is mainly due to the succession of privacies: the forecourt, the first arch, the main court, the tower arch, the lawn, the orchard. All a series of escapes from the world, giving the impression of cumulative escape.

VITA TO HAROLD   *Sissinghurst*

9 November 1948

Darling, it was such a lovely rich sunset this evening—the woods looked like tapestry, all brown and green, and the poplars on the way to the lake were bright gold. Then there was an extra bit of enchantment, because all the younger Jacob's sheep were playing a game round the big oak. They scampered round and round after each other, and sometimes they tried to run up the trunk of the oak, and then fell off again, and ran round again, and butted each other when they caught each other headlong. They played the game not knowing that I was watching them, all unselfconscious they were—it was like a Greek thing, an idyll, or like a frieze—it reminded me of Keats and the Grecian urn, only there was no urn, just our Sissinghurst field and the woods beyond.

Oh how happy I was—oh how happy—for that brief suspended moment. I felt so wildly happy that I had to tell you about it—like a sort of sharing.

Your Mar

HAROLD TO VITA   *10 Neville Terrace*

7 January 1949

I sent you a wretched little scribble yesterday as I was hurrying off to Windsor. My visit there was a great success. I climbed up the hill and the policeman directed me to the entrance to the Library. There I met Owen Morshead, who was kind indeed. He first showed me the diaries [of George V]. They are really little more than engagement books and not at all revealing. But they are invaluable for checking dates. There are also those extracts from Queen Victoria's diaries which Princess Beatrice preserved. She burnt all the rest. Wicked old woman. Morshead tells me that he does not think that the King or the Queen or even Queen Mary will be difficult so long as I do not attack the principle of monarchy, which I assuredly have no intention of doing. But he fears that all the old aunts and people will descend upon them and bully them. Luckily there are few aunts left. He says that the difficult thing to treat will be King George's handling of his children. "The House of Hanover, like ducks, produce bad parents—they trample on their young."

Thereafter he took me to the Round Tower, to the muniment rooms where I was received by Miss Mackenzie, a formidable woman who has all the appearance of being the Principal of Girton [College, Cambridge]. There is one room devoted entirely to George V. It has a small window with a lovely view over the river. This will be my room, and Elvira [Niggeman] can come and type with me. The documents are sufficiently numerous to provide me with masses of original material but not so vast as to be unmanageable. If I go there three days a week, I should be able to get through the lot in four months. I was cheered by this. I then lunched with Morshead and his wife and daughters. A happy, decent, cultured family. I came back here feeling zest about the book. It will really contain material of importance.

VITA TO HAROLD　　　　　　　　*La Tour St Loup,*
　　　　　　　　　　　　　　　Longueville, France
1 March 1949

Violet's [Trefusis] car met me at the Gare du Nord. We drew up at the Meurice, and there was Violet herself, with plumes waving all out of her hat, looking like a dowager duchess. So we drove out to St Loup together and had a perfectly delicious dinner (champagne), and talked. What worries me is the way that V. persecutes her charming old maid. It reminds me of B.M. It's really more than a little mad. She curses her *all* the time. If I spoke to Rollo [her dog] like that, he would run away and never come back. She (Alice the maid) poured it all out to me this morning, says her health is breaking down (V. even wakes her up at all hours of the night), and that she will have to leave. Of course V. doesn't believe it, but the day will come when Alice will really go, and I don't know what V. will do without her. It is a sort of lust for power, I think: she must have someone to bully. I cannot explain it in any other way, but it is most painful and horrid.

VITA TO HAROLD

10 March 1949

Parador de San Francisco, Alhambra, Granada, Spain

I have had an odd experience today. I have been to the street where Pepita was born.[1] Oh such a slum it is—very narrow, you could almost shake hands from one little balcony to the other overhead—crowded with people and children, but there can be little doubt that it was exactly the same when Pepita played there as a little girl. A Malaguerian poet called Munoz Rojas took me there. He has been looking up all the places and found the hotel where the Consul locked Granpapa into his room.[2] We lunched with Rojas after seeing the cathedral and the Alcazar. He was at Cambridge, and is now a farmer as well as a poet.

HAROLD TO VITA

1 June 1949

10 Neville Terrace

The Brains Trust was not, I felt, a very good one.[3] Such silly questions. Enid was so terrified of saying something silly that she scarcely said anything at all. I had to jab at her. Crowther was angry that the question about the devaluation of the pound was left in. He thinks that it is something that should not be mentioned. He is quite

1. In Malaga in 1830. Her mother was gipsy-born and her father a barber.
2. Lionel Sackville-West was so desperately in love with Pepita that he intended to marry her although he knew that she was already married. The British Consul prevented him by locking him into a hotel bedroom for three days.
3. Harold was a frequent quest on the BBC's prestigious radio program, "The Brains Trust." On this occasion his partners were Geoffrey Crowther (editor of the *Economist*), Enid Bagnold (the novelist), and Julian Huxley. Donald McCullough was always the Chairman.

sure that it will be of no benefit to anyone. I said that people had felt exactly the same in 1931 and that when we devalued, everybody was delighted and trade revived. He said that this was due to special circumstances. I said that it was odd that a terrible crisis arose in order to keep us on the gold standard, and that when we were off it, everybody was delighted. "It is a familiar experience," he said. "When we were boys we were told that certain practices were worse than death. And when we at last indulged in those practices, we found them rather pleasant." "I am glad you didn't say that on the air," Donald McCullough said: "It would have meant the end of the Brains Trust for ever."

VITA TO HAROLD   *Sissinghurst*

5 July 1949

I am not at all sure that we oughtn't to make the Erechtheum garden all grey and white.[1] It would then be nice all the year round. This would entail millions of cuttings, but I think it would be worthwhile, and by 1951 the cuttings will have grown into reasonably large plants. We will talk about it. It would mean leaving the *Night* roses there for another summer, or it would really be too empty, so we must make 1951 the year of triumph.

HAROLD TO VITA   *10 Neville Terrace*

6 July 1949

I agree with you about the Erechtheum garden being all grey. For next year we must keep *Night* where she is and prick in grey things all round her. We shall also have to take a vast amount of *regale* seed this year although it will not make big bulbs till 1952. We must think this out carefully. It will require *some* colour. I incline to pink as in the China roses. You prefer yellow. I am quite prepared to agree to

---

1. This was the White Garden, the most original and best known of all the separate gardens at Sissinghurst. The Erechtheum was a columned outdoor dining room that they made in a corner of this garden.

yellow since I feel that it is more original, and you have a better colour taste than I have. I quite see that those big pale yellow things in the cottage garden (Evening primroses?) would look very well. They must be faint pallid yellow—nothing that shouts or raises its voice. Yellow roses perhaps here and there. But all faint. We must aim at making it look pretty by 1951.

VITA TO HAROLD   *Sissinghurst*

28 September 1949

Darling, I did so enjoy reading *George V*. Not only because it was by my favourite author, but because it was so skillfully done. I do like good craftmanship in literature, even as I like it in a good carpenter or thatcher or bricklayer. I like things well made. I feel only, if I may speak as a reviewer and not as your worshipping fan, that you are getting a bit too frightened of what you regard as the too-personal touch. I know what is producing this cautiousness in you: it is the flood of cheaply vivid biography of recent years, the Philip Guedallas and so on. You are reacting; and it is a wholesome reaction. Think, all the same, of Stefan Zweig's life of Balzac: there was nothing cheap about that—he got the solidity as well as the highlights, the little points of light that touch up the character as in a Rembrandt. You are getting cautious and I think it is a pity because you are denying your own special gift. I know that *George V* is a serious book, so don't imagine that I am judging it from a light, frivolous, or what is called 'feminine' aspect. I am only asking you not to abjure your own particular genius, which you seem in some danger of doing because you are frightened of it.

VITA TO HAROLD   *Sissinghurst*

8 November 1949

The two people I miss most are Virginia [Woolf] and Geoffrey [Scott]—not that Geoffrey wasn't an awful nuisance to me—he was—and an anxiety—but I still think sometimes, "How that would amuse

Geoffrey!" and then I remember that I can't tell him. And Virginia even more so, because she was never a nuisance, only a delight. An anxiety of course—and I still think I might have saved her if only I had been there and had known the state of mind she was getting into. I think she would have told me, as she did tell me on previous occasions.

V I T A T O H A R O L D   *Sissinghurst*

14 December 1949

I am somewhat agitated, because the police telephoned for me to take a rather complicated case this morning.[1] I rather hate these cases, although the human aspect of them always interests me objectively. I don't like it when I am the only Justice, as I was this morning, and have to sit in a large armchair behind a table, while the wretched delinquent stands before me, and the room is full of police officers and the Clerk of the Court and his Clerk and the Detective Superintendent, all bringing charges and evidence against the prisoner, and all the ponderous weight of the Law and its apparatus of which I am a part. I always feel that here is a wild animal trapped and caged, and that if it sprang suddenly at my throat it would be seized and restrained by a dozen strong hands; and above all I feel, "There but for the grace of God and B.M.'s Marriage Settlement, go I."

"Take your hands out of your pockets when Her Worship speaks to you!" Oh darling, it makes me feel like a character in a Galsworthy play.

V I T A T O H A R O L D   *Sissinghurst*

7 March 1950

It has turned into the heavenly day we anticipated. Oh how I wish you were here! I walked down the spring garden and all your little

---

1. Vita had been appointed a Magistrate (Justice of the Peace) for the Cranbrook Bench in October 1948.

flowers bit and tore at my heart. I do love you so, Hadji. It is quite simple: I do love you so. Just that.

I look forward to the weeks when you will be here, loaded as a bee, and will stay put for a bit.

I faintly regret the French party.[1] I would have liked to see all the nobs—e.g. the Cabinet ministers, and the Queen for whom I cherish a scullery-maid passion, and I would have liked to wear my little medal [the C.H.] with its cherry-coloured ribbon, but on the other hand I wouldn't have known anybody there and I would have felt and looked oafish and been ashamed of my hands. No, it's better for me to stay down here and talk to the Women's Institute in Sissinghurst.

One has to choose.

HAROLD TO VITA   *10 Neville Terrace*

26 July 1950

Oh my God! Those Sitwells! Edith made the main speech at the London Library meeting yesterday. It was more conceited and egoistic than anything I have ever heard. She began by saying how shy and frightened she felt. She then launched an attack on people who made anthologies. And she then said something about how one was bound to suffer if one wrote great poetry. She then sat down suddenly. It was about the most incompetent thing I have ever seen. What made it all worse was that Lord Ilchester (who in his best moments is not good at managing a meeting) is getting I fear terribly gaga.[2] He made a deplorable chairman and I am sure everyone left the room feeling that the whole thing had been embarrassing and confused. I hate those things being muddled. It requires so very little arrangement to make them go properly.

I asked Edith how Osbert's gout was. She said, "Gout? That is but

1. A reception given on 8 March at the French Embassy for Vincent Auriol, the French President, who was on a State visit to England. Vita had been invited, but pleaded that she had nothing suitable to wear.
2. Harold succeeded Lord Ilchester (who was seventy-six in 1950) as Chairman of the London Library in November 1951.

a slight matter. What worries me is the state of his nerves. And can one wonder when one thinks of the ceaseless persecution to which he has been exposed these thirty years!"

VITA TO HAROLD   *Sissinghurst*

27 July 1950

I was amused by your description of Edith Sitwell—you remember that they are true neurotics; only, unlike most neurotics, they have got away with it, and have managed to impose a reign of terror on their contemporaries. Even Stephen Spender told me he would not dare to write a not-agreeable review of any of them. Thus the persecution of thirty years has been reversed.

All the same, Edith is a fine poet—I took down her *Song of the Cold* a day or two ago, and was uplifted in the way one is uplifted only by the best. You know, that sense of exhilaration . . . which has its counterpart in the sense of depression induced by bad poor thin stuff.

HAROLD TO VITA   *10 Neville Terrace*

17 August 1950

"What fun for you to go by river to Windsor and sleep on a boat." That was what Mar thought. But this is what happened.

Robin Maugham[1] had told me on the telephone that he specially wanted me to come that Tuesday as there was a Tangier friend of his coming who wanted to talk to me. The plan was that the Tangier friend and her little daughter should come down for tea and be taken a trip on the river; that I should arrive by train at 7.45 after they had got back; that we should all dine at the Hotel and then see the Tangier friend into her train; that we should sleep at Wargrave and start at

---

1. The novelist, playwright, and nephew of Somerset Maugham. He succeeded his father as 2nd Viscount Maugham in 1958.

dawn next day. He promised to get me to Windsor or at least Maidenhead by 10 a.m. But fate willed otherwise.

When I reached Wargrave Station I was met by Ken Long, who is Robin's assistant. Such a nice youth. He told me that on their return from their trip up the river the engine had conked out and the houseboat was stranded some miles up the stream. He had come to row me there. So I got into the tiny dinghy, draped myself in oil-skins and sat there in the pouring rain while he rowed me up the stream. The battery had run out and the only light on board were three candle stumps. The Tangier friend was a Mrs Dunlop—a nice woman—with a darling little daughter aged eleven of the name of Hughine. Had Robin and Ken realised in time that the boat was immovable and that the only thing was to row the Dunlop pair across to the hotel while there was still some light in sky and on river, all might have been well. But they conceived the *idée funeste* of towing the houseboat itself across the half mile of open stream which separated it from the hotel on the opposite bank. It was pouring with rain and there was a strong wind blowing up the river. Therefore after two hours grunting and towing by the dinghy they were obliged to abandon the project.

It was by then 10.0 at night and very dark. There was no food in the boat except bread and cheese and a cake. They decided to get some supper, and then to embark Mrs Dunlop and the child in the dinghy and row them across to the hotel where with luck they could get a taxi to take them to the station. Thus after supper they dressed the child up in Robin's huge army coat and lowered her gingerly into the dinghy. Her mother then handed down her coat and bag and climbed down herself. The night was wet and dark and they had no torch. Ken was in the boat helping them in. As Mrs Dunlop disappeared into the darkness I felt a bit uneasy and immediately there was a loud splash and spluttering and shouting.

The dinghy had capsised and there was the child weighted by this enormous coat in the water. Luckily they were not far from the bank and Ken was able to rescue her, and Mrs Dunlop swam to the shallow edge. The dinghy had meanwhile righted itself and drifted away down stream. By pulling on ropes hard we were able to edge the houseboat into the shallow water and Mrs Dunlop walked and the child was carried to the point where their dripping clothes wetted everything

around. They went into the wash-place and took off all their clothes
and dried with towels. They were then lent Pyjamas and wrapped in
blankets (of which luckily there were a huge quantity), were put in
the cabin and given coffee and hot rum. Mrs Dunlop behaved splendidly as did the child. The only remark that the little elf made was,
"This is what comes of knowing Robin." But Mrs Dunlop had lost
her bag in which was her passport and her savings bank-book for £150
and loose cash. The accommodation problem was serious. Mrs Dunlop
and her child were put in the cabin which had been meant for me. I
had to share Robin's cabin and the boy had to lie on the floor. It was
all very wet. Robin snored all night. I did not sleep very well. At 6.0
the next morning Robin got up and plunged into the river. He came
back towing the errant dinghy. He had also rescued the oars. Then in
the cold light of dawn he again plunged into the water and came up
after a few minutes clasping Mrs Dunlop's bag—muddy, sodden but
still intact. Ken rowed himself ashore in the recovered dinghy and from
there ran across to a boat-house and obtained a motor boat. With that
we started to tow the houseboat back to its base. It took a long time.
At one moment the dinghy sank, but we were able to recover it as it
was tied on to us by the tow rope. Finally at 10 a.m. we got back to
the landing stage. I left them drying their clothes. I caught the 10.28
and was in my room at Windsor by 11.30.

HAROLD TO VITA   *10 Neville Terrace*

12 December 1950

I went down to Shaw's house yesterday.[1] We drove down in a
car which was very rich and American—a Plymouth, bouncy seats,
central heating and so on—and we lunched at a Road House near.
Then we went to the Shaw's Corner house. It is a loathesome little
building. A small red brick 1880 vicarage with a sloping lawn, some
conifers masking the road, and some elongated flower-beds in the shape

---

1. Bernard Shaw died on 2 November 1950, and bequeathed his house, Shaw's Corner, near
   Ayot St Lawrence, Hertfordshire, to the National Trust.

of kidneys. A large kitchen garden to provide Shaw with his food. In the garden a hut in which he worked. The furniture was lodging-house. Not a single good piece. In every room pictures of himself everywhere. The Public Trustee was there and then Mr Löwenstein arrived, and Mr Horowitz representing the Shaw society. I took against them.

The Trustee man told me that Shaw had left the whole of his fortune to the Spelling Bee.[2] He was a discreet man, but he just hinted that it might be contested. Not on the grounds that Shaw was mad, but on the grounds that the spelling bee is not a charity. You heard the story of the man in 1650 who left £10 to accumulate for ever at compound interest? It was discovered that if that Will held, he would own something like £200,000,000,000 by 1850. Thus they brought in an Act to prevent that sort of legacy. It is under that Act it seems that Shaw's will could be contested.

But darling, it was thrilling. Shaw was there, in the garden. Still in the shape of ashes. It was difficult and indeed impossible to tell which was Shaw and which was Mrs Shaw as their ashes had been mixed.[3] But there on the rose bed and garden paths were these white ashes just like the stuff Mar puts down for slugs. I could easily have picked some up and taken it home in an envelope. But I do not admire Shaw all that. Besides Jim [Lees-Milne] might have thought it in bad taste. But it is a lesson not to leave in one's will that one's ashes must be scattered over the garden. They remain there for weeks and weeks.

VITA TO HAROLD   *Sissinghurst*

19 October 1950

Wasn't Ben charming this weekend? I go such a see-saw over him: he gets me into a state when he arrives in one of his moods, and then when he is in a good mood I *love* him. I often feel I should be nicer

2. A great part of his fortune was left to a society for the propagation of a new English alphabet.
3. His wife, Charlotte, had died in 1943, and her ashes had been preserved until they could be mixed with his.

to him, and I long to be, but he makes me so dreadfully shy some-times—I can't feel at ease with him, I feel like a motor-car with a clutch that won't get into gear. It grinds and nothing happens—the car won't start off.

VITA TO HAROLD   *Sissinghurst*

4 January 1951

I have been writing all morning. I re-read the beginning of my book [*The Easter Party*], and it doesn't seem so bad as I had thought. You know what ups and downs one has. Perhaps one is never able to judge oneself. One gets so easily dejected and then so readily elated, but the elation goes and the dejection returns. And of course the fact that one's own book, during the process of writing it, is so living and absorbing a part of one's existence, is in itself misleading: one has so immense a background of ideas that never get down on paper (because one must be severely selective) that one is apt to imagine that the reader will be sharing the whole of this cloudy experience, and will under-stand what is implicit as well as what is explicit.

I suppose this would not apply to a biographical or historical work like George V, but it certainly applies to fiction.

HAROLD TO VITA   *10 Neville Terrace*

17 January 1951

My mother is too pathetic for words. She just sits and cries. She is also rather irritable and suspicious. In fact, I fear her mind is giving way. People ought not to live over 85. I think it such a terrible thing that one should go on living and cease to be oneself—leaving a different picture of oneself behind. Life can be very hard and tragic.[1]

I have no news. I went to Windsor yesterday. The Thames was

---

1. Lady Carnock died on 23 March, aged ninety.

very full and quick and angry. I am reading Roy Harrod's book on Keynes[2] which I find entrancing. Really that Cambridge set were more gifted than anything we have seen since. They make Balliol look like an old cart-horse.

HAROLD TO VITA   *10 Neville Terrace*

12 June 1951

No my darling, I am not hiding anything from you. I have not become involved in a spy ring nor have I become connected in any way with Guy's disreputable habits.[3] I have not seen or heard of or from him for two years.

If I was depressed this weekend it was due to a combination of circumstances. In the first place my visit to the South of France showed me that I had really become an old man [he was 64]. I did not want to bathe, being so fat, and I was clumsy and slow getting in and out of boats. That depressed me, but I shall get over it. Then I was depressed by my conversation with Roland de Margerie[4] and others. They really feel that France is done for as a Great Power. Then, above all, I was upset by the Maclean-Burgess business. It is not only that I hate my old profession being made a fool of and degraded. It is not only that I am really sorry for Anthony [Eden] and all Guy's friends. It is not merely that I hate to think that Philip Toynbee had the same sinister effect on Donald Maclean (politically and morally) as he might have had on Benzie. It is that I am shocked to see how this terrible infection assails even the most well informed people. It is as if, during a cholera epidemic, even those who were immune began to contract the disease. If people such as they with education and a position in the country can throw over everything in their hysterical love for holy Russia, then what can one expect will be the effect on less informed people? Guy and Maclean KNEW that most of the Russian stuff was

2. *The Life of John Maynard Keynes,* 1951.
3. Guy Burgess had defected to Russia with Donald Maclean in May 1951.
4. Of the French Foreign Office. He had been in the London Embassy before the war.

lies. Why should they have become infected? It will do such dreadful
harm. And in the third place, I am constantly, persistently, deeply
worried by the fear that the cold war may turn into a hot one.

That is all, my sweet. Niggs has rather cheered me by saying that
he dined with Ben on Friday and found him really "speechless with
horror and disgust." He feels of course that Guy has betrayed Anthony
and the boy Jackie. I do not think that Ben would be as horrified as
I am by someone betraying his COUNTRY, but it is terrible to him
to think of someone betraying his friends.

So I feel a little easier about it. But what a curious mystery it
all is!

HAROLD TO VITA   *10 Neville Terrace*

2 January 1952

I dined with Raymond [Mortimer] yesterday at the club. I asked
him whether he thought it would be wise to get an injunction against
the publishers to prevent them republishing the Roy Campbell attack,
or at least to threaten the publishers with a solicitor's letter saying that
we would take action if the passage were reprinted.[1] He begged me
earnestly to do nothing of the sort. A libel action would be insane since
it would lead to nothing and create a vast scandal. But if we were
rightly determined not to bring a libel action, then any action short
of that would do more harm than good. Roy would be able to boast,
"They tried to frighten my publishers with vague threats, but they
never dared to bring an action." Tray begs us very earnestly to do
nothing at all. I think he regrets now that he ever reviewed the book.
He thought it the best way of saying what he thought. But on *second*
thoughts I think he wishes he had left it unmentioned. Anyhow he is
perfectly certain that all we can do is to adopt an attitude of silent

---

1. In 1931 Roy Campbell had published in his poem *The Georgiad* a satire on Vita and Harold,
which was particularly vitriolic about Vita's affair with Roy's wife, Mary. They took no
action at the time. Then, in 1952, Campbell returned to the attack in his autobiography,
Light on a Dark Horse. Harold wrote a letter of protest to the publisher but took the matter
no further.

disdain. I shall bring the book down with me. I would rather you did not read the passage, which is fiendish, but after all I suppose you must read it. What a bother for you, my poor darling Mar.

HAROLD TO VITA   *British Embassy, Copenhagen*

21 January 1952

It was dull and drizzly yesterday, but none the less I did some expeditions. The coast of Sweden appeared shining through the rain and finally we got to Elsinore. Mr Jerichow[1] is quite sure that Shakespeare came there himself with a company of English players and acted before the Royal Court. Does not the reception of the Mummers suggest personal experience? And how else could Shakespeare have known those two Danish names Rosencrantz and Guildenstern? I admit that the latter point always struck me as strange. Anyhow we went on to the bastions where a Danish soldier in a tin hat was gazing fixedly at a tanker steaming slowly across the Sund. The wild swans that frequent these waters had come into the moat of the castle since the open sea was too rough. Those that remained (and one could see them from the bastion) had their feathers all blown backwards by the howling N.W. wind. I thought of my return journey on Wednesday night.

In the inner bastion there is a plaque with a reproduction of the portrait of Shakespeare in the first folio. Underneath an inscription in Danish records that the saga regarding the Prinz Amleth of Juitland was used by Shakespeare in such a manner that the name of Elsingore or more accurately Helsingør became famous throughout the world. A true statement and to me, in the drizzle and the gale, with the wet swans struggling with their feathers, rather moving. Mar would have been moved; my mind and heart flashed out to her.

Then we visited the palace of Fredensborg, celebrated in the early diaries of George V; the little palace of Sorgenfri or Sans Souci; and the huge castle of Fredericksborg. We only descended from the car at

---

1. Harold's host. He was a very wealthy Anglophile Danish brewer.

the last place and then only visited the Chapel where are hung the shields of the Knights of the Elephant. Then we arrived, a little late, at the house of Mr Per Federspiel (or Peter Featherplay). He was educated at Harrow, got a C.B.E. for his assistance during the German occupation, and is legal adviser to the Embassy. There were many Danes there. A nice wife. The two little boys helped to hand round the food and drink. I noticed that the younger (aged 10) held the beer bottles in a most ungainly way. His mother whispered to me to explain. The beer they contained came, not from the brewery owned by Mr Jerichow, but from that of the rival Carlsbad Brewery. Thinking that Mr Jerichow might be hurt, the boy had decided to hide the label by putting his hand over it even at the risk of splashing beer.

I then retired and read a few pages of *Les Ambassades* [by Roger Peyrefitte]. It ought to be suppressed by the French censorship. It confirms everything I hate about the French: their meanness, their lasciviousness, their graspingness, their disloyalty, their cruelty, their egoism, their belief that anything said brightly and smartly must be true. Moreover I think it terrible to write about one's own amorous adventures in so stark a way, merely pornography. It is a revolting book; one cannot put it down.

HAROLD TO VITA   *Hotel Internazionale, Brindisi*

25 February 1952

I took the train [from Rome] for Brindisi. I had a first class compartment and luckily the British Council had reserved a seat as the train was packed. For nine hours, until ten thirty at night, did I sit tight on a hard red velvet seat. I read Simenon. I read Agatha Christie. I looked at the scenery, which really was not too good after one left the coast. It was of course dark when we reached the Adriatic Coast and I munched the cold chicken the Mallets[1] had given me and sipped the bottle of Chianti they had provided.

Oh my darling! How vivid to me was that journey we took

---

1. Sir Victor Mallet, British Ambassador in Rome.

thirty-nine years ago![2] Do you remember the sick woman and the husband who kept on jumping up and giving her sips of medicine? And how when in the autumn dawn we reached Bari and they got out, how you said with your sweet gentle smile, "I hope you will soon be better." And she cast back at you a look of utterly resigned despair? There we were, my sweet, so young, so healthy, embarking on what was a long life of love and action and success—and she must have been dead now these almost forty years and no more than a pinch of dust!

I walked out into the station square at Brindisi to find only a one-horse brougham. Anyhow, I bundled into it and drove through straight streets to this hotel. It was the last Sunday of Carnival and a few youths and maidens were parading the boulevards dressed in fancy dress and masks. But how dead it all was! Never have I had such a sense of absence of *stimmung* and *entrain*.

VITA TO HAROLD   *Sissinghurst*

27 February 1952

At the R.H.S. show there were the most lovely little spring things, crocuses, irises, scillas—in fact, a sort of idealised My Life's Work at its very best. I felt completely intoxicated.

People didn't begin to arrive for about twenty minutes. It was heaven.

At dinner I sat between the Chairman, Patrick Synge, whom I don't like; and David Bowes-Lyon,[3] whom I do. He wants us to come and see his garden. I met heaps of gardening friends and enjoyed myself very much. Jim Russell then gave a talk, with lantern slides, on the old roses; Graham Thomas was to have given it, but was ill. I was made rather a fuss of; they made me speak—but you know, Hadji, *I don't like it;* I hate getting credit for the wrong things; and I felt that there I was, an amateur amongst real experts;

2. On their honeymoon.
3. Sir David Bowes-Lyon was President of the R.H.S. His garden was at Hitchin, Hertfordshire.

and all because of my thin little *Observer* articles I had an undeserved reputation, also because a lot of people in the audience had been to the garden here. I felt a fraud.

H A R O L D   T O   V I T A   *British Embassy, Athens*

10 March 1952

   Oh my word there was such a posh dinner in the evening! The King and Queen of the Hellenes, the Queen of Rumania and Princess Nicolas, with attendant gentlemen and ladies in waiting. I sat next to the Queen. You know, she was a German (a Hanover princess, I think, name of Frederika), and she is generally supposed to be rather bossy and managing. Although they agree that she has been excellent in charitable work and in encouraging industries and so on, they feel she interferes too much in politics. I daresay that is all very true, but the Greeks are never contented with anyone. She is pretty for a Queen, not very well dressed for a Queen, easy to get on with for a Queen, out-spoken for a Queen. But I did not really like her. I suppose she had been told that people said she bossed the King, so she was doing the silly but devoted little wife stunt which always makes me want to yell aloud. She told me she liked being a Queen; she told me that she would not mind being poor if she could have two hot baths a day; she told me that she has a cushion which fits onto her bath; she told me she believed in God; she told me that Queens could always tell when people were flattering them.
   After dinner I had a talk with King Paul. He is an old pansy really, I suspect, but he adopts the manner of a bluff and hearty sailor. He tried on me the stunt that the Americans interfered too much with Greek politics. I did my stupid stunt of not knowing anything about nothing. But I rather liked him, I must say.
   After dinner we had a film of the King's funeral[1] as Princess Nicolas had asked to see it. Then we had *cercle* again. They stayed on till twenty minutes to two, regardless of my bed-time. But after the

---

1. King George VI had died at Sandringham on 6 February 1952.

film I had a long talk with the Queen of Rumania, who really is a nice woman, and who is coming down to lunch at Sissinghurst.

You can imagine how glad I was to get to bed.

HAROLD TO VITA   *10 Neville Terrace*

12 June 1952

In the morning we had the Historic Buildings Committee of the National Trust. We have a new member, the Earl of Euston. You know I am always rather worried that this Committee, which actually decides whether we take a house, is composed almost entirely of peers. Well, we are now to have a man called Mr John Smith. When his name was put up Esher said, "Well it's a good thing to have a proletarian name on the Committee—anybody know the man?" "Yes," said Lord Euston, "he is my brother-in-law."[1]

Then I had the Royal Literary Fund which rather depresses me. It is what people on the Actors Benevolent Fund must feel when they give assistance to the broken down chorus girls of the 'nineties': "I may end that way."

I dined at the Beefsteak and sat next to Richard Molyneux.[2] He had decided that his courtier days were over and all that remained was to retire to his rooms in Pall Mall and die. But then he was summoned to Windsor for a whole fortnight by the young Queen, just as an old family friend. He was beside himself with pleasure, and said that of all his many visits to Windsor he had enjoyed this one most. He says the Queen is very much the sovereign. She enters the room at least ten yards ahead of her husband or mother. I asked him whether the Queen Mother objected to being thus put in the shade. "Not at all," he said, "her attitude is one of adoring admiration." He says he asked the Queen whether Winston treated her as Lord Melbourne treated the young Queen Victoria. "No, not a bit of it. I find him very obstinate."

---

1. Viscount Esher was Chairman of the National Trust; Harold was Vice-Chairman; the Earl of Euston (later 11th Duke of Grafton) was Chairman of many amenity societies; John Smith became Deputy Chairman of the National Trust in 1980.
2. Sir Richard Molyneux (1873–1954) had been a soldier and Equerry to Queen Mary.

HAROLD TO VITA   *C.1. Albany, Piccadilly*

30 July 1952

My George V is to be published on August 14. They sent me round
four copies. One I gave to Tommy Lascelles; one I sent with a really
charming letter to the Queen Mother at Sandringham; one I sent with
a rather stiff letter to the Queen herself at Buckingham Palace; and one
I wrapped up in brown paper and took out to luncheon with Tony
Rothschild. He always hurries one out at 2.30 as then the work begins
again and the great wheels of the Maison Rothschild revolve. So
grasping my brown paper parcel I went by bus to the Travellers. I
washed and tidied there (I had got on my best suit with a white shirt)
and went on to Marlborough House to which I had been summoned.
The dear old lady [Queen Mary] is rather groggy on her pins now.
She tottered across the room. I bowed and presented the book, bowing.
She sat down with me in the window seat and looked at every page.
"What a lot of hard work!" she said from time to time. "How
dignified," she said. She looked at the picture of the King when he was
a young boy. "How like he was then to my poor silly son [Edward
VIII]." Then she chattered away for half an hour and then Princess
Margaret came in. So I went away. But it was a strange visit and the
last time I shall see the old monument.

Never in my life have I been as comfortable as in my son's flat.[1]
It really is delicious in itself and so convenient in its location.

HAROLD TO VITA   *C.1. Albany*

4 September 1952

I brought myself to tell Niggs about the K.C.V.O.[2] He was
absolutely horrified. He said that it would be "so unlike you, Daddy,
and even less like Mummy—poor dear Mummy," he said, as if you

---

1. Harold had left Neville Terrace, and was now sharing rooms with Nigel in Albany, the
   Regency apartment building off Piccadilly.
2. Harold had been awarded a knighthood for his biography of King George V.

had lost an arm. "Oh my God!" he said. "That is a frightful thing to happen." But being a sensible lad he quite saw that it would not be possible for me to refuse without appearing churlish, snobbish and conceited. But how much more I would have liked a Regency Clock.

HAROLD TO VITA   *C.1. Albany*

25 September 1952

I went to the Aberconway party. I was rather late in arriving, and the Amadeus string quartet had started playing Mozart's K.464 Quartet in A. So as not to interrupt, I sat on a little chair by myself outside the door. On and on they went. Mozart is just like Bunny.[1] He says, "Well, I must be going now," and then thinks of something else to say, and goes on and on till I could have struck the door with angry fists. Then the Amadeus were let out for a drink, and I was found by Christabel [Aberconway] on my little chair alone. So she dragged me into the room where there was a large selection of the nobility and gentry. The Amadeus quartet returned and I bolted, foregoing a rich supper awaiting the guests and taking my hat and coat away with me. I did not feel that I had dealt with this situation with much skill. I felt an untutored boob, a rustic, provincial.

---

1. Mrs. Cynthia Drummond, a Sissinghurst neighbor.

The success of King George V *gave Harold Nicolson more pleasure than the knighthood that resulted from it, and Vita was displeased at being addressed as Lady Nicolson when she wished to remain V. Sackville-West. Harold immediately began research for his next book,* Good Behaviour, *and as soon as it was finished, he embarked on his biography of the French critic Sainte-Beuve. He ceased writing his weekly column for the* Spectator *but continued his broadcasts on Foreign Affairs for the BBC's Overseas Service. He stood unsuccessfully for the Oxford Professorship of Poetry. Vita, meanwhile, was writing* Daughter of France. *Both their sons married, and in 1954 their first grandchild, Juliet, was born. The most important public events of these years were the death of Stalin, Anthony Eden's succession to Winston Churchill as Prime Minister, the end of the Korean War, and the coronation of Queen Elizabeth II.*

HAROLD TO VITA   *C.1. Albany*

20 November 1952

Oh my darling, when you get this I shall be 66, the mark of the beast. I do so hate growing old and the only thing to do is to bear the calamity with calm and resignation. But I was not intended to be old. I mean, for me there are no compensations at all in being a veteran and a grand old man of letters. I have no pleasure in being grand or important, or a K.C.V.O. Not that I am anything but delighted at the success of *George V,* or that I do not enjoy praise and being taken seriously as a writer. Of course I do. But I do not like being 66, so there.

James [Pope-Hennessy] gave a farewell party last night. He is off today in a cattle or at least a cargo boat to Dominica in the Antilles. He will be away five months. He told me such a funny thing about Gerry [Duke of] Wellington, who really is going mad with avarice. After dinner Gerry asked James to drop him on his way home. So they shared a taxi. James said to the driver, "Go to Apsley House," but Gerry said crossly, "No—certainly not, stop opposite on the park side." He then explained that if he drove to his own house, the taxi had to go round by St George's hospital which meant another 6d on the metre. Then when they reached the point opposite where Gerry was to be dropped, he jumped out quite crossly and said, "You would have taken a taxi in any case, so I needn't contribute." I really think avarice is the strangest of all obsessions. It can give no pleasure to oneself, and is a cause of dislike and contempt to others. I am not an avaricious man.

VITA TO HAROLD   *Sissinghurst*

31 December 1952

Well, when you get this letter you won't have time to read it, because your telephone will be starting to ring.[1] What a funny day for you, my darling. *I* know you don't like it. But what you must surely like, my sweet, is the realisation that you have made a real, solid, monumental contribution to English biography. I know that external appreciation means very little to you (except in so far as you are human, and praise from the right people is always acceptable, as they say in hospitals when one sends a brace of pheasants), and that the only true satisfaction one ever derives comes from within oneself, in the knowledge that one has done a job of work to the very best of one's ability and made a respect-worthy job of it, and given of one's best, both in conscientiousness and effort and even a kind of self-dedication to the task imposed.

This you have done, and you must know it, *dans ton foi intérieur,*

---

1. On the following day Harold's knighthood was announced in the New Year's Honours.

whatever you may pretend even to me, in your so-loveable diffidence and reserve and modesty. Then you must also know that *Marginal Comment* [his weekly article for the *Spectator*] has been a remarkable achievement.

Yes, looking back on this going year, I see what an enormous stride you have made, not only in your public reputation but in the satisfaction you must have given to your curly self.

And then, as you say, there are the boys: Niggs getting into the House and Ben happy at the Burlington[2]—and their affection for us, and the ease we all found together over Christmas. My only sorrow, and it is a deep one, is Nigel's appalling hair-cut.

VITA TO HAROLD   *Sissinghurst*

17 February 1953

Oh my darling Hadji, how much one dislikes growing older! I know how you hate it. You know how much I hate it. But I think the reason we both hate it is a double reason: the superficial reason is the physical reason, that one gets fat and bald and what-have-you, in the American phrase, but the real deep reason for us, you and me, is that we hate the idea of leaving Life, as we must, twenty to thirty years hence, and we both love life and enjoy it.

HAROLD TO VITA   *C.1. Albany*

7 May 1953

I lunched with the Austrians and the Queen of Spain[3] was there. After luncheon she took me aside and sat me down on a sofa and talked

---

2. Nigel was elected M.P. for Bournemouth East on the day the King died, 6 February 1952, and Ben became editor of the *Burlington Magazine,* the leading journal on the history of the fine arts. He remained editor until his death thirty years later.
3. The daughter of Princess Beatrice (youngest daughter of Queen Victoria) and wife of King Alfonso XIII of Spain. In 1953 she was aged sixty-six.

for half an hour much to the fury of everybody else. The odd thing is that she reminds me the whole time of Violet [Trefusis]. She has the same sort of waddle and the same sort of voice. I am writing to Violet to tell her how like the Queen of Spain she is—but I shall not use the word 'waddle': I shall say 'Démarche'.

When I got back from the clutches of the Queen of Spain, Elvira said, "Honours are showering upon you." And there was a letter from the Master of Balliol saying I have been elected an Honorary Fellow. How strange and impossible that would have seemed when I was there! But if there was one honour I should like above all else it is to be an Honorary Fellow of Balliol. I was so pleased that I telephoned to you three times but each time it was number engaged.

HAROLD TO VITA   *C.1. Albany*

10 June 1953

I lunched with Violet yesterday. It was not a success. She has a maddening habit of summoning the waiter, and forgetting all about him when he stands beside her awaiting instructions, but launching out on a long and boring story of her own. Pat Balfour was there and Osbert Lancaster and Loelia [Duchess of] Westminster. But it was not an easy luncheon somehow, and they spent their time telling mean little stories about their friends. Only one of them amused me. It was Maurice Bowra's[1] comment on being asked whether Rosamund Lehmann [the novelist] was as beautiful as reputed. "Meringue-outang," he answered. But my darling, life is such a difficult and cruel thing, so why make it more difficult by gossiping about people's faults? There is beauty, and love, in this world, and intelligence and faithfulness, and happiness and virtue—why lunch at the Ritz and spend your time picking out the ugly things? I felt all angry.

---

1. The Warden of Wadham College, Oxford, 1938–71

HAROLD TO VITA   *C.1. Albany*

3 November 1953

My own darling Mar,

Oh it was a gale, and rain slopped among the bricks—but I was so happy with my home and my darling and dear Benzie. I know Sissinghurst to outsiders may seem a bleak and ruined sojourn, but to me it is mellow and warm and welcoming always and the haven of peace.

I can't get over Virginia's diary—so self-pitying, so vain in a way, so malicious.[1] The envy is difficult to understand. One realizes that she must have been far more mad than that calm exterior suggested. It doesn't make me admire or like her less. But it will surely create a bad impression on those who never saw her great dignity or witnessed the wit and curiosity that rendered her animated. It really has left me with a puzzle.

VITA TO HAROLD   *Sissinghurst*

2 June 1954

Never again will I write in *The Observer* about being ill. Besides I wasn't ill; it was simply that I couldn't think what to write about. It brought me so many deeply concerned letters of sympathy and enquiry. How false and fleeting is journalistic popularity! I often think how empty and lonely some people's lives must be, that they project themselves into the lives of unknown people. One can understand the glamour appeal of film-stars or Princess Margaret. But why us?

VITA TO HAROLD   *Sissinghurst*

31 August 1954

I miss you! It is dreadful, getting so used to your daily companionship, my most perfect companion, whether travelling or at home.[2] But

---

1. Extracts from Virginia Woolf's diary had just been published by her husband, Leonard.
2. They had been on a motoring tour of the Dordogne in search of literary and historical sites, including the Lascaux caves and the Château de Montaigne.

we *were* happy weren't we? And we can think back on that lovely
country with the poplars and the green grass and the hanging woods
and the quiet river and the strange caves and the patient pious oxen
and the castles and the *manoirs*. I can't tell you how happy it makes
me to think that you liked and understood the Dordogne in exactly
the same way as I do. It is horrid to have to communicate with you
by letter instead of just shouting "Hadji!" whenever I want you. But
as a result we have stored up a great cellar-full of vintage happiness
and love—as we always do when we get away together alone.[3]

VITA TO HAROLD   *Sissinghurst*

14 September 1954

I got into such a rage. I listened to a BBC Home Service programme about myxomatosis, and it was all from the point of view of
the farmer or the tame-rabbit breeder whose trade might be threatened.
And *not one word* about what the rabbits might suffer—just profit,
profit, profit, or loss of profit. That is all men think of—just their
purses—and I do think it is disgusting. It makes me sick with life. I
know you will think me silly and sentimental, but I don't care if you
do. I *know* there is something beyond material profit in this beastly
utilitarian world. You can't deny this. It is the thing that makes me
love you, and you love me. It is what takes the place of religion in
people who are not that way inclined. It is all the same thing: all paths
meet at the end of a long converging perspective—whether the end
of it is what is called science, or God, or the Creator—that is what
I profoundly believe.

Sorry, darling, I got carried away on a storm of temper, thinking
of those wretched swollen rabbits I had seen in our lane. I think I had
better stop now. You don't like it when I take up lost causes, although
you can take them up with violence sometimes yourself. Only then
it is something like Cyprus and ENOSIS, or the reconstruction of
Germany—shaking hands with bloodstained murderers, who would
start it up all over again if they saw a chance.

---

3. Harold wrote on the top of this letter, "Keep this dear letter, always."

HAROLD TO VITA   *C.1. Albany*

13 January 1955

I went to give the first of my Mau Mau talks.[1] Miss Fuller presided
and I was cross (a) because they had put a huge picture of me on *London
Calling* without asking my consent; (b) because it had been cold at
Stationers Hall; (c) because Miss Fuller had asked me to come 15
minutes earlier in order to "settle down," whatever she meant by that.
Then when I arrived, she asked me primly if I would change the
opening words. They were, "When a man reaches the age of 68." She
explained that my talks in this series were being put on discs and sent
to the Mau Mau to play over to themselves on winter evenings and
must thus have no date-mark. Would I say instead, "When a man is
approaching the age of 70"? Then having gained my consent to this
outrageous mistatement, she mumbled something about "having left
my handkerchief upstairs" and left the room. So to pay her out I
climbed under the table and hid there. Unfortunately the young man
in the control room saw me doing this, and when Miss Fuller came
back he said to her, "He has got under the table." So when she entered
the room she said coyly, "I see you," and I had to climb out looking
Oh! so foolish.

HAROLD TO VITA   *C.1. Albany*

9 February 1955

At the Literary Society I sat next to Tommy Lascelles. He says that
your Queen made a wonderful job of her dull shy husband. But he
would willingly commit suicide for her daughter. He admits that she
has not got the public charm of the Queen Mother, but says that she
is really a sweeter nature and a far better mind. He says people will
not realize for years how intelligent she is, but that eventually it will
become an accepted national fact. He says that Winston always comes
away from an audience with tears in his eyes. Silly old buffer.

---

1. His overseas talks for the BBC, which he called Mau Mau after the Kenya tribe that was
   then in revolt against the British.

VITA TO HAROLD   *Sissinghurst*

5 April 1955

My very own darling Hadji

You have gone away again, and oh the difference to me! I have
got so used to having you here safe, that I cannot re-orientate life
without you at all. Somehow I feel that these 3 weeks have brought
us so close together; so although of course I hate your suffering pain,
I cannot help feeling that something valuable has come out of it.[1]

All I hope is that Dr Hunt will urge you to spend as much time
as possible down here in future. I do so love having you here, and being
able to look after you in little ways—and you would be better able
to write your books instead of Mau-mauing[2] so much—I know you
like your London Library, National Trust, National Portrait Gallery,
and your London life, *grand lever* and so on, and I would be the last
person to want you to stop all that—you know that, don't you?—but
I do estimate your own books so high, the Manners book [*Good
Behaviour*] is one of your very best, and if you spent more time down
here you could write another book—oh please, Hadji, consider my
plea, which is half selfish and half reasonable. The selfish part is that
I do so love having you here; you are all my happiness; the reasonable
part is that I think you ought not to drive yourself so hard as you do,
and waste your wonderful gifts on Mau-mau when you might be
writing a book on—Bad behaviour?

Anyhow, darling, you know I love you absolutely and completely
and for whatever remains of our lives.

Your Mar

HAROLD TO VITA   *C.1. Albany*

24 May 1955

I got a simply frightful supertax demand, approaching £2,000. It
does mean that no author can save for his old age in these days unless

---

1. Following visits to Germany and Portugal, Harold had suffered two minor strokes, on 11
   March and 15 May. He was less affected by them than by an acute attack of sciatica.
2. See note, p. 414

he lives in a garret in Soho. I have no wish or desire or intention of living in a garret.

Oh my dearest, how lovely it was when we went out into the orchard last night! So calm. So gentle, and the ducks following. And now my dear silly Fanny [duck] has returned! What happiness you and I have derived from that garden—I mean real deep satisfaction and a feeling of success. It is an achievement—assuredly it is. And it is pleasant to feel that we have created a work of art. It is all your credit really. Mine was just rulers and bits of paper.

HAROLD TO VITA   *C.1. Albany*

16 November 1955

But I *do* know about the R.H.S. Medal in gold.[1] I know it is among the highest honours one can receive in the shrub world. It is like being made a Fellow of All Souls. Now it is nonsense you saying it is owing to *The Observer* articles. They may have helped, since people know that they have been uniformly instructive and have exercised a wide and long influence. But it is really that my darling is a very very good gardener and that at Sissinghurst she has planted so wisely and so well. I cannot think of anything that has pleased me so much since you got your C.H. and I was made a fellow of Balliol. It is a long long time since the day when you and I dug up a primrose in full flower and shoved it into the bank at Long Barn.

VITA TO HAROLD   *Sissinghurst*

31 January 1956

My Hadji

Such a cold, white Sissinghurst—but I'm so snug in my tower with your lovely fur tippet round my shoulders, keeping me warm like

---

1. Vita had been awarded the Veitch Gold Medal of the Royal Horticultural Society.

love—so I thought I would write you just one last January word
before retiring in the somewhat Amazonian embraces of Mademoiselle
[*Daughter of France*] for the evening—and tomorrow it will be February, and although we may be in for a horrible wintry time we shall
know that spring is always round the corner.

Darling, I love you so; you are my eternal spring.

I suddenly thought, supposing you were found poisoned one day
when we were here alone together, and I was accused of poisoning
you. Then there's an inquest, and it is discovered that I have been
buying cyanide of potassium, ostensibly to destroy wasps' nests, but
I cannot account for it: where did I put it? what have I done with
it? did I give it to the gardener? wouldn't that have been the natural
thing for me to do? people aren't so careless as all that with a deadly
poison, surely, Lady Nicolson? Come now! You can't expect us to
believe that . . .

And then my Counsel produces our letters to each other, years and
years of letters full of love.

What a silly story. That's what comes of reading too much
[Georges] Simenon.

                                                    Your Mar

HAROLD TO VITA   *C.1. Albany*

8 February 1956

Oh I had such fun just now! A woman telephoned asking whether
I was Fergus & Fergus, and would I have her fiancé's kilt ready by the
first of March without fail? I said that we were an old Scotch firm,
perhaps a wee bit old-fashioned, but we did not think that a young
woman should mention her fiancé's kilt. She gasped in astonishment.
I said, "I am afraid that I cannot answer so delicate a question, and you
must get your fiancé to write to us himself." "But he is in the
Cameroons!" she wailed. "Oh," I answered, "I thought you said he
was in the Black Watch." By then she was getting suspicious, so I
replaced the receiver.

HAROLD TO VITA   *C.1. Albany*

29 May 1956

Alas—May is leaving us and how superb it has been. I walked round the garden last night between 7.0 and 7.25, absolutely drinking in the beauty of the sunset and the soft lights playing across the Weald towards the downs. I felt that no garden has ever been so beautiful as our garden, no May ever so beautiful as this May, no duck ever possessed of such personality as Fanny, and nobody ever so showered with love and happiness as I am. So I entered into a mood of UNIVERSAL GRATITUDE and then a little worm came and said I was being selfish about the Canaries.[1]

But, darling, it really is a combination of negatives, of which my extreme prejudice against Franco is the easiest to abandon. We must face the fact that it is probable that before long and at any time I shall have a serious stroke. I have got so much out of life that the prospect of death fills me with no apprehension. Of course I want to live to see Carlo become a person, Juliet a little girl,[2] and our relations with Greece placed upon a footing of amity. Of course I loathe the prospect of being separated from you and all those really very numerous people whom I love. But I shan't be there to feel sorrow. Thus I concentrate my worry on the situation I shall leave behind and dread a complicated death or extreme squalor at the end. That is the worst of those who have no belief in the life hereafter: they do not want to say goodbye ungainlily, since death-bed scenes and circumstances may leave sad memories and I should wish to be remembered only as a person who was alive and happy. It is for this that I fuss about crematoria, not wanting my darling to be faced, as Diana[3] was faced, with the problem of how to dispose of the corpse. Thus if we went to some remote island in the Canaries, I should be worrying about this corpse business even as I worry about wasps. I know this is irrational, but one is irrational

---

1. He and Vita had discussed taking tickets for a cruise to the Canary Islands, which had been a Spanish possession since 1476.
2. Carlo was Ben's putative son (in fact, a daughter, Vanessa, was born on 8 August) and Juliet was Nigel's actual daughter, born in June 1954.
3. Duff Cooper died on 1 January 1954 while on a voyage to the West Indies. His body was landed in Vigo and buried at Belvoir Castle, the home of his wife's family.

about some things, and my holiday would be clouded by my fuss and I should feel only that we had spent more money than we can afford and derived no pleasure. Thus I do not want to go to southern islands and would much prefer to remain even in February at home where there are lovely quick crematoria waiting to receive me. I should like us to have a motor trip in France or even Spain in October when the wasps are few. And then face the winter at home with solemn resolution.

HAROLD TO VITA   *C.1. Albany*

15 August 1956

I do so love it when you come to London and bless these rooms with your presence. You are like a country-bred puppy on a lead, seeking to escape up some side street from the crowds upon the pavement and the fierce traffic in the streets. Your hand was trembling with panic when we crossed Piccadilly. Oh my dear dear Mar! How one does love the odd corners of people whom one loves!

I did not dare to ask Ken[1] how *Good Behaviour* had sold in the U.S.A. Now why was I so gawky about that? Was it just shyness and a feeling that when one lunches with a man one should not talk business? Or was it an odd pride, which made me suggest to this dollar magnate that as a Knight of the Victorian Order I was indifferent to money? I really do not know. All I know is that I am an ODD FISH.

---

1. Ken McCormick, the president of Doubleday, the New York publisher.

In 1957 Harold, then aged seventy-one, described himself as "getting very old, decrepit, gaga, forgetful, deaf and aphasic [speechless]." In fact he wasn't. His slight deafness never became a serious problem, though it caused him to retire from the chairmanship, not membership, of his Committees, and the two minor strokes he suffered in 1955 scarcely diminished his social, literary, and gardening energy. Politically he was aroused to his former fervor by the Suez crisis of 1956, and he wrote three more books, The Age of Reason, Monarchy, *and* Journey to Java. *The latter took the form of a diary written on one of the winter cruises that he and Vita enjoyed during the last six years of her life, and she based her last novel,* No Signposts in the Sea, *upon another. It was during the last of these cruises, to the West Indies in January–February 1962, that she first noticed the symptoms of abdominal cancer, from which she died at Sissinghurst on 2 June of that year.*

HAROLD TO VITA   *C.1. Albany*

30 October 1956

I read in the newspapers this morning as the train sped through Kent the statements made by Anthony and Selwyn Lloyd on Hungary.[1] I was revolted by their cant. When people rise against the Russians they are hailed as heroes and patriots; but when they rise against us, they are called terrorists and hanged. I do not see that it was

---

1. On 29 October, Israel launched their attack against Egypt (in collusion, as it later transpired, with Britain and France), and the Soviets crushed the Hungarian revolt in Budapest. Anthony Eden was Prime Minister, and Selwyn Lloyd his Foreign Secretary.

at all necessary for Anthony to indulge in such hypocrisy. He went out of his way to do so. He is a rotten creature, vain and purposeless, and I hope he is soundly defeated at the next election. A Prime Minister should give some idea of principle and consistency; Anthony is just all over the place all the time.

HAROLD TO VITA   *C.1. Albany*

15 November 1956

Eden's policy was not only morally wrong but a costly failure as well. People will talk less about keeping the Canal open and safe-guarding our oil supplies when they have to have petrol coupons. But for the moment all Tory opinion, bemused though it be, is in favour of Eden. Simple minds work simply. The ladies of Bournemouth do not like the Russians, the Americans or Nasser; Eden has dealt a blow to these three enemies; therefore Eden must be right. It is as simple as that. Nigel and I have always believed that there was some collusion between the French and the Israelis to which we were a consenting party. It now seems that some American journalist[1] has got hold of the story and has obtained documentary proof. If the story gets out I do not see how the Government can survive. It is an utterly disgrace-ful tale.

HAROLD TO VITA   *C.1. Albany*

11 July 1957

The Prime Minister [Harold Macmillan] appeared at the Grillions [Club] dinner last night. He seemed bursting with energy and high spirits. One of his many headaches is that under the new scheme for

---

1. Not American, but the French brothers Merry and Serge Bromberger, in their book *Secrets of Suez* (1957). Nonetheless, the revelation did nothing to change opinion in Bournemouth, and Nigel was disowned by his constituents for his opposition to the Suez operation and eventually lost his seat.

economising on the army, some county regiments will have to be fused and this will arouse fierce resistance. Will the West Kent agree to being called the Kent and Surrey? No they will not. Macmillan is thinking of dropping the county names altogether and inventing new regional names such as "The Weald Regiment," "The Regiment of the Tweed" and so on. But he says that the life of a Prime Minister is spent between successive waves of indignation, and that he must accept that fact.

VITA TO HAROLD   *Sissinghurst*

1 October 1957

I write to you on this the 44th anniversary of that happy day [their wedding], and love you even more now than I did then (which is saying a lot) and please forgive me all my trespasses.

I have finished those American proofs and am filled with loathing for my *Observer* articles, but must now finish arranging the latest lot for publication in a fourth book—but what on earth am I to call it?[1] It makes me rather cross to have had this (may I say?) success with those wretched articles and to have gained a reputation of a kind I never desired or deserved. You will understand this, so I needn't enlarge. It's rather like you not liking to have your voice recognised by taxi-drivers who have heard you on the wireless.

And so goodbye, my precious most precious Hadji—I return to my galleys—a galley slave, in fact—but you are there in the background always, filling my heart with love.

VITA TO HAROLD   *The King's Arms, Hadleigh,*
                                         Suffolk
9 October 1957

We went to Layer Marney[2] which I had always wanted to see. It is *very* odd, but far bigger and less ugly than I expected and there

1. *Even More for Your Garden*, 1958.
2. In Essex, where there is an eight-story Tudor brick tower, the tallest in England. Vita was motoring with her friend Edith Lamont.

is a lovely little church next door, of the same date, with Crusader tombs, and all the decorations of their harvest festival—sheaves of corn, marrows, apples, masses of flowers, baskets of eggs—very charming and real.

Then we went to Lavenham [Suffolk], famous as a beautiful village, with a really magnificent church like a small cathedral—the churches everywhere are beautiful as I had always heard—and through other unknown villages, all perfectly charming—and on to Hadleigh with a red sunset on one side and a full moon on the other—by lanes, through absolutely *uninhabited* country, Hadji, except for an occasional farm homestead—it might be France, you see nobody, and no new houses, and lots of water in little streams and lakes, and a church tower on a distant hill.

This is a very nice tiny hotel, spotlessly clean, boiling hot water, no other guests, very nice people, Rollo a great success ("you can leave your dog behind when you go, madam"), and as it seems quite near everything I want to see, we have decided to stay here the next two nights.

HAROLD TO VITA   *C.1. Albany*

13 November 1957

Oh my sweet, I had such a bloody afternoon yesterday. I told you I was doing my advert on independent T.V. for *The Observer.* [1] So I went to the studio in Ebury Street at 2.0. My piece was only to last 3 minutes but it took three hours and a half !!!!! First a man in a green jersey made me up—smearing beige grease over my poor face and then powdering the surface lightly. He touched my eyebrows with kola and then smeared my eyelashes which have never in seventy long years required such surrogation. Then the interviewer arrived and we had to rehearse the piece four or five times. Then the lights were turned on and they measured distances with long tape-measures and kept on fuss, fuss, fuss. It was 3.30 before they had arranged the thing to their

---

1. A television commercial, for which Harold was not paid. He contributed to it out of loyalty to the newspaper, where his weekly book reviews were published.

liking, moving the property ornaments backwards and forwards along the property chimney piece, and then I and the interviewer began our silly little dialogue over again. At 4.0 the lights were turned out and the electricians and camera men left us alone. That was the ten minutes tea interval. At 4.20 they came back and I thought that it would be terrible had I been doing a love scene, and made to rehearse passionate embraces over and over and over again. The falsity of that world is really terrifying. Anyhow at 5.20 I got away into a darkened Ebury Street with all those arc lights making brown circles in the pavement and on my retina. But one must learn to suffer without complaint.

VITA TO HAROLD   *Sissinghurst*

26 February 1958

Oh Hadji, my book [*Daughter of France*] is so bad. It really is. I am not imagining this: I *know* it is bad.

I am writing this to you late at night. I haven't been over to have my supper yet.

I did take trouble over that book. I read a lot, but I haven't been able to synthesise or compress it as I hoped. It is just a mess. I had a clear picture when I started, but now it has all got muddled up with detail and the outline has got lost.

HAROLD TO VITA   *C.1. Albany*

9 April 1958

As my train drew out of Etchingham station I looked down on the graveyard and there were three men in greatcoats and cloth caps shovelling clay on top of Eustace's box.[1] It struck a cold horror to my heart. I felt the whole thing was the grimmest, coldest funeral I had

1. The funeral was that of Lord (Eustace) Percy, who had died at Etchingham, Sussex, on 3 April, aged seventy-one. He was one of Harold's oldest friends, his contemporary in the Foreign Office, and became Rector of the Newcastle division of the University of Durham.

ever attended, and at least to be cremated (apart from other advantages) is warm. I thought how terrible it was to be dressed in a night-shirt, nailed in a box and then put deep in the cold clay. And I thought back on the days when Eustace was young and regarded as among the most gifted and promising of my generation. What has he done with his life? I daresay he did much good at Newcastle, but what pleasures or adventures has he enjoyed? His life has been as cold and bare as the church in which he was funerated (by the way, the Church as seen from the Railway is a truly splendid bit of architecture). At least when I die nobody will think I failed to make the most of life.

VITA TO HAROLD   *Sissinghurst*

10 April 1958

I drove back from Sevenoaks through the park at Knole. I had taken my key with me, and let myself out by the Mast-head gate.

Oh Hadji, it was such an odd experience—it seemed as though I had never been away—it was all so familiar. I think I had better not go on writing about it, because it is making me cry, but I might tell you some time. I hadn't really meant to go and yet I think I must have or I wouldn't have taken my key. Edie [Lamont] was so tactful, she never spoke—she just let me look.

Oh Hadji Hadji—why do I love Knole so much? It's stupid—and I hate that beastly Nat. Trust symbol. Knole should have been mine, mine, mine. We were meant for each other.

VITA TO HAROLD   *Sissinghurst*

23 September 1958

I am sorry I was tiresome to you, getting upset about Edie [Edith Lamont] yesterday morning. I know you hate emotional manifestations, and shy away. But sometimes one's feelings overcome one, and one bursts out. You see, if Edie died, I should really feel rather desolate.

For one thing, she is about the only person who understands how much I love you, and would know what I would feel if you got ill or died. She is my only close friend. I haven't got many friends, and I don't want them, but it is nice to have one friend to whom one can talk openly, and if I lost Edie, I should have nobody left.

VITA TO HAROLD　　　　　　　　　　　　　　　　*Sissinghurst*

12 May 1959

You have been so good to me,[1] so patient, taking trays away, taking Dan [dog] out, sending me champagne and God knows what else, and then your readiness to trot about fetching Aristotle. You and I are so unaccustomed to being ill, that when illness does descend on us, we regard it with astonished resentment and don't quite know what to make of it.

HAROLD TO VITA　　　　　　　　　　　　　　　*C.1. Albany*

14 July 1959

I have still not disinfected myself from the slime of *Lolita*.[2] It is nonsense for Niggs to assert that it is a "great" work of literature. Literature will not experience any loss if it is not published. I think it a very clever book and well written. But I also think it 'obscene' in the sense of 'liable to corrupt'. It is absurd for Niggs to contend that it is a 'cautionary tale' and will deter those who have this temptation from wishing to practise it. Perverts of that sort are obsessed by the physical appeal and do not mind if Lolita was a horrid little minx. Nabokov has stressed the physical appeal with such licentious insistence that the pervert will be encouraged in his passion rather than discouraged.

---

1. Vita had been ill for two months with viral pneumonia.
2. The novel by Vladimir Nabokov, which Weidenfeld and Nicolson published in 1959 in defiance of much controversy. Vita and Harold were among those who considered it obscene. Today it is regarded as a minor classic.

HAROLD TO VITA   *C.1. Albany*

8 September 1959

What a lovely morning! Sun coming through mist. It was pleasant sitting on the catalpa bench with my darling and discussing why so many of our friends were discontented or unhappy. I still maintain that it is worse to muck up one's life by one's own fault than owing to an act of God or someone else's fault. You see, it adds self-reproach and guilt feelings to misfortune. Thus I am sure Cyril Connolly is more unhappy at being lazy and wasteful of his own great gifts if he could attribute his indolence to anything but himself. You and I can at least feel that we have got the most out of such talents as God gave us. But I believe what I appreciate most about my gifts is the gift of seeing beauty. Why should I experience such a spurt of pleasure at seeing the tower of Staplehurst church catch the sun through the fog? And why should that pleasure be doubled if you are there to share it? Oh bless you my saint for giving me such a happy life.

VITA TO HAROLD   *Sissinghurst*

27 October 1959

My own darling Hadji,

I was thinking this morning how awful it would be if you died. I do often think that; but it came over me all of a heap when I looked out of the bathroom window and saw you in your blue coat and black hat, peering into your scoop.[1] It is the sort of sudden view of a person that twists one's heart, when they don't know you are observing them—they have an innocent look, almost as a child asleep—one feels one is spying on some secret life one should not know about. Taking advantage as it were, although it is only the most loving advantage that one takes.

Anyway, the scoop would be the most poignant coffee-cup [relic after death] ever made.

I often think I have never told you how much I love you—and

---

1. The "scoop" was a hollow in one of the paving stones in the Cottage Garden at Sissinghurst, and Harold used it as a rain gauge.

Tuesday
Oct. 27.
1959

Keep

My own darling Hadji

I was thinking this morning how awful it would be if you died. I do often think that; but it came over me all of a heap when I looked out of the bathroom window and saw you in your blue coat and black hat, peering into your scoop. It is the sort of sudden view of a person that twists one's heart, when they don't know you are observing them. They have an innocent look. Almost as a child asleep. One feels one is spying on some secret life one should not know about. Taking advantage as it were, although it is only the most loving advantage that one takes.

Anyway, the scoop would be the most poignant coffee-cup ever made.

I often think I have never told you how much I love you — and if you died I should reproach myself, saying Why did I never tell him? Why did I never tell him enough?

Your Mar.

if you died I should reproach myself, saying, "Why did I never tell him? Why did I never tell him enough?"

Your Mar

HAROLD TO VITA   *C.1. Albany*

22 March 1960

I may see you during the course of today but I do not count on it. I rather want to see you, more than usual, as I want your advice on what literary figure should be awarded the O.M. Edith Sitwell has been suggested and I repress all jealousy and try to view the proposition wholly objectively. I feel that the O.M. should only be given to poets likely to be esteemed by successive generations, and I cannot rid myself of the idea that Edith is just a momentary or contemporary fashion. I should prefer, if the Arts are to be considered, to give it to Kenneth Clark.[1] The O.M. is a tremendous order and I do not wish to diminish its prestige.

I dined at the American Embassy. We were twelve at dinner. The two Whitneys[2]; the Queen Mother and lady; the Prime Minister and Lady Dorothy [Macmillan]; Heathcoat Amory, the Chancellor of the Exchequer; Mr and Mrs Profumo[3]; and Jeremy Tree, the racing son of Ronnie: he is a great race-course friend of the Queen Mother's. I sat between Mrs Whitney and Mrs Profumo, and thus was able to talk to the P.M. who was on Mrs Whitney's other side. He was delighted by what I had said to the *Daily Express* about his election.[4] He was in splendid form and really talked sense about the summit conference. He is annoyed at people calling it 'the' summit conference, and would prefer it to be called 'a' summit conference. He foresees that if we can have these summit conferences say once in every four years, we shall not perhaps achieve a complete settlement, but shall avoid momentary blocks and disagreements. He quoted me as saying (I suppose I did

---

1. Kenneth Clark was awarded the Order of Merit in 1976.
2. John H. Whitney, the Ambassador, and his wife.
3. John Profumo was then Minister of State for Foreign Affairs. His wife was Valerie Hobson, the actress.
4. As Chancellor of Oxford University.

somewhere) that the greatest of all diplomatic assets was the passage of time. If we could, by recurrent summit conferences, gain twenty years of peace, then by that time Africa and Asia may have settled down and Russia become more bourgeois. He dreads the disappearance of Khrushchev, since he is personally pledged to peace and his successor might be more militarist.

I had a long talk with Lady Dorothy afterwards. She says that at Rambouillet[5] there was a wonderful chef and about fifty servants with silver chains, but no soap in their bedroom and so cold that she had to sleep in a woolly. She asked Mme de Gaulle whether there was anything special she wanted to do when she comes on a State Visit and she said she wanted to go to Gorringes. I talked to the Queen Mother for about half an hour. I had to leave in the middle to go wee wee, but she took it well. As always, she asked after Mar and the garden. She did not offer to come down again and I did not press the suggestion. She was wearing a superb necklace of diamonds and pearls and a lovely pink taffeta dress. She really has the most wonderful skin I have ever seen. I could not detect in it a wrinkle. I enjoyed my dinner very much.

I have written to Mrs Whitney to say so.

They are nice people.

V I T A　T O　H A R O L D　　　　　　　　　　　　*Sissinghurst*

13 April 1960

What a delightful article about de Gaulle. Darling, there's nobody like you for doing that sort of thing so gracefully, so amusingly, so originally; and, in the conclusion, so nobly. You always achieve the perfect balance between the light and the serious. Your article reminded me of Virginia's remark that a phrase ought to be like casting a line in fishing, which I have quoted to you before now: it should describe a graceful parabola and come to rest in a solid plomp. Only Virginia was talking about a phrase; and I am talking about a whole article. Her metaphor (or simile?) applies to both.

---

5. The imposing château outside Paris where François I died and Macmillan met de Gaulle to discuss Britain's entry into the Common Market.

HAROLD TO VITA   *C.1. Albany*

1 June 1960

No darling—the reason I was depressed was not financial worry (an obsession to which I am not addicted) but merely that I had felt exhausted in the morning and too slack to write. Hitherto I have got tired when standing or walking too much, but have never been tired by reading or writing. I felt it a portent, and that I might cease to be able to earn my living and might have to fall back on my heiress and become a charity child. That prospect is enough to sadden any man. But I recovered all right and yesterday I felt quite spry again.

In fact I did a lot. I had myself shaved and manicured at Delhez. I lunched at the American Embassy. They have erected on the terrace a shamyana or palenquin or tent, the paving stones covered by a thick grey pile carpet and tables with drinks. The occasion was the conferment on Maurice Bowra of the diploma as honorary Academician, such as I have got. I wore my button in my lapel. The Ambassador made a halting allocution and Maurice said nothing—not a single word of thanks—in reply. There were leading university figures there—Noel Annan, Dadie Rylands, Mortimer Wheeler[1] and so on. I told Wheeler that I regarded him as a traitor to sacred Greece for extolling the harsh Romans. "I do it," he said, "with my tongue in my cheek." Now people ought not to discuss and expound such serious subjects unless sincerely. I always thought Wheeler a fraud.

VITA TO HAROLD   *Sissinghurst*

23 November 1960

I don't really look forward to our trip this year[2]—and I don't believe that you look forward to it either. Anyhow, I am sure we shall get some pleasure out of it—as we always do.

---

1. Sir Mortimer Wheeler, the most distinguished archaeologist of his day.
2. Their cruise in January–February 1961 was to Rio de Janeiro and Montevideo. Violet Trefusis did not, after all, join them.

I pray to God that Violet does not really come, whether escorted by a new prince or not. I simply cannot envisage Violet on a ship with us. We should have to control her very strictly, and bolt our cabin doors against her all through the morning and evening when we want to be quiet, you with Tikki and me with foolscap.

Isn't life odd?

There was once a time when Violet and I were so madly in love, and I hurt you so dreadfully—and now how dead that is, passion completely spent—and the true love that has survived is mine for you, and yours for me.

I think it was partly your fault, Hadji. You were older than me, and far better informed. I was very young, and very innocent. I knew nothing about homosexuality. I didn't even know that such a thing existed—either between men or between women. You should have told me. You should have warned me. You should have told me about yourself, and have warned me that the same sort of thing was likely to happen to myself. It would have saved us a lot of trouble and misunderstanding. But I simply didn't know.

Oh what a very unexpected letter to write to you suddenly. You won't like it, because you never like to face facts.

HAROLD TO VITA   *C.1. Albany*

30 May 1961

Did you see that Sidney Bernstein[1] has sold some of his shares for four million pounds? Lucky person. We could pay all our wages, clean the moat, have a forester and mate to clear up the wood, and live happily ever after. But I don't believe that money brings happiness although it may diminish worry. I am a happy man. I have you and Niggs and Benzie, and Juliet and Adam [Nigel's children]. I shall never forget Juliet running down the path between the big yews and flinging her arms round me. The charm of those two children is hot sunshine to me. I do like good manners. I do like affection. I feel all comfortable

---

1. The film producer, who had rented Long Barn in the 1930s.

inside when I think of that happy, happy day. Oh my darling, how lucky I am!

HAROLD TO VITA   *C.1. Albany*

23 August 1961

I went to see your grand-children in Limerston Street. The door was opened by Juliet in her dressing-gown and pyjamas. She bounded down the staircase and flung herself into my arms. She insisted on showing me her homework, and I must say she seems to have done very well, scarcely ever getting a sum wrong. Then Adam came in very solemn in his new scarlet dressing-gown. They clambered onto my knee as usual, and made me tell them stories. Most of the tales of my youth end up by my being beaten by my father. "Dadda," they chimed in chorus, "has never beaten us. He has never said cross things to us." "I don't believe it," I said, but they nodded their little fair heads in unison and repeated, "He never gets cross"—implying that Mumma often does. I am afraid that Niggs is what you call 'mild'—you think it a beastly thing to be. But I should like to see you with someone who wasn't mild. It would be hammer and tongs all the time. It is merely because I submit patiently that no crockery is broken in anger at Sissinghurst.

The children were still on my knee when the following conversation took place:—

Adam: Grandpapa, I shall be four next month.
 H.N.: Yes, I know, Adam.
Adam: I shall soon be quite grown up.
 H.N.: Yes, but don't hurry to get as grown-up as I am.
Adam: You are very very old, aren't you, Grandpapa?
 H.N.: Yes, Adam, I am very very old.
Adam: You will die soon, Grandpapa, won't you?
 H.N.: Yes, Adam, very soon. And I hope you will always
        remember me.
Adam (a look of devil mischief on his face): No I shan't. I
        shall forget all about you at once.
Juliet (flinging her arms round my neck): But that's rude,
        Adam. I shall remember Harold all the rest of my life.

Adam continues to grin like a little imp. He truly is adorable, since
he has so unconventional a mind. They were both looking so well.
Juliet's teeth have returned, and she is much better-looking and as
graceful as ever.

H A R O L D　T O　V I T A　　　　　　　　　*C.1. Albany*

27 February 1962

My darling,
　　I enclose the order for Daimler saying they will be waiting in the
forecourt. I am so relieved that dear Edie [Lamont] is coming with
you. I could not abide the idea of Mar with her little suitcase going
alone to Holloway Prison. Edie's tact and discernment and reticence
about the tragedy in the boat-train has wiped out all trace of jealousy.[1]
It was ridiculous of me to feel jealous, and Edie, I know, suspected
it and was wonderfully considerate. But I *was* jealous, idiot that I am.
　　I do not allow myself to get worried, and in the watches of the
night I forbid myself to brood in misery and concentrate my mind on
our happiness together, on great moments like Kermanshah [in 1926],
and above all on our deep love for each other which no catastrophe
can ever take away.
　　Thus my heart is filled with pity for you, knowing how you hate
hospitals and bedint sisters, and hospital beds and foods, and being
mucked about, and leaving our lovely house. We have both got to go
through a nasty time and must face it like square-jawed Janes. You are
so brave that you can be calm and self-contained. But I am not as brave
as you are, and I miss my Mummy who could comfort me. Knowing
your secrecy, or more accurately your love of privacy, I shall not tell
anyone and merely say that you are in hospital 'for observation'. Even
that I hate, since I know how you loathe being spied on.
　　I doubt whether you will get this, but I shall come to the hospital
soon after six tomorrow.

---

1. Vita had suffered a haemorrhage in the train at the outset of their cruise to the West Indies
　with Mrs. Lamont, and on her return she was advised to undergo an operation at the Royal
　Free Hospital, Canonbury, in north London.

VITA TO HAROLD   *Canonburg Hospital*

27 February 1962

My own darling Hadji,

   This is not a nice patch for us to be going through, but I think
the only way to take it is to realise that as one gets older these bothers
do come upon one.

   I am not going to indulge in self-pity, and I am not going to be
more of a bore and a worry than I can help. I have an absolute horror
of being a bore and a worry to anybody, but more especially to you,
my sweet, who are not a person who ought to be worried.

   So I hope that within a few days I shall be home, and all gay and
happy again.

                                                           Your Mar

HAROLD TO VITA   *C.1. Albany*

24 April 1962

   I am sorry to have annoyed you by insisting on a night nanny, but
I do so dread the idea that you might fall down in the night and be
ill for another six months.[1] She is a competent woman and I don't
really mind her. But I am seeing far more television than ever before
since it aids conversation at meals. Oh dear, I hope it is warm today
and that you sit a bit under the catalpa. It is so lovely there.

   I feel that people are under the impression that I don't know how
ill you have been, or that, if I do know, I don't care. How little they
understand! Why bother poor old Hadji? As if I hadn't been worried
enough! But they *mean* well—how astonishingly well they mean!
What is odd is that Bunny [Drummond] is the least hysterical of the
lot. But all the others say that I have never been accustomed to grave
operations and don't UNDERSTAND. I wish Glen [dog] could be
taught to bite all well-wishers.

---

1. Vita had survived the operation for abdominal cancer, and returned to Sissinghurst in a
   very weak condition.

VITA TO HAROLD   *Sissinghurst*

2 May 1962

My own darling Hadji,

I am going to get up and go into the garden: it is quite warm. I am glad that you have got away from all those boring nurses and atmosphere of sickroom: poor Hadji, you are so uncomplaining. My handwriting is better, don't you think? I shall try to get as far as your life's work [Spring garden] today, and can take one of the nice light garden chairs along with me. Also I shall put on some clothes which may make me feel a little more human. What I find one grudges is the appalling waste of time and not seeing to the things one wants to see to.

HAROLD TO VITA   *C.1. Albany*

24 May 1962

I hope it is all right about Philippa, Niggs and the children coming to luncheon on Sunday. I shall see to it that they do not trouble you too much. Oh my sweet, how I long for the day when you get well again. I don't like the idea of that vast dog keeping you awake. He means so well, but he can't reduce his size nor does he understand how ill invalids can feel. I shall be down by tea tomorrow and shall remain all the week.

V ita died at Sissinghurst on 2 June 1962 at the age of seventy, and her ashes were placed in the Sackville family vault at Withyham in Sussex. A tablet to her memory is in the church above.

Harold was profoundly shaken by her death. Although he continued to write his weekly book reviews for two more years, and once traveled to Greece, once to Italy, and once, for two weeks, to the United States, his energy slowly declined. He gave up writing and gardening, and in his last years scarcely read more than news-paper headlines. He became very silent, but would occasionally reveal flashes of his old, self-mocking humour, as when he said to me after the success of his published diaries, "It is rather sad to think that of all my forty books the only one that will be remembered is the one I didn't realise I'd written."

Of course this wasn't true. Scarcely a week passes when I do not see quoted by a journalist, politician, or fellow author some saying of his, and Some People, his biography of Tennyson, and King George V: His Life and Reign have in their different ways become classics. Vita's reputation, too, has long survived her death, far more of her books remaining in print than Harold's, and her garden at Sissinghurst, now a property of the National Trust, has become one of the best known in England.

They are remembered, too, for their unusual marriage, which since their deaths has been celebrated in print and film, but never more sympathetically than in the present volume, where they tell their own story. My fear has been that some readers might find it sentimental. Reiterated expressions of mutual love between husband and wife are said to be unnecessary if it is genuine and strongly rooted, but Vita and Harold felt the need to reassure each other constantly of what both profoundly believed, so amazed were they that *their marriage had survived its first traumatic ten years to become for both of them a life-enhancing success in the remaining forty.*

Harold died at Sissinghurst, aged eighty-one, on 1 May 1968 of a heart attack as he was undressing for bed, and his ashes were interred in the cemetery of Sissinghurst parish church, which looks across the woods, fields, and orchards of the Weald of Kent toward the rose-red house where both had given and experienced so much happiness.

INDEX

Abbreviations: V.S-W or Vita for Vita Sackville-West, HN for Harold Nicolson

ABOUT THE AUTHOR

NIGEL NICOLSON still lives at Sissinghurst Castle in Kent, where his parents created a garden that has become one of the most famous in England. He has been a Member of the British House of Commons and a founder-director of the publishing firm of Weidenfeld & Nicolson. He is the author or editor of many books, including the six volumes of Virginia Woolf's letters, biographies of Field Marshal Alexander of Tunis and Mary Curzon, and *Two Roads to Dodge City,* which he wrote with his son Adam.

SOUTH POLE
STATION

SOUTH POLE STATION

ASHLEY SHELBY

Picador | New York

SOUTH POLE STATION. Copyright © 2017 by Ashley Shelby. All rights reserved. Printed in the United States of America. For information, address Picador, 175 Fifth Avenue, New York, N.Y. 10010.

picadorusa.com • picadorbookroom.tumblr.com
twitter.com/picadorusa • facebook.com/picadorusa

Picador® is a U.S. registered trademark and is used by
Macmillan Publishing Group, LLC, under license from Pan Books Limited.

For book club information, please visit facebook.com/picadorbookclub
or e-mail marketing@picadorusa.com.

Ashley Shelby is a fiscal year 2010 recipient of an Artist Initiative grant from the Minnesota State Arts Board. This activity is made possible by the voters of Minnesota through a grant from the Minnesota State Arts Board, thanks to a legislative appropriation from the arts and cultural heritage fund.

MINNESOTA
STATE ARTS BOARD

Map by Rhys Davies

The Library of Congress Cataloging-in-Publication Data is available upon request.

ISBN 978-1-250-11282-8 (hardcover)
ISBN 978-1-250-11285-9 (e-book)

Our books may be purchased in bulk for promotional, educational, or business use. Please contact your local bookseller or the Macmillan Corporate and Premium Sales Department at 1-800-221-7945, extension 5442, or by e-mail at MacmillanSpecialMarkets@macmillan.com.

First Edition: July 2017

10 9 8 7 6 5 4 3 2 1

For Hudson and Josephine, always.

For Manny, without whom this book would not exist—and
who once advised me to relax my shoulders.

And for Mom: this one's for you.

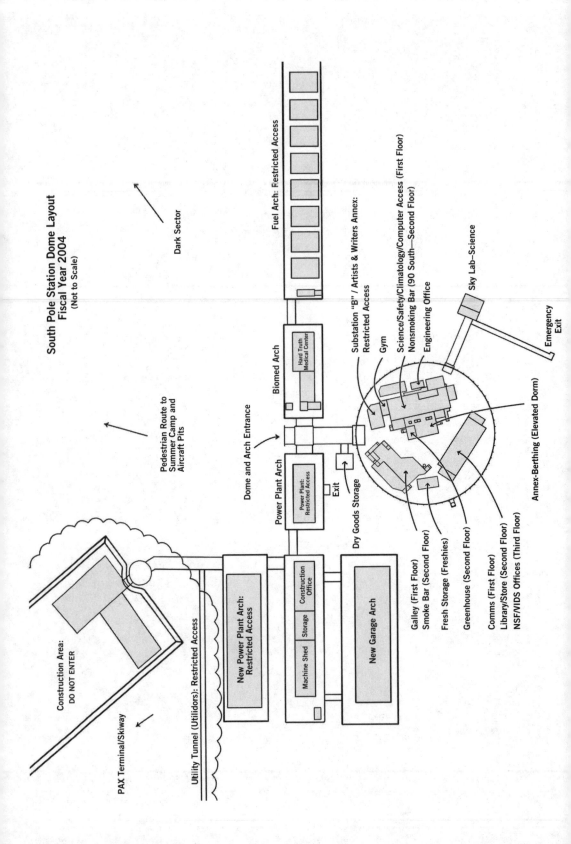

South Pole Station Dome Layout
Fiscal Year 2004
(Not to Scale)

Dark Sector

Fuel Arch: Restricted Access

Substation "B" / Artists & Writers Annex:
Restricted Access

Gym

Science/Safety/Climatology/Computer Access (First Floor)
Nonsmoking Bar (90 South—Second Floor)

Engineering Office

Sky Lab–Science

Emergency
Exit

Annex-Berthing (Elevated Dorm)

Biomed Arch

Hard Truth
Medical Center

Pedestrian Route to
Summer Camp and
Aircraft Pits

Dome and Arch Entrance

Power Plant Arch

Power Plant:
Restricted Access

Exit

Dry Goods Storage

Galley (First Floor)
Smoke Bar (Second Floor)
Fresh Storage (Freshies)
Greenhouse (Second Floor)
Comms (First Floor)
Library/Store (Second Floor)
NSF/VIDS Offices (Third Floor)

Construction Area:
DO NOT ENTER

Utility Tunnel (Utilidors): Restricted Access

New Power Plant Arch:
Restricted Access

Machine Shed | Storage | Construction Office

New Garage Arch

PAX Terminal/Skiway

AMUNDSEN-SCOTT SOUTH POLE STATION GUIDE
2003–2004
FY04

The National Science Foundation welcomes you to the Amundsen-Scott South Pole Station. This handbook describes facilities, procedures, and safety reminders that will help you during your stay at South Pole.

This year's science, construction, and airlift schedules are the most ambitious in our history, and we have a talented group of people to make it all happen. Our success will depend on our commitment to safety and community involvement.

Located at 90 degrees South latitude, Amundsen-Scott Station has an average annual temperature of -56.7 degrees F, with a record low temperature of -117 degrees F. It rarely snows at South Pole; however, a relatively constant wind speed of 5–15 knots compounds the accumulation.

Most station buildings are located beneath an aluminum geodesic dome, which provides a windbreak for the living, dining, communications, recreation, and laboratory facilities. The main station can accommodate twenty-seven people under the Dome. Additional personnel are housed in modular hypertats and in Summer Camp—a collection of canvas Jamesways, a short walk from the main station.

A series of steel arches houses the power plant, biomed facility, garages, artists' & writers' studios, and main fuel storage. The Dark Sector is located grid west of the station and houses facilities for astronomy and astrophysics research. The Atmospheric Research Observatory lies 300 feet upwind of the station, but the majority of climate change research takes place at the West Antarctic Ice Shelf (WAIS), also known as The Divide.

Please read this handbook thoroughly and don't forget to visit the Geographic South Pole during your stay!

Welcome Aboard,
Tucker Bollinger
South Pole Area Director

polie

Do you ever have pain in your chest unrelated to indigestion?
Are you often sad?
Do you have digestion problems due to stress?
Do you have problems with authority?
How many alcoholic drinks do you consume a week? A day?
Would you rather be a florist or a truck driver?
True or false: I like to read about science.
True or false: Sometimes I just feel like killing myself.
True or false: I prefer flowers to trucks.
True or false: Voices tell me to hurt people.
True or false: I am an important person.

Five months before this pelvic exam of the mind, Cooper Gosling had received a letter on embossed government stationery assessing her application to the National Science Foundation's Antarctic Artists & Writers Program. From it, Cooper learned that her portfolio of paintings featured "interesting juxtapositions that suggest an eye particularly attuned to the complexities of human habitation in Antarctica" and "superior technical skill that still leaves room for interpretation," as well as "a frenetic color palette within mainly controlled compositions." There was, the letter had noted tartly, "potential for improvement over the course of the fellowship."

She had been accepted, pending successful completion of physical and dental exams, fire training, and a psychological assessment at the Denver headquarters of Veritas Integrated Defense Systems, the contractor currently running the show in Afghanistan, and also in charge of basic operations at South Pole. The acceptance letter had come with an airline voucher—they expected her in Denver in three weeks. She was advised to travel light and to pay special attention to hygiene.

The night she received the letter, Cooper had driven directly to her father's house to apprise him of these developments. She imagined him falling to pieces, his joy resplendent. Bill Gosling was into this stuff: polar exploration was his deal. Sure, he preferred the heroics of the North Pole explorers, the drama of the Northwest Passage, the cannibalism of Franklin's lost expedition. But his "polar library" included memoirs from the South Pole boys, too: Shackleton, Amundsen, Scott, all first editions. Now that he'd retired from 3M, where he'd been part of the second-string Post-it team, he'd begun work on a memoir of being a polar enthusiast. It would, Cooper could only assume, include many scenes set in armchairs. They'd connect on this South Pole thing, Cooper was sure. He'd offer more than the smile her older sister, Billie, had always described as "faint." He'd confess that she now possessed the skeleton key to his soul.

Instead, he offered her another book: Apsley Cherry-Garrard's *The Worst Journey in the World*.

"The definitive account of the Scott expedition, written by a survivor," Bill said as he placed the book in Cooper's hands. "Make this a priority." (It was in this manner, incidentally, that Cooper had managed to slog her way through Everyman's Library of the World's Most Boring Books.) Cooper searched her father's face, but his expression remained as mild as always. Was it possible he'd forgotten? Or was he trying to tell her not to forget why she was going? Cooper had, of course, already read *The Worst Journey in the World*, had long ago committed entire paragraphs to memory. In fact, the book had been, throughout 1981, Cooper and her twin brother David's deranged bedtime reading. They were eight when Bill shelved Nancy Drew and opened *Worst Journey*. Night after night, he sat on the edge of the bed Cooper still shared with David, and narrated the adventures of what sounded like a rejected Marvel superhero team—Cherry, Birdie, Titus, Uncle Bill, and Captain Scott—as they slogged their way across Antarctica. The saga was the kind of monomyth Cooper would later read about in her comparative mythology electives but would never encounter in real life—Trials! Atonement! Apotheosis! Birdie, Cherry, and Uncle Bill (the fine doctor Edward Wilson), who had set out on the Winter Journey to retrieve an emperor penguin egg, became a holy triumvirate.

Cooper treated each reading as if it were a poetry slam, leaping out of bed during the exciting parts, and falling asleep on David's shoulder during the boring "Spring" chapters, which featured light polar housekeeping and a broken George Robey record spinning on the gramophone. David, on the other hand, listened quietly but intently to everything. It wasn't Cherry's myopia or Edward Wilson's rendering of penguin fat that captured his imagination. It was Titus Oates, the one who walked into the blizzard, his frostbitten foot black and grotesquely swollen. Titus had asked to be left behind; he knew he was slowing them down. Scott and the others refused to leave him so he begged, like a child, and they put him to bed in his sleeping bag. He prayed, loudly, to die before morning, and when he awoke to discover he was still alive, he decided to do it himself. He didn't bother to put his boots on. This time no one stopped him.

The idea of philanthropic suicide was too abstract for Cooper to understand (their mother, Dasha, who felt explorer lit documented "man's endless quest to enlarge his penis," claimed the idea itself was impossible, not to mention inappropriate for elementary-age children). But David was gripped by the notion. Titus's honorable death figured into their play on winter days, David devising scenarios where he'd walk into the woods that ringed their suburban home in order to disappear, leaving Cooper to await his return. When Cooper played Cherry to David's Scott or his Titus, she did little more than hang around expectantly, just as Cherry had. Hoping for months to see the Scott party emerge from the Beardmore Glacier valley, Cherry was always certain the men were just over the rise. As a result, Cooper came to identify with him, this aristocrat who'd bought his way onto the *Terra Nova*, the Scottish whaling ship that carried the Scott party to Antarctica. Twee and myopic, Cherry was a hothouse flower; Cooper was sure everyone must have doubted him. Over the course of the journey, however, he'd become indispensable, and, eventually, its most eloquent witness.

But that was years ago now, and neither Cooper nor Bill had so much as glanced at *The Worst Journey in the World* in a decade. In fact, after the divorce, Bill had begun selling off his rare book collection volume by volume, and Cooper had always assumed that *Worst Journey* had been the first to go. It was burdened by memories that had never made the promised transition from unbearable to bittersweet. The only other copy in the house, David's own heavily annotated mass-market edition, had disappeared.

Cooper took the book from her father and chose to say nothing. Bill gazed out the window at the lightly falling snow. The flakes were fat and hairy, and they descended at an angle. Bill apprised the snow cover. He signaled his approval with a curt nod, and told Cooper to get her coat. Five minutes later, they were outside. It was after ten, but the freshly fallen snow illuminated the backyard as cleanly as moonlight. "Snow is one of the best insulating materials, if used properly," Bill said as he assessed its moisture content by rubbing the soft flakes between his fingers. "The quickest way to die is to stop paying attention."

Winter survival training dictated that you did not travel in a blizzard, he told her. You stop and dig a snow trench or make a snow cave with a hand shovel. *What hand shovel?* You travel with a hand shovel. If you are an amateur and don't carry a hand shovel on your person, you can use your snowshoes. *What if you aren't using snowshoes?* If you are sans snowshoes, you are a dipshit with no business traveling overland in winter. But if you are a dipshit traveling overland in winter with no snowshoes, you use your hands.

Bill and Cooper spent the next hour digging out a trench, a coffin-shaped cavity carved out of the snow. Cooper marveled at her father's efficiency, the certainty of his movements. How well he seemed to know how to do this.

When the specifications were just right, Bill slipped under the lip of the roof by sliding down the snow ramp they'd built to facilitate entry. Cooper peered into the darkness and saw her father supine, his hands behind his head, smiling at nothing.

"What's so funny?" she asked. Bill shook his head, but the smile remained.

"This is how I'd like to die."

"In a snow trench in your backyard?"

"In nature, in winter. Climb in the trench, kick out the roof, and go to sleep. It's like Cherry said. If Death comes for you in the snow, he comes disguised as sleep. 'You greet him rather as a welcome friend than a gruesome foe.'" Bill peered up at Cooper. "Doesn't get any easier."

It didn't occur to Cooper then to ask her father if death was supposed to be easy.

*

The suburban campus of Veritas Integrated Defense Systems looked like a centerfold from *Maximum Security Prisons Quarterly*. Its cinder-block buildings were divided into quadrants and separated by LiftMaster Mega Arm security gates. A shuttle bus deposited Cooper, along with eight other Pole candidates, at Quadrant 9, where they were photographed and fingerprinted. They followed a Veritas employee down intersecting beige hallways in a disaffected clump. As they waited for an elevator, Cooper saw two men in royal-blue company polos in a break room staring up at a suspended television, watching a recap of Bush's State of the Union speech from the night before. "The British government has learned that Saddam Hussein recently sought significant quantities of uranium from Africa," Bush was saying.

"Holy shit," one of the Veritas guys laughed. "I mean, at this point, you have to go loco on Hussein, right? You have to bomb the shit out of Baghdad." He looked over at his companion. "He's gonna, right?"

The man clutching a vending-machine latte replied carelessly, "Relax, we already submitted a bid."

Cooper and the other applicants were led to a large conference room with a view of Parking Ramp Alpha (parking ramps Beta, Charlie, and Delta were a short shuttle ride from the main complex). Cooper took a seat at the table and looked around at her fellow Pole candidates: all men, all self-consciously hirsute, and all engaged in silent contests over who could fit more carabiners on their stainless-steel water bottles. They avoided making eye contact with Cooper, so she turned her attention to the stack of paperwork in front of her: hundreds and hundreds of questions that had no good answers.

Two hours and five hundred questions later, Cooper and the eight men were allowed to grab a coffee before returning to watch a mandatory video from the Veritas Integrated Defense Systems president. The video commenced with a synthesizer version of "My Country 'Tis of Thee" playing behind scenes of waving flags and purple mountains majesty. The fruited plains dissolved into a shot of a man in a company polo of slightly better quality than the ones Cooper had encountered in the break room. He wore an American flag pin on his lapel, and was looking just off camera.

"I'm Daniel Atcheson Johnson, president of Veritas Integrated Defense Systems, or VIDS. For over seventy-five years we have worked to develop advanced technologies that help planes navigate, reduce traffic congestion, even land astronauts on the moon. With such diverse capabilities, VIDS is much more than a defense contractor. We are a global citizen invested in our collective future. Defense technologies with civilian applications, and the building of bridges between the defense industry and the people we protect. That is our commitment to you. The guidance chip in a medium-range ballistic missile shares the same technology found in your car's airbag. Think about that for a moment, and you'll realize that the future is VIDS." After a brief pause, during which someone behind the camera seemed to be instructing him to continue, Johnson added, "VIDS—the first line of defense and your trusted partner for a better tomorrow."

The door rattled open, and Cooper turned to see one of the psychologists beckoning her toward the door. Together, the women walked down the hall and into a windowless room. Inside were a desk, two chairs, and a limp spider plant with no hope of achieving photosynthesis.

Once they were seated, the psychologist offered Cooper a sympathetic smile. "Glad that's over, right? I mean, what a drag, all those questions."

"You have to ask them, I guess," Cooper replied, cautious.

"Why do you think we have to ask those questions, Cooper?"

"Why do you ask those questions?" *Christ, why was she repeating the questions back?* "My guess would be to weed out people who may not be mentally fit for polar service," she said.

"Do you consider yourself fit for South Pole?"

"If I didn't, I wouldn't be here," Cooper said, even though she had no idea what made a person "fit for South Pole." But she realized that to a psychologist looking for a problem, she sounded impatient. "I can clarify, if that's allowed."

"Relax"—the psychologist consulted her papers—"Cooper. This isn't a test. It's a conversation."

"I guess what I was trying to say is that I'm going down on an artist fellowship. It's not like I'm an astrophysicist or someone really important on the support side."

"You don't consider yourself important?"

"I just mean that it will probably be easier for me. It's not like people's lives depend on whether I complete a painting or not." *Just mine*, she thought.

The psychologist pulled a piece of paper out of a file, read it, then looked up at Cooper. "Are there any emotional or psychological traumas you feel could impact your potential for success at Pole?" Cooper was irritated by the psychologist's work-around of the obvious trauma—the emotional liability—that she had disclosed on her paperwork. It was as if the woman were trying to extract a confession.

Cooper tried to rearrange her face in a way that conveyed both sadness and stability. That it was bad, yes, but that the jagged-glass edges of it had been smoothed over by the last nine months, even if they hadn't. Cooper had never known a jagged edge to become smooth, not unless it was broken off completely.

"You're talking about my brother, right? I mean, if that's what you mean by emotional 'trauma.' " Cooper made quote hooks around the word *trauma*, and the psychologist frowned. "Sorry," Cooper said, and added, "Trauma," this time without the quote hooks.

"Suicide is a major emotional trauma." The psychologist paused, waiting. "Would you like to talk about it?"

Cooper stared into the woman's face, a Glamour Shots advertisement come to life. Did she want to "talk about it"? Did she have a pressing need to unburden herself to a woman wearing faux leather knee-high boots in a building on the campus of the world's second-largest defense contractor? How could she explain that this was the only way you could talk about it, by disclosing it in paperwork, by putting air quotes around it, by gliding along the surface? Cooper knew that explaining this would make her unfit for polar service. That, and telling the truth about David, because if there was a gene for what he had, for the schizophrenic madness that boldly announced itself one day like a Mary Kay saleswoman, then maybe it was somewhere in Cooper, too. Unexpressed, perhaps, or merely waiting for a trigger.

She braced herself for more probing, more note-taking, but suddenly the psychologist shifted gears and told Cooper they could come back to the David question. Cooper knew from months of sliding-scale therapy that the sudden shift away from what her therapist called Cooper's "dominant story" did not bode well for her chances of landing at Pole. She was overwhelmed by the feeling of having been summarily dismissed. She wanted to go to Pole. She had to go to Pole. Cooper had no idea where the sudden desperation was coming from, but she knew she'd rather lie down in a snow trench and kick in the roof than not go to Pole.

The psychologist handed Cooper a sheaf of papers.

"Here are the results of those tests, by the way."

"Already?"

"We have a machine."

Cooper folded the papers in half without looking at them. This caught the psychologist's attention.

"You don't want to see your results? It's actually very interesting. It takes your answers and graphs your responses, showing where you fall in several categories of human neuroses." She turned her copy of Cooper's test toward her. "Take 'tendency toward delusional thinking,' for example."

It seemed to Cooper as if the earth had tilted slightly, by degrees. She gripped the arms of the chair in a way that didn't suggest panic.

"Here is the center line," the psychologist continued, "which represents a statistically 'normal' person. This x here shows us where your answers indicate you'd fall. No one falls right on the line." Cooper did not look up from her hands to see where the x was.

"Cooper?"

"I'm sorry," Cooper replied. "I'm not much into explanations." The psychologist stared at Cooper for a moment, the tests limp in her hand. *Look her in the eyes.* "I just want to paint at the bottom of the earth," Cooper heard herself say.

The psychologist surveyed Cooper as if she were a thrift store evening gown.

Finally, she said, "Just sit tight for a minute, would you?"

Once the door clicked shut, Cooper pulled at the fabric of her shirt from beneath her armpits, trying to get some ventilation. She fished a compact out of her bag and began studying the swollen zit under her nose. A moment later, she heard the door open.

"People will pity a person with rosacea or shingles," a voice said, "but there is no sympathy in the world for a person with acne. I'm living proof of this." Cooper twisted around in her seat to see a man wearing a tight thermal shirt tucked into what looked like very expensive jeans. "I'm being sympathetic," he added, "not judgmental."

Cooper had never seen a human enter a room in this way, like an android whose design hadn't included joint flexion. After his confident pronouncement on acne, the man shuffled in, head down, and offered her a painful-looking smile. "Miss Gosling," he said in a faint Southern accent, "I'm Tucker Bollinger, your friendly South Pole area director."

He was a black man with eyes a color she'd never seen before, a mix of yellow and green—Golden Beryl, if you were going by a paint box. He had three piercings in his left ear, all of them empty. His cheeks were hollow and acne-scarred, and Cooper saw there was a kind of beauty about him; yet it was a beauty that had been coaxed into existence. He seemed as guilty as if he'd stolen it, as unconvinced of its authenticity as someone who'd witnessed its creation and knew it to be false.

"They brought in the big gun," Cooper said, snapping the compact closed.

"Am I a big gun?" he replied. "I've been told I have a big gun."

"You just told me you run South Pole," Cooper said. "In terms of guns, that qualifies as an assault weapon."

Tucker moved toward the chair next to Cooper, and seemed to consider sitting for a moment, before placing his hand on the back of it, as if posing for a Matthew Brady portrait. "I'm more of a matchlock musket," he said thoughtfully. "In fact, the parallels are nearly complete."

"So, you're here because I wouldn't look at my test results."

"Sometimes the contract psychologists get responses that aren't on their protocols, so they call somebody from the Program in to double-check. One person's tendency to hole up in her room with Proust is another person's schizoid isolation. Not that I speak from experience." He glanced over at the paperwork on the desk, his hands now thrust into his pockets. "You're in the Artists and Writers Program." He looked up from the pages. "Says here that you've been a live-event artist."

"My first job out of art school."

"Bat mitzvahs?"

"Weddings, mostly. The brides carried kale."

"Better than a caricaturist-for-hire," Tucker replied.

"Barely."

"Well, we don't get a lot of traditional visual artists anymore," he said.

"Conceptual?"

"No, they stopped coming in the early nineties. Now it's mixed-media artists, collagists, and found art. Last season, they had a guy doing paper clips. He made a uterus. He called it a feminist conduit to tactile interaction. There was one sexual harassment complaint."

Cooper felt her limbs relax, and her muscles immediately ached from the tension they'd been holding for the past three hours. Clearly the bar for artistic achievement was low at South Pole.

"Do you have any talent?" Tucker asked.

"Maybe," Cooper said.

"Maybe?"

"It's kind of like psychological exams, I guess. Subject to protocols." When Tucker didn't reply, Cooper added: "I've been told I have talent."

"If you don't agree, then why are you here?"

"I don't know why I'm here. But I'm here."

Cooper could see this wasn't enough. "What if I promise to just be your typical aimless thirty-year-old looking to delay the inevitable slide into mediocrity?"

"That rolls off your tongue easily."

"Yeah, well, I've said it before."

Cooper thought she detected a slight smile somewhere on Tucker's face, but he didn't let it crack open.

"Then you will fit in very well," he said. "But can you, just for paperwork's sake, give me one line that I can write down on this form? One line about why you want to go to South Pole?"

"I put that on my application."

"That thing about 'new horizons' and 'fresh perspectives'?"

Cooper sighed. "How about to further my creative journey?"

"Insincere."

"For adventure's sake?"

"There is no adventure, only a grind."

"I like cold climates?"

"Stay in Minnesota."

"I want to be somewhere else."

"You're getting closer."

"But if I say that, you'll think I'm running from something," Cooper said.

"It's not 'running from something.' It's turning aside." Tucker thought for a moment. "Or looking askance. Looking askance at civilization. If you apply to go to Pole because it seems 'cool' or because you're looking for 'adventure,' then you'll crack up when you realize it's not a frat party. If you don't fit in anywhere else, you will work your ass off for us. This has been proven time and time again."

He clicked the pen attached to his clipboard and scribbled something. Then he stood up and indicated that Cooper should, too.

"I'll have to meet with the program directors this afternoon to go over the borderline cases."

"I'm borderline?"

"Sorry."

"What about my one-liner?"

"What about it?"

"You're going to use that thing about the personal journey?"

"Unless you have something better. The paper-clip guy said something about a personal journey, and he scraped in." Tucker waited a moment, rubbing his left earlobe between his fingers, but Cooper could think of nothing to add. As she gathered her things, Tucker said, "Listen, shrinks worry about fresh death. Especially a suicide. Unresolved grief does sometimes lead to breakdowns, especially in extreme environments. But then so do delays in booze shipments. I'm sorry for saying 'fresh death.'"

"I don't mind. I guess it is."

"You'll know by tonight," Tucker said. Cooper smiled weakly and watched as he left the room. She could hear his footfalls in the hallway. It sounded like South Pole itself was receding. As she closed her eyes to deny tears an exit point, she realized that she had underplayed the importance of this whole thing. For the first time, she understood it wasn't the lark she'd been telling herself it was; Cooper knew that the jagged edges would continue to lacerate her unless she did something drastic. She didn't quite know why she believed this, but she did. In fact, it was one of the only things she believed in now.

As she stared at the pale, sickly leaves of the office plant, Cooper understood that her chance was slipping away. She was on the verge of being rejected, as Scott had rejected Cherry.

Cherry.

She leapt to her feet. "I've got one," she called down the hallway, where Tucker was talking to a VIDS employee. "A reason to go."

Tucker dismissed the man, and waited as Cooper jogged toward him. "It's a quote, but it's why I want to go down."

"Quoting others suggests avoidance," Tucker replied when she arrived.

Cooper shook her head. "No, it only means that someone more articulate than me has been in my shoes. It only means"—Cooper could hear the hitch in her voice—"that someone else said it better than I could. But it's why I want to go."

Down the hall, someone began brewing a vending-machine latte, and Cooper realized she was holding her breath. Tucker finally clicked the pen again and held it poised above the clipboard. As she spoke, Cooper tried to keep her voice steady.

＊

That night, after a "trust-building" exercise at Applebee's involving Tabasco sauce and 7UP, Cooper returned to her hotel room to find the red cube on the phone blinking. It was Tucker calling to confirm that the shuttle for "fire school" would arrive at the hotel promptly at seven a.m., and that she was expected. Cooper listened to the message twice. She wanted to assume that an invitation to fire training meant she was in, but earlier at the restaurant, over double-crunch bone-in wings, some guy from Spokane told her a story about a woman who'd done the tests, completed fire school, flown to Christchurch,

New Zealand, and been allowed to pick out all her extreme cold weather (ECW) gear, before being denied a berth on the flight to Pole because of a "clerical error." It was best to assume nothing.

The next morning, Cooper boarded a shuttle bus with twenty other sleepy people and three highly caffeinated officials from VIDS. She chose a seat next to a pale, heavy-lidded man of about forty. He had poorly maintained ginger mutton chops, a high-and-tight, and the face of a hamster. He was examining a chain wallet with his name, Floyd, spelled out in tiny strips of duct tape. She imagined him straining over this project, fat pink tongue sticking out, Lit'l Smokies–esque fingers arranging the strips in the letters that formed his name. He glanced over at Cooper, so she said, "Hi." He turned away, or possibly askance.

"I've done this three times," he said to the window. He drew a penis with a cartoonish scrotum in the fog his breath had made on the glass.

"You've done fire training three times or you've been to South Pole three times?" Cooper asked, to be polite.

"Was I talking to you?"

"I'm pretty sure you were."

"It's a mistake to be 'pretty sure' of anything," he said, using quote hooks. Cooper remembered her earlier use of quote hooks and burned with shame.

"Excuse Floyd. He's saying, in his typical incoherent way, that he's been to Pole three times."

Before Cooper could turn to get an eye on the man seated behind her, a VIDS official wearing Ray-Bans atop his salt-and-pepper crew cut whistled to get everyone's attention. "Get ready, folks. This is team-building time," he shouted as the bus pulled into the Centennial State Fire Academy, which was located a few miles from the VIDS corporate campus.

Once everyone had shuffled down the aisle and off the bus, the prospective "Polies" lined up against a chain-link fence. Cooper noticed the guy next to her was stretching, linking his fingers and reaching for the sky. After two days of mingling with the marginally attractive,

Cooper was startled to encounter someone whose looks were above average. He was built like a basketball player, at least six-four, with lean limbs and fierce hazel eyes in an otherwise relaxed and confident face. She wondered about his Pole occupation—carpenter, engineer, forklift driver? Cooper decided he was a carpenter, because he had that rangy look that she associated with woodworkers.

He glanced over at her. "You a Fingy?" Cooper recognized his voice as the one that had asked her to excuse Floyd earlier.

"A what?"

He laughed. "You've answered the question. Fingy—stands for 'fucking new guy.' "

"Is that an official term?"

"Official enough. I'm Sal," he said, sticking out his hand.

"Cooper."

"Science or support?"

"Uh, I'm not sure—I'm down on the A-and-W grant."

"Ah, you're an *artiste*."

"I detect sarcasm."

Sal grinned. "Never."

Cooper turned to watch as a squat two-story building disgorged smoke while people dressed in fire gear ducked in and out, rescuing dummies and laying them on the grass about ten yards away.

"After these cadets finish, we'll start suiting up," the VIDS official said.

"What's this guy's name again?" Cooper whispered to Sal.

"Just call him VIDS. That's what we call all the Denver-based admins. They're interchangeable. It's easier that way."

"VIDS sounds like a venereal disease you'd catch at Blockbuster."

"Good one."

The VIDS official clapped his hands to get the Polies' attention. "While we wait, I'd like to take this opportunity to welcome you to the United States Antarctic Program, also known as the Program. You may be going down there as a cook, a geologist, a custodial engineer, an admin—"

"Astrophysicist!" Sal coughed into his hand. Cooper snuck another look at Sal. It strained her credulity to believe that an astrophysicist could be both physically attractive and supremely self-assured—not that she'd ever met an astrophysicist, which had always sounded to Cooper like a made-up job title.

"In whatever capacity you come down here," the VIDS official continued, "whether you're on the science side or the support side, you hold your colleagues' lives in your hands."

A small woman wearing a pink bandanna raised her hand. "Excuse me but I have a thing with fire masks. For example, I wasn't a good scuba diver because the mouthpiece freaked me out. I could see myself being someone who would take it out underwater, against my better judgment, you know, just because it's a foreign object in my mouth. So I'm just wondering how this, um, tendency, I guess, is going to impact fire training." Scornful chuckles all around. The woman looked at the group. "What, is that a dumb question?"

"All questions are good, all questions are good," the VIDS official said, rubbing his hands together nervously. "What's your name, honey?" Cooper noticed her stiffen at this. Apparently so did the VIDS guy. "I mean, your name?" he stammered.

"Pearl."

"Pearl, I think because the fire mask doesn't actually go into your mouth like a scuba regulator does, you'll be pleasantly surprised by how nonintrusive it is."

Pearl nodded. "Good. Nonintrusive is always welcome."

Over the next four hours, the Pole candidates donned helmets, fire jackets, overalls, boots, and face masks, and endured every worst-case scenario known to man. Forced entry using a halligan and an ax. Extinguishing vehicle fires with dry chemical powder. Crawling through an eighty-foot plastic tunnel called the Gerbil Tube in order to "get used to tight spaces." Some of the applicants folded under the pressure and were hastily wrapped in shock blankets. Pearl did, in fact, find the face mask obtrusive, to the tune of a panic attack in the Gerbil Tube, and so was officially reassigned to the Trauma Team, which, at Pole, would muster to provide CPR or splints in case of catastrophic injury. Some of the Polies, Cooper noted, were studs. Sal had been the only one to locate the "infant reported to be in the building" and drag the miniature dummy out by the scruff of its neck, only to pretend to breastfeed it as the others scrambled to safety.

The last exercise of the day was in the Maze, a smoke-filled, two-story house. Cooper was expected to perform a sweep-search and rescue her victim—a scientist who had joined the group late. She had already seen several other veteran Polies, at fire school for recertification, complete this exercise; they'd exited the synthetic fires laughing and slapping one another on the back. It wasn't easy, Cooper reasoned, but it was probably doable. She awaited the fire chief's whistle, and when she heard it, sprinted into the building.

As soon as she stepped into the Maze, though, she realized she was fucked. The place was a carnival funhouse of stairs, dead ends, and walls of fire. It turned out synthetic smoke wasn't all that different from real smoke—and it obscured everything, so Cooper began crawling. Room by room, she searched for the scientist. Sweat began to dribble down her forehead and into her eyes, steaming up the glass of her fire mask.

"Where are you?" Cooper cried. It sounded as if she were shouting into a pillow. She climbed up the stairs on all fours, and turned into the first room she came to. The ceiling was on fire. Cooper thought she could make out something lying motionless halfway across the room. She got to her feet and scuttled over to the body. It was one of the CPR dummies. Cooper began kicking it mercilessly, her fear and frustration mounting to panic. What if this was a trick? Some kind of test? Maybe there was no one in the Maze awaiting rescue. Maybe the scientist had entered the building and then slipped out the back door, and Cooper's score was based on how long it would take her to realize this.

But then, through the groans of the generator that was powering the smoke machine, she thought she heard something. Someone was humming. Cooper crawled down the hall and pushed open the second door. There, next to the window, was a man in fire gear, on his haunches, cowering. For a moment they stared at each other through the smudged Plexiglas of their masks. Then Cooper kicked his boot with hers and he slowly got to his feet. She took hold of his arm and forced him down the stairs like Lennie Briscoe on an episode of *Law & Order*.

By the time they burst through the front door, a crowd had gathered around the Maze, and it exploded into applause. Cooper pushed the man away from her so hard that he fell to the ground. She tore off her fire mask and tried to get a good breath.

"You were never in danger," the fire chief said, marking something on his clipboard.

As the crowd dispersed, Cooper watched while a medic attended to the scientist, who was now draped in a shock blanket. When he turned his enormous china-doll eyes toward her, she couldn't stop the scowl that formed on her lips.

"Congratulations," Sal said, handing Cooper a bottle of water.

"Thanks," she said. "You think I'll pass?"

"You'll pass."

She looked up into Sal's face, surprised. "Really?"

He nodded, then tilted his head toward the scientist. "So will he."

"Isn't he the one who abandoned the CPR lady-dummy in the bathtub on his first Maze run?"

Sal shrugged. "This is a formality for him. His ticket was punched a long time ago."

"Who the hell is he?" Cooper asked.

Sal glanced at the man. "He answers to 'The End of Science.' See you at Ninety South."

*

Four months later, Cooper was standing on a slice of sea ice just outside of McMurdo, the American polar station set on the hairy fringes of Antarctica. To the north, the bare volcanic rock of Hut Point Peninsula sloped toward McMurdo Sound in glossy black sheets. Short-stacked dorms, repair barns, and warehouses seemed locked on the basalt as if petrified midslide. Diesel fumes burned her nostrils.

The sun hung low in the sky, an ornament that swung from east to west, never disappearing, until the day it did. On the C-17 that had ferried them from Christchurch, an electrician had told Cooper that when the month-long sunset ended in March and the sun finally hooked around the Earth, leaving South Pole in total darkness for months, she'd forget what it looked like almost at once. "You'll live for civil twilight," he said mysteriously.

As she waited for the National Science Foundation rep to finish gossiping with the pilot, Cooper looked around at the raggedy group of artists loitering a few hundred yards from the humorously big-wheeled bus that was waiting to take them into town. Which one, Cooper wondered, was Harold? Back in Denver, the NSF had assigned each grantee a buddy—a "fellow Fellow"—and instructed them to exchange regular e-mails up until the date of their departure. It was important, the grant administrator had impressed upon the artists, to be supplied with an existing friend at Pole. Cooper had been paired with a biographer named Harold. When she'd asked him about the subject of his book, he had been evasive. After four months of correspondence, all Cooper knew about him was that he was a British ex-pat from Sacramento who fancied peach melba and foxhounds, and who suffered from mild eczema. Harold's knowledge of Cooper was limited to two facts: that she felt hotdish had never received its gastronomic due and that the fake Minnesota accents in *Fargo* were the blackface of regional phonology. Pictures had not been exchanged, so Cooper had no way of picking Harold out from the collection of fur-lined hoods and balaclavas arrayed before her.

Finally, the NSF administrator, wearing UV goggles and an impossibly large parka, walked toward the group, looking as buoyant as the Stay Puft Marshmallow Man. "Seventy-seven degrees, fifty-one minutes south," he boomed, each word accompanied by a steam blossom. "One hundred sixty-six degrees, forty minutes east." The historical novelist, who'd vomited into his hands on the plane, sighed in recognition, letting everyone know he'd done his homework.

"Welcome to McMurdo, everybody," Stay Puft said. "Welcome to Antarctica." The sound of heavy mittens clapping followed this pronouncement, and someone attempted a whistle, then quit halfway through, winded. The high altitude and thin air did not offer enough oxygen for carefree whistling.

"All right, guys," Stay Puft continued, "I know you're moving on to South Pole Station tomorrow morning, but I think there's still time for you to enjoy what Mactown has to offer. We always treat the artists to a game of bowling before they head for Pole, mostly because we put a little money on the game and because you guys are notoriously bad bowlers." *Ha-ha-ha,* the group laughed. *We're bad bowlers.*

"Oh, hey," Stay Puft said to a tall, stone-faced man who was briskly passing the group on his way to the Terra Bus. "Goggles really aren't optional down here, brother. I mean, unless you want to light your corneas on fire."

"Noted," the man said, his consonants tinged with unmistakable Russian frication. "But I'm not Fingy, and McMurdo is not cold."

"What's a Fingy?" someone asked. Cooper felt no need to provide this person with the secret knowledge she'd been given at fire school—she suspected any advantage, no matter how small, could be helpful to her. Stay Puft turned to everyone else and clapped his mittens together: "Terra Bus time! Grab your bags and let the festivities begin!"

Cooper dragged her bag past the other artists, and caught up with the tall Russian, who was carrying his enormous duffel as if it were a lunch box. He'd been seated across from Cooper on the flight from Christchurch, and was imperious and massively bearded. Once or twice during the six-hour flight he had consulted a notebook, but had otherwise barely moved. When he noticed Cooper was keeping pace with him, he looked down at her.

"Hello," he said.

"Hey," Cooper said. "Are you a writer or a painter?" When he didn't immediately reply, Cooper added: "Muralist?"

"You mistake me for artist," he finally said. "I am not here to paint pretty pictures of penguins."

"Carpenter?"

"Now you confuse me with construction personnel. Those are assholes. Science is only reason for people to come here." He looked down at Cooper again. "You are one of these artists?" Cooper nodded. "I do not understand why you are here."

Cooper saw herself reflected in the man's mirrored aviators, which he'd donned in place of the goggles everyone had been issued back in Christchurch. Reflected in his sunglasses, Cooper's head was bulbous, her body a tube. She was ridiculous.

*

That night, the artists crowded into the bowling alley at McMurdo, Mactown Lanes, which was located in a Seabee Quonset hut that also housed a ceramics studio, and was a gathering point for exactly the kind of people one might expect to find in bowling alleys and ceramics studios. The bowling alley consisted of two lanes and the last existing Brunswick manual pinsetter system in the world. A woman in a bikini top and board shorts was the designated "pin monkey."

As she waited for her turn to bowl, Cooper learned she'd be heading to Pole with an interpretive dancer who hoped to choreograph a show based on the mating rituals of the hydrocarbon seep tubeworm; two novelists, traversing the same ground as the novelists who came before them (*The Catcher in the Crevasse, Fahrenheit-98, The Sun Never Rises, Love in the Time of Snow Blindness*); and Cooper's pen pal, the biographer named Harold.

Cooper watched as the interpretive dancer threw a gutter ball and danced back to her seat under the pink and green strobe lights pulsing to the beat of "Heart of Glass."

"It's rather quaint, isn't it," the man sitting next to Cooper said as they watched the heavily tatted pin monkey get up from her folding chair at the end of the lane and reset the pins. Cooper took in the man's pink jowls-in-training and his friendly, constantly blinking eyes. A portrait would focus on the broad, Truman Capote forehead abandoned by the hairline. These features, and the British accent, could only mean that this was Harold.

"Actually, I'm surprised how ugly this place is," Cooper said. "You think Antarctica is going to be the purest place in the world—like the last pure place on earth—and you get here and it's like Akron." She offered him her hand. "I'm Cooper."

The man's face flushed, and he offered a gap-toothed smile. When he took her hand, his was predictably moist. "I'm Harold, your pen pal!" He giggled. "Now, is there a ghost of a chance that you'd allow me to perform my best Minnesota accent, or would that just send you into a rage? I've been working on it for weeks."

"I'll try to control myself," Cooper replied. "Go ahead."

Harold squared his shoulders and straightened his posture, affecting the standard Minnesotan-at-the-wheel-during-rush-hour position. "Oh geeeee, yoooooo betcha!"

"Not bad, but if you're going for cinéma vérité, you might want to try the phrase 'I'm headed over to Lindy's for the meat raffle.'" Harold positively glowered. "Anyway, nice to finally meet you, Harold." Cooper wasn't sure she'd ever spoken the name Harold out loud before; it came out sounding a little sarcastic.

Harold winced. "As I've been told incessantly since we landed at Christchurch, Harold is a perfectly awful name." He paused, thoughtful. "I don't believe they're naming children Harold anymore. I've settled on Birdie for the duration."

"Birdie?"

"It's the nickname of the bloke I'm writing a book about. I've simply co-opted it."

"Birdie Bowers?" Cooper said.

Birdie went pinker. "You know Birdie? Americans never know him."

Cooper shrugged. "My father's a frustrated explorer, so I'm on a first-name basis with a lot of dead men."

"Yes, there's a whole generation of those kinds of fathers, isn't there? Men cut out for Shackleton's adventures but forced to work as accountants or teachers." He ran a hand across his pate. "It's a bloody shame, actually. There's nothing left for them."

The overheads suddenly dimmed and were replaced by the swirling colored lights found in Cosmic Bowling systems across the globe—Antarctica, apparently, included. Birdie made his way to the bowling lane, and as Cooper watched him test the weight of several bowling balls, she put her hand in her parka and touched the vial she'd carried with her from Minneapolis. As she did so, she imagined Cherry in his bunk on the *Terra Nova* as it neared this continent, and a jubilant Birdie Bowers hauling him out to give him a celebratory dig in the ribs.

*

The next morning, as Cooper stood on the McMurdo ice runway waiting to board the plane to South Pole, the sun hovered on the horizon, looking as runny as an undercooked egg. A few weeks earlier, in mid-September, it had risen for the first time in six months. According to the breathless reports Cooper had overheard in the dining room, penguins had gone into hysterics, which had promptly sent a National Geographic cruise tour group into hysterics.

The sea-ice runway was busier than O'Hare, crowded with C-17s and a gaggle of LC-130s from the New York Air National Guard. All of the planes had been outfitted with skis instead of wheels, as well as jet fuel that wouldn't turn to Smuckers in sixty-below temps. It was into one of these LC-130s—everyone called them Hercs—that Cooper climbed, along with the rest of the artists, scientists, and support staff heading to Amundsen-Scott South Pole Station.

The interior of the plane looked like the digestive tract of a cyborg: the floor was littered with various cables, tie-down straps, and metal bars. There were no windows. Cooper strapped herself into a jump seat and, since there was nothing to look at besides red cargo netting and beards, she closed her eyes and tried to sleep.

Three hours later, the sound of the pilot's voice broke through the howl of the plane's engines. "McMurdo was Fiji compared to what you're about to experience," he shouted over the speaker. "And goggles are required, folks. We'll be on the ground shortly. Might want to grab on to something. Could get a little bumpy on the way down."

As if on cue, the plane fell a few hundred feet, before floating up again, and then dropping another hundred. It went on like this for ten minutes. The scientists and construction workers in the jump seats across from Cooper seemed unfazed, while next to her, the historical novelist yelped pathetically. Halfway down the row, Birdie had dropped his head between his knees.

The landing, however, went smoothly, and as the plane coasted along the ice, Cooper had the strange feeling of being on a seventy-seven-ton toboggan. Relieved cheers filled the cabin as they coasted to the end of the skiway. Almost before the plane had come to a complete stop, the doors were opened and everyone began filing out, but Cooper couldn't move. McMurdo had been the last exit, a place with bowling alleys and an ATM. This was the end. This was South Pole.

When she finally made her way to the exit, she stopped short, holding up the rest of the line as she stared into infinity—sheer white of a character she'd never seen in life or art. She felt light-headed.

"Your goggles," Birdie shouted over the din of the roaring engine. He pressed them into her hands. She pulled them over her head and onto her face, and began walking down the stairs, but on the last step she stumbled. As if in slow motion, she landed face-first on her bag, which had been thrown out of the cargo hold. Immediately, a mouthful of polar air seized her lungs, and she started to choke. It was as if her throat had instantly crystallized. Birdie hauled Cooper to her feet.

"Thanks," she croaked.

All around her was a landscape of snow without end; there was no horizon. She felt seaborne, bodiless. There was no edge, no crust to hold it all in. Crowded around the runway were groups of people wearing the green parkas that distinguished the Polies from the McMurdo-ites, who wore cherry-red. Again, the tall Russian scientist disembarked and carried his oversize duffel with ease, his aviators glinting in the sun. Cooper watched as other hoodless men in aviators surrounded him, clearly excited to see him. Beyond them was a large silver geodesic dome: South Pole Station.

"How was McMurdo?"

Cooper peered into yet another fur-lined hood and saw Tucker's face. Relief washed over her.

"We bowled," she said, her body beginning to shake from the cold. "Two games."

"Put on your hood," Tucker said, and Cooper complied. "I'm glad you're here. You were missed." The passivity of the sentence only underscored its weirdness. "Come on, let's go inside."

The entrance to South Pole Station had nearly been swallowed by drifting snow. The ramp leading into the dome sloped down into the frozen earth like a long, swollen throat. Cooper stopped to watch a group of people shoveling out a trench that encircled the dome like a moat. On seeing the artists pass into the tunnel, one of the workers stopped and leaned on his shovel. He pointed toward a wooden sign speared into the ice. In handwritten letters, it spelled *Caution! Crevasse of Death*.

"Live it. Learn it. Love it," he said.

As the Fingys inched farther down the tunnel, a town the color of a safety-hazard cone materialized beneath the frozen Spaceship Earth dome. A collection of ugly, two-story prefab buildings sprouted from the dirty ice. One of the novelists began hacking uncontrollably as a tractor and forklift rumbled past them coughing exhaust that wreathed the buildings in smog. Cooper glanced at an enormous digital thermometer hanging over the entrance to one of the trailers. Inside the dome it was thirty-five degrees below zero. Outside it was negative fifty. This, Cooper knew from the station guide, was a balmy summer's day.

Tucker led the artists into the galley, located on the first floor of the largest trailer. As they shuffled in, a pair of guys playing chess looked up at them, then looked at each other, and flashed the international sign of cultural superiority—the *Star Trek* finger-split.

Tucker stopped near the soda dispenser. "This is the galley. This is where you'll come to eat," he said. "Our production cook is Miss

Pearl here." The woman in the pink bandana Cooper had seen at fire school now stood in the middle of the kitchen. She was smiling, both hands on her apron-wrapped hips, her ash-blond hair gathered in a short ponytail, the same bandanna wrapped around her head. A small cadre of galley workers buzzed behind her, preparing for lunch.

"Hi, *artistes*, welcome to South Pole! I'll give you a quick run-down of how the eats work around here, and I'm sorry if I'm short on details—we're in the middle of the lunch prep and also, this is my first year so I'm going by what the binders tell me." In the kitchen, soups bubbled in industrial-size pots and a couple of guys in hairnets chopped vegetables. "I'm told food is really the only unequivocally nice thing about institutionalized life down here," Pearl said as she led the group between prep tables. "We really try to make it special, make it nice. Lots of people have told me that they haven't eaten bet-ter food than the food they ate here on the ice." Pearl slipped past the meat slicer, where a thin guy was running a ham across the blade. "And this is Kit. He's our rock star DA."

"District attorney?" one of the artists asked, and Cooper caught Tucker rolling his eyes.

"Nope, here DA stands for dining assistant," Pearl said cheerfully. "Everyone say hi to Kit." Everyone murmured a hello, and the group moved through the kitchen. As Cooper passed him, Kit began mov-ing his pelvis in rhythm with the slicer, tongue hanging out, eyes half closed.

"Your zipper's down," Cooper whispered. Kit shrugged and con-tinued slicing.

Pearl was now standing in front of a stack of cabinets, saying that there were three squares a day, six days a week. "If you need to eat at Midrats, let me or Bonnie know," she said, gesturing to a heavy-set dark-haired woman working the stove across from the cabinets. "Bonnie's the head cook."

"Excuse me, but what are Midrats?" Birdie asked, smiling stu-pidly at Pearl. Cooper could see he was already enamored.

"*Midrats* is the term we use for our midnight meal cooked for the workers on the graveyard shift. It's short for 'midnight rations'—Midrats! Does that answer your question?" Birdie signaled his assent with a thumbs-up. "Anyway, leftovers are stored in the white fridge over there, and you can warm up whatever you want in the microwave. But if you're seriously unmotivated, you can check out the cabinets." She turned around and pulled open the door to a large cupboard. A pile of ramen noodles and plastic-wrapped Melba toast tumbled out. Cooper picked up one of the ramen soup packages from the floor.

"This expired in 1996," she said.

Pearl shrugged. "We're at the end of a long supply chain."

*

Across an expanse of snow a quarter mile from the Dome, the James-ways lay atop the ice like giant prehistoric grubs. This tent city, called Summer Camp, was where most of the Polies slept. The rest bunked in the Hypertats, closer to the station, while a select few had rooms in the elevated dorm under the Dome. Cooper was halfway to camp with her bag—bag-drag was an individual sport and a rite of passage for Fingys—when she heard the sound of footsteps, which, on dry Antarctic snow, sounded like boots crushing Saltines.

"Hey," a familiar voice called. Cooper turned to find Sal walking toward her, his rose-red parka a Pollock drip against the starched sky. He grinned at her, and Cooper noticed for the first time a deep dimple in his right cheek. "Technically, I'm not supposed to help you bag-drag," he said. "It's a time-honored tradition to force the Fingys to haul their luggage out to camp." He reached for Cooper's duffel. "But I'm feeling charitable today."

"Except I'm too proud to take handouts," Cooper replied, moving the bag out of his reach with her boot. She hauled the strap back over her shoulder, hoping to give the impression that she found the duffel featherlight.

"Do you even know where you're going?"

"E6."

"Ah, E6. That's where they found the body last season." He grinned again and gestured to the Jamesway farthest from the station. "Last one on the left there." It looked miles away. Cooper groaned, and let the duffel strap slip from her shoulder. Sal slung the bag over his shoulder easily, and together they walked toward Summer Camp in silence.

When they arrived at E6, it suddenly occurred to Cooper that the only things that would be standing between her and minus-56-degree temperatures were plywood and vinyl-coated cotton duck. "I can get it from here," Cooper said, taking the bag from Sal. "Thanks for the good deed." Sal tipped an imaginary hat. As Cooper watched him walk away, she considered how much she hated guys who tipped imaginary hats.

She pulled the Jamesway door open and kicked her bag into the darkened interior. The door sucked shut behind her, and the walls breathed in and out with the Antarctic summer winds. Canvas curtains separated the sleeping quarters, leaving a narrow hallway running down the middle of the Jamesway. Light snoring came from all directions, along with the faint sound of death metal leaking from someone's headphones. All at once, the heater—a massive metal monster set at the back of the tent—kicked on with a congested roar.

Using a flashlight she'd been given back at the station along with two towels and a set of bedclothes, Cooper scanned the doors until she found her room at the end of E6. It was the size of a closet, nothing more than a single bed, a dorm-style desk, and a chair. Cooper clambered onto her bed to peer out the plastic-paned window cut high in the wall. More white without end. She craned her neck and saw that a huge snowdrift hugged the other side of the Jamesway wall. She glanced down at the floor and saw the foot of the drift ended under her bed.

Kicking her snow-crusted bag closer to the dresser, Cooper pulled off her fur-backed mittens before removing layer after layer of clothing until she reached her thermal vest. This she unzipped, before removing her money belt, where she'd been keeping her oil paints since landing in Christchurch three days earlier. The visual arts coordinator at the NSF's Artists & Writers Program had suggested she transport her paints this way if she "insisted" on using oils instead of the obviously more practical tempera; the warmth of her body would keep them from freezing and losing integrity. Titanium white. Yellow ochre, burnt umber. And the workhorse of polar artists, cerulean blue. Cooper rarely opened new tubes—the firmness and fullness of the paints felt as strange as the first time she had held an erect penis in her hand. She was more comfortable using the twisted, deformed soldiers, often capless, found in high school art rooms. So when her sister, Billie, had handed her the bag from Utrecht Art Supplies, Cooper had been shocked. Inside was a set of Winsor and Newton oil paints, and two small containers of turpentine.

"The guy said these were the best," Billie had said. "Something about pigment load. I assume this is a painting term and not a porn sequence."

"I'm not worth these paints," Cooper said, and Billie had grown impatient.

"Stop cringing. Just take them. As we both know, the clock on talent runs faster than regular clocks. Tick-tock."

As with most things, Billie was, of course, right: in art, as in life, your innate talent was valued in inverse proportion to your age. For Cooper, the clock had ticked off almost fifteen years. She'd been plucked from obscurity while in high school by the "Holy Order of the Precocious Child," as Billie called it, when a curator for MoMA, in town for a lecture at the Minneapolis Institute of Arts, had deigned to look at the lobby display where the winners of the Minnesota High School Visual Arts Competition had their pieces set up. Having discovered in junior high that she had the technical skills of a hyperrealist, Cooper had gone all Charles Bell and produced a series of paintings depicting vending-machine charms. The curator was particularly taken with Cooper's absurdly detailed study of a tiny roller skate on a lead chain. "You've brought a sense of allegorical wonder to the obviously tawdry," she'd said.

Within two months, Cooper and her vending-machine series had been featured in *The New York Times Magazine*, alongside the work of three other visual arts prodigies (the title of the article had been "Could These Young Artists Save the American Art World?"). Cooper was bewildered to read that her "preoccupation" as an artist was not just on "gifted creations of likenesses, but also the instigation of psychological states in the observer," when all she'd been trying to do was not look too closely at the things around her that actually mattered. Like what was happening to her brother.

It was around that time that David had gotten worse—though by that point, using the word *worse* was like gilding one of Monet's water lilies. The "Weisman Incident" had made the ten o'clock news on all three local stations (in Minnesota at that time a teenager flailing incoherently on the roof of a modern art museum was sweeps-worthy). That was when the painting stopped. Cooper wasn't sure why she'd stopped, only that nothing seemed worth painting. She knew even then that to adults this sounded truculent, but representation suddenly seemed a cheap way to comment on ideas. Interpretation seemed hubristic. Better, Cooper thought, as she watched her parents grapple with David, to leave life in its native language. So the planning had stopped, too. Everything did. And Cooper was glad. She was relieved to once again be unexceptional—but of course said nothing to her family and concerned mentors about this relief and instead stockpiled their pity like she was building up treasures.

But then, some months after one of David's institutionalizations, when it seemed that David, back in high school again, was doing better, Cooper did start to paint again. Small things, mostly for friends, and mostly staying in the well-worn ruts: a butterfly, a still life, a tree. Nothing that had any real meaning to her. Such things were still too dangerous. Eventually, though, she set the crutches aside, and tried to pick up where she'd left off when David had first gotten sick, quietly enrolling at the Minneapolis College of Art and Design after graduation.

She had showings at small local galleries, where people who didn't know her name sipped white Zin and praised the kind of art they could afford while denigrating the kind they couldn't. She sold a few canvases at art fairs, had a couple pieces hanging at the Uptown Caribou Coffee ("Man Staring into Latte" and "Untitled Meditation on

Shade-Grown Beans"), and had even been commissioned to paint the skyline of St. Paul for a professor from Hamline University (although she'd blown it after she asked: "What skyline?").

Armed with a BFA and a spotty résumé, Cooper worked as a substitute art teacher, but had been laid off when the Minnesota legislature cut all "nonessential curriculum" funding. She turned to community ed and began teaching "Adventures in Acrylics" to retirees far more motivated than her. Then she turned thirty, and saw that the years behind her were littered with part-time jobs, newsboy hats, half-finished canvases, and visits to the psych ward at Hennepin County Medical Center to see David. She quickly ran out of money, and began work at the same Caribou Coffee where her canvases were still hanging, unsold. She started dating a fellow barista, a twenty-three-year-old emo named Forrest, to whom she lied about her age.

Then one day, the professor from Hamline who'd canceled her commission called to tell her about the National Science Foundation's Antarctic Artists & Writers Program at South Pole. "It's a unique opportunity to experience humility and accountability on a visceral level," he said. "When the paperwork crossed my desk, I thought of you immediately." The words—*South Pole*—had pierced her. Cooper thought she had buried those two syllables and everything they signified long ago. When David became sick around their sixteenth birthday, their fondly recalled playtime heroics had given way to hallucinations and obsessions. To David, South Pole was no longer a place where men went to become lions, a landscape that spawned a thousand daydreams. It was instead a viper's nest of secret civilizations. It was a Nazi hideout. It harbored a portal into a hollow earth, where men like Arthur Gordon Pym and friends sailed into a milky wormhole and vanished. David wanted desperately to be there, and sometimes, when things were bad, thought he was. Cooper felt strongly that she would have been able to handle it all better if *it*—this chemical Grendel that had replaced her brother's fine mind—had allowed Titus and Cherry to stay at South Pole. But these paladins had been erased from the continent—and when they disappeared, Cooper did, too.

She looked down at the tubes of paint in her hands. None of them had lost integrity, so she wrapped them up in the bath towels and put them in her battered green canvas Duluth Pack with the rest of her supplies. Next, she set her books on the desk—a polar library in miniature, with Shackleton, Amundsen, and the ancient copy of *Worst Journey* her father had given her back in Minneapolis (all of which she'd decided to bring after Tucker assured her little polar literature would be found on the continent itself). On top of the books was where she placed the antique pocket compass Bill had snuck into her duffel, and which she'd found while searching for a tampon during the layover at McMurdo.

Finally, she plunged her hand deep into the pocket of her parka and pulled out a Tylenol travel vial, the *Extra Strength* rubbed out by her constantly searching fingers. It was four and a half inches long, point-eight ounces light, though, of course, the packaging data no longer reflected the vial's contents. Cooper set this next to the compass and lay down on her bed. After a few minutes, the heater cycled off, revealing the sounds of a couple having sex on the other side of the Jamesway. A moment later, they stopped. A woman's voice, dripping with sarcasm, said, "I'll guess I'll just finish myself off then." It was the first familiar thing Cooper had encountered since stepping foot on South Pole.

*

The second familiar thing was South Pole's computer lab, referred to at the station as the Cube Farm. It looked like any second-rate college's computer science department, with a half-descended projection screen dangling against a whiteboard and three rows of candy-colored iMacs. The lab was half full when Cooper walked in to check her e-mail, and aside from rapid keyboard clicking, mostly silent. As she walked down the least-populated row of computers, she saw one of the Polies was scrolling through photos of disgruntled cats dressed up as circus clowns.

The only e-mail in Cooper's in-box was from Billie.

2003 October 11
00:13
To: cherrywaswaiting@hotmail.com
From: Billie.Gosling@janusbooks.com
Subject: Working the Pole?

C.,
How's Pole? Life at the World's Most Mediocre
Publisher remains mediocre. Mom just acquired a
book on divination by punctuation and set me up
with the author of said masterpiece. I agreed to
the date because of my long-standing fascination
with the Oxford comma. Our first date ended with
an exchange of punctuation-related insults. He
finds commas guilty of crimes against humanity.
I told him double spaces after periods or I
walk. If you're in the market for some reading
material, I can provide. Illuminati conspiracies?
The Book of Thoth? Labyrinth literature? Mom's
been on a spree. Meanwhile, I sit here and write
rejection notes all day. (Yes, Janus Books does
sometimes reject things.) Oh, and I'm supposed to
say that Mom misses you terribly and sends you her
blessing.

Billie, your sister,
The World's Oldest Editorial Assistant™

*

2003 October 12
09:50
To: Billie.Gosling@janusbooks.com
From: cherrywaswaiting@hotmail.com
Subject: RE: Working the Pole

B.,

I can only e-mail when the heavens and the sat-
ellites align, and the sword is in the stone.
I've been here for eight hours and have already
lost all sense of time. It's strange down here.
Like a strip mall at the end of the earth. There
are only nine women. When winter starts in March,
there will be four. I'm told that while the odds
are good, the goods are odd. The guy at the computer next to me is starting to get really excited—
like, bordering on sexually excited—by a cat
video, so I need to sign off now. More later.
C.

As she sent off the e-mail, Cooper wondered again why her older
sister chose to spend her days photocopying new-age manuscripts
and preparing their mother's morning yerba mate. Billie claimed
nepotism was her only chance at gainful employment after years of
failed attempts, and perhaps this was true. Their mother, Dasha, had
climbed the ranks at Janus Books after becoming interested in the
questions of "The Seeker." The Seeker was on a journey for meaning,
and stuffed into her tribal-feather double-fringed medicine-bag purse
were books like the *Tao Te Ching*, *the Tibetan Book of the Dead*,
Thus Spoke Zarathustra, and Ernest Holmes's collected works. After
several years in middling editorial positions at Janus, Dasha had
learned the hand grips, the passwords, the ritual work, whatever it
was that launched a former paralegal into a position of Masonic power,
and was now executive editor. In the decade she'd been there, Dasha
had transformed Janus Books from a quiet publisher of self-help
books, a kind of lapdog for the self-actualizing, to a frothing Aquar-
ian beast. It hadn't escaped Cooper's notice that this ascent took
place as David succumbed to mental illness. This fact bothered
Cooper—she wasn't quite sure why. Clearly selling self-help books
was her mother's coping mechanism, and didn't we all need coping
mechanisms? Still, as a rule, Cooper avoided Janus's myrrh-scented

halls. But she also understood you had to say goodbye to your mother if you were departing for the seventh continent—even if your mother was wearing a dashiki.

It was Billie who met Cooper at Reception. Her older sister was imperious, angled, beautiful, and cool. Bette Davis in army-navy tactical cargo pants and a black tank top. Even though she couldn't snow camp, Billie had been, until recently, the Goslings' Best Hope: the one with the brains, the Algonquin wit, the ability to produce obscure Jack London references at the perfect moment. These were traits that were highly valued by their father, and so Billie honed them until she could wield them like a prison shank to keep Cooper, and her talent, at bay. Of course, Billie had talent to burn. She'd gone to New York on a playwriting fellowship, begun dating an artisanal tobacconist, and after eighteen months found herself in the midst of fleeting success—a run at the Lortel with the play she wrote between waitressing shifts, an Obie nomination, and the inevitable inability to pen a second play.

Soon, Billie was back in Minneapolis, living in the guest bedroom of Dasha's warehouse-district loft, humiliated by her failures and determined to play out that narrative for as long as possible. In the meantime, she assisted her mother by logging copyedited changes to *The Visigoth Manager: Germanic Paganism in the Workplace,* and pretended nothing hurt.

As Billie walked Cooper down one of the hallways toward Dasha's office, she'd said, "Did you know that when you do book deals with certain lady folk singers from the sixties, you have to put into the contract that her hotel rooms will be outfitted with reiki candles and a synthesizer?" She stopped in front of a door and knocked. "Such wisdom I have gained while working here."

"Come in," Dasha commanded. Billie pushed open the door, and promptly disappeared around a corner. Cooper found her mother leaning back in her Herman Miller Aeron chair, feet on desk, glasses atop forehead, Sontag stripe gleaming in the cold glow of energy-efficient lights.

"Hello, dear."

"Hello, Mother."

"Please don't call me 'Mother.' "

Cooper did jazz hands and shouted: "Hello, Mommy!" This, at least, produced a smile.

"Sit down, honey." Cooper sat in the chair next to the door and waited. Dasha only stared at her, smiling, so Cooper said, "I am now seated."

Dasha looked at her searchingly. "Ant-ar-tica?"

"Antarctica. There's a C in it."

"Polar bears."

"Penguins."

"Clearly, I need to brush up on my geography skills."

"It doesn't matter," Cooper replied.

Dasha sighed deeply. "I want you to know that I understand what you're trying to do, and I give this venture my—"

"Mom, please, no blessing, no benedictions, no burning sage. I just came to say goodbye. Can we just do 'goodbye, good luck, I'll miss you'? I don't even need the 'I'll miss you.' "

"You have my blessing."

"Don't need it, Mom," Cooper half-sang.

"Sweetheart, for me, a blessing is not approval."

"Then what is it? Because it sort of sounds like you're giving me the okay. I don't need an okay."

"Well, for me a blessing is a sincere wish that you get what you want out of this experience. When will I see you again?"

"Next September."

Dasha seemed genuinely surprised. "A year?"

"That's what I signed up for."

Dasha placed her fingertips together and looked up at the ceiling. "Blessing or not, I need to say this before you leave or else I won't have done my job as a parent: you are an exceptional talent, but you are also a thirty-year-old woman who has never held a long-term professional job in her life. You're thirty, Cooper. I need you to hear the starkness in that. At thirty, routes begin to disappear. And at some point you have to answer for what you are—whether that's a success or a failure."

"What if I'm a Seeker?"

"I'd like to be validated by hearing an answer from you," Dasha snapped. The tone of the conversation—the way it resonated like a faint echo of the kinds of conversations Cooper had had with her mother before the Seeker had absconded with her—soothed Cooper's nerves.

"Let's see what it looks like when I return," she said. Dasha's face fell. These words must have been lodged in some capsule in Cooper's brain, ready to be deployed at exactly the wrong time: David's parting words to them on Christmas, when they'd let him drive himself back to the group home because he'd been so good about his medication, so lucid, that it was almost like he was restored. ("Louie DePalma is back!" Billie had shouted after two glasses of Shiraz.) He'd asked about Cooper's painting, about Billie's writing. He'd been funny, brilliant—beautiful. Cooper had felt guilty tailing him in her Tempo until he got to the intersection of Forty-sixth and Blaisdell, a couple of blocks from the Damiano House, the group home where he'd been living since his last 5150. When David's counselor had called Bill and Dasha to let them know he hadn't come home that night, and later, when the police put out the "Missing Vulnerable Adult" flyer, Cooper realized she'd failed him a million different ways.

"I know you and Billie choose not to talk about him with me," Dasha said, her voice brittle. "I know you blame me for not being more in tune with what was happening, and I think—"

Cooper felt her stomach begin to churn. "Mom—please."

"Honey, at least let me say this—"

But Cooper couldn't. She couldn't hear this, just as she couldn't forgive her mother for telling mourners at his funeral service that David had been a "bleeding tree." Cooper stood up and walked out of Dasha's office, and it was only when she was in the lobby and saw Billie's face that she realized she had her hands over her ears.

*

"Gimme a minute," the station doctor called out to Cooper from behind a dirty white vinyl curtain. "Okay, so—that sound fair?" she said to a patient.

"Yeah, that works," the man said. "I can't, like, get lice or anything, can I?"

"Friend, if we had a lice problem on station, I'd be the first to hear about it. Wash the pillowcase if you're nervous."

"I don't want to use up my water ration."

"Then go, live on hope."

The curtain slid back to reveal a man clutching a pillow. The doctor emerged from behind the curtain with a half-empty bottle of Robitussin. This, Cooper knew, had to be Doc Carla, a weathered, lean woman in her late fifties, with thick brown hair pulled into pigtails, a wind-chapped face, and lips that glistened with Vaseline.

"Bartering for the return of unused medication is the work of saints," she said to no one. Then she glanced at Cooper, and cringed. "Well, you look like hell. Come on in, lady."

When Cooper had awoken in her cell-like room in Summer Camp that morning, she'd discovered her right eye was Super-Glued shut and her eyelashes had become a petrified forest of dried pus. She felt like shit. One of her nostrils was stuffed up; the other was flowing freely. Her bones ached and her skin felt clammy. Her South Pole handbook indicated that she should visit the station doctor at the clinic—a place Cooper now knew went by the name Hard Truth Medical Center.

Doc Carla pointed to a metal exam table that looked like it had come down on the *Terra Nova*. "Take a seat." As Cooper shimmied her way onto the table, she surveyed the room: two ward beds, a red standing Snap-on "Intimidator" toolbox, two green oxygen canisters, and an enormous gawking army-issue exam light.

"You probably got the Crud."

"The Crud?" Cooper asked, squinting like a deranged pirate.

"An illness found at the outposts of civilization," Doc Carla replied. She opened an industrial-size tackle box and began digging through piles of medication. "It's like the flu. Most Fingys get it when they arrive." She shook her head in disbelief. "You'd think they'd tell you guys this stuff. Until the doors close for the winter, those human petri dishes from McMurdo are going to keep me in business." All sickness, it seemed, came from McMurdo. This was one reason Polies hated McMurdo-ites, but only one.

Doc Carla tossed a box of medicine on a small metal tray on wheels, then came at Cooper with a penlight. "Probably a bacterial infection of the soft tissues," she said as she peered into Cooper's right eye. "I'm going to give you a course of antibiotics and some drops for the eye." She turned around to fish the drops out of the dorm fridge. "Don't feel nauseated, do you?"

"No."

"Stiff neck?"

"I don't think so," Cooper said, rubbing her neck, which suddenly seemed a little sore. Doc Carla handed Cooper the eyedrops and the box of pills. "Take these so it doesn't turn into meningitis. And lay low for a few days. No sex until the eye gets better. And if you start puking or you can't move your neck, get yourself over here *tout suite*. I might not be able to save you but at least your family can't sue me."

After leaving Hard Truth, Cooper started to meander up the tunnel toward the main station when she was almost run over by a forklift. "Open your eyes, dumbass," someone shouted at her in passing. Cooper watched as the forklift careened up the tunnel, stopped suddenly, and unceremoniously dropped its cargo of crates onto the snow with a crash. Immediately, a crowd of people materialized around the boxes. By the time Cooper arrived, a scuffle had broken out between the forklift driver and the attendant crowd. Several Polies stared sadly into one of the crates.

"You just pulverized an entire case of Cabernet, dickweed," one of them snapped. Cooper recognized the angry Polie as Kit, the DA from the galley. By this time, the driver's insouciance had been replaced by unmistakable fear. He stammered an apology, but it went unheard. Cooper had the feeling that punishment would be meted out later. For now, the group had moved on to more important matters, like getting the crates of booze into the station store before it froze.

"You," Kit shouted at Cooper. Cooper hastily slipped her goggles over her eyes in order to disguise her disfigurement. "Be a pal. Take this Coors Light to the store."

The South Pole Station store was located on the second floor of the comms pod. At McMurdo, the station store offered souvenirs, scented soaps, and *New York Times* best-sellers. Here at Pole, nearly the entire inventory was 90-proof. Besides tampons, chocolate bars, and toothpaste, the stock was comprised of Jägermeister, Crown Royal, and Jack Daniel's available for purchase—and below cost—along with Apple Pucker and Stoli vanilla vodka. Cases of Budweiser were stacked atop cases of Red Stripe. Rows of pale Chardonnay and scarlet Merlots lined the walls, while silver kegs haunted the corners.

Cooper maneuvered her way around the frantic cargo handlers, who were desperate to keep the new shipment from freezing, and deposited the Coors Light next to a crate of sambuca. A Polie elbowed past her and fussily set three vials of angostura bitters on the shelf above her. When he noticed Cooper looking at them, he shrugged. "For the fancy drinks," he said.

*

Cooper was relieved to discover that wearing snow goggles inside the galley was the kind of eccentricity that could go uncommented upon. She pushed her tray through the cafeteria line, regarding the steaming metal tubs of gelatinous Salisbury steak suspiciously. She recalled

Pearl's assertion that many Polies claimed the eats at Amundsen-Scott were second to none.

As she stood at the exit point of the lunch line, a reedy man in glasses and a T-shirt that read "Denialism: Science for Morons" dropped a note onto her tray. "Could you give this to that guy over there, the one in the Confederate-flag bandanna?" Before Cooper could ask him why so many Polies wore bandannas, he'd slipped away and rejoined a group of other bespectacled men wearing the same shirt. She glanced down at the folded note on her tray, then back at the men, two of whom now clasped their hands and shook them in supplication. She sighed. The possibility that anything other than sexual disappointment and second-rate computer labs might become familiar to her seemed remote.

"What's this?" the man donning the Stars and Bars growled when Cooper handed him the note.

"They asked me to give it to you," Cooper said, trying to make out his face through her goggles. "Those guys over there." The man leaned back in his chair and looked behind Cooper at the knot of scientists. After a beat, he smiled and, without reading it, handed the note back to Cooper. "I know what this is about. Tell them to fold it up lengthwise, roll it into a tiny tube, and shove it deep into their asses. Tell them to pass it like an ass-joint."

As Cooper walked away, she pushed her goggles onto her forehead and read the note. It was a plea to join a pool tournament, addressed to someone named Bozer—presumably the proud son of the South with whom she'd just spoken. She shrugged at the scientists, who looked crushed.

Across the galley, the scientist she'd rescued back in fire school during the partner exercises sat alone at a table, studying a book without turning the pages. Around him, guys in Carhartts and feather boas wolfed down mac-and-cheese casserole and talked about how the load of grade beams that had arrived on a flight the day before had maxed out the vertical cargo space.

"Can I sit here?" Cooper asked the scientist. He looked up, startled, then gathered in his utensils as if they were taking up too much room.

"Yes," he said.

"What're you reading?" Cooper said as she attempted to cut into the rubbery Salisbury steak. The man gently closed the book and placed his hand over it, but Cooper had spotted the title: *Alarmism and the Climate Change Hoax.*

"I find reading as I eat relaxing." He slid the book off the table and dropped it into the bag at his feet. "One has to eat, right?" he continued. "It's inconvenient, this need to eat." He finished off his juice in a long gulp. "You look familiar."

"Yeah, I saved you from the burning synthetic fires of hell, remember?" He looked at her for a moment, as if he were translating her words into his native language. Cooper marveled at the utter strangeness of his face: too long to be comprehended at a glance, and too finely cut to be traditionally handsome. Red patches marred the pale skin of his cheeks.

"Yes, that's it," he finally said. "I failed fire training."

"I thought they DQ'ed everyone who didn't pass."

"Not everyone, apparently," he replied. "And you—you're an artist Fellow, correct?"

Cooper was surprised. "Yes. Though it's been implied that we're parasites that contribute net zero to the station."

"Scientists say that because they can only quantify the value of a Monet by giving you a rough estimate of how many quarks might be in it." Before Cooper could process this, the man gathered his dishes onto his tray and then departed with an awkward wave. Cooper turned to call after him, but realized she didn't know his name. It was as if they'd both silently agreed not to bother with them.

When she turned back to her tray, Cooper found a flyer lying atop her mac and cheese. She looked up to find Sal staring down at her.

"Pick a side, Fingy," he said. Cooper lifted the flyer off her food, and shook toasted bread crumbs from it.

SCIENCE   DENIALISM

— COLLECT DATA   — START WITH CONCLUSION

— DRAW CONCLUSION   — PRETEND YOU HAVE
                                       DATA

I, THE UNDERSIGNED, DO DECLARE THAT I

SUPPORT THE SPREAD OF:

                ———— SCIENCE

                ———— FAIRY TALES
        (CHECK ONE)

        SIGNATURE : _____

Sal hovered over her, one hand gripping the back of her chair, the other palming the table. Cooper returned the flyer to him. "Yeah, I'm not signing this."

"Why not?"

"There's no box for Sasquatch Studies," she replied, shoving a forkful of meat into her mouth. She looked up and met his eyes, which had widened in disbelief. Luminescent hazel, with depth. Not like Forrest's, whose mud-brown eyes seemed affixed to his face only because they were required to be there. "Seriously, this is dumb," Cooper said. "You scientists really put too fine a point on things." Sal looked amazed for a moment, and then he laughed. It was a nice laugh, Cooper thought, and the dimple sweetened the pot. Still, he was a little too pleased with himself. Cooper piled her tray with her dirty silverware and headed for the dish pit.

"You are strange," Sal called after her. Everyone turned and looked at her. Pearl took Cooper's plates with a pitying smile, and whispered, "Everyone here's strange."

*

Armed with her South Pole Station handbook and map, and her painting supplies, Cooper made her way to Substation B, the trailer near the elevated dorm, where the artist and writer studios were located. At the top of the metal stairs leading to the door was a large sign that read *Off Limits/Restricted Access*. She pulled the door open anyway and nearly ran into Tucker. He seemed unsurprised to see her, and peered into her face.

"I heard it was the Crud," he said. "How bad is it?" Cooper slid the goggles onto her forehead. Tucker recoiled and began laughing behind his closed fist.

"I'm overwhelmed by your compassion," Cooper said, sliding the goggles back down.

"I have nothing but compassion for you, having been afflicted by acne and facial tics for most of my life."

"Well, I'm already on antibiotics, so don't worry yourself sick over me," Cooper said.

"Antibiotics. Well, you are now officially a Fingy."

"God! If I hear that term one more time I am going to rub my infected eye all over you—sorry, that was bitchy."

"It's okay. I like bitches. I seek them out. You have a ways to go, though."

"I'll do better next time," Cooper said, thinking that would make for a very accurate tattoo.

"Come on, I'll show you to your studio," he said, ushering her down a short hallway. "By the way, I hear you've already become enmeshed."

"Enmeshed?"

"You ferried a note between Beaker and Nailhead at lunch."

"What the hell are Beakers and—you know what, never mind."

"Beakers are scientists. Nailheads are construction. But if anyone asks, the Beakers are the prophets and the Nailheads are the patriots."

Cooper growled at Tucker.

They stopped at a door. Someone had taped a postcard portrait of Foucault's cheerful face just above the doorknob. "I'm so glad Denise is back," Tucker said. "You'll like her!"

"Who's Denise?"

Tucker began whistling ominously and sauntered back the way they had come.

When Cooper unlocked the door to her studio, she found it was a small, square room with no window, just a desk, a couple of chairs, and an old easel lying on its side. Someone had carved *Don't eat the yellow snow* into one of the legs. A web of frost grew on the south wall of the room, and in the corners, clear ice collected like tiny frozen waterfalls. The lighting, Cooper noted with disappointment, was abysmal—*On the Waterfront* without the symbolism. On the desk, someone—Denise?—had left a green canvas bag and a pile of books (*The Sociology of Isolation, Sociological Materialism in Remote Communities, Achieved Status in Areas of Limited Resource*). Cooper let her roll of canvas fall at her feet and began unpacking her supplies.

As she was examining her palette knife, the door opened and a dark-haired woman walked in. "Hi," she said. "Just popped in to say hello. You must be Cooper."

"Yep, that's me," Cooper said. The woman's eyebrows arched questioningly over her cat's-eye glasses.

"Interesting name for a woman." She paused, and turned her eyes to the ceiling. "Cooper. Barrel maker. Lunar crater. D. B. Cooper." She glanced at Cooper. "I'm making associations. Not a mnemonic device, exactly, but I lay these associations down in my memory palace, which should lead me to your name, Cooper, if I become toasty over the course of the winter. I'm Denise. We'll be sharing a studio for the duration."

"Toasty?"

"It's a slang term that covers a whole range of psychological disturbances brought on by the extreme environment here." Seeing Cooper was confused, she added, "I'm a sociologist by trade."

"I thought this was the Artists and Writers' Annex."

Denise shrugged. "Well, this is where I was assigned. I'm not offended by being housed with the artists, if you're wondering—though it does suggest that my field of study is viewed as one with less precision than, perhaps, cosmology. But then that idea would be offensive to artists, wouldn't it? As if they are not precise in motivation. But is art about motivation?"

Cooper wanted to roll her eyes. Of course it was about motivation. But she only said, "I don't really think about those things." Denise, Cooper learned, was on sabbatical from Columbia and was supposed to be in a favela in Rio, living among transitioning transgendered men who injected industrial-grade silicone into their bodies to give themselves hips and breasts. She'd received institutional encouragement to delve deeper into this point on the gender matrix, but here she was, at Pole, four thousand miles away from her research subjects.

"I take it there are one or two transitioning men here to study in isolation?" Cooper asked.

"I like that you're confident enough to joke with a new acquaintance about a sensitive topic. No, after traveling here a couple years ago, I simply lost my passion for my work in Brazil. I felt it best to hand off the research to my younger colleagues. I'm now studying the population here."

"I guess anybody who'd voluntarily come to South Pole is probably worth studying."

"Yes, it's fertile ground," Denise said. "The station population is most analogous to a penal institution—I mean, on a macro level. For a social scientist, it's a dream. I have it all here—defended neighborhoods, degradation ceremonies, a chance to test the contact hypothesis."

"Examples?"

Denise had allowed her glasses to slip, but she pushed them back up now, her face flushed with excitement. "Let's see—defended neighborhoods, that's easy: Beakers are not allowed in the fuel shed or power plant, except for one or two exceptions, while the Nailheads are only allowed near the scientific equipment when occupying narrowly prescribed roles, such as repair and logistical support. Degradation ceremonies would be something like the bag-drag for the Fingys, where they are forced to transport their own luggage to Summer Camp. It's like a perp walk. Something to introduce the novitiate to a total institution and prepare them for external control."

"Christ," Cooper said.

"I know, intense stuff, right?" Denise said. "But I'm most interested in how the scientific community here is going to cope with the arrival of a climate change denialist." She used her pen to scratch a spot on her scalp hidden by her prodigious brown curls. "Hmmm. I keep adopting the terminology of the dominant group. The more appropriate term here would be *skeptic*—climate change skeptic." She pulled on one of her curls until it was perfectly straight, then released it. "Although that, too, is problematic. The scientists here would object to that term. I'm still trying to parse this one out. Anyway, let me know when I lapse into group jargon. It has the potential to affect my neutrality if I'm not careful, and I don't want to go all Margaret Mead."

After Denise left, Cooper realized she'd worn her goggles the entire time they'd been talking, and Denise hadn't batted an eye. She decided she liked Denise very much, and turned to her sketchpad with some optimism. She put on an Etta James CD to drown out the roar of the machines rumbling through the fuel arches downwind from her studio and picked up her pencil.

*

2003 October 28
20:40
To: Billie.Gosling@janusbooks.com
From: cherrywaswaiting@hotmail.com
Subject: Changing the subject line

B.,

What are you and the High Priest of Divination by
Punctuation doing for Halloween? It's apparently
a big deal here. You are expected to wear a costume. Some people bring their costumes to Pole.
Others just cobble something together. In other
news, I got an eye infection and experienced the
finest in frontier medicine. Drinking is an endurance sport, scientists included, who, by the way,
are currently pitching a collective tantrum about
a climate change denialist doing research here.
The overall literary aesthetic can be summarized
as Tom Robbins Rox. Haven't heard from Mom or Dad
yet. Write back. I'm told that after about three
months down here, the letters and e-mails stop
because loved ones forget you exist.
C.
p.s. Don't ask me if/what I'm painting.

*

2003 October 29
00:43
To: cherrywaswaiting@hotmail.com
From: Billie.Gosling@janusbooks.com
Re: Changing the subject line

C.,

The High Priest of Divination by Punctuation and
I have agreed to disagree about the semicolon
and have moved on to dry humping on my loveseat.
Afterwards he consented to letting me call him
Phil. When I asked him what his plans were for
Halloween, he indicated that he'd be honoring
the ancient roots of the holiday with cocktails

at the Minnesota NeoPaganist Society. Apparently, Minnesota is a hotbed for paganism—Phil
referred to it as Paganistan, which I thought was
in poor taste, considering our current military
commitments. I had dinner with Dad on Sunday. He
says he'll write you a letter. He doesn't "do"
e-mail, which he believes is written E+MAIL, and
which is also how he pronounces it. I choose not
to correct him for obvious reasons.
B.
p.s. See, I didn't ask you what/if you're
painting.

*

"And so she comes up to me—now keep in mind, I'm in a hostel in
Cheech and I'm in boxers with one of those half-staff morning boners.
Anyway, she asks me if I've heard of Larry McMurtry."

It had escaped Cooper's notice that day on the bus in Denver that
Floyd looked positively Minnesotan, with the kind of round, ruddy
face you'd find in Sauk Centre or Fergus Falls. However, he had
made it clear, loudly and often, that he was a proud Floridian, and
this, it seemed to Cooper, explained a lot. As she took a seat at the
far end of Floyd's table with her lunch tray, she noticed his mutton-
chops looked even more unkempt than they had in Denver. His
sleeve was pulled back just so, revealing a forearm tat of a woman
straddling a power pole. Sparks emanating from her bare boobs
suggested she was being electrocuted, but in a sexy way.

The group of men sitting with Floyd didn't seem overly interested
in his soliloquy.

"McMurtry, right? So, yeah, I cringe," he continued, "but I say,
sure, I've heard of him, but I've also heard of Zsa Zsa Gabor.
What's your point? Well, she says she's reading one of his books. I
say, 'So?' and she goes, 'I think he won the Nobel prize for cowboy
writing.'"

Floyd let loose a huge belly laugh, but his friends continued eating in silence. "The Nobel prize for cowboy writing?" Floyd tried again.

Finally, a skinny guy in a stained University of Oregon sweatshirt said, "I thought there was, like, only one big Nobel for writers. I didn't know they had one for Westerns."

"Shut up, man," Floyd said bitterly.

"What did I say?"

"Just stop talking."

Tucker quietly took a seat on the bench next to Floyd and waved Cooper over to join him. As she scooted her way down the bench, her plastic cup of Dr Pepper wobbled, then spilled the length of the table. Everyone burst into applause. Sheepishly, Cooper mopped up the spill with her napkin. Tucker watched but offered no help.

Because everyone was still staring at her, Cooper decided to throw in her two cents about McMurtry. "I think *Lonesome Dove* actually won the Pulitzer," she said, as she balled up the sodden napkin. She glanced over at the skinny guy, who now seemed unwilling to make eye contact with her. Tucker, too, avoided her eyes. She'd done something wrong, but she wasn't sure what. She thought of Denise. Had she just trespassed into a "defended neighborhood"? Quietly, she added: "I'm just saying that'd kind of be like winning the Nobel prize for cowboy writing."

After an excruciating silence, Floyd extended his fish-white hand toward her. Cooper took it lightly—as she had anticipated, it was clammy and damp. "Hi, remember me? I'm Floyd. I'm important." He dropped her hand. "First of all, nice of you to invite yourself into this conversation and offer a pearl necklace of wisdom. We're always looking for fresh Fingy insight."

"Be nice, Floyd," Tucker said, pushing his salad greens around his plate, but also, Cooper was annoyed to discover, stifling a smile.

"This *is* me being nice," Floyd replied stonily, turning away from Cooper.

"And second?" she said.

"Huh?"

"You said, first, it was nice of me to insert myself into your conversation. I was just wondering what part two was."

"Part two is fuck off."

Floyd picked up his tray, followed by his friends, who quickly swallowed what was left of their food. At the dish pit, they dumped their plates into the sink simultaneously, sending waves of soapy water all over Pearl's apron.

"Come on, Floyd," Pearl shouted, "be a person!"

"Interesting," Tucker murmured, when the men had departed.

"What's interesting?" Cooper replied.

"Just that people tend to treat the power plant manager with kid gloves," Tucker said. "You know, because he's in charge of keeping the heaters going and stuff."

"I had no idea *Lonesome Dove* was such a lightning rod."

"There are hidden sensitivities everywhere. They're like land mines," Tucker said. "Floyd's basically a good guy. *Basically* being the operative word here. He's under a lot of pressure with the construction of the new station, and sometimes he relieves his stress with poorly informed but weirdly elitist literary critiques of popular authors. Best to think of him as our resident Kim Jong-il: wildly unpredictable, with the power to annihilate his neighbors. Helps that Floyd looks a little like him." He glanced over at Cooper and seemed relieved to find her grinning. "The eye looks better."

"Doc Carla told me even if antibiotics are past their expiration date, they can still work. But five years? I was doubtful."

"How's the work going? Has inspiration struck yet?"

Cooper quickly spooned a lump of the potato gratin into her mouth in order to avoid answering the question. Despite her hopeful start in the studio after meeting Denise, she had ended up with nothing. Nothing except a hasty sketch of the *Terra Nova*, which she'd begun out of desperation. Drawn from memory, it was a mess of flying jibs and mizzen sail, and it hadn't been born of inspiration. It had been a product of a stubborn but useless memory.

Sal sauntered over from the caf line and dropped his tray onto the table across from Cooper. "I miss tots, Tucker," he said. "I want tater tots. Fancy potatoes aren't my speed." Then he looked over at Cooper as if he'd just now noticed her. "Oh, hey, it's the strange person who won't sign the petition. You're the dancer, right?"

"Painter," Cooper replied.

"I want to meet the dancer. Is she hot?" Cooper examined Sal the way she had examined the endless still lifes she'd had to paint in art school. He seemed haphazardly arranged, but there was some underlying cohesive structure that she had to tease out. His unwashed, dark auburn hair was boyish-looking, but she could tell he kept his hair longer than he might otherwise so that it would fall over his forehead and hide his slightly receding hairline. He had a nose that, as he aged, would widen and grow almost bulbous and become more visually interesting. His conversation, however, left much to be desired. It seemed as if he were only playing the role of the bro-dude, not living the life. Still, Cooper thought, there was no law that said an astrophysicist couldn't have the personality of a bro-dude.

"You don't look like a Sal," she said.

"What do I look like?"

"Brock? Josh? Colton?"

"Keep it coming," Sal replied.

"Edison. Keegan. Chase."

"So what you're saying," Sal said, swallowing down a mouthful of gratin, "is that I look like the rush chair for Sigma Chi."

Decently handled, Cooper thought. The table next to them erupted in laughter, and a group of smart-looking guys, including the tall Russian scientist Cooper had met at McMurdo, got up and left en masse.

"There's gonna be a Beaker-Nailhead cage match before the winter's over," Sal said, watching the men file out.

"No, cooler heads will prevail," Tucker said soothingly.

"I doubt it," Sal replied. "Alek has the capacity to go Unabomber on people. It's all that Marxist scientific determinism bullshit." Cooper looked at the next table over; it was occupied by a crew of brawny men in various stages of male-pattern baldness. Seated at the head of the table was the Confederate-bandanna-wearing man—Bozer—

who'd coined the "ass-joint" phrase that had already found its way into Pole's lexicon. ("Stop being such an ass-joint, Chuck!") Cooper longed to ask Tucker whether Bozer's bandanna bothered him, but something told her to keep the question to herself.

"It seems like the Nailheads rule the roost. I wonder if it's the beards," Cooper said.

"Do the Nailheads draw their power from the beards or do their beards grow lush because the Nailhead is powerful?" Tucker mused.

"Those beards are the result of several years of ice-time," Sal said. "Nick over there—the guy in the Fleshgod Apocalypse T-shirt—this'll be his fourth winter-over. His beard's as old as that. Tuck, remember last year when he let that girl build a hanging fairy garden in it?"

"Four seasons?" Cooper said, disbelieving.

"No—four winter-overs. There's a difference. If you winter-over, you're here for the entire year, including the polar night. Six months of total isolation. No flights in, no flights out."

"Why would anyone do that four times?" Cooper asked.

"You will know the answer to that question before you leave here," Sal said. He stretched his arms over his head and interlaced his fingers, just as he'd done at fire school. "I need coffee." He stood up and looked down at Cooper. "Want some?" Cooper shook her head no. Tucker headed over to the coffee tureens with Sal, and, as if on cue, Denise slid into his seat.

"I'm having a ball watching Tucker claw his way from ascribed status to achieved status," she half-whispered. "Speaking of him as the only man of color at Pole."

"What about all those guys from Hyderabad?"

"They don't count. There's nothing like observing an American black man in an environment in which he'd not be expected."

Cooper thought it wise to change the subject. "What's the word on this guy Sal?"

Denise thought for a moment. "Sal Brennan. Scientist. Cosmology, I think. He's a veteran—been here a few times before. I have heard he's in the final year of a rather important experiment, though I don't know the details." Denise unfolded her napkin and carefully arranged it on her lap. "I'll have to check my notes. The scientific staff seems to avoid me, so my knowledge of his background is meager. Oh, now this is interesting."

Cooper turned to follow Denise's gaze, and saw two gaunt men walking through the galley toward the chow line. Both were draped in Swedish national flags, with cross-country skis on their shoulders, and the Polies they passed were slapping them on the backs and smiling. A VIDS staffer jogged after the skiers.

"See," Denise said, pulling out her notebook. "This is the kind of scenario I find fascinating. What benefit is VIDS protecting by denying visitors food?" As Denise scribbled, Cooper watched the Swedes carefully return the trays and listen politely as the admin explained to them why they couldn't eat in the galley.

"Who are they?"

"They arrived at the station last night—Bozer said they're skiing across the continent. They came straight from Vostok. The Russians apparently treated them like kings. VIDS is only letting them pitch their tent outside the Dome." Cooper knew VIDS tried to keep tourists and adventurers away from the station—people were always trying to cross the continent by ski, by snowshoe, by fat-tire bike. One summer an ultra-marathoner made an attempt but went hypoxic three miles outside of McMurdo and had to be carried back on a snowmobile. People still talked shit about ultra-marathoners as a result.

Denise and Cooper watched as the Swedes walked out of the galley with their gear. Out of the corner of her eye, Cooper saw Bozer approaching their table. When he arrived, he put his hands on Denise's shoulders and began rubbing them.

"Hey, chicklet," he said.

"Bozer," Denise said warningly. "Don't cross the boundary." Cooper felt he'd already done that with the Confederate bandanna, but said nothing.

"I'm Bozer," he said to Cooper. "I'm sleeping with her." For the first time, Cooper saw an expression of displeasure pass over Denise's face.

"Your lack of discretion is becoming a problem," Denise said. Bozer discreetly laid his fat, crooked middle finger on the table between them, and wiggled it. Cooper tried not to laugh. "There is an unspoken code of conduct here regarding relationships on the ice," Denise said. "At least before winter starts." She turned to address Bozer directly. "You don't formally acknowledge the person in public. You don't sit next to them at meals, and when a transgression takes place, you say 'you've crossed a boundary.' When you say that"— she peeled off Bozer's left hand, which had migrated from the table back to her thin shoulder—"they're supposed to stop touching you immediately."

"Okay, honey, but you know I don't subscribe to that kind of bullshit," Bozer said. "We all have an ice-wife, fuck buddy, whatever. What's to hide? Other people get weird about that, but I'm an open book."

"Is *ice-wife* just another term for a hook-up?" Cooper asked.

"So-called ice marriages aren't necessarily commitments down here," Denise said. "But the perceived permanency provides much-needed emotional support, particularly as the season grinds on." She lowered her voice. "Some people in ice relationships even have spouses and families off the ice."

"You're making it complicated, darling," Bozer said. "Alls you gots to do is figure out who's a dyke, who's married, who's open-married, who claims to have a boyfriend, and who wants continual action. Go from there."

"Typically these courtship rituals are kept offstage, à la Goffman," Denise said. "In this social environment, and at this particular time in the institutional cycle, it's important that this basic need be broadcast. You will see this change over the course of the season."

"So that's how you guys got together?"

"Repeat offender program," Bozer said, gazing over Cooper's head.

"Bozer's been on the ice nine times before this," Denise said.

"Nine times?"

"There's a quaint saying down here," Denise said. "The person who coined it has been lost to history: 'The first time is for the adventure, the second time is for the money, and the third time is because you don't fit in anywhere else.' "

"What's the ninth time for?" Cooper asked, looking at Bozer. He returned her gaze, a scowl on his lips but amusement in his eyes; however, Tucker's voice rang through the galley before he could answer her. "Hello, attention!" Tucker shouted between cupped hands. Everyone quieted down. "Fellow Polies, I regret that it's come to this point so early in the season, but I need to make an announcement. Our fearless communications and logistics director, Dwight, has informed me that our GOES satellite link, which has been overburdened for a week, has just had an irreparable failure. Too much usage. His investigation leads him to believe that a few individuals are using up most of the bandwidth that is shared by the entire station." Some people giggled. "I appreciate the fact that some of you need contact with the outside world in order to have contact with yourself, but it's overloading the system. So, bottom line, get your porn on, but just not over GOES."

Cooper took this opportunity to say goodbye to Denise and Bozer, and approached the galley kitchen with her tray. Pearl was piling a stack of them onto a cart. "Excuse me," Cooper said. Pearl brushed a stray lock of blond hair out of her face with the back of her wrist and looked at her. "What about those skiers?"

"What about them?" Pearl replied.

"They're camped outside. VIDS won't let them eat in the cafeteria." Pearl frowned, uncertainty darkening her normally sunny face. "They have to eat," Cooper pressed.

"I know, but I could get in trouble," Pearl said.

"What about the expired ramen? The Melba toast?"

Pearl leaned back and glanced over her shoulder. "Let me ask Bonnie first."

As Cooper waited for Pearl to get the head cook's okay on the mission, she noticed the VIDS staffer watching her from the coffee tureens. Pearl returned and gave Cooper the high sign, before noticing the admin's owl-like glare. She cleared her throat conspicuously and said somewhat robotically, "Oh, you want to eat at your studio? Let me give you a to-go container." Together, the women shoveled gratin, slices of meatloaf, canned fruit salad, and carrot sticks into to-go boxes, and eventually the admin turned his attention to a commotion at the tureens: a Fingy cryogenics tech had just learned that neither tureen contained decaf, which had annoyed him, and was then told there was no decaf at the station at all, which destroyed him. While this was happening, Pearl placed the containers into a small cardboard box for Cooper and passed it across the counter. Cooper slipped out the door without being noticed.

Outside, about a hundred yards from the station, Cooper saw a ski planted in the snow with a Swedish flag tossed over it. The flag hung limply, looking hungry.

Cooper kicked at the bottom of the tent with her boot—the winter camper's doorbell. One of the men unzipped the flap. His windburned face took Cooper aback: his skin looked like upholstery.

Inside, it was quickly established that the Swedes' English was perfect, but they seemed unsure of Cooper's, so initially they thanked her effusively with much hand-steepling and half-bows. She took a seat on a pack while they devoured the cold food. The younger one wiped his mouth on his sleeve, then apologized for his bad manners. "Will you get in trouble for this?" he asked.

"Maybe," Cooper said.

"You are a very kind person," he replied.

"Not really," Cooper said.

"No, Americans are very friendly," the older Swede said with conviction, "except for your bureaucrats. But that's true everywhere." He rummaged through his pack and pulled out a package of biscuits. He offered it to Cooper; after months of eating these Swedish cookies, his taste for them was lost forever.

"So, why are you guys skiing across Antarctica?" Cooper asked.

The older one gazed back at her. "Why are you here?"

"I'm an artist. I'm here to paint." Cooper didn't mention the fact that she'd painted exactly nothing since arriving.

"You must come to South Pole to paint?" the other Swede asked, grinning. Cooper was about to reply when she heard footsteps. She cursed softly, and the Swedes quickly boxed the food back up and slid it under their sleeping bags. When Cooper moved to unzip the tent, the younger Swede motioned her toward the rear. He lifted up a sleeping bag and indicated that she should hide under it. Cooper crawled beneath the bag, nose-first into a rucksack containing their dirty laundry. She tried not to gag.

"Excuse me, fellas," she heard VIDS admin say. "I'm just looking for a station member." There was a pause, and Cooper realized the Swedes were pretending not to know English. She envied this ability to disappear from a conversation. "Look, guys, I know she's here."

Cooper pushed the sleeping bag off her head and struggled to her feet. The admin rolled his eyes. The Swedes moved closer to Cooper, like protective older brothers, and she nodded at them, letting them know that it was okay. As she inched her way toward the opening, the older one, noticing Cooper had left behind her Swedish biscuits, slipped them into her parka pocket.

The VIDS admin—Cooper saw from the stitching on the front of his parka that his name was Simon—helped her out of the tent, then took her arm, as if they were going for a stroll across the English countryside. "It's hard to know which end is up when you're down here for the first time," he said. Cooper peered into his parka hood, but his face was deep in shadow now that they were outside in the relentless sun. She could only see his pale lips moving as he spoke.

"I'm figuring things out," Cooper said.

"Yes, I see that. But it's my job to ensure that you're figuring them out right. Taking food out of a federal research facility, for example, is against protocol."

"The Beakers take lunch out to their labs all the time."

"Please don't call them Beakers. It's disrespectful. And the scientists are eating their own lunches, not stealing from our limited food supply and giving it to every foreigner who happens to be passing by." Cooper looked at him uncomprehendingly. Simon sighed. "Look, I know you were trying to do the right thing, but the protocols are in place to protect life and government property. What if we get into a fix where our food supply flights are delayed and we're facing a shortage? That food you just gave away could have fed a couple of our support staff. Would you be able to look them in the eye if they had to go hungry?"

By now they had reached the Dome. "Did you receive help from anyone in the kitchen?" Simon asked.

"It was all me," Cooper said quickly.

"Are you sure?"

"Yes."

"And the to-go containers?"

Cooper hesitated. "I—I took them from the kitchen."

"You mean you stole them," Simon said, with the exhaustion of a put-upon parent.

"I guess."

Simon released her arm. "Cooper, you're an NSF grantee, so I can't write you up—I only oversee the support staff, not the feds— but I will have to send a memo to your grant coordinator about this. I'm sorry."

"What does that mean?"

"It just means that there will be a flag on your file, and if you violate any more policies, they may revisit your grant status." He stared at Cooper for a long minute, and she realized he wanted her to plead with him not to do this, that the only reason he'd brought up the memo was so he could hear her beg him not to send it. She'd given up begging after David died, so she summoned her inner Bartleby and remained silent as the wind picked up around them. Finally, Simon shrugged his shoulders and walked up the entrance tunnel.

Cooper waited until he had disappeared, and then walked across the ice in the opposite direction. She passed the ceremonial South Pole marker—a line of international flags snapping in the breeze, representing the twelve signatories to the Antarctic Treaty, and a mirrored gazing ball set atop a barber's pole. This tourist stop wasn't her destination, though. No, she wanted ninety degrees south—the geographical South Pole, the Pole of her imagination, of David's.

She could see it in the near distance, a polished copper star set atop a stake rooted to an ice sheet. From orientation, Cooper knew that on New Year's Day, this marker would be ceremoniously repositioned to account for its annual drift, as the entire station population looked on. The copper star installed the year before would be replaced by another symbolic work of art wrought by one of the Polies. This year, Cooper had learned via the *Antarctic Sun*, the honor would go to Sal.

But Cooper didn't care about polar tchotchkes. Back in Denver, Tucker had told Cooper that here she could find some of Robert Falcon Scott's words printed on a sign speared into the ice. She gazed at the large square sign now. On the left were Roald Amundsen's bland platitudes, the kind of banalities uttered by those who won races. On the right was a quote from Scott, the words of a man who had given everything, including his life, in his attempt to reach the Pole, only to come in second place to Amundsen: *The Pole. Yes, but under very different circumstances from those expected.*

Son,

I hope your decision to send me the book was not an attempt to gain my acceptance for your lifestyle choice. You won't get it. We've shared some good times in the past—you always did know how to make me laugh. But that's all behind us now. You've made your choice and now I've made mine. Our conversation tonight was our last. There will be no more of them. No communications at all. I will not come to visit, and I don't want you in my house. Have a good Christmas and a good life.

Goodbye.

Leon (Dad)

borderline-borderline

When the contract psychologist told Tucker there was a "border-line" applicant waiting in the office, he took her literally. After all, the job site was almost custom-made to attract people with personality disorders: narcissists, anti-socials, avoidants, dependents. Border-lines. The well-adapted chose McMurdo, the Hampton Inn of Antarctica. The slightly less normal picked Palmer Station. Only the margin-dwellers looked farther inland, toward Amundsen-Scott. It was the most remote research station on the planet, a place you went to become unreachable. This, of course, diminished the pool of applicants, so only those with a documented history of psychiatric disorders were rejected out of hand.

There were three widely accepted behavioral predictors that distinguished a successful polar applicant: emotional stability, industriousness, and sociability. But these traits had to be finely balanced against the necessary component of "crazy" required of a person who would choose to spend months upon months in Antarctica. Furthermore, that person had to be interesting enough for others to want to spend large amounts of time with, but not too "interesting." Over the years, Tucker had learned that some social skills were more highly valued at Pole than others: intimate familiarity with Settlers of Catan, detailed knowledge of nonconformist zombie-apocalypse scenarios, and the willingness to grow facial hair competitively, to name a few.

As he looked through the applicant files each season, Tucker would wonder how he had slipped by. Not only slipped by, but climbed the ranks quickly, going from site manager to area director in a single season without the relevant experience typically required for a promotion. He knew nothing about carpentry. Less about logistics. Zero about the allocation of limited resources. The Pole veterans assigned to positions under him knew far more than he did about how the station was run, but they had showed no bitterness at his appointment. This worried Tucker, until he realized that he hadn't been hired for his technical skills. When Karl Martin had offered him a job five years earlier, he'd mentioned Tucker's "cool gaze" and his powers of observation—both key attributes, apparently, for a successful South Pole station manager. It struck Tucker as bizarre that he had not had to submit to a psychological exam himself.

"Not borderline-borderline," the psychologist said to Tucker now. "Borderline, as in she's right on the cut-off."

"Reason?"

"Fairly recent death in the family."

"Cancer?"

"Suicide."

"That's an automatic DQ."

The psychologist wrinkled her nose and grimaced. "Yeah, but she's one of the Artist and Writers Fellows. You know the parameters are a little wider on those applicants. Also, she wouldn't look at the results. Technically a red flag."

"That's a red flag?"

"I know, I actually had to look that up in the manual. No one's ever not wanted to look before."

"What did the manual say?"

"That it suggests avoidance."

Tucker pinched the bridge of his nose. "Naturally. I'll go see her."

"Room two twenty-one."

Tucker walked down a hallway in the Systems and Solutions wing, which was lined with framed photographs of VIDS's various work sites—the U.S. military's "enduring bases," like Kosovo's Camp Bondsteel, Bosnia's Eagle Base, and Bagram Airfield outside of Kabul. South Pole Station was considered by VIDS to be part of its "Hostile and Developing Regions" branch, but Tucker was far removed from the military ops. Still, it was not uncommon to see military types— mostly black-ops CIA agents—going into the VIDS offices with the contract psychologists for their own exams. Tucker admired the agents' taut bodies, their set jaws, their bristle-brush hair.

When Tucker walked into Room 221, he found the borderline case hunched over a compact, attempting to dispatch a zit. It was an image so devastatingly familiar that Tucker felt as if he'd just walked into his childhood bedroom. Her name was Cooper—the kind of unexpected gender flip he found endearing. Tucker looked at her face, the intact blemish, the right eyebrow ever so slightly shorter than the left, her lips pink and full, her rich, dark eyes full of fear. Even with the pimple, she was pretty, but in a took-you-a-minute kind of way.

Before she spoke a word, he knew this would be a close call. But that's why they'd hired him. He knew how to make close calls. All but one had been successful. There was the metalworker with Asperger's— VIDS psychologists had argued his eccentricities and wooden personality would cause problems. Instead, the guy had been the most productive metalworker on the team, and was so popular that he'd been voted Equinox King. Then there was the highly skilled maintenance specialist who was a diagnosed bibliomaniac—Tucker had assigned him librarian duties, and filled out thirteen forms, some in triplicate, so the man could sleep in the library. The guy had alphabetized the library within the first week. Bozer, their veteran construction chief, who had been red-flagged one year because of several complaints about his Confederate flag bandanna—both VIDS and the NSF had decided to make Tucker the final arbiter on the matter, because (and of course this was only implied) he was the Only Black Person at South Pole. In interviewing Bozer, Tucker knew he had on his hands a red-blooded clay-eater from the poorest part of South Carolina. But he also knew Bozer was smart and steadfast, a man whose long years of experience in war and on the ice made everyone at Pole safer. Tucker knew that if he gave Bozer an ultimatum—the bandanna or his job—the man would've come to Pole with a naked pate, but angry as an adder. He didn't do that. Instead, he approved Bozer, and his bandanna, and let the admins wonder.

But while VIDS trusted Tucker to make the close calls, even they were worried about Doc Carla. They had not been keen on her. She was considered a "high-risk investment" despite the fact that finding candidates for this particular posting was so notoriously difficult that Karl Martin had called it "a janitor at the porno theater kind of a gig." The type of board-certified physician who was willing to sojourn in Antarctica for six months, preferably a year, for paltry pay and under extremely difficult work conditions was one whose personality might not be described as "charming." Tucker assumed this was a known fact, but thanks to the complicated tenure of Jerri Nielsen, the Pole doc who'd diagnosed her own breast cancer and who was widely considered a personable "normal," the threshold for minimal sociability had been raised (along with the number of release-of-liability forms).

It had not helped Doc Carla's case that the majority of her practice had, in the years leading up to her posting at South Pole, been focused on drug-addicted prostitutes. It was through this work that Tucker had gotten to know her almost twenty years earlier, and it was how he'd known she'd be the right person for the job. He had been working as a production assistant for a famous documentary filmmaker in New York when he read a short article in the *Times* about a woman doctor who drove a van around the city, handing out condoms and McDonald's vouchers to girls who worked the worst strolls. "Check it out for me," his boss said when Tucker showed him the article. "See if there's anything there."

But when Tucker cold-called Doc Carla's office and mentioned the word *documentary,* she hung up on him. He called back the next day and, disguising his voice, made an appointment for a hepatitis test. A week later, he arrived at her office, which was located in a brownstone in Alphabet City. Sitting in the window was an orange cat, its tail whipping this way and that, its face impassive. When the cat opened its mouth to meow, no sound came out. For some reason, Tucker had always remembered that.

"How old are you, Tucker?" the doctor had asked as Tucker took a seat on her exam table. She tied a piece of rubber hose around his left arm.

"Twenty-five, Dr. Nicks," he said, keeping his eyes on his veins.

"Call me Doc Carla." As she tapped the underside of his forearm, she examined his face. The Bell's palsy, which would render half his face slack and droopy from time to time, had gone away for now, but the acne had not. Tucker averted his eyes from his ugly blue veins.

"Do you engage in high-risk behavior?" she asked.

"What do you mean?"

"Do you have anal sex with men, do you share needles, do you sleep with hookers?"

"No! I mean, no, I haven't done that before."

"Which one?"

"All of them, I guess. Any of them."

The doctor ran her fingers over the inside of his forearms, looking for good veins. The feel of hands on his body was almost arousing, and Tucker felt ashamed.

"But you're gay, right?" she said, in a tone Tucker would come to realize was her version of gentle.

"I guess so." He hated when people could tell at a glance.

"Don't guess so—know so!" she replied.

"Yes, I'm gay."

"But you don't engage in homosexual behavior?"

"Sometimes. Just not that thing you mentioned—not that way. Yet, I guess." He wanted to disappear into one of those magician's dry-ice plumes.

"A gay black man," Doc Carla said. "You sure got it easy, kid." Suddenly, she exhaled—it was almost ecstatic—and said: "Look at these veins. Oh, my. They are just pristine. And look, I don't even need to really coax."

The time seemed right, so Tucker cleared his throat. "I read about your work with prostitutes. In the *Times*."

She rubbed his skin with iodine. "They check in with me every couple years. I almost didn't talk to them this time."

"Why?"

"Every time they write about me, the do-gooders come out of the walls. I've gotta peel 'em off. They're useless. I can't take their checks because I'm not a charity and if they volunteer one night, they never come back. Their tender sensibilities and all. I just lost my van driver."

"Yes, I read about that in the article."

Tucker closed his eyes as Doc Carla slid the needle into his vein; the initial prick gave way to a dull ache. After a moment, he opened his eyes and saw her attach a small vial to the tubing. Tucker watched as his blackish blood rushed through the needle. He felt dizzy. Doc Carla noticed.

"Jesus, stop looking, honey! Focus on Lulu," she commanded, pointing to the cat, who was still sitting in the window. "It'll help. She's one of the stations of Brahma. What do you do for work, Tucker?"

He hesitated. "I work in film."

She withdrew the needle and prepared a second one. "I've heard that before."

"It's not like that. Legitimate film. I'm just a production assistant."

"Gotta get that foot in the door. I better give you an AIDS test, too, even though you tell me you're a monk."

She removed the second needle from Tucker's vein and held a piece of cotton over the tiny wound.

"Could I go with you once?" Tucker asked.

"On one of my runs?" Doc Carla asked. She studied his face again, the way she had when he first sat down on the exam table. "Do you drive?"

"I've driven before."

She snapped off her plastic gloves. "You ever been around hookers?"

"No," Tucker said.

"You squeamish?"

"No," Tucker lied.

"Then meet me here tomorrow night. And wear old clothes, not this million-dollar shit," she said, flicking the wide lapel of Tucker's Goodwill jackpot find, a purple paisley Calvin Klein dress shirt.

When Tucker met Doc Carla the next night, she'd braided her thick, almost mangy hair and rolled it into a bun at the nape of her neck. The van was parked out front. "You know how to drive shift?" she asked.

"Yes, ma'am."

"Don't call me ma'am. Makes me feel old. And I'm not old. I'm not even forty. Jesus H. Christ."

"I'm sorry."

Doc Carla handed him the keys. "Eleventh, Twelfth, and Thirteenth, mostly between Second and Third. Full of IV-drug users."

"That's where I live," Tucker said.

"Bad blocks," she said. "How'd you end up there?"

"It's where I ended up," Tucker said.

"You know any of the girls there?"

"No."

"They all seem alike when you first meet them—bad makeup, bad skin, neon green or pink high heels, black stretch pants, usually got a hole in 'em. But they've all got their own attitudes. They say finding a specific hooker in New York is like finding a needle in a hay factory, but it's not true. I can find anyone. I've got to. Somebody's got to start keeping track of how many girls this thing kills. They need condoms and doctors and they need food."

The van was outfitted with a little kitchen and a miniature examining room, separated from the rest of the van by a *Peanuts* bedsheet tacked to the ceiling. There were venipuncture and butterfly needles, plastic cc vials, stacks of McDonald's vouchers for free meals, sanitary wipes, tampons, and condoms. Boxes and boxes of condoms.

They pulled up in front of a tenement building on East Eleventh, and within minutes a tiny woman with black hair, half of it in her face, walked up to the side of the van.

"Hey, Doc, you got some tissue or something? I want to get this fuckin' cum off me." Tucker almost retched, but Doc Carla didn't even blink.

"You need to start carrying hygienic supplies, Renata," Doc Carla said, handing the woman a handful of tissues. Renata ran the tissue down her pant leg, then shoved it into her pocket. "Got any free McDonald's, Doc?"

"If you got time for a test," Doc Carla said. Renata sighed, but walked back toward the sliding door and waited for Doc Carla to unlock it. "I give 'em these vouchers and ten bucks if they take an AIDS test. It's about twice as much as they get for a blow job down here." She walked to the back of the van and opened the door for Renata. "When was the last time I saw you, beautiful?"

"I don't know, Doc," Renata said as she climbed into the van. "The nights all get sort of smushed together. Don't know what's a month anymore."

After Doc Carla drew Renata's blood, other women began materializing like specters out of darkened doorways. An hour later, Doc Carla had Tucker drive into Brooklyn, to an empty lot near the waterfront, in the industrial badlands around the corner from Bush Terminal. The lot was surrounded by a tall metal fence, with a van-size hole in it.

"I made that hole a year ago," Doc Carla said. "There's another one on the other side, but it's girl-size; that's how they get in here." It had recently rained, and the mud was a cesspool of candy wrappers, gloves, scraps of paper, used condoms, and the amber shards of broken beer bottles. Tucker tried to ignore the pins-and-needles feeling taking over the right side of his face.

"See that clump of ailanthus trees?" Doc Carla said. "Pull the van up under those ugly things, by the Dumpsters."

"The Tree of Heaven," Tucker said, easing the car forward.

Doc Carla laughed darkly. "Can't polish a turd, Tucker."

As they approached the Dumpsters, women began appearing from behind them. A few even came out of the Dumpsters themselves, some of which had been turned on their sides and made into rude shelters. Tucker wanted to put the van into reverse and speed away before he saw any more. Instead, Doc Carla opened the passenger-side door.

"There's Sandy," she said. "God, I've wanted to test her again for three months. Sandy!" The woman wandered over. "Did you know what I meant last time when I said you tested positive for HIV?"

"I don't know which one that is," Sandy said.

"It's one of the newish ones," Doc Carla said. She reached into the glove compartment and handed Sandy the same brochure she had given Tucker the day before when she'd sent him home. "You know I never tell you girls to get off the streets. That's not my call. But Sandy—sweetheart—you gotta stop working, honey, because you're going to start killing people. And please come see me. I can help you."

"But I'm feeling good, Doc. I'm getting fat. I don't think I'm sick anymore."

"Who's watching the baby tonight?"

"Oh, the state took her already," she said.

"What'd you call her?"

"Daphne." When she saw Doc Carla writing this down in her notebook, she added, "But they probably already changed it, Doc."

Later, after they finished their rounds, Tucker stole a glance at Doc Carla as he turned the van onto Houston Street. Her bun had come undone, and the braid now lay across her right shoulder.

"Do you do this every night?" Tucker asked.

"Every night." She looked at him sleepily and reached over to touch his face, half of which now hung slack. "Bell's palsy. Have you had it before?"

"Yeah," Tucker choked out. "But not for a long time. Tonight's the first time in a long time."

They drove down Houston for a while. As they waited for the light at Avenue A, Doc Carla said, "It's stress that brings it on, the palsy. It won't last long. But you probably know that." She sighed. "This may be too much for your tender sensibilities, honey. It's almost too much for mine, and mine are damn blunt instruments."

A sob swelled in Tucker's throat. All he could manage was a thick, "Please."

He could see her studying him, and tried to hold it together, but his need at that moment was depthless. "Your parents," Doc Carla said. "Do they both hate the gay thing, or is it just your dad?" Tucker tightened his grip on the steering wheel, and she noticed. "I'm sorry, honey. I have a bad habit of letting my mouth run."

Two stoplights later, Doc Carla was asleep, her chin on her chest, and her braid falling over the seat belt and across her shoulders. Having her hand on his face had made Tucker feel less alone. Her question, though he'd left it unanswered, had made him feel human. He felt seen. And now he wanted nothing more than to remain forever in this metal beast loaded with condoms and coupons hurtling down Houston on a string of green lights.

Over the next six months, Tucker worked for Doc Carla after work, driving her van and getting to know the girls on the strolls. He never mentioned the doctor to his boss, and his boss forgot about her. When the film crew began work on a documentary about a cadre of squatters in a Lower East Side tenement, Tucker was tasked with locating archival footage at the Museum of Reclaimed Urban Space. That was when he began writing, in the five-minute stretches it took for the museum's archivists to locate the requested VHS tapes. It had started as a diary, but soon became a story, then a novel.

Little in Tucker's life had come easily, but the novel did: he wrote a complete draft in eight weeks. The filmmaker hooked him up with a literary agent, and the agent sold the book. A year later, it was published as *Unfortunate*. The summer after it came out, Tucker had been named the third tine on a trident of "promising" young male writers, christened thusly by *New York*. But Tucker always knew it was Doc Carla they were interested in, not him—the story, not the writer. He tried to forget this. He found that he couldn't.

Tucker waited to tell Doc Carla about the book until he had a copy to give her; he had dedicated it to her. She was not happy. "You lack imagination and integrity. You mined me for material. You took from these women the last things they had—their dignity and their anonymity. This is real life, Tucker, not art. I thought you cared. You're not an artist. You're a voyeur." She took the keys to the van and stopped answering his phone calls.

At first, Tucker ached for her presence as if she'd been a lover. He couldn't sleep. He barely ate. It faded, over time, but there hung about him always a heaviness. For a while, he lived off his advance, but soon he had to beg the filmmaker for his job back. He spent the next few years logging archival footage, applying for licensing rights, and, later, proving his genius for administrative work, as a unit production manager on several well-received documentaries. He found he was unable to write. Doc Carla was right. He was not an artist.

In 1997, after managing a documentary about the birth of the National Science Foundation, Tucker was offered a job as a speechwriter with the NSF's Office of Legislative and Public Affairs. He'd become friendly with a number of admins during filming, including the head of the NSF, Alexandra Scaletta. Tucker moved to Washington, D.C., where he was told to write pithy, diplomatic, "accessible" speeches for her. After the midterm elections, when the speechwriter position was eliminated due to congressional budget cuts, Scaletta decided to take Tucker with her on a trip to Antarctica. She wanted him to suss out the federal research stations, get status updates from the Program's support contractor, and to meet Karl Martin, VIDS's head of Hostile and Developing Regions.

It was during that first jaunt, a visit that took them to all three U.S. research stations in a single weekend, that Tucker had an hourlong tryst with a welder in the comestibles storeroom at Palmer Station. It was his first physical encounter in three years, and he had tried to pass off his inability to work his way through the man's layers of ECW gear as a seductive burlesque. But eventually the welder grew anxious and wrenched off his overalls, his jeans, and his long underwear, and pulled out his well-insulated dick himself.

Although Tucker knew full well the unexpected rendezvous was a fluke, it colored his perception of Antarctica, infusing it with hope. He applied for the assistant manager position at South Pole Station as soon as he got back to Washington. Despite Scaletta's letter of recommendation, Tucker was turned down the first time, due to a "lack of relevant experience," but after his third try, he received an invitation to VIDS's Denver campus, where he was deemed "exceptionally well-suited" for polar service.

One day, several years later and between Pole assignments, Tucker picked up *The New York Times* and read that the city had shut down Doc Carla at the urging of the American Medical Association and sex worker activists, who found her work with prostitutes greatly concerning. The doctors abhorred the McDonald's coupon swap. The activists didn't like the implications of the tests—they infringed on the sex workers' human dignity. And so, after citing her for numerous violations, the Department of Health had confiscated Doc Carla's van. When she refused to turn over the medical records she kept on the women she tested, they suspended her license and took her to court. No one came to her defense because no one she had cared for had a voice.

To Tucker's relief, there was no awkwardness when he got ahold of her. She acted as if there had never been a break between them. He encouraged her to begin seeing private patients again, but she told him she was done. "This was the only thing that kept my work meaningful, Tucker. They've taken it from me now, and I'm done."

"Well, I need a doctor," Tucker said.

"I told you—"

"It's a tough assignment, though."

There was a pause on the end of the line. "Go on."

"It's a clinic that sees injuries and illness not typically encountered in regular medical practice."

"Go on."

"It's a lonely outpost. Populated by difficult patients. Impossible environment. Far from civilization. Lots of drunks. Lots of red tape. Poorly supplied. Plus, you'll be responsible for any dental emergencies."

"Is it in hell?"

"It's at South Pole."

*

The woman in Room 221—Cooper—was lying to him because she hadn't prepared. The other artists and writers knew the game. They'd applied for enough grants and fellowships to have become adept at crafting the bloated prose required of artists in search of funding. But

Tucker had been at the game long enough himself to know that the less slick the self-presentation, the better the artist. And then there were the eyes—anxious but penetrating. Tucker wasn't concerned about the brother's suicide, even though the contract psychologist was. She was paid to be. He was paid to be intuitive, and he sensed that Cooper was coming from a place of strength. She wanted to go to Pole for the reason he had gone: to avoid becoming a tragic figure.

Still, she was officially borderline, and Tucker would be expected to present some evidence at the final psych meeting that night which counterindicated the initial red flag. One thing that typically smoothed the way in these cases was a coherent, thoughtful reason for wanting to go to South Pole—one that didn't include heroics or escape fantasies. But so far she had nothing for him and, by the time he was halfway down the hall, he had almost given up on her. Still, he wasn't entirely surprised when he heard her calling his name from the doorway of room 221.

"I've got one," she panted when she reached him. She told him it was a quote. History, Tucker thought. No good, and he told her so. But she insisted, and so he acted as if he was going to write it down.

"'If you are a brave man, you will do nothing; if you are fearful you may do much, for none but cowards have need to prove their bravery.' Apsley Cherry-Garrard. Of the Scott party." There was no imploring gaze, no clasped hands, no more fear in her eyes—just her frank, open face. "I'm a coward. Let me prove I'm brave."

For some reason, Tucker thought of Doc Carla asking him if he knew how to drive, all those years ago. She seemed to be saying then, as Cooper seemed to be saying now, that if you were a coward and knew you were a coward, you would do fine in this life. Maybe that, along with regular chemical peels, was why Tucker had made it this far.

*

Doc Carla was sitting on one of the metal steps leading to the clinic, smoking a cigarette through her filthy balaclava. Only her tired face was visible. Tucker kicked some snow over a frozen mound of vomit, and took the seat next to her. Doc Carla glanced down at the puke and took a long drag off her cigarette. "Poor guy almost made it to the can."

Tucker watched a grader grind down the entrance tunnel on its way to the work site and noticed Cooper walking across the long expanse under the Dome, alone, hood off but goggles on. She didn't see him, and he restrained the impulse to call to her, to check on her. She had made herself scarce since getting lost a few days ago in the Utilidors—the underground utility tunnels through which Floyd had been leading Fingys on a tour. Her humiliation touched something deep in his being.

"The Crud's rampant, Tucker," Doc Carla said. "Got four of 'em beating down my door this morning." She took one last drag off the cigarette, then dropped it in the snow. "But the Crud I can handle." Tucker looked over at the doctor; they were not even to Halloween yet and she already seemed preoccupied. Tucker wanted Doc Carla to remain content, but he still wasn't sure if diagnosing hematomas and treating cracked hands with Super Glue was going to keep her happy.

Doc Carla coughed. "So, you think she must've come here knocked up."

"Maybe. But if she was, she didn't know. She wouldn't have come if she'd known."

"That one would come if her legs and arms were chopped off. And you know it."

Tucker thought back to the incident at the comestibles berms two days earlier that had kicked off this whole drama. He had come into the galley after Pearl had radioed him for help—she and Bonnie were making lamb ragout for dinner later in the week, and they needed two lamb carcasses from the berms, which were located a quarter mile from the station. When he'd arrived in the kitchen, Marcy and Cooper were slouched over the metal prep table, having also been summoned. Cooper had been on house-mouse duty all week, a rotating job each Polie undertook at least twice a season that had him or her at the beck and call of the galley.

"About time," Marcy snapped, peevish.

"'He who forces time is pushed back by time; he who yields to time finds time on his side,'" Tucker replied. "Talmud."

"I don't care what he said, I just don't like sitting here with my thumb up my ass when I could be out helping Bozer on A3." Marcy was Bozer's right-hand woman, a skilled heavy machine operator with four winters under her belt, more than any woman in polar history. She wore stained Carhartts, her dishwater-blond hair tucked into a rainbow-colored knit cap, and she could replace the suspension system on a thirty-year-old tractor with her eyes closed.

"You're in a sweetheart of a mood, Marce," Tucker said.

"I just want to get this show on the road," she growled.

Ten minutes later, Tucker was straddling a snowmobile, his arms around Marcy's waist, with Cooper seated behind him. The engine roared as they sped out to the comestibles berms, rounded mounds of snow that stretched like dikes along the plowed paths. There were berms for many things: wooden spools, obsolete scientific equipment, construction debris. Tucker remembered seeing the berms from the air on his first plane ride in, laid out like Morse code in the snow.

Marcy suddenly gunned the engines and pulled the snowmobile sharply into a doughnut, sending up a sheet of ice crystals. Tucker felt Cooper tugging desperately on his parka in an effort to stay on. When Marcy pulled up to the berm, she braked hard, and Cooper was thrown off the snowmobile before it had come to a stop. To Tucker's great relief, she got to her feet, brushed the snow from her parka, and headed to the berms without even glancing back, barely limping.

Tucker looked at Marcy. "That wasn't very nice."

"Just wanted to give the Fingy a thrill," Marcy replied.

"Or a compound fracture."

Suddenly, Marcy's shoulders convulsed, and a great wave seemed to roll up her back. She listed to the right and vomited onto the ice.

Tucker saw Cooper turn at the sound of Marcy's retching. Veterans seemed immune to the Crud, and Tucker had never known Marcy to be sick. He had a bad feeling about this, but knew it was better to wait on Marcy than to press her. He waved Cooper back toward the berms. A few minutes later, he joined her, and together they chopped away at the snow and ice surrounding the lamb carcasses. "She okay?" Cooper asked. Tucker nodded, but said nothing.

After a few minutes, Marcy finally got herself upright and motored over to the berm. Tucker and Cooper dragged the two lamb carcasses to the cargo hauler attached to Marcy's snowmobile. Without a word, Marcy revved the engine, and as Tucker and Cooper climbed onto the back, she casually vomited again.

By the time they were all walking through the galley, though, Marcy had regained some strength, and even joked with some of the Nailheads on her way to the bathroom. Both Tucker and Cooper followed Marcy into the restroom, however.

"Get this parka off me," she said. Tucker clawed at the Escher landscape of zippers on the heavy coat and yanked it off, just in time for Marcy to launch herself toward the toilet. He backed up against the wall until he was almost a part of it, but Cooper headed straight for the stall and gently pulled Marcy's hair out of her face. This was good, Tucker thought. First, she'd done a tuck-and-roll after being thrown from the snowmobile and hadn't blinked. Now she was helping Marcy puke with dignity. She could be useful. It was good to be useful, especially for a Fingy. Especially for an artist Fellow. Good, good, good! As his thoughts devolved into one-word declaratives, a bigger thought wormed its way through the cracks: Marcy didn't have the Crud. Marcy was knocked up.

As she retched, he kept his eyes fixed on a Robert Crumb Tommy the Toilet poster taped on the wall above the sink. *Tommy Toilet sez: Don't forget to wipe your ass, folks.*

Tommy the Toilet was who Tucker thought of now as he listened to Doc Carla tell him that she'd have to send Marcy home. "NPQ," she added. He winced. No acronym in the polar lexicon was more feared than this—Not Physically Qualified. He knew sending Marcy off the ice was their only course of action, but he also knew that an NPQ on her record would make it very hard for her to return to the ice. If the cause was recorded as pregnancy, she'd never be back.

"Who have you told?" Tucker asked Doc Carla.

"Who have I told? I'm a vault. I've told no one. But she has to go."

Doc Carla waited for Tucker to reply. When he didn't, she said, "I'm glad we agree." She shifted on the metal steps leading to her clinic and craned her neck to look at the frost fronds hanging from the ceiling of the Dome. "Ah."

"What?"

"I'm just thinking how fun it'll be telling her she's going home. The woman has nothing in life except this shithole." Tucker thought but did not say that this was one thing he and Marcy had in common.

After leaving Doc Carla, Tucker took a walk around the outside perimeter of the station to think. He stopped at the construction site for a while to watch Bozer and his team, which included Marcy, assemble the mezzanine stairs to the A3 module. He wondered what it would be like running the new and improved South Pole Station while watching this one sink under the snow. For a moment, he was overcome by sadness.

Just beyond the site, he saw Cooper and Sal talking out on the road to the Dark Sector. He almost smiled; he liked when the young people got together. Back in Denver, Sal had announced that he was planning on celibacy this time around. Everyone knew how much he had at stake this season, even those Polies who had failed science. Tucker had made a point during training to explain to the support staff that this was an unusually important season for the Dark Sector—one cosmology experiment in particular was in the final stages of long-term research that could possibly confirm or destroy the inflationary theory of the universe. It was, Sal had told Tucker, unprecedented that physicists researching two different models would work on the same experiment: Sal and his team from Princeton were working jointly with the Kavli team from Stanford, both looking for something called b-modes.

The Californians, who moved about the station as a unit, were disciples of Sal's father, the great physicist John Brennan. They were Big Bangers. Sal, on the other hand, had thrown his fortunes in with another pioneer scientist who fervently felt that the evidence pointed toward something called the cyclic model, in which there was no Big Bang, but rather a series of collisions between membranes—the universe being one of those "branes" and the other being just a hop, skip, and a jump across an invisible dimension. There was more, of course, but Tucker had forbid further discussion when Sal started talking about "pre-Planckian predictions of dust."

The radio squealed. It was Comms. Dwight shouted something—every other word was lost in static. But Tucker had heard enough to get the gist of things: there was a phone call for him in the office, and, as all phone calls to the station manager typically were, it was urgent.

"I've got two unhappy congressmen on my ass," Karl Martin said when Tucker finally picked up the satellite phone in the communications office. "You need to open the kimono and tell me what the hell is going on with this—what's his name?" Tucker could hear Karl searching through some papers.

"Pavano. Frank. There have been some minor tensions between the scientists, but nothing out of the ordinary," Tucker said. "Standard territorial posturing."

"Well, I don't know what the hell that means, Tucker, but these guys, they floated the term 'hostile working environment'—at which point I brought in Legal. What's going on down there?"

"I've received no complaints. The grantee has been assigned a lab and is taking full advantage of the facilities." Tucker chose not to mention the T-shirts, the petition, and the ruthless ostracism at meals. He heard voices in the background and the moist sound of a sweaty palm squeezing the mouthpiece of the phone. "I've gotta run into this meeting," Karl said, "but get Scaletta on the horn—she's been getting an earful, too, but she's not returning my calls. See if you can put this fire out."

Tucker had tried for months to get Scaletta's input on the situation with Dr. Frank Pavano, but the NSF had remained silent on the matter. Tucker had thought it wise to add diversity workshops to the mandatory training for research techs who supported the major experiments. Turned out it was far easier for white male scientists to accept colleagues with dark skin or vaginas or both than it was for them to accept the presence of a climate denier in their midst. In fact, all the scientists, regardless of ethnicity or gender identity, hated Pavano, even before meeting him. Meeting him personally, it seemed, was beside the point. As a result, resistance to the training sessions tailored to prepare the support staff for Pavano's arrival was intense, and buy-in was nonexistent. To make things worse, Pavano had been unable to secure a research tech, which meant he'd be responsible for all aspects of his research project, including operations, repairs, and soul-crushing amounts of paperwork.

Pavano himself had been given extra counseling by one of the senior psychologists, and when Tucker had asked how it'd gone, she'd said, "He's basically autistic."

"That," Tucker had replied, "will work to his benefit."

It was only when the two congressmen who'd sponsored Pavano's efforts to get to Pole held a joint news conference that Tucker received a call from Scaletta.

"I dropped the ball on this one." She sighed. "Bayless and Calhoun promised to keep the grant on the down-low. Now they're on fucking *Fox & Friends* talking about methane isotope variability in deep ice cores—a concept I can assure you they don't understand, much less pronounce correctly."

"I think we have it under control," Tucker said.

"I knew you would. But I do need to say this: it's vitally important to the Program and to the NSF itself that Dr. Pavano's research is unimpeded, and that all previously agreed-upon resources be made available to him." She paused. "I know that's not technically your purview—"

"I understand."

"I'd also like to minimize media interest in his research. I'm hoping this will die down."

After handing the sat phone back to Dwight, Tucker stared at the collection of *Star Wars* figurines that the comms tech had arranged fussily on his desk. He imagined Dwight reverently bubble-wrapping Yoda and Darth Vader before placing them in the corners of his duffel bag for the trip to Pole. The thought cheered him briefly.

"Everything okay?" Dwight asked.

Tucker picked up Darth Vader. "Do you think he was a good manager?"

"He commanded authority naturally," Dwight replied. "He asked penetrating questions and listened to stakeholders." When Tucker raised an eyebrow at this, Dwight conceded that perhaps Darth Vader wasn't all that good at listening to stakeholders.

Instead of heading out of Comms and back to the admin pod, where he had hundreds of e-mails waiting for responses, Tucker decided to head upstairs, to the library. He found it deserted. He flipped on the fluorescents and walked over to the bookshelves. The maintenance specialist's alphabetization efforts had mostly held, although he did see David Baldacci living with Stephen King.

Tucker let his fingers dance over the wrinkled paperbacks one by one until they reached a glossy, unbroken spine. He knew which book it was by touch alone. Slowly, he pulled it from between Baldwin and Bradbury. It was clear that it still hadn't been read. As he always did, Tucker turned the book over to look at the author photo, a broody Ettlinger. It seemed like a daguerreotype—limpid, light eyes; snug-fitting white undershirt; a subtly flexed bicep; airbrushed skin the color of weak coffee. The man in the photo was unknown to Tucker now.

DEFENDED NEIGHBORHOODS AND DEGRADATION CEREMONIES IN REMOTE POLAR COMMUNITIES

Denise Notebloom
Department of Sociology, Columbia University
New York, NY 10025

ABSTRACT

Utilizing eight months of direct observation of the sociocultural issues inherent in prolonged isolation and confinement in a remote location, this paper examines the process of psychosocial adaption to an outsider whose presence enhances the in-group's mechanical solidarity. In a social environment in which "monopolistic access to particular kinds of knowledge" (Merton, 1972) is a hallmark feature and *Gesellschaft* a guiding principle, the arrival of a scientist whose views are in direct opposition to mainstream scientific opinion presents a unique opportunity to observe in-group/out-group dynamics. Based on observations recorded in the context of the four distinct characteristics of human behavior unique to the "polar sojourner"—seasonal, situational, social, and salutogenic (Palinkas, 2002)—the in-group's foundational *Gesellschaft*, when confronted with an outsider whose presence threatens the social ecology, transforms into mechanical solidarity. This is manifested in a more vigorous defense of "neighborhoods" against the outsider, as well as more frequent degradation ceremonies. I argue that such strategies are strained to the breaking point in reestablishing social equilibrium.

Keywords: *ANTARCTICA, MICROCULTURES, ADAPTATION, COPING*

the dance of
the anxious penguin

The Gore-Tex mitten Cooper was trying to sketch was in bad shape—a small rip discharged yellowed insulation material while the tip looked as if it had been dipped in barbecue sauce ten years earlier. Cooper had found it in the skua pile—a repository for random shit abandoned by current and former Polies. Named for the opportunistic brown seabirds that haunted the Antarctic coasts, *skua* functioned at Pole as both a verb and a noun: you could skua something—either by adding it to or removing it from the skua stream—or you could seek out skua. At McMurdo, the skua took up an entire shed. At Pole, it was located in a cardboard box. Cooper had spotted the mitten after breakfast, and, artistic desperation clouding her judgment, had seen in it great potential to create a work that "accurately reflects your time spent at South Pole," per the NSF directive. As she looked at her first attempts, she felt that although it was shitty work, it was at least better than the fourteen sketches of her own mitten she'd done up to this point. When she returned stateside, she'd have to present her output to a joint National Science Foundation/National Endowment for the Arts committee. She suspected that a study of various polar mittens would not suffice, not that she wasn't trying. She'd completed one panel of a planned triptych—of mittens.

She was trying to remember what grass looked like when someone knocked on the door. She found the *Alarmism and Climate Change Hoax*–reading scientist from the galley on the other side. "Hi," she said.

"I realized too late that we did not exchange names the other day. Tucker told me your name and where to find you. I'm Frank Pavano." The name sounded vaguely familiar to Cooper, like the name of an Italian food company based in Weehawken, but she couldn't place it.

She pulled the door open a little. "Well, Frank Pavano, do you want to come in?"

"I don't want to interrupt your work," he said, glancing over her shoulder.

"There's no work going on here, I assure you." Cooper held the door open wider, and Pavano strode past her, directly to her easel. Cooper was unused to the frankness of his interest in her art—most people looked everywhere but the work. Instead, Pavano leaned closer to her canvas to study the Gore-Tex mitten drawing she'd transferred from the sketchbook. "You seem to have an interest in protest art. Capitalist sublimation specifically."

"You got that from a mitten?"

He shrugged. "I took some art criticism courses in college to break up the biochem curriculum. But I got C's, so you can take my observation for what it's worth."

"It's worth a C," Cooper said, "speaking as someone familiar with C's." She smiled, and to her relief Pavano smiled back. "You're a Beaker, right? Sorry—scientist. What are you doing down here?"

"Broadly, I'm studying methane isotope variability in deep ice cores," Pavano replied, still studying the canvas. "My early career work was in heliophysics, but I've cultivated an interest in climatology over the years. I received some unexpected funding this year to go a bit outside the scope of my previous research." He scratched the side of his nose with delicate precision. "What about *your* objectives while you're down here? What are the parameters? Do you have to deliver a statement of results?"

Before Cooper could answer, someone knocked on the door. She glanced at her watch. "That'll be Denise. My shift is almost up. Do you want to grab lunch?"

Pavano seemed alarmed by the invitation. "No, I have to get back to the lab. I just wanted to formally introduce myself. On reflection, I realized I'd repaid your interest and kindness with a hasty departure, and I thought I'd apologize." He opened the door, and slipped past Denise wordlessly. A moment later, he reappeared. "Thank you for the invitation, though."

Denise raised an eyebrow at Cooper as she walked in. "I'm curious to see how, or if, he is going to integrate into the scientific community," she said, as she pulled out her laptop and set it heavily on the desk.

"He's nerdy enough to fit in," Cooper said.

Denise shook her head. "No, he's a walking example of the Black Sheep Effect. In cultural groups, like the one here, people will upgrade certain group members based on culturally desirable traits or likability. Look at Marcy, the heavy machine operator, for instance. Because years on the ice are culturally valuable, Marcy is a high-status individual. Off the ice, that might not be true." She opened her laptop, and Cooper saw the background photo was set to a photo of Bozer standing on a beach in thermal socks and sandals. "The flip side is that the 'in-group' will keep group members who threaten the group's cohesion on the outside, making them into a separate out-group. A black sheep."

"Why would this guy be a black sheep?"

Denise looked at Cooper, confused. "A climate-change skeptic working at the world's foremost climatology and atmospheric science research site is not likely to be warmly welcomed by the existing group."

So *Alarmism and the Climate Change Hoax* wasn't the opposition research material Cooper had assumed it to be. It was actually research material. *Pavano.* Suddenly all those outraged comments on the "South Pole Pals" message board she'd scanned six months earlier made sense. "Wait, is this the guy who's trying to prove that the ice under the Pole isn't all that old and could totally fall in line with the whole Noah's Flood thing?"

Denise stared back at her blandly. "No, I believe that's the working hypothesis of a biblical climatologist in Australia whose name I don't recall. I don't know much about Pavano's research yet, only that his findings set him in direct opposition to the vast majority of climate researchers around the world. The rumors surrounding the provenance of his funding only add fuel to the fire."

Everything was coming together now, and Cooper was cheered by the fact that some of the weird social interactions she'd witnessed were starting to seem a little less puzzling. At breakfast a week earlier, for example, people had been talking about how one of the head climate researchers, a paleoclimatologist from Madison named Sri, kept "forgetting" to get "the Denier" a username and password for the West Antarctic Ice Sheet data server. When Sri and his team had hopped a plane for the research camp—known as the Divide—they had removed the Denier's name from the manifest. It was treated as a joke, and no one was disciplined. But the Denier—Pavano, Cooper now realized—had contacted his congressional sponsor, a Republican senator Cooper thought she'd heard of named Bayless, who promptly called his contact at the NSF, and Pavano was immediately shuttled out to the camp and given full access to the ice archives, the lab, and, at Bayless's request, Sri's research site.

Cooper dropped her brushes in a can of turpentine. "Well, it sounds complicated," she said as Denise sat down to begin work.

"All social interaction is complicated, of course, but down here it's even more so, which is what makes my job so fun," Denise replied. "I'm waiting to see if metaphorical effects are amplified at a place like Pole. You know, the idea that holding a cup of hot tea makes people feel warmly toward others, or that a person in a high place, like a cherry picker, is seen as being situated farther up the hierarchy. Last year, Lee and Schwartz found that when exposed to a fishy smell, people actually grow suspicious." Denise glanced over at Cooper. "In sociological terms, you might say that Frank Pavano is a just-opened can of tuna."

A very slight smile was the only indication that Denise had made her first joke.

*

Back at the Jamesways, Cooper found a note under her door from Birdie indicating that there was an artists' meeting in thirty minutes. Cooper groaned, but she knew Birdie was counting on her to be there. Before leaving her room, she saw her *Terra Nova* sketch had fallen from the canvas wall, where she'd pinned it. She set it on her desk and studied it for a moment. Her sketches were often the products of procrastination, but Cooper kept coming back to this one—so many times, in fact, that she had completed it. Who knew what it meant? All Cooper knew was that looking at it made her feel better. She pulled on her balaclava and parka for the trek back to the station.

As she hurried out, she accidentally nudged her pee can with her boot. She heard sloshing and realized she'd have to empty it. If she waited another day, she could have a biological disaster on her hands. Pee cans were one of the many secrets veterans kept from Fingys, but after Cooper's act of civil disobedience with the Swedes, she'd apparently garnered some social capital; Pearl had left an empty #10 can, once filled with industrial-grade cling peaches, outside the door of Cooper's room, with a note thanking her for not selling her out to Simon. Now Cooper no longer had to venture outside the Jamesway to use the bathroom, which was located in a separate structure a hundred yards east. However, she still had to walk over there to empty the can into the communal pee barrel.

Reluctantly, she picked up the can with her mittens and pushed the door open with her shoulder. She immediately collided with a man dressed in full ECW gear and watched as at least a quarter cup of her urine splashed onto his bunny boots. His woolen face mask and neck gaiter muffled his angry roar, and Cooper hurried past him before he could get a good look at her, grateful for the anonymity provided by the balaclava and the darkness of the hall.

After emptying the can into a barrel and tucking it into a corner to avoid having to return to the Jamesway, she turned to the warped mirror, and cleared a swath through the condensation. It was time to see how she was faring in terms of polar aesthetics. The rule of thumb, she now knew, was that someone who was a "five" off the ice was easily an "Antarctic Ten." Cooper squinted at her reflection: her infected eye, which had looked like a gelatinous bead for a week, was totally healed. Her hair was so oily it had darkened a few shades—two-minute showers twice a week meant thorough shampooing was now a luxury. Her shaggy bangs fell across her eyes. As she stared at her reflection, she felt she embodied the very definition of the word *mediocre*. She noticed a waffle crumb in the corner of her mouth, and as she flicked it free, her brother's face suddenly seemed to inhabit hers, staring back at her through her own eyes. She gripped the sides of the sink to steady her suddenly weak knees and quickly closed her eyes against the image.

"You meditating or something?" Cooper opened her eyes to see Marcy.

Cooper brushed her bangs out of her eyes. "Sort of." It wasn't three days ago that she'd held Marcy's hair off her face as she'd puked into a toilet. Cooper thought she looked better.

"Well, for a second there, I thought you were doing the rosary," Marcy replied. She seemed as if she wanted to say more. Talking to Marcy was helping. Studying her face helped even more—analyzing the angles of another face obscured David's—and Cooper saw that although Marcy was only in her late thirties or early forties, her skin was already worn and craggy from her cold weather adventures. Yet her mouth had a sweet downward droop to it, like a baby's pouchy lips. Her small eyes were almost as dark as Cooper's, and the lines that radiated from them made her look like a happy Buddhist deity. But right now, the eyes were sad.

"Thanks for the other day," Marcy said. "It wasn't my finest moment."

"No worries. I've had my share of not-fine moments, too. You're feeling better?"

"Yep, fit as a fiddle," she said tightly. "You got your costume ready for tonight?"

"Costume?"

"The Halloween party?"

"Is that tonight?"

"Well, it *is* Halloween."

"I lose track of the days."

"Just wait until winter, honey."

"I don't have a costume."

"Scrounge one up from skua, no biggie."

Marcy reached past Cooper and plunged her hand in the plastic bin containing condoms that was replenished daily. "Tonight's the night to land an ice-husband," Marcy said. "If you want one." Cooper thought she saw the sheen of tears in Marcy's eyes, but they were quickly blinked away. She dropped the condoms into Cooper's hand. "Get laid, honey. It takes the edge off."

*

Like everything else at South Pole Station, the gym was located in a trailer. On the outside door was a handwritten poster announcing the first meeting of the American Society of Polar Philatelists: *The Harvis Collection in Da' House at Our Next Meeting! Be There or Be Filled with Aching Regret.*

Inside, Birdie had arranged the folding chairs in a circle. Cooper took the one directly beneath the net-free basketball hoop, and watched as the historical novelist and the interpretative dancer walked in together, not quite holding hands. The literary novelist entered alone, listening to his Discman.

"Does anyone want to run the meetings?" Birdie asked, brandishing a clipboard. "The Program insists on a group leader." No one replied, and Birdie tried to hide his pleasure at taking the helm.

"Could I say something before we start?" the interpretive dancer asked, and Birdie reluctantly granted her the floor. "I'd like to start off this meeting with a haiku that I believe may put this whole strange adventure in perspective.

"The man pulling radishes

"*Pointed the way*
"*With a radish.*"

Birdie looked over at Cooper, but she turned her gaze to the climbing wall to avoid his eyes; she understood that laughter would diminish the power of the radish. Still, the dancer grew frosty at the lack of appreciation, and said crisply, "What are we supposed to be doing at these meetings anyway? I'd like to get a handle on what's expected of me. I tend toward anxiety, and anxiety is not conducive to creativity."

"It can be," the literary novelist said, fiddling with his Discman. The dancer looked at him with disdain and flicked her long braid over her shoulder.

"Yes, well, it isn't for me," she said.

"So far as I can tell," Birdie said, "the Program wants us to meet in an official way once a month and to keep minutes, and then submit them to the officers at the end of this adventure. Why don't we go around the circle and talk about what we're working on?"

"My work deals with the cartographic imperative," the literary novelist said. The dancer leaned over her knees to look at him.

"Cartographic imperative? Like, the desire to map things?"

"Yeah, exactly. Like, why do the people who come down here feel like they have to, you know, name it? Or claim it for their country? I'm really interested in what is behind that motivation."

"And what's the title of your book?" Birdie asked.

"I'm calling it *Mapping the Breath.*"

"Profound," the dancer said, punctuating her point with the kind of dreamy sigh she'd expected for the radish haiku.

"Yeah, I was thinking that, like, mapping the breath is pretty much impossible. And cartography in general is such a hubristic endeavor that it's almost as ridiculous."

"But the book itself sounds self-aggrandizing," Cooper said, before she could stop herself. The tenor of the room changed at once, like a writing workshop suddenly infused with candor. "I mean, at least the title does," Cooper added. Birdie shook his head slowly, stifling a smile. The literary novelist, loose-limbed and squinty-eyed, squinted at her harder. "Yeah, no, I want feedback," he said. "I mean, that's good. In many ways the desire to put a cartographic imprint on land that belongs to all humankind finds a parallel in the canine impulse to mark its territory."

The door to the gym opened and Denise walked in, followed by a blast of cold air. Her glasses instantly turned opaque with steam. "Sorry I'm late," she said as she pulled off her hood. "I'm Denise."

"She's a sociologist," Cooper added as Denise wrestled off her parka.

"I was told this would be a closed meeting," the dancer said stiffly. "I have no interest in being studied."

Denise's plain face radiated serenity. "You needn't worry—my research interests lie elsewhere, though I do have a casual interest in the Artists and Writers contingent because they have, historically, been even more isolated due to their low social status at the station."

"Low social status?" the dancer asked.

A sound somewhere between a snort and a cat trying to clear a hairball exploded from the historical novelist. "So we're pariahs," he said acidly, picking at a mole on his neck.

"Perhaps I was a little too general."

"But low social status means no one likes us," the dancer said.

"Well, in layman's terms, I suppose that would be a fair characterization," Denise said. "Though the term *superfluous* would be more accurate."

"This makes me really anxious," the dancer said to the historical novelist.

"Put it in your work," he said soothingly.

Cooper smiled. *Put it in your work*. This had always been her father's standing advice. Maybe this was the standing advice all exasperated relatives or spouses gave to agitated artists. My first date ever stood me up, Dad. *Put it in your work*. I made a really bad decision having to do with a vending-machine salesman/artisanal tobacconist/urban shaman last night. *Put it in your work*. And it was true,

Cooper thought. You *could* put it in your work, and you did, but then the work itself became nothing more than a hall of mirrors, reflecting back all the crappy things that had happened, or which you had made happen, in your life. That was why she'd stopped painting when David was sick. Who needed a mirror when the only thing reflected was loss after loss? She dropped her hand into her pocket, her fingers searching for the vial. She found it and ran her thumb over the serrated edges of its childproof cap.

"Cooper?" Birdie said. She withdrew her hand quickly and looked up. The artists were watching her expectantly. Next to her, Denise scribbled something in her notebook. Out of the corner of her eye, Cooper saw *Thousand-yard stare—already?* written in the margin.

"Sorry," she said. "So, I'm a painter, though since I got here, I'm not sure anymore." There were a couple of appreciative chuckles. "Actually, I probably shouldn't even call myself an artist. A professor once told me that you can't be cynical and artistic, that these traits are diametrically opposed. He said I was cynical. And I guess I am." Hard, actually—"hardened by premature success" were her professor's exact words. Artists had to be porous, he'd said, like sponges, capable of soaking things up and releasing them. If you were a stone, you could do nothing but take up space. And while a sponge could become a stone, a stone could never become a sponge. "So I'm finding the polar landscape challenging to capture because I don't want to do dead-explorer stuff or glaciers, and I definitely don't want to go the route of putting incongruous, unexpected man-made stuff on the ice, like I've seen in other polar art. That feels sort of didactic."

"I actually think that sounds interesting," the literary novelist said. "Like painting a Walmart on the polar cap to make a point?"

"Too obvious," Cooper said.

The literary novelist looked at his nails. "I didn't realize visual artists were interested in subtlety."

As the conversation continued around her, Cooper began wishing that someone *would* appear and point the way—with a radish, a compass, a finger, it didn't matter. She just wanted someone to tell her how to move forward.

*

After the meeting ended, Cooper stepped out of the gym, and saw a commotion near the door of a construction office at the other end of the trailer. A knot of people, including Pearl, were doing a little dance. Cooper noticed Sal standing with them. "I'll come to the recital but I'm not taking the class," she heard him say.

"What's happening?" Cooper called down to him.

He seemed surprised to see her, but quickly assumed a look of nonchalance. "Hey, it's Frida Kahlo," he said, walking toward her. "Make yourself useful and paint me something I won't want to drop-kick to Vostok."

"Something with tater tots?" Cooper replied.

"Oh, if you got into tot art and you were any good, I'd marry you."

"Why are the girls all excited?"

"Dave's in from McMurdo."

"Dave?"

"Dave's dance class? The most popular rec class in the history of the Program?" He noted Cooper's skepticism. "It's kind of a big deal. Starts Thursday, if you're interested."

"Nothing could induce me to go to Dave's dance class."

"Fingy, when you can't walk your dog, mow your lawn, get a coffee at the place where you know the guy who makes it, you will begin to find dance class with Dave appealing. And if Dave doesn't show up for the dance class, you'll go apeshit. You have the expectation that he will be there and he better well keep his fucking commitments, because Dave's dance class is all you'll have to hold on to down here once those doors close for the winter."

All this bluster, but he was grinning. "And now I have to keep my own commitment to show up at the Smoke Bar and get wasted before the Halloween party. Adios." He turned and began walking away.

"Where's the Smoke Bar?"

"Winter-overs only," Sal called over his shoulder.

"Come on."

He stopped walking. "All right, Fingy. Follow me."

Smoke Bar was located on the second floor of the galley trailer. Cooper had heard about the Smoke Bar, but had never been able to suss out its exact location. All the summer workers and most of the scientists congregated at the other bar, 90 South, which was the Señor Frog's of Antarctica. Smoke Bar was Chumley's—back when you had to be somebody to get in. Gaining entry to the Smoke Bar was, Cooper understood, a privilege.

When they reached the top of the metal stairs, Sal blocked the door and turned to look at Cooper. "You're about to enter a very delicate ecosystem, so when we get in, go sit with Tucker, who will be drinking vodka neat at the table under the dart board. I'll introduce you to the Beakers when it makes sense. They get excited and weird around ladies, seeing as they're in such short supply here. I have to manage their expectations." Cooper knew Sal was bullshitting, but she didn't mind. He pushed the door open with his shoulder and let Cooper enter.

As she walked in, The Smithereens' "A Girl Like You" was playing at max volume. Cooper took in the foosball table, a disco ball, and the stripper pole. Twinkling fairy lights hung from the ceiling, along with at least twenty purple Crown Royal sacks, below which ashy clouds of cigarette smoke created a small weather system. The bar itself was a piece of plywood on crates, behind which a man in a George W. Bush mask was dispensing drinks from a series of minifridges lined up against the wall. Everyone bought their own liquor at the station store, or shipped their own booze down to Pole before the season started. Cooper had settled for the cheap New Zealand beer that came in cases on every flight in, but her supply was down at 90 South with the rest of the Fingys'.

Cooper spotted Tucker at a table with some galley workers and assorted Wastees—the people who handled garbage and sewage—and she and Sal silently parted ways.

"I know a guy whose credit card was stolen," a guy without a chair was telling the table. "The thief ordered a really expensive cell phone and also sent him a Lobstergram. Guy cancels the card, and Lobstergram didn't want the lobster back. The guy was allergic to shellfish so he gave it to a friend." This raised no response, and no one offered him a chair.

"Anyway," a tall man with Cher-like hair and a sparse, preadolescent-style mustache said. "As I was saying before I was so rudely interrupted: you play the Antarctica card off the ice, you're laid ninety-nine times out of a hundred."

"Doesn't work for women," a dark-haired woman said, her feet on his lap. Cooper recognized her as Pearl's boss, Bonnie, the head cook.

"Why?" her cloak-wearing companion asked.

"No man sitting at a bar is gonna get his dick hard if a woman tells him she's just back from the ice chip, except maybe another Polie. And in that case, it's just a reflex."

Tucker took Cooper's arm and simultaneously pulled out a chair from another table. "Congratulations on gaining entry," he whispered. Then to the group, he said: "This is my friend, Cooper." Cooper cringed. The first thing she'd understood when she'd arrived was that introductions were for the desperate; the fewer you required, the stronger you appeared. Pole was a place where people simply became known.

"You tell us you don't have friends, Tucker," Bonnie said, "that you're a lone wolf."

"Well, Bonnie, I'm starting fresh," Tucker said. Cher then introduced himself as Dwight, "the wizard-god of Logistics and Comms." Too late, Cooper realized Tucker had slipped away.

"Judging by your attire," Dwight said, "you are neither Beaker nor manager, neither galley slave nor Wastee. Reasonably attractive, yet with no obvious male companion." He paused and looked over at Bonnie. "Wow, this is exactly like cosplay."

"No, I recognize her. You were in the kitchen the other day," Bonnie said, scrutinizing Cooper's face. "I think you're a VIDS psychologist, trying to blend in with the population."

"I'm a painter," Cooper replied.

"They sent people down to paint the walls?" Dwight asked, incredulous.

"Artist," Cooper clarified. "The NSF sends artists down each year to do . . . whatever."

Bonnie reached across the table and offered Cooper her hand. "Well, let me formally introduce myself—I'm Bonnie, the head cook." Cooper took Bonnie's chapped hand for a shake, but Bonnie grasped Cooper's and pulled it toward her, caressing it. "Dwight, honey, feel her skin." Dwight ran a bored finger over the top of Cooper's hand and withdrew it, nodding.

"So pink and soft," Bonnie cooed.

"That's how we find the Fingys when there's a blackout and we need fresh meat," Dwight said in a monotone. "Their soft, infant-like skin."

Cooper excused herself to beg a beer off George W. Bush. She cursed softly when she noticed, again too late, that the man sitting to her left was Floyd. "Who's more heroic," he asked his companion, brandishing a glass of whiskey, "a woman doc who got a common disease, but who was also trained to deal with it, or the pilot who successfully landed a Herc in the middle of a polar winter to evac her?" He paused here, letting his rage build. "You tell me which demands more bravery. You tell me who risked their life. Do you even know the pilot's name?"

"Dude, I'm just trying to have a drink," the guy said wearily, pushing his fingers in and out of a plastic jack-o'-lantern's mouth.

"Major George R. McAllister," Floyd said. "You remember that name." He glanced over at Cooper. "You, too—George R. McAllister. Oh, hey, I know you. You're the McMurtry apologist. Who the hell let you in?"

Luckily, death metal began blaring through the speakers at that moment and Floyd skipped over to the stripper pole and started gyrating. While everyone guffawed at this, Cooper noticed Sal was watching her, but he quickly looked away. She watched Floyd for a while—he was surprisingly agile—and finished the Canterbury ale Bush had loaned her, but it gave her a headache. She was about to leave when Birdie walked in, his thick glasses reflecting the lights from the revolving disco ball. He carried a bottle of Dewar's bearing his name on a piece of masking tape and two highball glasses pinched between his thumb and fingers. He took a seat next to Cooper.

"Who told you?" she asked.

"Told me what?"

"About this place—who let you in?"

Birdie smiled and opened the bottle. He poured out two measures, then handed a glass over to Cooper. "She did." He nodded toward Pearl, who was throwing darts with a couple of dining assistants.

"You're kidding me."

"This strains your credulity? I'm not offended. It strains mine. Look at her. She's gorgeous." Cooper looked over at Pearl. For the first time, the pink bandanna was off, and Cooper saw that both sides of her delicately shaped head were shaved to the skin, leaving only a thatch of blond hair, which had been pulled up into a ponytail. She was wearing a black headband with glittery cat ears, and when she laughed, Cooper could see what Birdie meant.

Cooper clinked her glass to Birdie's. "Cheers."

"How's it going, then?" Birdie asked. "The painting, I mean."

"Mittens," Cooper said. "All I've got is mittens. And there's no way to justify that as art." Not that she hadn't tried. *The mitten is a talisman, an image of worship in a place where god is dead. It's a study of both the humility of the simple garment and the hubris of our belief that it protects us from this savage continent.*

"You?" Cooper asked.

"I'm having a hard time pulling things together myself. Now that I'm here, Bowers grows elusive." Cooper could feel Sal's eyes on her again, but didn't risk a look in his direction this time.

"I can't imagine caring enough about a person I've never met to spend years researching his life and writing about him," she said. "You'd have to be obsessed."

Birdie nodded. "Biography is not a genre for the lukewarm. Bowers was just a sledger, like me, head down, strap over his shoulder, the only one on the Scott expedition without skis. He was optimistic to the point of being demented. Cherry said there was nothing subtle about him. He wasn't complex like Cherry, who was a head case. He's not intrinsically interesting like Scott either, nor a hero like Titus, and thank god he wasn't a narcissistic ass like Teddy Evans.

There are no scandals to unearth on this fellow, no dark side. I suppose I'll need to find a dark side. I'm told we all have them."

"Except me," Pearl chirped as she passed. She leaned down between Cooper's and Birdie's chairs and slung an arm around them both. "Dark sides are for moons, not people."

Birdie nearly snapped his neck watching Pearl continue on to the bar top. Cooper told Birdie she had to hit the john. She passed Sal's table on the way to the restroom, and he reached out as she walked by and hooked his fingers through one of the belt loops on her Carhartts. He was leaning back, his chair resting precariously against the wall—sodden, and more attractive for it, a feat Cooper had never seen achieved before. Next to him, his Russian cohort, Alek, looked up at her with bleary eyes.

"Where you going, strange person?" Sal said.

"To the bathroom."

"I come with?" Alek said thickly.

"Sure, that's going to happen."

Alek fist-pumped toward the sky. "She says this will happen."

Sal squeezed Alek's shoulder with his free hand. "Alek's drunk on moonshine."

"Samogon," Alek growled.

"Sorry—samogon. It's a moonshine they make in the Urals. NSF thought it was isopropyl alcohol and let it pass. You met Alek, right? You can call him Rasputin."

Alek frowned. "Always Rasputin. Why not Gorky or Pushkin?"

"Because you're an evil monk, not a literary genius," Sal replied.

Alek extended his middle finger and thrust it skyward. "Why do I allow you?" he bellowed.

"What do you actually do, Alek?" Cooper asked.

"I am here to help Sal win Nobel."

Cooper was intrigued enough to hold her pee. "This is important research season for our team," Alek continued. "For world." He lifted his glass of clear liquid. "I drink to it."

Sal looked embarrassed. "Samogon makes Alek sentimental," he said. "Ignore him." He gestured to a chair. "Sit down. I want to talk to you about something." Cooper took the chair, and Sal leaned over the table. "I hear you're getting cozy with Frank Pavano."

"Cozy? He visited me at my studio the other day." Sal leaned his chair back again, resting his knees against the edge of the table. "Does this have something to do with your petition?" Cooper asked.

"I can't hear of this man anymore," Alek said, and took his samogon to the table where Birdie was sitting with Pearl.

"His work must be legit if the NSF funded his research," Cooper said.

Sal made a guttural sound in the back of his throat. "Look, last year, a couple of Republicans in Congress got letters from their constituents saying that they couldn't get the literature on alternate explanations for climate change in the schools, they couldn't get federal funding, they couldn't 'teach the controversy.' Then one of these morons—guy named Bayless, out of Kansas—realizes that serious science is done at Pole and not one scientist is down here trying to prove climate change is a hoax. He gets constituents to flood the NSF with letters, joins forces with another Bible-thumping congressman, Calhoun, goes on *Fox & Friends*, they do their thing, open inquiry, whatever. Of course, this has absolutely nothing to do with the fact that Bayless and his own personal Lennie Small are up for reelection next fall."

"So the NSF caved to political pressure?"

Sal shook his head. "Officially there was no 'political pressure.' In fact, NSF rejected Pavano's application initially. Then all of a sudden he's funded and NSF releases a statement that says they support the general principle of academic freedom and inquiry and are sending Pavano down here to disprove climate change."

"Is there anything there? What's his science?"

"Let's not use *science* and *Pavano* in the same sentence, okay?" Sal said. "Pavano is collecting ice-core data from the Divide that he'll use to dispute the models that indicate Earth is going to become a giant Bunsen burner. At the same site, I might add, where the real climatologists are extracting and analyzing ice cores that will prove that it is. His presence on the ice means that somewhere a real climate scientist did not get his grant approved." He raised his glass. "And so, my darling painter person, the fact that Frank Pavano is at South Pole Station is officially a sign of the end times."

"You're not a climate scientist. Why do you care so much?"

"If you were a scientist, you wouldn't ask that question."

All around them, people were starting to leave to get dressed for the Halloween party. "You coming?" Sal asked. "Everyone comes. It's a polar spectacle."

Cooper looked over at Birdie—his face was rosy and tears were streaming from his eyes. Pearl rubbed his shoulders as Alek held an empty glass of samogon above his head triumphantly.

"I guess so."

Tucker appeared at their table, his hands clasped in front of his body. "Frosty Boy's back," he said. Sal threw his head back and punched the sky with both fists. Tucker turned to Cooper. "Frosty Boy is a soft-serve machine that delivers flaccid ice cream in a continuous stream."

"He's probably spent more time under the loving, quasi-sexual ministrations of the maintenance specialists than he has actually dispensing soft serve," Sal said.

"Why keep it around if it doesn't work?" Cooper asked.

"You can't just come in here and replace things like Frosty Boy with something that works better. We grow attached to these temperamental pieces of crap. They're rejects, just like us."

*

A half hour and scavenged costume later, Cooper found herself standing in the darkened gym wearing a Freddy Krueger mask and surgical scrubs while a five-piece band calling themselves Coq au Balls covered an Avril Lavigne song as a joke. No one was laughing. On the booze table beside her, a jack-o'-lantern vomited seeds and pith. Cooper watched as the VIDS and NSF administrative staff jogged onto the dance floor, singing along to "Sk8er Boi." She worked her straw through a slit in the Krueger mask and drained her screwdriver. A ghost-memory flickered in Cooper's mind of Billie, at four-teen, advising her that *liquor before beer, you're in the clear and beer before liquor gets you there quicker*. Or was it *never been sicker?* Whatever. Next to her, Dwight groomed his Chewbacca mask with a small comb. When he noticed Cooper watching, he trilled at her.

Halfway through her third screwdriver, everything in Cooper's line of vision began to take on the soft edges of a high school senior portrait. She scanned the crowd. There was Bozer, dressed as a hobo, a play on Tucker's widely adopted moniker for him, *hobosexual*, a man who was the opposite of a metrosexual, a man who gave not two shits about his appearance. ("Like Michael Moore," Tucker had said helpfully.) Holding a woman's purse on the end of a stick, and wearing torn culottes, Bozer was showing off a handmade bird-house to a Fingy meteorology tech, who apparently believed his story about the rare "glacier sparrow" that nested at South Pole. Across the gym, the interpretive dancer was sporting a rainbow clown's wig and enormous novelty sunglasses in the shape of hearts, and Electric Sliding with the historical novelist, who really was just shuffling.

Cooper turned away from the stage in time to see a woman from McMurdo walk purposefully toward Sal and grab his hand, pulling him back toward the dance floor. Through the eyes of Freddy Krueger, Cooper considered the woman: so that's what Sal liked, she thought. Women who wore oversize football jerseys, hot pants, and slightly off-kilter trucker's hats and called it a costume.

"This is the annual start-of-the-season hook-up," Tucker said, stepping next to Cooper. "Whoever you hook up with becomes your ice-wife or ice-husband for the season." He looked out over the crowd of bearded Britney Spears and wobbly space cowboys. "Choose wisely."

"I'm trapped in a bad remake of *Meatballs*," she said.

"One wonders if a *Meatballs* remake could be good?"

"What is the sound of one hand clapping?" Cooper replied.

"I know it seems like a frat party, but it won't last. The beginning is always like rutting season on the Great Plains."

"What about you? Do you have an ice . . . person here?" Cooper asked.

"As Calvin Coolidge once said, 'I have found out in the course of a long public life that the things I did not say never hurt me.'" With this, Tucker wandered away, and Cooper finished off her screwdriver. Now she was sufficiently drunk. She pulled off the Krueger mask and threw it high into the air, not bothering to watch it fall in the middle of the makeshift mosh pit by the stage. She spotted her parka hanging on the NordicTrack that had been shoved into a corner of the gym. On her way over, she passed Birdie and Pearl, who were deep in conversation. "And they have these things called 'meat raffles,'" Birdie said, his face still flushed from Alek's samogon. "Meat raffles!"

As Cooper made her way to the door, the lights suddenly dimmed—everywhere she looked, jack-o'-lanterns leered at her, their crooked mouths illuminated by battery-powered votive candles. By the door, she had to force her way through a knot of Beakers dressed as approximations of Christ's apostles (bedsheets and beards). "Finally, the waiter leaves," one of them was saying. "And that's when she leans over and whispers, 'I don't believe in carbon dating.' So I said, 'I don't believe *we'll* be dating.'"

As soon as she stepped outside the gym trailer, the icy air wrapped itself around Cooper's midsection, and she realized she hadn't zipped up her parka. When she tried to join the zipper parts together, the world tilted and she felt certain she could feel the speedy rotation of the earth on its axis. She leaned against the tire of a forklift and steadied herself. Below her boots, though, the ground circulated like a frothy whirlpool. She raised her head and stared in wonder at the sunlight pouring into the long entrance tunnel; she knew it had to be well after midnight, but it was as bright as a Folgers morning. The thought of fresh air pulled her forward.

Halfway down the tunnel, she took a deep breath—the cold air rinsed through her lungs and the world stopped spinning for a moment. Then she saw the row of metal folding chairs blocking the entrance. A large handwritten sign had been taped to a chair. It read:

*NO, YOU CANNOT GET SOBER BY GOING OUTSIDE! RE-
TURN TO PARTY YOU DUMBSHIT.*

Cooper remembered her studio—it was technically under the
Dome. Maybe she'd be a better painter drunk than sober. They said
Hemingway was. Hemingway wasn't a painter, Cooper reminded herself. And who was "they"? *Hemingway wasn't a painter. Hemingway wasn't a painter.* She chanted this line out loud as she circled
back to the artists' annex. A couple making out in the cab of a Caterpillar stopped to stare at her.

When she arrived at the door to her studio, she tapped the postcard
of Foucault for good luck. Upon walking in, though, Cooper came
face-to-face with her *Mitten in Winter* canvas, and her heart sank. The
painting now struck her as revolting. She glanced over at Denise's desk;
a large cardboard box had been set atop a stele of textbooks. Cooper
knew it was filled with slightly less than twelve gross Blue Razberry
Blow Pops; the candy was circulating among the station population as
currency. (Someone had already been called into HR for simulating
fellatio on one of them during the sexual harassment training video.)
But Cooper wasn't looking for candy. She wanted the box cutter Denise had used to open the package. When she found it, she pushed the
blade up and watched as its geometry changed the farther it extruded.
She lay it flat against her forearm to test its sharpness and discovered
that a slight change in angle could draw blood.

She turned to her canvas and thrust the blade into it. It didn't rip
cleanly—the canvas resisted and the first cut frayed. It was only when
she retracted the blade a few degrees that it became an efficient tool
of destruction. Cooper ripped long, jagged lines through the mitten,
and the fabric peeled away from the gashes, dropping fiber at her
feet. Every sound—the thrumming bass from the party next door, the
vibration of the power plant, the creaking of the ice—faded, save her
own thumping heartbeat. Then, slowly, she realized someone was
pounding on her door. She froze, hoping whoever it was would walk
away, but the knocks continued, taking on a percussive quality.

"Who is it?" Cooper called.

"Herbert Hoover."

Cooper unlocked the door and opened it a crack to find Tucker's pockmarked face. He was holding two steaming cups of black coffee. As he handed her one through the gap in the door, his eyes traveled to Cooper's shredded canvas. "Ah, killing your darlings tonight, I see." Cooper opened the door wide and let him pass through into the room.

She sat down heavily on the stool and sipped the bitter coffee while Tucker took off his parka and hung it on the back of the door. He kicked the ribbons of canvas into a pile and removed the frame from the easel. In its place he put one of the blank canvases Cooper had stretched and prepped the week before in a fit of optimism. As he tidied the room, Cooper could feel the high-octane coffee sobering her up, sip by sip.

Finally, Tucker turned to her, his muscular arms hanging awkwardly at his sides.

"You didn't mention it on the application," he said.

"Mention what?"

"That you were a prodigy. *The New York Times Magazine* thing. Whether you had or had not saved the American Art World at age sixteen. Incidentally, according to my online research, it's still at risk."

Cooper's head swam. "That person no longer exists."

"Don't be dramatic."

She fixed Tucker with a glare. "Would you trade on fleeting success fifteen years after the fact?"

Tucker winced.

"I am not an attractive person but I am an honest one. You can ask me anything. I will tell you I am single and a homo. I relate to you because when I was your age, I was also someone who had hopes and dreams. I find as I grow older that I like to give the young people advice. And my golden rule is this: If you are going to be self-conscious, try to be funny about it or insightful. Otherwise, and I'm guilty of this, it is nothing but self-indulgence. And smile more—easier said than done if you have had Botox and a job like mine."

He picked up her sketchbook and held it out to her.

"What?" Cooper said.

"You're going to paint my portrait."

"I don't do portraits."

"Just pretend you're at a wedding. I can get some kale from the kitchen if it would help."

Cooper looked at Tucker's face, ruthlessly pitted by years of acne, and yet strangely smooth from all the chemical peels. Despite its imperfections, though, his face was a limpid image, perhaps the only truly clear image she'd seen since she'd arrived at this confusing place. She was starting from zero anyway, so she selected the sharpest pencil from her pencil cup and pulled her sketchpad onto her lap.

"Do I seem straight to you?" Tucker asked as Cooper began to work. "I mean—am I queeny?"

"Why are you asking me that?"

"I've been advised several times to 'be a man.' In corporate scenarios, mainly. It's made me question my masculinity."

"Well, whoever said that is an asshole."

"You didn't answer the question."

With the side of her hand, Cooper blended the outline she'd drawn of Tucker's head. "Why are you down here?" she asked. "Give me a one-liner."

"Smartass."

"I want to know."

Tucker looked down at the cup of coffee in his hands. "One day, I decided to embrace a new manifesto, and I say this without being glib or self-deceiving: always look for the positive in all situations. This credo is also self-serving, since in my case, anyway, negativity causes facial afflictions."

As she sketched, Cooper thought the eyes would be most difficult; the eyes always were. But Tucker's were uniquely challenging. The startlingly green irises disappeared beneath his upper and lower lids, but the eyes themselves had a slight downturn at the corners. Sometimes, there was a flatness to them, as if he had checked out. Other times, rarely, they looked almost manic. Still, as she worked, she felt a kind of peace, as if her brain were cooling off. All she had to do right now was draw a picture.

"Here's what I learned, Cooper. If your current environment is not conducive to a satisfying life, then you change your environment. That well-worn advice about your problems following you wherever you go? Patently false. I find I can live well at South Pole, which is good, because I want to live long enough to find out if John Cougar Mellencamp gets buried in a small town.

"Hey."

Cooper looked up from her sketchpad.

"You're working."

Cooper grinned. "I guess all I needed was coffee—and Herbert Hoover."

"I am but a humble servant," Tucker replied.

As she worked, looking from her paper to Tucker's gentle face and back again, Cooper was overcome by a feeling she hadn't touched since David was alive, since she'd stood on the edge of the woods and waited for him to return—the conviction that the world could become known if only you looked hard enough.

*

```
2003 November 01
06:23
To: cherrywaswaiting@hotmail.com
From: Billie.Gosling@janusbooks.com
RE: Changing the subject line


C.,
My Internet research tells me that you have to
take another psych eval in a couple months
because you're staying through the winter. My
guess: you have to fail the psych exam with flying
colors in order to stay. Would crazy people, if
collected together, actually form a unit of
sanity, their respective psychoses canceling one
another out? Dad drove up to Grand Casino Hinck-
ley last week. He and some other 3M retirees got
```

schooled at the poker table by a bunch of elderly Hmong men who literally had no tells. Afterwards, they went to see Styx at the Events
Center. OK, I have to go—there's a manuscript by
Carlos Castaneda's last lover waiting to be pho-
tocopied. Mom acquired it last year and now has
"buyer's remorse." Question: Did you ever wonder if Christ wore the cloak of the Illuminati?
Me either. But Mom assures me that a huge "sub-
sub-segment" of the New Age population wants an
answer to this burning question, and I live to
serve. Dad tells me the real money is in explorer lit anthologies. I didn't have the heart
to tell him the market for explorer lit died with
"talking machines" and lineament.
B.

✷

2003 November 03
11:08
To: Billie.Gosling@janusbooks.com
From: cherrywaswaiting@hotmail.com
Re: Changing the subject line

B.,
The Halloween party was a bust. I got drunk and
left early. In other news, I completed a triptych. Mittens. Actually, one is a glove. Which
means I can assign it meaning. It was originally
supposed to be all mittens, but I destroyed one
of the panels in a fit of Artistic Angst. Tucker,
the station manager, convinced me to "start fresh
or become a tragic figure," so I also started a
portrait. In other news, there's a guy. He spoke

to me at length about the dangers of politics intruding on science, but all I could think about when he was talking was how weird it was that an astrophysicist could be extremely physically attractive. That never happens. Why does that never happen?

C.

*

When Cooper woke the next morning, her left eye was encrusted with dried pus. Cursing, she hauled herself out of bed and felt around for her ECW gear. She was embarrassed to have to go see Doc Carla about her eyes again—it was her fault for not taking the entire course of antibiotics.

She pulled on her parka and, out of habit, thrust her hand into the depths of the pocket to touch the old Tylenol vial. To her horror, she realized the cap was loose—not detached, but nearly. She removed it from her pocket, and after checking to make sure nothing had escaped, pressed the top down firmly. She held it in her hand and stared at it through her good eye for a minute. What the hell was she doing, carrying this around like a talisman? And what was her plan for it anyway? She'd only ever gotten as far as getting it down here. She hadn't considered what she'd do with it once she arrived. She set the vial on her desk, next to the compass. She'd have to deal with it at some point, but not now.

As she walked down the entrance tunnel toward Hard Truth, she passed yet another guy holding a large pillow to his chest. He stopped short and looked hard at her. Suddenly, he began fumbling in his pocket for something. "Hey," he said, shoving another folded note at her. "Will you give this to Bozer?" In a place where Beakers were peering into the beginnings of the universe, how could a pool table be so important? Tucker had so far refused to intervene, hoping the situation would resolve itself with a frenzy of broken test tubes and bent

levels that would allow the hostile energy to dissipate without causing bodily harm. Denise, on the other hand, remained convinced that
only when one of the groups established dominance would equilibrium be restored. Cooper snatched the note from the pillow-clutcher's
hands without a word. *Bozer*, it read, *The cases of Schlitz will arrive
on the morning flight from McMurdo. We expect reciprocity.*

When Cooper got to the clinic, the door was locked. She knocked,
and heard Doc Carla bark, "Wait!" After a minute, the door opened
just slightly and Tucker's face appeared. He took one look at her,
then slammed it shut. Cooper could hear people talking on the other
side. Suddenly, the door flew open and Tucker pulled her in.

Toward the back of the room, Marcy huddled on a chair, a blanket pulled over her shoulders. "Oh . . . I can come back later," Cooper said.

"Stay," Marcy said. "Learn from my mistake." Tucker had his
head in his hands. The feeling in the room was familiar—Doc Carla's rugged bedside manner a little too forced, Tucker's silence, Marcy's resignation. This was the Trinity of the Unfortunate Event.
Cooper had been through its rigors before. It had been present during David's third 5150 hold—the day Cooper had run out of her
shift at Caribou Coffee when he'd been found on the roof of the
Weisman Art Museum, flapping his arms and walking in tight circles, unresponsive to the museum's security officers, and then, later,
the police. "That's what happens to everyone who sees the Damien
Hirst exhibit," Billie had said at Hennepin County Medical Center,
where they had traveled to meet the cops. Bill had laughed at this.
Cooper still couldn't forgive him for it. That was the only thing she
had left to forgive him for—the laugh. When Cooper had glimpsed
David as the orderlies walked him down the hall to the back ward,
he looked like a mannequin, his arms bent at weird angles, his legs
stiff. Cooper, still wearing her latte-stained barista's apron, had
watched in horror as he'd hobbled down the hall until he and the
orderlies stopped before a set of white doors. With a swipe of a key
card, the doors opened and swallowed him up.

Cooper was still standing there, frozen, when a nurse shoved something at her. "He was waving this around when the cops got to him. Most of 'em, if they're raving, they got a Bible. Never seen this one before." Cooper took the book without looking at it. She knew which one it was. Only when the nurse was halfway down the hall did Cooper dare to look: the ghostly image of three men—Edward Wilson, Birdie, and Cherry—silhouetted in the mouth of an ice cave.

Every night that week, Cooper stood outside in the backyard with Bill, staring at Hale-Bopp through the telescope. It was March, and for three months the comet had been a smeared fingerprint on the sky, but now, as it approached second magnitude, it grew brighter, it grew tails—one yellow, one blue. It had split at the root. Toward the end of the week, Cooper overheard Bill in the kitchen saying *care facility* and *Clozaril* and *menial jobs* and Dasha saying, "In some cultures, schizophrenia is a form of shamanism." Billie, uncharacteristically, remained mute for days. And the book that the orderlies had had to rip from David's hands, with its crenellated spine and its portrait of their men, remained Cooper's secret possession; the *Worst Journey in the World* was now the most important thing in the world.

Doc Carla gripped Cooper's upper arm roughly and propelled her to the sink. "I don't have time for this shit," she snapped. "You should've finished the whole course of antibiotics." She forced Cooper's eye open like it was a clam and squeezed eyedrops into the seam.

"I have such a good pee can," Marcy said thoughtfully. "I mean, it's the best one on the station. Epoxy-lined steel. Substantial volume. It even has a top. Damn. I take that pee can home with me between seasons. I use it when I'm off the ice." She looked over at Tucker. "Sometimes I become immobilized on a toilet. I don't know why." She shook her head. "No, you know why, Marce. You know. You know it's because you have no idea how to be outside of this place." She laughed bitterly. "You know what's funny is that about a week in, some guy in the machine shop, some asshole loaner from Mc-Murdo, was telling me how he didn't think women should be on the ice at all. He tells me that in the military there's this 'phenomenon' of female service members getting knocked up so they can be relieved of their duties. Says, 'It's an easy out, like a no-fault divorce.' And you know what? I agreed with him."

Marcy looked worn and tired, her wild hair pointing in all different directions. "Well, it's my own damn fault." She shook her head. "It's dumb to say it out loud, but, Christ, I thought I was too old to make a baby. I haven't bled in a year. I thought it was over for me. I guess I got lazy. If anyone else finds out, especially the guys, my long and storied career here will go down in flames."

"It's happened before, Marcy," Doc Carla said. "And it will happen again. Human nature."

"If it were some other chick, Doc, I'd be standing there with everyone else wishing she was dead. As it is, I'll be the only one wishing I was dead, but at least I'll be off the ice when everybody finds out."

"You're leaving?" Cooper asked.

"This shit's an automatic NPQ," Marcy replied.

"Couldn't you come back? Afterwards, I mean."

Marcy looked from Cooper to Tucker and Doc Carla and back again. "Afterwards?"

It took a minute, but Cooper's question finally penetrated, and Tucker pushed himself off the wall. "After your R-and-R trip. To Cheech."

"What the hell do I want in Cheech?"

"It'd be tough to find a provider in New Zealand who could help," Doc Carla said casually, "but let me work on that. Only if you're interested of course."

Marcy understood now. She leapt up and looked at Tucker. "You'd take me back? No NPQ?"

Tucker caught Doc Carla's eye. She nodded, and Tucker put his arm around Marcy's shoulder. Tears began leaking from Marcy's eyes, and she wiped them away angrily. "Then put me on the fucking manifest," she croaked. "Next plane out."

"You should still do your seasonal meeting, Marce," Tucker said.

"Yeah?"

"If you don't, there will be talk after you leave. Act like nothing's changed. Meet with the girls, and people will know you're coming back. You'll just have to come up with a reason why you're taking your first-ever R-and-R."

Marcy nodded. "I can come up with something." She turned to Cooper and thrust out her hand awkwardly. Cooper took it uncertainly and let Marcy pump it a few times. "Hey, man," she said. "Thanks."

"For what?"

"I was driving so hard, and so fast, I missed the exit ramp. You didn't. I owe you."

Cooper shrugged. "I guess there's a reason I'd rather be a truck driver than a florist."

*

A few weeks later, a rumor began circulating about a reporter from the *Miami Herald* on his way to the ice, having been thoroughly vetted and approved by the NSF based on his prior friendly coverage of the Program. NSF thought he was likely to produce a piece that would put a shine on things, and therefore safeguard the Program's budget from conservative freshman congressmen, all elected in the recent midterm elections, and whom Sal described as "Tracy Flicks with dicks."

"God, I hope he's Cuban or something," Bonnie said as a group of Polies, including Cooper, settled in to watch a VHS of the 1987 World Series. "I want to see someone other than Tucker who has skin with melanin, for chrissakes." She looked over at Dwight. "No offense, honey."

"None taken," he replied, arranging the tail of his cloak behind him as he took his place on the sofa. Cooper fell into one of the La-Z-Boys and watched as Tom Brunansky made his way to home plate. Pearl was knitting another pair of leg warmers for a woman in Dave's dance class, and had just frogged her last row of stitches when Sal and Alek stalked in toward the middle of the third inning. Alek was holding another bottle of samogon.

"Turn on game," he said.

"It *is* on, Einstein," Bonnie snapped.

Sal took a seat on the arm of Cooper's recliner and said nothing. Pearl caught Cooper's eye and gave her a quizzical look, but let the awkward silence go.

Finally, after an inning and three glasses of samogon, Alek stretched his mantis-like arms and sighed. "So," he said. "Information. I have some. Pavano agrees to debate."

"Who?" Pearl asked.

"The climate skeptic," Cooper said.

"Please don't call him a skeptic," Sal said. "All scientists are born skeptics. Pavano is not practicing science."

"Debates are against regulations," Dwight said. "If he's going to talk, he has to call it a lecture."

"This would be incorrect term to use," Alek said, as Kirby Puckett adjusted his cup on the edge of the batter's box. "Pavano doing presentation on climate change would be like lecture on baby dolls."

"I did a lecture on quilt making last month," Pearl offered.

"Yes, but you didn't advertise a lecture on quilt making that was really a lecture on Bigfoot," Sal said.

"I'd go to a lecture on Bigfoot in a hot second," Dwight said.

"I'd go to one on baby dolls," Pearl replied.

"Guys, you're not helping," Sal said.

Cooper knew from *Worst Journey* that there was a great tradition of lecturing at South Pole. On the Scott expedition, everyone had been expected to produce a discourse on a topic that could be considered a specialty. In addition to being a fine physician, Edward Wilson was a brilliant artist, and he lectured on sketching. Debenham on volcanoes. Titus on "horse management"—even after all the ponies had died, his ideas on equine caregiving were apparently still worth hearing. Eighty-plus years later, lectures continued to be popular events at Pole, except now the talks were about things like "Subglacial Lake Properties on Polar Plateaus" and "Crafting with Crown Royal Bags."

Alek informed everyone that Sri had approached Pavano at Midrats and asked if he'd consider a lecture on his ongoing research so the rest of the station could understand what was behind the "controversy." Pavano had refused to go into specifics, citing his sponsoring university's confidentiality policy, but had agreed to a big-picture presentation, with time for Q&A. This kind of setup could easily be turned into a debate if the moderator was game.

As Dwight and Pearl were discussing the ethics of this bait-and-switch, Sal suddenly sat up and said, "I have a new rule: if you refuse to accept the central tenets of science and insist on trying to destroy science education in our schools, then you don't get to benefit from it. Turn in your iPod, throw away your computer, and no more vaccines for you. Live by your principles. Also, no synthetic fibers. That's in the Bible."

"Well, I don't even believe in vaccines," Dwight said.

"You had to get them before you came down here," Pearl said.

"I know. I'm just saying I don't *believe* in them."

On the television, fifty thousand homer hankies waved in unison as Kirby Puckett chugged around the bases.

*

It wasn't until mid-December that Cooper next saw Frank Pavano, fumbling with his parka in front of the clinic.

"Hey," she said. He looked up at her, startled. "I've been looking for you. You've dropped off the face of the earth."

"I've been out at the Divide for much of the last month," Pavano said. He successfully zippered his parka. "I'm on my way to the shortwave carol sing. Do you want to carol?"

"You like caroling?"

"I find I'm in the Christmas spirit."

Together, they walked to Comms. This trading of carols was another Antarctic tradition, along with the Christmas tree the iron-workers built out of metal scraps, a collection of aluminum glistening in the twenty-four-hour sunlight. When Pavano and Cooper arrived, they found twelve other people in ridiculous hats crowded around a shortwave radio. This motley crew of Polies, named the Singing

Skuas, sang mangled hymns into the radio to the McMurdo station choir—the Mactown Madrigals—who had been rehearsing since September and were therefore tools. Both groups hoped their carols also reached some of the field camps scattered across the continent, including the ice-coring climate camp on the Divide.

A man wearing angel wings and a halo on a wire handed Cooper and Pavano sheet music, and the group began singing. "The Twelve Days of Christmas" to modified lyrics. "Twelve berms a-growing, eleven carps a-siding, ten waste pallets weighing, nine galley slaves cooking, eight smokers lounging, seven loaders loading, six congressional delegations, FIVE FLIGHTS A DAY! Four tourist herds, three expired condoms, two thermal gloves, and a glacier sparrow in an aluminum tree!" Cooper was surprised to learn that Pavano had a beautiful, crystalline singing voice.

"Are you coming to my presentation this weekend?" Pavano asked as they pulled on their parkas.

"I'll be there. Are you going to talk about your research?"

"I'm going to talk about my ice-core analysis and the so-called climate crisis. The scientific staff offered me an opportunity." He halted and analyzed her frowning face. Cooper was reminded of the smoking computer icon her Macintosh would display during an irreparable failure. "You seem skeptical," he continued haltingly. "Don't worry. I'm used to hostile audiences. Perhaps I can change one person's ideas about my work."

But Cooper thought his words came out like a series of deflated balloons. "You don't have to do it, you know."

"I want to," Pavano insisted. He looked at the ceiling and seemed to be searching for a thought. Finally, he said, "I'm clued in. I've seen the T-shirts, I've seen the drawings in the game room. I know what they say."

"So you know they're trying to trap you into a debate," Cooper said.

Pavano nodded. "In fact, I'm glad people care so much. Climate change will become a central policy point in the next few years." He pulled on his reflective snow goggles.

"Come on, let's go look at the Christmas tree."

They walked down the entrance tunnel in silence for a few minutes, the sounds of their breath coming through their face masks almost in sync. Outside, Cooper blinked against the sun, then looked across the ice through her goggles, toward the great invisible boundary that separated the six-month day from the six-month night. She thought about the catalog of polar art she'd studied on the flight from Los Angeles to Auckland—some of the painters had chosen to paint the explorers, but they made certain their work underscored the great hubris of these adventurers, not their heroism. The painter who'd depicted Shackleton's ship listing in the hard-packed blue ice had taken care to emphasize the continent's triumph over the "cartographic imperative," by making the men translucent. But, in fact, the vast majority of the work deemed resonant enough for inclusion in the catalog had been nearly featureless, experiments in light, shade, and variations of blue and white using acrylic and ink. Oil, it appeared, was passé, as was chiaroscuro: the place was too flat, too dead-seeming, for body.

"Let me ask you a question," Cooper said. She pointed at the horizon with her mitten. "What do you see when you look out there?" Pavano gazed at the smoking ice—a light wind had lifted the top layer of snow. "I'm supposed to see something profound," Cooper continued. "I'm supposed to translate this profound thing through art. But to me, it just looks like snow."

Pavano considered the plateau, his arms hanging slack by his sides. In his stillness, his profile seemed to Cooper to take on the aspect of bas-relief. He was Lincoln on the penny.

"Just as I thought. Impossible," she finally said, and began walking again. Pavano didn't walk with her.

"Wild horses," he said.

"Wild horses?"

"Yes, to me, the sastrugi over there looks like a herd of wild horses. Running into the wind, just about to leap into the high prairie grass. Frozen, naturally."

Cooper looked at Pavano, surprised. "I'd give that a B-plus."

"You're a tough grader."

"Should I grade on a curve?"

"Only if it's not the Keeling Curve," Pavano said, and chuckled. Cooper resolved to look up the Keeling Curve later. They walked a little farther in silence. "Have you been out to the ice-coring camp yet?" he asked. "Ah. No, of course you haven't. What I meant to say was that you should come out to the ice-coring camp. It's a slightly different icescape. It might jog something loose, perhaps provide some inspiration."

"That'd be nice, but they're not handing out Airbus rides to tourists like me."

Pavano seemed to think about this for a moment. "Then come as my research assistant." Cooper laughed, but Pavano continued. "I'm entitled to one, though they haven't exactly made it easy for me to find a willing volunteer. Currently, I've been assigned one of Sri's research techs, though she's made it clear that she has no interest in being part of my project."

"I don't think they'd allow me to get anywhere near the site. And anyway, I don't know how to do research."

"Isn't this research?"

"What, taking a walk?"

"Metaphorically, all research is a long walk."

"And all great literature is set in Madison County," Cooper replied.

They reached the Pole marker. Just a few feet downwind was the Christmas tree. At the very top, a snowflake of aluminum nuts sparkled in the sunlight.

"I find myself thinking of that tree as I fall asleep at night," Pavano said. "It's one of the most beautiful things I've ever seen."

Cooper regarded the tree for a moment, then Pavano. "If you can get me on the manifest, then I'll go," she said. Pavano turned his radiant face to Cooper and smiled. His smile plucked something deep inside her, and a feeling—familiar and yet out of reach—washed over her. Her heart began to pound and she silently recited, *The urge to jump reaffirms the urge to live.*

She left Pavano without saying goodbye and hurried toward the machine shop, praying to find it empty. It was deserted, and she slunk between a grader and a bulldozer. Her face was numb and her fingers felt only half there: she could bend them, but even bent they felt as if they were straight. She rubbed her mittens together, but this did little to distract her from the powerful feeling that had overcome her as she stood with Pavano. The urge to jump, she told herself again, affirms the urge to live. This had been drilled into her head by different therapists, who told Cooper the feeling was common, that it even had a name: high-place phenomenon. The desire to throw oneself off a building was the brain's misinterpretation of the instinctual safety signal. But at the time she had first encountered the impulse, it did not feel like a signal. It seemed very much like a voice. Cooper and David had just turned eighteen. He'd been strange for two years, but had not yet been accurately diagnosed. The first diagnoses—attention-deficit disorder, generalized anxiety, bipolar disorder—had initially inspired hope, but had faded like fireworks. This was the twilight time, before things became clear. They were, all of them, standing atop the Dahl Violin Shop in downtown Minneapolis—Billie, Dasha, and Bill in the background, Cooper and David standing at the edge of the roof. Below them, the Aquatennial parade streamed past. The Queen of Lakes sat perched atop her float like a doll.

The impulse to leap off the edge seized her without warning. It was a drumbeat, a song. Her mouth went dry, and it felt as if her limbs were filled with sand. It was the most powerful feeling she'd ever experienced. She gripped David's hand, and he looked over at her in surprise.

"What's wrong?" he asked.

"I kind of want to jump off," she whispered. "I don't know why."

David turned back to the parade. "Because he's telling you to," he replied coolly. "Don't worry—I hear him, too. There's only one way to make it stop, you know."

Goose bumps rose on her forearms. Here was confirmation. The faceless thief had taken him.

A snowmobile careened through the shed, sending a shower of snow crystals over Cooper's head, and she forced herself to begin walking back toward the station. Nothing about Pavano was like David. Nothing, except their loneliness.

*

Cooper spent the hours leading up to Pavano's presentation trying to realize in oils a sketch she'd made after her walk with him. The colors combined to create too-dark grays and Disney-like blues. Everything was contrasty and obvious. And, again, everything was flat. She turned to the portrait of Tucker she'd begun on Halloween. She'd sketched most of the painting out on the canvas already, and had gotten as far as the right eye with her oils. But now the eye was too big: it dominated the canvas grotesquely. After staring at it for a few moments, Cooper realized that of course it was supposed to be grotesque. She grabbed her eraser and briskly removed the rest of the sketch, including the weak attempt to capture Tucker's sharp facial structure, the unintentionally cubist lips, and the left eye that was not only smaller than the right, but also oddly shaped. In erasing, she felt she'd accomplished enough to soak her brushes in turpentine and head to the galley for Pavano's presentation.

When she got there, the room was packed with Polies—even the artists had shown up. Cooper took an empty seat next to Sal and Sri, whose messy thatch of black hair and tired eyes suggested he had clearly spent too many hours squinting at ice cores. Dwight, who was handling the moderating duties, tapped the microphone twice, then said, "Icebreaker to start." When everyone laughed, he looked around, puzzled.

"Dwight is deaf to puns," Sal whispered to Cooper.

Dwight cleared his throat, and tried again. "Tell us a personal thing about yourself, Pavano. And by the way," he added, looking out at the audience, "each questioner will have to do the same when he asks his question."

"I enjoy Rollerblading," Pavano said.

"What's the worst thing about Rollerblading, Pavano?" Floyd called from the back, where he sat with Marcy. "Telling your mom you're gay!" The room exploded with laughter.

"Careful, Floyd," Simon, the VIDS admin, warned.

Dwight pulled a scrap of paper from a small pile on the table in front of him. "Okay, first question goes to my lovely companion, Bonnie."

Bonnie got to her feet. "My name is Bonnie and a personal thing about myself would be that I am the head cook here and that I hate vegetarians because they make my life difficult. And then my question is: What's up with ice cores, and why is everyone mad?"

The audience tittered.

"I think I understand your question, Bonnie," Pavano said, with a voice that possessed all the treble and pitch of a window air conditioner. "You are interested in the controversy surrounding ice-core analysis."

"Sure," Bonnie said. Next to Cooper, Sri bounced in his chair, and Sal placed a hand on his friend's knee.

"Prevailing scientific opinion states that ice cores will reveal patterns of climate change," Pavano continued, "even evidence of volcanic eruptions. However—"

"Look, most of us understand basic ice-core analytics, right?" Sri burst out, wrenching around in his seat to look at everyone in the audience.

"Here we go," Sal murmured.

"Drill down a million feet, take out an ice core, look at the rings, analyze. Summers get warm, so the ice melts and you get clear layers. Winters, no melt, you get snow layers, a milky layer, and you look at the air bubbles trapped in the layers. People who have dedicated their lives to analyzing these cores know what they are looking at; they know how to interpret the data."

Pavano cleared his throat. "What Dr. Niswathin is saying is that it is widely assumed—and I use the word *assumed* intentionally—that each ring pair, the clear ring and the milky ring taken together, account for a single year: the clear ring accumulates during the summer season and the milky ring appears at the conclusion of a winter season. That's how you get estimates of a hundred thirty-five thousand years of ice data. But on what evidence do we base our assumption that each pair represents a year?"

"It's rather obvious," Sri said.

"That is the fallback position of the researcher with bad data," Pavano replied with a smoothness that Cooper hadn't thought possible. "I'm not here to debate geology, of course, but if the earth is billions of years old," he continued, "why isn't there more ice at the North and South Poles? Is the earth, as you posit, billions of years old, or is there any chance the polar ice cores show us that other models might have some validity? If they do, what does that say about your team's climate-change research?"

One of the climatologists on Sri's team raised her hand. "Before this, you were a vocal proponent of intelligent design. Intelligent design is not a scientifically accepted theory. You don't even believe in the validity of radiometric dating."

"I am often surprised by the parochialism of mainstream science," Pavano replied.

Sal leaned forward in his seat. "And I'm surprised that the oil industry landed a bought scientist at a federal research facility."

"Are you suggesting that I manipulate my conclusions to align with the financial interests of my funding source?"

"I'm saying that you and whoever signs your checks are making a cottage industry out of global warming denial because the money's good."

"If I were willing to alter my views to ingratiate myself with a funding source, I'd be an extremely vocal proponent of so-called global warming, seeing as most of the grant money seems to go to researchers who take man-made causation as fact. As I've argued with you before, there is nothing unscientific about looking for other explanations. But let's step into your line of expertise: the origins of the universe."

For a moment, the men shared a look that betrayed some level of intimacy, and everyone in the galley caught it.

"Sounds like a desperate ploy to distract from your poor science, but go ahead," Sal said.

"Time and time again, scientists like you have failed to provide any meaningful explanation of how the universe began. You can tell us what it looked like; you can tell us how it was done. You can't tell us why."

"Why? This is all about god?" Sri exclaimed. "Of course! It's what you do. I mean, look at your paper on the structural dynamic stability of Noah's ark. I read that." He looked over at Sal. "We all did."

For the first time that evening, Pavano looked flustered. "That was an early publication, and one that I regret. And I've said so in print. I will add, just for interest's sake, that some models of ice cores do suggest significant quantities of snow accumulated immediately after the Flood, that perhaps as much as ninety-five percent of the ice near the Poles could have accrued in the first five hundred years or so after the Flood—"

The room fell quiet, as if Pavano's words had gone beyond the pale and could never be taken back. Cooper and the other nonscientists looked at one another, confused.

"Holy shit," Pearl whispered. "I think he just said Noah's flood is a scientific fact."

"Sri, you're wrong," Sal said. "This isn't about god. This is about money. Frank Luntz is why Pavano is going to become a very rich man."

"Frank Luntz?" Bonnie asked. "Sounds like a hot dog company."

"Frank Luntz advises the Bush administration about various policy decisions. Last year somebody got hold of a memo he'd written about how to handle what he called this 'global warming problem.' Luntz and everyone else in the White House knows global warming is real, that it's man-made. Luntz told them the scientific debate is closing against them, but isn't fully closed—that there's just enough time to keep the public uncertain, to keep it thinking that there's no consensus in the scientific community. No big policy changes need to be made if the public thinks there's widespread disagreement. Pavano enters stage right."

Pavano shuffled behind the podium—his face had drained of color.

"So you're saying, what?" Pearl asked, her brows furrowed. "That he doesn't actually believe what he's saying? That he's gonna make stuff up while he's down here?"

"To believe in climate change—" Pavano tried, but Sal interrupted him.

"See, look at his language. He's talking about Santa Claus, the Easter Bunny. Scientists don't believe in things. They either know things or they don't."

Cooper could tell that Sal had just walked into a trap, because Pavano suddenly seemed very focused. "Just like those who once promoted the Big Bang as fact—as the gospel of how the universe began—suddenly change their minds? Tell me if this sounds familiar, Dr. Brennan: 'Humanity's deepest desire for knowledge is justification enough for our continuing quest.'"

"Don't take Hawking's words in vain," Sal said.

"So Stephen Hawking's your prophet, and yet you desecrate what many others find sacred."

"And now we've fallen down the nerd-hole," Bonnie groaned behind Cooper. "In like, a minute, they're gonna start talking Elvish."

"He's putting up a good fight, though," Pearl murmured over her shoulder.

"You guys have gone way off the rails," Dwight said, exasperated. "Can we get back to Bonnie's question about ice cores?"

"Yes, tell us what research you're trying to thwart while you're down here," Sal said.

"Unlike other grantees on the ice this season, I'm not trying to thwart anyone's research," Pavano said. "Alarmists are finding it difficult to explain away the fact that Antarctica's sea ice is at record levels. It's not melting. To the contrary, it's quite robust."

"The record amount is only three-point-six percent over the 1981 to 2002 mean," Sri cried. "I mean, this year the edge of the ice extends out only thirty-five kilometers farther than it does in an average year. It's actually getting thinner."

"In climate science, it seems to me, anything is possible," Pavano said.

"Could Antarctica melt?" Pearl asked. Cooper noticed a couple research techs roll their eyes.

Pavano chuckled. "I think the scientists in this room would agree that even if man-made climate change was real, it would take thousands of years for it to grow warm enough for the Antarctic ice shelf to melt. In fact, that kind of catastrophic ice melt would require heat of apocalyptic proportions. But because I dispute the assumption that the earth is warming, it's nothing I worry about."

"So what you're saying," Pearl replied, "is that the earth is not warming up like everyone says, that global warming isn't real?"

"What I'm saying is that very little research has ever been funded to look for natural mechanisms for climate change. It has simply been assumed, by the scientific community, that global warming is man-made."

"I would actually prefer that the earth was not warming," Pearl said.

"It may not be," Pavano said.

"That makes me feel better."

"No, Pearl," Sri shouted, "don't go over to the Dark Side!" This resulted in a chorus of protestation. Amid the shouts, Cooper noticed Sal quietly stand up and walk out of the galley.

That night Pavano pinned to the large bulletin board in the galley an abstract from a just-published paper by Willie Soon from the journal *Climate Research*, which claimed "the twentieth century is probably not the warmest nor a uniquely extreme climatic period of the last millennium." By the next morning, it was gone, and in its place was a hand-drawn flyer: *Breaking News Update: Climate Change Jesus super-excited about new developments, says "you're getting warmer!"* Next to this was a muscle-bound superhero Jesus, with a bubble coming from his mouth containing what one of the Beakers later told Cooper was the Schrödinger equation. Climate Change Jesus was set upside down, coring ice with his crown of thorns.

PRODUCTION COOK: 5:00am–3:00pm and 4:30pm–10:00pm

PREPARES HOT BREAKFAST: including pastries, fills juice machine
and breadbox

PREPARES LUNCH. Soup Daily
Assists with dinner.

Shops for own menu items on regular basis and general kitchen use
items every other week on rotating basis with Head Cook (Bonnie)

Menu will be provided. Both cooks are accountable for the food
and adhering to the APPROVED menu. Special occasions/holidays
are excepted from the menu.

Food is to be used from Berm B first. Call in items from Berm
A only after ensuring they are not available from Berm B. Food
rotation is very important to its quality.

COOKBOOK KEY
EBF: Enchanted Broccoli Forest
MW: Moosewood
MWC: Moosewood Cooks for a Crowd
SL: Still Life with Menu
SP: South Pole 3–Ring Binder

BASIC ROTATIONS
Pasta 2 x week
Mexican 1 x week
Italian 1 x week
Seafood 1 x week
Alt every other cycle: Italian chicken fingers with patty, Tuna
Melt with Seafood Croissant

enchanted broccoli forest

There were many ways to make things disappear at South Pole Station. After all, there were twenty-three different categories of waste. "Dormitory biological waste"—bloody bandages, used tampons, snot soaked Kleenex—was stored in fifty-five-gallon open-top drums. Galley food waste—like onionskins, uneaten oatmeal, and trimmed fat—was packaged in Tri-Walls lined with three layers of polyethylene gusseted bags. But the category that Pearl found most relevant to her purposes was the "domestic combustibles," also known as the "burnables." This category included paper towels, cigarette butts, food wrappers—and cookbooks that had been carefully dismantled, page by page.

Enchanted Broccoli Forest was the first to go.

Still Life with Menu was the second.

Pearl wasn't sure if *Still Life* would be missed, but she knew *Enchanted Broccoli Forest* would. It was a go-to. Vegetarians sometimes requested *EBF*-specific dishes. But a week had passed, and still Bonnie said nothing about the missing cookbooks. Pearl couldn't have known that Bonnie would lose the kitchen over the inedible Carrot-Mushroom Loaf from *Moosewood Cooks for a Crowd*. She only knew Bonnie would lose the kitchen eventually. It was why Pearl had agreed to take the job in the first place.

No one knew that Pearl had been waiting for a Carrot-Mushroom Loaf moment since she landed at South Pole in late September. She'd been hired as production cook, the junior position to Bonnie's head cook. Pearl had applied for the top position, of course; she hadn't spent ten miserable years in various eateries and ship's galleys to become second fiddle in an institutional kitchen. (Nor did she go to Antarctica to become Alice Waters, but you had to pay the bills and government work paid well, especially when room and board was free).

But Bonnie was a lifer; and after a certain number of years on the ice, lifers received the privilege of turning jobs down rather than having to reapply for them. Bonnie would never turn down a job at Pole, and it took only a couple of days on the ice for Pearl to understand that the woman would not be easily overthrown. She had allies. Those allies were other lifers, and they'd lost their taste for edible food some years earlier. Calling Bonnie to account for the state of the food at Pole wasn't going to be an effective strategy. The operation would have to be subtler than that, requiring the actions of a person exhibiting the traits of monomania. Not all of the traits, of course—that kind of psychological profile would be peremptorily red-flagged by the VIDS team. Just a few of them.

"Can you focus obsessively on a single thing?" Tucker had asked Pearl back in Denver after the psych exam. "Can you be insane when it comes to this single thing—improving the food—and be rational about everything else?"

"What do my results say?"

"That's why you're in my office."

"Then you already know the answer."

Pearl had arrived at Pole in the midst of an overhaul—a new station was being built just hundreds of yards from the current one. The National Science Foundation had been soliciting and rejecting plans for a new geodesic dome for years. Six months before Pearl came to Pole, they'd finally approved a plan. It was a matter of some irony that the firm that had won the design contract was based in Honolulu.

One of the modules under construction would house the new galley with what Tucker had promised Pearl would be state-of-the-art appliances, stainless-steel prep tables, and more capacity—however, it wouldn't open until next season. The kitchen in which she'd be working this season—the old kitchen—would present challenges. The galley on the Icelandic herring boat she'd crewed the summer after high school had been better equipped.

September 30, 2003

Perhaps the cramped conditions are what killed Bonnie's creativity. Or maybe it's the six-packs she puts away at the Smoke Bar every night. We'll see. There's a galley staff meeting tonight to go over the season's menu. I'll observe and say nothing.

By the time Pearl was aproned up and scrubbing her nails for the first meal of the season, she had only seen Bonnie a couple of times since that trust building exercise back in Denver. Bonnie had come into training hot. She was pissed. Pissed that she'd had to go through fire school again, and even more pissed that she'd have to deal with a Fingy production cook. Her previous production cook had left for the cruise ship circuit, and Pearl sensed that the parting had not been amicable. The trust-building exercise had done little to improve Bonnie's outlook on the season to come. Granted, the "trust facilitator" contracted by VIDS had made a poor choice when he'd picked the "eye contact with touch" exercise. Pearl and Bonnie stood across from one another in the meadow adjacent to the fire school, eyes locked, hands clasped. But Pearl saw the pride in Bonnie's angry eyes. Pride was easily exploited.

March 12, 2003, at training

Met her today. Big woman—my height but weighing in at about two bills. Wouldn't tell me anything about what to expect, says all "Fingys" have to fend for themselves. Wouldn't

*tell me what Fingy means either. She hates my undercut, said
it was "punk, fifteen years late." I'm trying to be friendly, but
she's not having it.*

The first days in the galley were like any of the first days Pearl
had spent in a new kitchen, be it on land or at sea—getting used to
her surroundings, examining the supply lists, memorizing her duties, and getting to know her co-workers. Kit, a skinny guy with
lank brown hair pulled back in a ponytail, was the main DA—the
dining assistant who was responsible for everything from cleaning
tables and filling the milk machine to stocking the napkin dispens-
ers. As head cook, it was Bonnie's job to write up the menus and
manage all kitchen operations.

"Bonnie is a loner by nature," Tucker told Pearl the first week in.
"Being at Pole goes against every fiber of her being."

"I thought Pole was like the loner's Disney World."

Tucker shook his head. "You have to at least possess the capacity
to enjoy the company of other loners."

"Then why is she there?"

"Dwight, our comms tech. They met at a Sheraton in New Or-
leans. He was the IT guy, she was buffet cook."

"She followed a guy down here?"

"It's not all that uncommon. Like two negative electrons, two
misanthropes can bind together with the force of—"

"Negative electrons repel each other," Pearl said.

Tucker paused. "Huh. Well, that explains why Sal Brennan has
banned me from the Dark Sector."

Her days began with a 4:30 a.m. alarm. The sun shone as brightly
then as it did at noon, which made getting up fairly easy. She'd make
her way from her room in the elevated dormitory under the Dome
(the galley staff received superior accommodations) to the kitchen,
where she'd prepare hot breakfast for 105 people and put her proofed
pastry and bread dough in the oven.

At first, Pearl adhered slavishly to Bonnie's menu. Huge warming
trays filled with bright yellow scrambled eggs, vats of gluey oatmeal,

white and wheat bread. The Polies seemed unperturbed by the monotony, although Pearl did notice that those who took oatmeal loaded their bowls with raisins, brown sugar, and nuts, as if trying to bury it under an avalanche of condiments. One guy even used salsa.

October 15, 2003

Bonnie says it is acceptable to bake in quantity and freeze items after they have been double-wrapped and dated. This is bullshit. She says "acceptable" but she means "required." I don't freeze my pastries. It does a disservice to me, to the pastries, and to anyone who tries to choke them down. Plus, the freezers smell like fish. Trying to figure out a non-confrontational way to handle this—too early in the season for a fight over breakfast foods. I plan on bringing up the oatmeal issue soon, though. It's pretty low-stakes. A little seasoning, cinnamon and nutmeg, maybe, or even a couple teaspoons of vanilla or almond extract—hell, even a dash of salsa—could go a long way.

Between meals, Pearl had to make the rounds of the storage units, recording temps and noting stock levels. The units outside of the galley trailer, in dark corners of the Dome, were the worst—the air was as cold there as it was outside. The giant freezer where they stored the meat products actually had to be heated. As she scanned the shelves, Pearl marveled at the quantities required for every meal. Thirty pounds of orange roughy for fish and chips. Nothing less than twenty-eight pounds of ground beef for Texas Tamale Pie. Grilled Reuben called for twenty pounds of corned beef, and the veggie Reuben needed five pounds of tempeh. Pearl glanced down at the monthly menus on the clipboard—it was like an endless repetition of the same twelve meals. She knew she could do better than polenta pie and fucking tofu nut balls.

Pearl thought the station greenhouse was a nice touch, though. It was a steaming shoe box set atop the stairs on the annex berthing building. When Pearl opened the door, she had to break about fifty pounds of suction force, but once she did, she was treated to the smell of soil and green things, smells that Pearl had already forgotten—earth, compost, ripe melon.

October 19, 2003
I told Kit I'd take over greenhouse duty and he looked like he wanted to kiss me. The greenhouse will be the key to my success. That and getting rid of the cookbooks.

Personas, not personalities, were important at Pole, so Pearl settled on being a flaxen-haired scrub with a penchant for pink bandannas and self-deprecating jokes. Her requisite edge came from her undercut, which she kept up using a pink Bic twice a week, an operation that required two mirrors and an hour of her precious time. She was a small woman with what Sal had called the "face of a Pilgrim." The scar above her right eyebrow—courtesy of a two-hook herring rig—suggested the correct amount of toughness and allowed her to affect kindness, solicitude, even motherliness, without losing credibility. She took up knitting again, and her wares became quite popular. She knit during Movie Night, she knit at the Smoke Bar, she knit during the station lectures. The station was clearly in need of a Goody Two-Shoes. Pearl could be that Goody Two-Shoes. She could be whatever she wanted.

Meanwhile, she continued her quest to run the kitchen, which included feigning respect for the VIDS bureaucracy. But it wasn't until the two Swedes came through the lunch line that Pearl realized the bureaucracy could help speed Bonnie's exit. As soon as the Swedes showed up in the galley, Simon had had his eye on them.

"I'm sorry, but station rules prohibit us from serving you meals paid for by American taxpayers," Simon told the Swedes. "If you have foodstuffs you'd like to cook in our kitchen, you are by all means welcome to do so after the kitchen has closed."

"It's okay, Simon," Pearl said, "I have no problem giving them some food."

"That's very kind, Pearl, but that's against protocol."

"I'll give them my meal—they can split it."

"Again, that's kind and selfless, but simply not possible."

The Swedes smiled at her and set their trays down. Pearl had turned away in time to catch Bonnie searching the bookshelves for *Enchanted Broccoli Forest*. She watched as Bonnie's fingers danced from spine to spine and back again.

Soon, lunch drew to a close, which meant it was time to stack the dirty trays on a dolly. Cooper approached Pearl with her tray, and asked about the Swedes. She wanted to ferry some food out to them. It took Pearl a minute to see the possibilities of such an operation— it wasn't until Cooper mentioned the expired ramen that it hit her. Pearl could facilitate this breach of "protocol," but as head of the kitchen, Bonnie would get the blame.

"Let me get the okay from Bonnie on this," Pearl told Cooper. She walked to the back of the galley, past Kit, who was going through boxes, looking for the missing cookbooks, all the way to the back door. She stood there for a respectable amount of time, then returned to the caf line, where Cooper stood waiting.

"She says it's okay," Pearl said.

*

October 28, 2003

Bonnie got called in by HR yesterday. They said she'd violated protocols by authorizing the delivery of station food to the Swedes camping out on the plateau. She denied it, of course, blamed it all on Cooper. Cooper won't talk, thinks she's protecting me. VIDS can't do anything about her—she's NSF— so they wrote Bonnie up. Bonnie told Kit and me that it was the first violation on her record, ever. Still hasn't mentioned the missing cookbooks to me, though. I plan on dissembling the three-ring binder (SP) tonight. There's nothing of value in it anyway. I volunteered to take the Midrats shift from Bonnie.

She seemed surprised and actually thanked me. She told me the
swing shift gets harder on her as she gets older.

One day, Bonnie mentioned that Marcy had called an all-women's
meeting in the library.

"What's it for?" Pearl asked, as she prepped for lunch.

"Seasonal Staking of Claims," Bonnie replied, whipping a vat of
minestrone into a ruby froth. Her greasy dark hair had escaped from
her hairnet and was plastered to her forehead.

"What claims are we staking?" Pearl asked.

"It's how we parse out who's hooked up, who isn't, and who's fair
game. It gets hairy when somebody steals someone else's man 'cause
she didn't know there was a claim."

Pearl didn't have a man, unless you counted the British ex-pat,
Birdie. He'd been making eyes at her since he arrived. There was
nothing wrong with the guy—he was a little soppy, but his accent
made him rather endearing. In fact, he was almost lovable, in a
goofy kind of way. Unfortunately, he wasn't much of a looker—
balding, with beady eyes and ruddy cheeks—but that didn't matter.
Even if they struck up a friendship, they likely wouldn't be swapping
bodily fluids. Pearl had been celibate for five years on purpose. She
felt that she'd reached the Bodhi Tree of sexual enlightenment, and
this stint at Pole might make her a Buddha. It wasn't that she was
asexual—there had just been too many disappointments for it to
be a coincidence. She felt misled about sex. *They must not be*
doing it right, she'd thought at first. Then, *You must not be doing*
it right. Then, *Maybe you're gay.*

She'd given her virginity to a seasonal cannery worker in Cordova, Alaska, the summer between her sophomore and junior years
of high school. Without her foster parents' permission, she had
followed a school friend from Portland up to Alaska to crew on a
herring fishery. The friend hooked up with a deckhand, which, in
hindsight, had been a far better bet. Pearl noticed too late in the
game that the cannery worker had a womanish nose that quivered,

and a tiny, timid mouth. When he brought her back to his rented rooms on the harbor, he told her he was an art student at University of Alaska. Later, she realized that this disclosure should have prompted a hasty exit, but she was sixteen and not well versed in the portents of bad decisions. They stood around in his rooms awkwardly, looking at his canvases. Each was a rendering of SpongeBob SquarePants engaged in lewd acts. "A concept run amok," he told Pearl. When they finally got into bed, he went limp and would not touch her anywhere below her waist.

Back home in Portland a few years later, Pearl ran into a baseball player from high school she'd had a crush on (he was playing for Lewis & Clark College now) and after an hour-long conversation at Starbucks, he brought her back to his off-campus apartment, where they had sex: the first time to get it over with, and the second time because maybe it would be better. The sex felt to Pearl like a battering ram trying to breach a cervix. How funny, she thought as he grunted behind her, that all the electricity between them in high school—the furtive glances, the long stares—translated into this National Geographic special on the mating rituals of bonobos.

When a psychologist at VIDS headquarters had warned Pearl not to get pregnant—"selfish and avoidable," he'd said—Pearl had announced her celibacy with pride.

The psychologist had just laughed at her. "Yeah, I saw that on your questionnaire. There's condoms aplenty down there, but just do me a favor and pack birth control. A pregnancy puts everyone at the station at risk," he said.

When Pearl ventured to ask how a pregnant woman put the station at risk, the guy smiled and leaned forward in his chair, as if recounting the details of an NFL game. "Spontaneous abortion. Massive blood loss. Early labor. Hypertension. You want the menu? 'Cause there's more."

"I don't need the menu," Pearl replied. "I was just curious."

"Well, now you know."

"Do you offer this menu to your male applicants?" Pearl asked.

The psychologist laughed again. "When men develop the ability to get pregnant I'll consider it."

*

Marcy's meeting took place on the fourth floor of Skylab, an orange tower connected to the Dome by an underground tunnel. It housed laboratories, a music rehearsal space, and Bozer's pool table. When Pearl arrived with Bonnie, most of the other women were already sprawled on the Naugahyde sofa. Pearl was unable to tear her eyes away from the sofa—its very presence meant that a Naugahyde couch had been approved on a cargo list, loaded onto a C-17, and ferried down to South Pole. Surely, such things could not be possible, she thought.

"You okay, Pearlie?" Marcy asked, tapping the chair next to her. Marcy's appearance was even more disturbing than the sofa's—her face was drawn, her eyes sunken into her face, limned by purple shadows. Her unexpected R-and-R had sparked rumors of a cancer diagnosis.

As if reading Pearl's thoughts, Marcy yawned. "Shit, I'm tired. Bozer has us pulling double shifts three times a week." Pearl quietly took a seat.

"Let's lay it all out on the line tonight, girls," Marcy said once everyone was seated. "Time to stake claims."

"Aren't some of you already in relationships?" Cooper asked, rubbing her swollen eye with a ball of Kleenex.

"Honey, I'm not trying to play a game of Clue here," Marcy said. "I don't want to end up fucking Colonel Mustard in the Library, only to find out that Mrs. Peacock blew him in the Ballroom. Look—most of you know I do this every year. There's nine of us and about a million of them. It's easier if we know the score before we get too far into this magical mystery tour."

"Obviously, Dwight's off-limits," Pearl said, glancing over at Bonnie.

"Obviously," Marcy said. "What about Floyd?" When no one replied, Marcy nodded. "Yeah, poor Floyd."

"Sri would be cute with a different chin," Cooper offered.

"Sri is married," his lab tech replied sadly. After a pause, she added: "I like his chin."

Someone knocked on the door.

"Who is it?" Marcy barked.

"Denise."

"Enter."

Denise pushed the door open with her shoulder. "Sorry, everyone. I lost track of time." As Denise struggled out of her parka, Bonnie leaned over to Pearl. "When she's in the room I feel like a lab rat," she whispered.

Denise heard this and held her hands open, as if to show Bonnie she wasn't carrying recording equipment or a gun. "I'm just here as a Pole female. Is that okay?" Bonnie grunted and crossed her arms.

"Back to the matter at hand," Marcy said. "What about the men artists?"

Pearl felt her stomach turn over.

"The historical novelist is hooking up with the interpretive dancer," Cooper said. "And the literary novelist has a thing going with one of the cryo techs. That leaves Birdie."

"That the one with the birthmark on his face?" Marcy asked.

"No, that's the historical novelist. Birdie's the one who's constantly mooning over Pearl," Cooper said.

All of the women turned to look at Pearl, and her face burned with embarrassment. So others had noticed his attentions. She tried to gauge the women's interest in him without asking outright. No one had leapt up at the mention of his name. And he seemed harmless, didn't seem the type to wheedle or plead for sex. Pearl imagined him growing old waiting for her to take his hand—even his name suggested the gentle flutter of wings. And anyway, the Polies had advised her to ally herself with a companion for the duration; as a woman, she would have her pick, so she picked Birdie because he looked like a man who could be strung along. Pearl remained silent, but knew her raging blush made it obvious.

"Okay, Birdie's taken," Marcy said. She nodded at Denise. "Bozer's spoken for. Floyd, nobody wants, and besides, he has that mail-order bride out of Novosibirsk. Sri's got a chin problem—also, married. Everyone else is fair game, right?"

As Marcy looked around at the women, Pearl could see deep sadness etched on her face. She could see the other women saw it, too, but they said nothing. "That's it, right?"

"What about Sal?" Cooper said quietly.

Marcy smiled for the first time since she'd walked into Skylab. "Sal's all yours, honey," she said. Pearl was relieved to see she wasn't the only one whose cheeks were on fire.

*

Running Midrats gave Pearl a distinct advantage, though it was not without its drawbacks. On the plus side, there were fewer mouths to feed, so Pearl could spend more time on the food. The con was that the Midrats crew was made up of staunch Bonnie allies—grizzled old hands who'd formed an ironclad bond over this midnight meal. It took a few weeks before their irritation over the change in personnel faded.

Pearl hewed close to the set Midrats menu at first—irregularities raised eyebrows at Pole. Routine was vitally important to the operation of the station and to the minds of the people working there, and curveballs were not appreciated. So Pearl started by cooking exactly what was on the menu. *Sloppy Joes on a Bun (Tempeh Joes on a Bun). Honey Dipt Chix with Mashed Potatoes, Gravy (Pilaf). Texas Tamale Pie (Veg. Tamale Pie). Turkey Club Sandwich w/Pasta Salad (Szechuan Rollups w/Tempeh).*

Once the Midrats meal had been served, Pearl would hunch over her notebook, trying to meld flavors in her mind, to imagine what dishes might revive the long-dead taste buds of the veterans without creating resentment. She identified the foodstuffs that were lowest on the totem pole: dates, Melba toast, lentils, capers, tempeh.

November 4, 2003

 Found out Bonnie has hated the plantains we get in bulk ever since she tried a Sweet Potato and Roasted Plantain gratin (Still Life p. 123) to bad reviews. She told me she tried to get the plantains off the shipment list but VIDS says they're a cheap source of potassium and don't get mushy as quickly as bananas do. Typically she sautés them in butter and brown sugar once a week and serves them as a breakfast side. I already have three potential dishes in mind, but since I'm charged with the daily soups, I'm going with a plantain sopa. Tucker has warned me about the "parochial tastes" of Polies, but I think he's only talking about the repeaters. The fresher Beakers and support staff still have taste-memories of halfway decent food. Won't take much to reawaken that.

When Bonnie had been running Midrats, she lumbered in a half hour before service, pulled the prepped ingredients from the fridge, and started cooking. Pearl rarely left the kitchen after dinner service now. She took her time with the meals, and the meals on the menu not only tasted better, they also looked better. The presentation was nothing out of the ordinary—fussiness would have resulted in ridicule. But it was just different enough to create a sense of beauty that was almost invisible.

She also started pickling vegetables. This activity was an acceptable use of the station's vinegar stores because the supply of fresh produce would run out about a month after the station closed for the winter. Pearl pickled everything from carrots to the tiny gem-like chili peppers grown in the greenhouse. To be festive, she tied ribbons around the jars and displayed them near the condiment tray. One night, she canned an entire shipment of damaged peaches, and set one jar aside for Birdie. When she handed it to him, he was so happy, he kissed her. To Pearl's surprise, it wasn't horrible.

For the first meal swap, Pearl decided to start with the vegetarian meals, since they'd likely arouse less attention and because the vegetarians tended to have a more forgiving palate. The scheduled Lentil-Walnut Surprise (p. 147, *MW*) was bypassed in favor of a black-pepper-glazed tempeh, served with sherry-braised leeks, fried capers, and hoppin' John. The sherry was cooking sherry a year past its expiration date and the hoppin' John was made from a five-year-old bag of dried black-eyed peas that Pearl found in the pantry. Still, Pearl thought it stellar. No one at Midrats said a word.

A week before Thanksgiving, Pearl served her Plantain Sopa—a cream-based soup made from ripe plantains—and her pickled chili peppers. She paired it with a buckwheat flatbread. This time, three people came up for seconds, including a non-veggie maintenance specialist.

November 15, 2003

Bonnie came into the kitchen this morning furious. Someone told her about the plantain soup. I couldn't ask if the review was good or bad because she was like the Tasmanian Devil. She said all menu changes had to be approved by VIDS, and went on and on about the importance of proper authorization. I spoke to Tucker about it this afternoon, and he hemmed and hawed for a while, but then said he'd make some calls. Tonight, right in the middle of dinner prep, he came in and told Bonnie that VIDS had authorized me to make any menu changes I wanted during Midrats. She walked out, leaving Kit and me to deal with the rest of dinner service.

Word quickly spread that Midrats meal was by far the best meal served at Pole. The ranks of midnight diners swelled, and the graveyard crew complained that they couldn't get a table. For them it wasn't about the food; it was about the company. For the new arrivals, it was the opposite. Pearl's changes to the Midrats menu had now extended beyond the vegetarian option and into the main entrées. One night she took the leftover Cornish game hens from the previous year's food stock and broiled individual birds with a glaze made from her own stash of homemade sour cherries. The desserts were beyond anything anyone had seen at Pole before: buttermilk panna cotta (in which Pearl could hide expiring milk—a perpetual problem), lemon chiboust, pumpkin tiramisu. Meringues and souf-flés were out of the question due to the elevation, but Pearl could live without them, and the Polies didn't know what they were missing.

Thanksgiving was turkey three ways—smoked, fried, and roasted—with Kit smoking seven birds outside, on the far side of the Crevasse of Death. "Fifty fucking below, ladies," Kit reminded Bonnie and Pearl. "I think that's enough selflessness for a day off."

"Dream on, honey," Bonnie replied, in a decent mood for the first time in weeks. But then Pearl felt a piece of her die as she watched Bonnie spoon jellied cranberries out of aluminum cans; the sound they made as they plopped, can-shaped, into the serving dishes was as gross as an overdubbed movie kiss.

Yet Bonnie surprised Pearl with other culinary efforts. From out of nowhere, she produced a jar of fermenting kombucha. She also delighted everyone with an enormous batch of real mashed potatoes—Bonnie had pulled some strings to get a crate of russets from McMurdo. For the holiday meal, Pearl had been relegated to pastry chef, and she did well: pumpkin and pecan pies, of course, but also a pear galette and 105 servings of pot de crème.

As Pearl looked out at the darkened galley, at the Polies stuffing their faces, at the paper turkeys and Pilgrims hanging from the ceil-ing and the twinkling fairy lights, she felt something strange. Not peace—the job was still unfinished—but a kind of serenity that she had not experienced in years. The feeling that, if she could make it hers, this kitchen could become a home.

*

After Thanksgiving, the main meals reverted to the usual, but now people were talking openly about the superiority of the Midrats meal. Bonnie was only left with the two Moosewood books: *Moosewood* (MW) and *Moosewood Cooks for a Crowd* (MWC). Pearl continued to find it strange that she said nothing about the missing cookbooks. She'd watch the woman sitting on an upended crate in her tiny office off the galley, squinting at online recipes. From time to time, she'd shout out, "We got pistachios?" or "Any starfruit from Cheech?" Invariably, they were always a few ingredients short.

One morning, during the lull between breakfast and lunch prep, Pearl was crouched in the freshie shack, tearing up pages from *Moosewood* and shoving them into the pockets of her parka, when the door flew open. She clumsily shoved the cookbook onto one of the produce shelves, but it was too late. Bozer had seen.

"What do you want in here?" Pearl said.

"I gotta measure the shelves for the new freshie shack," he said, a smile playing at the corners of his mouth. He brushed past Pearl and reached up to the shelf where she'd hidden the cookbook. When he pulled it out, several of the torn pages fluttered to the ground. He started laughing. "I knew it. Knew it from the minute Bonnie told me those books was missing." His narrow, unknowable eyes traveled the length of Pearl's body. He scratched the side of his face; the sound of his nails against the wiry hairs of his reddish beard sent a shiver of disgust down her spine.

"You planning on sticking around?" he asked.

"What are you talking about?" she said, trying to sound tough.

Bozer placed *Moosewood* back on the shelf, next to a crate of Spanish onions. "If you're going to run a lifer out of a job, you best be prepared to become a lifer yourself." Pearl's cheeks burned. "Now, I'm not saying the old girl is any great shakes in the kitchen. Maybe she done run her course here. I'm just saying that you oughta plan on making this a multiyear gig if you're gonna go to that kind of trouble. Now, meantime, here's what I need to see from here on out: barbecue once a week, make it ribs."

"Or what, you tell everyone I forced Bonnie out?"

Bozer spun a level in his hands. "And make it come with corn-bread and potato salad."

"We don't get cornmeal here."

"Then use back channels."

"And if I refuse?"

"Honey, if the Polies find out you double-crossed Bonnie, things won't go well for you. My requests are small."

Pearl was annoyed, but if this was the price of intrigue, it was cheap. She nodded at Bozer, and stepped aside so he could begin measuring the shelves. On her way to the door, she reached for *Moosewood*, but Bozer casually moved it beyond her reach.

That night, Pearl invited Birdie to her room for the first time. She wanted to show him the notebook—not the pages in which she'd documented her plan to take over the kitchen. Just the recipes. The book had been with her for eight years. It was hardbound, indestructible. Green leather, strong binding—pockets on the inner boards that bulged with scribblings, recipe cards, and other detritus from her various gigs. It was her book of tricks. It had every recipe that had ever worked, including the ones she'd written herself. She didn't know why she was showing it to Birdie. She hadn't shown it to anyone.

With the clean, pink nail of his index finger, Birdie pointed to a handwritten table written in the margins of the first page. "'Oven, liquid, sugar'—what is this?"

"A chart of high-altitude adjustments. Baking at elevation." She leaned closer to Birdie and placed her own finger next to his. "Take sugar, for example. Because the elevation is so high at Pole, I have to remove a tablespoon of sugar from every cup I use or else everyone's teeth will fall out. Increased evaporation increases the concentration of sugar. It makes everything taste too sweet, plus it weakens the structure of whatever I'm baking." Gingerly, she picked up Birdie's hand and set it in his lap so she could begin turning the pages. She flipped until she got to the recipe she wanted.

"I made this one up when I was a set-net deckhand on a tender out of Nome."

"Seawater Bread?" Birdie said.

"It's really basic. Dry yeast, a little sugar, four cups of flour, and a cup and a half of warmed seawater. I got it right off the deck. Let it proof overnight, drop it in the oven around five a.m., and voilà, fresh bread in the middle of the Norton Sound."

Birdie took Pearl's hand and placed it on his chest. "You're the most remarkable woman I've ever met," he said.

"Why, because I can make bread from seawater? Anyone can do that."

"No," Birdie said. "Because you did." Pearl didn't know why she felt embarrassed; she tried to pull away, but Birdie held her fast. Maybe it was all the things he didn't know. The things no one knew. She thought back to the day she walked onto that longliner docked at Cordova Boat Harbor on the Orca Inlet, a seventeen-year-old foster-home runaway. She'd just talked to Captain Whitty about crewing on his March halibut trip, and she was halfway down the dock before she remembered she couldn't take no for an answer. Not without fighting for a yes, anyway. It's what she'd been doing her whole life by that point: seventeen years spent fighting for a yes. The ones in Cordova who didn't fight—the former highliners, the ones who collapsed along with the herring fishery after the oil spill in '89—they walked around town like half-people. Pearl knew she was too young to be a half-person, so she'd turned around and marched back up toward Captain Whitty's boat and pounded on the door with her fist. "Open the door, Captain," she'd shouted. "I gotta say my piece." She heard him curse, but the door eventually opened, and with it came the unmistakable odor of a ruined dinner.

"Well, say it, then," the old man growled.

"I can work on no sleep and still have a smile on my face. I can splice line, I can cook, I got a strong back and a good head on my shoulders. And I make the best damn coffee in the state. And if you don't like how I work, you can throw me overboard. I don't care. But you'll give me a chance."

They'd stood facing each other for a minute, the only sounds the waters of Prince William Sound slapping against the side of the boat.

That was when Pearl glanced over Whitty's shoulder and saw the remains of his dinner smoking on the galley stove. "Plus, it doesn't look like you know how to cook," she said.

"I do okay," Whitty grumbled, but he stepped aside to let her pass. She walked into the cramped cabin and glanced at the frying pan. A black lump of something emitted a thread of smoke.

"What was it?" Pearl asked.

"Spam and white bread," Whitty replied, as though he were saying "filet mignon."

Pearl grabbed the pan and tossed its contents out the galley window and into the harbor. "I'll cook for you," she said, "but I also want to fish."

"You're too small," Whitty said quickly. "Not strong enough."

"Try me."

After making the captain a proper dinner—chicken à la king—Pearl had walked home that night in the gathering dusk of evening, gainfully employed and free. The ghostly outline of the Chenega mountains rose up in the gloaming. And up on the hill above the harbor, the lights of Cordova turned on one by one.

*

Bonnie's final mistake was the Carrot-Mushroom Loaf, a culinary disaster that occurred the third week of December. The thing sat on the serving platter like a hunk of human feces, the warming lights bouncing off its gelatinous exterior, giving it an unnatural sheen. It went untouched. The fact that Bonnie now had only one cookbook excused nothing: that the recipe was buried in the back of the book, as if even the Moosewood Collective knew it was a crime against carrots, only amplified the mistake. The kitchen at South Pole Station was built for desperate circumstances, but Carrot-Mushroom Loaf was an indisputable sign of surrender.

The next morning, Pearl and Bonnie were summoned to Tucker's office. Pearl whistled as they walked across the Dome toward the admin module, but Bonnie remained silent. Her dark hair hung limply around her face and she kept her eyes on her boots. Pearl started in on "Free Bird," just to see if Bonnie would say anything. It took a full minute, but Bonnie finally raised her head. "Shut the fuck up," she said, though it sounded halfhearted.

Inside Tucker's office, Pearl could barely sit still. Her knees bounced at sixteenth-note intervals. Bonnie sat slumped in the other chair, her hands clasped over her belly. Tucker studiously avoided looking at Pearl, and instead focused his gaze on Bonnie.

"I made a mistake," Bonnie said sullenly. "It won't happen again."

"This isn't about the Carrot-Mushroom Loaf, Bonnie," Tucker said. "I imagine that carrots and mushrooms suspended in aspic have an interesting mouthfeel." Pearl noticed the corners of Bonnie's mouth turn slightly upward at this. "This is about scheduling. You know we're constantly tinkering with schedules."

"Not in the galley."

"There's a first time for everything."

"That's why she's here, I guess," Bonnie said. Pearl felt her heart begin to race. Now that the moment was at hand, it was proving excruciating. Tucker kept his eyes fixed on Bonnie. "You need a break from this relentless schedule. You and I both know that with construction of the new station, we've seen an explosion in the transient population. We've got staff coming and going from Palmer and McMurdo, and the fluctuations have had a major impact on kitchen operations."

"So?"

"I think letting Pearl take on the head cook responsibilities for a while will give you a much-needed opportunity to relax, refresh— reflect."

"I think Bonnie's handling the kitchen just fine," Pearl said. "I mean, with the missing cookbooks, anybody would have to get creative."

Bonnie shot a withering look at Pearl. "Funny thing about those missing cookbooks. I never had a problem with them until you came."

"Bonnie, this isn't a demotion," Tucker said. "Your salary remains the same, your contracted job title does not change. It's just a change of pace. It's less work for the money."

Bonnie sat forward in her chair. "I don't come down here to do less work, Tucker. I know this has been the plan from day one. You want me out."

"Bonnie, please—"

"You think I'm an idiot? They tried to DQ me on the physical. Morbidly obese? Borderline hypertension? Never a problem—for four years, never a problem—and then suddenly Richard Simmons is signing off on the VIDS physicals. The union had to get involved." Bonnie jerked her thumb at Pearl without looking at her. "So you bring her down, have her hide my cookbooks, and deliberately turn the crew against me. Her fake-ass sunshiny bullshit is unmistakable. She's a sociopath." Bonnie hauled herself out of the chair. "You both are."

After Bonnie left, Tucker dropped his head into his hands. Pearl felt immobilized. Her legs had stopped bouncing. The nervous energy now seemed to bind her to the chair.

"Can you handle the winter alone?" Tucker said into his hands.

For a moment, Pearl was tempted to say, "Isn't that why you hired me?" Instead, she nodded. "No problem."

After leaving Tucker's office, Pearl returned to the kitchen, where Kit was peeling radishes and humming along to his Discman. Wordlessly, she walked past him and stepped into what used to be Bonnie's office.

It was a mess of papers, file folders, and dirty dishware. Pearl cleaned off the desk where Bonnie had mapped out so many meals, and took a seat on the wooden crate she'd used as a chair. She picked a food scab off the cover of *Moosewood Cooks for a Crowd*. There were so many colorful Post-its attached to the pages that it looked like a small parade float. Pearl was about to close the book and toss it on the pile of papers on the floor, when something caught her eye. An inscription on the inside of the cover.

Someone once said, "Cooking is like love. It should be entered into with abandon or not at all." We've abandoned our sanity already by going down to Pole. All we've got is each other, and this book. Make 'em drool, honey.

Your man, Dwight

From: Warren Slownik (wslownik@nsf.gov)
Date: January 18, 2004 3:30:58 PM EDT
To: Tucker Bollinger (tbollinger@vids.com), Karl
Martin (kmartin@vids.com), Carla Nicks (cnicks@
vids.com), Simon Murphy (smurphy@vids.com)
Cc: Alexandra Scaletta (ascaletta@nsf.gov)
Status: URGENT
Subject: CONFIDENTIAL: Injury Incident

A quick thank-you to everyone who provided input
during today's conference call. I've passed your
questions and concerns on to Alexandra. In the
meantime, I want to reiterate the importance of
protecting our grantees' privacy by keeping this
incident out of the media for as long as possible. An e-mail has been sent to all VIDS support
staff and NSF grantees regarding the incident, so
please be prepared for questions. I'm certain
there will be many from this group. In the meantime, any press inquiries should be directed to
Alexandra's office.

I've attached the injury incident report, prepared by Dr. Nicks.

Warren

the divide

2003 December 26
03:13
To: cherrywaswaiting@hotmail.com
From: Billie.Gosling@janusbooks.com
Subject: Beakers

C.,
I am sorry to report that Phil and I are no longer
an item. He said he needed a partner with more of
a "buy-in." He said my cynicism is "poisonous."
Mom promised not to sign him up for another book.
She launched a jeremiad in editorial board yesterday about climate change and polar bears and
how ironic it was that most of the world's research on global warming is taking place smack-
dab in the polar bear's natural habitat. No one
besides our new intern chose to remind her that
there are no polar bears at the South Pole, but
that's only because he doesn't yet know fear.
B.
p.s. What the hell is a Beaker?

*

```
2003 December 30
20:34
To: Billie.Gosling@janusbooks.com
From: cherrywaswaiting@hotmail.com
Subject: RE: Beaker
```

B.,
A Beaker is the South Pole term for a scientist,
even though I've never seen any of them handling
beakers. I'm sorry about you and Phil. Put it in
your work. The climate change denier did a Q&A
and the whole station turned out for it. I didn't
really understand what was going on, but the
Beakers were frantic by the end. I'm told this
Denier—his name is Pavano—is down here because
of "Congressional interference." Anyway, the guy
invited me to go with him to the ice-coring camp
as his "research assistant," probably because
I'm the only person who's nice to him. He's
definitely not trying to put the moves on. The
guy comes across as sort of asexual. I imagine
him genitals-free. Anyway, we leave in a couple
weeks. I'll report back.
C.

The morning after Frank Pavano's lecture, Cooper met Sal and Sri in the cafeteria line. They both looked hungover. "My brain hurts," Sri said as he spooned Pearl's Orange Walnut Spice Oatmeal onto his tray. "It spent all night looking for those IQ points I lost to Pavano's ravings." Cooper picked up some buckwheat pancakes and poured Pearl's chokecherry syrup over the stack.

At the table, Sal set his tray down heavily and stared at his food. The early consensus was that while he was clearly a bought man,

Pavano had put on a good showing. Several Beakers were convinced he was actually an atheist—overnight they'd dug up speculative Internet posts from 2000, when Pavano had been questioned at some conference-on-a-cruise-ship about irreducible complexity. He'd indicated then that faith in a higher power was not a prerequisite for accepting the theory of Intelligent Design. These atheistic tendencies were noted and puzzled over—was he pandering, trying to play both sides against the middle, or was he the Sasquatch of the Intelligent Design debate, an atheist Creationist?

"Don't be sad, man," Sri said, slapping Sal on the shoulder. "Pavano shall be defeated."

"Maybe in the long run," Sal said. "But by then it might be too late."

"I know why you're upset," Cooper said. "It's Pearl." Sal looked across the table at Cooper, a half smile on his face. He looked tired; Cooper saw for the first time that his auburn hair was tinged with wiry grays.

"Pearl what?" Sri said. "What does Pearl have to do with anything?"

"No, she's right," Sal said, still looking at Cooper. "She is exactly right. Pearl is the test case. She was buying in last night. She was feeling guilty about participating in a consumer economy that is leading to the destruction of the earth. Remember what she said? 'I don't want the earth to be warming.'"

"So? None of us do," Sri said.

"But when Pavano told her it wasn't, she said that made her feel better. She was relieved. Pavano gave her the out she was looking for."

"Pearl is Everywoman," Cooper said, through a mouthful of pancake.

Sri looked from Sal to Cooper and back again, his black unibrow furrowed. Suddenly, his eyes widened. "And it took Pavano two-thousandths of a second to plant doubt in Everywoman's brain." He stared at the wall. "Shit. People are so dumb."

"Pearl's not dumb," Cooper said.

"No, sorry. I didn't mean Pearl literally," Sri said. "Her oatmeal is awesome."

"The problem isn't brain power," Sal said. "It's hope. They're hopeful. Deniers provide hope. We don't. We're doom and gloom, and that's what makes it so easy for Pavano to convert."

"What the hell does hope have to do with science?" Sri asked.

"Nothing. That's the point. Pearl doesn't want to believe that the earth is going to burn to a crisp because human beings are assholes. Pavano can offer a different story, rainbows and lollipops," Sal said.

"And Pavano can also sound science-y," Cooper said. "Or science-y enough."

Under the table, Sal nudged her boot with his.

"I just wish I could get into Pavano's head," Sri said. "I bet the blueprints for world domination are in there."

"Or Exxon's annual report," Sal said.

"Well, maybe I can help," Cooper said. "Pavano invited me to the ice-coring camp. On the Divide." The men stared at her uncomprehendingly. "We were talking about painting and sastrugis and stuff, and I just told him that I was hyper-focused on mittens and not because I want to be." Cooper decided not to tell them about her portrait of Tucker or the one she'd started of Bozer. "So he offered to get me on the manifest for a flight to the Divide when he heads back in a couple weeks. To get some ideas. Different vistas."

"Well, isn't that generous," Sal said.

"But you can't go to the Divide!" Sri exclaimed. "Only approved scientists and techs go." He looked over at Sal. "Hell, I'm the head climatologist and it took me two weeks to get my paperwork processed."

"I'd be going as a 'research assistant.' He says he doesn't have one," Cooper said.

"That's because he shouldn't have one," Sri growled. "However, he's supposed to be borrowing one of mine." He tapped Sal's forearm. "NSF put him on my project budget. Like a leech."

"At least he's just looking at the core archive," Sal said.

"No, man, they're talking about letting him core," Sri said. "And not only that, they want my tech to fire up the Badger-Eclipse drill for him." He sighed. "Well, luckily NSF will never approve a non-grantee as a research tech."

"Actually," Cooper said tentatively. "About that. Apparently I'm already approved. They can't call me a 'research tech' but I'm allowed to go to the site with him as an 'assistant.' Something about a congressional override? I had to sign a bunch of release-of-liability forms."

The men stared absently at their oatmeal, looking sick.

Cooper took her tray to the dish pit before beginning the long walk to Summer Camp—Denise had the studio until noon, so Cooper thought she'd grab a nap. She was zipping up her parka outside the galley trailer when she heard Sal calling her name.

"Wait up," he shouted from the stairs, where he was fumbling with his parka and mittens. He half-jogged to where Cooper was standing. "I almost forgot. I have something for you. Come with me."

Sal had a room in the elevated dorm with the other physicists, who were mostly from Palo Alto or Madison, cities that were apparently hotbeds for astrophysicists who liked ice-time.

"Yo, Sal," a guy in a toolbelt said as they passed him. "What's the word on the new Pole marker? You come up with a design yet?"

"If I did, I wouldn't tell you, sweetcheeks," Sal said.

"Just don't disappoint us. All eyes are on you, my man."

"I thought the Nailheads hated the Beakers," Cooper said after the man had passed them.

"Unlike the vast majority of my Beaker brethren, I respect the Nailheads. We wouldn't be here without them. I let them know that on a regular basis." Sal pushed open a heavy steel door. "Therefore, I am not hated."

An overwhelming stench of body odor hit Cooper full on. "Oh shit," she choked.

"Welcome to the Beaker Box. I should've warned you. Scientists smell worse. No one knows why."

Cooper looked down the narrow hallway at the solid doors, the absence of enormous heaters, and the comparatively luxurious quarters of the Beakers and senior Nailheads. "Why do you guys get the nice rooms?"

"Because we're important," Sal replied.

As they walked down the hall, men in various states of undress sat hunched over tiny desks, studying papers or working on their laptops. "Skirt alert," Sal called. A few doors slammed shut; others flew open, and were followed by shaggy-haired heads.

Sal's room was much bigger than Cooper's, with a large desk and an Ethernet connection. Their beds were the same size, though, she noted with satisfaction. Against the back wall, a small window looked out onto the runway and, beyond that, the Dark Sector. Sal crouched down and began flipping through books stashed in a bookcase fashioned from an apple crate. Finally, he pulled a hand-bound book from the shelf and handed to her. It was plain, *White Album*–style, and the length of a novella. The cover was torn and the pages had been stapled together. It was titled *The Crud: Or How to Deal with All the South Pole Bullshit*.

"I have to say, I'm already intimately familiar with the Crud," Cooper said as she flipped through the book.

"This is about the existential Crud. It's full of stuff not found in the *South Pole Station Handbook*. Think of it as a secret resource for coping when things get hard. And they will get harder, trust me. There's a sequel waiting for you when you finish."

"Why are you giving this to me?"

Sal reached for his anorak. "Because I'm invested in your mental health, as it relates to the tot-art you're working on for me," he said. "But be careful with it. VIDS would give up two antiballistic missiles to get a hold of this book. This is the last remaining copy on the ice. The rest of them are in Al Gore's lockbox."

"Right next to my ability to produce decent art," Cooper said, tucking the book under her arm.

"Art's easy," Sal said. He pulled on the anorak. "Just present a subject and make a statement about it." He grinned at her. "Don't get mad. I'm kidding." He picked up a stack of papers from his desk and waved them at her. "By the way, everyone completed the survey, except you, Tucker, and Pavano."

"For someone with such big cosmic questions to deal with, you seem really worried about weirdly inconsequential things."

"Inconsequential? I don't like politics in my science. Do you?"

"I don't have politics or science."

"Well, that's your problem, then. All art is politics." He pointed at *The Crud*. "Do not let this fall into the wrong hands."

"That may have already happened," she said.

"No," Sal said, tapping the book gently, and brushing Cooper's fingers as he did so. "It's definitely in the hands of the person who needs it."

*

When she finally arrived at her room in Summer Camp, Cooper found a piece of paper attached to the door, flapping in the draft. *To the (wo)man who spilled his/her piss on my boots and then fled (piss-and-run): Identify yourself. Otherwise I'll be forced to spend the rest of the summer looking for you. Signed, Super Angry but Willing to Forgive at the Right Price Electrician in D3.*

She tore the note off the door, grateful once again for the anonymity provided by polarwear, and opened the door. After removing her ECW gear, she got under the covers with *The Crud*. The table of contents included chapters like "The VIDS Clusterfuck," "How to Score a Shower Curtain and Keep HR from Confiscating It Because for Some Reason They're Illegal," "Surviving DVs: Distinguished Visitors and Other Annoying VIPs," and "Why McMurdo Sucks." The book indicated, for example, that McMurdo-ites were mostly unfit for true polar service. Apparently, the fact that Discovery Hut was within walking distance of McMurdo, and that this historic site was a preferred location for clandestine blow jobs, caused the polar philatelists no end of grief. (It was also why Cooper had not felt moved to visit Discovery Hut during her layover at McMurdo—that, and the fact that it had been mobbed by cruise ship passengers, all of whom were still wearing life jackets.) McMurdo-ites also sucked because of their obsession with penguins; they were not above slithering across the ice on their bellies to get photos of indifferent Adélies.

Cooper's reading was interrupted by a commotion in the hallway—the canvas-duck walls rippled with the constant opening and closing of the Jamesway door. By the time she'd scrambled out of bed and opened her door, a squirming mass of bodies had filled the hall. Everyone was getting into ECW gear. Suddenly All-Call—the station's public address system—crackled on, and a robotic Speak & Spell voice began chanting: "A fire alarm has been reported. Please stand by for further instructions." Before Cooper could fully process these words, Kit grabbed her arm.

"You're on the fire team, right?" he said. Cooper thought for a moment—yes, back in Denver she had been assigned to the fire team. She scrambled back into her ECW gear and was almost out the door before she thought to grab the vial. She was stuffing it into the deepest part of her parka when Kit yanked open her door and pulled her down the hallway.

Outside, a flock of snowmobiles awaited them, piloted by the heavy machine operators who'd been on shift at the time of the fire call. Kit helped Cooper onto one, then climbed on in front of her, and they zoomed off toward the Dome.

"Do you see anything?" Kit called over his shoulder. Cooper pulled her face out of Kit's parka to look. Nope—just the half-sunk diamond dome and the orange Skylab tower behind it. No plumes of smoke, no sign of fire, besides the insect-like agitation of the Polies Cooper could now see mustering at the station entrance. The snowmobile they were on zipped past the Pole marker and entered the tunnel.

Under the Dome, the fire team was pulling on bunker gear and hauling air tanks off the ground and onto one another's shoulders. Bozer and Floyd were leading a group of Nailheads down the entrance tunnel to Skylab, where Tucker stood wearing a massive amount of firefighting equipment. "I got another one for you," Kit shouted above the din and pushed Cooper into Sal, who was spewing acronyms into his radio, which was promptly spewing them back. Sal pointed urgently, and Cooper wandered off in the general direction where he'd pointed, joining Birdie, who was already outfitted. He slammed an air tank against Cooper's back and pulled the shoulder straps around her arms.

Cooper's heart pounded and she realized she was sweating. She lifted her nose in the air, like a dog scenting the wind. The only smells she could detect were gasoline, exhaust, and, somewhere on the edge, the scent of Pearl and Bonnie's evening meal prep drifting out from the kitchen. "We'd be smelling smoke by now if it was bad, wouldn't we?" Cooper said to Birdie. He only blinked at her.

Suddenly, the activity level slowed down. The chorus of muffled walkie-talkie voices diminished to occasional solos, and the robotic All-Call voice was no longer chanting like a Gregorian monk. One by one, snowmobiles roared down the entrance tunnel. As the din subsided, All-Call came on again, but this time it was Dwight's voice that was chanting: "This has been a false alarm. A false alarm. Please return your equipment to the stations. Repeat: This has been a false alarm. Please return your equipment to the stations. Postmortem at All-Hands Meeting."

Cooper's legs began trembling. She kicked the air in front of her, as if to remind her legs that they were functioning limbs, but this only made things worse. A prickly heat climbed up her torso, up her neck, all the way to the top of her head, causing her face to flush; it felt as if someone had placed a cinder block on her chest. She lowered her body to the ground, trying to maintain some semblance of control. When the tears came, she was only half surprised.

She didn't know how long she'd been sitting there when someone slid their arms under hers and hauled her to her feet. When she pulled off her goggles and wiped her eyes, she saw that it was Pavano. His face was obscured by his balaclava, but his limpid eyes were unmistakable. By the time Cooper had gathered herself enough to mumble a thank-you, Pavano was already halfway down the entrance tunnel.

*

"I want to see a bird," Dwight said.

"I want to smell a new book," Pearl replied.

"I want to fondle a fresh bell pepper, and then eat it," Cooper chimed in.

"I want to pet my cat."

"What does cat hair feel like? I forget."

"I want to hear a child laugh."

"I want to go barefoot."

"I want a drink."

Everyone turned at this, like a litter of kittens following a tracking light, to see Marcy standing in the door. Or a weak facsimile of Marcy. She was drunk. Cooper knew this because Marcy was holding herself steady against the door frame leading to the Smoke Bar. Old Marcy never needed anything to steady her gait. She never showed up at the bar already drunk. But now here she was, her normally proud shoulders slumped. It was as if one of the major structural supports holding up the geodesic dome had suddenly sunk ten feet into the ice. Everything still standing, but the building was catawampus.

Cooper and Sal got up from their chairs at the same moment and helped Marcy to a seat. Floyd threw his head back and laughed. "Oh, this is rich," he said. "She's back. The case study for Why Women Shouldn't Be at Pole."

"Says the shapeless mass of existential impotence," Sal muttered, as he returned to his seat next to Bozer.

Floyd ignored this and focused his piggy eyes on Marcy. "So is it true?"

"Is what true?" Marcy said without raising her eyes from the table. Her voice sounded bruised.

Floyd continued looking at Marcy for a minute. "You stupid slut," he said. Sal stood up from his chair so fast his knees hit the edge of the table and sent the beer bottles wobbling. Cooper saw Bozer grip Sal's arm and hold it firm.

"So who's the daddy?" Floyd said.

"Mechanic at Palmer," Marcy replied.

"Oh, so a one-and-done."

Marcy finally raised her eyes and looked at Floyd. "My specialty." Cooper saw something change in Floyd's face—a minuscule shift in the angle of his eyebrows, a faint tightening of his lips. Before he dropped his eyes, Cooper could see they'd changed, too, had widened, child-like, with pain.

The silence of the room felt alien. Cooper watched Bozer calmly sip his Schlitz, his hand still gripping Sal's forearm. Finally, Floyd hauled himself out of his chair and walked over to Marcy. No one spoke as he leaned down and whispered something into her ear. She nodded, and Floyd stroked her messy hair before pulling her head toward his.

*

When Cooper walked in the gym for the second artists' meeting later that week, the interpretive dancer was not sitting next to the historical novelist, and he was clearly pissed off about it. She, on the other hand, was exuberant. "That false alarm last week was just the kick I needed, because I'm swimming in inspiration," she said. She flicked her Joni Mitchell hair over her shoulder. "I actually think I'm on the verge of a breakthrough." She leaned toward Birdie, the only person who appeared to be listening. "I met this Argentinean gentleman online who's doing research on Weddell seals at McMurdo—something about their estrus cycle. I'm thinking about transferring down there. Since it's mating season, there would be a chance for me to observe contact improvisation in the wild."

"But wasn't your project based on the movements of the hydrocarbon tubeworm?" Birdie asked.

"Yes, but I didn't realize how difficult it would be to interpret its vascular plume. This seal research is brimming with possibilities. I learned from this Latin genius that in order to do the research you have to capture the female Weddells by drawing a canvas hood over their heads, tying it closed, and then taking a vaginal swab."

"You can dance about that?" Birdie asked, incredulous.

"I see it less as a dance than a choreographed crime scene," the dancer replied.

"I hate Argentina," the historical novelist said from across the room, his arms crossed. "Full of Nazis." It occurred to Cooper for the first time that the historical novelist bore a striking resemblance to Karl Rove.

"He's quite spiritual," the dancer said thoughtfully. "Shaman-like, really. I like how he can summon sacred energy. I can actually feel it in my heart."

"You know what I feel in my heart?" the literary novelist said from deep within the hood of his University of Iowa sweatshirt. "I feel nothing. It's contracted like polar ice." He groaned. "Christ, even my similes are stale."

"You feel disconnected from yourself because you have put all that you are into your manuscript," the dancer said. "You do not exist outside of your work."

The literary novelist retreated further into his hood.

Birdie cleared his throat. "This is our second meeting, so I think it would be wise to assess what we've produced since being on the ice as a way of holding ourselves accountable. Seeing as I've been quite unproductive since arriving, I will yield the floor."

The literary novelist raised his hand. "I wonder if we can talk a little about the world-building that goes on here. I mean, we've been here for a few months now, and the novelty of, you know, living at South Pole quote-unquote has worn off, at least for me. Taking this from a literary perspective, I feel as though"—he cast a sidelong glance at the open notebook on his knee—"there's this completely separate reality that people down here have constructed for themselves. I definitely still feel like an outsider, like I haven't been fully embraced. I mean, no one even came and got me during that fire drill. If it had been a real fire, I would have been charcoal."

"They didn't come get you because you're a freak," the historical novelist snapped. "All of you are. I haven't met one normal person yet. Not one." He stood up and began pacing.

"And why exactly are you here?" the interpretive dancer asked him. "Have you figured that out yet?" Cooper heard frost in the dancer's voice for the first time since the unfortunate radish haiku.

The historical novelist snorted. "To keep my head down and write."

"And you couldn't have done that back in Poughkeepsie?"

"As I've explained to you in great detail, it's impossible to situate a speculative World War Two battle set at South Pole without actually being here. Why is that so hard to understand?"

As the dancer and the historical novelist bickered, Cooper realized that the literary novelist was actually on to something: the Pole community was, in fact, a parallel universe in miniature. It was a place you could go where people weren't flying planes into buildings or shooting up schools. They were just bickering about Poughkeepsie and satellite phone calls and pontificating on the hydrocarbon seep tubeworm's vascular plume. Most people off-continent didn't even remember this place existed, except maybe a handful of bored newspaper reporters and the schoolchildren in De Pere, Wisconsin, with whom Sal corresponded.

Cooper tapped the literary novelist on the knee. "Hey, when you were a kid, did you ever lock yourself in the bathroom and pretend it was a house?" He stared at her uncomprehendingly. "You know, like a cottage in the Black Forest: bathtub for your bed, sink for your cooking needs, the cabinet beneath the sink for your oven?" Nothing. "Look, I guess my point is that for me, South Pole is like my fantasy bathroom-cottage. You can pretend you have everything you need here. People might pull on the doorknob and threaten to kick the door down, but you know they won't do it, and you can be safe here until you're ready to face whatever ends up being on the other side of it. I like it here because this isn't the world. It's somewhere else."

"And it also has a toilet, so the parallel is complete," the historical novelist barked. "Christ. I'm counting down the days until I can get out of here."

"You're just mad that the Argentinean swabbed your girlfriend," Birdie said, and held out his pink hand to Cooper for a high-five.

*

Cooper finished *The Crud* the second week of December, having learned important things like where all the waste from the toilets went (a "lake" beneath the ice), and was ready to read the sequel, *Skua Birds in Paradise: Wintering Over at SP*, which Sal kept hidden in his room. Knowing Sal always skipped game night, she decided to venture over to El Dorm with *The Crud* to find him and *Skua Birds in Paradise*.

When she approached his door, she could see that it was half open, and that there was a woman in the room. The banter was intimate, the low lilt typical of people who have recently swapped bodily fluids. Cooper tried to turn back silently on her bunny boots, but the right one squeaked on the linoleum and brought the banter to a stop midsentence. The Frosty Boy tech in the hotpants and trucker hat who'd flown in from McMurdo, and who, Cooper thought irritably, might never leave, appeared at the door.

"Who is it?" Sal called out to the tech.

"A girl," she said flatly. This was a rare enough occurrence in El Dorm that Sal came to the door himself. His shirt was off. Cooper tried not to look at his chest, but ended up staring directly at it and quickly took in the details: no hair, some definition, not too much, nipples symmetrical and the color of strawberries. Sal edged past his visitor and closed the door against his shoulder.

"Don't tell me you already lost *The Crud*."

Cooper handed him the book. "To the contrary. I'm ready for the sequel."

Sal's demeanor immediately shifted. "Meet me in the library in ten." He closed the door in her face.

In the library, Cooper perused the shelves, noting that there were duplicate copies of every Douglas Adams book ever written, as well as the compulsory copy of *Zen and the Art of Motorcycle Maintenance*. She was pleased to find that Tucker was wrong— there was a copy of Shackleton's *South*. It just had never been opened.

"This will generate gossip," Sal said when he walked in. He locked the door behind him. "Now, it goes without saying that you do not read *Skua Birds* openly. Admin has a bounty pool on both books— winner gets an extra R-and-R off-continent, so motivation is high. Now turn around."

"What?"

"I can't let you see where I keep it."

"Fuck off," Cooper laughed, but she turned to face the back wall, on which hung every winter-over group portrait in Pole history. She stopped counting at thirty. As Sal shuffled around behind her, she studied the photos. They went from sepia in the 1950s to black-and-white in the '60s to color in the '70s and beyond, and yet the composition of each was remarkably similar: beards abounded, one person in a cowboy hat, another eschewing his parka for a flannel shirt, someone caught midsentence.

Just below these photographs was a lighted display case filled with brass sculptures—the old geographic Pole markers, which were replaced each year on New Year's Day. The 1999 marker was a gleaming copper bottle cap with the continent etched on top; 2000's depicted the South Pole under a wavy magnetic field, with the words *To Inspire and Explore* running the perimeter; another, its year un-mentioned, was a rotating sextant.

"These are beautiful as hell," Cooper said admiringly.

"The Pole markers are works of art," Sal said behind her. "Each year someone gets to design the new one. It's a huge honor."

"Who gets it this year?" Cooper asked, even though she knew. Sal placed his hands on her shoulders and turned her around to face him.

"Yours truly."

"Why you?" Cooper asked. "Oh, right—your super-important experiment."

Sal handed her a paperback with a black cover. This one didn't even bother with the title.

"Well, this is certainly inconspicuous," Cooper said.

Someone pulled on the door of the library, and after a momentary pause, pulled on it again and again. Cooper wasn't sure why, but she found the length of time that passed before the person's hand told his brain that the door was locked hilarious, and started laughing. The door rattled in its frame as the angry Polie pulled and pulled on the doorknob, as if the door were only playing games with him and would open eventually. Cooper could not stop laughing.

"Open the effing door, you ass-joints!" the man shouted. This sent Cooper into fresh hysterics. Sal rubbed his face vigorously and held his hands over his eyes for a moment, trying not to laugh with Cooper. "After finding us here together in a locked room," he said, "people are gonna think you're my ice-wife."

"But you already have one," Cooper said with a hiccup. "I saw her in your room."

Sal tilted his head. "Beth? She's just an ice-friend. Who is returning to McMurdo tomorrow."

"Finally."

Without warning, he leaned down so that his face was an inch from Cooper's. "Does that ease your mind, Fingy?"

"I was very upset," Cooper said, hoping the obvious sarcasm obscured the truth of this statement. "When I saw her, I was afraid the Frosty Boy had gone on the fritz again."

Finally, Sal unlocked the door and stepped aside to admit the *Star Trek* finger-split guys Cooper had seen the first day. They stalked past Cooper, muttering imprecations, *Breakout: Normandy* in hand.

*

When the rumored journalist from Miami finally arrived at the station, he turned out to be a ginger with a germinating goatee. He arrived cheerful, walking the station with an NSF public relations rep who shadowed him like a junior high hall monitor. As Cooper passed the men on her way from the studio to the galley, she smiled to be friendly. Sensing the possibility for a positive encounter that could result in good press for the Program, the PR rep stopped.

"A and W, right?" the rep asked, assessing Cooper's paint-stained overalls. "What discipline?"

"I'm a painter," Cooper replied. The rep scribbled this down, then asked her name, and scribbled that down, too.

"Tim, this is one of our artist Fellows," the rep said. "The NSF sponsors writers and artists every year to come down and—"

"Right," Tim said vaguely, looking down the hall toward the exit. "I profiled that paper-clip artist two years ago, remember?" He glanced at Cooper. "But I guess I should cover my bases."

Tim fished out a reporter's notebook from his parka. "What do you think artists bring to the conversation about what goes on at the Pole?" He asked the question like a Red Lobster waitress about to go on break.

"Is there a conversation about what goes on at Pole?" Cooper asked. The PR rep shifted his weight.

"Apparently," Tim said, "or else I wouldn't be here. What are you painting about while you're down?"

"The imperative of the explorer."

"And how do you interpret that?"

"Mittens."

"Fascinating," Tim said, tucking the pen into the coil of his notebook.

The rep gave Cooper a withering look.

Cooper continued on to the galley for lunch, and found Tucker and Dwight engaged in a heated discussion.

"But wouldn't you time travel if you could, Tucker?" Dwight said as Cooper set her tray down next to him. Tucker shook his head silently as he separated the carbs from the protein on his plate. Dwight gave a huff of disapproval. "You're telling me that if you could go back two hundred years, you wouldn't?"

"Before or after the Fugitive Slave Act?"

Dwight pounded the table with his fist. "You always make it about slavery!" Cooper watched as Dwight stormed off with his tray.

"Do you want me to slip ex-lax into his coffee?"

"That's just Dwight doing Dwight," Tucker said, pinching his eyebrow. "I'm a little on edge."

"What's going on?"

"That reporter from the *Herald* is working an angle about Pavano and his research."

"I figured. What's the big deal?"

"The Program was hoping to keep Pavano's presence on the ice a nonissue. They don't want it to become political." He looked up at Cooper. "I once thought that all you needed to get by in this life was a pleasant phone manner. Of course, that was when I was a telemarketer."

When the *Miami Herald* published Tim's story a week later, it had nothing to do with mittens or the construction of the new station. Instead, the headline was "In World's Last Bastion of Objective Research, Politics Intrudes." As Tucker had predicted, the article focused on Pavano's work on climate change, and how two conservative U.S. congressmen had gotten him on the ice. Bush's approval rates were plunging, and both men were up for reelection in their home states the next year—they hoped the "global-warming hoax" and the federal government's reluctance to fund "skeptics" would whip their constituents into a lather.

Somehow Tim had lost the PR rep long enough to sit down with Pavano for an interview. Tim portrayed him as the kind of fool who would spend his career trying to make sense of Piltdown Man. There was mention of the remoteness of Pavano's lab space, an ad hoc office in the Dark Sector. It was, Tim noted, on the very edge of the Sector, far from the labs of the other climate scientists at Pole.

The article also revealed personal information about Pavano, which the Beakers seized upon: he had been an Indiana science prodigy as a youth and had been courted by Stanford and MIT. He'd chosen Stanford and received degrees in astronomy and physics, specializing in heliospherics, but had had difficulty placing his research papers due to a plagiarism charge early in his career. He had rehabilitated his reputation enough to land a position at a private Midwestern college, where he worked for nearly ten years before he was, again, accused of plagiarism.

Tim had tried to get Beakers to comment on Pavano, but they had, at the NSF's request, remained silent. The piece ended with a quote from one of the congressmen who'd been responsible for getting him to South Pole:

> When reached for comment, Senator Sam Bayless (R-KS) said, "In the real world, outside of the ivory tower, science is a vigorous debate, not a museum piece. Just as there is no scientific agreement about the so-called Big Bang, there is no scientific agreement about the causes of so-called climate change." Rep. Bayless added, "I'm proud of my role in helping the National Science Foundation understand that diversity in science is a good thing."

Cooper found the sidebar accompanying the article more interesting than the political implications of congressmen bickering with the NSF. In coming to South Pole Station for the research season, Tim wrote, Pavano was reuniting with a former college roommate: an astrophysicist named Sal Brennan, the son of a highly respected theoretical physicist from Stanford. Dr. John Brennan had, with Alan Guth, helped introduce the idea of cosmic inflation. He had also plucked Frank Pavano from the cornfields of Indiana and brought him to Stanford, only to have Pavano decline to work on Dr. Brennan's team.

Tim reported that, at the same time Pavano was studying heliophysics across campus, Sal had taken up the mantle of his father's uncompleted work—the search for b-modes, the gravitational waves that would, if found, prove the inflationary theory to be correct. And he'd come close once: in 1999, Sal had been part of a South Pole–based experiment that had discovered that microwave radiation was polarized. (Tim didn't elaborate on the import of this finding, and

Cooper assumed that, to minds more subtle than hers, the discovery spoke for itself.) But then something had changed. Sal lost confidence in the inflationary model and decided to leave Stanford in order to do his post-doc work at Princeton with Peter Sokoloff, a theoretical physicist who had developed a rival theory to the Big Bang. This theory suggested that rather than the explosive genesis that Dr. Brennan and others had posited, the universe had come about as the result of the latest collision with a parallel world.

"Sal Brennan now believes what his father calls the Big Bang is nothing more than an echo," Tim wrote. "The two men have not spoken since early 2000, when the younger Brennan left for Princeton." Tim went on to report that others working in cosmology—particularly adherents to cosmic inflation—viewed Sal's model, which was a novel refinement of Sokoloff's, with skepticism. However, Princeton's joint South Pole–based experiment with Stanford's Kavli team was without precedent, and could possibly result in the elimination of one of the models by year's end.

"None of the cosmologists working on the standard model at Pole this season would go on the record about Sal Brennan's research," Tim wrote, "but some indicated that he and Frank Pavano's research interests had more in common that one might think."

Cooper absorbed this information avidly. Her own disagreements with her father ran along the lines of whether oars and paddles really were two different things. In some circles, she now realized, it was possible that a father would disavow his son over a difference of opinion regarding the origins of the universe. Or maybe it was just in Sal's circle that such a thing could happen. Either way, it was now clear to Cooper that Sal was not just a bro-dude with a taste for tater tots. There was a whole universe behind his laughing eyes.

*

"Journalists never get science right," Sal replied when Cooper found him on the climbing wall in the gym that night.

"What about Pavano? Did he get Pavano right?"

Sal dropped from the wall and rubbed powder off his hands. "Pavano's so awkward he makes even theoretical physicists uncomfortable. He was always too much in his own head, so he could never collaborate with anyone on papers. Then he started plagiarizing—and trust me, you have to work really hard to convincingly plagiarize helioseismology research. He couldn't get tenure and got the boot. With no home institution, he couldn't get funding. Without funding he was fucked."

"But he's here," Cooper said, "so clearly he's not totally fucked."

"Well, lucky for him there are people who make a living looking for failed scientists."

"But what about the plagiarism? Wouldn't that tarnish his rep?"

"You keep forgetting—it's not about the science. Plagiarizing a couple graphs in an obscure research paper? No, that's nothing more than a love bite. It's about the messaging. Did you read the rest of the piece?"

"You mean where they talk about you and your research? I stopped reading after the part about the branes and the parallel universes. It got too science-y and I lost interest."

He rolled his eyes. "Of course that's the part that is going to change the world, but sure, god forbid it get too 'science-y.' " He picked Cooper's parka off the floor and threw it at her. "Come on, I want to show you something."

Minutes later, they were careening across the ice on a snowmobile, flying over sastrugi and hitting every frozen crest so hard Cooper could feel her fillings clattering. The wind was ferociously cold; Cooper thought her face was going to peel off. She looked over her shoulder at the Dome growing smaller and smaller as they sped toward the metal city where so much science was done at South Pole: the Dark Sector.

She pulled her face out of the back of Sal's parka in time to see two enormous funnels, open to the sky and surrounded by scaffolding, and a couple of large, blue prefab buildings embraced by metal staircases. She was amazed at how impermanent the structures of the Dark Sector looked, like a mutated, multilevel trailer park. The place seemed deserted. Once inside, Sal led her into a large room filled with humming supercomputers and servers and endless coils of cables, all feeding into a large enclosed cable tray. He showed her the calibration station, and his face flushed with geek joy when he took out the blueprints for the Arcminute Cosmology Bolometer Array Receiver (ACBAR, he called it) that would be installed on the telescope next year.

Cooper began to lose track of the number of flickering computer screens and exactly what was supposed to be happening, but that was okay. She was almost getting it. This was what the Beakers were always yammering about. This was, in fact, Sal's world, and she was weirdly drawn to it.

Sal brought her to a small, cluttered cubicle. Her brain immediately filled in the gaps of time when she didn't see Sal during the day. He was here, going over readings with Alek and the other research techs. Sal flipped through some papers on his desk and started to say something, then stopped. He flipped through more papers, and Cooper cast about for something to say but came up empty. Finally, Sal cleared his throat. "Yesterday, I was looking over measurements of CMB anisotropies, and I thought—where will she be sitting at dinner tonight? Will she be wearing that ratty Vikings T-shirt again? Will she come to my table or will I have to go to her?"

If not for the description of the Vikings shirt, Cooper wouldn't have known Sal was referring to her. He looked at her expectantly. Here again came that weird seizing feeling in her chest of being on a precipice, and she could not immediately figure out how to respond. Sal laughed, and looked away. "I'm sorry. Usually when I make women uncomfortable, it's on purpose."

"No, I'm sorry. I'm not uncomfortable. I'm—I'm surprised. One minute we're talking about telescopes and words I can't pronounce, and the next minute—you said that. Sorry."

"Okay, now we've both apologized for nothing." He pinched the bridge of his nose like an exhausted teacher. "Look, I'm not used to subtlety in polar courtship. This is me telling you I like you. This is me telling you that sometimes I wonder where you'll be sitting at dinner or if you'll come into the Smoke Bar afterward. And that, after finding out from a Florida newspaper that I'm a total disappointment to a world-class scientific institution, not to mention my own father, if you still want to talk to me, I can usually be found here." As Cooper struggled to take all this in, Sal gestured toward yet another door. "Come on."

"Where are we going?"

"The 'scopes. That's why I brought you out here."

After inching along a metal scaffold bridge, dusted with fine ice particles, they arrived at a wooden frame—not a window, not a door, just a portal. Cooper peered through it and saw yet another incomprehensible scene of metal, wires, and mirrors. But as Cooper looked at it, it seemed to take a shape. "It looks like a metal coffee filter," she said.

Sal blinked at her. "That's actually a completely accurate way of describing what this telescope does. Except instead of coffee grounds, it catches neutrinos and maybe b-modes, if I'm really unlucky."

"Unlucky?"

"The Kavli team from Stanford is looking for b-modes, which, if found, will confirm the inflationary theory—the Big Bang. Lisa Wu would lay down her life to get a five-sigma on the presence of b-modes worming their way toward us from thirteen billion years ago. Of course, if she does, then my model is eliminated."

"The one where the universe is just a bouncing ball?"

Sal considered the telescope for a moment. "Do you believe in the Big Bang?"

"Believe in it? I thought it was a done deal."

"Not a done deal. Not yet. I don't buy the inflationary theory of the origins of the universe. I like a different model. I like the one that says there wasn't a Big Bang. That the universe is not infinitely expanding. That our universe collides against another universe—a brane—every few trillion years and this spurs something that looks like a 'big bang' but is really a big bounce. The theory is completely

compatible with every finding now held up as evidence for the inflationary theory, completely in line with what the WAMP satellite has
detected. In fact, our models—the inflationary theory and the cyclic
model, which is what my model is called—are like twins. They share
99.99 percent of their DNA. Only their mother can tell them apart.
But if Lisa finds b-modes, the cyclic model is smoke."

"What if she doesn't find them?"

"If she doesn't, those waves are too small to measure, and all
those temp fluctuations and galaxy seeds were created in a process
gentler than the violent expansion the inflationists promote. The cyclic model is like the lover's kiss of cosmology. In my opinion, it's the
most compelling scientific theory outside of gravity and evolution."

"Then why does it seem like you're the only one who believes it?"
Cooper said. Sal looked discomposed.

"I don't *believe* it," he said. "That's not how science works. But I
find it compelling enough to devote my life to it. The inflationary
theory has serious conceptual problems. It's extravagant, for one
thing—about as fine-tuned as a Beverly Hills housewife. It also
dabbles in the anthropic—it takes life into account—and that moves
it from physics to metaphysics."

There was an opening here, Cooper thought, one she could slip
through by asking a big but simplistic question. She wanted to connect
with him in a way that went beyond their moment in the library. She
decided to go for it. "How can something come from nothing?"

It was clear at once that Sal was irritated, but Cooper didn't know
why. "And there's the metaphysics, right on cue," he said.

"I'm just asking a question," Cooper said, confused.

Sal looked at her for a moment. "Ah, I see now. You're not asking
me how it happened. You're asking me who pulled the trigger." He
turned away and tinkered with the telescope. "Shit."

"What?"

He looked over at Cooper. "Nothing. It's just—I think you're
spending too much time with Pavano. These are his questions, not
yours. Dumb questions are not attractive."

Cooper felt humiliated. Blistering heat coursed through her body.

"Well, since I live each day in service to what you find attractive, I'm devastated."

Sal stared at her in surprise—Cooper herself was surprised—and both fell silent.

"Why is it so hard to talk to you?" he finally said.

"You brought me out here so I'd ask questions, right? Or did you just want me to *ooh* and *ahh* over your big telescope? I asked a question because I'm interested. In this. In you. You're telling me you and Alek sit out here and talk about the minutia of the beginnings of the universe and it never occurs to you to ask how it started?"

"That's all we do."

"No, I mean how it started before it started."

"And I am answering your question with precision: the universe is cyclic, it is built and destroyed, and then it is rebuilt. It bumps up against another world, from which we are separated by a dimension, and this sets off a bounce, what inflationists call the Big Bang."

"Before that. Before any of it, Sal."

"These are questions every kindergartener asks, Cooper."

"Have they gotten an answer yet?"

Sal started pacing the metal scaffold. "You know what gets old real quick? People trying to ask if there's a god in about a hundred different ways. Do you realize how ridiculous that sounds to someone who knows what the universe actually looks like? Is it my job to pretend like we're all on equal footing here, that we're all smart and all of our answers are equal and we all get certificates just for showing up? That may work in art, Cooper, but that doesn't work in the real world. Science doesn't work that way."

He studied Cooper for a moment, and then seemed to grow remote. "Oh, I see. It's meaningless to you because it doesn't take you into account." He laughed. "I know exactly what you want me to say. That your precious 'Big Bang' was the eye of god opening. When I don't play your game, you ask me if I can prove that it wasn't. Here's a real question for you: Would you even want me to tell you if I could?"

Cooper and Sal stood staring at each other. Cooper could see both certainty and fear looking back at her, until Sal blinked, and only certainty remained.

*

At the Smoke Bar that night, Cooper sat in silence with Birdie, watching Floyd and a contract plumber grind against a dining assistant to the strains of Electric Hellfire Club.

"Quit hogging the girl," the plumber shouted at Floyd.

"Has anyone seen Sal?" one of his research techs called from the door.

"He's up in El Dorm fucking that cargo handler," Floyd replied.

"No, I just saw him in the library," Denise shouted from the bar.

"You're seeing things, then," Floyd said, "because he's definitely getting his cargo handled right now."

Sal's research tech grinned sheepishly and walked out.

If Cooper hadn't already been completely soused, the exchange would have stung. Instead, she turned her attention to a half-full beer on the table that did not seem to have an owner. She drained it and set it back down. Next to her, Birdie slowly pushed the bottle away with his index finger.

"Well," he said, "unless I'm much mistaken, I've just witnessed a moment of desperation," he said. "What's wrong, Cherry?"

Cooper responded by pushing back her chair and getting another beer from the bar. She wandered around, pausing at various tables, and after downing a Jägermeister beer bomb with the contract plumber, walked up to Floyd and began an impassioned but incoherent defense of Larry McMurtry.

He merely waved her off. "Go sober up, honey."

She sauntered back to Birdie's table, but he was in deep conversation with Pearl now, so she decided to lay down on the floor and rest her eyes. Some time later, she found Tucker looming above her like a monument—he was wearing sunglasses, and in them, Cooper saw herself, twice. She realized she was using someone's bunny boot—

Birdie's?—as a pillow. A new face appeared next to Tucker's—an unfamiliar pink face with a mouth like an earthworm. "Are you okay, love?" The face swam in and out of view, and it wasn't until she noticed the surplice that Cooper realized it was the chaplain in from Palmer Station.

"I'm okay," she slurred. "Just wanna sleep." She dropped her head back against Birdie's bunny boot with a thud. The next thing she knew, Tucker was hauling her to her feet.

"I'll escort her to her room," she heard Tucker say to the chaplain.

"Encourage her to come talk to me tomorrow, will you," he said. "Best to cut these problem drinkers off at the pass, I think."

"Come on," Tucker whispered in Cooper's ear. He dressed her in her ECW, and escorted her down the stairs and across the Dome. As she emerged from the entrance tunnel, the crisp, thin air seemed to slap her halfway sober. Like a riderless horse galloping over a hill, vague but searing shame appeared and overtook her. She summoned every shred of competence she had to put one boot in front of the other.

"I'm sorry," she said.

"Don't be. Public intoxication is an occupational hazard."

"You have my paperwork. You know I'm not a drunk."

"Situational alcoholism is a documented disorder," Tucker replied.

"And it's not even cold," Cooper cried, as she blinked into the sunlight. "I'm at South fucking Pole and I'm not even cold!"

"It's thirty degrees below zero."

Cooper shook off Tucker's grip and skipped across the snow. She stumbled and fell face-first, her reflexes too slow to break her fall. Tucker turned her over and looked down into her hood.

"I'm going insane," Cooper heard herself say.

"You know what Foucault says," Tucker replied. "Madness can be silenced by reason."

This comment hit Cooper like a steel-tipped ice chopper to the head. She scrambled to her feet and pushed Tucker with both hands.

"Take that back!" An expression of shock passed over Tucker's face, quickly replaced by sadness. Cooper pushed him again. "It's reason that is silenced by madness, and you know it. Take it back!"

Suddenly, Tucker gathered her into his arms, into a firm, bigger-than-the-sky embrace. "Forgive me, Cooper," he said. Then, just as suddenly, he pushed her away and turned back toward the station.

The Jamesway was deserted. At her door, Cooper found a small package, wrapped in brown paper. She tucked the package under her arm and shouldered her way into the room. She successfully un-zipped her parka on the third try before sitting down to work off her damp long johns and assorted underclothes.

Once she'd stowed her ECW, she opened the package. It contained a bottle of Scotch. A note was included, which was decorated by an amateurish but endearing drawing of two penguins. The penguins were regarding each other from across an ice crevasse. The note, written in immaculate but minuscule print, read, *In hopes of inspiration. (They say Scotch was the drink of choice at Scott's Hut.) Thank you for your kindness. My invitation to the Divide still stands. You're on the manifest if you want to be. Frank Pavano.*

Placing the note from Pavano on her desk, she picked up the old Tylenol vial. She ran her thumb over the cap, thought about open-ing it, then decided against it, setting it next to the compass. She lay down on her bed with her boots on to wait for the room to stop spinning, and after about an hour, it did. She staggered over to her desk and laid a blank piece of paper on it. She stared at its brilliant whiteness for so long that iridescent green specks began flying across the page. Finally, she picked up a sharpened pencil and began sketching.

Fifteen minutes later, she had a crude drawing of a vending-machine charm in the shape of Frank Pavano. It was the first drawing she'd completed since the last mitten in the triptych, and it was that fact, rather than any merit inherent in the sketch itself, that calmed Cooper's nerves.

She heard the door to the Jamesway open at the end of the hall. The squeak of bunny boots echoed down the corridor until the footsteps stopped at her door. The sound of heavy mittens being removed was followed by a confident knock.

"You decent?"

"Wait," Cooper said. "Just—hold on." She struggled into her thermals and tucked the sketch she'd done of Pavano between the pages of *Worst Journey*. Finally, she opened the door to find Sal in his green parka and gaiters, frost on his eyebrows and his beard. He pushed his hood off his head with his forearm.

"Tucker told me you got obliterated at the Smoke Bar. He asked me to check on you."

"He's exaggerating. I'm fine. As you can see."

"Well, I told him I'd check on you. So I'm checking on you." He glanced around her room. "Can I come in?"

Cooper stepped aside to let him pass. He spotted the Scotch and picked it up.

"Mackinlay's?" There was reverence in his voice. "Where'd you get this?"

"It was a thank-you gift."

Sal looked over at Cooper. "From who?"

"Pavano."

"Frank Pavano gave you this?"

"There was a note. It's on the desk."

Sal read it, then tossed the sketch back on the desk. "He offers you 'inspiration'?" The ice groaned beneath the Jamesway, shifting.

"I'll take what I can get," Cooper said.

"Why is Pavano sending you gifts?"

"I think this is his way of being human."

"In my line of work, sharing research is like swapping bodily fluids, so I'm sure it's the same with art. Not that this is art." Then he saw Cooper's sketch of the *Terra Nova* taped to the wall. "Now this—this looks like art," he said. He leaned close to it, his eyes roaming from the ship's figurehead to its masts and riggings. "This is fucking intricate, Cooper. You did this?"

Cooper stepped next to him. "It's the *Terra Nova*. The Scottish whaler Scott brought to Pole."

"Holy shit," he said softly. He turned to look at her. "This is good, Cooper."

"You can have it," Cooper said, not quite knowing why she said it. "I mean, if you want it."

"Of course I want it."

Cooper reached across him to remove the sketch from the wall, and as she did so she felt she was toeing the edge, the parade passing by below her. She handed him the sketch and he set it on the desk without taking his eyes off her face. He touched her cheek with his cold hands like she was the most fragile thing on earth. They stood like this for what felt to Cooper like hours, and yet she had no desire to break their silence, or even move. Suddenly, Sal inhaled sharply and shook his head. "I'm just going to say it: I think you're beautiful and I want to be near you. Can that be enough?"

Cooper responded by leaning into him and, hesitatingly, kissing his mouth. She pulled back to see if this had been a welcome gesture, but his eyes were closed.

She sat on the edge of her bed and watched as Sal dropped to a knee in front of her and began unlacing her bunny boots, unthreading the laces through the eyelets unhurriedly. Once he'd pulled off her boots, he held her feet in his hands and looked up at her. "You should be wearing your blue boots," he said mildly. "They don't get your socks wet."

Then he helped her pull her long underwear over her head, and each time his cold hands brushed her skin, it seemed like getting a good deep breath was impossible. A sense of urgency began to rise up and grip Cooper as Sal undressed her. She scooted back on the bed to make room for him, and watched as he pulled his overall straps off his shoulders, like Cooper imagined a lumberjack might.

But as he reached for his belt, something changed in his expression—he looked at her as if seeing her for the first time, and froze. His suspenders hanging off his waist, and his blue thermal stained with old sweat, the cuffs pushed up to his elbows, he pulled away. He shook his head twice, like he was shaking off a blow.

"Oh god, what?" Cooper said. She looked down at her bare arms and curled into herself, drawing her knees up to her chest. Sal's back was now against the canvas door.

"I don't know," he said, his voice strange. "Something's wrong about this. I'm confused."

His eyes searched the room, landing on everything but Cooper's face. Then they found the compass, the antique compass—baroque, incongruous, but necessary. "The compass," he said. "Who brings an antique compass to Pole?"

"Who cares?" Cooper said weakly.

"No, it says something. It means something," Sal said. "It's messing me up." Cooper didn't believe him. Of course it wasn't the compass. They both knew this was a lie. The compass, with its dumb glass face, was itself a lie Bill had told Cooper again and again since the day he'd dropped it in her hands—that it was all you needed to navigate yourself to safety.

As she watched Sal pulling his suspenders back over his shoulders, Cooper realized there was no longer a reason not to reveal that lie—no reason not to step off the precipice, and no one to stop her from doing it. So she told him about Saganaga, how it had been during the trip to the Boundary Waters with Billie and their father two months after David was found that Cooper had gone wandering, gotten lost. She'd stumbled back into camp around ten at night, her panic long since replaced by indifference to her fate. Billie was already in her sleeping bag. Bill had been chopping wood; he hardly looked up. "You had a compass and you had our coordinates," he'd said, as if she'd only been out to use the latrine. "Obviously, you don't know how to use either."

The next morning, Cooper awoke to find he'd designed a compass course outside of camp. There was a log. Then, ten feet away, a stone. About two yards from that was a Nalgene bottle. Past that, the small wooden box containing David's ashes.

"I decided last night," Bill said. "It's up to you to get us to Lake Gray. You have the map and you have the compass. If we're not there in two days, we turn back. He remains in the box." Cooper had no time to absorb her father's anger before he roughly shoved the antique compass into her hands. He then grasped her shoulders and positioned her until she faced the woods. "What does it say now?"

"North."

"Wrong."

"Who cares," Billie said sleepily from the door of the tent. "That's what GPS is for." But something inside Cooper, a half-buried but strong and relentless feeling, took hold of her and said, I *care*.

But they never got to Lake Gray, not that time, and Cooper held the box in her lap the entire drive home.

All this Cooper told Sal not because she wanted him to understand her—it no longer mattered what he thought about her—but because she wanted him to know that, even if the compass was a lie, she was not. She told him about Cherry and Titus, about her imaginary journeys with David, how Edgar Allan Poe had infected his vision of South Pole, and how she'd come here to make sure their first idea of Pole was the right one, to reclaim it from the lies. Sal listened to all this, his chin on his chest, but when she was done, he said nothing. Cooper felt completely alone.

"I'm sorry," he finally said, grabbing his parka from the desk chair. "I know I'm being a dick, but I really don't know what to say. I need to think."

Cooper understood then that she had unloaded her baggage at his feet and he'd kicked it once or twice before deciding it was too much trouble. She continued hugging her knees, head down, and listened to the rustle of his parka, the metallic étude of his zipper going up, catching, going down, then going all the way up to his neck, and, finally, the sound of his boots retreating down the hall.

Cooper got out of bed, moved her desk chair to the back wall, and climbed on it. She pushed aside the towel she'd hung over the small window, the one she'd looked out of that first day. It was nearly three in the morning, but stark sunlight poured into the room. Outside, the sky was a pale and taut canvas. She glanced down at her desk, and saw the *Terra Nova* sketch was gone.

*

Sal and the lead of Stanford's Kavli Institute experiment, the elusive Lisa Wu, had been persuaded to lecture on their teams' respective effort to determine the origins of the universe. Cooper had only seen Lisa on one other occasion—at Pavano's lecture a month earlier, watching silently with her research techs. She was a tall, plain-looking woman with completely horizontal dark eyebrows. Her wan bearing was relieved only by the aquamarine rhinestone stud she wore in her left nostril.

Once the crowd settled down, and someone had found Lisa a can of mineral water, she began outlining the basic tenets of the inflationary theory: that the universe grew at unimaginably fast rates during the first fraction of a second after the Big Bang, that the expansion has slowed down, but not stopped, and that the theory, as endorsed by Linde, Guth, and Hawking, along with most mainstream physicists, had achieved five of the six "milestones" that would settle the question once and for all. Cooper had zoned out during the exquisitely detailed explanation of these milestones, but she perked up when she heard Lisa acknowledge that the rate of expansion initially exceeded the speed of light.

At this, a meteorologist raised his hand. "I thought the whole point of the speed of light was that nothing can exceed it."

Cooper noticed Lisa glance at Sal, who was sitting in the front row awaiting his turn. She replied that the meteorologist was correct—technically—but that "in physics, we've learned to expect the unexpected."

"That sounds like a slogan for a beer," Pearl whispered to Cooper.

As she started to wrap up, Lisa glanced over at Sal once again. "Before I turn the stage over to Sal, I feel compelled to say something else: Sal's father, Professor John Brennan, is the reason I'm standing here. He's the reason my whole team is here, really. He believed in each and every one of us, and we consider it the biggest privilege of our lives to be part of this experiment that he designed more than twenty-five years ago. It was only recently that the technology advanced to a point where his theory could be tested." Her eyes darted back toward Sal. "Some thought, perhaps continue to think, that this theory was impossible to test and therefore not scientific. Professor Brennan showed that it is, in fact, testable. And it was Professor Brennan who first understood that the matter and heat in our universe are regularly distributed, that this is not chance, but a cosmological principle."

Sal shifted in his seat. "But that might not mean a lot to those of you who don't live and breathe the Cosmic Microwave Background. Inflation created a uniform and stable cosmos; it can happen again," Lisa continued. "Perhaps it already has. This theory offers a view of the universe in which we are not alone, suggests that there are other universes in pockets of space and time. That's the inflationary theory in a nutshell, and though it's a hard nut to crack, I'm confident that by the end of the research season, we'll have the answer to our most pressing cosmological question."

Everyone applauded, and as Lisa walked past Sal to her seat, Cooper saw him whisper something to her. She remembered what it had felt like as Sal held her foot in his hand. She pushed the thought away.

Sal wrenched around in his chair. "Do you guys mind if Alek tells a joke first?" No one objected, so Alek stepped forward. "This joke happens near Munich. Heisenberg goes for drive and police stop him. Police says, 'Sir, do you know how fast you go?' Heisenberg say: 'No, but I know where I am.'"

Approximately one-sixth of the audience burst into peals of laughter, while the other five-sixths remained silent. Once Alek had returned to his seat, Sal approached the podium. "The Beakers are laughing because they got the joke, not because it's funny—trust me. Anyway, I'm not going to get into a rigorous defense of the cyclic theory of the universe or an attack on the Kavli team's work, but I will indulge myself in delivering one brief roundhouse kick.

"Professor Wu said something that I have to correct, and that is the idea that some of you may have about what she means when she says 'regular distribution.' This makes the universe seem like a calm and orderly place. It is not. If the inflationary theory were true, then the majority of space is an uncontrolled, chaotic place undergoing brutally violent inflation, powered by the kind of energy that tells Einstein to fuck off. But they'd also have you believe that hidden in the folds of this cosmic Technicolor Dreamcoat are those 'pocket universes' that Lisa mentioned, where ponies run free, the wind whipping through their manes—or, the flip side, an alternate world where you are living the life that would have unfolded had you decided to run that red light in 1998 and killed your family in a car wreck. To make matters worse, the inflationary theory is the Intelligent Design of cosmology—"

"Sal, that's not fair," Lisa said.

"Let me finish first, and then see if it's not fair. The inflationary theory is the Intelligent Design of cosmology because it is heavily reliant on the anthropic principle, which is the idea that the physical laws that govern the universe must be compatible with the fact that life exists."

Next to Cooper, Pearl raised her hand. "What's wrong with that? That seems logical."

"Yes, it does, but in cosmology, and in Intelligent Design, it is being used to explain features of the observable universe that people like Professor Wu, and like my father, cannot explain. This is the sign of a deeply flawed theory."

"I don't get it," Pearl replied.

"Simply put: instead of physical laws explaining the complexity and diversity of life, they are using the very fact of life to explain the complexity of physical laws. That's not how science works."

The Kavli team began moving about in their chairs, and one of them seemed about to speak when Pavano rose from his chair in the very back of the room. "Your own mentor has said that just because a prediction is consistent with the evidence does not mean the theory is right," he said.

"Yes, and he also said that a scientist must show that the theory has correctly identified the root cause of the phenomenon. And the inflationists haven't." He hesitated and, for a moment, his eyes met Cooper's. "As I told someone just the other day, it's a question every kindergartener asks: What happened before the Big Bang? The greatest minds in inflationary theory cannot answer that."

"And you can?" Pavano replied.

"Not yet. But I believe my team and I will."

"Then let me quote Susskind," Lisa said, standing up now. "'The field of physics is littered with the corpses of stubborn old men who didn't know when to give up.'"

"You're right, Lisa—I don't give up easily."

"Then enlighten us, Sal. Tell them about your own personal *Hitchhiker's Guide to the Universe*."

"It's simple, and there's not a single fine-tune in it: the Big Bang was not the beginning, but was instead the seismic instant marking the separation between our current period of expansion and the cooling from a previous one. What we know as the universe is actually a membrane, or what we call a *brane*. We theorize that our planet exists in a universe that contains at least eight unobservable dimensions. Our brane is separated from another brane by one of these dimensions, and when these two branes collide, it creates what inflationists consider a one-off event—the Big Bang. However, we believe this event actually happens every trillion years. Like a child's sand castle on a beach, it is built and torn down with the regularity of an ocean wave."

The Kavli team snickered.

Cooper raised her hand. "What would that look like?" Without turning around in her seat, Pearl offered Cooper a thumbs-up. Sal walked to the whiteboard and drew an image that looked like two pancakes being used as cymbals. "Like this," he said.

"No. I mean, what would it look like if I were standing right here when it happened. I want an image, not a diagram."

Sal dropped the marker on the table. "You're asking what it would look like if you were there, in the middle of it?" Cooper nodded. "It would be the stuff of daydreams. The most beautiful thing imaginable. First, the approach: You wouldn't feel it, but something enormous would be moving along a dimension you couldn't see. Then, when you collided with it, space would be infused with a nuclear brightness, an ungodly burst of radiation, and it would become hotter than a billion suns. Everything else in the universe—the galaxies, the planets, the stars—everything would be evaporated in an instant. The quarks and gluons that made up everything in the previous cycle would join the flood of new quarks and gluons created at the moment of the collision." He met Cooper's eyes. "The cycle would be renewed."

"So if I'm made up of quarks and gluons," Dwight said, "and, of course, I am, you're telling me I will live again."

"What I'm saying is that in our model, the universe is not lost in a sea of multiverses, not one of countless and random possibilities. Instead, it's a single, cycling entity."

Pearl set her knitting aside. "So we just bang and crunch over and over again?"

"I'm saying that every trillion or so years, the universe remakes itself as an echo of its previous form. Controlled evolution. Every corner of space makes galaxies, stars, planets, and presumably life, over and over again. Instead of being a product of chaos and unexplainable beginnings, the cyclic model—our model—has an explanation for 'what happened before the Big Bang.' It's fucking elegant as hell that evolution works just as well for the structures of galaxies as it does for opposable thumbs." He looked over at Lisa and the Kavli team. "Now, all that being said, if we find measurable b-mode polarization this season, none of what I just proposed is true."

"And that would be bad," Pearl said.

"No," Sal replied, "that would be science."

Suddenly, the galley door burst open, and an empty Heineken went sailing through the air before shattering against the back wall. Bonnie stood in the doorway, unsteady. Cooper noticed pink blooms on Bonnie's cheeks and a milk-white beauty about her skin that she'd never seen before.

Bonnie brushed her lank hair out of her eyes. "I don't mean to interrupt, but I'm going on record right now that I'm glad this shit is over." As she propelled herself into the galley, knocking over a pair of empty chairs, Dwight sprung to his feet to stop her, but tripped over the hem of his cloak. "Get out of my way, you stupid-ass skill monkey," Bonnie growled. Cooper looked over at Pearl. She had drawn her pink bandanna over her eyes and was slumped in her chair as if trying to dissolve. Next to her Birdie stroked her knee soothingly.

"Bonnie, stop," Dwight pleaded. But Alek stood up and pounded the top of one of the dining tables. "You stand up here," he said. "Let everyone hear." He assisted Bonnie onto the table.

Once Bonnie was steady on her feet, she looked down at everyone. "I just wanna say that I'm outta here tomorrow. Tucker and the powers-that-be have decided to demote me but I refuse to spend an entire winter at South Pole chopping other people's onions." Pearl's face remained obscured behind her bandanna. "So this crazy adventure's over for me, but guess what? I'm glad it's over. I'm glad it's over, and here's why: it means the end of the bullshit I've been dealing with since October." She looked down at Dwight. "You don't come to South Pole to 'strengthen your relationship,' Dwight. You don't come here to push boundaries so you can exchange sex e-mails with a fucking mini-doughnut vendor you met in a cosplay chat room!"

Dwight sank down in his chair.

"Come on, Bonnie," Sal said, laughing. "Stay. We love your hoosh."

"Nah, Sal. My time has passed. It's time for you guys to eat another woman's hoosh." She soft-shoed her way off the table and walked out of the galley.

Birdie turned around in his chair to look at everyone. "What's hoosh?"

The lectures over, everyone filed out of the galley and into their respective bars and lounges, Cooper hung back and waited for

Pavano. "Someone slipped the flight manifest under my door last night," she said.

"Yes, everything's been arranged. They're expecting us." He scuffed the floor with one of his boots. "I take it you are still interested in coming?"

Cooper watched as Sal stalked out the door. "More than ever."

*

The West Antarctic Divide was one of the most remote locations on the planet, but it was also, Cooper was certain, one of the loudest. The metallic roar of industrial generators made the screams of the 319's engines sound like a kitten's purr. The site was strewn with communication flags of all colors, from lemon-yellow to Achtung-orange; these were attached to one another by lengths of rope, designed to guide anyone caught in a whiteout. A plywood admin building stood sentry at the entrance, with a communications shack attached. Beyond those stood what looked like a dollhouse version of the fuel arches at Pole: these were, Cooper gathered from the hand-drawn map Pavano had made for her during the flight from South Pole, the drilling arch and the core-handling arch. So it was here that the fate of the world, or the global warming hoax, would be decided. This was sacred scientific ground, but to Cooper it looked like any other stretch of Antarctic ice occupied by humans.

Cooper and Pavano stood at the end of a long line leading into the admin shack, manned by an effusive NSF field rep, whose guffaw seemed to echo throughout the entire camp. Cooper and Pavano hadn't exchanged words since leaving Pole; the flight had been uneventful and characteristically deafening. Conversation was out of the question, and Pavano had spent most of the ride staring at the cargo rack just above Cooper's head.

"Pavano, Frank—and research tech," Pavano recited when they reached the front of the line. The rep looked down at his clipboard for a moment too long. Cooper could tell he wasn't reading anything.

"Would you excuse me for a moment," he said, before disappearing into an adjoining room. Cooper could hear whispers and the sound of shuffling papers. The rep returned, looking sheepish. "Your, uh, research tech is not approved," he said, his eyes not quite meeting Pavano's. "She has not undergone basic safety training."

"I was told this requirement had been waived since she is an NSF grantee and underwent safety training in Denver," Pavano replied.

"I'm just telling you what I know," the man said. "You can talk to the site manager if you want, but for now, she can't touch any equipment. You're in Sector 4B." He pointed to a shelf stocked with bright neoprene bundles. "Tents and camp stoves over there."

"What are my access hours to the ice-core archive?" Pavano asked.

The rep looked embarrassed. He consulted the clipboard. "Says here that you will have access to the core-handling room at 0300 hours; you may access the archive freezer at that time." Three a.m., Cooper thought. Jesus.

"And the coordinates for my coring site?" Pavano continued, unperturbed.

"Well, yes, there's a bit of a problem with that, too, I see."

"What's the problem?"

"That request has been denied—it says here that there are some safety concerns." Behind them, the people in line sighed. Denied requests led to long delays and grumpy core techs, who were in the ice archives waiting to be spelled. But to Cooper's surprise, Pavano didn't argue. He thanked the rep, then gathered his bag and stepped over to the shelf where the tents were wrapped in neat, ornament-like balls. Astonished, the NSF rep watched as Pavano scooped two tents from the shelf.

"Sector 4B is this way," Pavano said as he led Cooper out the door.

"Wait, don't you want to—"

"Argue? I knew exactly what would happen when I arrived. People are reassuringly predictable. Which makes my job easier."

"It's your job to get railroaded?"

"In a sense."

Cooper laughed. "You are so weird."

"I find I am just weird enough."

The walk from the central site to sector 4B was comparable to the walk from the station to Summer Camp at Pole, but Cooper wanted to crawl the last twenty yards—the air was so thin it felt as though she were sipping air through a straw. Her whole body hurt. Sector 4B turned out to be a ghost town. Vacant tents dotted the landscape, their nylon flaps dancing in the wind. Pavano dropped the gear. "I'd say they put us all the way out in Antarctica, but we're already here, so I'll say they put us in Siberia instead." He gestured toward the perimeter of camp. "Take a walk," he said. "I'll put up the tents."

Cooper was bent over her knees, huffing. She cocked her head up at Pavano and squinted in the sun. "How are you breathing and talking at the same time?"

"I did some high-altitude cross-training in preparation before the season began."

"Well, goody for you," Cooper gasped. Pavano almost smiled. "I'll help with the tents. I'm pretty good at setting them up. Lots of practice."

Pavano shook his head. "No, go walk. Look around. Maybe you'll get inspired."

"Maybe I'll die of hypoxia."

"Either way, a different perspective."

As Cooper began trudging away, she heard Pavano call after her, "Follow the flags."

"I'm sick of following flags," Cooper muttered.

The sun was merciless—bright with burning hydrogen and helium but offering no heat. That the continent on which she walked was wrapped around the bottom of the planet—that rock and ice could adhere to a curve—suddenly seemed a ridiculous notion. Cooper squinted, trying to conjure an image of Cherry, or even Mawson—the redoubtable Aussie survivor of a different adventure, with his skin peeling off in thick sheets, his tongue swollen, and his gums black as ink. Several of the Program's past artist Fellows had painted images of these men haunting the ice, sometimes literally as ghosts. But when Cooper thought of them, they faded quickly, replaced by other, more familiar ghosts.

As she walked, she kept thinking of what she hadn't told Sal that night in her room, of what had happened after that trip to Saganaga. About how she and Billie had returned to the Boundary Waters a month later without Bill, and without his knowledge, to take matters into their own hands. At their launch point, a group of men had appeared, wearing Duluth Packs on their shoulders and many-pocketed cargo pants. As soon as they saw Billie pulling the canoe off the car rack, the packs had dropped from their shoulders, hitting the hard grassless soil on the edges of the launch point simultaneously.

"We're good, boys," Billie said, grunting as she lifted the canoe on her shoulders. Her curse-soaked stumble confirmed the men's initial impulse. Two of them walked over to where she stood, slipped their shoulders under the eaves of the canoe, and raised it off her shoulders.

"Thanks, guys," Cooper said. Billie turned to her and mouthed an emphatic *fuck you.*

"You two planning to portage?" a scrawny guy in shorts asked. "We-no-nahs are a bitch." Cooper said nothing, chastened by her sister's soundless curse. The big guy looked at Billie, down the length of her body and then back again, assessing her suitability to the task and finding it wanting.

"You guys aren't going in alone, are you?" he asked.

"We're meeting our old man at Saganaga," Cooper said. "It's a test." Billie said nothing to contradict Cooper's easy lie.

"A test?"

"A competence test," Billie said, picking up the lie with ease. "We do this every year. He marks up the map. He goes in two days before us. We find him." These words came out of Billie's mouth without cadence or emotion, and Cooper saw her sister's lively eyes had turned dull and cold. She wanted the men gone.

"Wow, that's hard-core," the scrawny one said.

"You know what's really hard-core," Billie said, and to Cooper's horror, she dug the baggie out of her pants pocket.

"Billie, don't," Cooper said.

The guy peered at the baggie, and broke into a grin. "Dope? Yeah, that's real hard-core," he said.

Billie walked up to him and dangled the bag in front of his Maui Jims. "Guess again," she said. From where Cooper was standing, the guy looked like the figure in Magritte's *The Son of Man*, except instead of a bowler he was wearing a bad buzz cut and instead of a green apple in front of his face there was a Ziploc containing David's cremated remains.

The guy took a few steps back. "Jesus. You can't do that, you know. It's illegal."

"You gonna tell on me?"

"No," the guy said, even more quietly this time. "I'm just saying."

Billie put the baggie back in her pocket and walked down the ramp, leaving Maui Jim gaping after them. The big guy had set the canoe on the launch point, and held it steady as Cooper stepped in, and when she did she felt like she was stepping off the edge of the earth.

Later, when the men's voices had faded to silence and the only sound was the whisper of the paddles whirlpooling the water, Cooper remembered how the tangled mass of streams and rivers on the navigation map became a single ribbon of clear water. You took it on faith that on the other side of the granite islands, with their forests of spruce looming over the clearings, another waterway, another lake, another body, lay glinting like steel in sunshine. Maps were promises.

They paddled across the lake in silence, except for Billie's occasional call to switch, or to draw left or right. Billie favored her left stroke, and they were continually listing east. As the sun rose higher in the sky, the extent of the damage from the 1999 blowdown was laid bare. Cooper had heard that Ogishkemuncie and Seagull lakes had gotten the worst of it, nearly every mature tree felled by the wind. The patches of flattened forest made Cooper fearful; the open, endless horizon seemed to her like death.

But, still, the route was so familiar, it was like walking around the block. This was their circuit, the Gosling circuit, their route, their road, the only place David was ever truly serene. The annual trip where, invariably, all was quiet, even his brain, an electrified reef teeming with strange thoughts. All around the canoe, the yellow grass in the channels waved in the breeze like flickering candles, bright against the black remains of the charred trees.

It had been Billie's idea to pull a permit and go back a month after the first attempt with Bill, when Cooper hadn't been able to navigate to Lake Gray, when David's ashes rode back to the launch point in a wet pack wedged in the center of the canoe. Billie had prepped everything herself, even spirited away the We-no-nah without Bill noticing. This time, Billie had the compass—not the antique compass that had failed Cooper, but a plastic one purchased at REI. On it, north was north.

Later, after they'd camped and eaten, and after Billie had climbed into the hammock, Cooper walked into the woods that fringed the campsite, the baggie in her hand. A few yards past the latrine, she fumbled in her jacket pocket for the empty travel-size vial of Tylenol that she'd hidden in her backpack before she and Billie had left Minneapolis. She opened the child-safety lid with her teeth and, using a birch leaf as a funnel, poured a teaspoon's worth of her brother's ashes into the vial. She wasn't asking for much, she told herself—just a fragment. Lake Gray could have the rest of him, but these motes, these particles. These were hers.

That night, she and Billie walked together to the outcropping on Lake Gray and tossed David's ashes into the water without ceremony. Billie went back to the tent alone but Cooper sat at the fire, feeding it until the sky began to lighten with the dawn, occasionally touching the vial in her jacket pocket. Veils of mist hung above the water, as if waiting to reveal someone. And, indeed, Cooper saw a yellow We-no-nah gliding soundlessly through them. She went knee-deep into the lake, her eyes straining to catch another glimpse. In a moment, the canoe emerged from the fog, revealing a faceless man, and a Husky wearing a lifejacket. The man waved and continued on, and was once again enveloped by the mist.

Cooper climbed back up the sloping granite outcropping and looked down at her feet, at the bones of the continent. It seemed as if everything around her—the spiny arms of the pines bent over the water, the crackle of the fire she hadn't let die in the night, even the persimmon clouds of dawn—had receded completely. The silence was crystalline. Then, all at once, the sun emerged from the horizon, an undulating smear of orange. Cooper closed her eyes against the light.

When she opened them now, she was surrounded by snow.

*

As Cooper approached their site, she heard a bright, resonant male voice singing "Famous Blue Raincoat." Pavano's voice quavered for a moment as it glided over the notes in the line *she was nobody's wife*, then fell silent. Cooper coughed loudly before unzipping the tent door.

Inside, Pavano was lying prone and tending a camp stove.

"How did it go?" he asked.

"It looks exactly like Pole," Cooper replied.

Pavano readjusted the Sterno canned heat with his mitten, and leaned back on his elbow. The expression on his wind-chapped face startled Cooper; peering out at her from the shadows, he looked almost macabre. His clear eyes took everything in, but betrayed nothing. Cooper felt something stir in her—possibly an idea. It was in Pavano's face; Cooper saw it in his strange eyes, in his angular features. As she gazed at him, committing each feature to memory, a noise issued from his mouth. It took Cooper a moment to recognize it as a laugh.

"What's so funny?"

"I was just thinking that it's been a long time since I've had company," Pavano replied. "I'm a loner, if you haven't noticed. Not always by choice. I'm afraid I have forgotten how to make small talk."

"No small talk necessary," Cooper replied. "When do we get to work? Do we get to work?"

"In time. I'm waiting for a piece of equipment."

"I thought you were going to talk to the site manager."

"That won't be necessary."

"Well, let me know when I can help," Cooper said.

"I should mention that if the site manager refuses to budge on your approval status, any help you give me will likely land you in hot water."

Cooper shrugged. "I've already got a flag on my file. What's another one?"

She sat back against her canvas pack and pulled her sketchpad from the outer pocket. Across the camp stove, Pavano watched her remove her mittens in order to retrieve her pencil. She laid her sketchpad across her knees and rolled the pencil between her fingers as she considered Pavano. She could sense an artifice about him, but couldn't pinpoint it. Maybe it was the way his eccentricities could come and go: Pavano couldn't meet her eyes in the galley but here on the Divide he could stare at her unblinking for whole minutes. At the station he skulked; here he lounged.

She turned back to her sketchpad. Started. Erased. The shape of his eyes was hard to reproduce—they were wide-set, but also deep in his face. She tried again, and, once more, erased the beginnings. On the bruised paper, she drew an outline of a penguin, but it looked morbidly obese, and she erased it, too. She tried a rendering of the Empire State Building with arms, but it looked like a Transformer.

"Problems?" Pavano asked.

"I've given up on you. You're hard to sketch."

"I'm flattered that you'd choose me as a subject. Who, would you say, might be easy to capture on the page?"

Cooper thought of the portrait she'd done of Tucker, how she'd sworn to herself that although it was turning out pretty well, it was a one-off, an exercise meant to get her across the bridge and into the land of polar art. After all the mittens she'd produced, she'd resigned herself to painting the standard skyscapes, cloudscapes, glacierscapes, and snowscapes that seemed to be the expected output for a visual artist at Pole. But then she'd started that portrait of Bozer. And then, last week—after Cooper had noticed the two-inch scar above Pearl's right eyebrow—the one of Pearl.

"No one is easy to capture on the page," Cooper finally replied.

Pavano gestured toward the sketchpad. "Will this become part of your portfolio?"

Cooper shook her head. "No, I'm here to make grand statements, not portraits. That's what they want: statements. A face is not a statement."

"It's a statement of existence," Paveno replied.

Cooper set her notebook on the floor of the tent and inched toward Pavano on all fours until she was at his knees. He watched her as she reached up and took the bridge of his glasses between her fingers and pulled them from his face. His pellucid eyes regarded her impassively.

"You want to know if I exist," he said.

"Yes," Cooper said quietly. For a long moment, they gazed at each other, and the moment grew taut. The longer Cooper studied Pavano, the more familiar he seemed. He leaned in, drawing closer to her, and the world roared back to life. Cooper moved away, her heart thrumming. A blast of wind shook the tent, sending the Sterno canister into a cartwheel. The time it took Pavano to set it right again gave Cooper a chance to collect herself.

"What did you gather," Pavano said, "from your peek into my soul?"

"I don't know anything about souls. They're a human construct, they're not real."

Pavano seemed discomposed, as if he were a translator who'd fallen hopelessly behind. "It's natural to say such things when you've been spending time with scientists," he finally said. "To them, everything is constructed."

"But you're a scientist."

Pavano hesitated. "I'm also a man of faith."

"You said you were an atheist."

"No, I didn't say that."

"You implied it."

His expression softened, and he sat back against his pack. "Yes, perhaps I did. I find implications give me just enough wiggle room to work in peace. May I have my glasses back?" Cooper hadn't realized that the glasses were still in her hand.

Pavano removed the teapot from the canned heat, and Cooper watched as he carefully selected two teabags from the outer pocket of one of his packs. "Sal says you don't believe your own research," she said. "That you do this for the money because your career in academia tanked."

"Like most of Sal's theories, that's only about half accurate. As I'm sure he told you, I made some mistakes in my career that pushed me to the margins of academia. When you're in the margins, you're impossible to see. You find new frontiers, and you join forces with the people who live on them."

"Like Creationists."

"Theistic science," Pavano said.

"God."

"Methodological naturalism is religion."

Cooper rolled her eyes.

"What I'm trying to say," Pavano continued, "is that it's all religion at the end, whether it's me making the teleological argument at a conference or Sal trying to parse out the beginnings of the universe through his telescope."

"Sal's not religious."

Pavano handed Cooper a mug. "Sal Brennan is one of the most religious people I've ever known. For many years he worked on confirming the main model of the cosmos. His work was a kind of chase after his father's—my wife used to call them Odysseus and Telemachus. Anyway, Sal played a major role in building on Hawking and Penrose's model and making the inflationary model a widely accepted theory among the general public. Now he rejects it. He thinks he's found something better. Think about that for a moment, Cooper—here is a man who spent the better part of his career looking at what is essentially the same data he now has before him, coming to a conclusion that he believes is fact, and then changing his mind. And now he is a paragon of nonstandard cosmology, not to mention a cast-out son, and he's in danger of becoming as marginalized as the proponents of Intelligent Design he abhors. He's a believer, Cooper. His faith is immense."

"But he might actually be right," Cooper said. "There's no possibility that the earth is six thousand years old, that humans walked with dinosaurs."

"Forget Young Earthers and dinosaurs. Those are distractions. The compelling argument is that living things are too well designed to have come about by chance."

Cooper laughed. "The world is the least-well-engineered thing ever."

"You go too far."

No, Cooper thought. She hadn't gone far enough. "Explain suicide."

"The intelligence I'm talking about doesn't deal in individual circumstances."

"It creates a machine only to have it self-destruct?"

"It is an engineer, and it engineered a creature that can intentionally end its life. Maybe in some people, when the wiring has gone wrong, suicide is instinctive. There are countless documented examples of this in nature—mostly birds, as it happens. Petrels that fly into campfires. Mergansers that seek out submerged roots and drown while clinging to them." He removed his glasses to wipe away condensation, and saw, with a start, that tears were leaking down Cooper's cheeks.

The welcome sound of an approaching snowmobile allowed Cooper to wipe her eyes while Pavano struggled to his feet and put his goggles on. After he walked out, Cooper leaned over his sleeping bag to peer through the tent door. Hitched to the snowmobile was a large pallet containing a small generator, several winches and cables, three long, skinny blue cylinders, and something that looked like an enormous tampon applicator. The man on the snowmobile looked nervous as Pavano handed him an envelope folded in half. As soon as he unhitched the pallet, he sped off back toward camp.

When Pavano returned to the tent, he was radiant.

"What's all that?" Cooper asked.

"It's an agile drill that can retrieve cores up to thirty meters," Pavano replied. "But since they integrated the new BID-Deep system, it can, theoretically, reach depths of up to two hundred meters." Cooper was startled to see how happy this made Pavano. "It has been signed out under another team's name and won't be missed for about twenty-four hours. Once I extract this core, it's mine. The lab will be obligated to store it, no matter how it was obtained, and then send it to Denver, where I will analyze it. It shouldn't take us too long to set up."

"You did a work-around," Cooper said.

"I did what I had to do."

"Let's get started, then."

"I'll only need you to help me erect the tripod and the double sheave. The rest I can handle. You go get dinner."

"Do you want me to bring you back anything?"

Pavano shook his head. "I've got a Cup o' Noodles."

*

The galley at the Divide was just a tent, and as she looked at the dinner offerings steaming away in the large aluminum warming trays, unrecognizable in various states of congealment, Cooper missed Pearl's cooking keenly. She held out her tray and a lump of something resembling meatloaf was dropped onto her plate. She picked a stale roll out of a plastic basket and scanned the room. Across from her, a man in a blond wig topped with a tiara sipped soup from a bowl. Next to him, Cooper noticed Sri and his team studying some printouts. Cooper tried to catch his eye, but he seemed to be ignoring her. She considered sitting at his table anyway, but decided instead to take a seat at an empty one.

As she was poking the meat product on her tray with her fork, Cooper felt someone staring at her. The ice-core tech Cooper sat next to on the flight in was scowling at her, a lock of purple hair obscuring her right eye.

"Why are you helping him?" she asked.

"Excuse me?"

"Frank Pavano. He's a pseudoscientist."

"I'm an artist," Cooper said, as if that explained everything.

"You his girlfriend or something?"

"Christ, no. I'm here for inspiration. A change of scenery."

The tech put her hand on her waist and cocked her head. "Artists and Writers Fellow?"

"Yeah."

"But you're on the list as a tech. They put you on his manifest?"

"I know, weird."

"And what exactly are you painting?"

"I'm here to sketch and observe the field camp. And the surrounding ice sheet plateau, also." She cast about for something believable. "I'm calling it 'Transparent Truths.'"

"Transparent Truths?"

Cooper knew she had to get jargony now—jargon was the strongest shield for the professional with nothing to say. "I plan to create a suite of etchings and paintings on this source material, using color and implied texture, and focusing on a postmodern application of serial imagery."

The core tech relaxed a little. "Okay, sorry to grill you. It's just—having a guy who thinks global warming is a hoax at a climate research site is sort of big deal. My name's Fern."

"Cooper. And believe me, I get it."

A couple of other people sauntered over to Cooper's table. "It's just weird that you came on his manifest. That's not how this is usually done. I mean, you usually have your own flight order."

Cooper shrugged. "I don't even know what that means. I just do what I'm told."

"You know that he's on Big Oil's payroll, right?" Fern said. "This is basically like giving an NSF grant to Exxon." She paused. "What's he like?" The crowd around Cooper's table had grown bigger, but everyone remained silent, as if what Cooper had to say was extremely important.

"He seems normal."

"There's no way he's normal," someone from the edge of the group said. "Not even Pole-normal."

"The NSF is a craven, cowardly agency run by mealy-mouthed pieces of shit," another voice shouted from the back, this one belonging to the wig-wearing male beauty queen.

"Randy has that on his business card," Fern said, finally cracking a smile. "So you're here to help him extract a core? You know how to do it, right? Because it's actually really dangerous. They have people here whose only job is to do shit like that, and none of them are on his tech roster."

"I think he's going to do it himself. Seeing as no one will help him."

The room boomed with laughter. Cooper had no idea why.

*

Once she came to, Cooper's first thought was, why is Pavano puking? A few yards away, he was leaning over his knees, an entire Cup o' Noodles pouring out of his mouth and onto the ice in a steaming pile. Her second thought was that her hand was warm, even though she'd taken her mitten off to help Pavano with the corer, and last she remembered it was basically flash-frozen. She got to her feet, wondering why she'd been prostrate on the snow. Now Pavano was wiping his mouth with the back of his hand, and now he was shouting at her: *Don't look.* As if in slow motion, Cooper turned to see what he was going on about. Was that blood on the ice? Was that her finger, half attached—no, three-quarters detached—to her right hand? She felt consternation upon seeing the dangling finger, as if it were something stubborn, like a hangnail, and reached for it with her other hand and pulled it off. It came off easily, and she tossed it into the snow.

That gesture—the toss—seemed to trigger a sudden response, as if the cosmos had been waiting for this act, and now that it had been completed, the world splintered into shards. Each shard reflected the sun, like waves on a lake. Saganaga. The lake at the end of the Gunflint Trail. You stayed in the possession corridor because you didn't want to face the wind. Cooper was in the canoe, alone now, driving it straight for the shore.

*

Her mind was a museum. Only dusty relics remained: her hands guiding the elephantine drill onto the spot Pavano had marked on the ice. The sensation of her right mitten twisting into an infinite spiral as the generator roared; searing pain that quickly gave way to numbness. Pavano's noodles. His startled face. The blood on the ice and Cooper's mangled finger, which had been dug out of the snow by a compassionate research tech—Fern?—once the drill had stopped grinding and help began arriving. The finger had been placed in a snow-filled Coleman. Cooper remembered marveling at the Coleman, that such a thing could be found both at a suburban picnic and also on the West Antarctic Ice Sheet. There was the med tent and the disembodied face of the medic, displaying teeth in some facsimile of a smile. This was followed by a stretch of blackness, studded by occasional bursts of light and scored by a ceaseless shriek. Someone had tried to peel open her eyes; she had fainted. Cooper had blinked against the assault and reluctantly focused her eyes until she realized she was looking at Doc Carla. That's when the pain arrived—decadent, laughably excessive. Cooper felt an intense desire to chop off her right arm.

Then there had been twenty-four hours in Hard Truth with Doc Carla—triage and treatment, including an awful irrigation of the "wound site." No one else had been allowed to speak with her. There had been one time when Sal—it was Sal, Cooper knew, because he'd touched her bare arm as she lay there, and she'd remembered the feel of his hand from that night in her room—sat next to the bed and read to her after Doc Carla had kindly slipped her a Vicodin when the expired Tylenol with codeine had failed. She couldn't re-member what book it was now—it was the sound of his voice that had penetrated, not the words.

Doc Carla told her there had been an accident, that a finger on her right hand—the "pointer," the CEO of the hand—was gone, that they'd been unable to save it. Because Cooper couldn't visualize the injury, and because Doc Carla refused to let her see the wound until it had healed, it didn't seem real. None of it seemed real. And because it didn't seem real, Cooper appeared to be taking it well.

Unfamiliar people showed up at Hard Truth. Men and women dressed in Pole gear who weren't Polies. They were from the Na-tional Science Foundation, they were from VIDS. Doc Carla sat in a folding chair while the admins interrogated Cooper—it was like a deranged version of *Inherit the Wind*. Again and again, Cooper went over every detail of her visit to the Divide. Her inability to be spe-cific frustrated the admins, and when she mentioned Pavano's name, they became agitated. No one would tell her what had happened to him or where he was.

On their next visit to Hard Truth, the admin guys leveled with her. The media already knew what had happened, and this had opened the door to scrutiny. Pavano's congressional sponsors were claiming harassment and discrimination. There was talk that the two con-gressmen who had lobbied to get him on the ice wanted a federal investigation. This would mean subpoenaing every grantee who had had contact with Pavano—including Cooper, Sal, Sri, and entire cli-mate research teams at the Divide. They would be expected to leave the ice to meet with investigators. The effect this could have on the ongoing experiments at Pole would be catastrophic. In an effort to stave this off, Alexandra Scaletta, head of the NSF, had invited the congressmen to Pole to assess the situation for themselves, as "a ges-ture of goodwill."

"So, am I being sent home?" Cooper asked the latest NSF admin to interrogate her, a stout, genial man named Warren.

"I know it seems like we've been asking you the same questions a hundred different ways, but we're just trying to figure out how this happened. Why you were there, why Dr. Pavano was working with equipment checked out under another team's grant number. Is there anything else you can tell us that will help us out here?"

"How is he?" Cooper replied.

"Dr. Pavano?"

"Is he still here or did they send him back?"

"I'm afraid we're not allowed to say," Warren said. His look turned pleading. "That's why we're asking you these questions. The sooner we can create a timeline of events, the sooner we can put this all to rest." Cooper smiled to herself. *Good luck with that.*

*

When she awoke in her own room, she found her desk piled with homemade gifts wrapped in fax paper. There was even a bottle of Crown Royal in a purple sack with a note signed by Dwight. Pearl had left a basket filled with knitted items and various baked goods. Hanging from the coat hook on the back of the door was a small wooden birdhouse from Bozer, accompanied by a little sign that said *Glacier Sparrows Only.*

She glanced up at her tiny window, as if the constant sunlight could indicate the time. She peed in her pee can, holding herself steady by gripping the desk chair with one hand, so she could skip the bathroom— even though she couldn't remember the last time she'd brushed her teeth. She noticed now that Sal had left a note on the desk. *Radio when you get up and I'll come get you. Do not walk to the station alone. Sal.*

As she struggled into her balaclava, she saw Pavano's Scotch on her desk. She grabbed it by the neck and shoved it into the deepest pocket of her parka, along with her painkillers. Doc Carla had been careful: there were only three in the bottle, but at least they weren't expired.

Cooper was halfway to the Jamesway door when she turned around and went back to her room. Next to her compass was the vial containing David's ashes. She placed them both in her other pocket.

Outside the Jamesway, Floyd sat astride a snowmobile arguing with a fuel tech about glycol levels. When he saw Cooper walking toward the station, he cut the argument short and offered her a ride, which she accepted. As the snowmobile careened across the ice, Cooper tried to sort out exactly how she was supposed to feel about this finger thing. The whole experience so far had been like living inside Picasso's *Guernica*. She wasn't dead. She hadn't lost an arm. This wasn't cancer or a stroke. It was a finger. And yet Doc Carla had called it a catastrophic injury. Cooper felt as if she had been anesthetized. Where was her fear? Her outrage? Why did she feel nothing about this, besides the pain and the constant throbbing? She was disfigured—a painter, with hyperrealist tendencies, who'd lost a finger on her dominant hand. Was she an abstract painter by default now? Was she a painter at all? She didn't know. And right now, she hardly cared. All that mattered was that she get back to the station. Floyd drove the snowmobile up the entrance ramp and idled in front of Annex B.

"Please don't be nice because you feel bad for me," Cooper said as Floyd helped her off. "I don't want pity."

Floyd gave her a wry look. "You've been around long enough to know there's no such thing as pity here."

Inside her studio, Cooper found her easel where she'd left it and the blank canvas with the roughly outlined polar landscape. It seemed to have come from another era. She pulled the compass out of her pocket and set them on her desk. Then she shook off the mitten on her left hand—the bandage on her right was so thick it functioned as a mitten. After a couple of attempts, Cooper gave up on removing her parka. That would require help, and she didn't want any more help.

She slowly lowered herself to her knees and unfurled a measure of drawing paper from her roll. Doc Carla had cut away the top of the bandage so her thumb and remaining fingers were exposed, which would, theoretically, allow her to pick up her pencils and her brushes. Cooper seized a charcoal nib between her thumb, middle, and ring fingers, which, when squeezed together, functioned as a single digit. It felt awkward, and it hurt like hell, and when she set the nib to the paper, it moved as if following remote instructions from someone else, skittering all over the page and leaving a greasy black trail across the paper. After a few more tries, Cooper sat back on her haunches. There would be no more detailed studies of vending machine charms, no more hyperrealistic portraits of landscapes or roadside cafés. What about faces?

The door opened behind her, and there was Tucker, in sunglasses with a silk scarf tied around his neck and pulled up over half of his face. He was holding a solitary cupcake. "From Pearl," he said, his voice muffled. He set the cupcake down on the desk. Cooper glanced over at it. It was absurdly baroque, way out of proportion to its surroundings. The frosting had been colored pink with valuable food coloring, and a tiny purple violet had been piped upon it. A marzipan bumblebee, with two sliced almonds for wings, perched atop.

Tucker removed Cooper's paints and brushes from her stool and sat down.

"When do I rejoin the gen-pop?" Cooper asked. Tucker didn't immediately reply.

"Or am I being sent home?"

"I am not currently in the loop on that discussion," Tucker finally said.

"Does this mean my quarantine is over at least? Since you're talking to me. Even Floyd talked to me on the way here."

"You know that wasn't my decision. The NSF wants you ensconced here, hermit-like, so the media can't find you, so you can't get online and tell the world what happened. The place is leaking like any number of doomed ships in history."

She rolled up her drawing paper. "Tell the world what happened? *I* don't even know what happened."

"This whole business is my fault. I shouldn't have let you go to the Divide. I rarely make mistakes, but when I do—"

"This isn't your mistake."

Cooper walked over to the corner of the studio, where she kept the canvases: the beginnings, the orphans. "I want to show you something," she said. She found the portrait of Tucker. She pulled it out and shoved it at him without meeting his eyes.

"What's this?"

"You. That night. The Halloween party. Remember?"

Tucker looked at the painting—an eye regarding itself in a shard of mirror that was cupped in a brown-skinned hand. In the background of the reflection were the dirty tiles of a subway bathroom.

"I remember," he said quietly. He cleared his throat. "However, for true verisimilitude, I'm afraid you'll have to revise." He carefully removed his sunglasses and handed them to Cooper. Then he unwrapped the scarf, and Cooper saw that the left side of his face now seemed to hang slightly below the right. The left corner of his mouth fell slack and the corner of his left eye looked as if it were being pulled downward by an invisible thread. The unnatural smoothness of his chemically sanded face had given way to dark sprouts of wiry hair. He seemed half sad; and the look of half-sadness struck Cooper as far worse than a look of complete sorrow.

Cooper started to say something, but Tucker put his hand up.

"Self-pity is vain," Tucker said. "Don't encourage it, and don't engage in it." He stood up. "Eat the cupcake. Act normal. Act like you want to be here, like you're strong enough to be here. And start painting. As soon as possible. If you don't start immediately after the blow, you won't ever start again. I speak from experience." He cleared his throat and lightly stroked his cheek. "And now you have a whole new face to inspire you."

After Tucker left, Cooper felt a wave of despair wash over her. Her wound pulsed with heat as the dull ache gave way to scorching pain. She pulled out the pills Doc Carla had given her and tapped one out onto her palm. She took it dry, then sat down, trying to get a handle on the pain. She examined her bandaged hand. It didn't make sense to wait for Doc Carla in order to assess her disfigurement, to quantify what she'd lost. She had to see her hand now. But first she needed fortification. She pulled Pavano's Scotch from her pocket. It took two minutes, and the assistance of her teeth, but she was able to twist the top open. The first mouthful was medicinal. It burned, the way a wound burns the first time you run it under cold water. The second drink was smoother—still astringent, but warm. The warmth filled Cooper's chest, and it, along with the sublime cooling effect of the painkiller, took just enough of the edge off to give her the courage to assess her injury.

First, she released the insect-like jaws of the metal clamp biting the elastic bandage and began unwinding it. Her arm grew tired— the bandage seemed endless. Eventually, she reached the sterile gauze wrapping her hand in layers as thin as phyllo. After three circum-navigations, Cooper began to see the bloodstains and the thin slice of plywood that supported her hand.

She removed the final layer of gauze, tugging a bit to release it from the scabs, and there it was, a bloom of pith and dried blood. The other fingers, the thumb, the middle, the ring, the pinkie, were white and shriveled, glistening with moisture, and Cooper was over-come by revulsion. The pain came roaring back, crashing through the narcotic. It was as if the wound had sprung to life, as if it had a heartbeat of its own, and was determined to make itself known. Cooper wiped sweat off her forehead and tried to steady herself by taking another mouthful of Scotch. The pain didn't subside, and although somewhere in the far reaches of her brain she knew all she had to do was wait—just wait—she shook out the two remaining pills from the bottle. Cherry waited, and no one came. Cooper had waited, too, and David hadn't come. She was done waiting. She swallowed the pills with a double swallow of Scotch, and as the burn in her chest subsided, Cooper remembered that David's ashes were in her parka pocket. She jammed her uninjured hand into its depths and withdrew the vial. She sat down at the desk and set it next to the empty bottle of painkillers, and laid her head down next to them. As she stared at both bottles, they seemed to merge until it was impossible to distinguish one from the other.

Eventually, her thoughts returned to the igloo that Cherry, Wilson, and Birdie Bowers had made at Cape Crozier, the endpoint of the "Worst Journey in the World," just as they had in the weeks after David went missing. As the police searched, as Billie turned cold and Dasha and Bill turned on each other, Cooper thought endlessly of Cherry, Wilson, and Birdie huddled together in their igloo, waiting out a blizzard in complete darkness, save for the flickering glow of the camp stove. *For twenty-four hours we waited,* Cherry wrote. *Things were so bad now that we dared not unlash the door.*

They did, though. They had to in order to survive, and so had Cooper. In the spring, when they'd found the tire marks on the shore of West Lake Sylvia, out in Wright County, Cooper was the only one in the family who would go downtown to identify David's body. When she got to the morgue, they warned her. They told her they only needed confirmation. They told her they hadn't taken off his seatbelt. They told her about the book found wedged between the dashboard and the windshield. Cooper knew him only by his thick brown hair. It looked so much like her own.

She stood up so suddenly her chair fell backward onto the cement floor with an ear-splitting crash. The sound seemed to come from miles away. The opiates and the alcohol had met in her bloodstream by this time, and were finally mingling. Cooper tried to make a fist with her right hand, and though she could feel some dried blood crack, she felt no pain. When she looked into the fluorescent lights hanging from the ceiling, illuminated commas dove in and out of her line of vision. She may never paint again, but she would do this one thing. This was why she had come to this place, this frozen, dead place. And it was time. She picked up the vial of ashes and walked out of the studio, unaware that her parka was still hanging on the back of the door.

Cooper found the Dome silent, all the machines asleep while the Nailheads ate lunch, and as she walked down the entrance tunnel, she had to work to focus her eyes and steady her steps. She could see her breath, but felt warm. After what felt like days, she finally reached the bottom of the entrance tunnel, and looked out at the drifts surrounding the station. The cornices atop them loomed nearly twenty feet high. This was the moat of death, the deep, circular crevasse that formed around the Dome as winter progressed, but now it seemed bottomless. She glanced down and saw whales. Hallucinations, she thought, and congratulated herself for being able to tell. She blinked once and the whales obligingly disappeared. A hooded figure appeared at the top of the entrance tunnel, and then disappeared, too. Cooper's body was pulsing but her limbs felt stiff. She heard her name coming at her from all directions.

Across the plateau, she could see the caution flags that marked the sinking old station now buried beneath thirty feet of snow, its bones slowly being masticated by the polar ice. A hooded figure appeared again, this time running. Cooper gasped, and a mouthful of thirty-below-zero air scalded her lungs until she thought she'd collapse from the pain. At the same time, though, she felt uncomfortably hot. The person was still running toward her, and it struck Cooper that for some reason he knew what she was about. Perhaps he was coming to stop her. She couldn't let that happen.

She fell to her knees and began clawing at the snow with her left hand, holding the vial in the remaining fingers of her right.

Suddenly, her pursuer was next to her. He stopped and removed his parka. Before she could get a good look at him, the wind changed directions all at once. The snow was rising off the plateau, as if it were alive. A burst of wind knocked her off her knees, but she struggled to her feet. No, this wasn't the right place, this polar vehicle superhighway. No, she knew the right place for this. Beyond the Pole marker and the flags of all nations, at the place where Scott spoke from beyond the grave. That's where David belonged.

A high-pitched scream sounded in her ear. She could see boots just in front of her, and thought she could hear a voice. The boots moved away. Cooper dropped her chin to her chest and lay still once more.

Climb in the trench, kick out the roof, and go to sleep. Doesn't get any easier.

It was as if all of her muscles relaxed at once, like a building settling onto its foundation in a single movement. Cooper found she was standing alone in a clearing. Before her, a forest, pines and oaks twining together, meeting the edge of the snow. She walked toward it cautiously. All was silent. But life wasn't silent, Cooper knew—not even here, so this couldn't be life. Then, all at once, another clearing, and the sun trembling atop the ice like a gazing ball. Cooper closed her eyes against it. When she looked up again, the sun was gone, and in its place, a sparrow.

DEPARTMENT OF THE ARMY

U.S. TOTAL ARMY PERSONNEL COMMAND

ALEXANDRIA, VIRGINIA 22332-0400

ORDER NO: 41-5

The President of the United States has reposed special trust and confidence in the patriotism, valor, fidelity, and abilities of CARROLL F. BOZER. In view of these qualities and his demonstrated potential for increased responsibility, he is therefore promoted in the Army of the United States from Staff Sergeant General to Sergeant First Class. Promotion is effective 1 May 1991 with date of rank 1 May 1991. The authority for this promotion is Section 601, Title 10, United States Code.

Format 307

BY ORDER OF THE SECRETARY OF THE ARMY:

MICHAEL K. VEASEY

LIEUTENANT COLONEL, GS

CHIEF, PROMOTIONS BRANCH

DISTRIBUTION:

EACH PSC (1)

EACH MAJOR COMMAND (1)

SFC BOZER (1)

ASSISTANT TO THE CHAIRMAN (OJCS)

WASHINGTON, DC 20310

man without country

I see her standing at the end of the tunnel. I let her go that far. I know the impulse, and I respect it. You don't survive here without putting your hands on it sometimes, but you have to know how to kill it before it kills you. This one doesn't know how to do that. That's why she got into this fix in the first place, why she came back from the Divide minus a fork.

She's not wearing a parka, and she's shaking like a hog on butchering day—but it's like she don't notice. She just keeps walking, and I see that I have to go after her. My radio crackles, and I consider calling Floyd, but Floyd's got a big mouth, so I figure this one's on me.

When I get there—and I run to get there—she's standing by the moat, her body seizing with the cold. She's looking into the ditch like she wants to jump in, and she's shaking so hard she might end up at the bottom even if she don't mean to. She sees me, and next thing I know she's on her knees, and not in a good way—she's digging, like she's set to bury something. When she sees me coming with my parka, she gets to her feet and takes off. It takes me a minute to catch her, and when I do, she fights me. I'm careful—she's ain't got her bandage on, goddamn it, but I end up catching her and wrapping her in my parka. I have to throw her over my shoulder, but it's done. We're going back inside. Christ, the cold, though. It's straight from hell.

Once we're inside, I take the bandanna off my head, snap it square, and wrap it around her hand. It's ugly because it's a fresh cut, but the fingerless don't scare me. In my line of work, they're a dime a dozen.

"What were you doing out there alone?" I say, once I've got her hand wrapped.

She says, "I'm not alone."

"Not anymore you ain't," I say, and when I put my arm around her shoulder, she sinks into it like it's a warm bed.

I steer her to El Dorm and try to get her to my room without running into any admins, but we run straight into Tucker. It's okay—Tucker understands how I work. I let him know with my eyes that I got this under control, but this girl's his favorite, so he watches me close as I walk her past.

Once we're in my room, I sit her down on my bed and look into her face. Her eyes are streaming tears from the negative fifty-degree wind, and her pupils look like pinpoints. I could take her to Hard Truth, but I ain't done that to anyone yet. The quickest way to get *NPQ* stamped on your dossier is a trip to Doc Carla. No one, not even the weak ones, wants that. But she looks only half here. Lucky for her, I'm all here. This is my quarter. I can bring them back. Done it a million times. Only sane one left on the mortuary team after we cleaned up the crash at Erebus in '79. Tourist flight from New Zealand—TE-901. They'd been running them over Antarctica for years—cocktails-and-cameras type of thing. The plane crashed in sector whiteout conditions. Two hundred fifty-seven on board, all dead on impact. They called us in from Fort Lee to help the Kiwis' recovery mission, the only army unit in a navy operation, and we spent a week camped in tents at the crash site. Body parts everywhere, no telling how the legs got separated, and sometimes even the feet, cut clean away. The human grease turned our parkas black. It soaked through wool gloves. I was eighteen, just enlisted, practically still a blue-head. First place they sent me was Antarctica. Figures. It was my first time on the ice. I didn't want to leave.

I can smell the alcohol on her breath. "You take any scratch with that booze?" I ask.

"I took all three pills, but don't take me to Doc Carla," she says. "She'll be mad. And I don't want to go home." Her wound is leaking—my bandanna is done for—so I pull out my supply kit. Pole docs get supplied like they was going on a Girl Scout trip, so I bring my own shit. I have hydrogen peroxide, two irrigation syringes, dental filling mixture, glucose paste, hydrocodone, antibiotic ointment, gauze, and four three-inch elastic bandages with hook and loop strips. I keep my own hospital, because someone's always getting scratched up at the site.

I crouch in front of her and unwrap my bandanna from her hand. She winces, but doesn't say anything. The wound's opened up. Looks like it's breathing. I see the finger's been cut off down to the proximal phalanx—a little beyond, because the joint's gone. There's lint and shit stuck to it, so I tell her I'm gonna wash the wound site, that it's gonna sting, and before she can say no, I pour the hydrogen peroxide over it in a good steady stream. It soaks my pants leg, but I don't mind. Cupcake, though, she's almost levitating. I tell her to stop moving. "Makes it worse." I want to tell her that after the deep frost of the burn will come a kind of clean feeling, but I don't know how to explain it right so I keep my mouth shut. As I work, I see she's looking at me, as if she's seeing me for the first time. Her eyes touch on every part of my face—mouth, nose, eyebrows.

I smear about a pound of ointment on the gauze, and wrap her back up. I ask her what she was doing out there. She doesn't say anything at first, so I ask her again, and she says, "You ever feel like pulling a Titus?"

"The fuck does that mean?"

"The guy in the Scott expedition. The one who walked out without his shoes on to save the others. Do you ever feel like walking out into a blizzard and never coming back?"

"Impossible," I tell her. "It don't snow at Pole." The snow here comes in on the wind from the coasts. To a Fingy it might look like a blizzard but it ain't. It's just snow on the wind.

Possible, she tells me. Been done.

"Not here it ain't." You can die a million ways here, but not by "pulling a Titus," the fuck that means. She looks at me like she wants a medal for not walking into a blizzard. She doesn't know about life. Example: It would mean nothing to her to learn that a soldier could win a Bronze Star without stepping foot on the battlefield, that all you had to do was bring coffee to a four-star general sitting in a cool underground bunker in the desert, where the air is filtered and smells sweet as spring hay. You would not win shit for a search-and-rescue mission for an F-16 pilot who'd been hit by Iraqi gunfire and who put the plane nose-first into the sand at 130 knots. If you were honorably discharged because you were an old fuck like me, you would, however, get a job with the defense contractor responsible for cleaning up the shit left behind by the three thousand Abrams main battle tanks, the Bradley Fighting Vehicles, and whatever crackerjack bullshit Ali Baba used during Operation Desert Storm. That's what I did. I'm no good at serving coffee, but I am damn fine at cleaning up. Example: Kuwait City. The sky was dark at noon with smoke from the oil fires. The power grids were shot—Hussein had destroyed the transmission lines and distribution centers. Floyd, who'd been moved off a secret project laying DEW lines in Canada, was working at Shuwaikh, trying to get the grids back online. I'd met him at the Defense Reconstruction Assistance Office, where he'd been pitching a fit over a newbie Corps engineer assigned to his team. All his bluster told me was that he was tender as a newborn babe and had no business being in a war zone. He was a mess for the first few weeks, and the suits almost sent him home. I took him under my wing, and though he acts like he don't need me, he's followed me to every godforsaken outpost I've been assigned ever since.

One day, about a week after the U.S. military sent Hussein packing, I get the call to escort some Kuwaiti sheik from the Plaza Hotel to the airport so he could catch a flight to Ta'if, where all the other sheiks were running the country out of a Sheraton ballroom. I get to the eighteenth floor and see the door's open already. He's standing on the balcony, smoking. When he sees me, he tells me to come in. So I do, but he wants me on the balcony. As soon as I step next to him, the hair on the back of my neck is up. This guy ain't happy.

"Look at this," he says, pointing his cigarette at the city below us. It's sooty and dark. I see the same abandoned vehicles I saw on my way in, the same Iraqi tanks lying on their sides, the same sea of broken glass I'd walked across to get here, and the same Jawas standing guard at the door, except now there's a shavetail with them, pointing at something beyond the smoldering skyscraper across the street. In the distance, the oil fires glow.

The sheik starts talking, and I'm only half-listening, but I perk up when he tells me he's the city's engineer. I don't know why it hits me like it does, that even here, in this backward-ass country where men hold hands like schoolgirls and women dress like ghosts, there's a man with the kind of brain it takes to build bridges—to build entire cities.

I'm still turning this over in my mind as he tells me how the Emir single-handedly turned a collection of mud huts into a city of the world. "And see what they've done," he says, sweeping his hand in front of him. The wind catches the sleeve of his dishdasha, fills it like a balloon. I can't tell if he's talking about Saddam's army or ours. I don't reply—I never do when these guys jabber on—but he turns to look at me, his eyes wide, brown, as pretty as a girl's. "Look!" he shouts. Then he's grabbing me. "I want you to look, soldier!" My standard course of action when anyone lays hands on me is to pull my gun, but I don't need a genius to tell me this guy is just another lost soul.

"The airport's done for, and your wells are a mess," I tell him. "But the rest ain't too bad. Four years and you're back in business."

He hears this, but says nothing. He only drops the cigarette on the cement balcony and snuffs it out with one of his thousand-dollar shoes. He grinds it for too long, as if he thinks he can make it disappear. I find the oil fires again; I can't stop looking, the way you can't stop staring at a campfire. I'm still looking when, beside me, I feel the sheik walk to the other end of the balcony. I consider telling him that a river of money, courtesy of the United States taxpayers, is about to flood his city, that it'll get fixed up good, even better than what it was. But you can't talk to these guys. They're too sentimental.

I turn in time to see the edge of his dishdasha as it fills up with wind. I hear him land on the broken glass on the street below, and then I hear people shouting. What I notice is his cigarette flattened against the concrete of the balcony—a little bit of smoke still floats up from it. I walk to the edge and look over. The Jawas and the recruits are hovering over the body, and the shavetail is on his way back into the hotel to make a call. The engineer is dead, kissing the street. I curse him. I must shout it out loud, because the boys on the ground look up, trying to figure out where the sound came from so I have to step back. There will be questions and paperwork and then more questions. I won't be on the line for this. I ain't a suicide hotline, and this wasn't a mission fail. But the paperwork and the shrink— I'd rather pull my teeth out with pliers than deal with that shit again. I didn't need their help after Erebus, and I won't need it now.

I carefully set my supplies back in the tackle box and snap it shut. The girl's eyes are big—scared-big—and I ask her what's up. She says she left something out there, but she won't tell me what it is.

"Old Bozer'll get it for you," I say, like she's a baby. "Just say what I gotta look for." She shakes her head at me. Even though she still looks like someone killed her puppy, her eyes can focus on my face now. She's coming back. I see the shame is getting to her. She's too embarrassed to talk much. Good. What happened to her on the Divide ain't her fault, but this silly shit—going outside without ECW and playing in the snow—that is.

I got something to show her, so I take my old Palmer parka from the hook and help her into it. "Where are we going?" she asks while I pull her bandaged hand through the cuff.

"Just follow old Bozer."

*

It's colder in the Utilidors than it is under the Dome. No one comes to this door besides me. I drop my shoulder and lean it; it's ice-encrusted and gets harder and harder to open each year. I got the flashlight in my armpit, and once I break the door open, I have to crouch down and sort of shuffle through. She's not following me, though. She's watching me from the Utilidor tunnel, like she's scared of me. Denise wasn't scared. She walked in like a champ, no hesitation. She went right up to where me and Floyd had him laid out, went right up to him and told me to take the plastic off his face. But then it was me hesitating. My brains told me that the Man Without Country would look as pretty as he did the day he died—hell, this continent's got a whole baseball team of frozen explorers sleeping in the ice—but I wasn't keen on it. Denise was, though—she was real keen. And by this time, I woulda done just about anything for the woman, so I did it. I blew on the plastic to get it to loosen a little, and after that it was easy enough. Denise held his head while I unwound the sheeting like I was taking off an Ace bandage. First to show was his beard. Next, his mouth, his white lips frosty. When I checked on Denise, making sure she wasn't too upset, I seen something that surprised me. A smile. First one I'd seen since she'd come down. Something was happening here. Didn't know what it was, but I wasn't gonna try to stop it. Not if it'd help her. And it did. It did help her.

I'd gotten the call right after Halloween 1999, from the U.S. Coast Guard, asking if I had any interest in visiting Newport, Rhode Island. A Boeing 767 had gone deep-sea diving shortly after takeoff from JFK, and the head of the recovery team—one of the boys from the Erebus crash site, Gluck, now a twenty-year navy veteran—had asked for me specifically.

I was a month into the season at Pole but VIDS put me on a plane the next day, and I was on board the USS *Grapple* within forty-eight hours. I hadn't done water rescue before, but I wasn't there to rescue. I was there to recover. Gluck told me the Atlantic Strike Team was young—half of them were raw. He wanted me there to show the youngsters how a man handles himself when the bodies begin to appear, how to lay out the remains on the deck, how to catalog limbs, how to see without seeing.

Some cracked, but most got it, and when the bodies started coming, we were a well-oiled machine. We didn't talk about what happened to this aircraft—not our concern—but it was hard to miss the people crowding the pier every evening when our shift ended. The families. Second day into the operation, I was walking to the hotel shuttle bus when someone shoved a photograph in my hands. Before I had a chance to look away, I saw it was a picture of a smiling man, all messy black hair and a mustache. "This is my husband." The voice was gentle—not accusing, like the others. It was almost as if she were introducing us at a party. I looked up and saw a short lady with frizzy brown hair and a pretty mouth. She wore a purple polka-dotted scarf 'round her neck. Her glasses made her big brown eyes look even bigger, and I noticed those eyes were dry. "Have you come across him yet?" she asked. I glanced down at the photo again before handing it back to her, and she told me his name. Didn't want to know his name, but now I knew it: Kevin. She told me he was on his way to Cairo, that he was a journalist. "For a very prestigious periodical," she told me, but I'd never heard of it. She seemed disappointed when I said this, but I told her not to worry, that I barely know how to read. That made her smile a little.

Gluck passed by with two of the divers and gave me a funny look. I knew I should leave, but I asked her name. I don't know why I did. I never ask. But I wanted to know her name, even if I didn't want to know her husband's. She told me, "Denise," and she asked mine. Before I knew what I was doing, I told her my Christian name, because suddenly Bozer didn't sound good enough. She told me mine is a nice name, but when I told her everybody calls me Bozer, she said that it was "more fitting." That's when the shuttle bus driver laid on the horn.

Next morning, Denise was there at the pier, with a cup of coffee for me. Gluck gave me another funny look when he saw us talking, but I ignored it. I knew what he was thinking, that I'm going soft, and later, on the ship, he told me just that. Said I was setting a bad example for the rest of the team, talking to the families during a recovery operation, making it personal. But when she was there that evening, too, I knew Gluck was wrong, because I was feeling strong as a bull ox.

I took her to one of the chowder houses on the wharf, and let her talk about her man. Guy sounded pretty regular to me but to her he was a king. So I listened. But then she noticed my tat—the one on my forearm, of Antarctica with a roofing nail shot through the middle—and asked me about it. So I told her about Pole, that I'd been there since Floyd and me cleaned up Kuwait City—six years and counting. I tell her I'm a lifer.

"If you're a lifer," she said, quick as a flash, "what are you doing here?"

"I'm here to find your man."

She needed time, and she had places to go. She told me what so-ciologists do and why they need to move around. At first, she wanted to go to Cairo, to see if she could understand why an Egyptian ex-military pilot would send a passenger plane into the Atlantic. "Per-haps he was traumatized by war," she told me six months later, when I called her from Comms to see how she was doing. By that time we were talking every week, and I could feel my heart winging around in my chest as it got closer to Monday, when I knew I'd hear her voice. "I learned that many members of his squadron were killed in the Yom Kippur War," she told me of the pilot who'd killed her husband. "I imagine there are many ex-military men grappling with the same awful memories." I told her not to go to Cairo. I told her to come south. "If you want something to study, study us. Won't find a weirder bunch of people anywhere else on earth."

It took a season to convince her—she went to Brazil first to work with streetwalking trannies—but she came down, and when she came down, everything fit. I knew that was all she needed: a place where people don't fly planes into the ocean just because. Me, well, I just needed her.

When I showed her the Man Without Country that day, she looked at him for a good long time. It had been five years since that day Floyd and me found him a mile off the skiway. He hadn't changed a bit. For a minute, I worried I did the wrong thing. We never found her man—only a shoe, which she had to identify in an airplane hangar in Newport. True, no one knew who this man was, but at least he was whole. At least he was here.

When Denise got up from her knees, that beautiful smile was still on her face. I asked her what. She smiled wider. "He is everyone anyone has ever lost."

That's what I need to get Cooper to understand. We've all got our shit—me, Denise, the Man Without Country, who's got the worst shit of all 'cause he's stone-dead and ain't nobody wants him. Everyone's got it, and it don't make you special. Still, she won't walk in.

"You think I'm gonna go Dahmer on you?" I say to her. "Get in here."

Now she's in and it's pitch dark, as it always is. I wave the flashlight around the room so she can see the four plywood walls, get oriented. I take her arm, and we walk toward the far wall, and she's not asking questions—usually they're asking by now. The flashlight ain't hit him yet, but when it does, she stops short. I let her eyes get used to him. The drop-kick lands, and she backs up into me—her boots get tangled up with mine, and I have to catch her arm so she doesn't fall.

Now she's asking questions. "Bozer, what is this?"

"Go ahead," I say, holding the flashlight on him steady.

"Go ahead, what?"

"Go look. He's perfectly preserved." She turns around and puts her face in my parka. No one's done that before. I let her do this for a minute, and then I peel her off and set her on course again, and this time she walks toward him. He's set on the berm we made back when we found him, snow and ice we scraped from the floor and walls. It was me who thought to wrap him in sheeting from Logistics, and it's held up good.

"Who is he?" she asks.

"This here's the Man Without Country. He ain't got a home so we're leaving him here in the Tomb until we get word." She don't understand, so I explain. "We found him about a mile off the skiway. He was wearing a Vostok parka, but the Reds said he wasn't one of theirs. China, Chile, the Kiwis—nobody. The Program can't claim him because he's not a U.S. citizen. So here he lies." She walks closer to him now, looks at him. I can tell she notices that he wasn't wrapped hasty; it was done right. "You can see his beard," she says. She asks me why I'm showing her this, and I tell her the Man Without Country is here to tell her something. She looks at me with those sad dark eyes and asks me what he wants to tell her. "He says you don't come down here to commit suicide, honey. You come here so you don't."

*

I'm about to head to Skylab to look at the pool table next morning when I remember what the girl said about leaving something out there. There's already been a lot of drift overnight, and I probably won't find it. Hell, I don't even know what it is—she won't tell me. But I'm on my knees at the entrance, sweeping snow away, looking for something that might not even be there. A couple of machinists walk by and make some smart comments; I only have time to flip them the bird before I spot it. A pill bottle. Size and shape of a Tylenol bottle, but the label's been taken off. I almost leave it where I found it, except the container's got that greasy look to it of having been searched for again and again in a pocket, or held tight like it was the only thing keeping a person alive. I pop the top with my thumb, expecting to find more scratch, but that's not what I find. I know as soon as I see it. Everything is clear as the new day.

When I get to Skylab, Floyd and a field engineer named Randy are looking at the pool table, beers in hand. "One drop on that felt and I cut off your balls," I say, and they step away from the table. There's already one here, in the game room, but it got brought down during Reagan's first term. Worse than that, the table ain't level. I been shipping materials down to build this one during my downtime—bundle it up with the three-quarter-inch plywood and snuggle it under a saddle truss or something. The delicate shit—the felt, the netting—used to come down with a cargo coordinator named Jose, but then Jose went Elvis one day on a toilet back home in Tulsa, and I had to start bringing it down myself. Anyway, this table is for the good old boys: no Beakers, no admins, just Nail-heads.

I pull Floyd over to the table. "Get me a three-eighth-inch bolt and a Fender washer. You put the rails on crooked."

"They look all right to me."

"Just get me the bolts and the washer," I say. Floyd mutters something and leaves. If the Beakers see that anything about this table is off—and they will—they'll sneak into Skylab late at night with their laser levels, and we won't hear the end of it.

"I heard they're sending that girl back," Randy says to me. I take a piece of sandpaper from Floyd's toolbox and start working the edge of the rail.

"Which one?" I say, though I know.

"The finger girl. The *artiste*."

"They ain't," I say.

"Why not?" Randy asks. I shrug. I don't know how the feds work down here. "Probably has something to do with the fact that Frank Pavano is the one who cut off her fork."

"Yeah, I hear we're getting a visit from Washington," Randy says. "They're all up in arms about the Beakers. They're saying the Beakers bullied him. Fucking Beakers." I brush the wood dust from my hands and then blow it off the rails. Randy looks at the table like he's gonna cum all over it. "She's a beaut, Bozer. When will she be ready?"

"Soon. Sooner if that asshole will hurry up with those bolts and washers."

I hear the sound of bunny boot on metal staircase, and extend my hand behind me, but someone, not Floyd, says, "I hear there's a pool tournament at Equinox." I turn and see it's a Beaker, that Indian one without the accent. Sri.

"There might be," I say.

"Is this going to be a station-wide event?"

"Huh?"

"What I mean is—is this going to be open to the entire station?

Can anyone enter?" I just look at Randy and smile. He's new to all this. He needs to learn how to make the Beakers squirm. That's how we keep the equilibrium around here. Sri shifts his weight onto his other leg. "Is there some kind of entry fee? A case of beer?"

"I don't drink microbrews."

"I can get you more Schlitz," he says.

Although this does sweeten the pot, I don't budge. "Look, you guys can keep buying me beer, but the tournament ain't open to Beakers."

"But that's not fair."

"What's not fair about it?" I say. "This is my table. Use the one in the game room."

"You know that one's ruined," Sri says.

"Well, you Beakers shoulda been more careful with your Shirley Temples."

It's hard to get a Beaker upset. Sri keeps coming up with reasons why he should be allowed in the pool tournament, like logic has any bearing on my decision. Floyd finally shows up with the washer and bolts. He's out of breath, huffing like a steam engine going up a mountain pass. "Jesus, Floyd. You fat fuck."

"Karl Martin's here," he eventually coughs out. "He wants to talk to you." I don't care for Martin. He's fussy. He wasn't the one who hired me, either—that guy was an ex-military man who'd spent years in El Salvador doing shit that was neither sane nor legal. He was pushed out when VIDS decided to merge with a robotics manufacturer in '98, and that's when Martin, this former diplomatic pouch slinger, took his place. I will say that Martin mostly lets me do my thing. He's never come down and stuck his nose in between any steel girders. But still, I don't relish the opportunity to talk with him.

All-Call screeches on, and Tucker's voice comes through the speakers: "Bozer, report to A3 ASAP. Bozer, report to A3 ASAP."

I find Martin waiting for me in the garage. He's trying to play it cool, even if he's made the fatal mistake of wearing the red parka of McMurdo. I can see the crew giggling at him, but he can't, and that's all that matters.

"Bozer, sir, good to see you," he says, slapping me on the shoulder with his mitten. "The new station looked great on the flight in."

"Just the bones, but we're set to put the last steel beam on B3 in ten minutes," I say.

Floyd pulls up on the snowmobile. Martin gets on like he's getting onto a stallion. This is a big moment. B3 will be the comms and admin pod for the new station.

We motor past the tourists cheesing for pictures in front of the Pole marker, and that's when I see the girl again, Cooper. She's standing alone, facing the opposite direction, her hands hanging at her sides. I pull up to where she's standing. She looks good—healthy, sober—and she smiles at me. I tell her we're putting the last steel beam on B3. "First of the new pods to get enclosed," I say. "History in the making."

"Where?" she says.

"Come on, I'll take you. All the bigwigs wanna take pictures." I feel Martin lean in behind me to make room. She hesitates, but when I gun the engine, she allows Martin to pull her on. We're at the site in no time.

There's a small crowd by the Mantis crane. The sun glints off its steel body. All around me, I see cameras pointed in our direction, little ones, the kind that Polies brought down in their luggage. All of them snapping a photo that no one else will understand, a photo that will always have to be explained to people who weren't here: installation of the last steel beam on B3—a state-of-the-art comms hub built at the world's baddest construction site.

Floyd moves away from the minder so that I can run the crane. The line is taut, and as I move that steel beast atop the structure, I feel as happy as a pig in shit.

Once I jump off the crane, Martin slaps me on the back, hard. He's giddy. He slaps me again, not so hard this time, and I can tell he wants to talk business. "How much faster can you move on this construction, sir?"

"We're moving as fast as we can," I say.

"No doubt," he says. The words come out as two separate clouds of frozen air. I wait for the rest. "We got a problem, Bozer. You been keeping on top of the news?"

"Two Fingys and a stolen ice-corer on the Antarctic Divide ain't never gonna end well," I say.

He leans in. I smell Pearlie's onion-fried hash browns on his breath. "They're gonna try to shut this show down, Bozer."

"I'm listening."

"Pavano's got two congressmen who are riding Scaletta hard. They can hold up the appropriations bill."

I shake my head. "Simple workplace injury, I've seen far worse."

"It's a shitshow, Bozer. It's politics. It's messy."

I don't need him to spell it out. I've been through budget cuts before, but there have always been ways around them. There's nothing a congressmen can throw at a Nailhead like me that I can't turn into a solid plan of action. I tell Martin this, but he shakes his head. Tells me this time they're going after the agency as a whole. They want to shut the whole place down in the middle of the research season, want to kill the experiments, kill the construction, put the station into caretaker mode until the Beakers and their bosses at the NSF cry uncle.

"You stop construction now, the entire thing's gonna be under snow in a month," I tell him. "They'll have to put up twice as many dimes to rebuild this bitch when they finally get their heads out of their asses."

"I know," Martin says. He looks like he wants to cry. "I'm calling a meeting tonight. Please be there."

Floyd pulls up and Martin climbs on the snowmobile. He waves as they pull away and head toward the station. It's lunchtime. I look around and see I'm the only one at B3 now. I take a long look at the site. Martin's right. This is a shitshow. But it's my shitshow.

NATIONAL SCIENCE FOUNDATION

4201 WILSON BOULEVARD

ARLINGTON, VIRGINIA 22230

Dear Ms. Gosling:

Please review and sign the attached addendum to your Release of Liability and Indemnity Agreement and Covenant Not to Sue contract, and return both to your Station Manager at your earliest convenience. Countersigned copies will be placed in your personnel file. I wish you the best for the upcoming winter.

Sincerely,

Alexandra Scaletta

Agency Director, National Science Foundation

a known issue

2004 January 31
09:11
To: cherrywaswaiting@hotmail.com
From: Billie.Gosling@janusbooks.com
Subject: MIA

C.,
Saw on the news there was some accident in Antarctica at a place whose name I've already forgotten but which isn't Pole. I trust this is
far from your strip mall at the bottom of the
earth.
B.

*

2004 February 1
16:10
To: cherrywaswaiting@hotmail.com
From: Billie.Gosling@janusbooks.com
Subject: MIA Redux

So . . . now they're saying that the accident involved a South Pole scientist and an NSF grantee, which leaves me wondering. I keep remembering you saying that if you died down there, we wouldn't know. Dad has been calling NSF on the hour every hour and is getting nowhere. Something about HIPAA and privacy. Mom has resorted to burning sage in the bathroom at work. Be a pal and write back, or at least have NSF send us your death certificate so we can collect your death benefits.

*

2004 February 3
21:02
To: Billie.Gosling@janusbooks.com
From: cherrywaswaiting@yahoo.com
Subject: RE: MIA Redux

B.,
Sorry. I'm alive. NSF said they contacted you guys. Right hand, index finger, down to the proximal phalanx, which basically means I lost the whole thing. I don't remember much, but I'm told that I was palming the ice in order to get a better look at Pavano's core-hole, and god that looks bad when typed. Pavano lost control of this massive ice-corer and apparently my finger was in the way. At first they were going to send me home, but because of some political algorithm, it's better for everyone, self included, to keep me at Pole. I'm glad I'm staying. No offense. I like it down here. Anyway, it looks like this thing has set into motion some politi-

cal crisis where Pavano is being framed as the
exiled "minority-views" scientist using inferior
tools because of the "culture wars," and now we
are prepping for a visit from some Washington
dignitaries, who will land at Pole in a week.
C.
p.s. It took me forty minutes to write this
e-mail. Tell Dad I'm okay. Tell Mom the polar
bears say hey.

In the Smoke Bar, the vets were telling old station tales about the ones who went crazy: The guy who'd crammed a backpack full of graham crackers and beer and tried to walk to Zhongstan Station for hot-and-sour soup. The lady doing ice-core analysis last season who went on a vodka binge and tried to shave her underarms with a butter knife. The biophysicist who had torn the stuffing out of his pillow, because it "made too much noise in the night."

"You're *all* gonna be looney-tunes before this shit plays itself out," Bozer boomed from his seat at the bar, and it was Bozer who noticed Cooper first. "Welcome back, cupcake," he said. All eyes turned to her.

It had been two days since her trip outside, since Bozer had found her, fixed up her hand, and showed her a corpse. Seven pairs of eyes blinked at her, and Cooper couldn't summon any words. Finally, Doc Carla hauled herself out of her chair, walked over to Cooper, and led her to a table.

"Bozer told me nothing," she whispered. "But from here on out, you only get Advil."

Cooper smiled gratefully and sat down. Pearl brought her a beer, but no one spoke.

"So," Cooper said, taking a sip and looking around the room. "What happened while I was gone?"

Dwight and Sri glanced at each other, and then sped-walked to Cooper's table, each with a fistful of faxes. Based on communications Dwight had received from his counterparts at McMurdo and

WAIS, as well as eavesdropping he'd done on the admin lines, he'd learned that Pavano had been triaged for shock at the Divide, and then put on the same flight as Cooper, which was supposed to continue on to McMurdo after a refuel. But once the plane landed at Pole, the trauma team—led by Pearl—decided to bring Cooper in to Hard Truth instead. Pavano had wandered out of the C-17 while Cooper was transported to the clinic, and commenced a "drunkvincible" walk toward the Dark Sector. Sal and Floyd had had to chase him down.

Cooper's ripped and bloodied mitten was currently in a Ziploc at McMurdo, along with the illegally procured corer. The tech who'd helped Pavano forge the sign-out had already been DQ'ed and put back on a plane to Missoula. That was the extent of the information they had about Pavano's whereabouts and his future plans.

Dwight shoved one of the faxes he'd been holding at Cooper. "The campaign has already started."

"Campaign?"

"Oh, you're famous, Cooper," Dwight said.

"As Jane Doe," Sri added. He shrugged. "HIPAA rules."

It was a small piece in the Associated Press daily digest, with the headline: "Injury reported at ice-coring camp in Antarctica." The reporter quoted a source as saying that Pavano had been denied use of the industrial corer to which all other climate scientists at WAIS had access. That same anonymous source indicated that Pavano's time at the ice-coring camp and at South Pole Station itself had been marked by open hostility, ostracism, and obstruction. In other words, climate scientists had made research impossible for him, so, out of desperation, he'd worked around them.

"And then these just came in tonight," Sri said, bouncing on the tops of his toes. He handed her additional news digests, the same ones that arrived every night, but Sri had highlighted the headlines, which included "Climate skeptic 'frozen' out at climate change camp," "Could Antarctica accident have been avoided?" and "Republican congressmen who pushed for climate skeptic say 'hostile working environment' to blame in Antarctic amputation."

SOUTH POLE STATION 241

"'Antarctic amputation' sounds like a Lovecraft novel," Cooper said, but only Birdie laughed.

"It's not funny, Cooper," Sri said. "This is serious. They're coming to Pole."

"Who's coming?"

"The politicians, the suits, the directors, the congressional aides, the media."

"I think it was all a setup from day one," Dwight barked. "This shit was orchestrated."

"Dwight," Pearl said warningly.

Dwight looked over at Cooper guiltily. "I mean, I don't know if the finger thing was part of it, or . . ."

Cooper wondered if Dwight was right. What if it was all a setup? She recalled Pavano's preternatural calm in the line that first day at the Divide, when the "freeze-out" had begun. The way he'd come prepared with an envelope full of cash and the technical know-how to erect a twenty-foot-high ice-core drill. It wasn't just that he expected the roadblocks; it was almost as if he'd welcomed them.

"So what exactly happened?" Sri asked as he paced under the dart board. "I mean, I know you're not really allowed to talk about it . . . but . . ."

"They didn't give him a tech. They didn't give him access to any drills, or give him any means of extracting a core. I wasn't approved either, as his research tech, even though Pavano forwarded me an e-mail the day before we left that said I was."

Sri scratched his head compulsively and muttered, "Oh shit oh shit oh shit."

"But he didn't seem too upset about it," Cooper replied.

"That's because he's incapable of showing emotion," Sri snapped.

"No, I just mean that he didn't seem surprised. He seemed—I don't know—prepared for it." Sri stopped pacing and stared at her for a minute. Then he slammed his beer on a nearby table and raced out of the bar. The beer was quickly claimed.

As the conversations picked up again, Cooper leaned over to

Pearl, who had resumed her knitting under Birdie's adoring gaze. "Have you seen Sal?"

Pearl shook her head. "I haven't seen him for days. I think he's sleeping in his lab. Alek comes and gets the team's meals. Must be important stuff happening."

*

The dystopian hum of the power plant rattled in Cooper's chest as she passed two arguing maintenance techs on her way to Hard Truth.

"What time is it?" one said.

"What *is* time?" the other replied.

"Shut up and tell me what time it is."

"But time is irrelevant here."

"I'm just asking if we're still on New Zealand time now or if we switched to Denver time yet."

"Where did the extra day go?"

"Smoke my meat, asshole."

As Cooper headed toward the entrance tunnel, she heard someone calling her name. It was Sal. She wasn't sure if she wanted to run to him or run away, but as he got closer to her, she felt her body grow lighter, as if she might float away. His gait bore no trace of that swagger that made him so easy to identify out on the ice, when everyone looked the same in their parkas and hoods. He walked as if he'd walk right through her, but when he reached her, he gathered in his arms and pulled her up against his body. She felt him take three deep, deliberate breaths.

"You didn't wait," he said. "You were supposed to wait. You were supposed to let me come get you before leaving your room. Fuck you for not waiting."

"I'm sorry, Sal," Cooper said, and meant it.

"Bozer told me what happened," he said into the top of her head. "Outside." His warm breath on her hair felt good. "He saved your life."

"I know."

"You should be on a flight home."

"I know," Cooper said. "Did Bozer tell everyone about what happened outside?"

"No, only me and Doc Carla."

"Why you?"

Sal pulled away and looked at her. "Because even he knows."

"Knows what?"

"Are you going to make me say it?" Sal said. She winced as Sal pulled her close again and her hand was caught under his arm.

"Christ, I'm sorry," he said. He glanced down at her bandaged hand. "How is it?"

"Doc Carla keeps telling me that it will start looking better, but right now it looks like bad sci-fi makeup."

"You shouldn't have been on the Divide—"

"Sal—"

"No, let me finish. You shouldn't have been there—but more important, like vastly, vastly more important, Pavano should never have been there." He let her go and ran his hand down his beard as he paced. "I don't know what to do. I mean, it's one thing for oil executives to pressure Congress to defund working groups on the human impacts of climate change, but to send someone like Pavano to the Divide, and then to dangle him on stage like a puppet." He stopped and looked at Cooper. "And then your hand—your fucking hand, Cooper!"

As Cooper watched him pace, she found she was becoming annoyed. "Why are you doing this?"

"Doing what?"

"This. This 'I'm outraged' act. The last time I saw you I was a mistake you'd made. You were confused. You were sorry. Is this you being angry at Pavano for hurting me or you being angry that some politicians are fucking with your sacred science shit?"

Sal looked at Cooper for a long minute. "I deserve that. All of it."

Cooper hated him for saying this. It left her nowhere else to take her anger.

Sal reached out a hand to her. "I have something to show you in the machine shed," he said. "Will you come?" Cooper looked at his mismatched mittens. One was black, a Gore-Tex, while the other—the one he was holding out to her now—was a fur-backed gauntlet with a large rip along the top. Cooper knew at once that the Gore-Tex mitten she'd found in skua, the one with the barbecue-encrusted tips—the one she'd painted months ago—was Sal's. For some reason, her anger dissipated.

She put her hand in his and allowed him to take her to the machinery arch.

When they got there, it looked like ground zero of a Scud missile attack. Cooper stepped over vehicle parts and long curling threads of metal and wood, toward the squeal of a lathe. A Polie in overalls and safety glasses stood hunched over the lathe, blue sparks flying from between her hands. Cooper recognized Marcy by her tangled blond hair. Sal walked around the machine so Marcy could see him, and she stopped working on the crankshaft she'd been repairing.

She pushed her safety glasses on top of her head and, using her sleeve, wiped the sweat from her forehead. "Jesus, you again? Get off my back, man. It's done." She grinned at Cooper. "This asshole has been on me like tie-dye on a hippie about the new Pole marker. Hold on, I'll get it." When Marcy disappeared into a small supply shed on the other side of the arch, Cooper turned to Sal. "What's this about?"

"Marcy's in charge of making the new Pole marker."

"The one you designed," Cooper said.

Sal nodded. "I want you to see it before the ceremony."

"I thought the ceremony was supposed to happen on New Year's Day."

Sal grimaced. "Thanks to the war of bureaucratic attrition, the powers-that-be told us to reposition the marker closer to the end of the summer season, in mid-February."

"Why?"

Sal shrugged. "It's a directive from NSF. Some congressional committee wrote it into an appropriations bill. Arbitrary interference—just letting us know that they can control the operations down here. But if that's all the interference we get from Washington this year, I'll dirty-dance with Floyd in the galley."

Marcy emerged from the shed carrying something bound up in a rag. She gestured toward one of the worktables and they gathered around it. A coughing forklift pulled into the garage and shuddered off. Marcy leaned back to look, and, seeing it was Bozer, called him over. "I've outdone myself, boss," she said. "Come look."

As they waited for Bozer to lumber over, Cooper wondered what Sal's design would look like. She imagined it first as Viper, the coffee-filter telescope he had shown her. But that didn't touch the history of the continent, which was important. Something more generally cosmic, perhaps—a constellation, the Milky Way. Cooper remembered Sal's horrible drawing of the two branes colliding—the two pancakes—and stifled a laugh, imagining the sketch transformed into the Pole marker.

Bozer arrived and slapped his hands on the table expectantly. Marcy gathered the fabric between her fingers, then stopped and looked over at Sal. "I just want you to know that this was the hardest design I've ever worked from and that I've wished you dead pretty much constantly since you brought it to me. That being said, it's the best thing I've ever done."

Bozer told her to can it, and Marcy removed the rag.

The bright shop lights bounced off polished brass, creating white bursts in Cooper's vision. Slowly, the marker's shape became clear—the sinuous upslope of a bow, the sturdiness of two masts, and a web of rigging, like spun silk. Etched into its body were the words *Terra Nova*. Cooper realized she was trembling.

"That's good shit, Marce," Bozer growled, squeezing Marcy's shoulder. "That's very fine shit."

Marcy pulled a crumpled piece of paper from the bib of her overalls and spread it out on the table. "Well, I had a good design. A fussy-as-hell design, but still, a good design."

Cooper looked down at her sketch of the *Terra Nova*. Sal's precise mathematician's handwriting was all over it—numbers, and arrows, and measurements in centimeters and in millimeters. Instructions to Marcy, Cooper realized. Sal leaned over the marker, examining its intricacies, his face bright with happiness and admiration. When he turned to see what she thought, Cooper found she was unable to speak. She didn't notice Marcy and Bozer quietly walk away.

"Well," Sal laughed. "What do you think?"

Cooper could only shake her head and choke out, "Why?"

"This is me telling you that you belong here, Cooper." He hesitated. "And this is me saying I think we should be together down here. I know I was a dick in your room that night, before you left for the Divide. It was just—when you were sitting on the edge of the bed like that, with your boots off, looking at me—" He looked away, frustrated. "Everything about that moment felt too important to be in my clumsy hands. I didn't realize how important it was until I was touching you." His brow furrowed. "This is hard to explain." He walked over to the forklift and back again. "Okay," he said, "I think I know how to say this to you. Math. It explains everything. There's a moment when every geek comes upon a mathematical equation that almost destroys him. For Alek it's the Mandelbrot set equation. For me it's the Riemann hypothesis. Whatever a great poem means to a poet, that's what understanding these things for the first time is to someone like me. I can't explain it to you. All I can tell you is that your face that night, that night in your room, it was like seeing the Mandelbrot for the first time, the Riemann. Like starting a single-variable equation and watching it turn into differential calculus before your eyes. It was scary. I was scared. I didn't know how to explain that to you, and I didn't know what to do, either." Sal reached for Cooper and drew her close. "Then when you left with Pavano, I got angry, because I wanted you to be with me, not him. I was angry that he had that time with you, and that's when I realized: I can't even be away from you for a day without feeling like every minute is an hour."

These words created an incision in Cooper, which caused both pain and immense relief. She took his mitten in hers. "Come with me."

They walked across the plateau in silence. Once they were in Cooper's room in the Jamesway, she sat on her bed and lifted her feet toward him. Sal kneeled on the floor and took off her boots. He undressed her carefully, slowly easing the thick cuff of her parka over her injured hand. He eased her back onto the bed, and brushed the hair off her forehead. He peeled off his thermal sweatshirt, only taking his eyes of her as he pulled the shirt over his head. He slid one suspender off his shoulder, then the other, and once his base layer was off, Cooper saw his body was sinewy and muscular, and very pale. It seemed to Cooper at that moment the most beautiful, most desirable thing she'd ever seen, and her heartbeat pulsed in her ear. Her body wanted to disintegrate beneath his fingers.

He leaned over her and kissed her mouth, and he lay down on the bed next to her. Pulling her hair away from her face, he touched his dry lips to her throat, and told her to let go, so she did.

It was only later, long after Sal had reluctantly left her bed to return to the Dark Sector, that Cooper saw the vial on her desk. There was a note.

You don't do this kind of shit alone. Do it with us standing beside you. Bozer here.

*

When Cooper arrived at the studio the next morning, she saw that Denise had cleared their communal desk of textbooks and papers, and had tied a number of Blue Razberry Blow Pops into a bouquet with a note signed, *Good luck. Your friend, Margaret Mead.*

With one of the suckers in her mouth, Cooper walked over to the easel. She pulled off the dropcloth: Tucker's eye stared back at her. Without the Scotch and painkiller cocktail, she could better see that it was objectively decent. Despite what Tucker had told her that night, it needed no revision. In fact, it might even be done. Then there was the painting of Pearl. The brown eyes stippled with copper and the plain freckled face that burned with ambition.

Then there was the one of Bozer. She'd been outside, ready to start fresh in order to avoid becoming a tragic figure, observing the white wasteland to the west of the station. She'd tried to look at the landscape critically, the way she hadn't been able to do out on the Divide. It was an ocean, with wind-sculpted waves frozen in time. No—that was too generic. It was a desert—blowout dunes, sand seas. No, not that either. There was a reason, Cooper could admit now, that her desert series—"Richat Structure"—had not impressed nor sold at Caribou Coffee. ("This one makes me thirsty," she'd overheard someone say. "I refuse to be thirsty in my own home.") Then she'd blinked into the sun, and had been startled to see it was encircled by a purple and gold halo. It seemed impossible, as if her unchanging Minnesota sun had been replaced by a pulsating counterfeit. Deep black to the west, Cherry had written, shading into long lines of gray and lemon yellow round the sun, with a vertical shaft through them, and a bright orange horizon. His foot on the edge of the Antarctic Plateau, and Scott told him to turn back. Cherry had peered through his myopia waiting for them as he winked in the sun's faint gleam.

A metallic clatter of a load of beams falling to earth had made Cooper jump. She'd watched as the various construction vehicles circled the beams curiously. Marcy had gotten her bulldozer running again, and Bozer was on a snowmobile with an admin, gesticulating like a traffic cop. Cooper had thought about her sketches of Bozer, back in her studio. She'd managed a few broad outlines before losing steam and resorting to the hesitation wounds of a doomed painting—slashes of paint here, pointless half-tones there. He saw her standing there, gaping at the gathering crowd in front of the B3 module; he motored over to her and told her to get on—something important was about to happen.

Whether it was important was almost beside the point—it had appeared to Cooper, once she was at the site with everyone else, that Bozer was simply placing a large steel beam on the very top of the new module. But then she'd seen his face, and she'd understood.

The canvas in front of her now was embryonic, but promising. A nose set in the middle of the canvas—the nostrils lined with flesh-pink and sprouting hairs, and burst blood vessels sketched in with pencil, unpainted, undecided. The overgrown, Bobby Knight eyebrows with their searching insect antennas had yet to be considered.

Ditto the stylized handlebar mustache and the incongruous lumber-jack beard, and the glossy pate hidden beneath a series of offensive bandannas. But she had figured out the eyes, which was the only way into a portrait. These eyes that told you, point-blank, that manning a trawler crane at the end of the earth was the only place her subject belonged. She started to paint.

*

2004 February 3
11:57
To: cherrywaswaiting@hotmail.com
From: Billie.Gosling@janusbooks.com
Subject: RE: MIA Redux

I can't tell if your last e-mail was an attempt at humor or if you are really a new member of the Nine Finger Club. I'll assume it's the for-mer, and I'll bite: my research indicates other members of the Nine Finger Club include Buster Keaton, Jesse James, Lee Van Cleef, Daryl Han-nah, and Galileo. Lee fucking Van Cleef, Coo-per. But to be completely transparent, I should add that Galileo lost his finger post-mortem, when someone took the middle finger of his right hand straight from his corpse.

I don't know what to say. How are you going to paint?
B.

The station populace grumbled its way into the gym—Game Night had been cancelled and the half-finished games of Settlers of Catan from the week before would have to remain half finished.

Once everyone had found a seat, Tucker walked onto the stage, where a crew of unfamiliar men, clearly not Polies, were leaning back in mismatched folding chairs, speaking to one another in low tones. Tucker, Cooper noted, was still wearing sunglasses.

"First, let me run through the week's Significant Activities." He consulted a notebook. "Two Twin Otters left to support the Chilean Antarctic Program—that was on Wednesday. In construction news, Bozer and friends have finished the siding trim on the upwind side of the new station and have installed SIP panels on the third section of the Logistics Facility."

"Footers for the second section were installed this morning," Bozer called out.

"Floyd, what's the status of the leak in the Emergency Power Plant right water tank?" Tucker said.

"Still exceeds," Floyd replied. "It's a known issue."

"Doc?"

Doc Carla stood up and recited from memory the week's sick calls. "One subungual hematoma, one thigh contusion, one mononeuropathy, one biceps tendonitis, one shoulder rotator cuff tendonitis, one thumb strain." She glanced sideways at Cooper, and added: "And therapeutics for one finger amputation." This was met with a rousing round of applause. Next, Pearl stood up with a file folder in hand.

"Here are the numbers from the Food Growth Chamber: nine pounds of green leaf lettuce; fourteen pounds of red leaf lettuce; and nothing else has sprouted yet. Water usage this week was nine gallons. And our dedicated produce maintenance volunteer is redeploying at the end of the month, so please come see me if you'd like to volunteer."

"Thanks, Pearl," Tucker said. "Finally, some of you asked me to update you on Changed Conditions Affecting Functional Operations. We've completed one hundred and ten LC-130 missions so far, but we remain seventeen missions behind schedule, which could affect our fuel supply." The room quieted down a little at this news. "We'll talk about this more at the operations meeting tomorrow night. Now, on to the matter at hand. As you probably know by now, we're going to be hosting some Distinguished Visitors shortly."

Someone in the back started a chant of "Tom Waits, Tom Waits, Tom Waits, Tom Waits." The rest of the room picked up it up.

"It's not going to be Tom Waits, obviously, although if you want, I'll sing his catalog to anyone who's interested after the meeting." The men in the folding chairs behind Tucker laughed indulgently at this.

"Two esteemed members of Congress will be traveling to the ice next week, and because of the circumstances there will be new protocols. I'm going to introduce Karl Martin, our fearless VIDS president of Polar Operations, who will explain what's going to happen."

A man in a three-day scruff-beard, Kangol hat, and Carhartt work pants slapped the knee of the man next to him, stood up, and walked toward the microphone. His corporate mien was unmistakable, despite his clumsy attempts at native dress. Until this moment, Karl Martin had been nothing more than a reference point to most of the Polies—a corporate PR photo affixed to the dart board in the Smoke Bar.

"Maybe I should have worn my full ECW gear," Karl said into the microphone. "I mean, I see the black and green parkas, which is—heh heh—let's just put it out there: they make you the badasses. Nothing like those red parkas at McMurdo."

No one in the audience appreciated the pandering: the distant roar of the power plant was the only sound in the room.

Martin cleared his throat. "I get the feeling that I should get to the point, so folks, I'm going to speak frankly. The last week has been difficult for everyone. The blame game, rumors flying, tension between coworkers. These are all things that can complicate a working environment. Our goal at VIDS is, and always has been, a safer and more secure global community. Whether we're in Kabul, Tripoli, or right here at South Pole, it's our guiding principle. So when something like this happens—the tragedy that unfolded at an NSF research camp—we're shaken. And even though the actors involved were not VIDS contractors, nor were they working at an official VIDS work site, we feel let down. And although no VIDS employees or VIDS-issued matériel were involved in this workplace incident—which, again, unfolded at a National Science Foundation research camp and involved NSF Fellows—we are reminded that safety is of the utmost importance. And our hearts go out to the NSF, which bears complete responsibility for this incident." People began murmuring, and Martin, sensing he was losing the room, reloaded.

"You know, this is tough, unprecedented stuff. I'm not going to stand here and pretend like I'm a great scientific mind, but I am a decent scholar of humanity—decades in various theaters of war will make you one. Now, I know we say that South Pole is the only apolitical place on the planet, a place where science trumps ideology. That's how we like it. That's why we're here. Nations collaborate, and have collaborated, here for many decades, overlooking policy differences to come together in order to advance science and human thought. I mention this because the individuals who will be visiting the station in the next week are, by any definition, political figures.

"As you know, our friends at the NSF typically restrict official visits to the station to dignitaries like presidents and ambassadors. However, due to circumstances, NSF has invited a couple of our national legislators to come see the station, have a look around."

"This wouldn't have anything to do with the fact that they're on the Congressional Budget Committee, would it?" Sal called from his seat next to Cooper.

"Mr. Brennan, right?" Martin said.

"Dr. Brennan."

"Sorry—*Dr.* Brennan, wouldn't want to neglect the honorific."

"It's not an honorific, it's an earned title."

The chuckles from the audience made Martin set his chin.

"Dr. Brennan, you'll need to take up your concerns with Alexandra Scaletta. The fortunes of the support staff who make your experiments feasible are tied directly to congressional appropriation. And that's my purview. In fact, let's talk about the support staff for a minute. I expect those of you down here on contract will represent VIDS in a positive manner. You are not to address the visitors unless directly addressed by them; and in that case, you do not express an opinion. You will restrict any comment to your everyday duties on the ice or your families back home. Any comments beyond that will not be allowed. If you choose to ignore this, your contracts will not be renewed. We decided to keep it simple."

"That's draconian," Floyd said from the front row. Martin looked down at him from the stage as if he were a pile of offal.

"I wonder if you know who Draco is?" Martin asked.

"A member of Devo?" Kit called between cupped hands.

But Floyd was seriously pissed. "I know what *draconian* means," he said. "I used the term intentionally. What you've just described is draconian." Onstage, Tucker remained inscrutable behind his sunglasses.

"I apologize," Martin said. "For a moment I doubted your grasp of the word's meaning because you said it like you think you're insulting me. In the places where VIDS operates, draconian systems are key to survival. Before Draco instituted his code of laws in Athens, daily life was governed by blood feuds. Draconian law gives members of a community clear expectations and consistent consequences. And if Lockheed Martin wins the contract next year because the NSF budget is cut, you'll be praying to Draco that they hire you. Based on your demeanor, I wouldn't count on it."

From the back of the gym, a lone voice called out, "Tom Waits."

*

First came a procession of lower-level VIDS directors in from Denver. NSF reps arrived shortly thereafter, recognizable by their clumsy attempts to blend in. Together, they prowled the halls and tried to chat up the workers, drove out to the labs to "hang out" with the scientists, crashed 90 South asking for IPAs, and handed out swag from the agency's last grant conference. Meanwhile, the *Antarctic Sun* newspaper, published out of McMurdo, indicated that the congressional delegation would include an assortment of political aides, as well as the two Republican congressmen who had gotten Pavano on the ice—Rep. Sam Bayless of Kansas and Rep. Jack Calhoun of Tennessee.

The Distinguished Visitors, known at Pole as DVs, arrived around midnight, blinking at the sun as they stumbled across the skiway toward the station. Cooper and the other Polies who had gathered to witness their arrival made their way up to the Smoke Bar immediately afterward to discuss.

The Polies were three drinks deep when Calhoun walked into the bar. His sudden appearance, and his shellacked coif, somehow unruffled by both his hood and the straight-line polar winds, caught everyone off guard. Even Bozer looked surprised.

Only Marcy spoke. "Congressman, you look like you need a drink."

"Make that plural, and we understand each other," Calhoun replied.

"One South Pole Highball," Marcy called to Alek, who was playing bartender.

"How'd you find us?" Doc Carla asked, carelessly winding a rubber band around her fingers.

"Nice Afro-American man told me I could get a stiff drink here."

Cooper and Sal exchanged an amused glance.

"So where's your security detail, Congressman?" Sal asked. "Your advance team know you're fraternizing with the enemy?"

"An honest man has no enemies," Calhoun replied, taking the seat next to Pearl, who was knitting another scarf for Birdie.

"Wrong," Alek barked from the bar, as he handed the drink to Marcy. "Honest man has more enemies than anyone."

Marcy brought Calhoun the glass and watched as he lifted it to the light. "What in the hell is in this?" he asked.

She clasped her hands in front of her and batted her eyelashes. "Try it, and we'll tell you," she said, pulling out an unexpected Betty Boop imitation that Cooper thought was damn good. Tickled, Calhoun took a huge gulp and immediately started hacking. He flushed red and grabbed at his throat. Cooper thought he was going to have a heart attack. He peered up at Marcy through watering eyes.

"Drain cleaner?" he coughed.

"Jet fuel," Marcy said. "Just a tablespoon's worth, but the best buzz on earth."

"Murdering a U.S. congressman is a capital crime, you know." But he took another, smaller sip. "It grows on the palate," he said. He held the glass in front of his face and swirled its contents around. "But if I were you, I'd conserve as much fuel as possible."

"What's that supposed to mean?" Sal asked.

Calhoun waved the remark away. "Nothing. I'm just saying you should conserve. I do. I'm green. Eco-friendly. I recycle. I compost. Well, shit, I don't compost, but I conserve. I'm a conservative."

Cooper could see that Sal was oddly charmed by Calhoun's deflection. "Conservative and incoherent," Sal said. "Amazing how often those two things go hand in hand." Calhoun raised his glass at Sal, and Sal grinned, despite himself.

"So you've got your eye on the JP-8," Bozer growled from the table next to Calhoun. Cooper noticed Denise quickly place her hand on Bozer's knee.

"JP-what?"

"The fuel. You plan on holding back supply until you get your way?"

Calhoun was surprised. He peered back at Bozer. "I plan on protecting the integrity of scientific inquiry."

"I don't know what that means," Bozer replied. "But I do know what it means when we don't got enough fuel to get through the winter. I've got a station half built out there and if anyone fucks with my fuel supply, it'll be buried under eight feet of drift-snow in a month."

Calhoun blinked back at Bozer, and Cooper felt a wave of compassion for the man. He had no business being at Pole. He was beefy Midwestern stock, about sixty. His dark eyes looked sad, even when he was laughing, and his second chin looked like another smile. The eyebrows were fuzzy, almost furry—black shot through with wiry white hairs. Cooper searched her pockets for her pen, found it, and painstakingly tried to sketch the congressman on a napkin. Sal saw what she was doing and smiled.

He turned to Calhoun. "What exactly do you guys want?" he said. "I mean, you come down here with your parade of imbeciles, squawking about scientific integrity, but in the meantime, no one knows what your point is. What's the plan? To hold the station hostage until you get reelected? To subpoena every climate scientist until there's no one left to do the research?"

Calhoun held Sal's steady gaze. "I have nothing to say on that subject. It is out of my hands."

"And whose able hands is it in now?"

"Scaletta's. We tried to compromise. She rejected it."

"What are you offering?"

"Basic fairness. Scientific integrity."

"Already built into the system."

Calhoun shook his head. "If it were, then Frank Pavano would have had freedom of movement while he was here, free access to equipment. He'd still be on the ice. The NSF ensures minority scientific views get a seat at the table. Equal access to taxpayer-funded research sites at the Poles."

A small, strangled scream caused everyone to turn. Sri stood in the doorway, his hood still on, holding a chess set with both hands.

"You want the NSF to fund research that tries to prove global warming is a hoax," Sri said, his knuckles whitening as he gripped the box. Calhoun finished off his South Pole Highball and set it on the table too hard.

"Young man, I'm not saying that's what I want. I'm saying that's the proposal on the table. Your bosses have said no. We will take advantage of the tools at our disposal."

"Including subpoenas? One of the WAIS researchers was subpoenaed yesterday by her state's attorney general. They're taking her off the ice because someone from your office called and—"

Calhoun rose from his chair unsteadily. "This shit's above your pay grade, and I've already talked too much. I was just looking for a nightcap and some conversation."

Sal stood up and took the congressman's arm. "I'll walk you to the DV barracks."

Calhoun yanked his arm out of Sal's grasp. "I can get there myself, son," he said, and, after putting on his jacket, haltingly made his way out of the bar.

After the congressman left, the room grew loud and raucous with discussion about the unexpected visit, and predictions about the intensity of his hangover tomorrow after Alek confessed to putting a double shot of jet fuel in his drink.

Cooper turned to Sal. "I'm going to bed. Wanna join me?" He hooked his fingers into her belt loops and pulled her close, but then noticed Sri was lightly thumping his head against the wall. "I gotta console Sri," he said. "I'll come by later."

Instead of heading straight to the Jamesways, though, Cooper decided to drop by her studio, maybe fill out the sketch of Calhoun a little. She'd seen something in his face that she liked.

She had just opened the door to the trailer, when she heard someone mumbling from what sounded like the far end of the hall. Speak of the devil—there he was, in a crumpled heap, sitting with his back against the wall. He startled at the sound of her boots squeaking across the linoleum.

"Thank god," he said. "I wasn't out of there two minutes before the earth started spinning. I can't get in my room."

"That's because your room isn't in this trailer," she replied, as Calhoun struggled to his feet, using the wall for leverage. "It's in a much fancier one."

"Where am I?"

"This is the Artist and Writers' Annex." She gestured down the long hall. "Behind these doors all of us geniuses spend our days staring at blank walls, contemplating a career change." The cheap joke raised a laugh, and Calhoun asked her what kind of art she did. When she told him she was a painter, he laughed again.

"What's funny?"

"I'm just thinking about how many times I've said something like 'The federal endowments for the arts are wasteful and elitist, and steal much-needed funds from the hardworking folks of the middle class.'"

"Might be right about the wasteful part, at least in my case," Cooper said. "I painted nothing but mittens for the first three months I was here."

"Mittens?"

Cooper pulled her keys from her pocket and opened the door to her studio, careful to keep her right hand in her parka. "And one glove. Do you want to see them?"

Inside, Calhoun was taken by the mittens. He loved the mittens: he wanted to own them. After Cooper gave him the spiel—*It's a study of both the humility of the simple garment and the hubris of our belief that it protects us from this savage continent*—he offered to buy all four of them, including the triptych, on the spot. "I don't know much about art, but these—they speak to me." He wandered over to the canvas on the easel, the one covered by a dropcloth. "What else you got?" He pinched the fabric between his fingers. "May I?"

"Sure, but I warn you—that one's not a mitten," Cooper said. Calhoun pulled the cloth from the canvas, revealing her portrait of Bozer. Under the harsh fluorescent lights, his shining face seemed to take on a Wizard of Oz quality, hovering over them like a strange apparition. The bandanna was gone, revealing a long-ago-receded hairline and a broad, veiny forehead; a pair of untidy eyebrows held court over 7Up-clear eyes that looked beyond the viewer. The mustache and beard had been shorn clean, and left behind pink skin in their place. While the underlying structure of his face was built of clean, strong lines—having been painted before Cooper's injury—the rest of the portrait had a soft, almost tremulous feel to it.

"That looks like the fella from the bar," he said. "Except I believe he had a beard."

Cooper pulled her right hand from her parka pocket to drape the cloth back over the portrait. "It's not finished; I didn't have time to get to some of the details, and I—"

"So it's you," he said. Cooper realized he was staring at her bandaged hand. "You're the girl from the Divide." He looked from her face, to her hand, back to her face. "They told us you were a painter." He furrowed his brow. "Why the hell haven't you left this place? Don't you have people?"

"I have people. My people are here."

"You didn't want to go home?"

Calhoun's question took Cooper aback. "Home?"

"Home," Calhoun said. "The place where you live? Where you've got roots? You got people waiting on you, don't you?"

Cooper had not thought of home for weeks. Not of her father, her mother, not even, aside from their e-mails, of Billie. They belonged to another world now—a parallel universe, one of Sal's branes. And while at some point that world would collide with this one, the long rebound pulling them apart was welcome.

"I am home," Cooper said quietly.

Calhoun shook his head, and moved on to the nearly finished portrait of Pearl, which Cooper had set against the back wall—she had only to strengthen the background and shadow tones. Calhoun snuck another glance at Cooper's hand. "Did the accident affect your ability to, ah, to do this kind of work?"

"I lost a finger on my dominant hand," Cooper said. "So, yeah, it changed things. I'm not able to be as precise as I used to be." She surveyed Pearl. "But now I know that precision rarely tells the whole story."

"Aren't you angry? I'd be as mad as hell." When Cooper didn't respond, he added, "Proverbs says, 'Good sense makes one slow to anger, and it is his glory to overlook an offense.'"

"I know a better one."

"What is it?"

"'If you are fearful, you may do much, for none but cowards have need to prove their bravery.'"

Calhoun seemed deeply moved. "Ecclesiastes?"

"Apsley Cherry-Garrard. Of the Scott party. He's sort of my spirit animal."

"Scott. They told us about him on the ride down here. Poor bastard. All that, just to come in second place. Never heard of this Cherry character, though. With that kind of name, he had to be a little—hey, you okay?"

To Cooper's surprise, the static of a developing sob was filling her chest; she tried, unsuccessfully, to cough it away.

"I'm sorry," Cooper said when she'd recovered. "It's just that talking about Cherry—" She glanced up at Calhoun and saw incomprehension on his face. "That talking about Scott makes me think of my twin brother. He was big into polar exploration. He died last year."

Calhoun's mouth quivered slightly. "I'm sorry."

There it was again—that thing in Calhoun's face that she had seen in the bar. Cooper had no idea what it was, only that she felt compelled to tell him about David, even if there was nothing that indicated Calhoun would even be interested. "We used to pretend we were members of the Scott party, back when we were kids. He was always Titus, I was always Cherry. Never made sense, because Cherry wasn't on the final slog—all he did was stand around waiting—but we never cared. Titus was the injured guy who walked into the blizzard in order to save the others—he was the hero."

"A true act of selflessness," Calhoun said. He clasped his hands in front of him and dropped his head, as if preparing to pray. "A true act of selflessness." Suddenly, he began fumbling with the zipper on his parka. He seemed to have no clue how it worked. "I want to show you something," he said earnestly. When he saw Cooper's skeptical face, he guffawed. "Nothing like that." So Cooper reached over and helped him unzip his parka. He pointed to the lapel of his new North Face thermal. A glittering brooch in masculine red, white, and blue rhinestones had been pinned on the left breast. Cooper noted that it spelled out the words *Let's Roll*.

"Bayless makes me wear this damn pin wherever we go," he said.

"United Flight Ninety-three," Cooper murmured.

Calhoun nodded. "He says it buys political and social capital. I was nowhere near when it happened. I was in Scottsdale, for god's sake."

By simply listening to him, Cooper had unleashed something in Calhoun. It was as if no one had ever listened to him before. He told her he was a widower, that his wife's death from ovarian cancer had helped his last reelection campaign, even though it had destroyed him and his kids. His campaign manager had felt it necessary to use his bereavement to his benefit, and it had worked. Still, he told Cooper he was a failure as a legislator. His bills went nowhere, his committee assignments were unimportant. He despised his constituents, didn't even really believe in his politics anymore, didn't understand why they cared more about teaching evolution in the schools than the fact that they couldn't find good-paying jobs. But what else did he have? He was a sixty-three-year-old man with nothing—no job offers from lobbying firms, no universities eager to get him behind a lectern. Then one day, his campaign manager had called him at his home, saying a large donor was interested in making a substantial contribution to the campaign. "And he says 'when I say "substantial," I'm talking seven-figs substantial.' I get these guys on the phone—they don't tell me who they are right away—and I say, 'What's the catch?' They tell me they need help protecting the integrity of science. Why would I say no to that?"

When Cooper looked at the congressman, she realized he desperately wanted her to give him a reason to have said no. "Who was the donor?" she asked.

Calhoun smiled and walked over to examine another canvas, which was obscured behind Pearl's. "You know I can't tell you that," he said. Calhoun pulled the portrait away from the wall, and suddenly, his smile faded. He studied the gaunt, angular face, framed in a fur-fringed hood. The lucent eyes were gone, and in their place were two black caves.

Calhoun tore his gaze away from the portrait to look at Cooper. "I know this man," he said.

With an ear-shattering scratch, the All-Call system suddenly came to life, and Tucker's sleepy voice spewed out a host of acronyms and directives.

"That's for you. They'll turn this place inside out looking for you," Cooper said.

"Of course they will," he said as he walked to the door. "Their lapdog took a walk."

Cooper picked up the antique compass from her desk. She was ready to let it go; though it had failed her in so many ways, something told her it wouldn't fail Calhoun. "Wait, I have something to give you." She handed him the compass.

The wrinkles in the corners of his eyes deepened as he examined it. "You use this for inspiration?"

Cooper shook her head. "No. It was given to me. Sort of like your pin. Take it," she said. When he hesitated, she added: "Please."

Calhoun accepted it, gazing at it like it was the most beautiful thing he'd ever seen, his face radiant with happiness. For a moment, Cooper felt like she was looking at her father. *There's a whole generation of those kinds of fathers*, Birdie had told Cooper back at McMurdo.

Tucker's voice came over the loudspeaker again, talking about sectors and annexes.

"You better go," Cooper said.

Calhoun looked at Cooper, his eyes wet. "This means a lot to me, young lady. I take everything said in this room to heart."

Later, as she prepared for bed, Cooper got on her chair and gazed out the window at the endless expanse of snow surrounding the station. She reached for her ruler from the bedside table, and set it on the bottom of the window frame. The sun had sunk a half inch since last week. It looked like a burning ship, disappearing into the seam between earth and sky.

*

The next morning, on the same stage where Coq au Balls had performed on Halloween, Congressmen Sam Bayless and Jack Calhoun sat between the undersecretary for Democracy and Global Affairs and the NSF liaison for the House Appropriations Subcommittee on Commerce, Justice, Science, and Related Agencies. The Beakers considered Alexandra Scaletta's absence "conspicuous," but Tucker assured them that she was back in Washington trying to negotiate with the more reasonable members of the House budget committee.

Bayless was a lean, whippet-faced man, with the kind of facial structure one typically only found in Manga. His hair, heavily gelled, gleamed under the fluorescents. Even seated, he exuded arrogance. But it was Calhoun whom Cooper studied. She'd expected him to look tired, perhaps even exhausted, after last night, but instead he looked wide-awake. He was even smiling.

As Bayless moved to the podium, Cooper remembered Sal telling her that these DV speeches were usually obsequious paeans to the brutality of polar life, full of admiration for the "unique" individuals who sacrificed all that was familiar to do important work under heinous conditions, and promises to safeguard the funding that made such work possible. All had gone as expected so far, except for that last point. And there had been no grand confrontation, aside from Sal's conversation with Calhoun in the Smoke Bar. The station population, which had been itching for a fight, had—save for cynical veterans who knew better—depended on the scientists to lead the charge. No matter how passionate the dishwashers and welders were about keeping politics out of science, they were still just support staff, not climate researchers or theoretical physicists on government grants. The former could be dismissed as the partisan harridans and Libertarians they usually were while the latter were recipients of taxpayer funds that were currently under threat. The sense of unrest in the crowd was palpable.

"I'm told that you folks are not used to the kind of media attention you've been getting over the last few weeks," Bayless began. "I apologize for that, especially if Representative Calhoun and I have been the cause of any disruption to the important work being done down here. We are as surprised as any of you by the way the media has shown such robust interest in what's happening here. Dissent is the healthiest state of affairs in any democracy, of course. And while the South Pole is technically a continent without country, I do consider it a democracy." Cooper felt Sal stir next to her. "I think that democracy is under attack. That in a bastion of scientific thought, the covenant of free thought has been broken."

"There is no such thing as a scientific covenant," Sal burst out. "You're using religious language to describe science."

Two NSF admins approached Sal's row from either end. But the congressman put his hand up. "No, it's okay." He gripped the sides of the podium and leaned over it. "Without god, science doesn't exist." Half of the room laughed. "Oh, did I make a joke? I guess it must be funny to people who believe time, space, and matter came into existence unassisted. That planets and stars formed from space dust, not the hand of an intelligent force. That matter created life by itself and early life-forms learned to reproduce like Sea-Monkeys." At this, the room fell silent. "Look, guys—gals—we're on the same side. I believe in science. I also believe all findings of science will eventually be found to agree with Scripture."

"Amen," Calhoun said, dipping his head.

"But I know you don't care about my thoughts on science. You want to know about money. I know there's a great deal of speculation about the status of the NSF's budget. And it's true that discussions about NSF's operating budget, particularly for its polar operations, have been ongoing for the last few weeks—but so have the budgets of a number of federal agencies. This is not a deviation, it's not a conspiracy. It's part of the process. That being said, I would be remiss if I didn't tell you that the hostile working environment experienced by scientists working on alternative theories of so-called climate change has figured into the discussions as well."

Bayless gestured to one of his aides, and the young man sped-walked to the podium and handed him a sheet of paper. "There's still time to avert an unfortunate situation, so I want to talk about Frank Pavano for a moment. Dr. Pavano has been the victim of a systematic and sustained pattern of harassment based solely on his research." Bayless consulted the paper. "On November sixth, he was denied a username and password to access the West Antarctic Divide server. This was blamed on a 'majordomo error.' The next day, a research paper he posted in the common area was defaced, and then later removed. On November fourteenth, Dr. Pavano found a threatening cartoon taped to the door to his room, which featured a crude drawing of Christ, sitting atop an Earth-like planet engulfed in flames. On December eighteenth, Dr. Pavano was notified by the climate research chief—in writing and on NSF letterhead—that due to budget constraints, he would not be assigned a drill tech on his final research trip to the West Antarctic Divide. This was later found to be a false statement, and Representative Calhoun and I intervened on his behalf. In the days leading up to his final trip to the ice-coring camp, he was removed from the flight manifest—twice. Both instances were blamed on administrative error. Finally, upon arriving at the camp, he was denied use of taxpayer-funded equipment necessary to his research.

"All of this culminated, as you know, in a tragic accident involving a South Pole citizen. An accident that can be laid squarely at the feet of liberal scientists who will stop at nothing to muzzle anyone who dares to challenge them. And now she sits among you." Bayless peered into the audience. "Cooper Gosling, will you please stand up?"

Sal grasped Cooper's hand. Alek, in the seat on her other side, shifted in his chair, but did not turn to look at her. Cooper said nothing, but noticed the NSF reps glancing at one another.

Calhoun, having been summoned to the podium, now scanned the audience.

"Cooper, are you here?"

Climb in the trench.

No one in the auditorium turned to look at Cooper; their eyes fixed on Calhoun and Bayless, they betrayed nothing. At the side of the stage, Tucker remained unreadable behind his sunglasses. Simon, the VIDS admin, and Warren, the NSF admin, pretended not to see her.

Kick out the roof.

Calhoun's eyes finally found her, and for what felt like an age, he gazed at her.

Finally, he leaned over and whispered something to Bayless, and returned to his seat.

"Well, it looks like Cooper is not in the room," Bayless said.

"Which is a shame, because I think it's important to underscore what needless collateral damage looks like. I understand this young woman is an artist. I imagine the kind of injury she suffered will have an impact on her future work. And it was completely preventable.

"I mention all this because there are factions in Washington calling for an agency-wide budget freeze because of this situation. Jack and I have smoothed a few ruffled feathers by proposing that some commonsense protocols be integrated into the NSF's grant-making processes. Rather than quashing scientific dissent, such protocols would ensure that those scientists with a minority view are given access to the same research sites and same taxpayer dollars as majority-view scientists. We've also proposed simple, straightforward guidelines aimed at preserving the integrity of the research station. Scientists hostile to open, honest discussions lose their federal funding. More than one violation makes the program ineligible for federal grants for one year. An OSHA rep would be stationed here to ensure compliance. This approach protects the American taxpayer's investment in science. However, the head of the NSF does not share my commitment to scientific integrity."

"That's a lie," Sal said loudly.

"This is not a Q-and-A," Karl Martin shouted between cupped hands. He gestured to one of his VIDS minions and then pointed at Sal.

"This the same guy as before? No, let him talk, Karl," Bayless said. "This must be the alpha male scientist, I imagine."

"Yeah, yeah, I'm the alpha male," Sal said to Bayless. He dropped Cooper's hand and stood up. "Before even addressing the fact that your science is a failure, let's examine the reasons why you're even bothering to take up this subject, since I assume you are not a climatologist. I would probably further assume that your experiences with higher-level science are fairly limited."

"It is indisputable that I am not a scientist. I make this point with some frequency."

"So you vigorously oppose any policy—even any research—

designed to halt climate change, while claiming that you do not know the science of climate change?"

"That's enough," Karl said, rising from his chair. Bayless put his hand up again, and Karl slowly sat down.

Sal continued, "Then you should be made aware of the fact that in the scientific community, there's virtually unanimous consensus that the earth is warming. It's not a matter of whether it's getting hotter, it's a matter of how hot it will get. I propose that instead of fearing this new knowledge, you accept it, and leave science to scientists. Please, Congressman, go home and let the grown-ups get some work done."

Bayless stood at the lectern, smiling. There was something to fear in his smile, Cooper knew, and when she looked back at Sal, she knew he'd seen it, too. But it was Calhoun she watched. He was smiling, too—but his lapel pin was gone.

*

As soon as the congressmen were wheels up and flying home, the NSF brought all of the scientists, including Sal, into a closed-door meeting, which Tucker said would likely have a passing resemblance to a Chinese reeducation camp. The funded agencies and institutions, including both Sri's and Sal's universities, had been spooked by Bayless's threats and the loud congressional support he'd received after the news stories started appearing. The universities ordered their grantees and fellows to shut their mouths, or else they would bring them back to do lab work and send other, more discreet scientists in their places. Funding was sacrosanct.

"Confidentiality agreements," Sal said, tossing the packet on Cooper's bed, before falling on top of it and landing face-first into her pillow. He turned his head to look at her. "It turns every scientific project and experiment on the ice into a classified operation. I'm considering adding an appendix to *The Crud*. I'll call it *A Scientist's Guide to Political Interference*." He sighed. "And now there's no point for you to read *Skua Birds in Paradise*, since no one will be here this winter to benefit from it if there's a shutdown."

"Too late," Cooper said, scanning the papers Sal had given her. "Already read it. I'm really looking forward to that naked midwinter run from the sauna to the Pole marker."

She began to read aloud. "'Details and results of NSF-backed experiments may only be released publicly after joint approval by the NSF and the scientist's home institution. Scientists and techs are prohibited from speaking to the press in any capacity, even educational, without prior approval. All media requests must go through the NSF's media relations offices.'"

"And they told me I had to stop e-mailing with those kids in De Pere."

"What happens if you don't sign it?" Cooper asked.

Sal propped himself up on his elbow. "According to NSF, the scientists and techs who choose not to agree to these terms will be sent back on the next available flight, 'no questions asked.'"

"What about all the experiments?" Cooper said.

"Done."

Cooper and Sal stared sadly at the confidentiality agreement. She could only think of one thing to say to Sal. "Tom Waits."

He nodded. "Tom fucking Waits."

*

As the clocked ticked down toward winter, more flights landed, carrying fuel but never enough. The pilots, who were typically gregarious and gossipy, worked closemouthed, offering hardly more than grunts and monosyllabic answers to questions. Whenever Floyd mentioned the stingy supply of fuel, they'd shrug and get back into the cockpit as quickly as possible. It was clear the station's fuel was already being rationed.

Cooper tried to immerse herself in her work. She offered to paint portraits to help distract everyone from the looming crisis. Initially, only a couple of people came up to her during mealtimes, but once she set Pearl's portrait up in the galley, the requests came in steadily—especially since Pearl was extravagantly proud of being Cooper's first publicly displayed portrait. The work seemed to Cooper easy and meaningful, two qualities that had never coalesced over the course of her career.

One by one, more portraits appeared in the galley—Pearl hung them at evenly spaced intervals on the walls: Floyd, his hamster cheeks mitigated by shadows, the anger in his eyes replaced by the softness Cooper had seen there once or twice over the course of the season, usually when he was looking at Marcy. Kit in his Halloween gorilla suit, his mouth half opened. Dwight, sans cloak, his head dropped to his chest, his silky black hair obscuring his face. Doc Carla without her knit cap, her eyes an Edward Wilson blue. Tucker, still just the eye in the mirror shard. One by one the Polies had come to her studio or hadn't, and one by one, she'd come to know them a little better. None of the portraits had the photographic quality of her vending machine paintings; hyperrealism was simply no longer possible. However, the inability to be photographically precise had freed something in her.

Cooper was on her way to another artists' meeting in the gym, when she saw a group of women and two visibly distraught men crowded around a piece of paper taped to the outer wall of the trailer.

"What's going on?" Cooper asked.

"Dave's dance class," someone said. "He left for McMurdo."

"He promised to stay for the last class," another replied sadly. Cooper noticed one of the women was weeping quietly, while the others just stared at one another in disbelief. It seemed to Cooper a bad omen, and she hurried past them and into the meeting.

Propelled by their essential feelings of social impotence, and Denise's insistence in their last meeting that the artistic process is profoundly shaped by social settings, the artists and writers, save the historical novelist, had decided to make a statement that summarized their thoughts about political interference in science. They were certain their statement would show solidarity with the scientists ("who are just artists working in a different medium," the dancer said) and send a clear message to the politicians that they hadn't forgotten Helms and Mapplethorpe, and wouldn't let the NEA controversy be repeated in "science-y" fashion on the ice. If none of the newspapers bit, they'd publicize it via a blog.

"But I don't think horses make sense, in context," Birdie was saying when Cooper arrived at the meeting. "Although you could stretch the conceit and make as if the ponies Scott brought down here to their deaths are akin to the scientists. Scott being the government." He shuddered. "But that kind of parallel goes against every grain of my being."

"I don't even know if this is worth the effort," the literary novelist said. "Politicians don't get art."

"Well, as an agnostic Buddhist-and-pagan who is deeply vested in the principle of plurality, I find this conversation really complex," the dancer replied. "I'm committed to freedom of ideas, even the ones we dislike."

"The man has a right to do his research without being harassed," the historical novelist barked. "This whole thing is the worst kind of liberal arrogance. A coordinated campaign to discredit Frank Pavano's work." He laughed. "But look at it bite them in the ass."

"The man sliced off her finger," the literary novelist replied.

"It was an accident," Cooper said.

"Oh, no, sister," the historical novelist said, waggling his finger in her face. "This wasn't an old *whoopsie-daisy* kind of thing. That how they're spinning it to you? Nope. *Drudge Report* says the only reason he was coring without a tech was because the staff at the ice-coring camp wouldn't give him the tools he needed. If he'd been allowed to conduct his research without political interference, he wouldn't have had to use makeshift tools and you might still be a whole person."

"I still am a whole person," Cooper said.

"Fine. You're a whole person who is missing part of her hand. You're splitting hairs."

"I think the scientists' objection to Pavano and his research has to do with the idea that beliefs have no place in science," Birdie said, trying to regain control of the conversation.

"Beliefs have a place everywhere," the dancer said. "The world is built on them."

"You probably believe that the world is supported by a turtle," the literary novelist replied, his face darkening.

The dancer stiffened. "It's called the 'world-bearing turtle' and yes, I find truth in creation myths. Why do you care what I believe? How does it affect you?"

"You can't come down here to do research on Santa Claus."

"Forget Santa Claus," the historical novelist snapped. "Let's talk money for a minute. You guys want to get blacklisted?" He looked around the room. "These grants are my livelihood. What exactly are the chances of getting an NEA grant after this?"

"Zilch," the literary novelist said, sitting forward in his chair now. He tapped the dancer's knee three times with his finger. "But your chances of getting a Guggenheim or a MacArthur just increased exponentially." He sang the last word.

"It was a rhetorical question," the historical novelist growled.

"Let's reconvene tomorrow after we've all had some time to think this through," Birdie said. The artists murmured their assent and walked out of the gym. Cooper stayed behind.

"I don't do protest art," she said to Birdie, once everyone was gone.

"Me either. I haven't the faintest idea what to do. Perhaps I can find something in the life story of Birdie Bowers that echoes this current impasse, but the British government has always been very supportive of scientific endeavors."

"Don't rub it in."

*

The announcement came the next morning. Dwight laid the *New York Times* printout on the bar, and the Polies crowded around it. Bayless and Calhoun had finally put their money where their mouths were; the article detailed a House resolution they'd co-sponsored that would freeze the station's budget by suspending the National

Science Foundation's polar regions department. Until the resolution got out of committee, additional funding requests would be in limbo. Because fuel was a fluid line item in the station's annual budget, each request was considered a request for new funding and would need to be approved, in triplicate. The fuel supply had essentially been halted. Even if the resolution got out of committee, the Program was facing a sequester: all Pole operations would cease—from the construction of the new station and the climate research taking place at the Divide, to the cosmological experiments in the Dark Sector, including the joint Stanford-Princeton experiment Sal was leading with Lisa Wu.

"'The South Pole is touted as a bastion of scientific activity,'" Dwight read, quoting Bayless, "'where minds converge to answer the most important questions of the universe. It is a place where open-minded discussion leads to breakthroughs. But that is changing; the time-honored tradition of intellectual debate is under grave threat from elements of the far left, and our ability as a nation to remain the leader in scientific achievement is now in doubt. Taxpayers are currently funding a number of scientists and scientific programs through the National Science Foundation, and I think they might be surprised to learn that their hard-earned dollars are going to support a liberal agenda rather than disinterested science.'"

Dwight looked up from the printout. Sri bent over his knees, his hands interlaced behind his head. His breathing grew rapid, and Sal placed a hand on his shoulder.

"I've got lawyers going through my research files back in Madison as we speak. My grants for next year are suspended pending further review," Sri said. "They've already forced Fern and her team off the ice. If they shut us down, I will lose three years of research. I can't have a gap in the data. I can't, Sal. I can't."

"What is he talking about?" Pearl asked.

"Sri just got subpoenaed," Sal said. "Bayless got the Wisconsin attorney general to initiate an investigation for violations of the Fraud Against Taxpayers Act. They're saying he manipulated his climate data to get federal grants. It's just an excuse to get Sri off the ice and interrupt his research."

"How is it possible that people like this have the power to shut down an entire research base?" Sri said to no one. "I mean, what about the medical science that makes it possible for them to go in for their triple bypasses and come out as fresh as a newly plucked daisy? Did a Jesus in scrubs float down on a cloud of ether and come up with the protocols for that shit? I hate humanity. And yet I'm down here because I want to save humanity from certain suffering and death once this planet bursts into fucking flames."

"You're a misanthrope with a heart," Pearl said cheerfully.

Cooper glanced over at Sal, who was still squeezing Sri's shoulder. "No," he said. "He's a scientist on a choke chain."

*

After breakfast the next morning, an announcement went out over All-Call directing the winter-over crew to meet in the library—the individuals who had been approved to spend the winter at Amundsen-Scott. When Cooper arrived, she surveyed the winter population— the individuals who had freely chosen to spent months of perpetual night at the bottom of the earth. There were the Nailheads, including Bozer, Floyd, and Marcy; the Beakers, who would monitor their experiments through the season, Alek, Sal, and Lisa, and assorted research techs; Dwight, who would continue to run Comms and provide general research tech help; Pearl and Doc Carla; and two NSF "non-science" grantees: Denise and Cooper. Everyone else was contracted to move to McMurdo for the winter, like Birdie and Kit, or off the ice entirely. (Birdie had made his arrangements for a McMurdo transfer before meeting Pearl, and had spent the last two weeks trying in vain to get someone to approve him for a winter-over.) Cooper noticed Simon, the VIDS rep, and Warren, the NSF rep who had interrogated her in the days after her injury, were also in the room. Both looked as if they'd been invited to a slumber party at Guantanamo.

Cooper took a seat near Sal. He reached across the plastic chair between them and took her hand. His face was drawn and his eyes sunken; there was little remaining of the usual fire in them. He seemed, for the first time since she'd met him, almost beaten. On his other side, Lisa sat twisting a Kleenex in her hands. Cooper knew if the shutdown happened, hardly anyone in this room would be allowed to stay for the winter.

Before Tucker or either of the admins could begin speaking, Bozer stood up, his meaty arms folded across his chest.

"We don't have enough JP-8 to get through the winter."

"Calm down," Simon said dismissively. "We'll get to that later." Pearl looked over at Cooper, with raised eyebrows. *This* was going to be good.

"Actually, no, son, we'll get to that first," Bozer said. "I've winter-overed for nine seasons, but I'll be *fucked* if I stay past station closing knowing we don't have enough fuel to last us. My bags are packed. I have a seat on the last Herc out if that shit ain't here by next week."

"You realize this is your own fault, right?" Sri said to Bozer from across the room. Sal nudged him with his knee. "No, man, it needs to be said. If construction had stayed on schedule, and the planes didn't have to haul all your construction shit from McMurdo, we could've made do with the fuel we already had, no matter what these politicians were trying to do." Cooper saw Floyd's entire body wince. "Oh, and your precious pool table? Everyone knows you've been illegally shipping materials for that since summer."

Bozer turned his gaze to Sri. "My dear swami friend, you are obviously a miserable worm in a lab coat, so I will keep this simple: fuck you. Here you are, jacking off into your beakers because I've been busting my balls down here for the last five years, building your lab. So go fuck another penguin, and I'll keep this station going in the meantime."

"This has nothing to do with construction, Sri, and you know it," Dwight said. "This is political. I mean, look at what you Beakers have unleashed! This whole thing is your fault! If you guys had been cool about Pavano instead of acting like eighth graders, none of this would be happening."

"What the F, Dwight?" Sri said. "You're the one who made him kiss your ring for satellite calls!"

"To be fair, Dwight does that to everyone," Pearl chimed in.

"Washington isn't worried about satellite phones, Sri!" Dwight shouted. "They're worried about—oh, what was it? Oh yeah— threats and intimidation." He pointed at Sri angrily, his Livestrong bracelet trembling on his wrist. "Threats and intimidation, Sri!"

"What threats? What intimidation?" Sri cried. "These are fairy tales Pavano and his conservatard congressmen are spinning."

"Everyone knows it was you who took his name off the manifests to the Divide, Sri. Everyone knows your research techs deleted his username from the server. And the petitions? The multiple printouts, Sri, where you guys defaced stuff and made comments about Jesus. That debate, and the way Sal got up in Pavano's face while he was trying to give his talk?" Dwight looked over at Cooper. "And holy shit, her finger? Her fucking finger?"

"It's not their fault this happened," Cooper said quietly. Sal shook his head. He seemed to know something about Dwight that Cooper didn't, that this outburst was necessary and that Dwight should be allowed to go on, the way Floyd had been allowed to castigate Marcy that night at the bar when she'd returned from Cheech. And, in fact, letting that drama play out had worked—there Floyd and Marcy were, sitting perpendicular to each other, Marcy with her legs propped up on Floyd's lap. Cooper looked around the room: Alek was sitting quietly, his demeanor as serene as if he were settling in for movie night. Pearl knit, while next to her, Doc Carla scratched her ankle. Tucker leaned against a bookshelf, carelessly flipping through a James Patterson paperback. Only the admin staff looked mortified.

"She says it's not their fault. Okay, that's good." Dwight nodded at Cooper. "King Beaker's ice-wife says it's not his fault, in her completely unbiased opinion. Look, Sal worked overtime being an asshole to Pavano and then he put on that show when Frick and Frack and the rest of the government suits came—don't you guys see? Don't you see what's gonna happen, what they're already doing?" Dwight was hysterical. "They're gonna shut us down! They're gonna stop payments, they're gonna close up shop. They're gonna send us home."

Tucker reshelved the Patterson novel and walked over to Dwight. He rubbed his shoulders, and to Cooper's surprise, Dwight let him. He turned to look up at Tucker. "I don't wanna go home."

Simon sighed, and hauled himself out of his chair. Cooper caught the eye roll he sent over to Warren, who appeared to have gone catatonic. "I'll address your question about the fuel supply," Simon said to Bozer, "despite your lack of manners. We expect the Hercs coming in over the next ten days will carry enough fuel to put us where we need to be."

"Negative," Floyd said. "Seeing as I'm actually the one who runs the power plant and observes the fuels, and reports back to you, I can say with, yeah, let's call it total certainty, that that's not what I reported to you last week."

"I didn't see that report," Simon said.

"According to my calculations, I believe that we would need twenty-seven air tankers ferrying nothing but JP-8 in order to survive the winter. All those 'delayed shipments' set us back."

"Send the Nailheads home," Sri said. "Stop construction and keep a small crew to keep the station and the labs going. We can live off the fuel we have. I need my data. Sal needs his data. I'm not leaving here without my data."

Floyd laughed. "You think you're gonna finish that shit?"

"I know I am."

Floyd shook his head, and muttered, "Moron."

Sri looked over at Sal. "What's he talking about, Sal?"

Everyone turned to look at Sal. Like Warren, he, too, had folded his arms over his chest and closed his eyes. Cooper realized both men were in possession of the same information, and that their demeanors matched because this information had impacted them similarly. "Sal?" Sri said.

"We have bigger problems," Sal finally said.

"Bigger problems than a fuel shortage heading into winter?"

"They have us—you, me, Lisa, everyone—going home in two days."

Sri paused for a moment. "Because we didn't sign the confidentiality agreement," he said, his voice dead. Lisa dropped her head in her hands.

"Just sign the goddamn thing, guys," Marcy said. "Everyone else did."

"They're research techs," Sal said. "Early-career scientists, some of them still post-docs. Most of them working on other people's projects. You expect me to sign away my life's work, my ideas? I can't." He looked over at Sri and Lisa. "We can't."

Cooper reached over and rubbed Lisa's back as she wept.

After leaving the winter-over meeting, Cooper stopped by the station post office to see if she'd received any mail. Along with the fuel shipments, postal delivery had slowed dramatically, further dampening everyone's spirits. The place was empty when she arrived, as were nearly all of the post office boxes. Halfheartedly, Cooper thrust her hand into her cubby and felt around. To her surprise, there was something there: a package, the size of a pack of cigarettes, lumpy and wrapped inexpertly in brown paper. There was no return address, and Cooper didn't recognize the handwriting on the mailing label.

She opened it and found something hastily wrapped in a page from a week-old *Washington Post*. With some difficulty, she was able to tear the paper away with her good hand. As she did so, something metallic fell to the floor. It sparkled under the fluorescent lights like a Fourth of July firework. When Cooper picked it up, she saw it was Calhoun's lapel pin. *Let's Roll.*

**REGISTER NOW FOR THE 2000 DESIGN IN NATURE CONFERENCE
HOSTED BY THE CENTER FOR COMPLEXITY AND DESIGN**

Meet the most influential thinkers in the world of Intelligent Design and Climate Change while cruising through spectacular Alaskan landscapes at the height of summer. This weeklong conference will take place aboard one of Telkhine Cruises' most luxurious ships, the *Fantasy*, and will leave Seattle to cruise the Inside Passage. Our ship will call at Ketchikan, Wrangell, Hubbard Glacier, and other breathtaking ports and features, before returning via the Outside Passage. Spend time in the company of some of the world's foremost scholars, scientists, and design theorists and learn more about the most profound scientific questions facing us today: How did the universe begin? How did complex life develop? What does helioseismology tell us about fluctuating climate patterns? Is climate change real?

Featured speakers include Dr. Patton D. Rodale, *New York Times* bestselling author of *Alarmism and the Climate Change Hoax*, renowned Cambridge University mathematician and clergyman Dr. Jeffrey Osterholm, and Dr. Frank Pavano, a widely respected helioseismologist whose nascent research on the effect of global solar variations on climate fluctuations is attracting a great deal of attention. In addition to daily lectures and seminars, opportunities for more intimate conservations with our speakers will be available each night during formal meals and dancing.

Register today and experience the Intelligent Design of nature while basking in it yourself.

complexity and design

I see now that the cruise was a mistake, the *first cause,* if you'll allow the joke, of my current difficulties. But Annie had wanted so badly to go, and I felt this was something kind I could do for her after everything that had happened. It also appeared to be a career opportunity for me.

The cruise would leave from Seattle, dock at Juneau, sail through Glacier Bay, and then return—its only guests the individuals registered for the 2000 Design in Nature Conference, sponsored by the Center for Complexity and Design, an organization with which I had, until this point, been unfamiliar. I had been approached personally by the center's senior Fellow, who had received my name from a former colleague (I suspected it was Fred Zimmer, but the man on the phone would not confirm this). He showed particular interest in my most recent work, which had to do with solar acoustic pressure waves, and urged me to submit an abstract for the conference. But when I asked him to give me a sense of the conference's focus, he was evasive. He would say only that the expected audience would be comprised of academics, politicians, policymakers, Fellows of the Center for Complexity and Design, and regular citizens with an interest in the topic of science. He hinted that the organizers had detected in their audience a burgeoning interest in global warming, but offered no further guidance. It is telling to me now that I cannot recall the man's name.

It would not be inaccurate to say that, by this time, things had grown desperate for me. It had been three years since I'd been forced to resign from my position as the DuPont Professor of Physics at a small private college in the Midwest after the provost discovered I had plagiarized entire paragraphs in several of my research papers. In my area of study—helioseismology, or the study of solar wave oscillations—plagiarism was unheard of, and so when the University Research Integrity Committee began its investigation, there was great internal interest in the outcome. At its conclusion, I was given the option of resigning or being fired.

Annie was bewildered. I told her I'd been sloppy, that I'd been overextended, that I'd put too much on my graduate assistant's plate, and that he had cut and pasted from several sources directly into my master documents, intending, of course, to flag those sections so that I might rewrite the material. It had happened to several academics in the last few years, and even some journalists. Contrite, they'd all slunk into the farthest corners of their professions, but had slowly been able to piece their careers back together. Framed in this manner, Annie found it plausible that there had been no intent to deceive on my part, and this made it harder for her to accept that I had been treated so roughly by the university.

I had lost the support of all but one colleague—Fred Zimmer, the chair of the physics department and the man who had hired me. He was a theorist who had spent forty-five years studying quantum chaos, specifically entropy dynamics. He was warm and gregarious in a department known for its austerity, and he wanted to believe there had been a misunderstanding.

But the truth was that it went far beyond a couple of plagiarized paragraphs. It was systematic, a compulsion I could not keep in check for reasons I could not fathom. I began seeing a therapist. I told Annie the therapy was for generalized anxiety resulting from my resignation and the subsequent ostracism, but in reality, I was unspooling a career's worth of lies. My therapist accepted these lies; in fact she seemed to extract them, winding them back on a distaff from her chair across the room. And the question that hung over every session was *why?*

I had no answers to this, of course—the therapist had many, but she would pose her answers as yet more questions for me to consider. Could it be that, as a former "child prodigy," I had a pathological fear of failure that created a tension so unbearable that I had to affect the failure myself in order to relieve it? Could it be I had an inferiority complex because I was a first-generation college student, surrounded by individuals who had "suckled at the breast of the ivory tower"? (When I pointed out the somewhat mixed nature of her metaphor, she indicated this objection was a way of diverting the conversation, but this did not stop me from spending the rest of that session imagining an ivory tower with leaking breasts, sustaining an entire generation of infant-academics.) Could it be that I felt everyone's work was inherently better than mine, even when mine was yet unwritten, and so the compulsion to integrate the work of others into my own without risking a single change was a manifestation of both primary and secondary inferiority? Perhaps it goes without saying, but my therapist was a devotee of Adler. I found Adler's approach wanting in many areas, and as a result, I wasn't, in the words of my therapist, "doing the work." We terminated our relationship.

Annie encouraged me to mount an attempt to return to the halls of academia. The gap in my résumé would be hard to explain—a plagiarism charge is notoriously difficult to work around. Instead, I continued my work on the solar neutrino problem I'd been working on prior to my resignation, but this time only as a private citizen. Annie went back to work at Pricewaterhouse shortly after I left the university, in order to replace the steady paycheck and health insurance I had lost.

*

I wasn't aware that the man sitting next to me in the cruise terminal was addressing me until Annie nudged me with her elbow. Unlike the majority of the men milling about the waiting area, most of whom were dressed in khakis and polos, this man wore a business suit. He was clean-shaven and well groomed, and the symmetry of his face was pleasing. The gel in his hair gleamed under the harsh terminal lights, giving it a slightly plastic appearance.

"Scientists are prone to herd thinking," the man said, with the air of someone who was conspicuously repeating himself. Annie nudged me again. I was unsure of how to address his statement. He seemed to sense this, and, to my relief, he offered his hand. "Eric Falleri," he said.

"Frank Pavano," I replied, as we shook hands.

"Oh, I know who you are. You're the reason I'm taking this cruise." He grinned. "I'm very interested in your work."

Eric did not look like the sort who would typically take an interest in helioseismology—and besides that, I wasn't even speaking on solar acoustic pressure waves, the work for which I was known. I had proposed a series of talks on this topic, of course, but when the man from the Center for Complexity and Design called me after receiving my proposal, he'd asked if I'd be willing to speak instead about the impact of solar variations on global climate fluctuations. Although I was well versed in solar irradiance, I had very little background in climatology or knowledge of how spectral distribution could possibly affect climate patterns on Earth. However, when I mentioned this to him, he seemed unconcerned, and offered to pair me with another scientist who was preparing to submit a paper on the theory that total solar irradiance was a significant cause of climate change. "Though," he added, "as an organization we are skeptical that the climate is, in fact, changing."

I knew both positions ran against prevailing scientific opinion, and yet I was intrigued.

Eric and I spoke a bit about my lecture topic, and I confided that I felt far more comfortable speaking on subjects with which I was more familiar. He, however, seemed very enthusiastic. "Our conference participants are eager to learn more about the global warming hoax," he said. As I tried to process this, he added, *sotto voce*, "One of our most prominent sponsors asked us to reach out to you specifically, Dr. Pavano."

Annie was thrilled to find that we had been booked into a junior suite. There was a large fruit basket on the table, which she found deeply touching—any kindness shown to me during this time she appreciated with great fervor. She walked onto the small balcony overlooking the terminal building—we had not yet left the docks—and remained there for some minutes, gazing at the Seattle skyline. When I gently reminded her that it was time to dress for dinner, she turned and smiled at me, her lovely brown eyes shining with happiness for the first time in months.

"If making small talk with people who believe the earth is six thousand years old is all it takes to cruise to Alaska in a stateroom, sign me up," she said. My stomach sank. The smile disappeared from her face. "Frank, you've got to start somewhere. You can shake these people off when the time is right." She walked over to where I was standing in my tuxedo, and put her hands on either side of my face. "Brilliance can't be contained for long," she said. Her face, as beautiful as the first time I saw it, looked angelic as she said this. And if it hadn't been for the tears standing in her eyes, I would have thought her beatific.

We saw Eric Falleri at dinner, dressed in a very fine tuxedo with gleaming monogrammed cuff links. Annie asked after his wife—she'd noticed his wedding ring back in the terminal—and he'd said she was "back home in D.C."

"What is it that you do, Mr. Falleri?" she asked. Something about Annie's question embarrassed me. Her curiosity, sharp as a blade, was sometimes mistaken as an attempt to injure, when it was merely a reflection of her deep interest in people. I, on the other hand, found people inscrutable, and relied heavily upon my wife's investigations to provide context for social situations. Eric seemed discomfited by her question, and it was obvious enough that even I noticed it. After taking a too-long sip of wine, he finally said, "I suppose you'd call me a consultant, Mrs. Pavano."

She asked him to call her Annie, and then asked him about the entities for whom he consulted.

"Various clients," Eric said, reaching for his wine again. "Mostly energy consortiums."

"Oh, you're a lobbyist," Annie said, and Eric's face darkened. I could tell Annie noticed this, too, but neither of us were sure of her transgression. (I've since come to understand that lobbyists do not like their intentions to be pointed out explicitly any more than does an Amway salesman.) Despite this, Eric's expression quickly regained its previous cheerfulness, and he said that he was on the cruise representing one of the conference sponsors, a private corporation that owned a few refineries, a handful of fertilizer plants, and other "industrial operations." He then turned to his neighbor, a schoolteacher from Oklahoma City, and Annie and I spent the rest of the evening making small talk with the other people at our table.

As the dinner was coming to a close and many of the conference participants and their spouses were heading to the dance floor, Annie excused herself to return to the stateroom so she could watch *Survivor*, a small vice of hers. As soon as she'd left, Eric moved around the perimeter of the table and took her seat. He pushed aside the remains of Annie's dessert and leaned toward me. "I've heard about your troubles, Professor."

As soon as he said this, I felt something in me break free, and I realized it was a tension that had been present since the moment the man from the Center for Design and Complexity had first called—I had been found out. It was the same strange feeling I'd experienced the day Fred Zimmer called me into his office to confront me with the plagiarism charges.

Eric placed a friendly hand on my shoulder. "Don't worry, Professor," he said. "I want to share an opportunity with you. I represent a client who is in a position to fund research into global temperature and climate patterns. This is a pressing issue that will likely dominate energy policy discussions in the years to come."

"Well, as I've explained to the organizers of the conference, my research focus is far afield from—"

"What you've done in the past is not important."

"I don't understand."

"Let me ask you a question: If I were to say that a free society requires open discussion of all sides of an issue, would you agree with that statement?"

"Naturally," I replied.

"Would you also agree that it has a chilling effect on science when those whose ideas go against the grain are demonized by fellow scientists?"

"Of course, though I suppose it depends on what you mean by—"

"My client is concerned about the fact that climate scientists are intentionally suppressing alternative findings regarding global climate fluctuations. He also believes the political response to climate issues should be based on sound science, not alarmism or emotions. As a scientist—even a disgraced one—you surely agree."

The barb stung, and gave the conversation a different tone. "Forgive me, Eric, but, again, I feel compelled to point out that while I find the discussion on global warming fascinating—"

"We prefer to use the term climate change. It provokes less emotion than *global warming*. Global warming is scary. We don't want to scare people."

It took me a moment to process this, and he took another long sip of his wine. Finally, I spoke. "While I am a curious bystander, my research interests are not aligned with this topic. Frankly, I'd be a bit out of my depth."

Eric opened his jacket and pulled the conference brochure from an inner pocket. He searched it for the description of my presentation. Once he found it, he tapped it with his finger.

"It says here you're speaking on the impact solar variations have on global climate fluctuations."

"My focus will be primarily on total solar irradiance," I said uneasily.

Eric slipped the brochure back into his pocket. "Perfect. This aligns with my client's interests."

"I can't imagine how."

"Dr. Pavano, my client is proposing an opportunity that would allow you to reenter academia, regain control of your career, and do meaningful research with the kind of financial support most scientists don't even dare to dream about."

Eric went on to tell me that his client was prepared to endow a professorship at a university to which he already had strong ties. This university would provide me with generous research grants for more study into the subjects about which we'd spoken. I quickly realized this would require a substantial shift in my current research interests.

As we spoke, I thought about Annie lying on the bed upstairs in our stateroom, watching *Survivor*, so grateful for the fruit basket that she hadn't taken off the yellow cellophane. The decision was not difficult.

*

My cruise ship lecture was so well received that within a week of returning home, I had six invitations to present the same talk at various conferences around the country. The fees offered were substantial. Until I'd embarked upon the cruise, I had had no idea that a parallel scientific world existed, one separated from mainstream science by a matter of degrees. It was a place where science was expertly mimicked and, at rare moments, even practiced. I was entering the fold. And I found the inhabitants of this world to be, without exception, kind, welcoming, in earnest, and thrilled to find a "real scientist" in their midst.

Eric Falleri kept in touch regularly, and by April 2002, although I was not affiliated with any accredited university, I was a fairly well established "climate change skeptic." In this parallel universe, "expertise" came quickly. Although some bloggers who had taken notice of my work referred to me as a "denialist," my reputation was bolstered by the fact that I did not entertain the conspiracy theories that had gripped some corners of this world—charges of scientific and criminal misconduct resulting in a general consensus that climate change existed and was caused by humans.

I made one misstep at this time, which was agreeing to counsel a young biblical archaeologist on a paper about the structural stability of Noah's ark. I considered it an interesting puzzle—how does one research the buoyancy and bilge radius of an imaginary seafaring vessel?

To my dismay, the student added my name to the subsequent research paper. Although Eric was vexed, he felt that the journal in which it appeared was so obscure that it wouldn't pose any problems.

In late May, I was booked on a flight to Washington for a meeting with the Client, whom by this point I had come to consider a proper noun. The meeting was held in the Royal Suite at the Washington, D.C., Four Seasons, at a long dining table and over an opulent meal. Falleri was there, but the easy insouciance that I had come to consider his trademark was nowhere to be found. Terse now, he asked for the confidentiality agreement he'd sent me the week before the meeting. Once I'd produced it, he grimly escorted me to a seat on the left side of the table.

Shortly after, a group of men emerged from an adjoining room. There was little to distinguish one from the other. They were of similar age—between fifty and sixty—and wore suits of a similar cut and of similar quality. Three were balding, two had full heads of silver hair. It would take a keener eye than mine to determine which one, upon a glance, was the Client. My only indications were the facts that he entered the room a full minute after everyone else and that he walked directly to the seat at the head of the table. His firm handshake lasted only the length of a breath, as if the ritual were inherently distasteful to him.

Throughout the first course, a Waldorf salad, the Client remained silent while the others spoke about trivial matters—golf scores, recent vacations, the Preakness. He finished his salad with astonishing celerity. One by one, the others at the table noticed and set their forks down, too.

In the break between the main course—Maine lobster thermidor—and coffee, the Client finally turned his eyes toward me. The table conversation dissipated at once.

"Dr. Pavano, we meet at a time of great change," the Client said. He looked at me steadily, waiting, as if I might contradict him. I decided to respond with "Indeed." This met with his approval, and he continued, "I trust Eric has given you an idea of where our interests lie." He gestured to the other men at the table without looking at them. "These men represent some of the largest energy companies in the world. We are here together tonight because we have agreed that the defining issue of the coming decades, not just in our industry, but also in federal and global policy, will be climate change. We are aware that the majority of the science emerging from this area of study indicates that the earth is warming, and that it's warming due to carbon dioxide emissions. The responsibility for this warming, and its attendant repercussions, will be laid at our feet." He paused here to take a drink from his ice water. "We would like to approach this issue proactively. One way we can do this is by directing our resources toward sound science that looks dispassionately at the data, which our own company scientists tell us do not support the idea of man-made climate change. Unfortunately, they are unable to place any research papers in reputable journals, so we are losing control of the messaging. This issue has become politically charged. And that's why you're here with us tonight."

To his right, one of the balding men gathered that the Client was finished for now and that he was expected to speak.

"Dr. Pavano," he said, "I represent Americans for Responsible Petroleum, a coalition of oil and energy companies. We are deeply concerned about the science coming out of the federal research programs, which is indicating, overwhelmingly, that climate change is verifiable fact and that its causes can be connected directly to our industries."

At this point, he pushed aside a vase of purple hydrangeas and laid out a map of Antarctica. Small red stars had been carefully affixed to various parts of the continent. "The majority of federal and university-funded climate change research takes place in Antarctica, specifically at South Pole Station and the West Antarctic Divide. This work is overseen by the National Science Foundation, a taxpayer-funded federal agency. To date, there has not been a single climate researcher who doesn't go down there already convinced that climate change is caused mainly by fossil fuel emissions."

"Of course you know that a consensus exists among climate scientists that the fluctuations are, in fact, human-caused," I said.

The man smiled. "And you've played right into their hands, Dr. Pavano."

Chastened, I said, "I admit I know very little about the kind of research undertaken in the polar regions."

"Which is the other reason why you are here tonight," the Client broke in. "This coordinated alarmist campaign could have a devastating impact on the U.S. economy and lead to destructive government regulations. Think about the other alarmist campaigns that have been much ado about nothing. The population crisis. The so-called energy crisis. The hole in the ozone. We've sat on the sidelines long enough. To do so any longer would be irresponsible."

By the time the dessert plates were cleared away, I had recovered enough to begin asking questions, and they began to lay out the Plan. It had five phases:

Phase One: *Apply for a National Science Foundation–funded research position at Amundsen-Scott South Pole Station and the West Antarctic Ice Sheet (known as WAIS, or, colloquially, the Divide).*

Phase Two: *When, as anticipated, the application is rejected, identify at least two of the 135 known climate change skeptics currently serving in the U.S. Congress who might be willing to make National Science Foundation bias a platform issue.*

Phase Three: *Argue, in a coordinated media campaign, that the National Science Foundation, as a federal agency, is bound by law not to demonstrate bias (if bias is verifiable), or imply bias exists among National Science Foundation leadership (if no documented history of bias is available). If necessary, launch local and national campaigns to support the placement of a nonconformist climate scientist at the research base at South Pole.*

Phase Four (assuming Phase Three is successful): *Receive federal funding from the National Science Foundation, along with additional private monies from the companies represented at the dinner, via existing pass-through organizations, to explore the idea that climate change is caused by solar variations, not CO_2 emissions. (It*

*had been previously concluded that countering the idea that the cli-
mate was warming at all was a "zero-sum game.")*

Phase Five: *Once funded and sited at WAIS, produce compelling
data and, if the data do not support the Plan, manipulate it. Expect,
and even welcome, obstruction from researchers and administrators.
Document these actions but do not resist them. At the same time,
disrupt the existing ecosystem in a manner that attracts the attention
of the national media and solidifies the message of bias.*

As I was mulling over the Plan (as with the Client, I gave it proper
noun status), the discussion took the turn for which Eric had prepared
me in the months leading up to this meeting: the Client asked if I was
a "god-fearing man." Next to me, I could feel Eric shift in his seat, expectant but nervous. In our conversations, the lie to which we'd both
agreed, and which I was about to tell the Client, had been difficult for
Eric to accept. I knew he was raised Baptist, but was not "evangeli-
cal," as he put it. He knew I was an atheist, because Annie had mentioned it in passing to him at one point on the cruise. But when Eric
told me what I would be expected to do—the spiritual mantle I'd
have to wear if I were to be successful—I had no qualms. The burden
of having failed to fulfill immense promise was substantial; I had
thought many times over the years of what John Brennan said to me
when I'd declined to join his department at Stanford: "No one is more
unnecessary than a man who has failed to realize his gift." I had done
many things since to escape the fact that I had failed to realize mine.
Being something other than a profound disappointment seemed to me
at that moment sublime, even if it required lying about something
that, to me, was wholly unimportant. Faith was not so odious an idea
that I wouldn't use it in the name of my own personal redemption.
At the time Eric first brought up the idea of turning me into a
"god-fearing man," I sensed he was both relieved and repulsed by my
easy acquiescence. "We'll have to build a narrative," he warned.
"Otherwise, it will be too easy for the press to pick the story apart."
This narrative-building required a crisis—an atheist scientist who has

been thrown out of the halls of academia because of moral and ethical failings directly attributable to his lack of faith. A series of meetings had been arranged with a Pentecostal church in northern Virginia, which, Eric told me, had been chosen because it was fundamentalist in nature but modern in approach. I shared my manufactured narrative with the assistant general bishops, both of whom were deeply moved by the story of a scientist wrestling with his faith. I then met with the general bishop, who, toward the end of our meeting, grew animated and insisted I attend Sunday's service. "You are," he told me, "our Prodigal Son."

At the service, I was brought to the front of the church and surrounded by several individuals, including the general bishop, and experienced what I later learned was the "laying on of hands." I became a member in good standing of Olive Grove Christian Fellowship.

Annie had watched this unfold with growing unease. Being an atheist herself, she openly ridiculed my new membership at Olive Grove. She even spoke critically of the Client. Eric soon noticed that she was not, as he put it, "on board." This, he indicated, was a problem. In fact, things between Annie and me had grown strained since I'd undertaken the Plan. Annie had become distant—during the weeks I was in Washington and Virginia, she chose not to fly out on the weekends to join me. In the meantime, Eric wanted to know what could be done to influence her to become a more visible part of the narrative. I decided to ask her myself, and our conversation transformed into a fairly intense domestic squabble, in which Annie said things along the lines of "I don't know who you are anymore." Eric and I agreed to leave the Annie question alone for the time being, but I continued my active participation in Olive Grove, and even came to find the spiritual work invigorating, if not convincing. So by the time of the dinner in the Royal Suite at the Four Seasons, I was able to answer the Client's question with an assertion that I was an active member of Olive Grove Christian Fellowship. He then said that he understood I had been an atheist (specifically, he used the term *irreligionist*) and felt this was somewhat inconvenient, but acknowledged that it was difficult to find a reputable scientist who was a believer. Eric told the Client about my religious redemption, and how the story of an atheist scientist coming to Christ would be far more powerful than that of a churchgoing man experiencing an intensification of his faith.

"Luke fifteen," the Client said approvingly.

In the cab to the airport, Eric handed me an envelope containing a check. It was more than I'd made in the last five years combined.

When I submitted my proposal to the National Science Foundation, I chose Kibsairlin's ice cores as my research subject, with a secondary focus on methane levels in the Antarctic sedimentary basins. I suspected, or said I suspected—I wasn't yet sure what I wanted to suspect—that the levels were not as high as had been reported. I remained surprised at the speed with which I had become an expert in the world of climate change denial. In other disciplines, my lack of published and peer-reviewed articles would preclude me from such a rapid ascension. My reliance on meta-analysis rather than original research would be seen as a grave liability. In this collegial community of like-minded individuals, however, meta-analysis was the most effective tool for picking apart inconsistencies and sowing doubt.

"The idea," Eric told me, "is to make people think that there is controversy within the scientific community on whether climate change is human-caused. We won't be in trouble until the public thinks the conversation is closed." It was my job to keep the conversation going.

In early September 2002, the expected rejection letter from the NSF arrived, citing an overabundance of quality proposals. It was now time to move onto Phase Two of the Plan. In mid-November, I answered the door to find Fred Zimmer standing on my stoop. I managed to hide my shock, and invited him in. He asked after Annie, and I told her she was visiting her parents in Bismarck—going into the details about why she was no longer living in the house felt too complicated. I brewed a pot of coffee and we sat together at the kitchen table. I noticed how frail Fred was looking, how sunken his cheeks were, as if he'd been hollowed out from the inside and his skin had collapsed to fill the spaces. His thick glasses magnified his pale blue eyes so that they seemed to overtake his face, and his lips had curled inward, threatening to disappear completely.

"Colon cancer," he told me. "Metastatic. But I didn't come here to talk about that." He scraped his chair forward so he could lean on the table with both elbows. "I got a call from the *New Scientist* yesterday, asking me about the circumstances of your resignation. What the hell's going on, Frank?"

When I feigned incomprehension, he hit the table with his fist. I mopped up the spilled coffee with a napkin, and noticed Fred's hands were shaking. I felt gripped by something—compassion, perhaps, or pity—and I gently laid my hands on his.

He kept them under mine for only a moment before snatching them away angrily. "What's happened to you, Frank, that you're running around with these tinfoil-hat-wearing reptiles?" Although I was used, after all these years, to Fred's candor, I winced at this and he noticed.

"*Cui bono*, Frank?" he said.

"Taxpayers want disinterested science, Fred, not political alarmism."

Zimmer's eyes widened and a look of inexpressible sadness crossed his old and gnarled face. He said nothing for some minutes. "The stealing, the plagiarism—did you do it?" For only an instant did I consider lying to my old mentor. I could tell that the question was merely a formality, even though Zimmer was not known to stand on such things. He already knew.

I looked down at the coffee spoons, which I had set on top of one another, the bowls and the stems in perfect alignment. I didn't raise my eyes again until I heard the front door slam shut.

*

The Plan steadily grew in scope. The Group (the consortium of energy companies with whom I'd met that night in the Royal Suite) had started meeting with the two conservative legislators who'd been chosen to take up the cause, in exchange for several generous campaign donations. I met the men once—a representative from Kansas named Sam Bayless and a representative from Tennessee named Jack Calhoun. Bayless was the younger, and more serious, of the two men—

groomed, handsome, but not oleaginous. Calhoun was a husky man with crooked teeth, but a more sincere bearing. Bayless's participation was clearly an act of opportunism, while Calhoun's seemed like a last gasp. Both expected formidable challenges in the 2004 elections, and were eager to develop a major platform issue that would speak to their constituents.

Meanwhile, the promised endowed chair position was arranged for me with the kind of speed I'd thought impossible in academia—perhaps because Freedom University of Northern Virginia wasn't exactly a principal player. In fact, I had never heard of it, despite its bloated enrollment logs. Nor did it have an established research track record, but the faculty and administration were remarkably enthusiastic about my work. I'd only been living part time at home since the Plan had been implemented, spending much of my time in a corporate apartment in Silver Spring, Maryland, but taking the Freedom University position would require a move from my sleepy Midwest college town. Annie and I agreed to put the house up for sale. She had no interest in moving to Virginia, so she rented an apartment a few miles away from our old home, while I drove the U-Haul truck to Fairfax alone. We formally separated a week after I arrived in Virginia.

I was put up in a spacious but sterile campus apartment, and began lecturing on my quickly evolving research. Along the way, I was introduced to the concept of irreducible complexity by a fellow professor at Freedom, an idea that proved useful in my ongoing work with Olive Grove. Twice a month, I delivered lectures via videoconferencing, which were always well attended (Olive Grove was an unusually science-minded congregation). I found my fellow congregants deeply excited by the science of Intelligent Design.

The Client had no objection to my delving into this area—he called it a "side gig"—so I began adding to my public appearances, speaking not only on solar irradiation and climate fluctuations, but also on topics of interest to adherents of Intelligent Design—who were also, I came to understand, very receptive to the idea that climate change was a hoax. I learned from Eric, and sometimes the Client, in our rare phone calls, that there were ways to frame the climate change issue that would appeal to the deepest fears and biases in human nature. I found this fascinating. We began to capitalize on the mistakes of the environmental movement, which seemed unable to effectively raise the alarm about the changing climate. We countered the science that indicated the arctic ice and permafrost were melting, and found more and more people rallying to our cause. Such ideas gave them hope that polar bears had a future. In fact, hope was our top commodity.

It would be going too far to say I began to believe in the research as a whole, but there were elements of the science that I found convincing enough. I spent more and more time with Representatives Bayless and Calhoun, and was eventually hired by both campaigns as a "senior science policy advisor." I was made to understand that the demographics in Bayless's district had been changing in ways that could be considered unfavorable to him—the population was younger, "browner," in the words of one of his aides. The only way to counter this was to "double-down" and "fire up the base."

My first ever television interview was with Fox News. According to the media consultant hired on behalf of the Group, I played well to my strengths. I had appeared awkward, she said, while also managing to underscore the talking points we had gone over prior to arriving at the studio: the scientific weaknesses of current climate research; the importance of airing a full range of scientific views; the lack of consensus among scientists regarding not just the cause of climate change, but its very existence (*consensus* was the term favored by climate scientists, a mistake upon which we capitalized—its inherent imprecision allowed us a thousand ways to move); and, most important, the obvious bias demonstrated by the National Science Foundation's refusal to fund any climate change research that did not take man-made causation as its starting point.

My blond interlocutor was outraged on my behalf. "I find it interesting," she said, tapping her pen on the desk separating us, "that the very same scientists who bemoan political interference in their own work are so blind to their own biases." No less than four minutes after the interview concluded, as Eric, the media consultant, and I were sitting in the green room, a CNN producer called.

Over the next week, I became so comfortable giving interviews that Eric warned I was losing my awkward demeanor. The *Washington Times* invited me to pen an op-ed about political interference in science. I wrote about the National Science Foundation's rejection of my grant application in detail.

The Client was pleased with our progress.

Soon after my initial media appearances, Representatives Bayless and Calhoun began joining me on camera. Eric warned me that as the story picked up speed, Democratic political operatives, along with enterprising journalists, would begin to dig into my past and reveal the plagiarism charges. This of course made me uncomfortable, but he assured me that it was part of the narrative, and that the mainstream media's refusal to allow me, a man of faith, to be "born again" would only increase the public's support. Again and again, the media underestimated the importance of the lost lamb to the churchgoing American.

*

I was not entirely surprised to receive Annie's e-mail asking for a divorce, but it marked one of only two times during my preparations for South Pole when I doubted the wisdom of this entire endeavor—the first being the hours after Fred Zimmer's unexpected visit. I found myself unable to focus on my papers. The research that had so engaged me now seemed uninteresting. Instead, I thought a great deal about Annie, and naturally dwelled upon our happier years. Again and again, an image of her walking out of the Electricity and Optics building at Stanford, talking to Sal Brennan, came to me. She was beautiful, with a gap between her two front teeth.

Later, I found Sal in his father's lab, and asked about the girl with whom he'd been talking after class. He told me her name was Annie and that she was a classics major who sometimes took science classes as electives. He said he'd introduce us—"I happen to know she has a weakness for idiot savants," he'd said. He added: "Too bad I'm not an idiot." I appreciated the offer very much, but I was wary. Sal and I had only known each other for a year, but we already had a fraught history. He was John Brennan's son, a beloved professor emeritus at Stanford, and was quite popular on campus himself because of his own extreme erudition, his good looks, and his easy manner. This was not a combination often found in the physics and applied physics departments. To complicate matters, the year prior we'd had a falling out, and although Sal was no longer ignoring me when he saw me on campus, he was uncharacteristically reserved when we spoke. At the time, Sal's father had spent a great deal of energy trying to convince me to join the astrophysics department. Although John Brennan was one of the world's foremost scientists, I'd demurred for many reasons, but the most salient had been the fact that Dr. Brennan was clearly suffering from early-onset dementia. I suspected Alzheimer's, and I had made the mistake of saying so to Sal.

Despite this, Sal, it must be said, was as good as his word about Annie. A week after I saw her laughing with him on campus, I was sitting across from her at the Student Union, talking about Ovid and Apuleius. She was smiling at me, as if she was glad to be there. Later, she told me I was staring stupidly at her the whole time. I imagine I must have been, because I don't remember a word she said, only the look on her shining, happy face. After we were married, I asked her why she'd agreed to a second date. Because, she told me, "you were brilliant, and unabashedly weird and yet completely oblivious to it."

When he heard that Annie had filed for divorce, Eric visited me at my campus apartment. He tried to convince me that these domestic developments only deepened the theme of the misunderstood scientist. He suggested leaking to the media the fact that Annie was a professed atheist. At the look on my face, Eric fell silent. A few minutes later, he suggested another tack—the marriage could be framed as a casualty of a coordinated attack against my professional research interests. I admit that at this point I was beginning to fatigue of the falsity of the endeavor—what had initially appealed to those darker impulses that had pushed me toward plagiarism now seemed too costly. When I mentioned this to Eric, he told me he had the perfect solution: "Begin to believe in it. Stop acting. Buy in."

After he left, I sat on the edge of my twin bed for an hour considering his advice. Faith had seemed anathema to every endeavor I had undertaken in my life; I found solace in fact, comfort in evidence. I was patient enough to wait for data. When personal tragedy touched me— as when my parents died within one month of each other when I was seventeen—I turned to probability density to parcel out the likelihood of such an event. That a likelihood could even exist brought me the kind of comfort that the well-meaning words of believers did not.

Still, I couldn't ignore the fact that I had summarily dismissed the very idea of faith; summary dismissal, I knew, was not something in which a true scientist engaged. I began to grapple with the idea proposed by some of the senior members of Olive Grove that scientific research and "sound reason" consistently supported the truth of a loving, transcendent god. I knew I would never accept the Bible as a work of literal history, and my church mentors accepted this, but the idea of a sovereign "creator"—for so long an idea that had nothing to do with me—became a great comfort.

For the first time in my life, I began to believe in something other than my love for my wife. I wasn't a true believer yet, but I was on the road to Damascus.

*

On January 30, 2003, I received a call from Representatives Bayless and Calhoun. There were sounds of celebration in the background. "I have news, Dr. Pavano," Bayless said. "We just got out of a closed-door meeting with the head of the National Science Foundation." The line seemed to pause for a moment, creating a parenthesis in the celebrations, and I pulled the phone away from my ear, only to realize that Eric was calling me on the other line.

"Pavano, you there?" Bayless shouted.

"I'm here," I called back into the mouthpiece.

"Pack your bags, Doc, you're going to Antarctica."

It was only as I heard the hard *c* in Antarctica, which no one seems ever to notice, that I realized how badly I wanted to go.

The New York Times
March 21, 2004
South Pole Station: No End in Sight for "Occupation"

With the ambush of its personnel in Fallujah and an "illegal occupation" in Antarctica, the defense contractor Veritas Integrated Defense Systems is struggling to contain what could be a substantial blow to its operations. Citing the occupation of Amundsen-Scott South Pole Station, where Veritas provides support staff, as a "major and unnecessary distraction to global operations," CEO Daniel Atcheson Johnson has sent a team of lobbyists to Capitol Hill to help end the shutdown of the U.S. research station.

Last week, Republican Sam Bayless of Kansas and his colleague on the Congressional Budget Committee, Representative Jack Calhoun of Tennessee, delivered on a promise to freeze the station's budget if no agreement could be reached with the head of the National Science Foundation, Alexandra Scaletta, over proposed changes to the agency's guidelines that would make it easier for scientists skeptical of climate change to gain access to federally sponsored research sites.

At the heart of the shutdown is Frank Pavano, a heliophysicist who has voiced skepticism about global climate change. On a grant from the NSF, Pavano spent four months at Amundsen-Scott Station and the ice-coring camp at West Antarctic Ice Sheet before he was involved in an accident with another NSF grantee that Representative Bayless claims was a result of a consistent pattern of harassment.

It was in response to the alleged harassment, initially reported last fall, that Representative Bayless and Representative Calhoun demanded the NSF adopt formal protocols to ensure that "scientists with minority views" are provided with equal access to federal research sites and grant dollars. Ms. Scaletta, however, has refused to yield, and with the White House unwilling to enter the fray, the standoff has led to a temporary shutdown of operations at America's most remote research facility, which is currently being illegally occupied by ten individuals, a mix of NSF grantees and Veritas contractors.

The president has so far resisted calls to send in the National Guard to forcibly remove the individuals who refused to board the last scheduled flight out of South Pole. Sources familiar with the situation indicate that, with operations in Iraq intensifying, the president wants to avoid distraction. Others, however, argue that this is precisely the reason why he may be open to intervention.

operation deep freeze

The sky began changing in early February, as the sun began its month-long descent. Shadows were weirdly elongated, stretching toward a horizon that consumed the sun bite by bite. Once the sun had fallen out of sight, Cooper knew from the handbook, it would lighten the sky for two more weeks of "civil twilight," when Venus would be visible. Nautical twilight would follow, draining the sky of its pink blush. By the end of March, after the last flights had departed, all would be dark. This process was typically of great interest to the Polies, capped off, as it was, by the annual Equinox Feast, but anxiety over the possible shutdown had cast a pall over everything. Tucker decided to move the feast forward by five weeks in order to boost station morale—and, Cooper suspected, because he knew that in five weeks, there was a very good chance that no one would be here to celebrate the true equinox.

Preparations had been under way for a week when the letters from the NSF arrived in Tucker's in-box, with instructions to distribute to the grantees immediately. Cooper and Sal, who had been in Tucker's office when the letters had arrived, were the only other Polies who knew about them. All three agreed it made no sense to ruin the Equinox Feast with news that the station, and all the ongoing experiments, was going to be shut down.

On February 10, the galley transformed into Le Cirque. Pearl, Denise, and Doc Carla had hung strands of ice-blue Christmas lights across the ceiling that twinkled in the wineglasses set on the long table. The support beams were festooned with cheap silver tinsel, and battery-powered votive candles flickered in the corners of the room. The cloth napkins were removed from storage, and Kit had folded them into bishop's hats before placing them on the plates. Bonnie's absence—she'd flown to McMurdo the day after the bottle-throwing incident at Sal's lecture—was noted, and a place was set for her at the table, next to Dwight.

Everyone arrived in the one nice outfit they'd packed—Birdie wore his kilt, Dwight his formal cloak, and even Floyd had donned a polka-dotted tie. In the galley bathroom, Marcy lent Cooper her four-year-old purple metallic eye shadow. After pulling on the floral empire-waist dress she'd rolled into a ball and shoved in the deepest corner of her duffel back in Minneapolis, Cooper pulled her hair into a low, messy bun at the nape of her neck, and impaled it with bobby pins.

When she walked into the galley, the ceremonial equinox haircuts were already under way. Four Beakers sat in chairs, Sal among them, while their research techs lopped off their unruly locks with crafting scissors. Cooper grabbed a glass of Pearl's hot wassail and watched as Alek roughly shoved his hands into Sal's nest of tangled hair. He pulled on it mercilessly in order to straighten it for an even cut. Once Alek started cutting, Sal stared at the wall unblinkingly as his auburn hair fell to the floor in clumps.

Denise stepped next to Cooper, blowing on her wassail. She was wearing a rhinestone-encrusted headband, magenta lipstick, and a leather mini-skirt. Cooper nodded at her approvingly. "Ceremonies are so important," Denise said. "They are the social glue that keeps a community intact—especially one under duress." She gestured toward the crowd of Polies gathered around Bozer's portrait, which Pearl had hung the day before. "That's social glue, too." She looked over at Cooper. "I hope you don't underestimate how important you've become to the group."

"I'm important?"

Denise nodded. "There are two things you possess which are valuable to this particular group. One, you are a survivor. Two, at times of extreme anxiety, your paintings will remind the people here that they are not just cogs in the machine."

Cooper gestured toward the portrait of Bozer. "What did he think, by the way? Bozer, when he saw it."

Denise surprised Cooper by dissolving into giggles. "Oh, he executed the best Goffman-esque display of faux outrage I'd ever witnessed. You should have seen him—he was raging around like King Kong."

"Oh no," Cooper said, glancing around.

Denise put her hand on Cooper's arm. "No, you don't understand—his response was strictly impression management, basic maintenance of expressive control. He and I came back to the galley late last night, after he was sure everyone else was gone, and he just stood in front of it, staring."

"How did you know he didn't hate it?"

"He didn't put his fist through it."

A freshly shorn Sal stood up and placed a bowler hat over his head. He did a little dance for Alek as the other winter-overs gathered around him, but Cooper could see it was an effort for him. Denise left to take her seat next to Bozer, so Cooper wandered around the table until she found her place card. Sal sat down beside her and reached across to steal an extra wineglass. He set it next to his and looked at Cooper. "You look pretty tonight," he said.

Before Cooper could reply, Pearl leaned over her shoulder, bearing wine. "Red or white?" she said.

"Both," Sal said dully, tapping both of his glasses. "And leave the bottles here."

From across the table, Doc Carla—dressed in a peasant shift and long feathered earrings—lifted her wineglass to Sal. "Bottoms up to the bottom of the world, Doc," she said. Next to her, and dressed in a beautiful blue tuxedo, Alek raised a glass of samogon. "To our lady doctor," he said, "may you heal pain well." He turned to Cooper.

"And to you, *artiste*, who completed lovely paintings with no penguins."

As soon as everyone was seated, bishop's hats unfurled on their laps, Tucker took his place at the front of the galley, flanked by Pearl and Kit. "Working against the political odds, and a dire shortage of freshies due to the current difficulties, tonight's Equinox Feast is the work of two dedicated Pole civilian contractors who are so famous they need not be named." The room shook with applause and cheers. "We are here tonight, honoring Pole tradition, to mark the coming equinox, when we probably won't have the kinds of provisions we have here tonight."

"Or the fuel," Floyd grumbled.

"After dinner, we will go outside to move the flag and unveil the new Pole marker. There's a menu under your plates. All the artwork is courtesy of our fearless artist Fellow Cooper." The synchronous sound of plates being shifted arose from the table, followed by appreciative murmurs. Cooper watched as Sal looked over the menu card she'd designed—there was a sketch of the South Pole Telescope in the left-hand corner, the skyline of the Dark Sector in the right-hand corner, and an outline of the entire Antarctic continent in the middle. At the bottom were three images of men trekking through a blizzard—Wilson, Cherry, and Birdie. Sal smiled for the first time all night and pulled her in for a long kiss, which was met with applause completely devoid of sarcasm.

"Excuse me." Cooper looked down the long table and saw the interpretive dancer was on her feet, her Afghan tribal coin belt tinkling. "These momentous circumstances are so personally inspiring, that I'd like to perform a segment of the dance I've been working on since I've been here, a piece of nonverbal storytelling that encapsulates my experience at South Pole. I call it the 'Dance of the Anxious Penguin.'" Perhaps it was the wine, or the twinkling blue lights, but Cooper—and, to her surprise, everyone else—could not take her eyes off the interpretive dancer as she spun wordlessly around the room.

Once the performance, and dinner, ended, the Polies swapped their dining clothes for their ECW gear, and gathered around the geographic Pole for the ceremonial moving of the marker. With the sun hanging low in the sky, a pale compass rose, the Polies fell into line and one by one passed the American flag hand to hand from its former position to the new, drifted, but true South Pole. At the end of the human chain, Bozer removed the stake and installed the flag next to Sal's sheet-draped marker.

The Polies crowded around it, expectant, with cameras raised. Sal and Marcy each took a corner of the sheet and, at the count of three, pulled it off the tiny *Terra Nova*. Cooper remained on the fringes of the group, watching while everyone pushed and shoved to get a better look. Her heart was full. Above her, parhelions flanked the slowly sinking sun.

*

The next morning, everyone arrived at breakfast with their letter from NSF, which had been slipped under the doors in the Jamesways, Hypertats, and El Dorm overnight like hotel bills.

The exodus began almost at once. That evening, Cooper said goodbye to the literary novelist and the interpretive dancer, and even helped them bag-drag with her good hand. The historical novelist had been forced onto an earlier flight after an unfortunate incident with his manuscript. Cooper had heard the summons over All-Call that afternoon, and was halfway up the entrance tunnel when she saw the commotion. The historical novelist was wild-eyed—Rove in a rage—and pressed a huge manuscript to his chest. Polies began to appear from various parts of the station, and soon they had made a ring around him. Birdie approached Cooper and asked what had happened. She shrugged and the two watched as the historical novelist lifted the manuscript above his head.

"It's done," he shouted hoarsely.

Tucker took a step forward. "May I see it?" The novelist abruptly turned and began speed-walking down the tunnel, the pages peeling off the manuscript in his wake. Cooper and Birdie scrambled to catch them, but the wind blowing up the tunnel sent the pages skyward.

As Floyd and Tucker tackled the historical novelist, Cooper managed to grab one of the pages before it flew away. It was blank. She snatched another one from the air as it gently fell, swaying side to side. It, too, was blank.

She looked over at Birdie—the pages in his hands were blank as well.

*

Lisa Wu told Sal her team was going to comply with Stanford's directive to follow the evacuation order and return stateside, and would have to abandon the joint experiment. Upon hearing this, he disappeared to the Dark Sector, kicking even Alek out. Cooper knew Sal had received the same directive from Princeton.

That evening, he burst into the Smoke Bar, where Tucker was comforting Alek and the rest of the remaining Polies. Sal locked the door behind him and looked at them.

"I'm staying. I won't abandon this project. I'm going to caretake the experiment for both teams." He looked over at Tucker. "Lisa knows."

Tucker tugged on one of the low-hanging strands of fairy lights, loosening it so that it swayed just above the table. "Does the NSF know? Scaletta?"

"No comment."

"I assume you understand the potential consequences of defying an evac order."

"I can always seek asylum at CERN."

Without thinking, Cooper said, "What if we all stayed? Like Alcatraz but in Antarctica."

Someone pulled at the door a couple of times. Tucker, who was leaning against it, reached behind him to unlock it. A new VIDS admin who'd been flown in the week before from Denver walked in, her brow furrowed.

"Why's the door locked?"

"Sorry," Tucker said. "Sometimes it sticks." Cooper noticed the woman's eyes were searching the room, as if she were looking for a fugitive. Distractedly, she handed Tucker a manila envelope and exited the bar.

Everyone watched as Tucker opened the envelope and pulled out the caretaking roster—the names of those who would be allowed to stay at the station in order to keep basic operations running.

"Floyd. Bozer. Pearl. Doc. Marce. The rest are on the last flight out." Denise's child-like sobs shattered the silence, and Bozer pushed all of the darts into Karl Martin's face and went over to comfort her.

Tucker handed the roster to Sal. "Scaletta wants me in Washington. Let me know what you decide."

As soon as Sal had locked the door behind Tucker, Floyd said, "If we do this, none of you will get paid. They'll stop depositing your paychecks."

"I don't care," several people said at once.

"Can't they force you onto the planes?" Pearl asked.

"They're not going to walk us out at gunpoint," Dwight said. "They trust us to follow the rules. By the time they realize what we've done, it might be too late."

"What do you mean 'too late'?"

"Every hour we delay, the closer we get to the event horizon," Dwight replied. "Too cold to fly. No flights in, no flights out. If we can wait this out—"

"And create enough confusion and administrative chaos," Cooper added.

"—if we can do that, then there will be no chance of flights to haul us away. It will be too late."

Cooper noticed Sal watching her closely.

"What?" she asked.

"You sure you want to stay?"

Cooper rolled her eyes.

"No, this is serious, Cooper," he said. He looked around the room. "This has to be worth it to every single person here. If you violate this evac order, you probably won't work here again. You may even face federal trespassing charges."

"And what about you, Doc?" Bozer said to Sal. "You've got more to lose here than any of us."

Sal shook his head. "Me? It's this or nothing."

"When's the last flight?" Pearl asked.

"Monday," Dwight replied.

"That's Valentine's Day."

Dwight looked stricken for a moment. Then he shrugged. "So?"

"I'm just saying that locking ourselves into the station and occupying a federal research facility isn't exactly in the spirit of the holiday," Pearl said mildly. "It's like getting a Dear John letter."

"Nah, Pearlie," Floyd said. "You've gotta think of it more like a box of chocolates hand-delivered to the Congressional Budget Committee. Except instead of chocolates—"

"We get it, Floyd," Sal interrupted.

Bozer turned to Cooper. "You didn't answer your man's question. What about you?"

"What about me?"

"No finger, and no prospects after this is over. You good?"

Everyone in the room turned to see what she would say. She looked from face to face. Floyd's poorly groomed mutton chops and Doc Carla's slightly askew Yankees cap. Bozer's veiny nose and Alek's Fu Manchu 'stache. Pearl's white-blond eyebrows, Marcy's laugh lines, and Denise's frizzy curls. Sal's beautiful but tired eyes. Here were the faces that would surround her for the next six months, the brains with which she'd have to contend.

"Right before Halloween, I asked Sal why the station didn't just replace Frosty Boy instead of sending techs in every season to rebuild it," Cooper said. "He told me 'We grow attached to these temperamental pieces of crap.' Well, let's just say there are a number of temperamental pieces of crap in this room that I'm oddly attached to."

Everyone laughed at this, and this laughter seemed to form an agreement. They'd do this thing, no matter the consequences. They agreed on a password to ensure secrecy: *Occupy or Die.*

*

Pearl went into a baking frenzy in preparation for the Valentine's Day Exodus. She didn't want the Polies who were being forced off the ice to go home empty-handed. She and Cooper stayed up all night baking trays of jam tarts, sheets of heart-shaped sugar cookies, raspberry linzers, a two-tier red velvet cake studded with fondant roses, and mini-cupcakes frosted in crimson and white. (Cooper had to talk her out of making pavlovas when she realized the effort would require almost all the eggs left on station.)

The Valentine's Day dessert buffet raised the morale of the departing Polies—the goodie bags filled with handmade pralines and Captain Morgan rum truffles almost made them smile. Birdie, who had been utterly broken since receiving notice that he was being ferried off the ice and who, thanks to Pearl's fear of the repercussions of a naturalized citizen getting involved in a federal crime, knew nothing about the plans to occupy, received extra goodies, including an extravagant peach melba that brought him to tears.

One other gesture of goodwill took place in the days before the evacuation commenced: Bozer had, according to Denise, "surrendered to the better angels of his nature" and challenged Sri to a game of pool before he left for Madison. Everyone crowded into Skylab, gorging on Pearl's homemade delicacies, and watched as Sri entered the room. He stood on one side of the pool table and gripped the polished top rails. His eyes were full of emotion. Finally, Bozer tossed a cue over the table toward Sri, who caught it smoothly. "Rack 'em up," he said.

For the next hour, Cooper and the other Polies watched as Sri and Bozer traded wins on the felt—to their delight, each man was an accomplished player—and for those sixty minutes, it almost seemed like nothing had changed. It was as if the entire polar winter lay before them, uninterrupted.

As Cooper finished off one of Pearl's chocolate cupcakes, Tucker pulled her aside. The sunglasses were gone, and so was the Bell's palsy. "You're better," she exclaimed.

"Doc Carla has been giving me prednisone. Sometimes it helps with Bell's palsy. Listen, I'm leaving tonight for Washington—Scaletta thinks I can help with the negotiations. Something about my cool gaze."

"I wish you didn't have to leave," Cooper said.

"You are in very capable hands down here." He took her bandaged hand. "Do you remember chasing me down the hall back in Denver to tell me why you wanted to come to South Pole?"

Cooper flushed at the memory and smiled weakly. "Yeah, and you bought it."

"No, you told me the truth. You told me you were afraid. That's when I knew you'd be okay here. For none but cowards need to prove their bravery, right?"

Tucker's radio crackled and Cooper could hear a tech sergeant barking orders, the sound of a plane's engine roaring in the background. "I might not see you before I leave."

"So this is goodbye, then."

"As Jimi Hendrix once said, 'The story of life is quicker than the wink of an eye, the story of love is hello and goodbye . . . until we meet again.' "

"As Tucker Bollinger once said, 'Quoting others suggests avoidance.' "

"A wise man."

*

The next morning, as the last LC-130 to land at Pole, the one that was meant to take the rest of them off the ice, idled on the skiway, Cooper climbed down a ladder into the Utilidors with the other occupying Polies. With each step down, the scream of the plane's engines grew fainter. Above her, Floyd pulled the trapdoor closed and locked it. Below, the core group stood waiting, silent, their eyes wide above their balaclavas. Cooper reached the last rung and dropped down next to Sal. "Can't they just open the door and find us?" she asked.

Overhearing this, Bozer snapped, "Not where we're going. Now follow me." Silently, they made their way down the dark tunnel. It appeared endless, lined with corrugated metal and lighted by caged incandescents. All species of wire snaked across the ground, appearing to meld into a single cable in the far distance. Running along the walls of the Utilidor were the sewer, electrical, and data cables—Cooper imagined e-mails and fax messages coursing down this metal helix as she passed it.

She paused for Sal, and they allowed themselves to fall behind. He pinched the zipper of her parka between his fingers and pulled it up so it was completely closed, and took her face in his mittened hands—to his delight, Cooper had returned to him the dirty black Gore-Tex she'd found in skua, which she'd used to complete that triptych all those months ago. "I would like nothing more than to hole up with you for the next six months in a place where nobody can find us," he said. "That being said, I have to ask you one last time: Are you ready to do this?"

Cooper placed her hands on his. "This is like the Malibu Barbie Dreamhouse of unreachable civilizations," she said. "Maybe it's wrong to say, but I'm not upset this is happening."

Up ahead, the others were obscured by a veil of steam, which made them appear ghost-like as the pale light filtered through the vapor. For a moment, Cooper was startled; it was as if the image on David's copy of *Worst Journey*, of the three men in a backlit ice cavern, had sprung to life. "Everything okay?" Sal asked. Cooper nodded, and together they headed toward the phantom figures.

By the time they caught up, Bozer had already opened the metal door leading to the Tomb, where the Man Without Country lay hidden behind stacks of empty crates, wrapped in plastic sheeting. When they stepped inside, Bozer started to close the door, then stopped.

"Last chance for losers," he said. "You can still make the plane."

The group, huddled together in front of what Cooper knew was a frozen catafalque, blinked back at him.

"Occupy or die," Cooper said.

"Occupy or die," Marcy replied.

"I refuse to shout slogans, but I'm in," Doc Carla said wearily.

"Then I will: Occupy or fucking die!" Floyd shouted.

"Lower your voice, you dipshit," Bozer said. "Come on, let's go deal with the feds now. Marce, Pearlie, game-time. Dwight's waiting in Comms."

Cooper watched as the officially approved caretaking staff—Pearl, Marcy, Doc Carla, and Bozer—stepped out of the room, leaving the rest of them in the shadows thrown by an electric lantern. "Once we're sweet, I'll come get you." Bozer looked at Cooper, Sal, Denise, and Alek. "Last chance."

"Go," Alek growled. Bozer pulled the door closed. A moment later, they heard the key turn in the lock. Sal pulled Cooper close.

No one spoke for a while. The silence revealed the faraway roar of the idling plane. Eventually, Denise cleared her throat. "Because of the unusual circumstances, no one underwent the mid-season psych exam. It'll be interesting to see how a control group wintering over without the psych assessment functions under stress."

Before anyone could reply, raised voices could be heard echoing through the Utildors. "Here they come," Sal murmured. Cooper tried to imagine the scene that would unfold if the tech sergeant and his minions found them in the Tomb, huddling behind a locked door, with a corpse for company.

The voices grew louder, followed by the sound of heavy boots hurrying through the tunnels. Next to Cooper, Denise fidgeted, her hands like birds that couldn't quite get settled. Cooper placed her hand on Denise's knee, but this only seemed to make things worse.

"Wintering-over exacts intense pressure on the individual psyche," she said, her voice strained. "We rely on social contracts more than we would in any other scenario you can conjure. One study shows that after a winter in Antarctica, at least five percent of people on station can be deemed clinically insane."

The footsteps were getting closer.

"Be quiet, woman," Alek said angrily.

But Denise seemed unable to stop. She stood up suddenly. "But of course that assumes a standard population, not self-selected potential felons."

"Sit down, Denise," Sal said soothingly. "Everything's going to be okay. Bozer will come get us once the plane is airborne. But right now you need to be quiet." Denise didn't seem to hear him. She approached the door.

"The point of sharing that is not to scare you guys, but to remind you of the stakes, and to encourage you to invest in sanity."

The footsteps slowed down and the sound of walkie-talkies became audible. When Denise began pulling on the door, Alek and Sal both leapt up, but Cooper was quicker. She gently took Denise's arm. "Just a little bit longer," Cooper whispered. Denise was trembling, but she allowed Cooper to lead her away from the door.

As Cooper tried desperately to think of something to distract Denise, her finger—or the place where her finger had once been—began to itch intensely. "Denise," she whispered. "I have a question for you. Lately I've been having this really strong feeling that my finger is back, like it's physically there. I can even 'move' it—I actually feel it bend. Do you know anything that can explain this?"

It worked. Denise seemed calm in an instant. "Phantom limb syndrome," she replied quietly. "The perception of pain in an amputated limb or digit. Yes, this is real. One-armed men have been known to utilize their phantom limb to masturbate."

Sal brought his sleeve to his mouth, his shoulders shaking with laughter. Suddenly, the door began to rattle as someone pulled on the knob. Denise turned her eyes to Cooper—behind her glasses, they looked enormous, and they were full of fear. "I promise, it will be okay," Cooper whispered.

She knew the plane was idling, burning fuel, and that the temperature was dropping; she imagined the pilot was not exactly happy at the delay. Bozer had told them to expect this search of the station by VIDS and the NSF admins and higher-ups—they just had to wait it out. The door rattled again, more insistently this time. Muffled voices—including Marcy's—conferred on the other side.

"This is a WC," she told the others.

"A what?"

"Waste closet. Shit storage. Poo pantry. It's where we keep the leaky sewage drums. I can unlock it for you if you want to look around, but I warn you: it smells like a shithouse door on a tuna boat."

The search party hastily moved on. After their footsteps had receded completely, Alek fell back in relief, muttering in Russian.

*

Seventy-two hours in, Pearl and Dwight were already nursing a beef that had started when Pearl whistled for an hour straight during dinner. Now, in the Smoke Bar, her whistling had become defiant.

"If I have to listen to your stupid whistling and stare at your Pollyanna face and your stupid greasy pigtails all winter I'm going to kill myself," Dwight said, gripping a nosegay of darts in his hand. "You will find me swinging from the rafters in a cold breeze."

"You know what, Dwight? I try to be smiley and nice to everyone, even if they're rude. I feel like people don't need grumps around all winter, especially under the circumstances."

"Don't pretend like you're some kind of angel, Pearl," Dwight said, sending a dart into the board. "The act gets old real quick." He turned to Sal. "Look me in the eye, Sal, and tell me that prolonged whistling isn't a form of torture."

"Can't you guys try bonding?" Doc Carla suggested.

"Over what?" Dwight demanded.

"Both of your ice-spouses are gone," she said. "What about the bond of broken hearts?"

Dwight scoffed, and drifted away to another part of the bar.

Cooper nursed a vodka tonic as she watched them bicker. She hoped Dwight's tantrum wasn't a harbinger of things to come. Whistling was a minor crime, and they had several more months of this, at best. Cooper hoped Dwight would just immerse himself in his comms duties, which included keeping track of the federal response to the occupation, via the Web, his ham radio, and satellite phone. It had taken the authorities two full days to understand what had happened at Pole. The U.S. Antarctic Program had operated with military precision for decades. That members of the Program would disobey orders came not only as a shock to VIDS and NSF adminis-trators, it also paralyzed them. The prevailing attitude among those who were in charge was disbelief and utter confusion. Word had not leaked to the media yet, but Dwight was seeing some blogs mention-ing rumors of an occupation at Pole.

Once the LC-130 with the tech sergeant, Tucker, and the last VIDS and NSF admins had gone wheels up, Bozer and Marcy cleared the snowdrifts from the perimeter of the Dome before shutting the outer doors. The temperature had dropped dramatically by now, nearing seventy below. Floyd assured everyone that no pilot would try to land at Pole at this point. Not even JP-8 fuel could remain liquid in these temperatures. The only unqualified positive aspect of the occupation so far, at least for Cooper, was that everyone now had a room in El Dorm—she'd taken over the room next to Sal's, which had previously belonged to a telescope maintenance tech. The convenience of not hav-ing to empty a pee can into a pee barrel was almost decadent.

Sal walked over to where Cooper was sketching Doc Carla awk-wardly holding knitting needles. Now that Pearl had abandoned her whistling, she was trying to teach people how to knit. "I have to go back to the lab now," Sal said to Cooper. "Will you walk with me?"

They walked down the entrance tunnel in silence, past the fuel arches, which were now strangely quiet, running on caretaking mode. When they approached the entrance door, Sal performed an intricate routine with the lock, and together they pushed the door open. Then they were outside, in the half darkness of near-winter. Sal scanned the sky before taking Cooper's arm. "I keep thinking I'm going to hear a C-17 looping back to force us out by gunpoint," he said.

"Actually, it would be an LC-130," Cooper said. "A Herc."

"Oh my god, you're officially a Polie."

"What would you do if they did come back?"

"I've thought about that a million times," Sal said, his brow troubled. "I can't get any farther than suicide." He gripped her arm harder. "I'm sorry, Cooper, I shouldn't have said that."

Cooper said nothing, but noted that the word, even the offhand way it had been mentioned, hadn't pierced her in the way it used to.

In fact, with all the commotion at the station, she hadn't even thought about David, or the vial, for days. She wondered if that jagged edge had finally broken off.

They were halfway down the road to the Dark Sector before Sal stopped. He pointed to the sky. The aurora australis, roiling ribbon-like sheaves of purple and pink light, filled the sky. They gaped at it in wonder. There was something else there, too, like a fingerprint on glass.

"The Milky Way," Sal said.

"Jesus, that's beautiful."

"It's cripplingly beautiful," he said.

Cooper looked over at him. "Even though it has a super-massive black hole in it?"

"Especially because it does."

As Cooper gazed into its frosty heart, she imagined the black hole, its density equivalent to a billion suns.

*

When the feds finally shook off their incredulity, directives began arriving via e-mail, fax, and satellite phone. It started with the NSF's assumption that this had all been a misunderstanding. In Comms, Cooper and the other Polies listened in silence as the South Pole NSF rep, Warren, back in Washington, D.C., now, played nice cop with Dwight.

"Perhaps we weren't clear," Warren said gently. "And I can own that, I can take the fall for that." He hesitated. "One might even argue that I've already taken the fall for that."

"There was no misunderstanding," Dwight replied. "This is intentional."

"Tell Karl Martin it's draconian," Floyd piped in.

Warren sighed. "Guys, I have no idea what you're talking about. All we're seeking is a peaceful resolution to the situation."

"What? We're not armed, dude," Floyd replied.

"Well, the FBI wants in on this."

Floyd cackled. "Yeah? Tell 'em to come on down. They can fly Southwest."

There was a long silence on Warren's end of the line. Finally, he cleared his throat. "Just tell me how we can resolve this, guys."

Sal stepped past Floyd and leaned over the speakerphone. "The Wisconsin DA is tearing up Sri Niswathin's lab in Madison. Frank Pavano is doing more interviews than a starlet on a press junket. Bayless and Calhoun are preening in front of cameras and pretending to be the defenders of science—"

"Sal—"

"You're asking us how this will be resolved, and I'm telling you that this is resolved when Bayless and Calhoun let the budget bill go through committee. This is resolved when the sequester ends. It's not complicated."

"What the hell do you think we've been doing, Sal!" Warren shouted. "We've been working every angle here. I don't think you people understand—you are illegally occupying a federal facility. There's jail time associated with this kind of thing. Not to mention the fact that you've put your lives at—"

The call cut out without warning, reverting to static, and everyone turned to Dwight. "Satellite moved off-grid." He shrugged and looked at Sal. "Time to start contacting the media?"

"Permission granted," Sal replied grimly. Dwight shooed everyone out and got to work.

*

The next morning Cooper headed back over to Comms, where she was scheduled to relieve Dwight for a few hours. She found him sprawled on his ugly brown sofa, already asleep, so she spent her first ten minutes sorting the papers that had accumulated on the floor beneath the fax machine: there were separate piles for NSF communications, VIDS-related missives and threats, and the media requests, which had been pouring in since Dwight had started contacting reporters.

She'd brought along a mini-canvas and was priming it with gesso (Bozer had requested a small portrait of Denise) when the satellite phone began to ring. Its strange, insect-like buzzing woke Dwight immediately. Cooper brought the phone over to him.

The person on the other end of the line began speaking before Dwight could answer. His face contorted with effort as he tried to understand what he was hearing. Finally, he was able to break in: "Wait—wait, hold on. Hold on! No habla Russian." He put his hand over the mouthpiece and looked at Cooper. "Radio Dark Sector and get Alek in here."

Soon the office was crowded with the Polies. Alek had the enormous phone pressed against his right ear, his other hand covering his left. Sal, who had come over from the Dark Sector with him, threw himself on the couch and instantly fell asleep. The plosives of Russian spoken at high volume were making Cooper feel delirious, and she sat down on the couch next to Sal, lifting his legs with effort and sliding beneath them.

It seemed like ages before Alek got off the phone—enough time for Pearl to go back to the galley, make a batch of instant hot chocolate, and return to Comms with a tray of still-steaming mugs. After hanging up, Alek took a long sip of cocoa and carefully wiped his mouth with his fingers. "They want to come get me," he said darkly.

"Who wants to come get you?" Marcy asked.

"Rossiya," Alek replied. Marcy stared at him blankly. "Mother Russia. They want to come and get their citizen."

"And take you where, exactly?" Doc Carla growled from the other side of the room.

"Vostok."

"That's halfway across Antarctica," Cooper said.

"Twelve hundred kilometers, exact," Alek snapped.

"I thought it was too dangerous to fly into Pole at this time of year," Doc Carla said, growing irritated. "I thought that was the goddamn point of this whole game."

"In 1982, Vostok run out of fuel in the middle of winter. They make candle warmers out of asbestos fibers and diesel," he replied. "Russia doesn't give shit."

"Have they talked to the State Department?" Sal asked, awake again but groggy.

"No, they say not necessary."

"Actually, they're right; they don't need to," Dwight said, flipping through the papers on his desk. "But Russia is a signatory to the Antarctic Treaty, so they'll have to go through the secretariat."

Alek shook his head. "No, I don't want to go. I gave them better idea: airdrop."

Sal sat up suddenly. "You're a fucking genius, Alek."

"Not an evil monk?"

"No, you've achieved sainthood."

*

The airdrop, which Bozer had christened Operation Deep Freeze, had everyone giddy with anticipation. Airdrops were not unheard of at Pole—most winters, if the weather cooperated, a C-17 out of New Zealand would make a pass and drop supplies from its cargo hold. That was out of the question this winter: the sequester was still in effect, the station illegally occupied, and the resident population was accused of federal crimes. But Russia, sensing an opportunity to improve its standing in the international community at the expense of the Americans, was ready to help a comrade whose sense of duty to science had left him in dire straits.

Floyd began building the wooden wicks for the smudge pots, fires burning in fifty-five-gallon drums that would demarcate the drop zone now that the polar night—twenty-four-hour darkness—had fully descended. Bozer and Marcy spent nearly six hours grooming the zone, while Floyd split up the remaining Polies into teams. Marcy tuned up the forklift she'd use to locate the dropped crates and dig them out. Cooper was designated "project manager" since Doc Carla still didn't think she was ready to do any heavy lifting. Everyone who was working the drop zone pulled on the insulated refrigerator suits that had been hauled out of storage and awaited the transmission from the Russian pilots.

Finally an announcement came over All-Call. The Russians were ten minutes out. Sal, Marcy, and Bozer hopped on snowmobiles and headed out to ignite the smudge pots. Cooper glanced over at the temperature gauge. Sixty-three below zero. This was, as Floyd had mentioned many times, the kind of cold that could turn hydraulic fluid into pudding if the plane landed for more than two minutes.

Then came the call that the bird was two minutes out, and everyone rushed into the darkness, the team leaders gripping sets of night-vision goggles. Cooper could feel the rumble of the plane's engines in her chest as its under-wing lights appeared like bright stars on the horizon. Its roar grew louder and louder, until it seemed that Cooper's eardrums were going to burst, and that's when the parcels began drifting down from the inky sky. They floated softly on miniature parachutes illuminated by the teams' searchlights; Cooper thought they looked like jellyfish. The plane made a graceful turn on the far west side of the station, and passed back over them, waggling its wings.

In the distance, Cooper could see two Polies—probably Sal and Pearl—silhouetted by Marcy's headlights as she followed along behind them, waiting for cargo with her forklift. Cooper retreated deeper into the entrance tunnel, and her walkie-talkie started to crackle. Sal's voice broke through the static. "Are the doors open?"

"Yes!" Cooper shouted.

"The machines are loaded," Sal said. "We're on our way."

Floyd arrived on a snowmobile, pulling a pallet, with Pearl sitting behind him.

"They gave us oranges!" Pearl exclaimed, waving a bag of what looked like frozen suns. "Oranges! Can you believe it? Fresh fruit! Oh, I wish Birdie were here to see this."

Over the next fifteen minutes, the teams arrived with the rest of the cargo, which included a box of medical supplies for Doc Carla, DVDs of Russian soap operas, thirteen cases of vodka, and more oranges, which had been a gift from the flight crew. As everyone arrived, Cooper tried raising Sal on the radio again, but got nothing except static. She began asking the others if they'd seen him. Denise claimed he was loading cargo, but when Cooper tried to radio Sal again, she got no response. She mentally checked off every Polie who'd walked by her. Everyone was in, except for Sal.

"Give me a body count," Bozer said, suddenly standing next to her.

"Sal's missing," Cooper told him. The words made it real.

Bozer brought the radio to his mouth and called for Sal. Nothing. He tried again. Cooper was now gripped by panic. She'd been here before. She'd stood in one place, dumb and mute, and waited for someone who hadn't returned. She refused to wait this time. Cooper made a dash for the entrance tunnel, but Bozer caught up to her easily and roughly yanked her back inside. He pushed her away and jabbed a finger in her parka. "Calm down."

"Go get him, Bozer," Cooper cried. "Go get him."

Bozer pulled his mittens back on slowly. "Where is he on the grid?"

"He's supposed to be on the northwest quadrant." Bozer gestured to Marcy, who pulled her hood back over her head and walked toward the nearest snowmobile. Cooper started pacing.

Then a figure appeared down at the entrance end of the tunnel, red in the lights, hauling a pallet. Sal. It took a moment for Cooper to notice the two men skiing up the tunnel behind him. They were wearing ECW gear and carrying astoundingly large packs. Each was sporting a headlamp. It took her a minute, but Cooper realized with astonishment that they were the Swedes—the two men she had fed all those months ago. Halfway up the tunnel, they stopped, expertly plucked off their skis, and laid them against their shoulders before continuing.

Cooper watched as Sal and the Swedes reached the top of the tunnel. Sal's triumphant smile disappeared when he saw Cooper's face. "What's wrong?"

"I just—I thought you were lost," she replied, trying to sound calm, trying not to throw herself on him. "You didn't answer your radio. We called for you over and over. I was worried."

"Shit, I'm sorry," he said. "I lost my radio somewhere between the north and northwest quads. Then I found these guys. When I saw them coming in, I thought I was hallucinating."

By this time, a knot of people had gathered around to get a better look at the skiers as they loaded their gear onto Bozer's snowmobile. One of them had pulled out the familiar Swedish flag that Cooper had last seen draped atop a ski. She and Sal continued toward the galley, where the supplies were being carried for inspection. "Why are they here?" Cooper asked, though she hardly cared.

"They were camping at the Japanese base when they heard about the shutdown," Sal replied. "They felt it was their duty as international citizens to show support—they say they're loaded with goodies from Dome Fuji. I hope they brought mochi."

But Cooper barely heard what Sal was saying. She couldn't stop looking at him. It was as if he had been raised from the dead, as if she had spotted a lone figure waving at her from across the Beardsmore.

Inside the galley, chaos reigned. The Polies ripped open the crates with crowbars and the handles of metal soup ladles. There were thirty-pound bags of yellow onions, tins of instant coffee, canned cheese, and an entire pallet of gold foil–covered military rations, each containing a half-pound of beef, dried biscuits, and dehydrated potatoes. Doc Carla picked through the medical supplies, while Dwight sifted through the various DVDs and produced an old cassette tape of the Red Army Choir's greatest hits.

Nothing had been packed especially well, and a box of powdered tomato soup in cups had exploded, covering its crate with a fine red dust. But in the last box, lovingly packed within three layers of bubble wrap and placed in a bed of straw, Alek discovered sixteen bottles of ice-cold Russian vodka—Green Mark. His joy was equaled only by his teary-eyed nostalgia at hearing the strains of the Red Army Choir's "Song of the Volga Boatmen" trudging out of the speakers.

*

It took twelve hours for news of the Russian airdrop, and the unexpected Swedish delegation, to hit the news cycle. The Kremlin was quick to trumpet its act of philanthropy, while the Swedish station on Dronning Maud Land sent out a press release praising its countrymen for their hardiness. Soon, offers of help were coming in from the Kiwis at Scott Base, the Uruguayans on King George Island, the Indian scientists at Bharati Station on the Antarctic Peninsula, and the French Polies working through the winter at Dumont d'Urville. The Brits at Halley Research Station were more circumspect, seeing that they were literally floating on an ice shelf in the Weddell Sea.

The Polies gathered in Comms, save for Sal and Alek, who remained bunkered in the Dark Sector, as Dwight read the statement from the Chinese Ministry of Foreign Affairs, which had come in over the wire.

" 'The world watches as a two-party government stalemate holds international science hostage. The People's Republic of China offers the scientists currently abandoned at the American research base in Antarctica full logistic and scientific support for its threatened experiments, many of which have global importance.' "

As everyone exited Comms, murmuring excitedly, Dwight pulled Cooper aside. "An e-mail came in for you," he said. Dwight's regular corpse-like pallor had gone ghostlier, and Cooper's stomach lurched.

"Is somebody dead?"

"No," Dwight replied. "But someone's charade might be." He handed her a folded printout.

```
To: Amundsen_Scott_Comms@nsf.gov
From: fpavano@freedom.edu
Subject: Attn: Cooper Gosling

Dear Cooper,
I've clung to the root for too long. I refuse to
drown. I've ceased my activity on behalf of Bay-
less and Calhoun. I know it's too late, but I hope
it helps.

Sincerely,
Frank Pavano
```

De Pere Post Gazette
March 24, 2004
De Pere Students' Correspondence with South Pole Scientist
   Comes to Abrupt End

Did you know that Antarctica is the largest desert in the world? Did you know that in winter, no planes can fly in or out of South Pole? Do you know how to build a snow trench?

Every year, the fourth grade students at Marshall Elementary School study Antarctica during their unit on the earth's polar regions. But this year, their studies had been enhanced with personal correspondence with a scientist living and working at the South Pole.

Dr. Sal Brennan, a thirty-six-year-old astrophysicist from Princeton, had been communicating with the students via e-mail since September. He sent pictures and answered questions about his life on the cold, desolate continent. However, the students found their Polar unit merging into their U.S. Government and Civics unit when Dr. Brennan told them that, as a federally funded scientist, his experiment would be shut down as a result of the current standoff between Congress and the National Science Foundation.

"The students were thrilled by Dr. Brennan's e-mails," noted their teacher, Carlotta Beardsley. "They were constantly thinking up questions for him, and they'd enjoyed sending him e-mails about what they've been learning."

When the students learned of the decision made by several scientists, including Dr. Brennan, to remain at South Pole Station in violation of the government's evacuation order, and federal law, a lively debate ensued in the classroom, Beardsley said. "We are all heartbroken that politics have affected his ability to conduct research, but at the same time, it's a teachable moment for the students. We debated whether Dr. Brennan had done the right thing by staying and about what would be lost to the global scientific community if he'd left."

According to student Griffin Wakefield, Dr. Brennan was putting himself and others in danger. "I just thought, you have to do what the government says. What if he runs out of fuel or food?" Fellow student Diani Soltau, however, thought Dr. Brennan was doing the right thing: "You can't just restart an experiment. I think I would do the same thing if I'd spent so many years working on something."

the riemann hypothesis

Sal hadn't been sleeping much. It was Sri, back in Madison, tussling with lawyers and subpoenas. It was Lisa and her team, who'd reluctantly left the joint experiment in his hands. It was his stake in the experiment—cyclic universe or bust—now in its final year, the third. *Three*. Pythagoras' "noblest" number—the only number to equal the sum of all the terms below it.

Both experiments rushed forward now, in their waning stages, like binary stars mid-collapse. The e-mails poured into Sal's in-box, an engorged river of inquiries. From Kavli at Stanford, from Lebedev in Moscow, from Princeton—even from CERN. From the journalist-geeks, from the bloggers, from *New Scientist* and *Scientific American*. And then the e-mails from the Russians at Vostok volunteering to provide telescope techs, even to travel overland to do it. Or the Chinese, who offered to send their own team of physicists from Zhongshan via sleds. Sal assumed the U.S. government would see these particular offers as posturing, but he knew better. This went beyond secretariats and embassies and politics—this was science. Everyone who mattered knew what was at stake.

Now Alek was sitting on a folding chair, his hands between his knees, tears trickling down his face. Sal looked around the lab. The fluorescents sounded like cicadas; one bulb flickered, trying to die. The hard drives hummed ceaselessly. And above him, the telescope clicked as it rotated on its plate on the roof, searching the sky, looking for the curls in the polarized cosmic background radiation that the inflationary theorists had been so desperate to find, and which he had, it seemed, found for them.

Sal and Alek had been up for forty-two hours straight. They had not eaten anything besides stale Chex Mix and Mountain Dew, and had ignored all faxes and e-mails, except one. Sal had just hung up after a four-hour phone call with Peter Sokoloff, his boss and mentor at Princeton, going over data Lisa and her team hadn't yet seen, because they were back in Palo Alto, waiting to hear from Sal. He knew the rumors had been flying for months already—particle physicists, cosmologists, and astronomers all over the world seemed to sense something big was going to happen at the Dark Sector. That the research station was officially shut down—in "caretaking mode" while simultaneously being "occupied"—only made the anticipation more intense.

Dwight had set up the call to Sokoloff, and had kept the satellite clear for the four hours it had taken for Sal to painstakingly read out the data, line by line, to his mentor. When he was done, there had been an excruciatingly long pause.

"It's five-sigma, Peter."

There was another long pause. "Does Lisa know yet?"

"No."

Sokoloff sighed. Sal imagined the sigh leaving Sokoloff's lips, then bouncing off the pockmarked MARISAT-F2 satellite two hundred miles above the Earth's atmosphere, before diving into the GOES satellite's terminal just outside the Dark Sector. "This could just be synchrotron radiation or light scattering from galactic dust," Sokoloff had finally said. "It's too early to hand out Nobels."

But Sal had heard the change in Sokoloff's voice. Uncertainty. Not of the scientific variety—hell, that was their native language. No, this was uncertainty of the personal kind. Before they got off the phone, Sokoloff had added, "Tell your father before anyone else. Let him be the first to know."

"You know he won't understand," Sal replied.

"No, Sal," came Sokoloff's voice from the satellite. "That is the one thing he will understand. I'll call Lisa and hold her off until this sequester business is resolved. Do this in person."

*

"There is a theory, which states that if ever anyone discovers exactly what the Universe is for and why it is here, it will instantly disappear and be replaced by something even more bizarre and inexplicable. There is another theory which states that this has already happened."

Sal tossed the Douglas Adams book onto his dorm bed. The man was creative, Sal remembered thinking as he swilled down the dregs of a warm Budweiser, but a scientific illiterate. It was only years later, when Sal had learned to take the long view, that he understood Adams's genius. And it wasn't until this season at South Pole Station that Sal realized how prescient Adams's words were, how they seemed to speak specifically to this experiment, to this shutdown, to the appearance of Frank Pavano. After all, it was Adams who had heralded Pavano's arrival into Sal's life, because the moment Sal had tossed *The Hitchhiker's Guide to the Galaxy* onto his bed had also been the precise moment his new roommate had walked into their dorm room at Stanford's Roble Hall. Gangly and skinny, with eyes wide and penetrating as an owl's, the kid had stood there, frozen, unsure of what to say. By this time, Sal was familiar with the common anxieties of the nerd, so he reached between his legs and drew another beer from the six-pack. "They're warm, but who cares, right?" he said, holding it out.

Down the hall, someone turned his boom box to maximum volume and indistinguishable heavy metal filled the hallways. This seemed to shake the kid out of his catatonia, and he stepped into the room and shut the door behind him.

"No, thanks," he said, his voice as raspy as a two-string violin.

Sal shrugged and put the beer back. He wiped his hand on the leg of his jeans and stuck out his hand. "Sal Brennan."

The boy set his duffel down gingerly, as if it contained a hundred Fabergé eggs, and cautiously shook Sal's hand. "I've heard of you." His gaze was unexpectedly direct, and it lasted too long.

"Everyone has," Sal replied. "I've basically lived here since I was a toddler."

"You're Brennan's son," Pavano said.

"That's me. You are?"

"Francis Pavano. You can call me Frank if you want."

So this was the prodigy from Indiana whom his father had been stalking for the past four years. He had expected a dark-haired Italian kid, not this cut-glass automaton. So this, Sal thought, was what Midwestern genius looked like.

He slapped the bottom bunk he was sitting on. "I took this one. You okay with the top?"

Pavano nodded silently and picked his duffel up again. "Don't you live in Palo Alto?"

"Born and bred."

"Why are you living in the dorms?"

"I spend twenty out of twenty-four hours with my father. I need to be able to escape for the other four."

Pavano nodded again and approached the bunk. Sal watched as he gripped the ladder and shook it, assessing its stability. Convinced it was structurally sound, Pavano set his bag on the desk under the window. He turned and gazed at Sal for a long, awkward minute. Finally, Sal took the hint. "I can come back."

Pavano seemed greatly relieved by the offer. "Thanks, I'll only be a minute."

Sal took longer than necessary to leave. There was something about the kid that held him there. He wasn't a thief. He wasn't a pervert. He was a ninety-nine-point-ninety-niner. Behind heavy-rimmed glasses, his round, girlish eyes regarded Sal as if he were a bibelot catching the light. He was a Jehovah's Witness without Jehovah, only the unsettling gaze of a witness.

Sal spent the afternoon at the physics building on Lomita Mall, where his father and the post-docs were feverishly trying to finish the last draft of a proposal for an independent lab, which had been in the works for a decade—it was going to be called Kavli Institute for Particle Astrophysics and Cosmology, after the major donor, and was tentatively sited in Santa Barbara on a cliff overlooking the Pacific. Professor Brennan waved Sal into his office, where the other favored undergrads were going over data from an ongoing joint experiment at South Pole that would, it was hoped, eventually confirm that dark energy had driven the universe apart at accelerating speeds. Sal worked on the outputs for a while, but his mind kept returning to his strange new roommate.

"You're distracted," his father said without looking up from his computer, "and now you're proving a distraction. What is it?" The other physics students looked up at Sal. He hated them—hated the way they quieted down whenever his father walked into the room, the way they guarded their words, the way they answered him with an upswing in their voice, as if they were unwilling, or afraid, to say anything with finality in his presence.

"Nothing," Sal replied. Simultaneously, the undergrads turned to look at Professor Brennan. The professor kept his eyes on his computer screen. "Speak or leave," he said. "I cannot have distractions."

"Met my roommate today."

At this, the senior Brennan looked over at his son. "Ah, so he's arrived."

"You know him?"

"Of course—I arranged it all with the bursar. Francis Pavano. We're trying to coax him into particle physics. He's a gifted science mind, Sal. We just need to convince him that inflation is far more interesting than plasma physics."

"He wants to do heliophysics?" Sal asked, incredulous. "Matthews is a crank."

"Your influence would be much appreciated."

Sal groaned. "I have enough eccentrics in my life."

"Please try to remember that in this world, you're the outlier."

Sal got back to work, but found, after a few minutes, that he still couldn't concentrate. He looked over at his father, who was perusing the latest WMAP results. "Fine, I'll talk to him, see if I can coax him away from Matthews."

His father turned slowly from his computer and said, "Who?"

None of the students dared to look up from their work. "Pavano," Sal said.

After a moment—no more than a second, but a second too long—his father nodded. "Yes, please do talk to him. Tell him more about Kavli. I imagine for someone of his caliber, it would be quite an inducement."

When Sal returned to the dorm, the halls were quiet—it was dinnertime, and everyone had left for the cafeteria. When he unlocked the door and walked in, he saw that Pavano was standing at the window in front of a desktop easel, shirtless, his glasses atop his head. Pavano seemed unsurprised to see him.

"You okay, man?" Sal asked.

"I'm painting," Pavano said, gesturing toward the canvas on his easel. "I hope that's okay."

Sal dropped his backpack under his bunk. "You paint?"

"Occasionally," Pavano said. "It's just a hobby."

Sal walked over to where Pavano was working and looked at the painting. The canvas was daubed in bright, almost blinding white oil paint. A tidy black line split the painting neatly in half. Sal took a step closer and squinted. The left half of the canvas was blank. The right half of the canvas was filled with tiny equations and mathematical formulas. Sal recognized Euler's equation, standard-model Lagrangian, an attempt to render infinite pi—the typical doodlings of a mathematics nerd in love with the most elevated equations in the discipline. He was about to walk away from the canvas when he spotted it: unmistakable in its beauty and impenetrability.

$$\zeta(s) = 1 + \frac{1}{2^s} + \frac{1}{3^s} + \frac{1}{4^s} + \frac{1}{5^s} + \ldots = \sum_{n=1}^{\infty} \frac{1}{n^s}$$

The hairs on the back of his neck stood up. The Riemann hypothesis, which extended Euler's zeta function to the entire complex plane. Sal had lost interest in the distribution of the primes when he was in junior high, but it remained one of the great unproved theorems—any mathematician recognized it the way others would recognize a stop sign at an intersection. Still, it struck Sal as overly fussy that Pavano had included it in whatever was sitting on the easel. No, it was more than that. It seemed a desecration.

"What do you think?" Pavano asked.

"What do I think? I think it's the work of a beginner," Sal said. "A beginner painter and a beginner mathematician."

Pavano gazed back at Sal, his face a pale lake. Sal sat down at his bunk. The painting haunted the room like a squatter, whose presence was impossible to ignore. He knew he was being a dick, and he wasn't sure why, but seeing the Riemann on Pavano's canvas disturbed him. It was like seeing a classmate doing a nude life study of his mother.

"Put on a fucking shirt, man," Sal said. Pavano complied immediately, retrieving his shirt from the back of his chair. "I hear you want to go into heliophysics."

"I'm considering it."

"You know, heliophysics is like one step up from cybernetics," Sal said, glancing over at the painting again. "And Matthews is a fringe-riding lunatic who is only here because he's a fossil." Pavano remained impassive. "My father says you turned him down. Why?"

"I have my reasons."

Sal scoffed. "You think choosing Matthews over my father is the best course of action?"

Pavano paused uncertainly. "I do."

"Why?"

Again, Pavano hesitated. "I don't think Professor Brennan can meet my needs as a scholar."

Sal laughed. "My father will win the Nobel prize when they find b-modes, and they will."

"It's not that. It's that . . ." Pavano looked at Sal for a moment before turning away.

"What is it?"

"It's just that—I've spent a great deal of time with your father now, and I believe he's suffering from some form of dementia. Early stages, of course, but it's there. I saw it most vividly last spring when I spent that weekend with the department."

Sal gripped the edge of his bunk. Something deep in his brain told him to run, to leave the room as quickly as possible and pretend he hadn't heard what Pavano had just said. But he was immobilized. "My father is the top theoretical physicist in the world, you idiot."

"Yes, of course," Pavano said quietly. "But Matthews agrees with me. As do other members of the faculty."

Sal realized he was now standing. His body ached with rage. He wanted to wrap his hands around Pavano's skinny throat, crush the protuberant Adam's apple, hear vertebrae crackle beneath his fingers. Pavano took a step back. When he saw Sal stalking toward him, he retreated even farther until he was up against the cool cinder-block wall.

Sal's eyes fell on Pavano's Riemann hypothesis again, and, without thinking, he grabbed the canvas off the easel and put his foot through it, throwing the ruined painting at Pavano. It landed with a thud. Pavano's eyes—freakish and clear as glass—merely gazed back at him.

Sal returned to the physics building that night. It was deserted, but the lab was, as always, open. He spent two hours going over the day's data coming in from the South Pole Telescope, but found it hard, once again, to concentrate. He hated Frank Pavano with every cell in his body—hated his unnaturally smooth face, his hollow cheeks, his cavernous, simian eyes. He hated how his father had pursued him with a cupidity that was embarrassing, and which stimulated in Sal persistent envy.

Mostly, he hated that Pavano was right.

*

Somewhere, melted snow dripped down an exterior wall; Sal could hear the quiet growl of Bozer's snow mover digging out the construction site. The roar of machines had diminished to occasional animal-like noises as Bozer, Marcy, and Floyd struggled to keep both the station and the site from being buried. Sal missed the din. Hearing the discordant sounds of construction had been a comfort to him over the last seven months. Here, in the lab, the sounds of progress were less straightforward—in fact, they were damn near inaudible. The only proof you were getting closer to the truth, it seemed, was the chatter of an overworked desktop computer with a stuck spindle.

His laptop pinged, and Sal scooted his chair past Alek to look at his e-mail. It was another message from the NSF. It was, like all of the missives since the occupation had begun, marked URGENT. Sal forwarded it to Dwight without reading it, same as all of the other e-mails he'd received from government agencies. He would deal with the fallout later. Right now, he had to take care of this.

Alek had fallen asleep sitting up. Sal stepped past him again and lay down on the floor. *The inflationary paradigm is fundamentally untestable. Hence, it's scientifically meaningless.* Sokoloff had said this so many times that Sal had told him it was going to be his next tattoo. As he stared at the ceiling, he tried to convince himself that his mentor was right, that they could play the uncertainty card and keep the cyclic theory on life support. But wasn't that exactly what Pavano and his ilk were doing? Promoting doubt in the face of uncertainty? Five-sigma, they'd found. Less than one chance in 3.5 million that those b-modes—those curls—were a random occurrence. Less than one chance in 3.5 million that the universe hadn't unfolded exactly the way the inflationists said.

God, the fucking inflationists. They hated the name—it was an insult—and although he used it with abandon, Sal knew this was childish. For some reason, he always thought of the inflationists as balloonists—foppish men in top hats gazing down at the rabble as they ascended, their bony hands gripping the side of the basket. Of course, that was ridiculous—most of the men and women who felt the standard model was as close to truth as science could get were just like him. The most passionate among them were his father's acolytes. And maybe that's why he hated them—the balloonists—the ones who were able to float away on the winds of a scientifically problematic theory.

He would stay here, rooted to the ice, and do whatever he could to dismantle it. The inflationary theory was unwieldy, made up of disparate parts, and covered with ugly surgical scars. One of the very first things Sal's father had taught him was that truth was elegant because it was simple. The universe itself was simple—fundamental physics was simple—and the theory could not be more complex than the universe it described. But the inflationists had fine-tuned their theory until it was a Frankenstein's monster. It was this half-dead thing that his father had expected him and the other bright young minds in cosmology to elevate to natural law.

Sokoloff had taught Sal that the truth does not need fine-tuning. This theory—the Big Bang—was not simple, and so Sal knew it was not true, no matter if they'd found "proof" of the b-modes. His model—the cyclic universe model—was so stunning, so elegant, that when Sal heard Sokoloff and Turner speak about it at the monthly Joint Theoretical Seminar at Princeton, he'd felt woozy. But when he looked around the room at the other physicists, he saw nothing but rolled eyes and open skepticism.

After the seminar, Sal had rushed down to the podium and grabbed Sokoloff by the sleeve. "Doc, it's a fucking phoenix." Sokoloff was amused. He even laughed.

"I've never heard it put that way," he'd said, "but you're absolutely right. Can we sell it like that?"

What Sokoloff and Turner were saying, and what no one in the room besides Sal was willing to at least consider, was that the universe built its own funeral pyre and stepped into the flames, destroying itself only to be reborn. It was engaged in an endless cycle with endless variations, of which this one—this moment, this life—was nothing more than chance, the result of a hip check with the universe on the other side of a minuscule gap.

At dinner that night, Sokoloff reminded Sal of the weaknesses of the inflationary theory—weaknesses Sal's father had brushed aside as trivial. The standard model could tell us what had happened between the Big Bang and the universe as we currently know it, but it could not tell us what would happen next. Perhaps more important, it could not explain, and in fact even disdained, the very idea of exploring what had happened before. Sokoloff and Turner's model could. Sal's father had, somewhat famously, no patience for questions like this. "Let's leave that to the preschoolers and the Baptists and focus on finding b-modes," he'd said when Sal returned from Princeton that summer. "Don't get seduced by contrarians. They exist in every discipline of science." But Sokoloff wasn't a contrarian. He'd actually been an architect of the inflationary theory himself. Sal's father was right about one thing, though—Sal had been seduced.

By this time, Sal was heir apparent at the Kavli Institute for Particle Physics and Cosmology, which his father had spent the last ten years trying to build. What Frank Pavano had seen five years earlier was now an open secret: the mind of the eminent physicist had slowly been spackled with plaques. Alzheimer's. Pavano, having chosen another university for his doctorate when Matthews retired, was now publishing on wave oscillations in the Midwest.

Sal opposed his mother's desire to hide the truth from his father's colleagues and devoted students, though he also understood the impulse. He allowed her to believe he was in agreement, but he knew better. He had to tell—otherwise the changes his father had undergone would become part of his biography rather than seen as the pathologies they were. Especially because it was no longer heterotic string theory that spoke to his father; it was strange pop culture conspiracy theories that sometimes seemed to share the same DNA. They had the resonance of fairy tales, and the deeper they resonated, the more plausible they became.

This was true: at South Pole an enormous telescopic mouth gaped at the heavens, swallowing invisible particles that tiny scientists then examined in the machine's underground gut. The particles carried information from a place 13 billion years away. They told, or would tell, of a universe sprung from a singularity, where equations break down and energy is infinite.

This was not true: a system of caves and caverns traversed the earth's mantle beneath the ice of Antarctica—polar voids where an anti-civilization thrived, where, if our civilization were to encounter it, the two would annihilate each other, like matter and anti-matter. Hitler was a believer of the Hollow Earth theory. In fact, some believe he is there now, having been escorted via U-boat by a German sailor, who located the narrow underwater passageway (wormhole?) on an expedition to South Pole.

Both were fabulist tales. Only one was true. Knowing which was which, Sal realized, was the difference between lucidity and dementia, and his father was now on the wrong side. After the now-infamous evening physics lecture, in which Professor Brennan had deviated from a talk on the Calabi-Yau manifold to consider the role that the Argentine naval base at Mar del Plata had played in Hitler's escape to the German Antarctic city-base buried deep beneath the ice, the provost had asked Sal to come up with a "plan of action." The "plan of action" was meant to allow Professor Brennan to retire "with some degree of dignity."

A year later, on the day of the phone call Sal had received from the MacArthur Foundation notifying him that his work at Kavli had earned him a "genius grant," Sal found his mother bent over the kitchen counter, trying to glue a plate back together. Her hands were shaking. Sal quietly picked up the remaining shards piece by piece and dropped them into the trash, leaving only the one, which his mother still had between her fingers and could not seem to let go.

Upstairs, Sal found his father ensconced in his study, a sun-filled room on the top floor of their California Mission-style home. He was standing at the large window that overlooked the pool, an unintentional infinity symbol filled with sparkling blue water.

"Your mother tells me you have good news," Professor Brennan said suddenly.

"MacArthur likes the new model for radiatively induced symmetry breaking I introduced last year." The words were bitter in Sal's mouth. He tried again. "The model plays," he said, hoping a joke would remove the taste, but his father didn't respond. Sal wondered if he could slip away unnoticed. Outside, a car honked, and Professor Brennan leaned into the glass, straining toward the sound. Sal noticed for the first time that the room smelled like old man. He looked around at the bursting bookcases, the crystal awards, the framed degrees; the photo of Sal as a boy in a baseball uniform, his hair a mass of red-blond curls, his smile a series of gaps.

Sal saw, then, that his father had turned from the window and was looking at him. His eyes were clear. They were fixed on Sal's face. Sal gazed back at the strong jaw, the broad, deeply lined forehead, the prominent but structurally perfect nose. He wanted nothing more at that moment than for his father to embrace him. Then the horn honked again, and the interstice dissolved.

Sal went down to South Pole for Kavli that fall, the fall of 1999, to work on Viper, the telescope run by the guys at the University of Chicago. Sal knew then that this would be the last time he'd look for proof that the standard model of the universe was correct. Later, when the first installment of the MacArthur money was deposited into his account, he wrote a check for the entire amount, made out to the Kavli Foundation. Now he was free.

Two days after writing that check, four months after returning from his first research season at Pole, eight months after Professor Brennan had quietly retired, and sixteen months after talking to Sokoloff that night in Princeton, Sal left Stanford. When his mother asked him where he was going, he told her he was following the phoenix.

*

Sal didn't hear Cooper come into the lab. He must have fallen asleep, because she was squatting down next to him, her fur-lined hood framing her beautiful face. "They've been trying to get you over All-Call for the last fifteen minutes. Something's happened." She looked over at Alek, who had awakened and resumed his silent weeping. "What's going on? Why's Alek crying?"

Sal rolled over on his side and from his back pocket pulled the folded paper Alek had given him ten hours earlier. He handed it to Cooper and watched her scan it, her dark eyes moving from word to word. He knew it would mean nothing to her, and he was envious of her ignorance—Alek's tears would do more than anything to tell her what was on this piece of paper.

Cooper sat down next to Sal and looked at him questioningly. He pointed to the symbol that Alek had circled three times in brown marker, the color of each ring growing deeper as his fury strengthened his grip. Together, they looked at it.

5

Σ

Sal looked again and again and, as before, he couldn't stop. It was the most beautiful thing he'd ever seen in his life, and it was also the most disappointing. "This is why Alek's crying and you're on the floor," Cooper said.

"Short of finding life on other planets or directly detecting dark matter, it's the most important discovery in astronomy. It supports a lifetime of theoretical work. And it eliminates my model."

As she absorbed this, Sal thought of her question that day she came to his lab, the one he'd dismissed because it was inconvenient: *No, I mean how it started before it started.* He thought, too, of her paintings, which she'd begun photographing for her NSF portfolio before handing them over to everyone: the one of Pearl, how her golden hair—always hidden under that filthy pink bandanna—coiled around her neck; how her eyes laughed, but how they also clearly belonged to a woman with insatiable ambitions. Doc Carla, startling without her Yankees cap, her eyes fixed on a point in the distance, her entire life, somehow, in those eyes. Bozer, stripped to pith. Denise's unmistakable sadness. Everyone else, even Alek, even Floyd and Dwight. Everyone else but him.

But he didn't wonder why his likeness was not among the portraits; it was obvious that he had not allowed Cooper to truly look at him. He had never minded if the others looked—they couldn't see like she could. Post-docs, research assistants, waitresses, lawyers. Some understood the work, or pretended to. Some didn't, and some didn't even feign interest. It was fine. It was all fine. He took what he needed without being a dick about it, and they got whatever they wanted in return. This history made Sal notorious at Kavli for what was regarded as his "charm"—though in the world of cosmology and particle physics, the bar for charm was admittedly low.

It helped that he'd taken after his father, with his strong features and tall build, and that from his mother he had inherited the sort of face that women considered attractive (though one girlfriend had assured him that "beauty is neutral"). But what set Sal apart from other cosmologists, particle physicists, astronomers, and all the others who so desperately wanted the world to understand the implications of their work, was that he was bold. He said nothing until he could say it with authority. He hated hedging—framing ideas with conditionals that annihilated them. Margins of error as wide as crevasses, and therefore too dangerous to attempt a crossing. These were the inviolable commandments of science, but they were also the reason that the public paid science so little attention. Scientists were lame messengers, often handing off their findings to their weakest practitioners to share with the world, celebrity scientists who performed a kind of homeopathy that distilled them to nothing, or nearly nothing. He refused to be like them.

Then Cooper pushed his stupid petition away that day in the cafeteria. Disdainful. Solitary. Like a particle that was also a wave, Sal's heart was both closed and open. He tried to ignore it, but then she was everywhere. She was in the lab, she was in the equations that Sal still did by hand, she was at the telescope, blotting out the cosmic microwaves. She was outside, walking alone, looking at the sky. Looking. Each day that passed changed something about her, made her more beautiful. A glance in the cafeteria. A very slight smile. A smudge of paint on her cheek. A smart remark. Nothing rational. None of it precise.

First, he laid her out for Alek, like she was a cadaver in a nineteenth-century medical theater, to prod and insult in every way imaginable. Alek soon tired of this; he felt Cooper was ordinary and therefore inoffensive. Still Sal's heart thundered for her. *You're distracted,* he heard his father saying to him, *and now you're proving a distraction.* He could not afford a distraction. Not this season.

When the feelings persisted, Sal eventually declared that his intense attraction to Cooper must be evolutionary biology at work. There could be no other explanation. Alek felt strongly that Sal's vow of chastity for the season was to blame. No, Sal insisted, it had to be biology—millennia ago, he and Cooper must have been part of the same tribe. They would simply have to fuck so he could get back to work. Masturbation would cure this reptilian-brain desire, he thought. But it didn't.

Time passed. In the evenings, he drank, and he broke his vow of chastity with that Frosty Boy tech from McMurdo. These encounters typically meant nothing; now they had the sharp taste of betrayal. Although there was no one to betray, the feeling was unshakable. He couldn't stop thinking of Cooper.

Then one day, out at the telescopes, as he raved about his cyclic model like a meth-fueled evangelist, she asked why he was the only one who believed it. The question had enraged him, and it was only later—much later, in fact—that he understood why, and then he was even angrier. He was an apostate. So was Sokoloff. And at conferences where he'd seen his old Stanford colleagues, he'd loudly congratulated himself for being one. After all, the fact that a scientist changes his mind is proof that the scientific method works—that they can overcome their affinities for their cherished ideas and thereby protect the integrity of the whole endeavor.

But when Cooper had asked him why he was the only one who seemed to "believe" in the cyclic model, he grew angry, because instead of thinking of the great apostates of science—Darwin changing his mind on pangenesis, Marcelo Gleiser repudiating his hopes of a unified theory, crusty Fred Hoyle and his steady-state universe foolishness, Peter Sokoloff—Sal thought of Frank Pavano. Pavano, who was unworthy of even speaking Sokoloff's name. No, Pavano was not an apostate; he was a fraud. He was paid for his conclusions. Worse, Sal was convinced that Pavano didn't even buy into the pseudoscience he was peddling.

But still, a thought began eating away at him. It filled him with shame first, and then with dread. Wasn't it right, he began to wonder—unquestionably right—that Pavano was on the ice alongside him?

*

It was a week after the accident out on the Divide, after Cooper's injury and after the media had picked up the story and after Bayless and Calhoun had scheduled their flight down, that Sal approached Sri with his thought about Pavano. Tucker had come out to the Dark Sector the day before to tell Sal that Scaletta had met with the congressmen and had been told that unless NSF formalized a process to grant "minority scientific views" a place at federal research facilities, they would hold up the agency's polar regions budget in committee, which would quickly prompt a station shutdown. Scaletta had refused, and asked Tucker to begin preparing the scientists for the possibly of a station shutdown.

So Sal went to the climatology lab and put his idea to Sri: let the skeptics come. There weren't many of them—it was a 90/10 split among climate scientists already—and their research wouldn't yield anything dangerous. He tried to sound confident—dismissive, even. Let the children have dessert at the adult table—the meal's almost over, anyway, right?

It didn't go well. Sri paced the eight-by-eight room over and over again, muttering incoherently (Sal caught words like *betrayal* and *end of science*). But it seemed the easiest way to make the threat disappear—and, in some tenuous way, it adhered to the principle of scientific freedom. But Sri felt Sal's plan was morally reprehensible, that his motives were suspect—"selfish"—and Sal wondered if his friend was right. He let the idea go, and tried to ignore the growing sense of doom in the labs. But, like his constant thoughts of Cooper, he found his mind returning to the question again and again.

"What do you think about my idea?" he asked Alek one day after the congressmen had returned to Washington. Alek only shrugged.

"You have no opinion whatsoever on capitulating to the demands of two science-illiterate congressmen? Sri says funding a climate skeptic would be like funding Bigfoot research. Or an archaeological dig for Noah's ark. He says I'll do anything to keep my experiment going."

Alck sighed. "I tell story. In Leningrad, 1987, I am seventeen years old. St. Isaac's Square is full of people, because the authorities just demolished Angleterre hotel. This place is sacred. The great poet Yesenin end his life here. Understand, for us, this is like destroying Shroud of Turin. So we must protest. But this time, there are no arrests. No one can believe this—*glasnost* was slow to come to Leningrad. So the protests continue for weeks. I visit and help distribute *samizdat*. One day someone comes running to tell us dissidents are giving speeches in Mikhailovky Gardens. This is new—such things did not happen. But when we get there, a military band is playing and no one can hear the speakers. We are told the authorities have sent the band to play so the dissidents cannot be heard. The speeches stop and an old man puts half a lemon in my hand. 'Suck,' he tells me, and points to the band. 'Make sure they see you.' Before I can say, I see everywhere people sucking on lemons. At the front, I see the crazy old dissident Ekaterina Poldotseva handing them out from a basket. When the old man sees I am not sucking on lemon, he slaps my hand, he tells me, 'Poldotseva says the band will stop playing once when they see everyone sucking on lemons.' Empathetic saliva, he tells me. 'They will not be able to play their instruments.' Ten minutes later, the band packed up and left. They never return."

Alek turned back to his computer.

As Sal stared at the back of his friend's head, he wondered if Alek was, in fact, insane.

*

When the subpoena from the Wisconsin attorney general arrived for Sri, Sal had watched his friend's research techs bag-drag to one of the LC-130s that were evacuating nonessential staff in advance of the shutdown. It was like watching someone toss Darwin's dead finches off the side of the *Beagle*.

Once the letters from NSF began circulating, Sal began spending hours away from his own lab in order to get up to speed on the Kavli team's work—aside from her outburst at the winter-over meeting, Lisa Wu had remained stoic, but as they went over the data together, Sal noticed her fingernails had been chewed to the quick.

As each scientist shut down his or her experiment—from the experiments in the Atmospheric Research Observatory to the seismology labs—Alek's words began to take hold of Sal. To his consternation, the story about the lemon wedges was beginning to make sense. A week into the shutdown, he already knew what had to be done. He started sending e-mails. He started with the National Academy of Sciences listserv, followed by one to the Intergovernmental Panel on Climate Change, proposing the idea he'd pitched to Sri: Let them come. There would be a provision for practical requirements that would seem reasonable, even to backwater congressmen—like a track record of peer-reviewed science—but which would be difficult for a denialist to acquire.

"Science is a mirror that reflects nature," Sal wrote to Alexandra Scaletta at NSF. "Experiments are attempts to polish that mirror. Not all of them rub off the streaks, but these don't hinder the experiments that do." Sal wasn't sure he believed this last part—he wasn't sure of a lot of things now—but he sent the e-mail anyway.

The initial response from his fellow scientists ranged from disbelief to actual horror. He heard nothing from Scaletta. He waited. He wanted to give the Pole-based scientists, whose experiments had been ruined, enough time to reflect on the idea.

Then came the phone calls, all of them asking for Sal. He was spending twenty hours a day in his lab, analyzing the readouts from his own experiment, so Dwight fielded things as they came and took messages. He brought these scraps of paper to the Smoke Bar each night, so Sal could go through them.

"What are they calling about?" Cooper asked.

"The shutdown. How to end it."

Alek scoffed at this. "No, he is buying lemons."

"Lemons?"

"Alek," Sal said, his voice hoarse.

"This is how shutdown will end," Alek said.

Floyd made his way over to where Sal was sitting. "And how are you going to go about doing that?"

Sal pinched the bridge of his nose. "I think NSF should agree to fund a climate skeptic on the Divide once a season."

"Wasn't that the opposite of what you were railing on about earlier in the season?" Pearl said. "I don't mean to sound like a jerk, but it sounds like you're just changing your mind because you don't want your experiment to be affected."

"You're right. But I think we should give Pavano the opportunity to fail. I think we should let all of them fail. That's all they want—the opportunity to be totally, unmistakably wrong. If we don't give them that opportunity, they'll just keep stirring up this idea about uncertainty—'we're not sure, there's no consensus, let us show you the science.' I say, let them try. And in the meantime, we can get back to the real work of science." This earned him a blank look, so he sat forward in his seat and cleared his throat. "Let me tell you a story about lemons."

That night, he'd awakened in Cooper's room to find her out of bed, standing at her desk. The room was dark and she remained frozen in the strange shadows cast by the seam of light under the door. Although her naked back was facing toward him, Sal could see she was looking at something, studying it intently. It took him a minute to see the pile of bandages and gauze on the desk.

"Cooper," he said softly. "Come here." He could see her stiffen, and she shook her head without turning around. Sal threw the blankets off and got out of bed. As he approached, she curled into herself, cocooning her injured hand. She shook her head again, as if, for the first time since he'd known her, she was unable to find her voice. When he wrapped his arms around her, she heaved a great sob.

"Let me see," Sal replied, pulling her closer. She had tucked the injured hand between her rib cage and her left bicep, as if keeping it warm. He gently pulled at her wrist until her hand came free, and in the fading luminescence of the twilit sky that stole through the tiny window, he saw, for the first time, how her right hand looked pale and wrinkled with moisture, and how the place where her finger had been was knobby and scabbed. It struck him as so uncommonly beautiful, so like a tesseract, that he felt tears spring to his eyes. But he could tell from the way Cooper hung her head, and the way her body tried to become small as he cradled her hand, that she considered it ugly, and for once, he knew the kind of incomprehension everyone else experienced when looking at the Riemann hypothesis. They couldn't see why its uncertainty made it beautiful. He couldn't understand their blindness. Maybe there was something ugly in Cooper's disfigurement, but he couldn't see it, no matter how hard he tried.

In his lab now, where his phoenix had incinerated itself, Sal looked into Cooper's face as she kneeled over him, her eyes wide and happy. Before he had a chance to speak, the sound of All-Call filled the room. Sal propped himself up on one elbow—there was cheering in the background.

He stood up, and he, Cooper, and Alek crowded around the speaker. The chants grew louder.

"What are they saying?" Sal asked.

Cooper turned to him, her eyes wide. "That's why I came out here to find you. It's over." She kissed his dry lips. "Listen," she whispered.

Sal, Sal, Sal, went the chant.

The lemon wedges had worked. Sal looked at Cooper and realized that while there was nothing left of his experiment but a pile of ashes, in the cinders the phoenix already stirred.

NATIONAL SCIENCE FOUNDATION
4201 WILSON BOULEVARD
ARLINGTON, VIRGINIA 22230

Cooper Gosling
PO Box 423
Minneapolis, MN 55410

Dear Ms. Gosling:

At the close of every grant period the Antarctic Artists & Writers Program assesses the output of each grantee following his or her return from Antarctica. We have now had a chance to review the portfolio you sent. What follows reflects the comments from our distinguished panel of artists and arts administrators.

While we by no means consider ourselves the arbiter of "good art," the panelists were confused by the complete lack of landscape in the collection. In fact, its absence suggested, as one panelist put it, "an act of will." As you know, the United States Antarctic Program is a science-based research program, which takes as its sole directive the interaction with and better understanding of Nature. The Artists & Writers Program was designed specifically to convey this directive to the general public through different media. The panelists felt that your collection of portraits, while quite fine technically, could have been painted, in the words of one panelist, "in any local bar."

There was one exception. We were particularly moved by the portrait you titled "David." That the subject's face was represented only by a smear of white seemed an appropriate homage to the courage and selflessness of the great polar explorers. The mitten cleverly embedded in the background added depth. We hope you build on this strength in your future work so you can provide, for yourself and others, a greater understanding of the heritage of human exploration in Antarctica. We also encourage you to consider applying for another Artists & Writers grant. Enclosed is an application for the upcoming research season, along with a preliminary psychological questionnaire.

Regards,
National Science Foundation Antarctic Artists & Writers Program

one ton depot

2004 July 10
20:46
To: Billie.Gosling@janusbooks.com
From: cherrywaswaiting@hotmail.com
Subject: Prodigal daughter's return

B.,
Thanks for all your e-mails. Tell Mom and Dad
we're all okay. I'm sorry I haven't been able
to respond sooner. Once the station shut down,
Dwight forbid all personal e-mail, since it took
up bandwidth during the satellite fly-bys. Whatever that means. Anyway, looks like this shitshow
is coming to an end. We got word last week that
Jack Calhoun decided to commit political hari-
kari and break with Bayless to end the impasse
on the budget committee. I guess once Pavano did
that interview with *60 Minutes* about the oil consortium, he had to cut his losses. I suppose it
helped that NSF says it's willing to talk about

formalizing a process to ensure grant money for
"non-traditional scientists." They're going to
insist on a robust body of "peer-reviewed science" from each applicant, and Sal tells me
there is no such thing as "peer-review" in climate denial—but don't tell the deniers that! So
we're free! (well, free until September when the
first plane can fly in.) We're basically eating
nothing but Ry-Krisps and canned tuna now, but
we still have a shit-ton of Russian vodka.
C.

By mid-August, nearly everyone knew enough Russian to sing all three refrains of "The Song of the Volga Boatmen." Cooper had learned how to use the rodwell to melt Antarctic ice for the station's water supply, learning, too, that the water swishing around in the station toilets might be made from snow that had fallen in the fifteenth century (if you dug down far enough). She had finished nearly everyone's portrait, except Sal, whom she found she didn't dare commit to canvas since his countenance burned so brightly and so beautifully in her mind. But it was time, she knew, to do the last portrait—the one of David. The one, she now understood, that she'd come down here to paint. And to do that she had to do something else first.

Cooper found Bozer and the others in the bar the night after the announcement of the sequester's end. When Bozer glanced up at her and saw the vial she displayed to him in her hand, he nodded and stood up. The ragged crew around him immediately understood. Sal gripped Cooper's left hand and squeezed.

The entrance tunnel was bathed in red, but outside the sky was black as ink, the cold winds rolling off the East Antarctic Plateau and the southern lights streaming across the sky in refracting sheets of color. When they reached the Pole marker, the crew gathered around its silver globe expectantly, and their reflections swelled and shrank. For an instant, Cooper saw herself just as she'd been that first day when she'd looked into Alek's mirrored aviators.

"Not here," Cooper said. She pointed toward the *Terra Nova*, the geographical marker. "There."

Bozer looked at her for a moment. "You know if you bury him here, he won't be here next year. He'll drift."

Cooper held his gaze. "I'm counting on it."

Bozer tucked the ice augur under his arm and they began walking toward the *Terra Nova*, their flashlights casting milky beams into the darkness. When they reached the marker, Cooper pointed at a spot of ice at its foot, and Pearl and Doc Carla trained their flashlights on it.

Bozer leaned on the ice augur. "We're all here because of some shit. Everyone's got it, but you ain't got to be alone in it." He grunted. "That's all I've got to say."

He looked over at Cooper, his balaclava obscuring all but his clear eyes, and she nodded. He drove the blade into the mark. The group watched the auger rotate in silence; to Cooper, the spiraled blade seemed a vision of infinity. It was only when Sal gently nudged her that she realized Bozer had finished coring.

She stepped to the edge of the hole and dropped to her knees. Sal helped pull off the mitten on her right hand. Carefully, he opened the vial and emptied the ashes onto the flat of her mitten. For the first time since that night on the edge of the lake, she looked at the gunmetal gray of her brother's remains. Her hand trembled. She couldn't move.

Then the others were kneeling beside her: Dwight, Denise, Floyd, Doc Carla, Pearl, Marcy, Alek, Sal—even the Swedes. Only Bozer stood apart, leaning on the auger. She closed her eyes and released David's ashes into the deep cut in the continent.

*

The sun was warm. The sound of birds had not yet become familiar again, and Cooper was thinking wistfully of the silent song of Bozer's glacier sparrow. Sal drove the rental like a kid on a learner's permit, hands at ten and two, his body taut, eyes fixed on the road ahead. As they drove through Palo Alto, the lush lawns—freshly watered and glittering under the sun like sheets of emerald—struck Cooper as about as probable as a McDonald's on the Divide. The piebald hills seemed ostentatious. The tidy parks were exquisite. The palms fronting the university looked as flamboyant as showgirls, and the occasional appearance of children seemed deeply strange. Cooper and Sal drove through the streets in silence.

They hadn't even stopped in Christchurch. The others had back-channeled hostel bookings and begun making plans online as soon as the end of the sequester had been announced. Floyd and Bozer sketched out an appeal to the New Zealand government to give the Man Without Country a proper burial; Denise went looking for a thrift-store wedding gown, having agreed, finally, to marry Bozer when they got off the ice. Pearl found Birdie waiting for her at the airport with a bouquet of daisies and a finished manuscript, and Dwight haunted Internet cafés until he found Bonnie in a cosplay chat room. Tucker was still in Washington, helping Alexandra Scaletta and Daniel Atcheson Johnson pick up the pieces, and lobbying for a dismissal of possible federal charges against the occupiers. The support staff arranged to meet in Denver to plead their cases to VIDS. One thing everyone had agreed upon was that they would all be back.

But Sal had to tell Professor Brennan *five-sigma*. The sixth milestone had been reached. Slithering toward the telescope like an army of infinitesimal Slinkys, the gravitational waves had confirmed what the inflationists had claimed all along: that space was a wild, chaotic place marked by violence, and that humanity occupied a remote pocket universe carried along by eternal inflation. There were no branes, no hidden dimensions, no hints of elegant cosmic evolution—there was only the vacuum, and a planet adrift in a multiverse. And he wanted Cooper with him when he did it.

The rumors continued unabated, of course, and by the time Sal had flown out, even *Science* was speculating. Sal told Cooper that he'd talked to Sokoloff one last time before leaving Pole, and that he'd told Sal that Lisa Wu had petitioned Kavli to wait on the announcement until Sal had returned stateside, so he could be the one to tell his father that the inflationary theory had been confirmed.

Now they were here, pulled up against the curb, and Sal was staring at the steering wheel.

Cooper put her hand on his shoulder. "Do you know what you're going to say?"

"All I have to say is 'five-sigma at point two.' He'll understand." He paused for a moment, thinking. "I hope he will." Sal looked over at Cooper. She saw fear in his eyes. She leaned over the shift and ran her hand over his now-lush auburn beard.

Sal tapped the steering wheel. "Sokoloff says it might be dust or synchrotron radiation from electrons in the galactic magnetic fields. He thinks Kavli shouldn't announce until they can rule that out." Cooper chose not to remind Sal that he'd mentioned this to her several times on each leg of the flight from New Zealand. She knew he wasn't really talking to her anyway. He chewed on his lip for a moment. "But I won't say that to him. No, not now. I'll just tell him." He looked over at Cooper again. "He was right, you know."

"Your father?"

"Pavano."

"Right about what?"

"That I believed. I knew it was wrong to believe, but I did anyway. From the first moment I heard Sokoloff speak, I wanted to believe this was true—I wanted what was beautiful to be true, rather than the other way around. That's why this hurts so much."

Sal looked over her shoulder, through the passenger-side window, and up at the house. Cooper turned and saw a figure looking out at the car, moving between panes, made faceless by the reflection of the sun on the front windows of the house. As they watched, the figure disappeared momentarily, and the front door opened. Backlit by the setting sun, the door looked like a portal, the figure like a ghost.

"Let's go," Sal said.

Cooper shook her head. "No, you go. I'll wait here."

She watched as Sal ascended the steps. When he reached the top, the figure in the doorway held out his arms. Sal fell into them like a little boy.

Yes, Cooper thought, *of course.* This was what Cherry had strained to see for six months, waiting for the Scott party to return. You waited at One Ton Depot, just you and the dogs, certain the men were just over the rise. You overcame your myopia and you navigated using the faint gleam of the sun. You blamed yourself, wondering if you had only laid better depots, if they would have made it.

And then someone appeared, pulling a sledge.

Acknowledgments

This book is set at the "old" South Pole Station, which was officially decommissioned in 2008. Although set at what once was a real place, this novel takes liberties with the station's layout. I also switched up the timeline of when certain telescopes in the Dark Sector were installed. There's probably other stuff here that will drive veteran Polies crazy. Sorry about that.

The late Nicholas Johnson wrote the first funny book about Antarctica, the brilliant *Big Dead Place*. Set largely at McMurdo, it captures the absurdity of life on the seventh continent, and will never be equaled. Dr. Jerri Nielsen's memoir, *Ice Bound,* gave me a peek into the world of polar medicine. My copy of *The Worst Journey in the World* by Apsley Cherry-Garrard spontaneously combusted the day I finished my last draft of this novel. The canon of Antarctic literature is immense. If you're interested in learning more, I suggest you contact my father.

Stories derived from this novel appeared in *Third Coast, Southeast Review, 32 Magazine, Lascaux Review*, and the *Los Angeles Review*.

I owe thanks to many people for their support and encouragement. I'm deeply grateful to Tony and Caroline Grant of the Sustainable Arts Foundation. Thank you, too, to these talented Minnesota writers: Maggie Ryan Sanford, Sara Aase, Frank Bures, Douglas Mack,

Dennis Cass, John Jodizo, Lars Ostrom, and Jason Albert, who introduced me to Breakout: Normandy. I'll also never forget the incredible generosity shown to me by Yona Zeldis McDonough, Elizabeth McKenzie, Julie Schumacher, and Robin Sloan.

I'm immensely grateful to the formidable and funny (or formidably funny) Lisa Bankoff, who immediately loved my hygiene-challenged Polies, believed in the story, and who makes me laugh every time I talk to her. She's the best in the business. My editor, the preternaturally gifted Elizabeth Bruce, is Maxwell Perkins with a penchant for temporary tattoos, an encyclopedic knowledge of college basketball, and a brain the size of Antarctica. I could not be more grateful for all she did to make this book better. The crew at Picador/Macmillan have been a joy to work with. Thanks to Declan Taintor, Kolt Beringer, Darin Keesler, Henry Sene Yee, Karen Richardson, Emily Walters, and, of course, Stephen Morrison, without whom this book would be in a drawer somewhere.

Per usual when it comes to all things explorer, it was my dad who introduced me to Cherry-Garrard. Mom wanted to know why there wasn't more sex in the book. I'm so grateful for their love and support. Delta Larkey read a draft of this book when she had much more important things to do, and her support means so much. Lacy Shelby is one of only a handful of women in history who have winter-overed at South Pole Station. She shared just enough of her own experience there to inspire this book while staying true to the Pole axiom that "what happens on the ice stays on the ice." This book would not have been written without her. Jeff and Scott Meredith gifted me with two great lines and would both be royalty at South Pole. I will always be grateful to my best friend, Starr Sage. *Vaya con CL.*

Finally, this whole thing is for my patient and understanding husband, Emmanuel Benites, and my funny, loving, straight-up amazing children, Hudson and Josephine. They sledged right along with me, and, when I faltered, they never considered leaving me behind. Guys—we're done. Let's get a pizza.

ASHLEY SHELBY is a prizewinning writer and journalist. She received her MFA from Columbia University and is the author of *Red River Rising: The Anatomy of a Flood and the Survival of an American City*, a narrative nonfiction account of the record-breaking flood that, in 1997, devastated Grand Forks, North Dakota. The short story that became the basis for *South Pole Station* is a winner of the Third Coast Fiction Prize. She lives in the Twin Cities with her family.

AshleyShelby.com